ARE YOU MAN ENOUGH?

by Doug McKim

and Richard McKim

SAME OLD STORY PRODUCTIONS

VICTOR FERUS, President and CEO

Are You Man Enough? Second Edition

SAME OLD STORY PUBLISHING 2016
Mount Juliet, Tennessee
1027 Posey Hill Rd.
Mount Juliet, TN 37112

10 9 8 7 6 5 4 3 2

ISBN: 978-1-9454500-0-6

Dear readers,

Allow me to get straight to the point.

What you've got in your hands is the Second Edition of a novel which was originally published in December of 2010.

Are You Man Enough? was a very difficult book to write. It took me five years to complete this massive novel, with its many characters, intertwining plots and story lines, and attempts to tell a story of war's effects on a corrupt, yet crumbling nation and society.

When I began working on this book, I thought it would be a rather simple project. My plan was merely to make a pointed and angry commentary on war and violence. I had lost a family member in Afghanistan, and hoped to turn my anger and outrage into literary action.

I never imagined how my own life changed, over the course of five years.

I lost an older sister and both parents during the time I wrote the first edition of this novel. Personal loss and tragedy are elements that played heavily within the story. The painful deaths of those dear to me had obviously affected me, and carried over in how and why I was determined to finish the novel, no matter how much life and writing had exhausted me.

When the book was finally published, I felt equally relieved and frustrated . . . Relief that I was finished with this tale, and frustrated that it wasn't told as well as it could've been. Surely, the product was very ambitious and grand in its scale and scope. Yet, I feared that it had occasionally lost it focus, meaning, and purpose. The story meandered more than it should have. It went on a few pointless destinations, along wordy and unnecessary roads.

I recall film director Howard Hawks' concerns that "movies aren't released, they escape." I often worried that "Are You Man Enough?" had swiftly, and hastily, fled from my shaky hands, before it was given an objective and thorough edit. Long term, it was my hope to eliminate a number of "literary offenses", rewrite it in a more clear and concise manner, and strive not to try my audiences' patience.

The Second Edition features a larger, easy-to-read font, and new artwork on the jacket. The First Edition claimed to have been written by D McKim and somebody named *Prospero D'Aisling*. Today, I'm proud to announce that the actual creators are brothers Doug and Richard McKim.

I don't know who this "Prospero" guy was. To paraphrase Stephen King, I imagine that he "died from cancer of the pseudonym."

I believe that the Second Edition is a major improvement over its predecessor. I'm satisfied that the story is now told in a manner which I first intended it, those many years ago.

Please sit down, relax, and make yourself at home. Enjoy this Second Edition of my first published novel 'ARE YOU MAN ENOUGH?'

You have my eternal gratitude.

Doug McKim

ORIGINAL AUTHORS' NOTE

We began working on this novel, in response to the sudden and tragic news of a family member who died while serving his country in Afghanistan.

Are You Man Enough? tells the story of war's effects on a number of young people in a mythological setting. Our story does not condone the practice of training children how to kill. However, it is dedicated to those servicemen and women who have given the ultimate sacrifice in the line of duty, and to their family and friends who fully understand the true costs of war.

The world in which our characters reside is known as the *Earth*. It is not to be mistaken with the planet we all share. Human history, as described in this novel, does not entirely resemble our own.

Our story takes place in a period and location similar to the Middle Ages of Europe. There are also dramatic elements inspired by the Victorian England of Charles Dickens, the Russia of Sergei Eisenstein and Boris Pastarnak, the Germany of Adolf Hitler, and even the American West. One may even find comparisons to modern times. Readers should not examine the story's history, religions, societies, or cultures in an honest or accurate sense.

May peace, prosperity, and happiness bless those who read our humble scroll.

We are forever grateful.

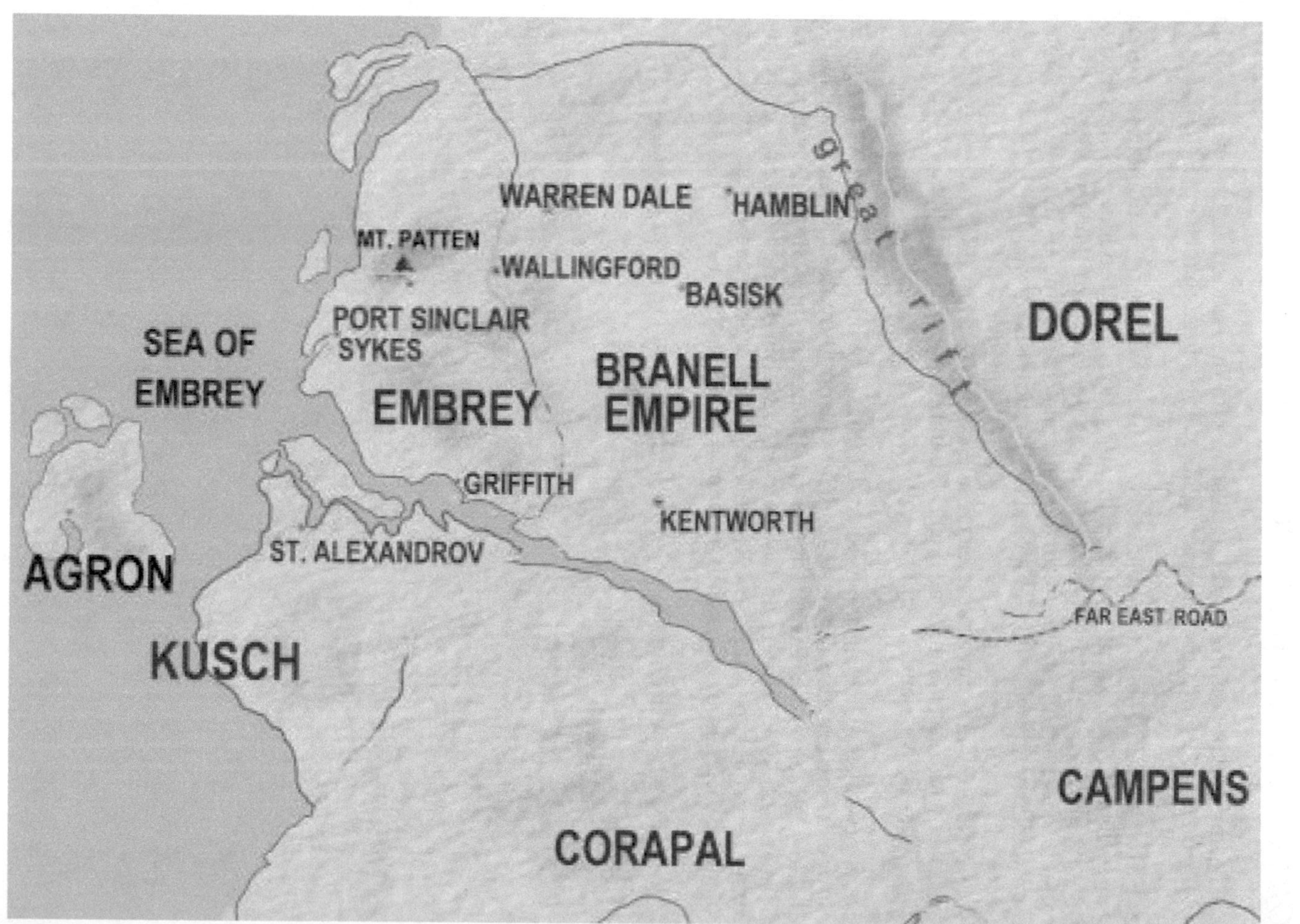
WARREN DALE
HAMBLIN
great rift
MT. PATTEN
WALLINGFORD
BASISK
DOREL
PORT SINCLAIR
SYKES
SEA OF
EMBREY
BRANELL
EMBREY
EMPIRE
AGRON
GRIFFITH
KENTWORTH
ST. ALEXANDROV
FAR EAST ROAD
KUSCH
CAMPENS
CORAPAL

ARE YOU MAN ENOUGH?

"Paransky," laughed Johanek, slapping the trader's tattooed shoulders. "Your wares never cease to amaze me!"

It was late August, as a balmy wind blew in from the south. Johanek relaxed in the living quarters of his private fortress, built from stone and mortar, overlooking acres of pastureland. On a calm Sunday afternoon, he shared a bottle of Campens Rose' with an Agronian trader named Paransky.

The two men enjoyed a dish of nuts and dried fruit. Across the room, a servant woman filled an opulent, iron tub for Johanek's annual bath. Johanek winked at Paransky, and turned his gaze upon the lovely young wench bending over the tub. Wearing a short skirt, the woman revealed her bare backside. Johanek licked his lips, in anticipation of his plans for that evening.

Born in poverty, Johanek grew wealthy by cashing in on a border dispute between Embrey and the Branellian Empire. He favored neither country, yet supplied both with armament. Business was brisk, as Johanek amassed a sizable fortune over the blood-soaked contest.

A bald, heavyset man with a graying beard, Johanek had much to show for his illicit activities. His greatest prize was an impressive home. Partially for security, but mainly for show, he purchased a small island in the Branell Straits, separating Corapal from the Branellian Empire. Through the efforts of his servants and bodyguards, he lived quite comfortably. His few guests, heavily monitored, bought arms or enhanced an exotic and valuable collection.

That day, Paransky delivered the stuffed hide of an unusual creature known as an *abarbeaus*. Resembling a cross between a simian and wild breed of cat, the strange mammal had long, dark red hair, and stood four feet tall from teeth to tail.

Johanek gently rubbed his fingers across the abarbeaus' maned neck and chest as it stood, harmlessly, in one corner of the room. With no one disputing him, he'd claim it was he who downed this new trophy. In truth, he killed nothing more than rodents and bugs. "Do people eat these things?" he asked Paransky. "I mean, hunt them?"

"Naw," chuckled Paransky, twirling his black mustache. "Not too many people eat them, but they'll damn sure eat you if they get the chance."

Paransky was a young, skinny fellow whose body was scrawled with tattoos, most depicting the female form in erotic poses. Though few knew his name, his physical traits were renowned throughout the Brindai Continent.

Along with the abarbeaus, Paransky sold dried meats and produce. There was a new item in this shipment, called tobacco. Rolled in thin parchment, tobacco was usually bought by those of a criminal or deviant nature. Slowly, it gained popularity among the upper class.

Johanek ignited the tobacco with a wax candle, and took a drag. Savoring the velvety taste, he gagged as thick smoke entered his lungs.

"Takes some getting used to," laughed Paransky.

Johanek carefully allowed the tobacco's aroma to linger on his tongue and gums, before exhaling. Happily, he asked to get in on the sale of it.

"You better talk to my partner about that," said Paransky, elusively.

"Well?" asked Johanek, impatiently. "Where is he?"

"In Sykes, on the second floor of Erickson's Imports."

"Bring him here, immediately! I'll sell your tobacco to the Branellian and Embrian armies!"

Paransky merely grinned.

"You'll see things my way, when you learn how much you can earn from those idiots," argued Johanek. "I love assisting them in their own undoing. Screw all Branellians and Embrians!"

"What do ya think about Agronians?" questioned Paransky.

Johanek especially disliked that rogue nation, but did not offend his guest. After all, it was Agronian smugglers who helped make him rich.

There were always disagreements on the cause of the Border War, and even greater dissent on which side started it. From most accounts, the conflict began centuries ago, when Campens, Branell, and Embrey were under one flag.

The last emperor of the Brindai Empire, King Sinclair, had triplet sons named Brandon, Anton, and Simon. Beginning in childhood, the boys' hunger for the throne was apparent. Sinclair forged a plan which, instead of reducing strife and tension, actually increased it.

Although the boys were born just moments apart, it was decreed that Brandon was to gain possession of the Brinde Provinces. Anton was given the Embria Province, while Simon reigned over Camensea.

Arguments arose concerning the border between Embria and Brinde. Both provinces had its share of mineral and agricultural resources, which the other needed. Instead of trading or bartering for goods, the two nations took what they wanted by force.

Brotherly love did nothing to halt animosities between Brandon and Anton. Minor squabbles evolved into all-out hostilities. The two rulers' deaths failed to alleviate their countries' bigotry and hatred, as battles grew more violent and bloody.

Camensea was eventually renamed Campens, the Brinde Province became the Branellian Empire, and the Embria Province was later known as Embria, or simply Embrey.

Paransky took his leave of Johanek, just prior to sundown. Johanek offered what he regarded as a fair price for the tobacco, then said his goodbyes.

Stripping off his heavy wool shirt and breeches, Johanek allowed a breeze from an open window to comfort him. Pouring a drink into a steel chalice, he crawled into the tub, filled with warm, soapy water. Johanek toasted the stuffed abarbeaus, sipped the liquor, placed it on small table, and closed his eyes.

Johanek nearly dozed off until a youthful voice said, "Greetings from the fairest of all nations, the sovereign state of Embrey."

Johanek snapped out of his trance, as a lad of fourteen approached the tub. This newcomer smiled cordially. He was dressed in a sky blue, plumed Cavalier hat, a white, silky shirt, and tights. Hanging from his leather belt was a dagger, adorned with a jeweled handle.

Even as Johanek doubled the newcomer's size, he felt endangered.

"Forgive me," the boy said, politely. "Did I come at a bad time?"

"Who are you?" growled Johanek. "Who let you in here?"

"Oh, I saw myself in," the boy said. "One mustn't be a bother."

"Are you with Paransky?"

"The tattooed man? Heavens no! Wouldn't be caught dead hobnobbing with such pirate rabble."

"Then who are you?" shouted Johanek, concealing his loins under soapy water.

"Oh, how rude of me!" The boy removed his hat, and took a chair next to the tub. "The name's Jesse. I arrived from Embrey on a . . . shall I say, *trivial* business."

Johanek stared at Jesse, as if he were an apparition.

Jesse frowned. "I say, old man . . . Don't tell me you've never heard of Embrey."

"Of course I have!" Johanek refused to shake Jesse's extended hand. "Now go! I've got the mind to call my guards in!"

"Unkind, unkind!"

"Damn it, I told you to go!" ordered Johanek, his voice echoing throughout the fortress.

"Oh, no worries," said Jesse, toying with the dagger's handle. "I'll go in due time. I shant overstay my welcome."

"You've got a lot of nerve coming here."

"Now, now, dear fellow. One mustn't get your dander up! I simply want to ask a few questions, then show myself the door."

"Then I've got a few questions for you," growled Johanek.

"Patience, my good man. Me first, me first!" Jesse cleared his throat. "One of our naval officers, Admiral Kraig, sent a diplomat named Macready into Kentworth to talk peace."

"Why would an Embrian naval officer want peace?" argued Johanek. "They're madmen and savages."

"You won't let me finish! See here, you made me lose my place. Now, where was I again?"

"Macready?" asked Johanek, searching for a way to disarm Jesse.

"Yes, of course!" Jesse crossed his slender legs. "While Macready was in Kentworth to chat with King Josiah, someone had the audacity to murder him."

"I . . . I don't know what you're talking about," stuttered Johanek, betraying himself with his own twitching eyes.

"Oh, I think you do know." Jesse eyed the stuffed abarbeaus. "I say, where in blazes did you get that?"

"Paransky." Johanek smiled, nervously. "The tattooed man . . . he sold it to me . . . You see, I . . . I'm a connoisseur of rare items."

"I should've guessed," mulled Jesse, feigning disinterest though his curiosity was aroused. "So you deal in dead monkeys? *Hmm . . .*"

Johanek had a strained smile.

"Well . . ." Jesse shook his head. "You may start now by answering my question. What about Macready's death?"

"I just told you," whispered Johanek. "I don't know!"

"Don't try me! You do know, don't you? It thrilled you immensely when Macready got carved up. After all, he worked to injure your vulgar enterprise, and naturally you couldn't stand by while someone adversely affected the bottom line, now could you?"

"I don't know!"

"I know you know who killed Macready," said Jesse, calmly. "And you know I know you know I know."

"*What?*"

"Quit stalling, fat boy! Just tell me, and I'll depart."

Johanek said nothing.

"Well, are you singing the aria for me?" insisted Jesse, coyly. "I won't go until you become conveniently . . . loose-lipped."

"I . . . I did pay someone to sanction Macready," admitted Johanek, shamefully.

"See!" cheered Jesse. "That wasn't so hard, was it?"

"Did Macready really think he'd stop the war?" argued Johanek, defensively. "The Branellians and Embrians aren't about to stop the killing!"

Jesse wagged the dagger at Johanek. "Did I ask you to change the subject, or make snide commentary? Don't justify Macready's murder in a pitiful moral debate. You paid to have him killed. I'm not here to see if it was right or wrong. You paid someone to stop Macready. Someone's paying me to find out who you paid to finish him off."

Johanek lowered his head. "Three . . . three of those kids that lunatic Maliek trained as hired swords for the Embrians."

"'Lunatic'?" protested Jesse. "'Lunatic,' you say? What a deplorable manner in which to speak of my dear Captain Maliek."

Needing a way to rid the world of Embrey's threats and annoyances, an Army officer shaped homeless and wayward boys into expert killers-for-hire. While many of Maliek's recruits proved useful, others terminated dignitaries not specifically marked for death.

"You're one of them!" cried Johanek. "I should've known!"

Jesse sighed. "And to think you'd never guess."

"You bloodthirsty little butcher!"

"Oh, please! Flattery will get you nowhere."

"I didn't ask who they were," said Johanek, wondering if he'd get through this interrogation, alive.

"I'm disappointed in you. Only an imbecile would treat me as an even greater imbecile. A man of your professional standing's got more sense than to hire swords without first getting their names!"

"If I talk they'll kill me!"

"And I'll kill you if you don't," said Jesse. "Take your pick, and be swift about it. I'm to be at a madam's house of joys in a few hours."

Johanek refused to speak.

Jesse snickered. "All right, war profiteer, I'll make you a deal. I'll give you a description of my former schoolmates, and you tell me if I've got the right men. Savvy?"

Johanek nodded.

"*Hmm . . .*" mused Jesse. "Was one of those dastardly butchers a lovely little Kuschan boy, with long blonde hair and the personality of a prissy flower girl?"

"He . . . he was the guy I made the arrangements with!" claimed Johanek.

"*Yuri?* Councillor Theo's darling pet? Are you sure?"

"If you . . . if you say so!"

"Good show!" Jesse stood, and put his Cavalier hat on. "I knew you'd cooperate."

"I played by your rules," whined Johanek, "now play by mine. You said you'd answer my questions!"

"Why, certainly. Ask me anything you'd like."

"Why didn't my guards stop you from coming in here?"

"They couldn't."

"What do you mean, 'they couldn't'?"

Jesse ran his fingers over the dagger's blade. "I shouldn't worry myself over the fate of your guards. At least, *I* shouldn't."

"Answer me! Why didn't the guards stop you?"

Jesse lacked emotion as he said, "I slit their throats, before conversing with you."

Jesse then drove his dagger into Johanek's hairy chest. Screaming, Johanek grabbed onto Jesse's shirt and dragged him into the tub.

As Jesse sent the weapon into Johanek's torso, over and over and over, the war profiteer held him under water. After a final, earsplitting shriek, Johanek floated dead above Jesse, and prevented him from escaping.

Jesse's thoughts sprinted, from spending a night in a nearby Branellian brothel, to his own self-preservation. He nearly lost his head. His heart beat like a drum, and his first impulse was to panic. Temptations to flail, uncontrollably, entered the mind like a phantom.

Think Jesse, think!

Get a grip on yourself!

Jesse reached for the fading light surrounding Johanek's murky, crimson silhouette, then latched onto the tub's lip. Throwing his awkward weight against the corpse, he slowly lifted himself to safety.

Soapy water burned his lungs and eyes, as Jesse crawled from the tub. Suds dripped from his hair, face, and clothing. Jesse gasped in deep breaths of fresh air. He came close, *too close,* to entering the Gates of Hell, where Johanek presently howled in horror and despair.

Jesse slapped clumsily at Johanek's body which drifted, face-down, in the tub. "You thought you had me, didn't you?" he giggled. "You thought you had me, but I had *you!* What have you to say about that, you fat, gluttonous oinker?"

His fear subsiding, Jesse finished Johanek's chalice of Campens Rose'. He then removed the bottle's cork and hastily swigged it. Knowingly, he ignored the humility he suffered from a debilitating phobia of water.

Jesse's beloved clothing, custom-made from a eunuch tailor in Corapal, was ruined. *Blast it!* Never would he make a good impression on the ladies, arriving at the brothel in such a deplorable shape.

My hat? Where's my hat?

Jesse reached into the bloody bathwater, and searched for his cherished Cavalier hat. He sobbed, realizing that it was damaged beyond repair. Wiping tears from his cheeks, he smelled the foul stench of defeat, even in victory. He had spent a fortune on his splendid apparel, and now it was destroyed!

Jesse removed the dagger from Johanek's chest, then slipped it into the sheath. He was alive, but at what cost? Jesse screeched like a madman, and caught the attention of those servants he let live, within the stone fortress.

Priding himself on his appearance, Jesse refused to wear cheap rags. Habitually, he lived beyond his means by purchasing only the finest duds, the best wines, and nights in bawdy houses. The only available clothes belonged to the bulbous pig Jesse had just slain. They were far too large and unsophisticated for his discreet tastes. Why, it was absurd to enter a sporting woman's parlor, dressed in a peasant's wool shirt and breeches that irritated his soft, delicate skin!

The evening was scrubbed! Though Jesse would be paid handsomely for this job, was it fair compensation for the loss of such pretty things?

Needing a target in which to vent his rage, Jesse repeatedly knifed the stuffed abarbeaus, until it was nothing but a ragged mess standing in the corner of Johanek's leisure area. Releasing a tirade of obscenities, he stormed from the fortress. *Slosh, slosh, slosh* went his shoes as he left the treasured Cavalier hat on a drab tile floor.

2

In a village with no name, on the Embrian-Branellian border, Yuri hid in a narrow ditch. His main concern now was treating a severe gash in his right thigh. A brisk wind swept in from a nearby canyon. Yuri tore open his breeches to examine the wound, which left a significant blood trail behind him.

It was a miracle that Yuri had crawled as far as he did, a mile from where a Branellian infantryman sent a knife into his leg. Yuri answered this aggression by then cutting the Branellian's head off. Ripping his shirt into thin strips, he tied a tourniquet around the injured leg, and bandaged it.

Yuri doubted whether he'd survive the brittle cold of early morning. There was no escape with the coming daylight, where he'd be target practice for archers on both sides.

Yuri was surrounded by dismembered bodies in the hazy moonlight, and the smell was atrocious. He risked passing out, freezing to death, or getting mauled by the dogs and buzzards who feasted upon the deceased from that night's battle.

Yuri appeared much younger than his fifteen years. His long, wavy blonde hair, soft voice, and effeminate nature made those he met wonder if he really was a boy. Turned away from a family who viewed him as "undesirable," Yuri was sold into bondage as a body servant to a cruel Embrian landlord. The landlord and his drunken friends took pleasure in mistreating the sensitive youngster.

One night, as the landlord played chess with a neighbor, Yuri murdered them both with a garden trowel. That next day, he made quick work of the constable and deputies sent to detain him. Over the following two weeks, Yuri was hunted like an animal, by those ordered to kill him on sight.

For twice what Embrian law enforcement was paying for Yuri's demise, a fisherman sold him to an Army officer named Maliek, who assembled a group of teens to handle the nation's dirty work. Like Jesse, Yuri was trained as an assassin at an unnamed school, in a remote corner of Embrey.

Yuri couldn't take the mischief and bullying his schoolmates meted him. Regarded as a sissy, he responded to his fellows' pranks and insults with fits of anger and crying. He was especially vulnerable, when it was discovered that he had a crush on a fellow trainee of the same gender.

Yuri finally lashed out and nearly killed another student. He was rated as too unstable and unpredictable by the instructors. Even Captain Maliek, who claimed never to fear anyone, was intimidated by Yuri's "unhinged mind."

Two days after being expelled, Yuri attempted to save the one man who gave him his walking papers. This, without the proper authorization. Held hostage by the Branellians, Maliek was to taken to Kentworth for interrogation and eventual execution.

Yuri was not alone in this suicide mission. The school chose fourteen-year-old Tim to reclaim Maliek.

Despite his removal from the school, Yuri volunteered to join Tim in the assignment. Was this to redeem himself, win back Maliek's good graces, or prove his worth to those who scorned him?

Or, as Tim suspected, to die alongside the object of his affections?

With the odds stacked against them, Yuri and Tim slowly worked their way through the Branellians' defenses. By stealth and distraction, they carved up any and all enemy soldiers unfortunate enough to get in the way. A Yuri staged a diversion, Tim sneaked through the Branellians' formidable barriers. In time, he spotted Maliek tied to a hitching post, and quickly removed him from harm's way.

Yuri paid for his loyalty to Embrey with a wound to his leg, administered by sharp Branellian steel.

Yuri was left to die. He'd earn no gratitude or thanks for his efforts. There would be no memory or proof of his existence, no gravestone to mark his passing, or kindhearted words on his behalf. Never would he be described as a hero. No one was to know of his sacrifices.

What heroism or sacrifices? Like all disciples of Maliek, Yuri was expected to kill himself, rather than surrendering.

Beneath the full moon Yuri cowered in a cold, muddy ditch. Did he have the courage to run a sword through his own beating heart? That was preferable to going off his head in pain, fear, or delirium. It was only a matter of time before the Branellians captured Yuri.

In truth, he deserved to die.

How many men had Yuri killed? Too many! Contemplating suicide, Yuri heard the sounds of mounted soldiers coming his way.

Yuri was surprised to see a contingency of armed Embrian warriors, escorting an overweight diplomat in his early fifties who traveled by open coach. Behind the contingency, their Branellian counterparts protested the two assassins' grisly raid, which took place during a meeting involving a prisoner exchange.

The diplomat caught sight of Yuri. "Who are you?" he asked, in curiosity and concern.

In a high-pitched voice and thick Kuschan accent, Yuri answered, "I'm just a boy, sir! I got lost, and the Branellians, they . . . they hurt me real bad!"

The diplomat, an Embrian Councillor named Theo, ordered a couple of soldiers to assist Yuri. Noting the weaponry that Yuri had on him, Theo gathered that the boy was not the innocent little lamb he so claimed to be.

Theo took pity on Yuri, and intended to hire him as a personal bodyguard. A lifelong bachelor, he also required an heir for the fortune he garnered over the years.

Though neither realized it at the time, Theo would come to accept Yuri as his adopted son . . .

"Young man?" a coachman said, shaking Yuri from a dreamlike trance. "Young man?"

"Y-yes?" stuttered Yuri, rubbing his tired eyes. "What? . . ."

The coachman smiled. "This is your stop."

Yawning, Yuri fetched a single bag at his feet, then stepped outside to a warm, sunny autumn day. Entering a dusty country road leading to a friend's home, he overheard a few passengers in the stagecoach whispering behind his back.

Walking at a steady pace, Yuri contemplated the "services" he provided his stepfather. Theo's idealism, speeches, and rulings were the ire of political rivals who sought to eliminate the legislator. As Theo granted him an appreciation of justice, altruism, and liberty, Yuri hoped to move beyond his violent tendencies.

However, his violent tendencies still came in handy, whenever Theo's life or interests were at risk.

By foot, Yuri came to a Kuschan house of faith, sitting on the outskirts of Sykes. The humble church, built from cottonwood and pine logs, sat near a dense forest. It held a meager congregation of fifty loyal followers.

Sitting down in a pew, Yuri awaited the pastor who resided in the backrooms with his wife and three children. There, he studied a painting above the church podium. The artwork depicted the unending battle between good and evil, involving the many human forms to assume the identity of the *Kued*. In the painting, the Kued was portrayed as a young male, pure even in his nudity, to die at the hands of an evil winged deity, the *Soraq*. Upholding a pledge to protect humanity the Kued perished, only to be resurrected by the highest authority in the Universe, the *Kuen*.

The Kued filled an esteemed, yet tragic role. Like the boy in the painting, impaled on Soraq's bloody sword, his devotion was placed upon the salvation of all mankind.

Similar to the Kued, Kuschans believed they were on Earth to protect others.

Yuri wondered if his work to Embrey, first to Captain Maliek, then to Councillor Theo, was worthy of the Kuen. Souls were easily possessed by Soraq. Were Yuri's deeds pleasing only to the source of misery and sorrow in the world? What if he died battling a foe, without redemption from the Kuen, or gaining respect in the hearts of his peers?

"Yuri," addressed Pastor Dimitri, leaving his quarters. He was a tall, handsome man with a thick, dark mustache and a black robe. Although Yuri rarely attended spiritual meetings, Dimitri treated him as a full-fledged church member.

"How are you, my friend?" inquired Dimitri.

Yuri sprinted into Dimitri's arms.

"Where have you been?" asked Dimitri, in the Kuschan language. "I haven't seen you in ages!"

"My father sent me to a leadership seminar at the University of Embrey," answered Yuri, also in Kuschan.

"Outstanding! Those of your social class benefit from that level of discipline."

Yuri said nothing. His 'social class' was purely accidental. He wasn't born into prestige, nor did he earn his status as a Councilor's son.

Once the two rested in a front pew, Dimitri asked, "When are you coming to dinner? My wife Yana would love to have you break bread with us, and our children absolutely adore you."

"Thank you." Yuri bit his bottom lip. "Dimitri . . . does Yana know what I do for a living?"

"If she did, you'd never be allowed through the door." Dimitri patted Yuri's knee. "Still, we Kuschans must stick together. Yana rarely speaks our language. We're Embrians now, or so she tells me. My wife forbids the kids to speak Kuschan, and she'll lay into me for speaking it with you, today."

Yuri snickered.

"I pray that your father's diplomatic ties with Kusch, along with your adoption, builds a stronger bridge to our homeland," said Dimitri. "You carry a tremendous weight upon your shoulders. I'm flattered that you came to visit me this morning."

"We'll always be friends." Yuri knew Dimitri since he was a small child in St. Alexandrov, Kusch's capital city. "I've always wondered . . . why did you choose to become a preacher?"

Dimitri smiled. "I didn't choose to become a preacher. It chose me. Those believing in the Kuen obey Him whenever He calls on us."

"Do you believe you'll make it into Paradise?"

"I don't know, Yuri. I'm trying! I've never been in a position to lay down my life for others. But that's not the only path to everlasting life. For example, feeding the hungry also defends those in need."

Yuri swallowed, nervously. "Do you think *I'll* enter Paradise?"

"It's not for me to say. What do you think?"

Yuri frowned. "No."

"Why do you say that?" questioned Dimitri. "Please, Yuri? Self-condemnation is in itself a sin."

"I've murdered people." Yuri looked away from Dimitri. "Lots of people."

"What you and I have done in the past stays in the past," said Dimitri, secretly. "There's no changing it. What do you hope to accomplish, as Councillor Theo's son? Will you end life, or uphold it?"

Yuri shrugged.

"What you've done isn't necessarily wrong, according to our faith," explained Dimitri. "Occasionally, the Kued was forced to kill, when it was justified for the good of all. Surely, some of your actions were justified."

Justified for the good of all . . .

Yuri wanted to think that he did right by removing evildoers, within Embrey and abroad. The initial thrill and excitement he had while completing an assignment was usually followed by guilt, self-loathing, and remorse. He harbored doubts of his value to the nation, as well as to himself

Justified for the good of all?

"Have you ever killed anyone?" asked Yuri.

"Well no, Yuri, but . . ." Dimitri paused. "Do you love Theo?"

"More than anything!"

"And you will kill again, if it means saving him?"

Yuri shifted uncomfortably in his seat. "I have."

"Theo's a decent man, though I don't agree with everything he says or does. I'm sure he's doing his best for Embrey. You should be proud of him."

"I am."

"Then your willingness to die for your father is honorable to the Kuen."

"What about those things I've done for Captain Maliek?" asked Yuri.

"What were his motives?" asked Dimitri. "What was in his heart?"

"I thought he cared for me."

"But he never stuck up for you when the other boys picked on you," assumed Dimitri.

"He encouraged it!"

Dimitri nodded. "Do you remember Colonel Eisenmann? He attended services here, prior to his death a few months ago. He was on General Gornick's staff when you were trained to . . ." Dimitri sighed. "Well, to do what you do. Maliek was not meant to be saved the night you and Tim entered Branell on his behalf. Tim was brought in to finish him, before vital state secrets were disclosed. For whatever reason, Tim had a change of heart and kept Maliek alive."

"Tim never said anything like that to me!" cried Yuri, in betrayal.

"He wasn't supposed to," said Dimitri. "Everything was taken from Maliek, and he was sent into Branell as a spy. Or so that's what Eisenmann told me."

"How can someone kill for a reason that's not permitted by the Kuen?" asked Yuri. "And how are we to know if it isn't?"

"I haven't experienced the life you have, Yuri, and I can't support everything you've done. Maybe there were some you . . . well, some who shouldn't have died. I can't say. I'm sure you've settled scores against some extremely evil men. With that in mind, perhaps you do meet the Kuen's approval. We've all made mistakes. Even the Kued has erred."

"How?"

"Because the Kued takes on the mind and body of a man, he too is prone to temptation and sin. We're in good company, Yuri."

"Was any of the Kued . . . different?"

"Different, Yuri?"

Yuri hesitated. "Yes. You know . . . *different?*"

Due to his femininity, Yuri was the object of ridicule and intolerance. This issue meant absolutely nothing to Dimitri. "Well, the book never said so, but there's a good chance that a few personifications of the Kued were like you." Dimitri smiled. "You know . . . *different.*"

Yuri thought less of himself for being 'different.' It troubled him knowing that Dimitri was aware of it.

"The Kuen created everything we see and hear," said Dimitri. "He created you and me. If it's the Kuen's plans for you to be 'different,' so be it. Accept it, Yuri. Accept yourself."

Yuri released a deep breath, and got to his feet. "I have to meet Father at *Luigi's,*" he sighed. "I'm so glad we had a chance to talk."

"It's my pleasure," said Dimitri, as he embracing Yuri. "My door's open to you, day and night."

"Thank you," answered Yuri.

Walking Yuri outside, Dimitri said, "Stop by anytime, and let us know when you can come to dinner. Remember, we Kuschans must stick together . . ."

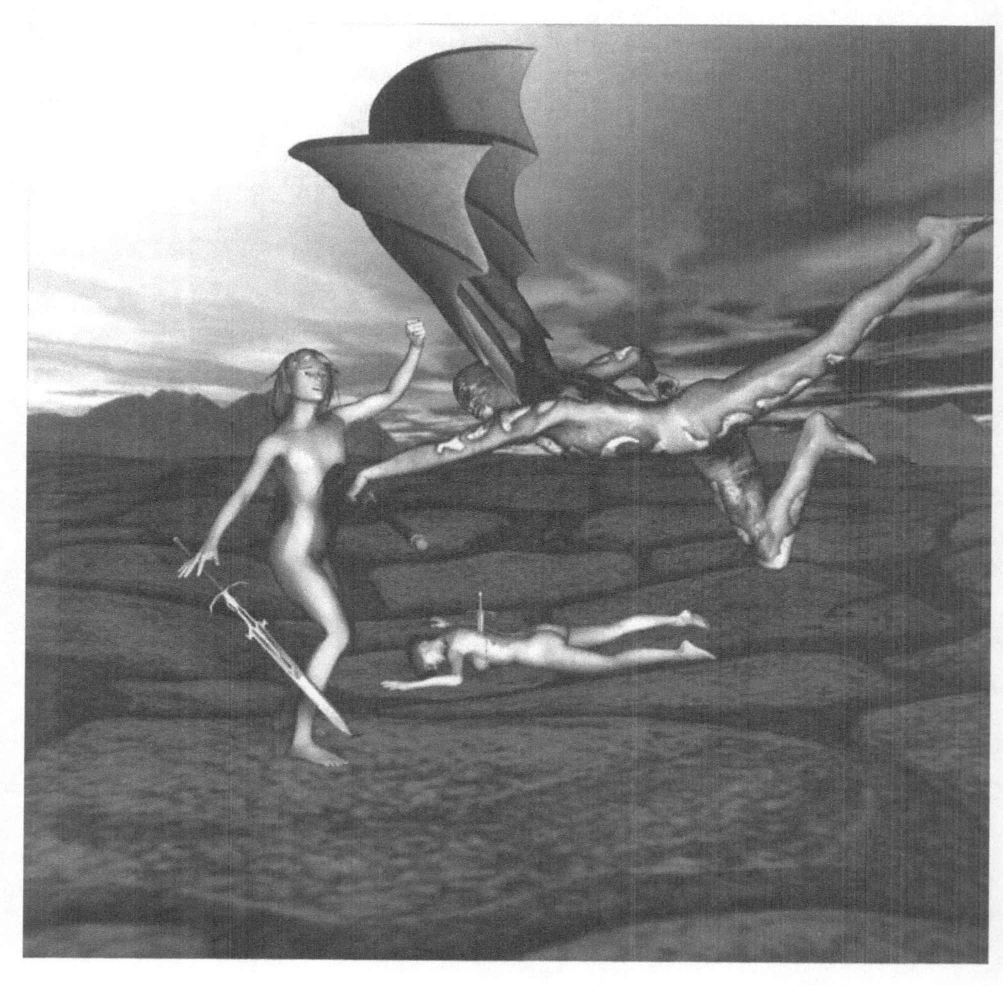

3

"So, the majority of your men lost their lives on Insula Infernus?" asked General Chang, chairman of the military tribunal.

"That is correct, sir," answered the defendant, Major Kohl.

"And, according to your own statement," said Chang, skimming through the indictment before him, "many of these fatalities occurred minutes after landing on the island's eastern shores."

"That is correct," repeated Kohl, nervously.

Chang continued. "And, according to your statement, these men were attacked by . . . pink simians."

Kohl's answer was drowned out by uproarious laughter and shouting.

Striking his gavel to the long, oak table, Chang called for order.

Even with charges of cowardice and perjury ranged against him, Major Kohl was among the most handsome and distinguished men in the courtroom. He stood six-five, with a trim, robust figure. Though his goatee featured more salt than pepper, he still had a full head of hair. His dark, blue beret rested upon one knee. His jacket boasted an eight-pointed star at the left shoulder, and was spotless. His tight fitting breeches were tucked into a pair of polished, black leather boots.

"Answer the question!" demanded Chang, an aging, potbellied man with a shiny, bald scalp. "Were these soldiers killed by pink simians?"

"They were . . . more red or purple . . . the *simians*, I mean," said Kohl, struggling to ignore the muffled giggling in the courtroom."Sir, please understand me . . . Those beasts were ferocious! My men were attacked from the trees and brush . . ."

"Do you expect us to believe that crap?" snapped General Gornick, a tall, bearded man sitting at Chang's right. "How stupid do you think we are?"

"With all due respect, General Gornick," interrupted Admiral Kraig, who presided at Chang's left. "I wish to hear Major Kohl's testimony."

"*Huh!*" barked Gornick. "You wish to make more excuses for your brother's damned, idiotic blunders!"

Kraig found himself in a predicament. Major Kohl was his older brother! Both men had spent their adult lives in the Embrian military. Kraig worked his way through the ranks to become the chief naval adviser to King Ogden. Highly respected and well decorated, he had the scars to prove his valor and courage.

Ten years older than Kraig, Kohl's wartime exploits rendered mixed results. Possessing a commanding presence prior to combat, he was notorious for retreating in minor skirmishes.

"I too wish to hear Major Kohl's testimony," ruled Chang. "You may continue, Admiral Kraig."

Kraig ran his fingers through his thick mustache and sideburns, and asked, "You also testified to a tribe of . . . winged men."

"That is true, sir," said Kohl, the courtroom's sweltering, claustrophobic atmosphere agonizing him. The long, rectangular room lacked windows. Iron candle lanterns, lining the four walls, lit the darkened space. There were more onlookers than usual at this hearing. Due to limited seating, several witnesses stood.

Kohl dealt with countless rivals throughout his military career. Many held important positions within the Ministry of War. Kohl despised few greater than the aristocratic Lieutenant Salazar, sitting behind General Chang. Salazar was decked out in a flashy Equestrian gear, his pencil-thin mustache well-trimmed and groomed. Born into wealth and privilege, his family owned and operated *Romero's,* one of the country's largest distilleries. Salazar had not yet tasted the harsh realities of combat, yet regarded himself as a master technician.

Kohl wanted to wipe the smarmy grin from Salazar's face. *Too bad the upstart wasn't with me on Infernus!*

This hearing began at six in the morning, and soon became an ordeal as everyone grew tired and restless. The courtroom was locked within the winding corridors of the War Ministry. During sultry, autumn days, it felt like a sauna.

"The tribunal will carefully examine the transcripts of this hearing," said Chang, believing it was Kohl's ineptitude and cowardice, while facing a hostile tribe in uncharted territory, which led to a massacre. No one, including Admiral Kraig, bought into stories of carnivorous monkeys or men with wings.

With a final strike of the gavel, the courtroom erupted in loud conversation as the crowd dispersed.

Despite their differences, Kraig wanted nothing more than to sit down over drinks with Kohl, discuss their childhood, and have a few laughs. It was not to be. Kraig thought it best to distance himself from his older brother. Clearly, Kohl had gone too far this time! He'd pay with his dismissal from the Army, an extended prison term, or *(regrettably!)* death by hanging.

Kohl left the stand, searching for a way to clear his tarnished reputation. As he stepped toward the exit, few made eye contact with him. He couldn't blame Chang or Kraig for their rulings. His account of this expedition of Infernus was out of reach for a mature, stable mind.

General Gornick was another story. Kohl never liked the hothead to begin with. Gornick's new uniform gave Kohl further reason to dislike him. Embrian Army officers usually wore stars on their tunics, similar to the one on Kohl's. Gornick came to the hearing wearing a symbol of a rattlesnake slithering around a sword. Proudly thrusting his chest out, he made sure everyone had a view of the insidious image.

Kohl turned to his one friend and companion, Sergeant Vix. "You might think about hitching your wagon to another star," he suggested, gravely.

"No, sir," said Vix, a burly soldier sporting a thick, black beard. "You told the truth. A man can't ask nothing more than that, from nobody."

Leaving the Ministry of War, Kohl and Vix mounted their horses and rode through the bustling avenues of Sykes. As they passed homes and businesses, citizens smiled and tipped their hats, unaware of Kohl's private and professional difficulties. The two soldiers kept at a steady pace, admiring the auburn colors and fall foliage.

Twenty years before, during a campaign waged against the Branellians in the Wilderness, Vix's arm was badly wounded by a machete. As infection set in, Vix grew feverish and delirious. Kohl moved Vix to a remote cave and stayed with him for more than a week. This, even with frigid temperatures and their foes' strength and proximity.

"Do ya think Chang or Kraig'll convict ya?" asked Vix.

"Don't get your hopes up," said Kohl, fearfully. "Come Monday, I'll dance a sweet little jig in the air, as my neck snaps."

"We'll swing together," responded Vix, angered at Kohl's joke. "Who says you'll get the death penalty? For all we know, you'll have to resign your commission, or get busted down to second . . ."

"I'm too old to be a gold bar lieutenant. And I'd rather die, than turn in my sword!"

Vix questioned if the major would back it up with stronger deeds and actions.

"You're a good soldier, Sergeant Vix," said Kohl, "and I don't want you jeopardizing your life any further. But I need your help. Are you man enough to go back to Infernus with me?"

Vix shook his head. "Why the hell you wanna do that, for?"

"If I . . . if *we* return safely home with a few specimens, I can prove my case in court."

"What kinda specimens? Them damn apes who pounced on us?"

"Yes, if I have to," said Kohl, unflinchingly.

Vix spit upon the cobblestone street. "You mean if *I* have to."

"Councillor Theo's offering to finance another trip to Infernus."

"Theo? Hell, I can't trust him, Major."

"Why not?" argued Kohl. "I've known Theo since we were boys. Not to mention that we're both living under his roof, if you haven't forgotten."

"Why's he gonna pay for another trip?"

Kohl laughed. "I told him there's a bundle of precious stones, hidden somewhere in the island's interior."

Vix sighed. "Look sir, we barely got outa there the last time, if you haven't forgotten. And just who do ya figure's dumb enough to come with us?"

Kohl shook his head, in disgust. "Fine, I'll go it alone."

"The hell you will!"

"You won't return to Infernus, and neither should I?" Kohl glared at Vix. "Damn it, I have to go!"

Vix and Kohl rode in silence until they reached *Luigi's,* a popular diner near the banks of the Ember River. Eight months out of the year, the restaurant sat beneath tarpaulins, allowing patrons to enjoy the pleasant weather. In the winter, Luigi's conducted their business in a large canvas tent. Dismounting from his horse, Kohl said, "I'm buying."

"No, sir," argued Vix.

"That's an order. It may be the last honorable thing I do for you."

The two men met their host, Councillor Theo, in one corner of the diner. Leaving home at fourteen, Theo enlisted as a merchant marine. Throughout his travels, he developed a knack for dialects and languages, and an appreciation for other cultures. He spent his free time studying, and was proficient in math and writing. He soon captained his own vessel, hauling goods from the Far East around the Horn of Actin. His wealth came from starting a publishing company in Embrey. Starting on a modest scale, he translated and published literature from around the globe.

Theo stood as he greeted Kohl and Vix. While Kohl shook Theo's hand with a tight, firm grip, Vix behaved coldly. As the trio sat down, a violinist played a medley of Embrian folk ballads and love songs. Several waiters dashed back and forth, tending to their customers. "How was your inquiry?" asked Theo.

"Not good," answered Kohl. "Not only did I have to put up with Gornick's badgering, I also had to cope with his sniveling little toady, Salazar."

"My proposal still stands," said Theo. "The same for you, Sergeant Vix. Give me the word, and I'll arrange passage and asylum for you, in Kusch."

"I've served the Army my entire life," said Kohl. "How can you ask me to leave the country, at this uncertain time?"

"Time may become even more uncertain," said Theo, "if Gornick has his way."

"Gornick," mumbled Kohl, disparagingly.

"Don't underestimate Gornick," warned Theo. "He's a very dangerous man. King Ogden thinks that Gornick's his lapdog. I see it the other way around. Once Ogden's back is turned, Gornick will move against him."

"Do you think Ogden can be usurped?" asked Kohl.

"I haven't spoken to His Highness in over a week," said Theo, sarcastically. "Our noble monarch alternates between his admiration of young boys, and making tearful confessions to that hypocrite Karl, from Lord Kelly's Academy. He has no idea how weak he truly is. If worse comes to worse, it'll spell the end to free speech, religious tolerance, and . . ."

"Your publishing ventures," snickered Kohl.

"Yes," said Theo, pointedly, "and *your* life, Major Kohl."

Theo's tense words wiped the smile from Kohl's face.

"You figure we oughta head back to Infernus?" Vix asked Kohl. "We oughta stay here and keep Gornick from taking over."

To retain a friend's good graces, Kohl said, "Gornick won't take over, as long as Councillor Theo's here to stop him."

"Yeah," said Vix. "As long as Theo's *still* here to stop him."

"Father!" someone called out, as the three men looked up to see a teenager approaching the table.

"Yuri!" cheered Theo. "My dear boy, I've missed you!"

"I missed you too," said Yuri, throwing his arms around Theo.

"I'm Major Kohl," the officer introduced, standing. "This is Sergeant Vix."

The boy shook Kohl's hand. "I'm Yuri."

"I'd like you to meet Yuri, my adopted son." Theo ran his hair through the lad's long, blond hair.

"Good lord," gasped Kohl. "He could pass for an angel."

Yeah, thought Vix. A fallen angel. Yuri was very attractive, indeed *pretty*. At first, Vix didn't know if Yuri was a boy or a girl. Yuri moved with the grace and poise of a gymnast or ballet dancer. The tiny voice and baby-face were deceptive. Yuri's hands suggested one unaccustomed to hard, manual labor. "I'm Vix," the sergeant spoke, hesitantly.

"I've heard many good things about you, Sergeant Vix," said Yuri.

Was Yuri's comment a sign of respect, or taken as a challenge? "What do they say about you?" asked Vix, unnerved by the boy's presence.

"Gentlemen, please!" said Theo. "Sit down, sit down! I sent Yuri to a leadership seminar at the University of Embrey. I expect great things from him."

Theo criticized Ogden for his "admiration of young boys." Vix wondered what the unmarried legislator gained from his companionship to Yuri.

"I assume you men refuse political asylum in Kusch," asked Theo, placing an egg roll in his mouth.

"Yes, sir," answered Kohl. "If I have to run, I'd rather make a second expedition to Infernus."

His eyes fixated on a freighter carrying imports into Port Sinclair, Theo recalled his days as a sailor on a similar vessel. "Have you recruited sufficient men for your adventure?"

Kohl loosened his collar. "Well . . . not yet."

"'Not yet'?" questioned Theo, harshly.

Vix gave Kohl an expression, as if to say *I told you so.*

"What if I raise a mercenary army for you?" asked Theo.

"I don't trust mercenaries or pirates," responded Kohl.

Theo laughed. "I don't care if you trust them or not, Major Kohl! I'm paying for this expedition, and I have the right to . . ."

"I'll go," said Yuri.

"What? . . . What did you say, Yuri?" stuttered Theo.

"I'll go," repeated Yuri. "Father, you say we should always accept challenges, if it's for a good reason."

Before Vix or Theo voiced their disapproval, Kohl praised Yuri. "That's the spirit! If I had two dozen men with your courage, I'd . . ."

"Out of the question," interrupted Theo, bluntly.

"That's right!" agreed Vix. "We can't go takin' no kids!"

"Why not?" asked Kohl, angrily. "If Yuri's man enough to come with me, I say . . ."

"Victory to Gornick!" someone shouted from the diner's north entrance.

A teenage boy, lacking a shirt, burst into Luigi's with a saber. The next seconds were surreal, as if to derive from a phantasm. Moments after his arrival, the teen decapitated a maitre d'.

Luigi's erupted into mass chaos, as the maitre d' dropped onto a table. Patrons ran in all directions, screaming. Before anyone stopped him, the teen laughingly split a female customer's head open. Blood and brains splattered upon his face and chest.

Lifting the saber above him, the teen turned to Kohl and Theo. Cowering like a scared rabbit, Kohl ducked under a table. Grabbing Kohl's arm, Theo swiftly dragged him away.

Vix drew his own weapon, a sword more than a yard long. Not fearing for his own safety, he dashed toward the crazed teen. "Drop the blade," he ordered, "or find yourself a head shorter!"

In the confusion, Yuri disappeared in the frightened crowd. Seconds later, his shrill voice sounded from the kitchen. "It's clear this way!" he called, urgently. "Hurry, Father, hurry!"

The crazed teen acted as if Vix wasn't even there. Pursuing Kohl and Theo, he was joined by two more armed youngsters. With a single-minded goal of fulfilling his sinister goals, the first teen failed when Vix gutted him. Staring at Vix in shock and denial, the first teen dropped to the ground. Theo led Kohl to the kitchen, as the other killers followed after them.

Vix watched as Yuri leaped through the air, like a cat chasing a mouse. Brandishing a dagger, Yuri slashed the second killer from groin to brisket. Without pausing, he then targeted the third killer.

The second killer shrieked while his entrails spilled onto mortified onlookers. Vix impaled him through the killer's heart, to get him out of his misery.

Moments later, Yuri's dagger found its mark in the third killer's lungs.

As the third teen released his weapon, gore splashed onto Yuri's clothing.

Attempting to speak, bright red bubbles gurgled from the teen's lips. As Yuri pulled the dagger back, the teen collapsed across a bench. Struggling to regain his weakened balance, the teen took a few clumsy steps to the bar, then fell dead.

Yuri and Vix glanced at each other. There was no point in explanations. Yuri had to prevent the three killers from slaying Kohl and Theo.

Justified for the good of all . . .

Though he never met him, Vix heard a good deal about Captain Maliek. He despised the notorious officer, as did many enlisted men in the military. Boys got no place in war! Yuri should have been home, helping his pa in the fields, or stirring his mama's buttermilk in the kitchen. "You was a Maliek boy," Vix accused. "Wasn't ya?"

"I don't know what you're talking about," mumbled Yuri.

"Get outa here," said Vix, tiredly. "I'll stay here 'til the law shows up."

Yuri whispered, "If anyone asks, you were the one to . . ."

"Get outa here!" ordered Vix. *"Get!"*

Yuri did as he was told.

As the commotion died down, few remained in Luigi's. The distraught employees mourned the maitre d', as a man wept over his wife's body.

Vix had witnessed so much violence and bloodshed in the Army, it became routine and commonplace. Those events happened on the battlefield, between warring nations. The citizens in Luigi's had no idea what was coming, and were undeserving in their fate. Vix considered on beheading the three young killers, for no reason than to vent his anger.

Major Kohl was nowhere in sight. Even with his posturing and rousing speeches, he often disappeared in a crisis.

Spitting upon one of the teens, Vix reevaluated his debt to Kohl. He was fortunate that the major had aided him, two decades back. But, at what point should he decide that he had repaid Kohl in full, then move on?

The three killers weren't probably a day older than fifteen or sixteen. Why were they filled with so much hatred? Why did they kill, randomly, without regard to human decency? Were they also graduates of Maliek's teachings? One thing was for certain. Vix remembered the words the first killer spoke, prior to his onslaught.

Victory to Gornick.

Vix noted a tattoo on one of the killer's shoulder, a cryptic image of a rattlesnake, slithering around a sword . . .

The steeple bells of Lord Kelly's Academy announced the hour of two in the afternoon. Scores of boys harvested the vast garden next to a three-story dormitory. It was a hot September day.

Occasionally, a few lads stripped naked to swim in the cool, swift waters of the adjoining Ember River. Lord Kelly's Administrator, Leader Karl, disapproved of this activity. Luckily he was away, and placed Leader Sven in charge. As a boy, Sven also basked in the winding tributary, while tending the acres of corn, spuds, and grapes. This produce was used for commerce, or supplied Lord Kelly's flock in the wintertime.

Among Lord Kelly's one-hundred-and-sixty students was Brother Bradley. At the age of sixteen, Bradley had fair skin, dishwater blonde hair, and a thin, slight physique. Entering the fraternity as an infant, he never knew his biological kin. Along with his schoolmates, he wore a brown skullcap, sandals, and a long-sleeved tunic draping a few inches above his bare shins and knees. The tunic's buckle and chest featured the school's insignia, a gold octagon featuring hands clasped together in fellowship. Bradley also sported a brass necklace of the symbol, a beloved gift from Leader Karl.

Bradley delivered a basketful of corn for Brother Trevor to shuck. At thirteen, Trevor's height already matched Bradley's. His curly, dark hair covered both ears. A newcomer, Trevor wasn't used to the hard work of Lord Kelly's daily routine. In the shade of a pine tree, he was slow in his chores and got buried in corn.

"Lagging behind?" asked Bradley, mischievously.

"It's too hot to work!" griped Trevor, wiping his sweaty brow. "How much longer do I gotta? . . ."

"Until sundown," said Bradley. Tossing his cap next to Trevor, he slipped off his sandals, then removed his tunic and silk undergarment, shaped as a loincloth. "I'm going in for a dip. Join me?"

Trevor turned away from Bradley's nude body, and blushed. "Uh-uh, I ain't taking my clothes off!"

"C'mon, Trev!" laughed Bradley. "It's just us guys!"

"What if girls catch us?"

"We're behind a ten-foot, rock wall! How can anyone see us?"

Trevor pointed at a two-tiered passenger boat, gliding along the vast waterway. As it passed by, more than a dozen travelers turned their attention to the students of Lord Kelly's.

This wasn't the first time Bradley got caught in his birthday suit. The vessel was more than two-hundred yards away, and moving at a swift, steady pace. Cupping his groin, Bradley figured they couldn't see much, anyway.

Bradley sprinted to the river. A number of boys were already in the water as he shouted, "Ready or not, here I come!" then jumped in with a thunderous *splash!* This impact disturbed other bathers, and even drenched a few lads toiling in the nearby garden.

"Hey!" protested Brother Andre who, at fourteen, shared similar traits with Bradley as hair and eye color. Bradley capsized him, as he floated peacefully with the current.

"Sorry!" apologized Bradley, with a grin.

"You ain't supposed to be in here, boy!" complained Andre. "Get out and go slave some more!"

"Me?" argued Bradley. "You never did an honest day's work in your life, *boy.*"

"'Ready or not, here I come!'" someone laughed, then dunked Bradley.

One moment, Bradley's head was above water. The next, he caught murky sights of his friends' legs and loins. Fighting to break free from his captor, Bradley flailed helplessly as, twice more, his head was shoved into the depths. Everyone laughed at him. "Stop it!" he cried, exhaling water from his nose and mouth. Rubbing his eyes, he looked around to see who had nailed him.

"Cool off?" chuckled Fritz, swimming away.

The same age as Bradley, Fritz was among the tallest kids at Lord Kelly's. His sinewy arms, legs, and chest made him appear as an Embrian version of *Adonis.* Even with the deep-set eyes and ruddy complexion, Fritz was quite handsome.

"Jerk," mumbled Bradley, dragging his skinny, pale shell from the water. Fritz had ruined this brief recess. It was just as well. Bradley's time and talent were needed by Giorgio, who chatted quietly with Trevor. "Good afternoon," he said, shivering, his skin pocked by goose bumps.

That morning, Giorgio had replaced his skimpy, immodest tunic for the more majestic robe, befitting his status as a Leader-Trainee at Lord Kelly's. His clothing resembled the Brothers' uniform, but flowed clear to the ankles. A foot taller than Bradley, Giorgio was eighteen, with brown hair, an olive complexion, and a pointy nose. He looked sophisticated and regal in his new clothing. "Nice," commented Bradley, enviously.

"Thanks," said Giorgio. "Too bad Karl's kind of mad at me."

"How come?"

"Even with a vote of confidence from the other Leaders, Karl opposed my promotion," explained Giorgio. "He disapproves of my friendship with Councillor Theo. I really want to stay at Lord Kelly's, but Karl's making it difficult!"

"Well, I want you to stay, too," said Bradley.

Giorgio sighed. "If this Leadership thing doesn't work out, Theo's offering me an internship with the Embrian Council."

Bradley was aware of Giorgio's pacifism. The Leader-Trainee's parents died as a result of the Border War. His father perished in battle, while his mother was executed for sheltering Branellian spies. A dedicated follower of Councillor Theo, Giorgio regularly attended the legislator's rallies, and was a frequent guest at his home.

Bradley loved and respected both Karl and Giorgio. Nightly, he prayed they put aside their differences and worked together for the good of Lord Kelly's. "Don't worry," he assured. "Karl will change his mind, when he sees the great job you're doing."

"You think I should stick it out?" asked Giorgio.

Bradley laughed. "I wish I was in your shoes!"

"I hope you're right." Giorgio motioned to the Administrative Building. "We've got another entry for you, Brad."

Among Bradley's obligations were to welcome enrolling students to Lord Kelly's. "Who is he?" he asked, dressing.

"Brother Kenichi," answered Giorgio. "He's waiting at Lord Sven's office."

"Kenichi?"

"He's Caucasian and Oriental," said Giorgio. "Sven thinks he'll be a great secretary, and so do I."

Giorgio and Bradley entered through an arched doorway into the Administrative Building. "I've read some of Kenichi's scrolls when he worked at Lord Charles'," added Giorgio, "and his writing skills are terrific."

The previous secretary, Brother Eli, died weeks before from consuming tainted poultry. His unexpected passing remained an open wound for students and staff, alike.

Giorgio and Bradley passed through a darkened, narrow hallway. Pottery sculptures and idols decorated the walls, sacred images the Brotherhood of Faith Church treated with importance. An older structure, the Administrative Building showed its age. The original logs, forming the inner skeleton, were decaying as the rock and mud skin eroded, then chipped away. Based on the year's income from wine and produce, Leader Karl planned to engage the students in a major restoration project. Bradley looked forward to this job. Not only would he learn a craft, but prove his devotion to Lord Kelly's.

Bradley strolled into Sven's office for his first glimpse of the school's latest disciple. Kenichi was slightly shorter than Giorgio. His dark hair, tied in a ponytail, dangled below the collar and was highlighted in streaks of blonde. Kenichi's frame was razor thin, his legs a chalky white from lack of sunlight. "Good day, Brother Bradley!" greeted Sven, staggering to his feet.

Giorgio and Bradley refused comment on Sven's drunkenness, yet worried that it gave Kenichi the wrong impression. They sought to present Lord Kelly's in the best possible light.

"Brad," slurred Sven. Saliva drooled from the corners of his mouth, into his red beard. "Say hello to Brother Kenichi."

Silence wedged the boys, as Kenichi made no attempt to acquaint himself. Such behavior was expected. New guys usually hesitated to endear themselves. This was often a hint of shyness, or trouble adjusting to a different environment. The boys generally made pals in due time, or remained guarded and reserved. Bradley recalled Trevor's arrival, days before. Separated from elderly grandparents who were no longer able to care for him, Trevor wept during his first evening at the school. He now got along with everyone, and did well in classes.

Bradley was ignorant of Kenichi's background, yet sensed a haunting past. "I'm Brother Brad. It's an honor welcoming you to Lord Kelly's Academy."

"Kenichi," the newcomer spoke, with a limp, lifeless handshake. *"Brother Kenichi."*

"Why don'tcha show Brother Kenichi around?" burped Sven.

"Sure," agreed Bradley. "What dorm room should we move him into?"

"Oh, just throw him with Andre and Bentley," said Sven. "In the basement."

Kenichi rolled his eyes back. "You mean the dungeons," he whispered.

"Brother Eli's old quarters," said Bradley, solemnly.

"That's appropriate," said Sven, "since Kenichi's our new secretary."

"Yeah," reminded Giorgio, "and I need to get my stuff into the Leader's dorm. It's good to meet you, Kenichi. It'll be fun working together."

"Thanks," said Kenichi, finally revealing his pearly whites in a strained smile.

"Follow me," said Bradley, determined to help Kenichi negotiate a smooth transition.

Both Bradley and Kenichi sighed as they left the Administrative Building. "It's nice today," said Bradley.

"Is he always like that?" asked Kenichi.

"Sven?"

"Yeah," said Kenichi, clearing his throat. "Guess I shouldn't say this, but our Leader at Lord Charles' wasn't a . . . a *lush*."

"I've heard of Lord Charles', but where is it?"

"At Lake Mather's, near the base of Mount Patten. It's really small. We only had one Leader. When . . . Lionel died, I got sent here."

"I'm sorry," said Bradley. "Were you guys close?"

"Very!" responded Kenichi. "I don't know where I'd be, without Leader Lionel."

"Where are your folks?"

"I never knew my father. I don't want to know him! Mom died when I was fourteen."

"I'm so sorry, Kenichi," said Bradley. "I never knew my parents, either. What did your mom do to support you?"

Kenichi said nothing.

Bradley noted Kenichi's animosity. "That's okay. It don't matter."

Kenichi was relieved when Bradley didn't pry. His mother looked after him, as best she could. At any rate, no one at Lord Kelly's had to know that his mom was a practitioner in the world's oldest profession.

Not long after Kenichi's fourteenth birthday, an Agronian sailor entered the brothel, requesting a night with an adolescent male. When Kenichi's mother denied access to her son, the sailor murdered her. As the sailor forced Kenichi's pants down, they boy ran a knife between the cretin's ribs.

For the next few months, Kenichi slept in makeshift shelters, sustaining himself on stolen and discarded food. This ended when kindly old Lionel, who shared the Word with a homeless congregation, adopted Kenichi upon enrolling him into Lord Charles' Academy. Lionel taught Kenichi how to collect and translate ancient scriptures. Kenichi now had a surrogate father, a good education, and a reason to carry on.

Bradley gave Kenichi a tour of the facility, which included a chapel, a cafeteria, a cemetery, and two dormitories. Kenichi was uneasy. Lord Kelly's was foreign and inhospitable. It was always tough being "the new guy." However, the stares which Kenichi got from various students made him apprehensive.

Kenichi disliked the community of Sykes, a city boasting a population of more than five-hundred thousand residents. He missed green fields, calm mountain streams, crystal clear lakes, and the sounds of crickets at night. He wanted a home built of wood, with openings to let in fresh air and sunlight. Above all else, Kenichi hated Lord Kelly's uniform! It was humiliating to reveal his skinny thighs, shins, and knees. At Lord Charles', he was provided a full robe.

And though he appreciated the education obtained from his spiritual training, Kenichi doubted the existence of an omnipotent being.

Leading Kenichi into the cramped quarters in the dormitory's clammy basement, Bradley said, "This is where you're staying. I hope it's all right."

"I guess," mumbled Kenichi, accustomed to a room to himself. He now had to share a room with two others!

Thin, straw mattresses rested upon oak chests, pieced together with iron bands. By removing the mattress, the chest became a desk, table, or couch.

Storage, personal items, and blankets were kept in the chest. A small table, single candleholder, and two benches sat in the room's center.

"You'll bunk with Andre and Bentley," said Bradley. "They're brothers . . . *real* brothers, I mean. And they're full of it too, so don't let them get you down."

"Who do you stay with?" asked Kenichi.

"Trevor and Derek," groaned Bradley. Trevor's thirteen, Derry's twelve. I feel like their babysitter."

"Too bad we can't have a room together," said Kenichi, feeling at ease with Bradley.

"You'll really feel that way, after a few days with Andre and Bentley. I'm sorry, Kenichi. It wasn't my idea moving you in here."

Kenichi would be eighteen in less than a year, and gladly bid *adios* to Lord Kelly's. "Well, since I'm your secretary, I'll be too busy to hang around much. I'm only in here to sleep, I guess."

Once more, Bradley shook Kenichi's hand. "It's nice meeting you," he said, pleasantly.

"I'll make the most of it," said Kenichi, his expressions stating otherwise.

"There's still a few hours of sunlight, and I've got to go out and work in the garden. Join me?"

Kenichi yawned. "If I've got any choice in the matter, I'd rather not. I need a little rest. I'm still a bit tired . . . from the long trip."

"The cafeteria opens at four-thirty," said Bradley. "See you there."

"Sure," replied Kenichi. "See you then."

As Bradley left, Kenichi found himself in a chamber of stone, narrow beds, and lousy furnishings. Shaking his head, he surveyed his prospects in this miserable hole. For the most part, he always viewed himself as an outsider. His mixed blood was something of a curse, as he remained uncomfortable with both the Caucasian and Oriental race.

Too 'white' for one, too 'yellow' for the other . . .

Kenichi peeked through the room's single window. There, he viewed his 'Brothers' sweat in the hot afternoon sun. Their beliefs were as distorted as the images through the dusty glass. Certain feeble minds willingly upheld superstitious gospels, while persisting in lowly squalor. Most of these guys were headed toward a dismal future. They'd see only hard labor and poor living conditions, at the mercy of greedy landowners. Their efforts would feed the mouths of those unwilling to share their hardship and misery. Their refuge from such toil came through sex, alcohol, and religion. Likewise, a few would carry a weapon for the King, who cared less if they lived or died. Still, their fates were preferable to long, grueling days at the end of picks, hoes, and shovels.

And yet, what price glory was there in the service of a wicked ruler? Not for me! Kenichi wanted to use his skills for all in need, instead of placing blind faith in an unseen entity.

A huge galley hauled freight to its destination across the Ember River, at Port Auric. In the distance, Kenichi saw the rugged, bald peaks of a mountain range. He yearned to see what lied beyond the steep shards, carved from earth and granite. I'll remove these silly clothes, escape from Lord Kelly's Academy, and paddle my own canoe!

I want to be free!

"Whatcha doing in my room, boy?" a stern voice asked.

Startled, Kenichi turned as two blonde boys strutted into the room. The oldest was around Bradley's height. The youngest was much shorter, with a tiny frame.

These must be the roommates, figured Kenichi. Better get them on my side! "I'm Kenichi," he introduced, smiling nervously.

"I'm Andre," the older boy said. "Who let you in here, boy?"

"I'm your new roomy," said Kenichi.

"You look weird," the smaller kid spoke, his mouth hanging slack.

"Don't listen to Bentley," said Andre. "He's a numbskull."

"I thought you both were," remarked Kenichi.

With a phony snicker, Andre slugged Kenichi's shoulder. "Good one, boy!" he said, disparagingly. "What are you, anyways?"

"A person," answered Kenichi, concealing his anger.

"I meant . . . are you a gook, or what?"

Kenichi held his ground. "What are *you,* boy?"

A bit intimidated with Kenichi's tone, Andre grinned. "Me? I'm just plain white."

Staring at Kenichi, the younger boy repeated, "You look weird."

"You're right, Andre," said Kenichi. "He is a numbskull. Is he 'just plain white,' too?"

"That's Bentley, my kid brother," answered Andre. "Whatcha say your name was again, boy? *'Itchy'?*"

"It's not 'Itchy,'" said Kenichi, tiredly. "And it isn't 'boy.' It's *Kenichi.*"

"Good to know ya, 'Itchy,'" taunted Andre. "And I can tell you're a gook, even if you don't sound like it."

Kenichi's temper flared. "What does that mean?"

"Well, don't your breed say stuff like 'me no like potatoes . . .me eat chop sticks' . . ."

Kenichi squeezed Andre's nose.

"Hey, boy!" screeched Andre. "Le'go!"

"My name's not 'Itchy'!" shouted Kenichi. "And it's not 'boy'! It's *Kenichi!* Got that, *boy?*"

As Kenichi led him around on his tiptoes, Andre's response came out as whines and gibberish. Wearing a blank expression, Bentley stood back with one finger up his nose.

"What's my name?" demanded Kenichi.

"*'Kenichi'!*" cried Andre, his eyes watering. "You filthy, slant-eyed gook son of a . . ."

"What?"

"*'Kenichi'!*" screamed Andre, desperately.

"Good one, boy!" cheered Kenichi, as he finally released Andre.

"What's going on in here?" someone inquired, from the door.

Turning on one heel, Kenichi saw another student of seventeen enter the room. Instead of the common brown, this kid's uniform was a forest green. He had coal-black hair, a tanned complexion, and a stocky build. "What's going on?" he again asked, carrying himself with authority.

"The name's Kenichi!" the new guy said, putting his arm around Andre's shoulder. "Just getting acquainted with my roomy!"

"Yeah," lied Andre, through clenched teeth.

"I'm Brother Geoffrey, your dorm assistant," the kid said, suspiciously.

"Good to meet you," said Kenichi, shaking Geoffrey's hand.

"Have you been shown around Lord Kelly's?" asked Geoffrey.

"Bradley gave me the tour."

"Give Brad my thanks when you see him," said Geoffrey. "If you need anything, I'm in Room Ten, at the end of the hallway. Getting along with your mates? I hope they treat you better than Brother Eli, God rest his soul."

"Oh, they *will,*" snickered Kenichi. "Don't worry about that."

"I help everyone living on this floor," said Geoffrey. "That takes in everything from homework, to daily chores, to girls."

"Yeah, right," whispered Andre.

"Well, I'll let you get back to what you were . . . doing," said Geoffrey, reluctantly leaving the room.

"Watch out for Geoff," advised Bentley. "He's queer."

"How would you know?" asked Kenichi.

Andre sneered at Kenichi. "Later, boy," he said, his cheeks a fiery red.

Kenichi wasn't afraid of these clowns. Still, he dreaded sleeping in the same room as them. Bentley posed no threat. Andre was the ringleader of their shenanigans. Once he earned Kenichi's fear and respect, everything would be fine.

Running his hand through Andre's unruly hair, Kenichi laughed, "Anytime! I'm waiting, *boy!*"

5

"Leader Royce, can me and Trevor go to a play, tonight?'

It was five in the afternoon. As the students dined in the cafeteria, Leader Royce relaxed in the lobby of the Leader's dormitory, penning next Sunday's sermon. Due to Karl's absence, he was drafted into handling the morning service.

Public speaking was not one of Royce's strengths. Quiet as a child, he was ridiculed for a weight problem he carried into adulthood. Despite his shyness, he was a brilliant bass tenor, and never hesitated in staging solo performances on holidays. The advisor for Lord Kelly's Choir, he had a natural talent for music.

In a few short days, Royce was leaving his post in favor of married life. He planned to make a living building cabinets and furniture for his future father-in-law.

Royce had nearly finished the project when Bradley interrupted him. "What did you say, Brad?" he asked, in frustration. "Can you and Trevor *what?*"

"Trevor's never been to a play before," said Bradley, "and I thought maybe we'd go to . . ."

"What does Leader Karl say about that?" asked Royce, his leniency often making waves. "You know his attitude about plays."

"Yeah, but you're not Leader Karl, and he's not here. Please, Royce?"

Royce sighed. "Brad . . . Karl will have my hide for this!"

"Oh, c'mon! Please!"

Royce rolled his eyes back. "What does Sven think about you attending this production?"

"I didn't ask. I think he passed out in his room."

"Imagine that," said Royce.

"Karl thinks that plays are nothing but dirty talk and sex. He's never even been to the theater!"

"Yes, but he's Leader Karl." Royce sipped his herbal tea. "So, what's the play about, and where's it held?"

"At the Falcon Theatre. It's a historical drama by Sir Roland Knox. *King Auric IV.*"

"Yes, but what's the play about?" asked Royce, impatiently.

"I just told you! King Auric IV, and his victory over Agron in the Twelfth Century!"

"Yes," said Royce, sarcastically, "with plenty of dirty talk and sex."

"Oh, c'mon Royce!"

"I'll let you go if you keep it a secret," said Royce, who hated being the villain.

"Of course!"

"Shh! It's a secret!"

"Sorry!"

"You may go, on one condition." Royce grinned. "Take Brother Fritz with you."

Bradley gasped. "Brother Fritz?"

"No Brother Fritz," lectured Royce, "no King Auric IV."

"But Fritz's a jerk!"

"He is not a jerk!"

"You wanna bet?"

"Look," breathed Royce. "Try to understand my point of view. Fritz doesn't get invited on many outings."

"Gee, I wonder why."

"I'm shocked," said Royce, appealing to Bradley's concepts of fairness. "I always thought you'd give everyone a break."

"I do!"

"Then give Fritzy a break."

"He never gave me one, Royce."

"Then maybe he will, from now on." Royce stood and patted Bradley's back. "I really don't think Fritz is a bad kid."

"You never seen him in the cafeteria."

"Actually, I *have*." Royce paused. "You know what I think? Fritz's tough-guy act is just that, an act. He bullies everyone around, because he's scared."

"Yeah, well, I'm scared of him," admitted Bradley. It gave him the shivers to be in the same room with the creep. "Do I really gotta take Fritzy with us?"

"Yeah, you really gotta take Fritzy with you," insisted Royce. "The younger boys look up to you. Who knows? Maybe you'll do more to turn old Fritz around than any of the Leaders can pray to accomplish with him."

"But Fritz don't even like me! He's a lost cause!"

"Will you say that, when you're a Leader?" asked Royce. "Then you'll have to deal with a lot of kids like Fritz."

Bradley dreamed of obtaining Leadership status at Lord Kelly's. The job demanded fairness to everyone, despite their pasts or personalities. Some of the Leaders, Karl in particular, habitually violated that rule. "All right," moped Bradley. "But I think it's a dumb idea."

"Oh? Didn't you tell me the other day that you loved everyone here?"

"I love Fritz, but I don't like him."

"Then maybe you will, after tonight." Royce gave Bradley a paternal kiss on the forehead. "I'll miss everyone at Lord Kelly's but somehow I'll really feel your absence. I hope we can write back and forth, and arrange visits during the holidays. It'll be exciting to see what changes you'll bring to the school when you're a Leader. How about it, young man?"

"I'd like that," said Bradley, holding back his tender emotions.

"Tell me how it goes, tonight. Let me know if Fritz gets out of line."

"I will," agreed Bradley. "We'll have fun . . . I *hope*."

As Bradley started to leave, Royce stopped him. "What all do you know about King Auric IV?" he asked.

Bradley shrugged. "Not much, other than he conquered Agron a long time ago."

"That's part of it," said Royce. "Soon after Auric usurped power from Agron's emperor, that nation staged a successful coup against him."

"Really?" asked Bradley. "Bet that's not in the play! So then what happened?"

"He returned to Sykes, but the Embrians didn't want him, either." Royce laughed. "That's when King Ogden's great-grandfather took over."

"Huh," mumbled Bradley. This was a subject few Embrian textbooks covered.

"Legend has it that Auric, along with his mistress and his bodyguards, set sail for Insula Infernus."

"Infernus?" Bradley's curiosity was aroused. "I've heard scary things about that place! What happened when they got there?"

"I don't know. I always wondered if they created a settlement on the island."

"They probably starved to death."

"It'd be Hell on Earth, all right. Still, I wonder if ol' Auric made a go of it."

"Wouldn't we have known about it, by now?"

"Good point, Brad," said Royce. "But, for the sake of an argument, what if Auric's descendants are over there, living as they always had, and they don't want us knowing about it?"

Filling a tray with a boiled potato and bean soup, Kenichi went to a long, narrow table for his first meal in Lord Kelly's cafeteria.

At Lord Charles' Academy. Kenichi was treated as an equal. In Lord Kelly's, everyone either ignored him or made small talk behind his back. Unable to spot Bradley anywhere, Kenichi kept a stiff upper lip and sat alone, near one end of a corner table. Food tasted better without chatter, anyway.

"Hey there, boy!" called Andre, sitting next to Kenichi.

Kenichi frowned.

"*Kenichi,*" said Andre, apologetically. "I don't mean nothing by calling you 'boy.' I do that with everybody."

"Okay," said Kenichi, grudgingly. "How's the nose?"

Andre snickered. "I had that one coming. Reckon we got off on the wrong foot. I thought it over, boy . . . *man.* Y' know what, buddy? We'll be laughing this over, sure enough!"

"Sure enough," groaned Kenichi.

Once Bentley placed himself to his left, Kenichi felt trapped between two dimwits.

"So, where you from?" asked Andre.

"The Earth," answered Kenichi.

"Good one, boy! . . . Itchy! . . . *Kenichi!*"

"I was born in a small town called Marks," said Kenichi. "For the last few years, I went to school at Lord Charles'."

"A lot of your breed in Marks?" asked Andre.

"My 'breed'?" questioned Kenichi.

"Aw, you know." Andre slanted his eyes. "Folks like that."

"No," answered Kenichi, circling his eyes with his thumbs and forefingers. "Almost everyone's like *that . . .*"

"Our daddy was a ship's captain," said Bentley, biting into a carrot stick.

"Too bad," said Kenichi. "Did he sink?"

"No," answered Bentley, unaware of Kenichi's sarcasm. "We heard he got caught by pirates and was hunged."

"We were supposed to go live with our Aunt Imogene," said Andre, "but she didn't want us."

"I can imagine how she felt," said Kenichi, turning to the younger boy. "So tell me, *Bent.* Do I still look weird, or are you over that?"

"No," said Bentley, lacking humor. "You still look weird."

"I told you Bentley's a numbskull," laughed Andre.

"I noticed," whispered Kenichi.

Scooping up a spoonful of soup, Kenichi found a dead fly in his meal. At first, he thought this was simply his bad luck. That was, until he noticed the guilty expression on Andre's face, as the troublemaker struggled not to giggle. Bentley, too, fought back mirth.

Finally, the two miscreants erupted into hysterical laughter. "Good one!" Andre told Bentley, in admiration.

"Do you think that's funny?" questioned Kenichi, his cheeks turning red.

Andre snickered. "What's the matter, *Itchy?* Don'tcha like your 'flied lice'?"

Without a word, Kenichi grabbed the idiot by the scruff of the neck, and shoved his face into the bowl of contaminated soup . . .

"Well, if you're coming with me," said Bradley, unhappily, "then let's go."

Intended as a special occasion, the evening evolved into a headache. Trevor had never watched a historical drama from a prominent playwright and Bradley looked forward in sharing that world with him. The last thing anyone needed was taking Fritz along. It wasn't a question whether Fritz would pull something stupid, but *when.*

"Have you ever seen any of Roland Knox's plays?" asked Bradley, trying to make Fritz feel welcome.

"Who the hell's Roland Knox?" asked Fritz, stepping through Lord Kelly's main gate. "I'm just glad to get outa there."

Bradley wondered why Fritz always made fun of others. As the hooligan's antics offended Bradley, Trevor thought they were funny. Fritz had a magnetic, harmful effect on the younger kids.

The boys' jaunt to the Falcon Theatre, on a street running adjacent to the waterfront, led through the seamier parts of Sykes. There was the hustle of independent street vendors, selling an array of merchandise and food. The area was also lined with public houses and sporting ladies. Soldiers, sailors, and ruffians from all corners of the globe streamed the crowded thoroughfares, looking for a good time. Fritz's lousy mood suddenly grew more jovial.

Bradley hated these streets. Many of Lord Kelly's students once lived on these very boulevards, and few wished to return. Several buildings were abandoned and decaying. The crammed lanes were littered with human sewage and horse dung. Large segments of the population were vagrants and homeless.

In the distance, the bells from Lord Kelly's steeple signified the time of six in the evening. With the sun dropping in the western horizon, the breeze grew increasingly chillier. Bradley and Trevor wrapped their school capes around their upper thighs and torsos.

"This is where I get off," said Fritz, heading toward an off-limits paradise known as *The Rooster's Beak,* where scantily-dressed women offered themselves for a price.

"In there?" asked Bradley. "Fritz, you're supposed to come with me and Trevor!"

"I never said that. *You* said that." Fritz strutted to a bright red sign, exhibiting a vulgar painting of a chicken. "Run along now, Brad. I'm staying here."

Bradley sneered. Had Leader Royce known of Fritz's true intentions, the lowlife would be expelled from school. However, Bradley disliked a snitch. Fritz withheld certain information from the Leaders, but not from the Almighty. He'd answer for it, in the end. "Fritz!" screamed Bradley. "Don't go in there! Come with us, please!"

"No can do," said Fritz. "I've got a night with Princess Chiachi. A boy like you would never keep a lady waiting, would ya?"

"What is this place?" asked Trevor.

"Never mind," whispered Bradley.

"Wanna find out, Trev?" taunted Fritz. "Great, I'll show ya!"

"Can I?" asked Trevor, eagerly.

"No!" yelled Bradley. "Fritz, I'll tell Leader Royce!"

"Tell Leader Royce, am I supposed to care?" asked Fritz. "Tell ya what, though. I'll make you a better deal. We'll all go in together, and not tell Royce squat."

"Yeah!" agreed Trevor. "We'll go to the play tomorrow night!"

"Shut up, Trev!" snapped Bradley. He, too, harbored thoughts of exploring The Rooster's Beak. Fear, along with his faith, upheld a decision not to.

"Aw, c'mon Brad," invited Fritz. "I'm buying. You never been with a woman before, and this'll . . ."

"That . . . that's none of your business!" stuttered Bradley.

Fritz laughed. It was no secret that Bradley was a virgin. If Lord Kelly's had its way, he'd go to his grave without ever getting laid. "A man can't live forever," said Fritz. "Hell, you wouldn't know what to do with a woman, if ya had one!"

Bradley was speechless. Fritz hit too close to home.

"Let's go to the play tomorrow night," said Trevor, following Fritz to the door. "Is that okay, Brad?"

Placed in charge of two schoolmates, Bradley failed in this appointment. He was angry with Royce, for insisting that Fritz tag along. He was angry with Fritz, for lying to everyone then tempting Trevor. He was angry with Trevor, for accompanying Fritz into that wicked establishment.

Finally, Bradley was angry with himself, for his inability to prevent a moral catastrophe. Trevor had no idea what awaited him, and the price was his very soul. "Trevor, please!" cried Bradley. "Come with me!"

"Don't worry, Brad," said Trevor. "It's okay."

"Oh hell yeah, Trev!" laughed Fritz. "Ever'thing's gonna be just fine!"

Bradley slouched. This ruins it for everybody, and look what's come of it! If Fritz wants to destroy himself, why drag Trevor down with him?

And in the process, destroy me too?

"Don't waste your time with *Brother* Bradley," Fritz said to Trevor. "He'll never be a man, but you're gonna be, real soon!"

As Fritz and Trevor entered The Rooster's Beak, Bradley nearly wept. Fritz condemned himself to eternal damnation! His spirit was weak and corrupted, anyhow. What about Trevor? He's got no idea how this will affect him!

What truly upset Bradley were realizations that he also thought of entering that house of ill-repute. His frustrations were directed at the world, in general. Trevor was too young to know pleasures of the flesh. His path was now set. Outside of forgiveness, his existence would be fraught with lies, scandal, and debauchery. He'd have no one to blame but himself!

Bradley didn't like Fritz one bit, but he loved Trevor dearly. It was his responsibility to look after that stupid kid. It was that same stupid kid who was afraid to skinny dip with his schoolmates! Now, he'd bare himself to a cheap strumpet!

Why are people allowed to buy sex? The Master intended it as a pact between a man and a woman, united in marriage. Fritz desecrated the Creator's will by tarnishing it. No matter. Bradley still fantasized about joining Fritz in this sin.

Yes, Bradley was still a virgin. This was as much God's decision, as anything. Bradley chose not to engage in sexual intercourse, until he was wed. However, if he qualified for Leadership status, that obligation required life-long celibacy. Upholding such principals, Bradley worked to honorably abide them. Regrettably, there was still a powerful hunger stemming from his loins. He hated Fritz and Trevor for what they were doing!

He also envied them.

Why go to the play, now? It won't be any fun. I should just go home, seek answers through prayer, then wash myself in the light and the love of the Lord.

Damn Fritz for his immorality! Damn Trevor for his lack of convictions! And damn Brother Bradley, for his jealousy of them both!

Bradley considered finding a dark, hidden corner of a building, where he'd pleasure himself with a clenched fist. He was diverted from this self-inflicted *torture* when he encountered three young men of similar age, who were members of a rival congregation. Unlike the Brotherhood of Faith, these lads were too much like the strict Leader Karl. They believed in nothing which brought happiness . . .

. . . and hated those unlike themselves!

The *United Westerland Brethren* wore long, black robes which concealed their feet. Their heads were covered by dark, wide-brimmed, pointed hats. Their long hair was braided in ponytails, hanging below the shoulder blades. Shaving was a sacrilege. Already, these boys had unkempt patches of hair, which smudged the lips, cheeks, and chins.

Once the Brethren members saw Bradley, they regarded him as a heathen. No words were exchanged, as they found humor in Bradley's skullcap, flimsy sandals, and tunic which showed off the legs. Disparaging laughter slipped from their mouths.

Bradley knew what it meant to be a minority, and therefore "inferior."

Minutes later, Bradley got in line at the Falcon Theatre. After placing a coin in The Box, he strolled through the vast entrance into a huge amphitheater. The Falcon held three levels of seating, circling an elevated oval stage below. Audiences in the upper level were protected by a small, overhead roof. Everyone else, including the performers, was at the mercy of the weather. The Falcon's capacity exceeded fifteen-hundred viewers. The decorations were archaic and gaudy, dating back more than a century. The facility exuded a touch of surrealism, the root of its appeal to Bradley. It was an escape from a world of work, duty, and struggle, a refuge where pretense was truth and dreams were shaped and fashioned. The stage props took on lives of their own, and were illuminated in the flickering light of torches and lanterns, focused upon expensive glass mirrors, and polished reflectors.

Bradley snaked his way to a seat in the third row of the theater's lower level. As darkness fell upon the city, he wrapped himself in the cape. Even with hundreds of patrons within the Falcon's walls, he felt alone. He hoped to attend this play with a friend, and suffered the stings of abandonment. The luster of his surroundings failed to shine so brightly, as the experience was rendered hollow and meaningless.

"Hey!" someone shouted out, in the drone of the massive crowd. "Why didn't you wait for me?"

Bradley was surprised as Trevor sat down next to him. "Trev," he said, noting a faint smell of alcohol on the boy's breath. "Why . . . how come you didn't stay at The Rooster's Beak?"

Trevor blushed. "You kidding? I don't even like girls! They was mostly fat and ugly! This one put her cold hands on my legs, reached under my uniform, and tried taking off my underpants!"

"What did you do?" asked Bradley, praying that Trevor didn't succumb to temptation.

Trevor giggled. "I ran!"

Overcome by tears of joy, Bradley embraced Trevor.

"What was that for?" asked Trevor, in confusion.

"Just because, Trevor!" cheered Bradley. "Just because!"

A chorus, buried under a fake beard and layers of face paint, stepped from behind a curtain to open a drama on the life, legend, and legacy of King Auric IV.

In response, the audience reacted with thunderous applause.

That next morning, Fritz woke alongside the woman who was his evening's companion. Princess Chiachi was not the "Pride of the Orient," as The Rooster's Beak so claimed. Even then, Fritz had no reason to complain.

Quietly, Fritz got out of bed and dressed. Bradley and Trevor probably squealed on him. Oh, well. Assuming he was kicked out of Lord Kelly's, Fritz was better off.

Theft was Fritz's stock and trade. How else could he raise the funds to visit The Rooster's Beak? Fritz stole from residents and businesses throughout Sykes, and wasn't above getting sticky fingered at the school. While the Leaders mistrusted Fritz, they were unable to indict him without proof. All they had to go on was Bradley's word! Hell, Brad might lie, just to see old Fritzy get the heave-ho!

With a grin, Fritz put that dumb skullcap on his head. He no longer thought of himself as a "Brother," but as a free man. He was more of a man than those pious Leaders, who allegedly had never slept with women their entire lives! The fools had no clue what they were missing! In truth, they were probably nothing but liars and butt-lovers!

As well, Fritz pitied cowards like Bradley and Trevor. To think he was willing to pay for their good time! Was that buying friends, simply to justify his own actions? *Whatever.* Brad and Trevor could go screw themselves, while ol' Fritzy diddled the ladies!

Fritz hoped to make a prosperous living on the black market. In time, he'd be a respectable trader in Embrian society, perhaps in the whole wide world!

Leaving Chiachi's room, Fritz went downstairs to a lavish tavern. The walls and ceilings were decorated in murals, many of grotesque or obscene images. The boisterous, jovial nature from last night had ceased. Only the saloon keeper, a couple of prostitutes, and Madam Flora entertained guests. "How was it?" asked Flora, a heavyset woman with red-dyed hair and greasy lipstick.

"Terrific," said Fritz. "It's a'ways terrific, here."

"Who was your young friend, last night?" asked Flora.

Fritz laughed. "Aw, just some dumb kid."

The bartender laughed. "Well, that dumb kid hightailed it out of Princess Claire's room, like he just saw the Devil."

"Do I get a refund, or do I gotta make it up to Claire?" asked Fritz.

"We'll give you a deal." Flora ran her wrinkled fingers along Fritz's sinewy legs and hips. "You've put on extra weight."

"Yeah, here," said Fritz, cupping his groin. This got a chuckle from everyone. "I gotta get home, before they gimme the walking papers." Fritz grinned. "Ya wanna know what? I kinda hope they do tell me to get lost!"

Leaning forward, Flora whispered in Fritz's ear. "That man in the corner, with his nose in a book? He's a master from Lord William's Academy!"

Fritz caught a shadowy glimpse of Van Owen, an older Leader from a nearby parochial school. Van Owen was known as a strict disciplinarian, for his especially harsh treatment of unruly students. "Yeah," mumbled Fritz, shrugging. "What of 'em?"

"He likes to watch," informed Flora, "and will pay for anyone putting on a show. You bang Claire on the bar, and you'll walk away with more coin than what you came in with. Deal?"

Fritz smiled in anticipation. "Deal!"

Fritz walked at a steady pace, with only a mild hangover slowing him down. Meanwhile, Van Owen had just sneaked out of The Rooster's Beak, grinning cheerfully with a bulging hard-on.

As a rule, Fritz's trip from the bordello involved the taking of high-priced items from their rightful owners. Not today. He now had a little extra spending money, and free nooky to boot!

Fritz strutted onto the school grounds, like he was in charge of his own destiny. Already, a few boys worked in the garden. Starving, Fritz stepped into the cafeteria where he found Bradley, wearing an apron and a scowl.

With Kenichi, Bradley spent the morning preparing meals. His tunic sleeves were rolled up, and both hands parched from lye soap, as he removed dirty dishes from the tables.

"How was the play?" asked Fritz, sarcastically. "Have as much fun as I did?"

"I got into trouble because of you!" whined Bradley.

"What for?" asked Fritz, playing the innocent.

"Leader Royce asked why you didn't come home last night with me and Trevor."

Fritz pointed at Kenichi, slicing potatoes in the kitchen. "What about him?"

"He got into a fight with Andre and Bentley. Right here, in the cafeteria."

Fritz roared in laughter. "Who won?"

"I wasn't here when it happened, but I heard that Andre and Bentley were bawling like babies when they ran outside." Bradley gave Kenichi a look of admiration. "I got a new roomy, too."

"What did you tell Royce about me?"

"Nothing!" Bradley sneered. "You ought to be happy that I kept my mouth shut, Fritz. Now I'm getting punished, on account of you."

"Oh well," commented Fritz, about to walk away.

"By the way, Fritzy," said Bradley, mischievously. "I almost forgot. Brother Geoffrey needs someone to put in with Andre and Bentley. I gave him the name of the perfect roomy for those two idiots."

"Who?" asked Fritz.

Bradley smiled. *"You."*

6

"Quite a splendid drink, Councilor Theo," said Major Kohl, relaxing in his host's study. "What did you say it's called?"

"Coffee," answered Theo, sipping from a china cup. "On a recent trip to Corapal, I found a restaurant that sells it as their house beverage."

Kohl refilled his cup. *"Coffee.* Sure hits the spot."

"I prefer it to Campens Rose'," said Theo. "It won't alter the senses, or give one the unforgiving morning-after which liquor does."

Major Kohl and Sergeant Vix engaged in an afternoon chat at Theo's spacious home, overlooking Sykes. Along with Yuri, the quartet rested on separate cots, dined on hors d'oeuvres, and sampled Theo's favorite beverages. Theo's property was surrounded by fruit trees and an evergreen forest. A large number of workers labored in the orchards. Theo's study was decorated by antique artwork and volumes of books. The house, formed from mud and stone, was shaped like a dome.

"The coffee's delicious," complimented Kohl. "We'll take some on our return journey to Infernus. What do you think, Sergeant Vix?"

Vix shared Kohl's sentiments of the drink, but dreaded thoughts of a second excursion to a hellish land, far to the west.

"I envy your trip to that new world," said Theo. "As it is, my responsibilities are here. I'm afraid that Embrey is on the brink of destruction."

"I do hope that civil war or a revolution is avoided," said Kohl, turning to Vix. "I don't care to meet more loons, like the ones we detained at Luigi's."

Vix and Yuri exchanged glances. Staying true to his word, Vix said nothing of Yuri's grisly handiwork.

"A swift sword changes the hearts of even the most fanatical," said Theo, implying that Vix alone put the three assassins down.

"Yeah," quipped Vix. "Puts deep holes in 'em."

"Enough of that, gentlemen," said Theo, struggling not to laugh at Vix's joke. "Please, let's forget the world's problems, and savor this tranquil moment."

The three men drank their hot coffee and sampled finger foods, provided by Theo's manservant Linus. The conversation remained warm and cordial, except from Vix, who had little good to say.

"Sir," an older man spoke, entering the room. "I beg your pardon."

"Yes, Linus?" asked Theo. "What is it?"

"Riders approach the estate," informed Linus, nervously. "They carry a state flag. I assume they're here on official business."

Kohl and Vix peeked through the study window. Four uniformed soldiers galloped their horses into Theo's outer courtyard. Kohl's heart skipped a beat. The lead horseman was Lieutenant Salazar, accompanied by a young aide named Reginald, and two guards. Kohl was to be at the Ministry of War on Monday, for the reading of his verdict. It was only Saturday, now!

Theo quietly escorted Yuri from the room.

"They mean to kill you, Major Kohl," said Vix. "They'll have to go through me, first!"

Kohl frowned. Vix was probably right. Salazar was no friend or ally. A member of General Chang's staff, Salazar had aligned himself with General

Gornick.

"You'd better go," warned Vix. "I'll hold 'em off, as long as I can ..."

"No, Sergeant Vix," said Kohl. It didn't matter what others thought of his shoddy military record. Kohl would die, bravely. Deep inside, he didn't know what frightened him more . . . to be savagely cut down, or to whimper like a child.

"Major Kohl!" shouted Vix. *"Move!"*

"Calm down," urged Theo, returning to the study. "They can't seize you, Major Kohl. You're in my custody."

"Who says they won't kill you, too?" argued Vix.

Unbuckling his sword, Kohl handed it to Theo. "Will you see to this?" he requested. "No Gornick man will dare grace his wall or person with it!"

Theo passed the sword to Linus. "Hide this!"

Obediently, Linus dashed to his own quarters, at the end of a narrow hallway.

Sucking in a deep breath, Kohl thrust his chest out like a bantam rooster, feigning nobility and courage. "If they're just after me," he said, anxiously, "there's no point in all of us . . ."

"If they take you, they'll have to take me, too!" said Vix.

"Wait!" ordered Theo. "Let me talk to Lieutenant Salazar. Maybe I can . . ."

A knock on the door told Kohl there was no way out. "I don't want either of you to risk your lives, on my behalf," he told his companions. "Put down your weapon, Sergeant. I . . . I'll do as they say."

"We're here to collect Major Kohl," someone said, in a voice to make Vix's blood boil. It was Salazar.

Vix was helpless in saving a man who was like a father to him. Reluctantly, he slipped his sword back into its sheath.

As Salazar stepped into the study, he was not alone. He was followed by Reginald and the two guards, each baring swords. "I'm here for Major Kohl," spoke Salazar, pleasantly. "My warrant is the will of King Ogden."

Unlike the majority of Embrian officers, who wore an eight-pointed star on their uniforms, Salazar's emblem resembled Gornick's at the hearing. It also matched the young assassin's tattoo at Luigi's, an image of a rattlesnake, slithering around a sword. "'Victory to Gornick,'" Vix breathed, one hand edging toward his weapon.

"Gornick?" mumbled Salazar. "No . . . I'm here on General Chang and Admiral Kraig's authority."

"That's a gaudy symbol on your jacket," commented Theo.

"That's none of your business," challenged Salazar.

"You don't have to go with them," Theo told Kohl, resenting Salazar's brazen attitude. "I'm an Embrian Councillor, and Major Kohl is my custodial charge, *and* my guest. I demand that you leave here, immediately."

Salazar removed a subpoena from his uniform pocket. "I've been given my orders," he said, in a huff. "I'm to deliver Major Kohl to the Ministry of War. It's my duty to carry that out."

Carefully, Theo examined the subpoena. While the scribe looked legitimate, he distrusted Salazar. Handing the paper to Kohl, he asked, "Is that your brother's handwriting? Does that signature belong to Admiral Kraig?"

There was no denying Kraig's eccentric penmanship. Yes, Kohl was placed under the War Ministry's jurisdiction. Kohl nodded, and returned the subpoena to Theo.

"I want to make sure Major Kohl gets into town, safely," said Vix.

"Out of the question!" stated Salazar. "Major Kohl, if you please? Do be a sensible old man, and . . ."

Vix stepped toward Salazar, furiously.

"No!" shouted Kohl, throwing himself between Vix and Salazar. He was still a soldier, and preferred to act like one. "Enough! I'll ride with you, Lieutenant Salazar. I don't want to, but I will."

Salazar snickered, knowing he'd get his own way.

Correcting his slouching posture, Kohl motioned to the door. "I'm with you, Lieutenant," he agreed, solemnly. "Please take the lead . . ."

"Nothing to worry about," laughed Salazar, as he and Kohl rode from Theo's home. "If you're man enough to fight pink monkeys on Infernus, then what's so frightening about a simple legal matter?"

Kohl lowered his head.

"Oh, I'd forgotten," added Salazar. "There are no winged men or pink elephants roaming the War Ministry's chambers."

"Shut up," growled Kohl, wishing to slap the smarmy grin from Salazar's face.

Mounted on a black stallion, Salazar headed the contingency like a hunter with a trophy kill tied to a packhorse. His next goal was to prove his mettle on the battlefield.

"Why am I called in, today?" asked Kohl. "My hearing isn't until ..."

"The tribunal wants to make sure you don't sneak away," informed Salazar, "on Theo's subsidy and support."

Kohl thought about breaking free from his captors. It was useless. Reginald and the two guards took the rear, staring at him like hawks.

Minutes after leaving Theo's, the five men entered a thicket. Bright rays of sunlight peeked through clumps of trees. Kohl suffered from sweaty hands, cold shivers, and a rapid heartbeat. Despite the written subpoena, he didn't think he'd reach Sykes, alive.

From out of nowhere, an arrow pierced Reginald's throat. Bolting, Reginald's horse threw its rider and sped away.

Witnesses initially viewed this incident with shock and bewilderment. The other horses were also startled. No one noticed the quill, protruding from Reginald's neck.

A second arrow struck a guard's chest, and zipped through the back. Somehow, the guard managed to stay in the saddle. Opening his mouth to issue a protest, blood seeped from his mouth, as he dropped to the ground.

"Take cover!" cried Salazar, drawing his sword.

Not knowing what to make of this situation, Kohl didn't await explanations. Squeezing onto his horse's reigns, he spurred the animal to a mad, forward rush.

"Kohl!" screamed Salazar. "Guard, pursue that man!"

As the remaining guard chased after Kohl, a third arrow nailed Salazar's horse through the chest. Staggering, the horse nearly landed upon its master. Clutching his sword, Salazar safely rolled away.

Though Kohl's mare was fast, the guard soon caught up with him. The guard made feeble swings at Kohl with his sword. While these advances made no contact, Kohl shrieked like each had inflicted bodily harm.

There was no escape. If the guard didn't slay Kohl, then an unknown assailant just might. Kohl screamed. Turning a blind corner, he met a lone, cloaked figure in the center of the road, aiming a longbow at him.

Clumsily, Kohl leaped from the horse. Catching his foot in the stirrup, he slammed into the gravel road, below. Stinging from the impact, he received a swollen cheek and a black eye. Momentarily, he saw lightning bolts and stars. A sharp pain jolted from his leg, as he jerked it away from the stirrup.

Pointing his sword at the injured officer sprawled upon the roadway, the guard chuckled, "Thought you'd get away . . . Eh, Major Kohl?"

"No!" begged Kohl. He motioned toward the cloaked archer, to warn the guard. "There! Over *there!*"

"For God's sake, get to your feet," the guard said, impatiently, "or I'll have no choice but to . . ."

Before the guard finished his sentence, an arrow struck his right eye. Blood spurted into the guard's face, clothing, and onto Major Kohl.

The lifeless guard sat on the horse, his face contorted in a bizarre comedy of death. Kohl followed the surreal, slow fall of the guard, which ended in loose gravel and flying dust.

As Kohl tried to stand, blood oozed into his mustache and goatee. Small stones embedded in the palms of both hands. His leg, while not broken, prevented him from running. His thoughts then returned to the mysterious archer. Throwing his arms above his head, he shouted, "I surrender! I give up!"

No answer.

"I surrender!" repeated Kohl, desperately.

Again, no answer.

Kohl's only safe haven was more than a mile away, at Councillor Theo's. Not a great distance, but a long, tough hike for a man hounded by assassins. Favoring his injured leg, Kohl limped slowly, painfully, toward the house. Yet, a killer was out there, somewhere, poised to strike.

Kohl turned a corner to find Salazar, grieving over the loss of three men and the stallion. Kneeling to Reginald, Salazar was tortured by the hopelessness of it all. An arrow, lodged in Reginald's throat, had collapsed the trachea. Gasping for air while clutching at Salazar's uniform, Reginald died in the lieutenant's arms.

Getting to his feet, Salazar refused to accept what had just transpired. Ambush, failure, and death were rolled in one terrifying, gruesome package, due to his own carelessness and arrogance. Not only had Salazar failed Reginald and the two guards, but his beloved stallion, as well. The horse was a gift from his big brother Enrique, for winning a commission in the Embrian Army.

Reginald was a recent graduate from Lord Conway's Academy, the same school Salazar had attended in his youth. He was the eldest son of a loyal employee at Romero's, the distillery owned by Salazar's family. Demonstrating his gratitude to one who had spent more than twenty years working there, Salazar assigned Reggie as his right-hand man and confidante. That evening, he had an especially difficult letter to write . . .

On the verge of tears, Salazar reminded himself that he was not only an officer and a gentleman, but a man. He had to face this tragedy, as such. The surviving horses had fled, leaving Kohl and Salazar afoot.

"I demand to know the meaning of this murder raid!" Salazar shouted at Kohl.

"I don't know!" answered Kohl, his voice echoing through the forest. "It was somebody, not far up the road!"

"*Somebody?* It was a lot of somebodies, if you ask me! No one man was responsible!" Salazar took a deep breath. Apparently, Kohl was not involved in this attack. He wasn't smart enough to stage a successful maneuver.

Salazar cautiously scanned the surrounding area. "It was probably an army of trained killers," he surmised. "They're still out there, so stop looking at me like an idiot!"

"Address me as Major Kohl, or sir, when you speak to me!" insisted Kohl. "Have you forgotten, Lieutenant Salazar? I'm your superior officer!"

"You're my superior officer, under my authority!" With a deep breath, Salazar swallowed his wounded pride. "Very well, then. What do you propose we do now, *Major* Kohl?"

"Return to Councillor Theo's. What else can we do, *Lieutenant* Salazar?"

"Right. I'm certain Theo had something to do with this butchery."

"He couldn't have! Theo's an Embrian Councillor!"

"Yes, and he wants the throne."

"Who are you to make such accusations?" questioned Kohl. "Everyone knows you're nothing but General Gornick's errand boy."

Clenching his fists, Salazar held back temptations of slugging Kohl. Ripping the emblem of the sword and snake from his jacket, he threw it at his feet. "Is that better, *Major* Kohl?"

Kohl smiled. "Yes, much better, *Lieutenant* Salazar . . ."

Vix's frustration was unbearable. Assuming Kohl died in captivity, he'd never forgive himself.

As Vix paced the study floor, Theo prepared an emergency trip into Sykes. There was need for a special meeting with his fellow legislators, on Kohl's behalf. Though his outrage paralleled Vix's, Theo had a more peaceful means to secure justice. Urgently, he scrawled a bill he hoped to present to the Embrian Council.

Entering the study, Linus announced, "Major Kohl and Lieutenant Salazar are back."

Vix glanced through the window to see two injured men stagger past the gates. It was incredible! Neither man was on horseback, while Kohl was helped along by an antagonist. Alarmed by the blood dripping from Kohl's head and hands, Vix ran outside. Putting one arm around Kohl, he carefully walked him inside.

Salazar bit his tongue. This wasn't the time or place to prefer charges against Theo. Salazar wondered why he was left standing, while three of his men lay dead. Once he reached the Ministry of War . . . *if* he reached the Ministry of War, he aimed to prepare a writ of warrant, then launch an investigation against Theo. Someone had ordered the murder of three men, and someone would answer for it!

"Sir?" a soft voice asked. "Sir, may I be of help?"

Salazar saw a lithely beautiful, blonde-haired boy step toward him. The boy, standing five-feet-nothing, calmly approached Salazar. "Pardon me, but we haven't met," responded Salazar, politely. "My name's Lieutenant . . ."

"Salazar." The boy shook Salazar's hand. "I'm Yuri."

"Yuri?" asked Salazar, noting the thick Kuschan accent.

"I'm Councillor Theo's adopted son, from St. Alexandrov."

"Yes," spoke Salazar. "I once traveled there, to worship in Lord Simon's Cathedral."

"I was an altar boy at Lord Simon's," said Yuri. This was a fabrication, a mere persona forged by Captain Maliek, invoking innocence where it did not belong. "We held mass and sang vespers six times a day. What a lovely church, Lieutenant Salazar!"

Salazar wore a lopsided grin. "Look Yuri, I can't stay. I've got to be in Sykes, assuming I make it."

"Won't you please come inside?" asked Yuri.

"I'm not wanted here. Major Kohl and I don't like each other." Salazar withheld his negative opinion of Theo. "It . . . it's a long story. I don't want to tell it, and you don't want to hear it." Salazar lowered his head. He had his first taste of warfare, and saw no glory or heroism in it. "And Yuri . . . I've got three men to bury . . ."

Yuri had the ability to kill Salazar, just as swiftly as he killed the aide and two guards. Yet, he spared the lieutenant. Occasionally, shame, humility, and ill memories were a worse fate than death. Yuri had just terminated three Embrian soldiers. In the back of his mind, he wondered if his actions pleased the Kuen or, as Pastor Dimitri had suggested, were "justified for the good of all."

Salazar was haunted by images of Reginald with an arrow piercing his throat, gasping out a final breath, holding onto a mere shred of life which ultimately refused him.

It was too late for Yuri to change the fact that he had sanctioned Salazar's men. What was done, was done. Still, Yuri wished he hadn't taken part in the bloodbath. When it came to the realities of violence, Salazar was a novice. Yuri doubted if the man had ever laid eyes upon a dead person, until then.

Guilt gnawed at Yuri. Was Major Kohl's life worth the price of three men? What was the Kuen to think of Yuri, now? More importantly, how did Yuri feel about himself?

"I'll help you bury your men," offered Yuri, apologetically.

"I can't ask you to do that," whispered Salazar. "I led them into a trap. Damn it, I should've been more careful. That area was so right for an ambush! It makes me feel so damned stupid!"

Yuri almost wept. Salazar blamed himself for everything. Although Theo was regarded as a compassionate man, he often resorted to more fatal solutions, in order to reach his goals. Yuri was simply the tool to execute those solutions.

Salazar's support of General Gornick endeared him to no one at Theo's. The man was either wrongheaded or naive. He had no idea of the hazardous political ground in which he tread. Unwittingly, Salazar found himself in a world where altar boys were actually mad-dog killers, and reform-minded book publishers were bloodthirsty murderers hiding behind mighty words.

Yuri had butchered those men, and now he'd help lay them to rest. "I'll fetch a spade and shovel," he said.

"*I'll* bury them!" insisted Salazar. Chang and Kraig gave him an easy assignment, and he botched it! "It's my duty, not yours. I should've been more careful."

"But I want to help!" cried Yuri, dashing into the house. Moments later, Theo and Linus hurried outside, both seemingly shocked and concerned.

Initially, no one exchanged words as Theo and Salazar stared at each other.

"I'm very sorry, Lieutenant Salazar," Theo said, breaking the silence. "Won't you please come in? Burial arrangements must be made, and I don't quite know where to begin . . ."

"I'll take care of it!" snapped Salazar, nearly accusing Theo of wanting to finish the job. For Yuri, he halted his charges against the legislator.

"I know you will," said Theo, "but . . ."

"There are snipers loose beyond those gates," reported Salazar, pointedly. "Aren't you beefing up your security, or do you already know you're not on their list?"

Theo glanced at Yuri. The sniper was someone he loved, more than Embrey itself! As a result, he chose his words prudently. "Security? Why, I have only a small household staff here, my warden, and a bodyguard. However, you . . . you're absolutely right, Lieutenant Salazar. We'd better take refuge inside, out of harm's way."

"But, Father!" cried Yuri. "Lieutenant Salazar wants to see to his men, and I promised to help!"

"You *promised?*" Theo caressed Yuri's hair. "But why? . . ."

"I owe a debt to my men," stated Salazar. "I hope to grant them the honor I so denied them in life. Whoever killed them may also kill me, too. I really don't care, anymore."

"Lieutenant Salazar needs me," said Yuri. "Shouldn't I be there for him?"

"That's not necessary!" yelled Salazar. "I'll attend to it. But I want you to know this one thing, Councillor Theo. Those were Embrians who died under my command. Allow an Embrian Army officer to bury his own soldiers."

Theo nodded. "I'll dispatch my warden to investigate this. He knows these woods, and can sweep through them undetected. I'll have Strunk tend to the burials." Although he disliked Salazar, Theo still pitied him. "It's a sad day for us all, Lieutenant Salazar."

"Thank you," mouthed Salazar, his throat tightening.

"We'll arrange burial in the south orchard," said Theo. "A fitting place for three brave men to rest . . ."

7

At the age of forty, Strunk boasted the physique of someone half his age.

Strunk was a short, stocky man, shaped like a whiskey barrel with sinewy arms and legs. Nature didn't bless him with a full head of hair. Daily, Strunk shaved those few strands with a straight razor. He shiny scalp, wrinkled head, and piercing eyes instilled fear in the faint of heart. The graying goatee and missing front teeth added to the nightmare, which he projected to friends, neighbors, enemies, and acquaintances.

Strunk was proud that he never ran away from, or lost a fight. His cruelty and swordsmanship made him stand out. He had the ability to decapitate an opponent with one bold swipe of the blade. More often than not, his victims went to their graves, minus a skull.

This "talent" caught the attention of the former monarch, King Marco, who granted Strunk a favorable position. The former sailor was one of only five men commissioned as state executioners.

While most in that elite group maintained their anonymity under black hoods, Strunk revealed his identity to the vast groups witnessing the gruesome craft. Prior to the "main event," Strunk entertained onlookers by shuffling his feet in a makeshift dance, telling bawdy jokes, and reciting barroom songs. Upon completion of the task, Strunk displayed the severed head, allowing blood to spray upon his grimacing face. It thrilled him to swing the ax into boney flesh, revel as the body twitched in a macabre fit, then hear the roar of spectators with their booming *oohs* and *ahhs*.

Earning an enviable wage, Strunk was never permitted into high society, which regarded him with contempt. He preferred his good times with those classes who appreciated his hijinks and antics.

Oh, but how times had changed!

Mortified by the debauchery of public executions, the Embrian Council, led by Theo, put a stop to public beheadings. As a consolation, Theo hired Strunk as a laborer, splitting fence posts and chords of firewood.

Life was never the same. Strunk missed the fame and infamy associated with his position. He earned a mere fraction of the money working for Theo, as he did as an executioner. Placed in a modest home on Theo's land (a tiny, one-room shed), Strunk never forgave the legislator for taking away his livelihood.

Strunk was born to an Agronian father and an Embrian mother. His father, Stossee, was a noted freebooter who commanded a small fleet. Strunk grew up on the decks of Stossee's ships, learning the art of piracy, brutality, and murder. By the age of seventeen, he was captain of his own vessel.

Briefly, Stossee dealt clandestinely with Embrey's King Marco. Once his treachery became too great a burden, the Agron Sea Council, which licensed the pirate trade, took action against him.

In a violent sea battle near the Kuschan coast, Stossee's fleet was annihilated in a joint Branellian and Agronian venture. Granted no mercy, Stossee's sailors perished in hails of arrows. Strunk realized that the foe gave no quarter, so ran his ship into the coastal shallows. As the enemy closed in on him, he went below as his crew continued working the sails. There, he hulled the ship with a broad ax, scuttling it to the sandy bottom.

Strunk retreated to the hold, where dozens of large, empty casks were stored. As the ship went down by the stern, the casks became floatation devices, and prevented him from drowning.

For two long days, Strunk remained in the damaged ship, before making good an escape. On the beach, he found the bloated, decaying bodies of his crew and companions, including that of Stossee's.

Making his way north, Strunk joined the Embrian Navy.

"That's no way to hold a goddamn pick!" Strunk hollered at Salazar. He didn't care about the lieutenant's social, economic, or military status. So what if the officer came from money and privilege? All Strunk saw was a young, dumb kid in a flashy uniform, showing no blisters or callouses on his hands.

Digging the graves of his fallen soldiers, Salazar had never once used a pick or shovel. In poor physical condition, he grew tired of the strenuous labor. Below the thick sod wasn't dirt, as much as an infinite number of rocks, some larger than his noggin. With sunlight beating down upon him, Salazar was exhausted. Recurring thoughts of the massacre played out, over and over, in his mind.

"Gimme that goddamn thing!" cursed Strunk, ripping the pick from Salazar's hands. "Don't choke it! Why hell, you had yer hands clear up *here!*"

Salazar backed away, as he wiped his sweaty brow. He was tired, humiliated, and angry. Strunk's language and behavior were salt in a very deep wound.

Many people disliked Salazar. Their criticisms were usually spoken behind his back. Rarely had anyone jumped in the middle of him. Salazar may have disputed Theo on several issues. They were in agreement when it came to the grotesque spectacle of a public beheading.

"Look you, here's the way you use it!" snapped Strunk. "The way you had yer grubbies on this handle, you'd never get done! Bear'd come along and eat them guys before you finished 'er up. Then prob'ly eat you."

Gritting his teeth, Salazar wanted to swing a shovel at Strunk's face, then allow bears and worms to eat him. It would've served the country to be rid of the most despicable person he had ever met.

While lopping criminals' heads off, Strunk obtained a large "fan base" throughout Embrey. He wined and dined his followers, engaged in a bar fight or two, then ended the night in a cheap cathouse. Salazar found no appeal, whatsoever, in a man like Strunk. Theo should've had more sense and dignity than to hire that ne'er-do-well.

Then again, who likely called the shots on Reggie and the two guards?

"Go on," said Strunk, leaning the pick against an apple tree. "Get that dirt out with that shovel."

Resenting orders from someone of Strunk's ilk, Salazar did as he was told, until . . .

"Goddamn it!" barked Strunk. "Who showed you to use a shovel like that?"

"Fine!" Salazar threw the shovel down. "You do it, then!"

"Why, don't that beat all?" laughed Strunk, baring his few, blackened teeth. "What's the Army coming to? How much did Mommy and Daddy pay for yer fancy commission? You for damn sure didn't earn it."

"Three of my men are dead!" yelled Salazar. "How do you expect me to? . . ."

"Them men wouldn't o' got killed, if you knowed somethin' about soldierin'. Go on, take a swing at me. Go on. Y'ain't doin' the Army no good by lettin' yer men get killed like that."

"Shut your mouth! It was a squad of snipers who attacked us! How do I know they're not about to kill me, this very minute?"

"It wasn't no squad o' snipers! It was only one guy. You got nothin' to worry about, he ain't bein' paid for you, or you'd be dead with the rest."

"How do you know that?" asked Salazar, in an accusation.

Taking a drink of bottled ale, Strunk wiped his hairy lip and chin. "I ain't no hired killer."

"What did you call it when the monarchy compensated you for disposing of Embrey's inmates and political prisoners?" questioned Salazar. "That makes you a hired killer, in my opinion."

"I ain't never killed nobody hidin' behind a goddamn rock or tree!" Strunk turned his attention to Yuri, who was even less qualified for digging than Salazar. While assisting Salazar, Yuri was joined by his ill-mannered black terrier.

The dog, Boris, was a gift from Omar, Salazar's childhood friend and the youngest member of the Embrian Council. The overactive canine excelled only at barking, chasing squirrels, and getting in the way. Through Salazar's urging, Yuri distracted Boris by playing fetch, not far from the dead stallion. With a high-pitched, feminine giggle, he issued Boris shrill commands in the Kuschan dialect.

For Salazar, the image of a boy and his dog represented the waning days of childhood. In a few short years, Yuri would enter the rigors and challenges of adulthood. For Yuri, playing with Boris represented a childhood he never had. This activity was preferable to looking Salazar in the eyes.

Though Yuri knew he should've helped Salazar, he didn't grant Strunk the same consideration. His thoughts of the cretin mirrored Salazar's. Not only was Yuri intimidated by Strunk, but his scary reputation.

The sight of the three dead men, along with the expression on Salazar's face, was a reminder of Yuri's crimes against humanity, the Embrian military, and the Kuen. For Theo's sake, as well as his own, Yuri maintained a facade of innocence. The pain in his heart nearly propelled him to make a full confession, then plead for Salazar's forgiveness.

"Yer green," Stunk told Salazar. "Ain'tcha?"

"Excuse me?" responded Salazar, puffing out his chest though the wind was knocked out of his sails.

"Whadda think o' Theo's baby-faced ghoul?"

"Yuri?"

"Spooky, if y'ask me."

Salazar admitted that Yuri was odd, a definite square peg. The kid probably had few chums, and was likely a constant target for bullying. Yuri was an outsider, but Salazar wouldn't describe him as *spooky*.

"*Kuschan!*" shouted Strunk. "You there, Kuschan! Get here. Me an' Lieutenant Salazar's got somethin' we wanna ask you."

Yuri dropped the stick he tossed for Boris, then wandered to Strunk and Salazar.

"That's close enough," said Strunk, as Yuri got less than two yards away.

"Yes?" asked Yuri, nervously.

"We got t' wonderin'," inquired Strunk, smiling. "What's it like, bein' you?"

"Me?"

"Yeah," said Strunk, a twinkle in his eye. "What's it like pokin' yer ol' John Henry up some guy's ass? Or are you on the bottom, willin'ly takin' the cock?"

Salazar gasped. Strunk's remarks were uncalled for. Though he heard it all before, Yuri didn't merit any guff from one of his father's employees. Salazar feared that Yuri would fly into Strunk. In his estimation, the outcome of that contest was apparent. Strunk had the ability and spirit to injure Yuri, without giving it a second thought.

Strunk grabbed the pick, and held it in a defensive position. "Do it, freak. Go on, do it. Take yer best shot at me . . ."

"Stop it!" shouted Salazar. "You don't have to mistreat him. He means no harm to you, me, or anyone else!"

"Yer green," said Strunk, in a self-satisfactory tone. "Y' don't know what yer dealin' with, but I do."

Whimpering, Yuri sprinted to a clump of trees, across the roadway toward the house.

"Yuri!" called Salazar, pursuing the sensitive teen.

About a minute later, Salazar found Yuri crouched under a cottonwood tree. The boy's eyes were moist, his cheeks a fiery red. The feisty terrier licked his lips, begging to play fetch. "Go home, Boris," moped Yuri, brushing the dog away. "Just leave me alone . . ."

"Are you all right?" asked Salazar, cautiously approaching Yuri.

Yuri turned away. "Don't worry about me. I'm just . . . mad."

Salazar knelt beside Yuri. "I don't have to worry about you, but . . . well, you worried about me, when . . ."

"Leave me alone," sobbed Yuri.

As Salazar put his arm around Yuri's shoulder, the boy refused his affections. It wasn't just Strunk's humor setting him off. Salazar had no idea who murdered those soldiers! In coming to Major Kohl's rescue, Yuri paid with his own conscience.

Justified, for the good of all? . . .

Unable to look at Salazar, Yuri concealed his face under the palms of both hands. "You shouldn't be here with me, Lieutenant Salazar."

Silence separated Yuri and Salazar.

"Where did your father find him?" asked Salazar, referring to Strunk. "Not much of a man. Maybe you should just consider the source, then forget it."

"I'd like to kill him," whispered Yuri.

"A good man to kill," snickered Salazar. Sitting down, he threw one arm around Yuri's torso. "Don't let him get the better of you. He's not worth it . . ."

"Leave me alone!" screamed Yuri. "Please, just leave me alone!"

Salazar's jaw dropped.

"Forgive me, Lieutenant Salazar," apologized Yuri. "I'm sorry. I didn't mean to be so rude."

"I know that," spoke Salazar, returning to his feet. "You want to be alone. Hell, I'm not doing any good, here. I'm doing no good for you, for my men, or my horse! I guess the best thing is for me to walk to town, with my tail between my legs." Salazar paused. "But, before I go, Yuri, remember this one thing. Don't let people like Strunk take advantage of you. You're a better man, than he'll ever live to be."

Theo, Kohl, and Vix rambled on about Salazar's cockiness and arrogance. Sure, when Salazar arrived to collect Major Kohl, he was showy and proud. Not now. Yuri and Theo saw to that! If Salazar was as bad as everyone described, why was he so concerned about Yuri? The foolish, ignorant, pitiful man! He really has no clue!

"Do you need a horse?" asked Yuri. "Father will lend you one."

"No," answered Salazar, sick to his stomach. "I don't need a blessed thing from your father."

"Why not? Don't you like him?"

"I don't know when I'll be able to return it," explained Salazar, muting his sour opinion of Theo. For all the lieutenant knew, he was a dead man, already! Snipers were still out there, waiting to fill arrows into him!

"Someone finished my men off," mumbled Salazar, an empty feeling in his stomach. "They'll soon do me the same way, Yuri."

His back slouched like a condemned man on his way to the gallows, Salazar began the slow, agonizing march into Sykes.

"I'll go with you," said Yuri, hopping to his feet.

"What?"

"I'll go with you," repeated Yuri, seeking Salazar's approval despite the legal and moral infractions against him. Nothing he did now made his acts of aggression right in the hearts of men, or to the Kuen. No matter. Yuri bore no ill-will toward Salazar.

Taking a deep breath, Salazar released it in a sigh. "I appreciate that. But you'd be wise to stay here. Away from this parcel of land, I can't guarantee your safety. Because of your relationship to Councillor Theo, you'd make the perfect hostage . . . and target."

"You'll be safe with me, Lieutenant Salazar," assured Yuri, with confidence. "I promise."

Salazar stared at Yuri. How could the boy's soft, harmless nature protect anyone?

On the other hand, taking Yuri along was advantageous. If Salazar was alone, Theo wouldn't hesitate to dispose of him. He'd think twice about committing another killing, with his fragile stepchild there to witness it.

After all, Yuri was oblivious to violence and bloodshed . . .

8

In the early afternoon, Bradley cleaned the last dirty dish from lunch.

Placing the dish in a storage rack, he glanced into the once boisterous cafeteria, which minutes before was filled with one-hundred-and-sixty boys. Now, it was empty and quiet. The only one there was Kenichi, who scrubbed the tables and mopped the floors. In a few more moments, their kitchen duty would be over, and Bradley could help move Kenichi into his dorm room. It'd be nice to have an older room mate, someone he could really talk to.

Bradley's stomach rumbled. The boys had started their punishment at dawn, with only a cold potato to sustain them. Drying his hands onto an apron, Bradley considered how unfair it was to pay for Fritz's disobedience. That's how it usually went at Lord Kelly's. Troublemakers got away with everything! Bradley never understood why Royce cared so much for Fritz. It was cruel to force that bully on Bradley and Trevor. Now, Bradley's record was tarnished. It served Fritz right to live with Andre and Bentley!

Kenichi dragged himself into the kitchen. Usually wearing his hair in a ponytail, that day he let it hang freely upon his shoulders. Beads of sweat dotted his forehead. He hadn't slept well the night before. The relocation to Sykes, then his fight with Andre and Bentley, kept him wide awake. Sleeping on the stone floor of Bradley's room didn't help, either.

"What should I do with this mop water?" panted Kenichi, his knees nearly buckling.

"We used to just throw it outside," said Bradley. "Now Sister Judith wants us to dump it in the hallway latrine."

"All right." Kenichi rubbed his weary legs. "Then what?"

"Tell Judith we're done, then get your room assignment from Geoffrey. I should be finished by then."

Storing the mop bucket in one corner of a pantry, Kenichi then entered a damp, dark cellar, down a flight of stairs below the kitchen. There, Sister Judith and Brother Eduardo sorted and inventoried produce from the garden, for the winter. As Judith examined that year's supply, Eduardo removed damaged fruits and vegetables from their cribs, and tossed them in separate boxes. They were used to feed the school's hogs and chickens. Eduardo made for a comical sight, his clothes and legs smeared with dust, dirt, and sweat.

An older woman, Judith was the only female member of Lord Kelly's staff. Her job also included supervising work detail for ill-behaved boys. She was a short, thin woman with a face like a horse. As she barked orders to Eduardo, her voice resembled the clatter of a rickety old cart on a cobblestone lane.

A scrawny, dark-skinned boy of fourteen, Eduardo was not a student, and never participated in the school's spiritual exercises. True to his father's dying wishes, along with a minimal payment, he was taken in by the more sympathetic Leaders, and earned his keep under Judith's guidance.

Distrusting those of "mixed blood" and heritage, Leader Karl initially denied Eduardo's entrance into Lord Kelly's. As Karl put it, the lad's mother was "as white as snow" while his father was "blacker than the pit of Hell." As well, Eduardo's religious background derived from the hated United Westerland Brethren.

Vetoing Karl's ruling against Eduardo, the other Leaders were obligated to "save" the boy from eternal damnation, through worthwhile labor. They also insisted that Eduardo wear the same type of uniform as the students, and reside in their dormitory.

As Kenichi went into the cellar, Judith and Eduardo had their backs to him. "Ma'am," he said. "Brad and I are done . . ."

Judith answered Kenichi with a shrill laugh. "Eduardo!" she shouted, grabbing her assistant's sleeves.

"Yes, Sister Judith?" yawned Eduardo, tiredly.

"This is the boy who settled Andre and Bentley's hash!" snickered Judith, excitedly.

"Good job!" cheered Eduardo. "You did something we all wanted to do for an awful long time! They sure had it coming!"

"It couldn't have happened to two ornerier brats," added Judith, patting Kenichi's back. "They turned poor little Eli's life into hell!"

Kenichi blushed.

"So, you boys done?" asked Judith.

"Yes, Ma'am," answered Kenichi.

"Then you're free to go." Judith winked. "Well done, young man. I'm very proud of you."

Kenichi never imagined that his anger drawn against Andre and Bentley was viewed as someone's guilty pleasure.

As Kenichi arrived in the dormitory basement to chat with Geoffrey, it was quiet. A few lads read from scriptures in the lobby, as twelve-year-old, twin brothers Sergio and Giuseppe checked the hallway's candles and lanterns. To Kenichi's amusement, Fritz hauled his stuff into Andre and Bentley's room. His dour expression said it all.

Approaching the slightly opened door to Room Ten, Kenichi heard muffled sounds from inside. Peeking into Geoffrey's dorm, he was shocked, humored, and embarrassed.

Geoffrey sat on the bed, as another boy straddled his lap. Both had their tunics lifted to their waists, and neither wore undergarments. Squeezing their partners' bodies, the two teens locked lips in a display of love and passion.

His stomach churning, Kenichi hesitantly pecked on the door.

Geoffrey was never in such a hurry to rid himself of this pleasure. Throwing his companion upon the bed, he urgently lowered his tunic and rushed to the door. "Can I? . . . Can I help you?" he asked, his voice revealing panic.

Kenichi resisted the temptation to laugh. "I just need to see you about a . . ."

"Room assignment!" interrupted Geoffrey. "I . . . I guess it didn't work out with Andre and Bentley."

"I guess not," mumbled Kenichi, knowing Geoffrey was afraid. Feigning ignorance, he added, "I never met Brother Eli. How could he stand living with those idiots?"

Geoffrey sighed. "It was just Eli's bad luck to get stuck with them, just like eating that spoiled poultry . . . I guess."

"I guess."

"We don't like having four to a room," said Geoffrey, his cheeks still flush. "In your case, I'll make an exception."

"How come?" asked Kenichi, glancing into the room at Geoffrey's companion, who reached to the foot of the bed for his silk loincloth.

"For one thing, Bradley's fond of you."

Kenichi smiled. "Well, I'm fond of him, too."

"I also think that Trevor and Derry need another positive role model."

"I can only hope I can be a positive role model." Kenichi smirked. "I'm not starting out so well."

"You're fine," said Geoffrey. "Andre and Bentley can start fights in empty rooms."

"Is that your roommate?" asked Kenichi, motioning to Geoffrey's partner.

Geoffrey and his partner turned to each other. How could they possibly explain themselves? If the truth of their relationship was disclosed, punishment involved shunning, spiritual "reawakening," or expulsion.

A similar incident years before led to the offenders' drownings, while being "cleaned of sin" in the Ember River. Fear clouded Geoffrey's thoughts. The other boy was even more agitated.

"No, no," said Geoffrey, tensely. "Dorm assistants don't have roommates . . . You see, this is my . . . best friend, Randy."

"Hi, Randy. I'm Kenichi."

Randy was slightly shorter than Kenichi, with a freckled face. His brown hair was trimmed neatly above his ears. "Nice to meet you," he said, in mistrust and apprehension.

"Randy and I were . . . practicing a recital for tomorrow's service," claimed Geoffrey.

"I look forward to it," said Kenichi. "I'm sure everyone will be . . . amazed."

Geoffrey escorted Kenichi from the room. "How . . . how's your job as our secretary?"

"I'm starting in the morning. I never worked at this large of a facility. Lord Charles' was really small, and my job there was a cinch." Kenichi sighed. "It'll be okay . . . I hope."

"Oh, you'll make out all right," assured Geoffrey.

"By the way," reminded Kenichi. "My room assignment?"

"I'm sorry, it's in my desk." Geoffrey ran to his quarters, then returned with the needed scroll.

"Thanks," said Kenichi, about to walk away.

"Kenichi," whispered Geoffrey, looking all around. "What did you see . . . a few minutes ago?"

Kenichi refused to make waves. If imbeciles like Andre and Bentley harbored suspicions about Geoffrey, then so did everyone else, and Kenichi wasn't about to bring this awkward incident to the Leaders' attention.

"See what?" he asked, strolling to the stairway. "I didn't see a thing."

Bradley left the cafeteria on a windy but cloudless day. The breeze swept cool, moist air from the river. This didn't dampen the festive mood created by crystal clear skies, above. A small group of boys completed harvesting the garden. Lord Kelly's had scheduled a rented donkey to plow the soil, later in the week.

Bradley spotted Kenichi lazing by the riverbank, staring dreamlike at the ships going to and from Port Auric. The sailors on those vessels were a tough lot, steeled by hazardous work on the seas. Home was the rolling deck of a freighter.

These were men from all races and origins, engaging in every imaginable vice, living as if each day might be their last. They drank too much, found solace in the arms of prostitutes, and told the worst lies.

And, occasionally, Kenichi longed to be one of them.

"That's where you're hiding!" said Bradley, sitting next to Kenichi on a large, sun-bleached rock. "Ready to move in with me?"

"I guess," Kenichi answered vacantly, in no rush to do anything.

"What are you looking at?"

"I'm just homesick, Brad. I'm not sure where home is, anymore."

"Maybe you're already home. I don't know about you, but I like it here. It takes a while to get used to Lord Kelly's. Not that long ago, I laid awake thinking about my folks, who I never knew. I spent the whole night crying my eyes out."

"If you think that'll help," said Kenichi. "I just want to get out and see the world, that's all. You ever feel that way?"

Bradley shrugged. Providing he had his friends, and the love of God, he was content.

"When I was at Lord Charles'," said Kenichi, "Leader Lionel and I hiked to the summit of Mount Patten."

Bradley was in awe. The highest point in Embrey, Mount Patten was more than nine-thousand feet above sea level. "You've been there?"

"Only four or five times."

"Is it a tough hike?"

Kenichi laughed. "What do you think? We'd start out at dawn, then spend the entire day on the trail. We reached the top just in time to set up camp and watch the sunset. You can see everything from up there!"

Though Bradley was happy for Kenichi, he was also jealous. Kenichi did something most students only dreamed about. Bradley had never laid eyes upon Mount Patten. He based his interpretations of it on sketches in school textbooks.

"We'd spend the whole night looking up at the stars, and talking," reminisced Kenichi. "That next day, we'd go fishing in Lake Mathers."

"Wish I could do that," moped Bradley.

"Well, why don't you?"

"*What?*"

"Why not?" laughed Kenichi. "Let's go next summer, just the two of us!"

Bradley didn't think he'd have time to visit the peak. His various responsibilities kept him too busy. "Aw, I dunno, Kenichi."

"Come on, Brad! It won't be any fun if I go by myself, and I'd like a friend there with me!"

Bradley was flattered. "Thanks, but what's the rush? That mountain's not about to sprout legs and walk away . . ."

"I . . . I've got to go visit Lionel's grave," interrupted Kenichi, his voice lacking emotion.

Bradley stared at Kenichi, in disbelief.

Fighting to maintain a stiff upper lip, Kenichi rubbed his moistened eyes. "During our last trip, Lionel's heart gave out. We were going home after a long day, when . . ." Shaking his head, Kenichi was unable to say more.

Bradley put his arm around Kenichi. "I'm so sorry," was the only thing he could come up with.

Despite his best efforts to do so, Kenichi failed to stop a few tears from seeping out of his eyes. Everything he had truly cared about, whether it be his mother or a beloved father figure, was gone. Deep inside, Kenichi wondered if he had anyone left. "I tried saving him, Brad," he said, staring blankly across the river. "Honestly, I *tried!* Just like I tried helping my mom!"

Sobbing, Kenichi buried his face in Bradley's tunic.

Bradley recalled how Kenichi was distant with everyone, upon his arrival the day before. Well, everyone at Lord Kelly's had a sad story in which to share. That afternoon, Bradley caught a glimpse into a small part of Kenichi's troubled past.

Bradley loved everyone at Lord Kelly's. He made an exception with Fritz, but Fritz was the exception, anyhow! Somehow, Bradley just knew that his relationship with Kenichi would become very special to them, both . . .

9

Fearing that snipers and assassins lurked behind every tree, every dark corner, and across every stream, Lieutenant Salazar led Yuri to a remote inn, between Theo's home and the community of Sykes.

Even though the proprietor never truly achieved the naval ranking, *Captain Harris'* was a noted stop for soldiers, sailors, merchant marines, and peddlers. Years before, Harris served with Theo on several freighters. Due to their friendship, Theo supplied the inn with various beverages, including a new, popular item known as coffee.

Upon their arrival, Salazar and Yuri spotted a tattooed man making a number of tobacco sales. Salazar detested the smoking weed, as much as he loathed the tattooed man. He regarded Paransky as a competitor, a criminal, and a parasite. Romero's, the distillery owned and operated by Salazar's kin, produced only legal liquors, and followed the rules and regulations of the trade. Paransky wasn't tied or obligated to such strict guidelines, and took advantage of established, legitimate companies.

More concerning to Salazar than a few pirates and smugglers, were thoughts that his life was endangered. Sitting down for a steak dinner and a pint of ale, he was unable to relax. Cutting his T-bone, his hands shook so badly that Yuri had to help him.

Salazar was expected at the War Ministry with Major Kohl. Regrettably, Yuri failed to make for the cheeriest of dinner guests. As the boy spoke of this childhood in Kusch *(mainly lies!)* he was torn by gnawing guilt. Salazar had bought him a meal fit for a king, and treated him decently.

Salazar had no clue who killed his three men. Words of kindness could not ease Yuri's conscience. Maliek told his recruits to never feel shame or remorse for completing a hit, regardless of the victim's nationality, politics, or spirituality. What difference did it make whether the target was innocent or not?

That worked for boys like Clive, Tomas, or Jesse. During dinner, Yuri nearly broke down and confessed his role in the murders. One could have easily argued that, due to his support of General Gornick, Salazar was a threat to Councillor Theo. However, Salazar was a true gentleman. Never once did he comment on Yuri's effete nature, or chide the teen for being "different." This, even as a few customers gave Salazar and Yuri disparaging looks.

Every night, Captain Harris' furnished entertainment in the vast dining hall. It usually involved a storyteller, balladeer, or dancing women. That evening, Harris provided three female Kokashima strippers. Despite their sensuality and beauty, Salazar regarded the show as a distraction.

After giving the waiter a bundle of coins for a bottle of brandy and a room for the night, Salazar wandered through a darkened stairwell to his room. By the flickering light of a single candle, and the full moon shining through a window, he proceeded to numb the pain by getting drunk and urged Yuri to join him in oblivion.

Yuri refused the brandy. Sitting in one corner of the room, he listened to Salazar's rants on the audacity of Harris' unwillingness to sell an excellent brandy such as Romero's, while promoting an inferior brand like *Galbraith's*.

Shifting uncomfortably in his chair, Yuri said nothing. As a mild draft chilled the room, he suffered from cold sweats. His fingers tightly clutched the arms of the chair. He fought back temptations to spill the beans, and even considered on indicting his father, who gave orders to wipe out the aide and two guards. It was one thing for Yuri to swing at the gallows. Allowing Theo to be executed would likely act as a catalyst for civil war and violence. His lips quivering, Yuri whimpered.

"What's the matter?" slurred Salazar, pouring himself another glass of the wretched Galbraith's, masquerading as brandy. "Hope I ain't boring you with all my harping and bitching over this second-class, fourth-rate, cheap-john substitute for a fabulous drink like Romero's."

Staring at Salazar's image through the candlelight, Yuri found it nearly impossible to speak. He hoped Salazar was unable to detect a teardrop, escaping from one eye.

"Not only is Romero's the finest damn brandy this side of Vladistan," burped Salazar, "it's also got the best damn people working for it! Why, just this afternoon, I helped bury the son of one of our most dedicated workers . . ."

Yuri turned his head away.

Salazar slugged the table. "Might not be Romero's, might not even be as good as Romero's!" he snickered. "But, come on, have a drink with me! Unless you're too good to drink with a measly second lieutenant, or think your pa will break me for giving it to you."

"No, thank you, Lieutenant Salazar," whispered Yuri.

"Hell, a measly little drop won't hurt you, little Kuschan altar boy. I promise not to tell, if you promise not to tell . . ."

The sounds of someone stepping through the hallway, followed by knocking at the door, nearly caused Yuri to leap from his own skin. He feared that he'd now answer for the murders at Theo, while Salazar thought someone delivered a second bottle of the dreadful, low-grade Galbraith's.

Laughing at the frightened look on Yuri's face, Salazar roared, "Come in, if your nose is clean!"

No one expected Major Kohl to enter the room.

One could hear a pin drop, as Kohl and Salazar stared at each other. For a brief moment, Salazar was compelled to reach for his sword, hanging from a chair. Afraid of Salazar, Kohl still managed to stand his ground. Yuri's attention switched from the major at the door, to the lieutenant sitting at the table.

Salazar harbored his own animosities about Kohl. He expected the coward to be accompanied by a couple of husky, pug-ugly guards, assigned to drag him to a stout tree limb and a reliable noose.

Alone as he reluctantly stepped inside, Kohl closed the door.

Aware of protocol, and his own well-groomed manners, Salazar motioned to an empty chair. "Please," he said. "Sit down, *Major* Kohl."

As Kohl hesitantly accepted Salazar's hospitality, the tension was unbearable.

"Did you come here to remind me that you're a high and mighty major, while I'm just a snotnosed second lieutenant?" asked Salazar, with a half-smile. "Or are you surrendering to me, after you fess up on your role in killing Reggie and my two guards? You and that self-righteous, pudgy friend?" Salazar stopped. For Yuri's sake, he halted his suspicions of Theo. "Brandy?" he asked Kohl, in a conciliatory tone. "It's not Romero's, but . . ."

"I had nothing to do with that," said Kohl, masking anxiety in his voice.

"And I was only to deliver you to General Chang and your brother, Admiral Kraig," stated Salazar, pouring his nemesis a glass of brandy. "You were in good hands with me, *Major* Kohl, or so I thought . . ."

"That filthy symbol on your jacket said otherwise!" snapped Kohl.

"What symbol?" chuckled Salazar. "I ripped the damn thing off and left it in the road beside my dear, departed horse."

"How can a man of your education and stature support a thug like Gornick?"

"And how can a lily-livered career officer support a book publishing, rabble-rousing, fat bastard? . . ." Once more, Salazar silenced his attacks against Theo. "Major Kohl and I need to talk, Yuri," he said, to protect the boy from a hostile, verbal exchange. "Can you make it home, all right? 'Concerned about the presence of a cloaked, hooded assassin in the vicinity, he added, "Come to think of it, you should stay downstairs, until I'm through . . . visiting with *Major* Kohl."

His heart beating rapidly, Yuri opened the door. "Don't worry. I know of a safe way home . . ."

"Are you sure?" asked Salazar.

"There . . . there's a shortcut to Father's," fibbed Yuri. "I should be on my way. Thank you for the meal, Lieutenant Salazar."

"Take care," said Kohl, like an uncle addressing a fond nephew. "I'll be there directly, after I have a word with *Lieutenant* Salazar."

"One more thing," slurred Salazar, staggering toward Yuri. "I don't know how you're going to manage it. Sooner or later, you're going to have to confront that Strunk character and prove that you're not afraid of him, even if you are. Remember what I told you . . ." Salazar put his hand on Yuri's shoulder. "You're a better man than that Strunk guy will ever live to be. Don't you dare forget it."

Unable to look Salazar in the eye, Yuri fled from the room.

Salazar let out a deep sigh. What he had to tell Kohl wasn't fit for the sensitive boy's ears. In truth, it wasn't worth getting into it with a man like Kohl. Salazar wondered if a trading of barbs was detrimental to his military career. His fear, rage, and intoxication had gotten the better of him. He'd forever be haunted by the sight of Reginald, dying slowly in his arms. Eventually, he'd have to share this terrible news with the aide's family, a task he dreaded. Salazar owed it to the dead, and to himself, to find out who called the shots on his men.

It was difficult to be alone in the room with someone that Salazar truly despised. He wasn't scared of Kohl, not at all! Kohl was nothing but a joke in the hallways and lavatories of the War Ministry!

On the other hand, both Salazar and Kohl had friends in high places. Kohl's younger brother was the Navy's head honcho, and Salazar couldn't afford to have Kraig as an enemy.

Kohl saw only a dumb kid in Salazar, and wanted to knock the hell out of him. Clearly, Salazar was badly stunned by that afternoon's massacre. The upstart was thrown out of his safe, "spoiled, rich kid comfort zone." Kohl even felt kind of sorry for him.

As Salazar returned to the table, his face spoke of the severe doubts now plaguing him. Kohl thought that maybe, just maybe, he had the upper hand over him. Leaning back in his chair, he sipped his glass of brandy. "It's a hard thing losing men," he said, quietly. "Isn't it, Lieutenant?"

Salazar didn't answer. His emotions ranged from empathy to contempt. It was embarrassing to view Kohl as anything more than a screw-up.

"So, what are you going to do?" asked Kohl.

"I know what kind of a man you are," Salazar spoke, looking away from Kohl. "I read your dossier . . ."

Kohl's gasped.

"You can't be trusted," continued Salazar, the brandy eliminating any inhibitions he had about confronting a superior officer. "And your rhetoric is as empty as your gutless soul!"

"Just who the hell do you think you are?" snapped Kohl. "I've served my country, long before you were even born. You don't know of the horrors I've seen!"

"Don't say that!" cried Salazar, his lips trembling as he recalled Reginald's murder. "You know what it is about you that grates me so much? 'Are you man enough to die for the honor and glory of Embrey? Are you man enough to follow me to hell and back?' Apparently, you ain't man enough to handle a goddamn thing!"

"What do you know?" argued Kohl, slowly easing his frustration and anger. "Who are you to criticize me? You're just an overgrown, thumb-sucking child who never worked an honest day in his life!"

"Maybe so," mumbled Salazar. "But you once had it all, Kohl, and then what? You wasted it! So many doors were open to you, and you turned them all away!"

"What are you talking about?"

Salazar smiled. "Twenty-eight years ago, in the Kuschan city of Anumun."

With a feeble smile, Kohl battled an urge to leave the room.

"It began as an estuary operation," added Salazar, "then evolved into a full-blown battle . . . Right, *Major?*"

Kohl was speechless.

Salazar chuckled. "You're the only survivor, out of twelve-hundred men. Because of it, you were honored as a state hero. But then what? You rode those dead men ever since, and never again will you be looked upon as a hero." Salazar grinned. "Right, *Major* Kohl?"

"You weren't there!" shouted Kohl, defensively. "How could you understand?"

"Then tell me about it."

"Why?" spit Kohl.

"Because now I *do* want to understand!" insisted Salazar. "Please? I'm listening."

Resenting the punk sitting at the table, Kohl still wished to get through to him. For the first time in nearly thirty years, he allowed the painful truth to get out.

"We went in to clear out what we thought was a small group of holdouts, in the Kuschan city of Anumun." Leaning across the table, Kohl pointed a finger at Salazar. "Allow me to set you straight, Lieutenant, before I go on. You say I rode those twelve-hundred dead men? Damn it, I was buried under them! There was no leaving the Army after that! Every year that passes, I've begged for a way to dig myself out from under those corpses!"

Salazar slammed his glass down upon the table, spraying brandy everywhere. "Just like I suppose you'll find yourself buried under the men you left on Infernus!"

Kohl laughed. "And you under the three you left this afternoon, not far from Councillor Theo's gate!"

"That's my concern," mumbled Salazar. "But we were talking about Anumun . . . weren't we?"

"Anumun didn't start out as a battle," explained Kohl. "We landed a force of two-thousand men into Kusch. Marching inland, we rounded up every local farmer along the way. As we set up camp outside of Anumun, we grilled our detainees for information on the rebels we hoped to destroy.

"In time, both our security and discipline broke down," the major continued. "The raping and looting of the detained Kuschans commenced in earnest. Our soldiers were no better than dogs!"

Salazar shook his head. "Such indulgences aren't permitted in the Embrian Army. What of the officers? Isn't it their duty to control their own men?"

"Like I said, you weren't there," answered Kohl, tiredly.

As Kohl gulped down his drink and poured another, he heard a few customers downstairs sharing an old Embrian folk song. Salazar also listened to the obscure piece of music, haunting even if it was slightly out of tune.

"I was an aide to Captain Lerner," said Kohl. "Unfortunately, it was a filthy scoundrel named Lieutenant Gornick who had General Cleftus' favor. The operation turned into a disorganized rabble, bent on carnal lust and depredation. Gornick and his cronies were right smack in the center of it!"

"I wondered when you'd get to that," groaned Salazar. "Go on."

"When the detainees refused to give up the information our interpreters sought from them, the executions began, followed by mass starvation. Captain Lerner and I attempted to regain control of the mission, and get it back on track. It was not to be."

"The official history of that campaign never mentioned such events!" countered Salazar. "Most of the dispatches I read came from your own personal account, Kohl!"

"And much of what was written was bullshit, detailed by blowhards and braggarts who weren't even there . . . Men like Gornick. Men like you."

Salazar sneered. Too often, Embrian history was laced with myth, legend, and outright lies.

"Our men ransacked Anumun," said Kohl. "There was lots of gold to be won. The more beautiful Kuschan maidens were ordered to serve the officers, and abused in every way imaginable."

Nursing his drink, Salazar quietly evaluated Kohl's story.

"We took everything of value, including food from the mouths of babes," said Kohl, like a distraught parishioner at a confessional. "We even used the Kuschans' horses for larder, as rations for our armies. Soon, the Kuschans were starving. One day, I found a young boy and his sister, weeping over their mother who'd been raped and murdered by a squad of Embrian infantrymen. I took it upon myself to look after those two children. A few days later, they too disappeared. To this day, I never knew what became of them.

"Lerner got so disgusted that he pulled our own troops out of Anumun, and established a new base next to the detainee camp," said Kohl. "Our boys guarded the Kuschan prisoners. By then, most in the company grew so disillusioned they spend their time drunk, even on duty. Lerner did nothing about it. He got so depressed over the reality of it all to care. In the end, I don't think he had any real power to remedy the situation.

"I did what I could to procure food to the prisoners." Filling his glass with

Galbraith's, Kohl swallowed it down. "My efforts were blocked by Cleftus' cruelty and degradation. When I was able, I used our finest men to lead the women and children into separate camps, where I hoped they'd be protected. Gladly, we shared our own rations with them."

Kohl went on. "There was an older detainee named Anatoli, who was a chief among his people. Repeatedly, he referred to me as 'Kohl Kued,' and begged me to set the detainees free."

"Did you?" interrupted Salazar.

"I couldn't," admitted Kohl, sadly. "However, I did establish s bit more control over the men, and procured decent rations to the camp. Days later, Cleftus and his staff, with Fourth Company, returned to Embrey. It was at that point when Lerner tried setting things right."

"But they got worse?" assumed Salazar, having difficulty remaining in his chair due to a cheap-john, second-rate brandy.

"I set Anatoli and a few other prisoners free," said Kohl. "Lerner knew about it, but failed to acknowledge my actions. He could not."

Despite his negative feelings about Kohl, Salazar's curiosity was aroused. "Then what?"

"Ten days later, the initial raid against us took place," said Kohl, in shame. "Mountain tribesmen attacked us from the southern perimeter of the detainment area. They were careful not to injure our troops, but more than a thousand prisoners escaped.

"Lerner was brought in for charges, for my part in releasing Anatoli." Kohl ran one finger along the rim of his glass. "With Lerner out of the way, I took charge of the prison compound, and was ordered not to lose another detainee."

"Not a word of that rings true to me, Kohl," argued Salazar. "You make it sound as if the Embrian forces were little more than thugs and bandits! I had an uncle who died at Anumun, and I doubt whether he conducted himself as you've described."

"Yes," mumbled Kohl. "It's easy to deceive oneself into thinking that we Embrians are better than other men. I myself kept a Kuschan woman as a servant. I convinced myself that she was properly looked after. A number of my fellow officers did likewise. We were nothing more than civilized brutes and rapists."

Salazar snickered.

"Well, there was a price for our ideal of civility," said Kohl. "One morning, we woke to face an army of four-thousand farmers and tribesmen. There was no parley, and their attack left us unprepared. Our sole comfort came in being better trained and armed. After losing more than five-hundred men, we somehow drove the Kuschans back, then retreated to the sea. Knowing our escape route, the Kuschans set roadblocks and traps for us. By the end of the second day, we were whittled down to less than a couple hundred men. With a few other officers, Lerner and I took thirty men and tried fleeing in the night. As we rode out, the Kuschans closed in on our makeshift outpost to kill those who remained. Lerner and I were apprehended early that very next day. There was no trial. One by one, the men were garroted, until I alone survived. It was then that Anatoli once again came to me. Once again, he referred to me as 'Kohl Kued.'"

Reaching into a pocket on the inside of his jacket, Kohl produced a small stone, mounted on a silver chain. "Anatoli gave me this," he said, displaying the stone to Salazar. "He told me this small piece of Kusch was the only thing I'd gain from my adventure into his homeland. Later, I was beaten within an inch of my life!"

Kohl sighed. "When I finally came to, I found no one around me except my companions . . . less their heads."

"Including Lerner's?" questioned Salazar.

Kohl nodded, yes. "I crawled to the beach, where a single ship awaited me. I've kept this stone ever since, though it's no one's idea of a treasure! It's a curse that I'll never free myself of, until I can somehow earn redemption. I hoped to do so at Infernus. I was just as blind during that campaign, as I was in Anumun, those many years ago."

Salazar smirked. "Am I supposed to feel sorry for you? Salute you? Kiss your ass? The Kuschans spared you because you aided them, which makes you a traitor! Right, *Major?*"

Kohl leaped to his feet. "You're a damned fool, Salazar! I do feel guilty, but only for trying to do the right thing. The honors bestowed upon me were not my request. My official reports were destroyed, and replaced by false documents written by Gornick. He knew the truth, but chose to hide it. I wanted out of the Army, but the powers that be refused to discharge me. I want to forget, but I cannot."

Limping toward the door, Kohl turned to the drunken, arrogant lieutenant at the table. "I need one last chance to salvage myself," he said. "Then maybe I'll have a truth I can finally live with. Give time and you'll understand, Lieutenant Salazar. Perhaps you do now, if you're man enough to swallow it. If you can handle the truth."

With that, Kohl stormed from the room and slammed the door behind him.

Left alone in the room, with only the dim light of a single candle flickering across the walls, Salazar poured himself another shot of the cheap-john, second-rate brandy. "Lies, *Major* Kohl!' he slurred, numbing his sorrows in the foul drink. *"Lies!"*

Exiting Salazar's room, Kohl started through the hallway, until he spotted a lone, solitary figure in the darkened corridor. Frightened by what he just encountered, Kohl soon realized it was Councillor Theo's stepson. "Yuri!" he exclaimed. "What are you still doing here? I thought you were on your way home."

Yuri's silence was taken as a sign of shyness and timidity. The boy heard every word between Kohl and Salazar. Vaguely familiar with the Embrians' campaign at Anumun, Yuri knew only Kusch's official version of it. He now viewed Kohl with a greater sense of admiration and pity.

"I don't think that fool understood a word I said back there," whispered Kohl, upset for baring himself to Salazar. "Some men have the luxury to gain courage through liquor. I do not."

Yuri shuttered. It was best never to eavesdrop on private conversations. As usual, he conveyed himself as a soft-spoken, childlike waif.

"Cat got your tongue?" asked Kohl. "Afraid to walk home, alone, in the dark?"

"No, no," stuttered Yuri, his eyes glued to Kohl's spit-shine boots, in the faded light. "I just wanted to make sure you're all right."

"H'm!" snorted Kohl, refusing to acknowledge his fear of Salazar, or concerns

of the lieutenant using his account of Anumun against him. "I can't stand Salazar, the punk," he mumbled. "But the man is right about one thing. The day will come when you have to stand up to that horrid executioner your father hired to cut fence posts and firewood. When and if you choose to do so, that's up to you."

"Yes, sir," said Yuri, barely audible against the sounds of revelry spilling from the dining room, below.

"Well, then do it," said Kohl, heading downstairs. "That is, if you're man enough to go through with it . . ."

10

After stinking up the outdoor privy, Strunk lifted his freezing butt from the cracked boards of the one-holer. Cinching his breeches, he fetched the oil lantern and stepped out into a brisk, moonlit evening.

Nights're gettin' cooler, thought Strunk, heading toward his tiny home next to a cluster of walnut and cottonwood trees, on the east side of Theo's property.

That lazy Salazar never hung around to see his men get a proper burial. Figures. One o' these days, the dumb lieutenant's gonna get himself and ever'one else killed on the Branellian border. The Embrian Army sure picks 'em, layabouts whose mommy and daddy get tired o' supporting. They buy their kid a military commission so the bum'll die gloriously in a stupid, useless charge against the enemy.

The sounds of an agitated hound grew increasingly louder. Mutt either treed a coon, or he'll catch a face-full of porcupine quills. Damn dog better shut up, so I can get some sleep.

Sure gettin' colder out here . . .

Blowing out the lantern in his right hand, Strunk enjoyed the bright moonlight illuminating the fields, orchards, and granite mountains. Expecting the season's first frost by morning, he wanted to stay outside, if it wasn't so chilly.

Strunk got them stupid soldiers buried by sundown. After receiving a generous bonus from Theo, he took a few shots of whiskey while consuming a boiled chicken and sliced taters. No job was too demeaning for someone who once earned a good wage easing the nation of its undesirables. His work was needed, wasn't it? Who else had the stomach for that kinda labor?

Lots o' morons claimed they killed condemned prisoners just as good as Strunk. After bein' given a chance, them amateurs only got the job half done, before barfing all over themselves and the guy getting his head lopped off. Goddamn it! I deserved every shilling they give me!

And just look where it got me . . .

Resting the lantern at the front door, Strunk fetched a few sticks of firewood on the porch when a familiar voice warned, "Don't move."

Strunk now had a dagger pressed into his Adam's apple.

Yuri . . .

Kuschan pansy, sneaking up on a man in the dark! Too cowardly to fight Strunk in a fair show! He can kill 'em good in the back, hiding behind a tree, rock, or bush. Craziness is what got him kicked outa Maliek's school. Pure Kuschan craziness.

Releasing a breath, Strunk debated on whether Yuri would hesitate in slicing his throat. He hated thoughts of dying at the hands of a fairy. Yuri couldn't take 'em, man-to-man, in a brawl. Why hell, of course not! Yuri had more sense than to challenge Strunk in a fair fight!

Strunk heard tell that, even after leaving the body, the brain still worked for a little while. It was a mess of hooey, but kept cowards and braggarts from approaching Strunk in a man-to-man head bashing.

Was Yuri fixin' to do ol' Strunk in? This was the time and place for it! Strunk's arms were tied up with a load of firewood. Even then, Strunk aimed to send one of them sticks into Yuri's face. With luck, he'd shove a nose bone into the fairy's brain, killing 'em right off.

Too bad, though. Yuri was real speedy with blades. "If yer gonna do it, do it," snarled Strunk, more annoyed than frightened. "Don't you go pullin' a blade on me, 'less you aim on usin' it. Hear that, Kuschan?"

"The only reason I don't kill you," said Yuri, with no jest or emotion, "is that it will upset Father."

Strunk smirked. "Does yer daddy know yer snakin' around, pullin' blades on his best slaves? Hell yeah, that'd upset 'em, goddamn it! Who'd chop all that wood? You for sure won't. Can't use a pick or a shovel. Can't use no ax, neither. And you ain't got the balls to slice me."

Strunk expected Yuri to come back with an empty threat. Nothing. Yuri wasn't fixin' to kill ol' Strunk in cold blood, was he? Loyal to Theo, he wasn't one to kill unless Daddy told him to.

What if he sliced ol' Strunk, just to salve his bruised ego?

Strunk smiled. Yuri was nuts! But was he nuts enough to contradict Theo's wishes, and do ol' Strunk in just for the hell of it? Yuri was scared of Strunk, so much so than to face him like a man!

Strunk banked on the idea that, through intimidation, he'd scare the fairy off. "Don't go shovin' a blade at my throat, and think you can get away with it."

"Stay away from me," whispered Yuri, "and I'll stay away from you."

"Hah!" laughed Strunk. "You like talkin' tough to me, Kuschan dog! Does it give you a thrill? The same thrill you got from humpin' that pageboy in Kentworth, before hackin' him to bits?"

"I didn't . . . I didn't kill him!" stuttered Yuri. "I just . . ."

Strunk hit a raw nerve on that crazy little son of a bitch. Did he go too far? Strunk refused to give in to Yuri's demands, or surrender to the weakling. "Yeah," he said, pushing Yuri to show his hand or leave the game. "You poked that Branellian kid with yer ol' John Henry, before pokin' 'em with a knife. Didn't ya?"

Yuri said nothing.

"Didn't ya?" questioned Strunk, riling Yuri despite his better judgment.

Yuri removed the weapon from Strunk's gullet.

Oh hell, yeah! Strunk knowed it all along! Yuri was a goddamn coward! Even with a clear advantage, he lacked the balls to kill a better, tougher man than himself.

Breathing a sigh of relief, Strunk turned around.

The last thing he expected was Yuri sending both feet into his grimacing face...

Leaving Strunk's modest home in the cold, moonlit evening, Yuri felt better *and* worse for putting the former executioner in his place. Well, wasn't that what Major Kohl and Lieutenant Salazar asked of him?

Strunk's saucy tongue was a reminder of what people usually thought of Yuri, who regarded himself as marginal and insignificant, an object of contempt and scorn.

Yuri sought respect, admiration, and acceptance from Embrian society. He hoped his relationship with Theo garnered him that. On the other hand, did he deserve such honors? Did his status as Theo's adopted son assure that he'd be afforded the same praises given to the families of the Embrian hierarchy? Try as he may, Yuri believed he'd never win the adulation of those who earned their parents' titles and property.

Many people despised Yuri, passionately. This was on the boy's mind, after knocking Strunk out cold in the doorway of his own house. Sure, it was gratifying for what he did to Strunk. Regrettably, Strunk was an unworthy folk hero in the hearts and minds in several Embrians, for his exploits on the battlefield, and career as an executioner.

Even if his violent past was justified, *for the good of all,* people often feared and loathed Yuri. Why? Was it because he was a foreigner, "different," or a hired killer, first for Captain Maliek, then for Councillor Theo?

Evaluating his place in the world, Yuri was nearly crippled by overwhelming despair. Tears welling in his eyes, he tried to compensate for the man he was, and the man he so wished to be.

Stinging from Strunk's curses and insults, Yuri permitted the pain to increase, until he could no longer turn the other cheek. As he escorted Salazar to Captain Harris', he failed to consider the source, forget about it, and move on.

Kohl and Salazar practically pushed Yuri to confront Strunk. With that in mind, was Yuri justified in paying Strunk back?

What agonized Yuri was that Strunk's remarks held some basis of truth. It was painful knowing that the one person to uphold Yuri should've condemned him, for the deaths of three Embrian soldiers.

Lieutenant Salazar . . .

Salazar didn't deserve to watch his aide and two guards die. Yes, Yuri disapproved of Salazar's support of General Gornick. Apparently, Salazar was as ignorant of Gornick's true character, as he was of Yuri's true identity.

Yuri had to wonder if he was nothing more than a bloodthirsty murderer. If he wasn't careful, that's all he'd ever be.

So many Embrians hated Yuri because he was a foreigner, because he was "different," and because he was a killer. He couldn't stop being a Kuschan, and would always he "different." Was it too late to change his path as an assassin?

Theo hoped to change Yuri into a man of prestige and honor. His considerable properties were warranted to Yuri, whether it be the publishing company, the land, perhaps even a seat on the Embrian Council. At the same time, Theo still required Yuri's services as an enforcer, in light of the instability within Embrey.

Jumping across a narrow spring, Yuri glanced through a window to see his father reading by candlelight, in the study. Was it possible him to explain his absence? What if Strunk protested Yuri's infractions against him?

Entering the warm house, Yuri began sneaking to his quarters. Theo met him at the study door. "What's going on, son?" he asked, holding a volume of fables and stories from Campensian folklore.

"Nothing," said Yuri, evasively. "I'm going to bed. Goodnight, Father."

Theo pointed toward the study. "Come in here, I'd like a word . . ."

"What's wrong?"

"Maybe nothing," said Theo, his tone stating otherwise. This wasn't so much a request, as it was an order. "Come on, Yuri. Let's talk."

Following Theo into the study, Yuri sat down on a small cot.

"You've been acting strangely since you left with Lieutenant Salazar," said Theo. "Come to think of it, why did you leave with him?"

Though he hated getting cross with Theo, Yuri responded with a question.

"Why did you ask me to kill Salazar's men?"

"Lieutenant Salazar supports Gornick," explained Theo, stifling his anger. "Can't you see that?"

"I like Lieutenant Salazar. I don't think he knows what sort of man Gornick really is."

"I heard from Major Kohl that Salazar already suspects who's responsible for those soldiers' deaths."

"And who is responsible, Father?" countered Yuri. "You, or me? They served the crown, and yet we murdered them!"

"I regret what happened, but Gornick's a dangerous man. I'm guessing so is Salazar. Because of that, I will regard him as a threat, and so will you. We can't be too careful. If Gornick does seize power, and I think it will be soon, the next time Salazar shows up it won't be for Major Kohl, but for me!"

"I know you don't like Salazar, but I do. He was very kind to me today, and I don't have that many friends." Yuri bit his bottom lip. "Salazar doesn't know it was me who . . ."

Theo gained a sense of warmth and comfort from Yuri's mere presence. Without giving it a second thought, he gave the boy a paternal hug.

There had been women in Theo's youth. Many women. Never once did the man think he'd have time for marriage, or to raise children. Now, in the autumn of his life, Theo wanted a son and an heir to receive his wealth and assume his political office. Yuri provided him with just that. He was the son Theo so yearned for, but never had.

"I've been worried about you, lately," said Theo. "I never slept a wink those days you were at the leadership seminar. Today, I worried myself sick when you left with Salazar."

"I worry about you, too," said Yuri, looking at Theo with two soft, sensitive eyes.

"So, where were you all this time? It's freezing outside!"

Yuri searched for an explanation to appease Theo. He hoped his evening with Salazar at the inn, or aggression against Strunk, didn't strain his relationship with the legislator. "The moonlight shining in our woods reminded me of my old home, in the northern Kuschan foothills."

"It isn't safe out there," warned Theo, sternly.

"Are you afraid of cougars?"

"I'm an important man in Embrian politics. Those seeking to harm me may also wish to harm you, too. I can't trust Gornick, nor will I trust those who curry favor with him."

"I don't think Salazar knows the kind of man Gornick really is," repeated Yuri.

"But how can we tell? From now on, Yuri, you and I had better stay close, just in case . . ."

"You need a bodyguard?" interrupted Yuri.

"Because you're my son." Theo caressed Yuri's long, blonde hair.

"I'm willing to die for you, Father, but I hate what I did to Salazar's men!" Tears streamed from Yuri's eyes. "Why did they have to die?"

"I had to stop them from apprehending Major Kohl!" snapped Theo.

"*I* had to stop them from apprehending Major Kohl! Is that what you mean? If you love me as much as you say, please don't ask me to . . . You told Major Kohl and Sergeant Vix that you expect great things from me. Such as?"

"I believe you have the makings to be a fine, decent man," said Theo. "You must understand, even I've had to make decisions which are morally wrong."

"By killing our own soldiers?"

Theo wanted Yuri to grow into a person of quality and courage. However, he still utilized the boy's bloody skills to further his own agenda. With his country on the brink of civil conflict, he required every tool at his disposal, to protect himself and his interests.

What was more important, Theo's position in Embrey, or the love of a child? The day was coming, when Yuri had to give up the sword. Was that day now upon them?

Theo kissed Yuri's forehead. "Since I've known you, I've always thought of you as my own flesh and blood. However, we've got to be more careful. I don't want you leaving the premises, unless it's absolutely necessary. And I don't want you anywhere near Lieutenant Salazar."

"I'm sure Salazar loves Embrey, the same as you."

"The same as me? Whose image of Embrey, mine or General Gornick's?"

"He may be swayed to our side," argued Yuri.

"*Hmm . . .*" Theo was skeptical. "I just wonder about that."

Throughout his life, from the merchant marines to operating a publishing house, then onto the Embrian Council, Theo had to surrender something, in order to gain something in return. Yuri's loyalty and devotion were unworthy of compromise. Theo knew he'd have to reconsider Yuri's service to Embrey and to himself, in exchange for a young man of virtue and honor. Was he truly willing to make such concessions or sacrifices?

"As much as I love Embrey," said Theo, "I love you that much more, Yuri."

Wiping his teary eyes, Yuri smiled. "I love you too, Father."

Even in the cold weather, Strunk slept well at the doorway of his shed, surrounded by slabs of firewood scattered like oversize matchsticks. By the time he woke up, minutes after sunrise, he found a number of chickens scratching at his weakened body. Strunk suffered from a fractured nose, two black eyes, and a mind-numbing headache.

Leaning against the porch railing to stay upright, Strunk didn't know what hit him. Seconds later, he couldn't accept the reality of it all. Retracing the steps from the outdoor privy to the shed, Strunk contemplated those few, short moments he was threatened, then assaulted, by the lowliest person he could ever imagine.

Strunk prided himself in saying that he never ran away from, or lost a fight. Until now. Knowing who had bested him made Strunk wish that the sorry, sawed-off son of a bitch had put him out of his misery. Strunk was cursed with realizations that he got whipped by Theo's cowardly, queer-eyed, shoot-'em-from-behind son.

Yuri . . .

That goddamn Yuri . . .

11

"I'm away on business for just a few short days," complained Leader Karl, early Tuesday morning. "When I get back, I find this entire facility in turmoil!"

Monday evening, as the sun dropped below the horizon, Karl returned to Lord Kelly's Academy. Rarely was he in a good mood. Upon his arrival, he was downright nasty with everyone. In his fifty years at Lord Kelly's, first as a student then as a Leader, he claimed never to have seen it in such disarray.

Sven blamed Karl's disposition on exhaustion, from travel and separation from home. Karl always griped at his colleagues for their leniency. But, by dawn that next day, he cracked down on students and staff, alike. "I get back last night," he harped. "Go to check on the boys in their dormitory, and practically get knocked down by their horseplay!"

The other three Leaders, Sven, Royce, and Sebastian, sat obediently as Karl lathered on about the poor discipline. They've heard this spiel, before. It was always like that, when Karl left to share God's word with King Ogden, simply to return in failure.

The Junior Leaders dealt with Karl's heavy-handedness in various ways. Sven lubricated himself in wine. Sebastian, the eldest Leader, let it go in one ear and out the other. Royce would soon be freed from Lord Kelly's, through matrimony.

"Now," said Karl, frowning. "Who assigned *him* as my secretary, without first consulting me?"

"Kenichi came to us with extremely high marks," said Sven. "From what I heard, Lord Charles' hated to part with him."

Royce, too, sang praises for Kenichi. "I never met a more conscientious worker than what you've got, sitting . . ."

"But no one consulted me about it!" yelled Karl, the veins in his neck protruding.

"You were gone," said Sven, with a silly grin, "and we needed a secretary."

"Give the boy a chance," said Sebastian, curling a finger through his gray, mutton chop sideburns. "Looks like he's doing a good job, to me."

"Who gives you the authority to explain my responsibilities to me?" questioned Karl.

Sebastian's seniority would've granted him the position of Head Leader. Advancing years and a weak heart motivated him to offer Karl the post, a decision he soon regretted. Sebastian's anger nearly caused him to pounce onto Karl.

Working at the desk outside of Karl's office, Kenichi heard everything said about him. No door divided his station from that of the Head Leader's. Appreciating the sentiments issued by the Junior Leaders, Kenichi was unable to tolerate Karl's hostility. Upon their introduction, he received bad vibes from Karl, who refused to chat with him except on matters affecting the school's finances. Kenichi never expected a cold reception from the administrator. He wished to plead his merits and qualities, but waited to hear the others' opinions before charging in.

"What exactly do you have against Kenichi?" asked Royce. "You don't even know him."

"And you do?" Karl fetched a dossier from a thick stack of papers on his desk. "Are you aware of his background?"

"What does that have to do with anything?" asked Sven.

"Well, look for yourself!" Karl handed the folder to Sven. "Not only is Kenichi of mixed blood, he's also illegitimate!"

"Half of the children at this school are illegitimate!" barked Sebastian. "What about Eduardo? Sister Judith's got nothing but good things to say about him."

"Yes," agreed Karl. "At least Eduardo's mother wasn't a strumpet!"

Embrian law stated that Kenichi had to reside at the school until he reached the age of maturity. No one said he had to be subjected to ignorance, ridicule, and bigotry. Kenichi stepped toward the Karl's office, when common sense took over. Repeatedly counting to ten, he slowly entered the office. "Leader Karl?" he spoke, concealing his outrage. "I just completed those invoices you gave me, this morning."

Royce said, "You're doing a fine job, son."

"Thank you," said Kenichi, touched by Royce's politeness.

"Take a few minutes, go outside, and get some fresh air," suggested Sven.

"Yes, sir," said Kenichi, inadvertently frowning at Karl.

"And Kenichi?" asked Karl, muting his criticisms. "Tell Brother Bradley I wish to see him."

Kenichi was torn. It was wise to remove himself from the Administrative Building, and get some needed sunlight and exercise. He'd never enjoy the cordial, loving relationship with Karl, as he had with Lionel. So be it. Kenichi hoped that, if nothing more, he and Karl merely *coexisted*.

"We've heard what Leader Karl thinks of Kenichi," said Sven. "Why don't we settle this now, by putting his appointment to a vote?"

"That's unnecessary," insisted Karl, knowing he was badly outnumbered in the room. Why give Sven the satisfaction by making him look foolish in the other Leaders' eyes? Although he had already made up his mind about Kenichi, Karl wouldn't win that dispute.

Shuffling through his paperwork, Karl cleared his throat. "Onto the next subject," he said. "Our records state that last month's sale of potatoes was down . . ."

"Sorry I'm late!" interrupted Giorgio. Dashing into the office, he looked like something the cat dragged in. Blonde whiskers dotted his face, while his robe was badly disheveled.

The Junior Leaders gave Giorgio a cautious glance. These men went to bat for him and, as with Kenichi, their views dissented from Karl's. Due to Giorgio's tardiness, no one defended him now. His strongest supporters now questioned his readiness for Leadership status.

"Did I miss anything?" asked Giorgio, nervously.

"Yes," said Sven. "The meeting."

Karl's displeasure with the young man was apparent. "I'd like to be alone with *Leader* Giorgio," he said. "Will you gentlemen please excuse us?"

As Sven, Royce, and Sebastian departed, Giorgio swallowed. This was the verbal equivalent to a trip behind the woodshed.

"A Leader is expected to be neat, tidy, and punctual," reminded Karl, angrily.

"I'm sorry about that," apologized Giorgio. "It's just that. ."

"Where were you?"

Giorgio said nothing.

"You know how I feel about Councillor Theo," said Karl, pointedly. "Giorgio, a Leader has no place taking sides in any political debate."

"Is that why you're so cozy with King Ogden?"

"Those visits have nothing to do with politics! I'm simply performing my obligations as the King's spiritual adviser."

"Why bother? We both know Ogden's a pervert who squanders hard-earned tax money on . . ."

"Shut your mouth!" yelled Karl. "How dare you speak to me like that? I've been a Leader for more than forty years!"

"So?"

"Perhaps I've learned something about my duties. I doubt you ever will."

"You opposed my appointment as a Leader-Trainee," said Giorgio, emotionally. "I want to know why."

"Despite what you might think," said Karl, "I don't dislike you. Indeed, you've got a lot going for you. The boys look up to you. And you're right about King Ogden. He is a degenerate, undeserving in his rule over us."

"Thank you," whispered Giorgio. "I value your honesty, Leader Karl."

"For the moment, I have Ogden's ear and I do my best to steer him toward a more wholesome and chaste life. It devastates me knowing that his relationship to children is an abomination. Whether you're aware of this or not, some of our boys were . . . well, enough about that."

"That doesn't surprise me," said Giorgio, in hushed tones.

"I deal with Ogden, because my role in his court helps us at Lord Kelly's," explained Karl. "Your association with Theo is a detriment."

"Why?"

"Because Ogden and Theo dislike each other, intensely. Much of our income derives from Ogden's own coffers. Will Theo make the same commitments?"

"I believe he would," stated Giorgio. "I have spoken to him about it, and with a few concessions . . ."

"Theo's disagreements with Ogden divide Embrey," interrupted Karl, bluntly. "You and I can't afford those same divisions, within Lord Kelly's or in our own hearts."

Giorgio squinted at Karl. "Why do you oppose Councillor Theo? He's done nothing wrong, and . . ."

"The man is a secularist, and I won't abide it. Either you forgo your allegiance to him, or I must ask you to leave."

Giorgio laughed. "Forgo my allegiance to Councillor Theo? Fine. You forgo your allegiance to King Ogden."

"Ogden is the monarch! Are you suggesting that we commit treason?"

"Theo is an Embrian Councillor," said Giorgio. "Are you suggesting that we forgive a pedophile?"

"I hear the word of God. Does Theo? He'll take this country into a civil war, with his upholding the rights of knaves and peasants."

"Theo opposes the Border War, sir. So do I."

Karl patted Giorgio's back, realizing he had tread too heavily. "I'm aware that your parents died in the war," he said, in a conciliatory tone. "Believe me when I say I am genuinely sorry for that."

"Thank you," said Giorgio, also seeking reconciliation. "Sir, the Border War is immoral, and runs contrary to the word of God. Embrey has encroached upon

Branellian territory, and at what cost? Thousands of men are slaughtered . . .”

"That's precisely what I'm afraid of," said Karl. "Your obsessive anti-war views, if expressed openly, will endanger this school."

Giorgio snickered. "Are you afraid of them endangering this school? Or that they endanger your obsessive rule over us?"

Karl's temper flared. "What did you say? I'm in charge here, and I'll not abide your insolence to me, or to any other Leader!"

"You say that Ogden subsidizes this school out of his own pocket," challenged Giorgio. "How much of that goes into *your* pocket?"

Kenichi gave Bradley the message to meet with Karl. Once the two teens reached the office, Karl and Giorgio were engaged in a wild screaming contest. Trying to ignore this explosive racket, Kenichi penned a letter to a nearby parish. It was futile. The name-calling and accusations proved too great of a distraction.

As Kenichi grew tired of the argument, Bradley was scared. He thought Karl would soon give him the same treatment as Giorgio. Removing his skullcap, he wiped sweat from his forehead.

"Enough of that!" demanded Karl. *"Enough!* I'll say this just once more, Giorgio. Forgo your allegiance to Councillor Theo, or leave this school."

"Maybe Sven, Royce, and Sebastian have other ideas about that," argued Giorgio.

"You were late for today's meeting. Do you honestly expect them to stick up for you, now?"

Giorgio had no comeback.

"I gave you an ultimatum, Giorgio," said Karl. "Either you're for me, or you're against me."

Even with his love for Lord Kelly's, Giorgio found it impossible to serve under Karl. He needed time for a realistic, mature decision. "I'll have an answer for you by this weekend," he informed, "if not sooner!"

Without acknowledging Bradley or Kenichi, Giorgio stormed from the office. He didn't want anyone noticing the tears in his eyes.

"Brother Bradley," addressed Karl, standing at the doorway. "Come in here, please? I'd like to speak to you."

Bradley turned to Kenichi for support, then entered the office. Sitting on a large oak chair across from Karl's desk, his spindly legs hung from the seat, as both feet barely touched the floor.

"Brad," said Karl, sitting behind the desk. "I admire your dedication to Lord Kelly's."

Bradley sighed. "Thanks."

"However, I heard you went to the theater, while I was away."

Now comes the reckoning! "Yes . . . yes, sir," answered Bradley.

"And taking swims in the river, during work?" pressed Karl, suspiciously.

Bradley nodded, his heart skipping a beat.

"Well, young man," said Karl, flatly, "that must stop."

"But why? Why can't I go to a play, once in a while?"

"You must give your full devotion to this school, and to your creator. Above all else, you must promise never to repeat anything from this conversation." Karl paused. "The monarchy verges on collapse."

Bradley's mouth gaped open.

"Giorgio was right about certain things," admitted Karl. "King Ogden's mishandling of the war, and his . . . moral digression, has lost favor with the Embrian Council, his military advisers and, more importantly, the rabble who want his head on a platter. Then we have malcontents like Giorgio's *esteemed* Councillor Theo speaking treason. Try not to worry, Brad, though we find ourselves in dire times. In moral terms, we must hold ourselves above everything else, so not to be affected here."

Bradley shook his head, in disbelief. How can we not be affected?

Stepping from behind the desk, Karl rubbed Bradley's shoulder. "I didn't mean to frighten you. It's just that . . . we must stand firm and strong. Whoever has control of the country, we can't draw their attention or ire. I'm not cracking down on Lord Kelly's because I want to, but because I have to. If we appear weak in our faith, or subversive in our hearts, we'll lose the school. I'll be ousted from this post on the mere hint of treason, and Heaven only knows what will happen to you, if Lord Kelly's even survives."

Panic, overpowering and inescapable, seized Bradley.

"That's why I demand Giorgio's loyalty," explained Karl. "His misplaced support of Theo undermines our mission to God. I pray that Theo doesn't gain control of Embrey. He's not supportive of our faith. I can't seem to get that through to Giorgio."

Bradley recalled those afternoons when Theo visited the school, to purchase produce and wine. Theo always seemed upstanding and friendly. Bradley wondered if Theo was unkind to Lord Kelly's, or simply toward Karl. "What do you want me to do?" he asked, nervously.

"Stand beside me," urged Karl. "Stand beside Lord Kelly's."

"But I'm scared!"

"Me, too. But we must be brave, and pray that God grants us the conviction and courage to endure this. We can't rely on Sven or Giorgio, anymore."

"How come?"

"Sven's too passive and easygoing, while . . ." Karl chuckled. "Well, Giorgio's like the wind. His loyalty won't remain with us, even if he wanted it to."

"But I respect Giorgio!" protested Bradley.

"Can we trust him?" asked Karl, suspiciously.

"I trust him."

After a long period of silence, Karl said, "I can't serve here forever. I still have to make sure Lord Kelly's stays in good hands. You care for our school, don't you, Brad?"

"Of course, more than anything! I want to spend the rest of my life at Lord Kelly's!"

"You know," said Karl, warmly. "I've been here since I was your age, and look where I am, today. I . . . I wish you could take my place as Head Leader."

"Me? I'm not even a Leader, yet! Who says I'm even smart enough to? . . ."

"Well, not yet, anyway!" laughed Karl.

"What about the other Leaders?" asked Bradley, a hollow feeling in his stomach.

"Leader Sebastian's older than I am, and his health's failing. Royce is getting married. Sven and Giorgio . . ." Karl stopped. What assurances were there that Sven and Giorgio wouldn't attempt to replace him?

"Why me?" asked Bradley. "What makes you think I'd be a good Head

Leader?"

"When it comes to our congregation, you're the best we got! You're the type of kid Lord Kelly's deserves! We need you, Brad. Believe me, we need you!"

Bradley examined his priceless necklace, a gift from Karl representing the school and its service to God and man.

"I'm sorry," said Karl. "I've overstepped my authority by suggesting that you'll soon be ready to take my place. However, I have reasons to worry about the school's future. I sincerely believe that, in due time, you will be our Head Leader."

Bradley grew faint. Me, the Head Leader of Lord Kelly's?

Legally, applicants were prohibited to begin coursework in Leadership, until age eighteen. It was a long, grueling process, testing their reliance upon self, along with blind faith in God. Hunger and isolation were two major obstacles. Applicants went days without speaking. They were locked away in rooms lacking windows or candlelight. Memorization of spiritual doctrine was essential. Depending upon the weather, a Trainee's quarters were like an oven, or an icebox. Applicants were grilled mercilessly on verses and teachings.

Eventually, they ventured into the granite mountains, overlooking Sykes. For a month, they lived off the land, with no human companionship or assistance. During this ritual, they were expected to make contact with the Almighty.

"I'm not supposed to do this," said Karl removing a book from a shelf behind him and handing it to Bradley, "but I want to give you an advantage. Share this with no one."

Bradley skimmed through a large, dusty textbook, titled *Guidelines in Leadership*. With no cited author, it was easily the thickest book he ever laid eyes upon.

"Give me your word you'll never repeat what we've discussed, today," concluded Karl.

Wondering what he was getting himself into, Bradley shook Karl's hand and, with a sigh, left the office.

Little did he know that Giorgio stood outside of an open window, hearing everything that was said . . .

Bradley spotted Kenichi toiling over mundane accounting and paperwork. "Kenichi?" he said, glancing into the office to see if Karl was eavesdropping. "Can you help me with this?"

During his time at Lord Kelly's, Kenichi grew to like Bradley, and was honored to give him a hand. Examining the textbook, he gladly accepted the job as Bradley's tutor. "Sure," he said, smiling. "When do we start?"

12

The topic may have been fascinating, but the details were excruciatingly dull.

It was in the early evening. Outside the gray, thunderous clouds threatened rain. Bradley and Kenichi sat in the dormitory study hall, reading the first chapter of Guidelines to Leadership. The anticipation and excitement, which they first met this challenge, quickly waned. Whoever wrote that dull book showed no enthusiasm toward the rights and responsibilities afforded Leaders. The anonymous author probably never achieved that lofty career, or had and grew to hate every minute of it.

Within the first few hours of scanning the text, the boys' thoughts drifted. Their chairs were uncomfortable, the lights were dim, and students streamed back and forth through the area. Bradley considered going into his room to study. The other roommates, Trevor and Derek, often turned it into a madhouse with their squabbles and pillow fights.

"Kenichi?" yawned Bradley, rubbing his eyes. "What are you going to do, when you turn eighteen?"

"After I climb Mount Patten again," said Kenichi, "I'm hiring on the first freighter leaving Embrey, and sail places I've never been before."

"Why don't you stay here, and become a Leader like me?"

Kenichi frowned. An honest answer could potentially damage his friendship with Bradley. "I'm not at home at Lord Kelly's," he said, a bit apologetically.

"But you're really smart! If Royce gets married, and Giorgio has to go, we'll need your help."

"I don't think Karl likes me."

"I know, but . . ."

"And I don't get along with some of the other guys," added Kenichi. "You're the only one who's that nice to me. You and Eduardo, I guess."

"It's just that you're the new guy."

"I was the new guy at Lord Charles', too. I hate being the new guy."

"I wish you'd just stick it out," moped Bradley.

"Come with me to Mount Patten next summer," begged Kenichi. "You said you would."

Bradley made promises he wasn't likely to keep. "Karl needs me here."

"Karl doesn't own you, Brad! It's a big world out there, and we should see it, the both of us! Come on! We'll visit every port city from St. Alexandrov to . . ."

Bradley shrugged. "And . . . I think I'm needed here, too."

"Then take a year or two off and work on a freighter with me."

"I can't do those Leadership courses without you! If we're both Leaders, it won't be long before we're running Lord Kelly's!"

Kenichi couldn't understand Bradley's devotion to the school. He'd never get shy of it, soon enough! With a sly grin, he mused, "If I was the Head Leader, the first thing I'd do is get better uniforms."

Bradley was offended. "What's wrong with our tunics?"

"Well, just look!" Kenichi stood. "Mine doesn't even reach to my knees! Anytime I leave the campus grounds I think everyone's staring at my legs! It's embarrassing!"

"But I like our uniforms!"

"Why?"

"It shows that we belong to Lord Kelly's, and that it belongs to us," stated Bradley. "We belong here, Kenichi. Don't you take pride in your school?"

"I'd take pride in *your* school, if only it took pride in me. I'll never like these uniforms! My legs get cold or sunburned, and I feel so naked!" Kenichi laughed. "Frankly, I think the United Westerland Brethren wear snazzier clothes than we do."

"You're not serious!"

"Yeah, Brad," responded Kenichi, flatly. "I am."

"Hey, boys!" cheered Fritz, storming into the study hall like a bull in a china closet. "Let's get us some women, tonight!"

Thanks to Fritz's arrival, the study session had drawn to a close. What upset Bradley was the entourage of younger boys, following the troublemaker into the room. He wanted to expel guys like Fritz, serpents bent on corrupting naive, impressionable minds.

"I'm sick of working in the garden," commented Fritz, his voice booming throughout the study hall. "I'd rather rake my hoe into something else!"

"Let's go," whispered Bradley, sneaking the textbook into a tote bag.

"C'mon, fellas!" roared Fritz, slapping Kenichi's back. "Wanna go to The Rooster's Beak with me?"

"No," groaned Kenichi.

"What about it, Brad?" taunted Fritz. "Ain't ya heard, boys? Brad's a regular ladies' man. Never turns down the chance to wet his noodle."

"Shut up!" cried Bradley. He regarded his virginity as a positive thing. Fritz made it sound so terrible.

"'Shut up!'" mocked Fritz, in a whiny voice. "Whadda ya say, Kenny? Y'ain't getting yer kicks with Brad! Wanna get laid tonight? I'm buying!"

"No," groaned Kenichi, who liked the name *Kenny* as much as having Andre refer to him as *Itchy*. Grinning, he asked, "So, Fritzy. How's life with Andre and Bentley?"

Noting a crack in Fritz's armor, the younger boys released nervous chuckles.

"The Rooster's Beak don't give a damn if yer white or yellow," said Fritz, struggling to recover. "They even sell darkies! Hell, the joint might even rustle up a butt-boy for Brad. You'll feel right at home!"

"Shut up, Fritz!" repeated Bradley.

"You shut up, Brad," ordered Fritz. "Why don'tcha go play with your hand?"

Bradley's face reddened. The boy did nothing against Fritz. His love of God, along with fear, kept him from taking a swing at the antagonist.

Fritz snickered. "Oh, I forgot. You don't believe in jacking off, do ya? Then let Geoff and Randy take care of it. They might even wrap their mouths around it, for shits and chuckles."

Fritz's lewd remarks garnered laughs from many onlookers. Bradley's pained expression caught Kenichi's attention.

"You know, Fritz," said Kenichi. "I should be right at home at The Rooster's Beak. I grew up in a place like that. And I've had enough of those women."

"So *that's* why Karl don't like ya!" cackled Fritz. "Sure didn't suck being you, growing up in a cathouse. Wish I lived in a joint like that. I'd never leave!"

"Maybe you can say that, but I can't," mumbled Kenichi, knowing his disclosure troubled Bradley. "I just had enough of women like that."

"'Enough'?" balked Fritz. "Man, a fella can't get enough pussy, at least I can't! How much is enough, Kenny?"

"Enough!" shouted Kenichi, tiredly. "How much have you had, tough guy?" Kenichi's tone intimidated Fritz.

"You know, Fritzy," continued Kenichi. "If one of the girls didn't have a client, they took *me* to bed."

Fritz upheld his swagger, though it was gradually fading. "Oh, yeah? How much that cost ya, Kenny?"

"Nothing, Fritzy, nothing. You see, unlike some of the customers, I never beat on the women before they took *me* to bed. I never proved my manhood by slapping them around. I slept with the girls, because it made them feel better. After I left the brothel, I sold myself to rich society dames to fill my stomach and sleep somewhere besides under a bridge, or in an abandoned building." Kenichi laughed, despite the misery this experience brought him. "Guess that made me the whores' whore, and the sluts' slut."

Bradley didn't know whether to respect, despise, or pity Kenichi. He only wished Kenichi was more like him; pure, innocent, and clean.

"It's easy for anyone with a little money," said Kenichi, thumping Fritz's chest with his finger. "It's just fun and games for loudmouths to brag about, go blundering in like they owned the place. For me, screwing got to be just another chore, like cleaning rooms, changing sheets, or emptying piss pots. So much of a lousy job that I loved it and I hated it, as I loved and hated myself for it. I'll tell you this much, hotshot. My mother was a whore, and I've got a lot more use for whores than I'll ever have for you. So, whatever you do, don't talk to me about whores. I forgot more about whores than you'll ever know!"

That was it. Fritz was knocked down a peg or two. Those watching this exchange kept score.

Lifting his tunic, Fritz cupped his scrotum in one hand. "Rooster's Beak, here I come!" he shouted, exiting the room.

"Where's he think he's going?" questioned Kenichi. "He's not permitted to leave campus."

It was wonderful that someone had finally countered Fritz. Yet, what were Bradley's opinions of Kenichi now? Was Kenichi any better than someone of Fritz's caliber?

Kenichi's personal history was far from honorable. There was no way to change it, in order to meet a friend's approval. Kenichi still rated Bradley highly. He didn't grant the school or its Leaders the same considerations.

"All right, *Leader* Bradley," said Kenichi. "Don't just stand there. Let's get to work!"

13

Fritz stormed from the dormitory, wanting to kick Kenichi's ass! He was more than willing to pay for the half-breed's good time, too!

Lord Kelly's was a jail. With Karl's return, it evolved into a concentration camp. Fritz once held dominance over most of the students. Things changed, when Kenichi refused to dance to Fritz's tune. Thoughts of pounding the slant-eye's nose in, over and over, grew obsessive.

Fritz sat on a bench, between the two dormitories. As the sun sank in the west, a cool breeze stung his sinewy legs. He didn't care. He needed a night on the town, rubbing shoulders with soldiers and sailors, before topping it off in the arms of a "princess."

Spying through a window at the Leader's dorm, Fritz caught a splendid sight. Sven relaxed in his room, with the good book and a bottle of Lord Kelly's wine, produced from its own vineyards. Fritz licked his lips. Lord Kelly's hooch was crap, but hooch was hooch!

Now, how to swipe a few bottles from Sven?

Trevor and a smaller boy, Brother Derek, left their dormitory and headed to chapel for prayers and meditation. Derek was a frail-looking child with sleepy eyes, spindly legs, and a ghostly skin color. Fritz smiled. Sven was easily diverted by the younger boys. Anyway, the drunken Leader had far too much booze on his hands! It was his social and moral obligation to share the wealth!

"Trevor, Derry!" called Fritz. "C'mere! I got a deal for ya!"

"What's going on?" asked Trevor.

"Think you can get Sven outa his room for just a few minutes or even . . ." Fritz stopped. "An hour?"

"What for?" asked Trevor, curiously.

"Never mind what for!" barked Fritz. "Just get him outa his room!"

"What're we supposed to do with him?" asked Derek.

Fritz sighed. "Aw, I dunno. Talk to him about . . . *God.*"

"What's in it for us?" hinted Derek.

"A fun night out with the boys," offered Fritz. "Or are we gonna sit around playing 'Twenty Questions'?"

"Okay," agreed Trevor, oblivious to Fritz's intentions.

"Remember," whispered Fritz, "you gotta keep Sven outa his room, until . . ."

"What're you gonna do in Sven's?" questioned Derek.

This is gonna take forever! "Fetch us some treats," said Fritz. "And if ya do really good, I'll share 'em with ya!"

"What kinda treats?" asked Trevor.

"Only the best," assured Fritz. "Just like what they gave you at The Rooster's Beak, before you chickened out and ran!"

Deviously, Trevor and Derek agreed to Fritz's bidding . . .

Sven read a few verses from *The Book of Dino,* and poured himself another glass of wine when a knock on the door diverted him. Staggering, he was surprised to see Trevor and Derek at the door. "Good evening, gentlemen," he slurred. "What can I do for you?"

"We . . ." Trevor swallowed. "We got a buncha questions . . . about God!"

"You came to the right man," boasted Sven. "Come in, and we'll discuss . . ."

"Can't we just go to the study room?" interrupted Derek, his wheezy voice cracking.

Sven frowned. "Why not just stay here?"

"Leader Karl might think something evil!" Derek twitched a nervous eye. "Like maybe you was getting all touchy with our legs and, y' know, other *nasty* stuff."

"Why would he think? . . ." Sven paused. "Good point, Derry. But who'd even know you were here? The mice?"

"Please?" whined Trevor. "I don't want the other kids saying bad things about me and Derry."

"Wait 'til I get my book an' bottle." Burping, Sven nearly knocked over his wine glass. Slowly, he led the boys to a study room. A single lantern, hanging from the ceiling, lit the small space with hard oak benches and a round table. Resting his wine on the table, Sven awaited the first question.

Trevor and Derek gawked at each other, expecting their buddy to begin.

"Well, let's not be in such a hurry," remarked Sven, with a clever smile.

Derek cleared his throat. "Does God see and hear everything?"

"Why yes, Derek," said Sven, warmly. "He does."

"But how?" asked Derek.

Sven hesitated. "He just . . . does. His angels check up on us."

"Where are these angels?" asked Trevor, peeking around the room.

Sven sipped his wine. "They're invisible."

"How?" asked Derek.

"They just . . . are, that's all," answered Sven. "They tell God what we're doing."

"Tattletales!" shrieked Derek.

"Well, something like that," snickered Sven. "It's their job to tell on us if we're bad."

"Do they get paid for snitching?" asked Derek.

Sven grunted. "Sort of . . . They get to live forever."

"How long is forever?" asked Trevor.

"Forever!" snapped Sven. "You know, Trev, an awful, *awful* long time. A'right?"

"What do angels look like?" asked Derek.

"Hmm . . ." pondered Sven. "Naked little babies, with white wings."

Derek's eyes widened. "That's horrible!"

"How do you know what angels look like," asked Trevor, "if they're invisible?"

"Ask Brother Bradley," suggested Sven, weakly. "He knows everything."

Trevor giggled. "Bet he don't know what's in The Rooster's Beak."

Sven spit wine across the room, wondering how Trevor learned about that wicked place.

"Where does God live?" asked Trevor, quickly changing the subject.

Sven stared at Trevor, suspiciously. "In Heaven."

"Where's Heaven?" asked Derek.

Throwing one arm toward the east, Sven said, "Oh, a long ways away, in . . ."

"The Branellian Empire?" questioned Trevor. "How can that be? Branellians are the enemy!"

Sven laughed. "No, Trevor, not the Branellian Empire! I meant ..."

"The Wilderness?" inquired Derek.

"Uh-uh!" disputed Trevor, referring to random, unexplained occurrences in eastern Branell, at a remote area plagued by strange creatures. "That's where the demons live, moron!"

"No it ain't, dummy!" yelled Derek. "Ain't you never heard of the Great Ripped?"

"Boys, boys!" cried Sven. "Cool it. There's no need to fight!"

"Oh, a'right." Trevor stuck his tongue out at Derek. "So,where do we live?"

"The Earth," said Sven, impatiently. "Just where do you think? The moon?"

"I dunno," Trevor said, with a shrug. "Where does the man on the moon live?"

"Where is the Earth?" asked Derek. "And how old is it?"

Sven drank straight from the bottle and sighed, "Welcome to my world . . ."

Fritz entered Sven's quarters through a hinged window. A single wax candle, placed on a night table, lit the modest room. A narrow bed and sets of mugs populated it.

Lifting the candle, Fritz noticed a door leading to a darkened corridor. His heart raced. It wasn't merely the reward which the thief sought, but the excitement of the hunt. Carefully, Fritz tiptoed into the room, holding the candle to his front.

Fritz overheard the conversation between Sven, Trevor, and Derek. Stifling a laugh, he didn't know what stopped Sven from slapping the snot out of the two youngsters.

With no time to lose, Fritz sneaked into the corridor to locate a drunkard's paradise. He entered a dank, musty cellar, crowded with various beverages from Embrey and the surrounding region. Fritz only guessed how much booze was in there, or the manner in which Sven acquired it. He nearly let out a cheer, but thought better of it.

Excitedly, Fritz almost snatched the nearest bottle, then ran for it. But no! The crook had gotten this far! What use was it to make off with a product of inferior quality? Most containers were filled with Lord Kelly's wine. Each boy got a glass of the slime with their Sunday dinners. Fritz figured Sven had a valuable concoction, secluded in the cobwebs and dust. Carefully, he searched for a diamond in the rough. There just had to be a hidden treasure which Sven hoarded like the fat, greedy pig he was!

The sounds of footsteps from the hallway sent chills down Fritz's spine. Holding back laughter, he sucked in a deep breath and stood motionless.

As the muffled drone of Sven's spiel carried from the study room, did someone just enter his quarters? Damn it! Fritz regretted taking this chance, no matter how worthwhile it was. He thought about grabbing a few easy bottles, then leaping through the window. The next few seconds were so thrilling, so crucial, so *dangerous!*

Fritz heard Karl's baritone drawl, which was answered by Sven. Gradually, the *clickety-clack* of footsteps faded away. A creaky door opened, then closed. Silence.

Fritz sighed. All was safe. Still, it was best to lift the best available hooch, then make a swift getaway.

Fetching a bottle of Kuschan vodka, Fritz started to scram, when a particular item appeared to him, as if by magic.

A quart of costly rose', from the vineyards of southern Campens, was more than Fritz could have hoped for, or expected. A chuckle slipped past his mouth. How did Sven manage to secure that bootleg bugger? The Campens Rose' far exceeded Fritz's wildest expectations! It was the gold at the end of a dark, dank rainbow!

Without hesitation, Fritz grabbed the Campens Rose' and shoved it under one arm. Only a fool would leave without that beauty!

Fritz was so ecstatic that he paid no attention to the large, black spider crawling up his left leg . . .

"Look, I really don't know how old the Earth is," said Sven. "Prob'ly five or six-thousand years old, according to Scriptures. But anyway, getting back to angels . . . I just happen to know of two little angels, in this very room."

"Who?" asked Trevor.

Sven laughed. "Don't you get it? They're sitting at this very table, and their names are Trevor and Derry!"

"What?" the lads cried out, in unison.

"We're no angels!" argued Derek.

"Why, sure you are!" claimed Sven.

"Uh-uh!" shouted Trevor. "We ain't invisible, we ain't naked babies, and we ain't got no white wings!"

"And we ain't gonna let you get all touchy at our legs!" added Derek.

"When I said that angels tell God about our conduct on Earth," explained Sven, "I didn't mean to imply they're tattletales. They're only looking out for us."

"Sounds like snitching to me," groaned Trevor.

"Very well, then" said Sven. "Let me ask you this. If Derek got into trouble, will you help him out?"

Trevor snickered. "He's always in trouble with Leader Karl."

"No, I ain't!" hollered Derek.

"No, no!" stuttered Sven. "That's not what I meant! We're all in trouble with Leader Karl. But imagine that Derek got attacked by a bear. Will you rescue him from certain death?"

"Of course!" Trevor put his arm around Derek's shoulder.

"And Derry," said Sven. "Imagine that Trevor is pursued by an army of Branellian soldiers. Are you willing to give your life in order to save his?"

"Oh, heck yeah!" exclaimed Derek.

"That cinches it," said Sven. "You're a couple of little angels."

"Whatever," mumbled Trevor.

"Anytime we give of ourselves to a friend, or even to a complete stranger, we're angelic," explained Sven. "That's what God expects of us."

"Really?" asked Derek.

"Lord Kelly's got a lotta angels," said Sven. "You're both angels, Bradley's an angel, Giorgio's an angel, even if Karl don't think so."

"Karl don't think anybody's an angel, except him," said Trevor.

"You got that one right," said Sven. "That new boy, the secretary, what's his name?"

"Kenichi," said Trevor.

"Yeah, Kenichi!" said Sven. "He's an angel, even if Karl don't think so."

"Andre and Bentley ain't no angels," said Derek, getting a laugh from Trevor.

"Andre and Bentley can both go to hell," burped Sven. "Them, and all that other demon spawn . . ."

"Yeah," chuckled Derek. "What about Geoff and Randy?"

"Geoff and Randy?" questioned Sven. "What about them?"

Trevor put a finger to his mouth, to hush Derek. "What about Fritzy?" he asked.

"Yeah," inquired Derek. "What about Fritzy?"

"Fritz's an angel, even if he don't think so," said Sven.

"Fritz?" gasped Trevor.

"Sure, why not?" laughed Sven. "That pea-wit thinks there's nobility in doing stupid stuff. But don't judge Fritzy. Judging's a sin, too. Why, I've seen kids a lot worse'n Fritz turn their lives around, and turn into pretty good guys. If ol' Fritzy puts his mind to it, it's the devil to pay to stop him!"

Neither Trevor nor Derek believed what Sven had just said.

"Aw, you never can tell," said Sven. "You boys might have to depend on Fritz, when the going gets tough. Tell you one thing, I've never seen a harder worker than Fritz, when . . ."

A high-pitched scream in the night ended this meeting. Breaking glass, swift running, and adolescent cursing brought Sven to his feet. "Stay put!" he ordered. "I'll go see what it is!"

Despite being told not to, Trevor and Derek followed Sven to his room.

As Sven entered his quarters, Karl was already there. An open window swung back and forth in the wind, as cool, damp air blew into the room. A smoldering candle lay on the marble floor.

The most disturbing sight was in the wine cellar. Sven and Karl found puddles of Campens Rose' everywhere, along with shards of glass from a broken bottle. Sven had some explaining to do. He saved the expensive drink for a special occasion. Now look what had happened!

The smell of wine on Sven's breath angered Karl. Sven's drinking problem began long before he entered Lord Kelly's as a student, years before. Karl harbored suspicions of Sven's dealings in the black market. The proof covered the cellar walls and floor. Karl believed that Sven was just as responsible for this crime, as the perpetrator.

There was little doubt as to the thief's identity. Who else was that thoughtless of stupid? The truth was especially disturbing to Sven. Similar to Royce, Sven had always defended the hooligan.

Prepared to make a sarcastic remark, Sven turned to Trevor and Derek. He saw something in the boys' eyes, which added insult to injury. Trevor and Derek wore expressions of shame and guilt. Sven was humiliated. How could I be so foolish? The boys' questions were not a sign of innocence, but a ploy to get him out of his room!

"I'll do this on my own," said Sven, kneeling down to clean the mess. He was in deep, hot water with Karl. A more pressing concern involved Trevor and Derek. Sven hoped that his animosities toward them were unwarranted. Still, his tone was fraught with menace. "Though I'd like a bit of help . . . from a couple of little angels . . ."

Fritz leaped through the window with a single bottle of Kuschan vodka, a bruised knee, and a spider bite on his butt. He failed to abscond with the cherished Campens Rose'!

After getting chomped on the rear, Fritz released a bloodcurdling howl, then fled from the scene. He didn't aim to drop the bottle of rose'. It was a sacrifice, indeed a casualty, in his quest to defy society's mores and norms.

Running from the Leader's dormitory, Fritz laughed hysterically. Nothing really worked out! Even then, Fritz viewed this night's caper as a success! He eluded capture, and obtained a small reward for his efforts. Mission accomplished! Fritz limped through a clump of trees and tall grass, to the school's remote cemetery. His knee and butt hurt like crazy! Oh, well. All wounds heal. Fritz had secured a pint of happiness! Nothing else mattered, other than he'd gotten away with exercising his chosen profession. Dark clouds, and the stinking rain, didn't diminish his spirits. Once more, Fritz was on top! The only thing to make it any better was screwing.

After urinating on a deceased Leader's headstone, Fritz stumbled to a gazebo to protect himself from the dismal weather. Relaxing on the floor, he screamed out a shout of victory. As a downpour drenched the world around him, he enjoyed the fruits of his labor.

Fritz promised Trevor and Derry a share of the goods. Too bad they weren't there to reap the benefits! Fritz thought about retrieving his partners in this crime. Was it worth it to go find them? Who says the twerps weren't already confessing their roles in this theft?

Fritz spent years at Lord Kelly's with a knife at his throat. His actions that night were likely his undoing at the school. *Great!* Fritz was sick of the strict rules, the hypocrites, and the lousy do-gooders! He hated the uniform, the endless rituals, and the superstitions. The only power in the Universe was wealth, and the means to get it! Karl, Sven, Brad and Giorgio could all go to that terrible place they constantly preached against!

As Fritz uncorked the bottle of vodka, he swore to kick Kenichi's ass!

So what if Fritz got booted from Lord Kelly's? *Thanks a lot, boys!* Yet, what price glory? His knee and butt were on fire! His leg was swollen, as he suffered from the unceasing, maddening throbbing! The spider bite was an itch not easily scratched. Rolling to one side, Fritz reached under his silk loincloth to caress the growing bump on his rump. Whatever that beast was, the son of a bitch had big teeth! Hopefully, Fritz stomped on it as he ran away.

Fritz drank, not only to celebrate, but to ease the pain. Rain now beat on the gazebo's roof. Though the vodka didn't add up to the trouble, mediocre hooch was better than no hooch at all!

Emptying the pint, Fritz tossed it carelessly into the darkness. He felt good, now! The only problem was that he couldn't move. Fritz lacked the strength to leave the gazebo. It was a dicey proposition, anyway. The cockeyed manner in which the gazebo spun in circles was scary as hell! Fritz feared getting tossed from the speeding platform, then land who-knows-where in the muddy boneyard.

Closing his eyes, Fritz smiled as he gradually blacked out.

14

"Karl thinks he owns Lord Kelly's!" yelled Giorgio. "He told me to follow his rules, or leave!"

"So, what are you to do?" asked Theo, concealing his amusement. He admired Giorgio, but regarded him as misdirected and naive. Giorgio was much like Theo, three decades back. The young man was driven, ambitious, idealistic, and full of himself. Youth often wishes to change the world. After years of disappointments and frustrations, dreamers painfully accept shortcomings, not only in human nature, but within themselves.

"I said I'd give him an answer by this weekend," said Giorgio, crippled by this decision. He spent most of his childhood at Lord Kelly's. It was there he first met Theo, when the statesman bought food and wine. Theo was impressed by Giorgio's interests in politics and government. Even after his parents' tragic fate, the lad possessed a strong sense of optimism. Theo encouraged Giorgio's participation in social discussion, rallies, and dissent.

Giorgio was torn. He wanted to stay true to his spiritual values, while taking sides in important issues. Were his political and religious ideas in sync, or did they contradict each other? Giorgio was blinded by the ultimatum which Karl gave him. He only had a few days to give the tyrant an answer.

Confused, Giorgio paid Theo a visit. The legislator recommended a relaxing stroll in the countryside. That morning, Theo and Giorgio explored the grounds, overlooking Sykes. Due to the overnight rain, the soil was wet and dewy. A calm breeze, fall foliage, and tranquil setting were therapeutic.

Theo disliked Karl. Their disagreements stemmed from the Head Leader's silence toward King Ogden's indiscretions. Ogden's father ruled Embrey with an iron fist. But the economy was stable, the roads were passable, and the military took pride in itself. Ogden's lust for children, his misuse of tax money, and overall weak, self-centered character, sent the nation down a ruinous path. Ogden could not avoid his countless errors by fleeing to a floating bordello on the Ember River. It took more than confessions to Karl to forgive years of abuse.

Theo believed the best solution was to remove the royal malignancy, at any cost. Certain members of Ogden's staff and family also wanted the throne taken from him. Theo hoped it was a bloodless coup, which didn't divide Embrey.

"Perhaps you're too smart for Lord Kelly's," Theo told Giorgio. "Maybe it's just too rigid for a freethinker, which you most certainly are. I think you're too open-minded to tie yourself to scrolls, written centuries ago."

"Don't you believe in God?" asked Giorgio.

"Yes, in my own image of Him."

"Your own image?"

"You've got your own ideals and values, which I believe are godly. Give yourself permission to speak out against injustice, even if it runs contrary to established laws of religion."

"But can't I do so through Lord Kelly's?" questioned Giorgio. "Shouldn't the clergy protest intolerance and hatred?"

"What if the clergy is intolerant and hateful? You'll never get anywhere, providing Karl's in charge. What have the other Leaders to say about this?"

"I'm sure they want me to stay, but are afraid to stand up to Karl. I'm surprised I was even chosen for the Leadership, since Karl hates me so much!"

"Oh, I'm not sure he hates you," said Theo, sarcastically. "He just doesn't like you very well."

"Did you know that Karl wants to appoint a sixteen-year-old as a Leader?" asked Giorgio, with indignation.

"That's against church policy, isn't it?"

"Yes! What's even worse is that Karl wants the kid to replace him as Head Leader!"

"Is the boy even qualified for Leadership status?"

Giorgio sighed. "No, not yet. Don't get me wrong, I love Bradley, but . . ." Giorgio frowned, ashamed of his own jealousy. "Brad will be a good Leader, someday. Right now, he's too mindful and afraid of Karl."

"So you think your friend Brad will obediently endorse Karl's ideology, without question or reservation?" asked Theo. "What are you to do, then? Do you stick it out at Lord Kelly's, just to find yourself in a losing battle?" Theo smiled. "My offer still stands. I'd like having you work with me in the Council Chambers. It'll be an introduction to a long, prosperous career. Omar was once my apprentice, and now he's an Embrian Councillor. Think it over. I've got an empty bedroom in my house, whenever you need it."

Giorgio still had a tough decision ahead of him. Thanks to Theo's kindness and generosity, he'd never end up on the streets. Assuming he was ousted from Lord Kelly's, Giorgio was determined not to be the only one to leave in disgrace.

Moments later, the two men were joined by Yuri and Major Kohl, who spent the early hours hunting with long bows. Despite his advancing years and an injured ankle, Kohl felt like a kid in Yuri's company. Though he was badly winded, his excitement and enthusiasm were evident.

"Your boy's terrific!" panted Kohl. "He's not much of a talker, but just look at this!"

Peeking in Yuri's game bag, Giorgio saw a half-dozen quail, a few squirrels, and a hare. Amazed at Yuri's marksmanship, he released a shrill whistle. "That's great!" he cheered. "How did you do, Major Kohl?"

"I only winged a few," admitted Kohl, tiredly. "I'll tell you, Yuri's definitely man enough to join me on any military campaign. I must have him with me, when I return to the island!"

"What island?" asked Giorgio, curiously.

"Major Kohl's staging a second journey to Insula Infernus," informed Theo, quietly.

"Infernus?" breathed Giorgio, in shock and surprise.

Theo nodded. "I'd appreciate it if you kept that under your hat."

Yuri's grin voiced approval of Kohl's plans.

Theo ran his fingers through Yuri's hair. "We'll talk about it," he said, with a strained grin. "Well, I'm so glad you had fun together. Yuri will be busy cleaning tonight's dinner. Do you like baked quail, Giorgio?"

"It's better than what they serve us at the school," said Giorgio, in anticipation.

"Certain lords prefer not eating meat until it becomes a tad *ripe,*" said Theo. "I like my foods fresh. What we don't serve right away is salted or smoked, like on fishing vessels."

Marching ahead of the others, Kohl and Yuri resembled an old man escorting a beloved grandson on a leisurely outing. "Where did you find him?" whispered Giorgio.

"Yuri?" asked Theo.

"Yeah. He's . . . *unusual,* isn't he?"

Theo snickered. "My adopted son and a delightful hand around the house. We . . . met in St. Alexandrov, on my recent mission to Kusch."

"Councillor Theo?" asked Giorgio. "Do you think Major Kohl can use me on his trip to Infernus?"

Theo was aghast. "But I thought you wanted to help mold Embrey's future, as my aide!"

Giorgio smiled. "Maybe . . . later . . ."

"It'll be risky," warned Theo. "Major Kohl lost most of his men on that last mission. You're a pacifist, Giorgio, not a warrior. Let professionals like Major Kohl and Sergeant Vix do the fighting. I urge you to stay here with me . . . *and* Yuri."

"But what an adventure!" said Giorgio, wildly. "What I wouldn't pay to set foot on Infernus! You traveled the known world, Councillor Theo. Aren't you the least bit curious about uncharted territories?"

Before Theo responded, Giorgio added, "I only hope that some of my buddies at the school could come, too! I'd die for an opportunity like that!"

Theo now had both Yuri and Giorgio to worry about. He understood Giorgio's desires to see faraway lands. As a merchant marine, he faced countless dangers on the high seas. Boastful talk didn't assure that Kohl's second expedition would be a picnic. "Youth," breathed Theo.

"By the way, Councillor Theo," said Giorgio, hesitantly. "As I walked up here this morning, I spotted three graves by your orchard. Was there an accident, or *what?*"

15

Anytime Lieutenant Salazar entered the Ministry of War, he was awed by its size and majesty. Built as a castle for an earlier monarch, the War Ministry was among the oldest, largest, and formidable structures in Western Embrey. Its highest point, displaying the nation's flag, reached nearly a hundred feet above the ground. The stone walls were more than a yard thick. Guards were placed at the rounded gate, in every window, and on the roof. Gargoyles, shaped like birds of prey and carnivorous animals, monitored staff and visitors.

Since word spread that Salazar had lost two guards and a trusted aide, colleagues and superiors distanced themselves from him. Salazar grew weary of constantly explaining and defending his account of the event at Councillor Theo's. It was the consensus that he failed in the simple task of delivering Major Kohl to General Chang and Admiral Kraig. Knocked down from his pedestal, Salazar had the single-minded goal in restoring his name, along with obtaining justice in the deaths of three soldiers.

Salazar was accompanied by a much larger entourage than before. Along with four guards, he was joined by two newcomers. To Salazar's right was Patrick, a lanky, fiery-haired young man assigned as his new aide.

To his left rode one that the lieutenant held at arms' length. As Salazar enjoyed a healthy rapport with Patrick, he refused to befriend his bodyguard, Jesse.

Jesse rode his horse with pride and confidence. That afternoon, he wore a white, satin cape, tunic, tights, and a plumed Cavalier hat, replacing the clothes destroyed in Johanek's bathtub.

Salazar, Patrick, and Jesse dismounted from their steeds in the livery stable, then entered a dark hallway leading to Admiral Kraig's headquarters. The chief naval officer's room was decorated by various forms of booty, claimed in past campaigns.

Without making eye contact, Kraig motioned for his guests to sit. "Sorry to hear about your bad luck," he told Salazar.

Though Salazar wanted to make excuses, he wisely avoided the subject. "Am I to retrieve Major Kohl from Councillor Theo's custody?" he asked, self-consciously.

"Not yet," said Kraig. "Taking into account the present state of our kingdom, we may require Theo and Kohl's allegiance."

Candid in his dislike for both Theo and Kohl, Salazar said, "I don't understand."

"My feelings for Theo are the same as yours," explained Kraig. "General Chang and I have postponed Major Kohl's sentencing for another date, despite General Gornick's objections. Now that we find ourselves lodged between a rock and a hard place . . ."

"You pledge loyalty to Councillor Theo," accused Salazar, "and not to General Gornick."

"Don't you?" asked Kraig, pointedly.

"General Gornick is an officer, and a tribunal member."

"Yes, and General Gornick is a butcher and a madman! Why should I lend support to someone who leads murder raids into the Branellian Empire, and whose atrocities against our own people are ...”

“What if Theo weakens our forces on the border?” interrupted Salazar.

“Your concerns are well-taken,” said Kraig. “And what if Gornick's unauthorized ventures into Kusch pushes us into combat on two fronts? See here, Lieutenant Salazar, I like you, and will not volley blame for what happened at Councillor Theo's.”

“Thank you, sir.”

“I joined the Navy to protect Embrey's interests, and the interests of our citizens. But I will not support a man who commits genocide.”

Salazar sneered.

“Don't give me that look,” growled Kraig. “Be happy to leave here with your head.”

It was an empty threat, and both men knew it. Even then, Salazar wiped the unflattering expression from his face.

“I don't care about Theo,” said Kraig. “However, I took an oath to support and defend the Embrian Council. I worry what Gornick will do, presuming he takes power from King Ogden. I don't know about you, but I've shed enough blood in defending Embrey.”

“Three of my men were killed,” spoke Salazar. “I can't pretend it never happened!”

“My brother wasn't responsible!”

Salazar nearly made a backhanded comment regarding Kohl's competency, but silenced it. “What if Councillor Theo is?”

Kraig learned early on that raw nerves rarely salved easily. “Embrey requires your devotion, more than ever,” he said, in a conciliatory fashion. “More than ever, we must assure that Embrey isn't thrown into a civil war.”

Whether civil war was inevitable, Salazar didn't want Kraig as an adversary. He sought only to stop those who carried out the attack on him. Clearly, he'd leave Kraig's office, empty-handed. “I appreciate your time,” he said, in disappointment.

“It's my pleasure,” responded Kraig, warmly.

Salazar looked at Patrick, then turned toward Jesse in disdain. “Admiral Kraig,” he said, secretly, “there's another issue I'd like to raise with you.”

Kraig ordered Patrick and Jesse to leave. This command upset Patrick. On his first assignment for the Army, the aide had sweat buckets of blood to appease Salazar. Grudgingly, he did as he was told.

Giving Kraig an impish grin, Jesse simply left the room.

“Is Patrick not working out for you?” asked Kraig.

“It's not Patrick!” exclaimed Salazar. “We've been friends for a long time, and I've never met a more loyal and honest man in my life. It's . . . the boy.”

“Jesse?”

“Yes, sir.”

“Jesse's your bodyguard. Surely you don't protest that.”

“I can't trust him,” stated Salazar, humbly.

“I'm not asking him to be your friend.”

“I won't befriend someone of Jesse's ilk! I don't want him near me!”

“You don't approve of his age, his demeanor?” asked Kraig. “Or is it his profession?”

“I don't approve of assassins! And I'll never approve of teaching children to kill, even for Embrey! It's a vulgar practice, sir, and I will not abide it! That kid should still be at his mother's breast!"

"Jesse's mother died long ago, he's an orphan," said Kraig, his grin agitating Salazar. "Nevertheless, whether to approve of Jesse or not, I personally assigned him to you. And if you don't like it, then you can hand me your sword, and your commission. Jesse is your bodyguard, nothing more."

"A rock and a hard place," whispered Salazar, in defeat.

"You made some very fine points today," said Kraig. "I'd like to station a number of soldiers at Theo's home to protect him and my brother. They are also to collect pertinent information, for our eyes only."

"Theo's no fool. He'll know exactly what's afoot, and kill those men, too!"

"I don't care if he does bear suspicions. Theo cannot harm, nor turn those men away. They're under my jurisdiction. As potential targets for harm, I'll treat them as such. Theo knows where the real power lies." Kraig snickered. "He can harp about it all he wants. It makes absolutely no difference to me."

Salazar nodded. He preferred having Theo and Kohl's heads on platters, but lost that one.

Salazar began to leave, but was halted. "Have you been dismissed?" snapped Kraig.

"Well, no." Salazar stood at attention. "Sir."

"There's one more thing, Salazar," said Kraig. "You've been reassigned to me. From now on, you'll do as I say, and live or die by my command."

"Why, I . . . I don't understand," stuttered Salazar. "My service is not to the Navy. I'm on the general staff, under Chang's authority."

"General Chang and I discussed this before your arrival." Kraig slapped Salazar's back. "You've been discharged from the Army, and I have written a naval commission. I admire your fire! It will carry you far, if you contain it."

Salazar didn't know what to say. What were Kraig's plans for him, exactly? To serve as a midshipman, or as a cabin boy?

"Now that you've been given to me," added Kraig, with a hearty smile, "I might help you along. You have the makings of a fine officer, and don't forget . . . You're doing a marvelous job, Lieutenant *Commander* Salazar."

After presenting Salazar with his new rank, Admiral Kraig met Jesse at a commissary, located in the War Ministry's courtyard. There, the young bodyguard sought to make a big splash with his delightful clothing, while choking down a stale pastry and low-grade burgundy wine. Instead, he found a cold reception in the nasty, dirty eatery. Personnel either ignored the flamboyant teen, or gave him unfavorable vibes.

Worse than the snobbish human company, however, were the multi-legged creatures swarming around Jesse's table. It was just like the Embrian government to allow its warriors to dine in such a deplorable site! Instead of enjoying his snack, Jesse used his hat to shoo flies away, while lowering himself to drink the crud which the War Ministry confiscated from a Mount Patten winery, charged with harboring Branellian spies.

Jesse smiled as Kraig approached him. "Did you get our bright-eyed, bushy-tailed lieutenant squared away?" he asked, with an air of superiority.

"Lieutenant Commander," informed Kraig. "I promoted Salazar after you and Patrick left."

"My, but you're getting agreeable in your old age. Won't that make Salazar's mum and big brother happy?"

"It makes me happy, too. Salazar may be inexperienced, but he'll do well."

"Truly?" questioned Jesse. "Even with his little mishap at Councillor Theo's? I thought maybe you and Salazar's mother were intimate years back, and now you're making up for neglecting a bastard child."

"*Jesse . . .*"

"Sorry, sir," chuckled Jesse.

"I never had the chance to congratulate you for handling Johanek," said Kraig, helping himself to a strawberry muffin.

"It was a labor of love."

"*What?*" snarled Kraig.

"It was a labor of love, *sir.*"

"Thank you." Kraig filled his chalice with wine. "However, according to your own report, Johanek almost handled you."

"Sir," whispered Jesse, evasively. "If you don't mind, I'd rather not discuss that."

"Too bad, we will discuss that. Did you enroll in those swim courses that I furnished you?"

Jesse's silence said more than he cared to admit.

"Your job is to kill, not to be killed," scolded Kraig. "You said that detaining Johanek would be a cinch. Then to hear that he nearly drowned you."

"Sir, the job was a success. Frankly, if you don't mind my saying, swimming wouldn't have been much of a help in that foul, heinous tub."

"As it now stands, your current position involves protecting a newly-commissioned naval officer. The Embrian Navy serves on the water, which means you serve on the water. Which means to learn how to swim."

"Sir, I have jobs to complete in Corapal and Branell."

"Didn't I just assign you to Lieutenant Commander Salazar?"

"But, sir . . ."

"If you recall, the sanction not only called for Johanek's termination, but for Volonte' and Howe-Fat's as well," said Kraig. "There was only one bird in that sack, not the three I asked for."

"Howe-Fat's in his castle, high in the Castellano Mountains. As for Volonte', he's in eastern Corapal, stirring up hate and discontent with the masses. I can't hope to apprehend those cads, unless I had a well-trained army, or two good men at my disposal."

"I asked for Howe-Fat and Volonte'," asserted Kraig. "Didn't you also promise me Copenhaver and Schlender, months ago? Obviously, that was more than what I should've expected from you."

"Sir . . ."

"It's out of your hands, now. I brought in your colleague Tomas to fetch me Howe-Fat and Volonte'. Maybe he'll bag Copenhaver and Schlender, while he's at it."

"Tomas?" laughed Jesse, disparagingly. "You'll never get anywhere with him."

"Oh? Why not?"

"Tomas was a crybaby when we served under Captain Maliek. He couldn't take the least bit of ridicule, direction, or chiding. Tomas was an even bigger boob than the Kuschan fairy residing with Councillor Theo."

"I assigned Tomas because I know he'll tend to business," argued Kraig. "He's not one to waste time in high-class bordellos, or blow government funds subsiding expensive tailors with their balls cut off."

"*Touche'*, Admiral Kraig."

"Take your mind away from Howe-Fat and Volonte', they're no longer your concern. Your job is to watch Lieutenant Commander Salazar's back."

"Babysitting," whispered Jesse.

"I don't care what you call it. If something bad happens to Salazar, you'd better hope something bad happens to you. Either that, or I'll make sure something bad does happen to you."

Jesse giggled. "Oh, but I do enjoy your idle threats, Admiral Kraig! They're so wordy and melodramatic. Like when you told Salazar he'd be lucky to leave your office with his head. *Brilliant!*"

"Are you sure you want to leave this table with your two heads? The one above your shoulders, and that wrinkly thing between your legs? Despite your insolence, you're under my command. Your success or failure falls on me. Is that clear?"

Jesse stifled a laugh. "Yes, sir . . . Very clear, *sir!*"

"It also means your life and death is also my responsibility. If I tell you to take swimming lessons, it's not an option but an order."

A chill ran down Jesse's spine.

Kraig rested his hand on Jesse's arm. "I don't know why you're so afraid of the water. But if you're to remain in the service of Embrey, you must conquer your fears. Otherwise, they're you're undoing. Then you're totally useless to me."

Misty-eyed, Jesse nodded.

"Understand me, Jess. Even with your fancy clothes, your endless primping, and your smart ass, I think very highly of you. Don't get yourself killed, without my written consent."

"I won't," whispered Jesse, touched by Kraig's sentiments.

Kraig sipped his wine. "So, what else have you gotten from your trip?"

"Something of particular interest to you. I may know who put the sock in Macready's mouth."

"Very well," said Kraig, leery of surrounding eyes and ears. "Let's have it."

Jesse grinned. "Yuri, of St. Alexandrov."

"*Yuri?* Councillor Theo's son?"

"You got it."

"I wasn't the only one banking on Macready. So was Theo! Jesse, my entire staff and every member of the Embrian Council hoped Macready might broker a successful deal between us and the Branellians! Why would Yuri sabotage it?"

"You don't know Yuri as well as I do."

"I know Yuri well enough to take note of his unfailing loyalty and devotion to Theo!"

"Yuri?" questioned Jesse. "Loyalty and devotion? What loyalty and devotion did he show us under Captain Maliek?"

"Theo gave Yuri a home! All you did was make his life miserable! I don't like Yuri, not at all. But there's no denying his love for Theo. He'd give his life for that man in a heartbeat!"

"*Maybe,*" mused Jesse. "Honestly, Yuri's unpredictable and most assuredly warped."

"I admit that he's not all there. In truth, he's a damned nut. Yuri wasn't the only lunatic to come out of Maliek's school."

"I'm not a lunatic," said Jesse, innocently. "I'm . . . *gifted.*"

"I just wonder about that. What makes you think Yuri took part in Macready's murder?"

"Johanek said that he hired Yuri and a few of my other classmates to shut Macready up, forever."

"And you believed him? People are liable to say anything when they're about to die. What other names did Johanek throw at you?"

Jesse shrugged. "He didn't give me any names, just a description of their top man."

"I'm skeptical," said Kraig. "It's not that I don't believe you. I just can't go on the last words of a cowardly arms dealer."

Jesse leaned across the table. "Isn't it at least worth looking into?"

"I'm posting a number of guards at Theo's home, not only to nursemaid him and my brother, but to eavesdrop on their conversations."

Jesse sighed. Kraig always played the part of the bureaucratic roadblock. "But, sir . . ."

"I've already been through that with Commander Salazar. You want the same thing he does, to storm onto Theo's land to kick ass and take names."

Jesse smirked. "Yes, sir. It's a start."

"Don't get me wrong, Jess. I'm not taking Theo or Yuri's side over yours. I asked you to find out who murdered Macready, and you told me what you know."

"Admiral Kraig," Jesse said. "I've known Yuri for a long time. Believe me, sir, he's whacko! I prefer not letting Yuri know I'm in the general vicinity. Then I'd have to sleep with one eye open."

Kraig snickered. "Sounds like you're afraid of him."

"I have reasons to be."

"Yuri was expelled from Maliek's school for trying to beat a classmate to death. It wasn't you he nearly killed, was it?"

"Don't insult me! How dare you question my abilities of defending myself, especially from that prancing sissy?"

"Then who?"

"A friend of mine named Marietto," explained Jesse. "We gave Yuri a bad time when he failed to block a simple move Captain Maliek demonstrated on him. Just a little harmless fun, no big deal."

"Oh, naturally," said Kraig, sarcastically. "A little harmless fun, no big deal. Then what?"

"By the time Yuri got done with Marietto, he might as well have ended him. The last I heard, Marietto sits in one corner of his madhouse cell, screaming and pooping his pants." Jesse swallowed. "Trust me, Yuri poses a threat to us all."

"We may be facing an even greater threat. If Gornick attempts to overthrow that pervert king of ours, and I'm sure he will, then we'll need everyone on our side to stop him. That includes Councillor Theo, my brother Major Kohl and, to our regret, your pal from St. Alexandrov."

"Yuri's no pal of mine. I despise him more than anyone. Sir."

"It's personal to you."

Jesse nodded.

"I've got no room for personal squabbles or vendettas," insisted Kraig. "What problems you may have with Yuri, bury them."

"I'd rather bury Yuri, sir."

"See here," spoke Kraig, angrily. "You strike against Yuri, you strike against Theo. *I* work for Theo."

"But you don't understand!"

"Then understand this. You work for me, Jess. Don't forget that! If Gornick makes his move, the last man I want opposing me is Councillor Theo, especially with Yuri under his wing. I'm not fond of Theo, but I get more done working for him, than without him. Can you accept that, or must I replace you?"

Crossing his arms, Jesse sat back like an insolent child.

"Wipe that look off your face," warned Kraig, "or this time it won't be an idle threat."

"Yes, sir."

"You're a fine soldier, Jess," said Kraig. "I appreciate your service to Embrey, and to me."

Jesse rolled his eyes back, and sighed. "Yes, sir. Whatever you say, sir."

Kraig reached into his pocket, then dropped a few coins on the table. "This should be enough for you to get drunk, and anything else you'd like to do."

Jesse was almost speechless. *"Moi?"* he whispered.

"A small bonus for Johanek," explained Kraig. "Enjoy yourself, tonight. Tomorrow you'll answer to Lieutenant Commander Salazar. Take good care of him . . . and Patrick, too! I'm sure that, once the three of you get acquainted, things will go smoothly."

Jesse slipped the coins into his tunic pocket. "Delights!" he cheered. "Chocolate-covered delights! *Delights de jour!"*

Kraig laughed. "Try not to act so pleased!"

"Oh, but I am, sir!" Moved to tears, Jesse wanted to kiss Admiral Kraig, but thought better of it. "Thank you very much! *Sir!"*

"You're so very welcome," snickered Kraig.

"Don't you worry about a blessed thing, Admiral Kraig!" assured Jesse. "Trust me, no harm will come to a single hair on Lieutenant Commander Salazar's lovely little head! You can count on me!"

"I have the highest confidence in you, Jess," said Kraig, like a father praising a son. "If you ever want to talk, don't hesitate coming to me. Good night and good luck."

16

"Let's call this meeting to order," said Leader Karl, sitting behind a long oak table in Lord Kelly's chapel. He was joined by Leaders Sven, Royce, Sebastian, his secretary Kenichi, and a student from a nearby school.

"I was unable to locate Leader-Trainee Giorgio," explained Karl, clearing his throat in disdain. "Therefore, I invited Brother Antoine from Lord William's Academy, in his stead."

"Thank you," said Antoine, with a smile.

"Antoine begins his Leadership training this week," said Karl. "He has no vote in the outcome of this hearing, but is free to question the defendant and witnesses."

Bradley sat in the front row of the chapel pews. He had known Antoine for many years. The two regularly chatted at church socials and conventions. Antoine was much taller than his last exchange with Bradley. He was now a blonde-haired, blue-eyed beanpole with slender, tanned legs.

Those attending Lord William's once dressed like Lord Kelly's students. Antoine came to this meeting with a different uniform. He now wore a shiny black beret, tunic, and leather boots. The insignia on his belt buckle and cape, of a rattlesnake coiled around a sword, gave Bradley reason to pause. This was anything *but* a spiritual symbol!

Sitting in the rear, not far from the chapel's doors, were two of Antoine's schoolmates, dressed in similar uniforms. Terry was fifteen, stood an inch taller than Bradley, and had brown hair. Lord William's secretary, Quinn, was sixteen, with curly red hair and freckles. Though Bradley personally disliked Terry, he had teamed with Quinn in a three-legged race at a recent school picnic, hosted by Lord Conway's Academy.

"This meeting is to determine the merits of an undisciplined student at Lord Kelly's," said Karl, somberly. "Does the defendant wish to make a statement?"

"Yeah, can we get this dog and pony show on the road?" asked Fritz, sitting alone on a stool. Facing the long table, his back was to the pews. "I got princesses waiting on me at The Rooster's Beak!"

Karl beat his hammer to the table. "Keep a civil tongue!"

That morning, Fritz was found in the cemetery's gazebo, chilled from the rain and cool autumn temperatures. His clothes were soiled from regurgitated vodka. He was placed in the custody of church officials, and risked expulsion from the school. The afternoon sun peeked through a stain glass window, blinding the unruly teen.

"Why are we even dealing with this crap?" questioned Fritz. "Can'tcha see I don't wanna be here?"

"That is for the Leadership, and not you to decide," spoke Sebastian.

Fritz scowled at Kenichi, who was busy penning a record of this hearing. "Who invited the half-breed?" he griped. "And what's that he's writing about me?"

"You are not to speak, unless spoken to!" shouted Karl.

"So whatcha gonna do about it?" asked Fritz. "Boot me out?"

"Quiet!" scolded Karl.

Fritz smiled, mischievously. "Sorry about the Campens Rose', Sven. Wanna tell me where ya got it? I always buy mine from a spinster woman named Ida-Joe . . . or somethin' like that . . ."

Sven leaped from his chair.

"Return to your seat," ordered Karl. "We've scheduled your case for later this week."

"What're they gonna do, Sven?" laughed Fritz. "Give you the old heave-ho, too? Wanna get drunk tonight and celebrate?"

"Why must I take this abuse?" whined Sven.

"Pay Fritz no mind," said Karl. "His words have no bearing on that particular trial."

"Yeah," replied Fritz. "The truth hurts, don't it?"

"Brother Bradley, come face the Leadership," said Karl, respectfully upholding the rules and regulations of this formal event.

Bradley was aware that his testimony spelled Fritz's end at Lord Kelly's. It was great to finally get rid of him! Yet, were Bradley's desires for vengeance correct, in evaluating Fritz? Bradley vowed to tell the truth, as the final decision was not up to him. Walking toward the Leaders' table, he stopped a mere yard from where Fritz sat.

"Brother Bradley," greeted Karl.

Bradley's voice was barely audible. "Yes, sir?"

"A few days ago, did you leave campus with Brother Fritz and Brother Trevor?" asked Karl.

"Yes, sir," answered Bradley, jittery.

"For what purpose?" asked Sebastian.

Bradley scratched his bare leg above the knee, and shuffled both feet. He turned to Kenichi, who gave him an encouraging smile. "To attend . . . to attend the theater."

"Did the three of you attend the theater?" asked Sebastian.

Bradley looked at Fritz. "No, sir."

"And why not?" asked Royce.

"Get to the point, a'ready!" shouted Fritz. "I went to a cathouse!"

"Not another word!" snapped Karl, pounding the hammer. "You may proceed, Bradley."

"Like he said," informed Bradley. "He went into a cat . . . into The Rooster's Beak."

"And did either Trevor or you follow Fritz into this establishment?" asked Karl.

Bradley refused to say.

"Answer the question!" bellowed Karl.

Bradley was shattered by Karl's pushy tone. "Trevor did," he whispered.

"Speak up," requested Sebastian.

"Trevor did," repeated Bradley.

"Trevor?" gasped Sebastian.

"But he didn't stay!" cried Bradley. "Trevor caught up with me at the Falcon Theatre!"

"That's all, Brother Bradley," said Karl. "You may return to your seat. Brother Trevor, please come forward to face the Leadership."

Trevor stood, and released a high-pitched giggle.

"Brother Trevor?" asked Royce. "Did you follow Fritz into The Rooster's

Beak?"

Trevor shrugged his shoulders. "I guess."

"Answer the question!" insisted Karl. "Did you, or didn't you?"

Trevor blushed. "Well, yeah."

Anything's better'n watching a dumb play," commented Fritz.

"Silence, Fritz!" ordered Brother Antoine.

"Well, it is!" said Fritz. "Just a buncha fairies dolled up in fluffy costumes, except them queer boys they get to play women. The Rooster's Beak's got the real thing!"

"Silence!" repeated Antoine.

"Who died and made you God, Pancake Head?" insulted Fritz. "Go back to yer own prison camp, pretty boy."

"How long did you stay at The Rooster's Beak?" asked Royce.

"I dunno," said Trevor. "About five minutes."

"Did you pay to go in?" asked Karl.

"No," answered Trevor. "Fritzy did."

"No good deed goes unpunished," said Fritz. This was met with muffled laughter.

"Why didn't you stay?" asked Antoine.

Trevor snickered. "This ugly fat girl got me into her bedroom. She reached into my underpants to play with my . . ."

"I see," interrupted Royce, stifling a laugh. "Then what did you do?"

"I ran outa there as fast as I could!" exclaimed Trevor. "I finally caught up with Brad at the theater."

"You woulda liked the fat girl a lot more," said Fritz. A few boys laughed.

"Now, Trevor, about last night," said Karl. "Did Brother Fritz coerce Brother Derek and you to divert Leader Sven from his room?"

Trevor wrinkled his nose. "What's 'coerce'?"

"Did he force you into distracting Sven?" rephrased Karl.

"Well, no. Fritzy said that if me and Derry got Sven outa his room, he'd give us some treats."

"Treats?" asked Royce. "What sorts of treats?"

"The same kinda treats I got at The Rooster's Beak," explained Trevor, "before that ugly fat girl tried playing with my . . ."

"No more questions!" interrupted Karl, urgently. "You may return to your seat, Brother Trevor."

As Trevor walked away, Fritz said, "Play yer cards right, and I'll getcha more treats. And this time, it won't be with the ugly fat girl."

"Brother Derek," summoned Karl. "Please face the Leadership."

The pale, sickly child slowly approached the table.

"Brother Derek," addressed Karl. "Did Brother Fritz coerce you to divert Leader Sven from his room?"

"No," answered Derek, absently. "He just asked a buncha times."

"Did Fritz promise you anything?" asked Sebastian.

"Just treats." Derek frowned. "He didn't say anything to me about ugly fat girls."

"I plead guilty to everything!" shouted Fritz, jumping to his feet. "Show me the door, boys, I'm outa here!"

"The Leadership doesn't recognize you!" shouted Antoine.

"Maybe you don't, Pancake Head. But everyone else does. I'm *Sister* Fritz!"

"Sit down and shut up!" commanded Karl.

Fritz threw his cap to the floor, then peeled out of his tunic. "Do I get what I want?" he demanded, tugging at his silk loincloth. "Or do I take *this* off, too?"

As most everyone erupted into hysterical laughter, Karl slammed his hammer into the table. "Order, order!" he shouted, slowly regaining control. *"Order!* Fritz, the Leadership has vowed to look after your needs, until you reach the age of maturity. What do you propose to do, assuming we grant you leave from Lord Kelly's?"

"Get drunk and get laid!" Fritz smiled, eagerly. "Wanna join me?"

Based on laws governing such matters, school officials had twenty-four hours in which to make their ruling. Despite the other Leaders' decisions, Karl had already decided Fritz's fate. "Meeting adjourned!" he called. "We will reconvene tomorrow. Fritz, you are detained at Lord Kelly's until the Leadership has voted. Now, put your clothes back on!"

Fritz did as he was told. While still under the school's thumb, he felt a tremendous weight lifted from his shoulders. He had one more thing to do, before starting his new life. He wished to confront Kenichi.

As Kenichi collected his paperwork and left the table, Fritz blocked his path. For several seconds, the two teens glared at each other. "You got something to say to me?" asked Kenichi, standing his ground.

"Meet me at the gate tomorrow, Kenny," said Fritz, "after Karl hands me my walking papers."

Kenichi slammed his scroll onto the table. "Why don't we go, right here and now? Invite your roommates, if they want another stab at me."

Debating the wisdom of fighting Kenichi, Fritz asked, "There something about me on that paper?"

"The truth. There's no point for you to look through it, since you can't read."

Kenichi's demeanor infuriated Fritz, who expected everyone to jump when he told them to. "I can read good enough to see that yer crapping yerself."

"Fine," Kenichi said, through clenched teeth. "If you want to fight, then let's get to it."

"That's too easy," said Fritz, unwilling to admit his fear of Kenichi. "Slant . . . gook . . . moo goo guy pan!"

"Moo goo guy pan'?" Kenichi smirked. "You idiot, do you even know what that is?"

Fritz beat a hasty retreat to the door. On his way out, he shouted, "I'll give you time to lose sleep over it. Kenny!"

Kenichi fetched his materials, and worked his way through a crowd to Bradley, who visited with Quinn and Antoine.

"Brad," addressed Quinn.

"Quinn," greeted Bradley, warmly. "How's life at Lord William's?"

Quinn's sour expression said it all.

"Hectic," sighed Antoine. Though he just turned eighteen, his appearance remained boyish, with a pimpled face and a pug nose. "I'm starting Leadership courses on Monday. Torres has to step down as Head Leader, so we're revamping our curriculum."

"Where did you get the new uniform?" asked Bradley, curiously.

"It's General Gornick's idea," informed Antoine, proudly. "Van Owen is our

Head Leader now, and he believes this change reflects Gornick's vision and ideals for Embrey. What do you think?"

Bradley liked the beret. Except for the dark color, Antoine and Quinn's tunics remained the same, its fabric and fashion resembling Lord Kelly's. Unsure of the heavy boots, Bradley disliked the menacing insignia, etched upon the belt buckle and cape. Apparently, Quinn also didn't care for it.

"General Gornick designed the emblem himself," explained Antoine, in a showy manner.

Bradley withdrew comment. "I think we'll just stay with our same clothes."

"Van Owen tells me that every school will have this exact same uniform, by next year," said Antoine. "I'm interested in talking to Karl about it. Do you think he'll mind?"

Bradley recalled Karl's urging to stay courageous and strong, despite an uncertain future. He already knew what Karl thought of Antoine's uniform. Students at Lord Kelly's had remained with the exact same style of clothing, since Karl entered as a youngster, decades ago. Any alteration would be vetoed!

Changing the subject, Bradley said, "I'd like you to meet our new secretary, and my new roomy, Bradley Kenichi."

"Glad to meet you," said Kenichi, extending his hand to Antoine and Quinn.

As Quinn shook Kenichi's hand, Antoine refused to do so. Kenichi represented an infected sore upon a nation which already had its share of foreigners. "I've got to go," said Antoine, avoiding eye contact with Kenichi. "I'll be back to discuss things with Karl, first thing in the morning."

"Wait," said Bradley, anxiously. "Just how are you revamping your curriculum?"

"We're much tougher and disciplined," said Antoine. "You'll agree that Lord Kelly's must be governed with a firmer hand. Just look at this hearing, Brad! Why did Karl allow Fritz to mock him, as he did? If I had my way with the knothead, he'd find my boot up his ass."

This was not the "good old Antoine" Bradley once loved and respected.

Rushing to the door, Antoine said over his shoulder, "See you later, Brad!"

"Wished I'd known you needed a new secretary," mumbled Quinn. "I would've applied in a heartbeat!"

Bradley's thoughts ran from animosity, to anxiety, to overwhelming fear. "What's going on, Quinn?" he asked, not as a demand but rather as a show of sympathy and support.

"You don't want to know," sighed Quinn. "I really can't stand it at Lord William's, anymore!"

"Why not?" asked Bradley.

Before Quinn answered, Terry strutted to the three boys. Examining Kenichi's ponytail with contempt and ridicule, he asked, "When did Lord Kelly's start letting girls in?"

"Drop it, Terry," whined Quinn, more as a plea than an order.

Terry reached out to yank on Kenichi's hair, with a mischievous smile. The angry look on Kenichi's face talked him out of it. Backing away, Terry aimed his caustic attitude at an easier target. "You coming," he asked Quinn, "or do I gotta drag you home?"

Quinn followed Terry to the door, like a disobedient child on his way to a paddling.

Bradley wanted to lash out against Terry, but was helpless in coming to Quinn's aid. This left him feeling both angry and saddened.

"Gee," Kenichi said, sarcastically. "I really impressed them, didn't I?"

"It's just that . . . they don't know you yet!" stammered Bradley, weakly.

"Yeah, well I'm not going out of my way to know them," commented Kenichi. "I've seen those looks they gave me, a hundred times or more. I might be used to it. It doesn't mean I have to like it."

"Sorry," whispered Bradley, in shame. Embrey was slowly going insane! Even Lord Kelly's would never be the same.

Kenichi patted Bradley's back. "Let's go to the river and talk."

"Sure," accepted Bradley, tiredly.

Bradley and Kenichi stepped outside to the warm afternoon sun, and sat under an apple tree at the edge of the Ember River. Neither spoke, as a constant flow of water beat against the sandy bank. After Fritz's inquiry, they both needed the peace and quiet.

Finally, Kenichi broke the silence. "Remember what we talked about, last night?"

"What?"

"I'm leaving Sykes, and I want you coming with me," said Kenichi. "First, we'll hike to the top of Mount Patten, then . . ."

"I can't!" argued Bradley. "I won't be old enough!"

"Who cares? Do you want Karl telling you what to do, for the rest of your life?"

"You don't understand, Kenichi!" screamed Bradley. "This is my home, and I love it here! Not only that, I love everyone at this school . . . except Fritz."

"What do you think of that new uniform?"

Bradley frowned.

"Will you still love it here, if you're forced to wear something like that, or told to work under a stricter curriculum?" asked Kenichi.

"I have to serve God, don't I?"

"Then become a missionary! If you stay in Sykes, you'll only serve General Gornick."

"Where did you get that stupid idea?" groaned Bradley.

"That ugly costume's Gornick's idea, isn't it? And so is their curriculum! Sounds pretty scary to me. Didn't Antoine say he was going to talk to Karl about it, tomorrow?"

"Karl's not going along with that uniform!" shouted Bradley. "Or their curriculum!"

"Maybe not," whispered Kenichi, doubtfully. "But what if Antoine doesn't give Karl any choice?"

17

"Damn dirty sons of whores!" roared Copenhaver, spitting his beverage in young Garry's face. "Dumb peasants been letting yer sheep piss in the ale again."

"Or was it their mammas?" laughed Schlender, shoving Garry into a second guide, Davy, as the two boys toppled to the sand and rocks. "Them dumb squirrel chasers don't know the difference between their old ladies and a cheap Kentworth strumpet."

Garry sat on the edge of the Ember River, examining his injured knee. Meanwhile, Davy glared at the smugglers in quiet protest.

Copenhaver approached Garry and Davy, brandishing a large oak club he called his man-killin' stick. "You know who's boss 'round here," he growled. "Lemme hear you say it."

"You are, Mister Copenhaver," said Davy, barely audible over the sounds of the wind and river.

Copenhaver waved the man-killin' stick in Davy's face. "Whatcha say? Couldn't hear ya! Who's boss 'round here?"

"*You* are, Mister Copenhaver," repeated Davy, his words laced with resentment.

Garry fought back tears.

Once the two smugglers laughed and walked away, Davy lifted Garry to his feet. "Chin up, Garry," he said, calmly. "We got work to do."

Instrumental in his friends' plans of breaking free from 'the trades' and starting life anew in Embrey, Garry was discouraged by the cruelty inflicted upon them. Davy gained inner strength and determination in their escape from an impoverished life in Branell, while Garry grew exhausted by it. Davy often figured he had to take care of Garry. "Come on," he urged. "You're all right. Walk it off."

Garry slowly limped to his fellow guides. As a sharp pain jolted through the knee, he tried getting tough about it.

"You're all right," assured Davy.

Garry bit his bottom lip. The knee would heal, in time. The boy was dealt far worse blows than that. More than anything, he simply had to rest. After a long, grueling hike along high-altitude trails, going any further seemed impossible.

Not that Garry and Davy hadn't already wandered a far distance, over steep mountain ranges and across swift, icy-cold streams from their rural home, to the Embrian coastline. Recruited by black marketeers to transport stolen goods in and out of the Branellian Empire, Garry and Davy were treated deplorably by their employers.

At age fourteen, Garry was a thin, lanky boy, standing more than six feet tall. His long, brown hair was unruly, his sensitive eyes resembling a deer's. He was dressed in a gray, wool turtleneck sweater, a red and blue, plaid kilt, knee socks and black brogans, the fashion for many citizens from northeastern Branell. Hanging from a belt, next to a leather sporran, was a dagger. Garry's hairless legs were a boney white, his face, neck, and hands chapped and tanned from the harsh elements.

The same age as Garry, Davy stood five-six, with short blonde hair. He also wore a sweater and kilt. The two boys came from Warren Dale, a tiny weigh-station between Wallingford and Hamblin, in eastern Branell.

Born into a family of smugglers, Garry knew of a safe passage through the Branellian Mountains, into Embrey. He and Davy were unwitting participants in a dangerous mission they knew little about. Both were experienced guides, having regularly taken men and supplies through a heartless, treacherous path from Warren Dale.

Their current employers were among the most ruthless crooks in the trades. Copenhaver was a stocky, broad-shouldered man with a thick, black beard and a bulbous nose. Skinny and scraggly-faced, Schlender often smelled of bourbon. Despite their criminal records, the two smugglers were recruited in a risky Branellian raid on the Embrian capital of Sykes. Their mission was to frighten their enemy with a sudden, devastating blow against the waterfront ports. The smugglers' greed motivated them to loot for pricy objects, kidnap women and children for flesh peddlers, and steal expensive liquor.

Beginning as messenger boys and carriers, Copenhaver and Schlender went into business for themselves. They soon became famous and infamous characters in the continent's underworld. Having earned the ire of political and military leaders, a steep price was placed on their heads. The smugglers somehow eluded capture. They planned to die wealthy in their old age, or perish gloriously in a hail of arrows.

Lacking the ability to read or write, Garry and Davy were forced into this dire existence. Their lives were based on cost, rather than on moral or humanitarian value. Garry was a mere commodity to satisfy another man's needs or whims. His mother and older sister happily benefited from his sweat, toil, and sacrifices.

Garry once felt an obligation to carry out his hazardous occupation. Now, he wanted out. He hoped that his pals, all in their early to mid-teens and dressed in similar clothing, won their freedom by escaping to the vast Embrian countryside.

With Garry and Davy, this small band consisted of a stoop-shouldered, redheaded lad named Marc, and a chubby, round-faced boy named Ivor. Harold, the twelve-year-old "baby" of the group, was prone to crying fits. He was especially vulnerable to the smugglers' vile humor and degradation. Schlender wasn't above dragging Harold to a remote area, and have his way with him. This was done, not for sexual gratification, but to exact dominance over a weakling.

When they were younger, Garry and Davy also suffered from Schlender's cheap thrills. Fear of death prevented them from fighting back, or running away.

This was Garry's fourth trip to the Embrian coast. He didn't like the mouth of the Ember River. The coastal winds didn't blow, they *sucked*. Still, Garry had no plans of returning to Warren Dale. He loved the rich, fertile farmlands surrounding Sykes, and wished to make a home there. Anything was better than hauling illegal freight across rough terrain.

Garry and Davy sat on the banks of the river, freezing their butts off as the cool, moist ocean air swept under their kilts.

As Branellian forces arrived from the mountains north of Sykes, they camped near the city. Their purpose was not the destruction of life, but rather to dampen the Embrians' will to fight. The conflict between Embrey and Branell had dragged on for too long, as soldiers and civilians on each side were slaughtered. There were no clear victors in the Border War, and nothing was resolved. It was hoped that, by taking combatants into the heart of the enemy nation, the Branellians could persuade their Embrian counterparts to cease fire.

In the early hours of the morning, three vital players entered this drama. One was a man of war, the second man delivered a message of peace . . .

. . . while a third brought death.

Captain Shimura was the skipper of the Branellian frigate, the *Browning*. At seven feet in height, he had a large, brawny physique. His piercing eyes, black goatee, and self-assured manner extracted nervous sweat from his ship's crew.

Sirro was a dark-skinned man from the sandy deserts of Vladistan. Like the majority of his countrymen, he was a member of the United Westerland Brethren. He wore a pointed hat, a black robe, and a long, flowing beard. Unlike the more radical followers of his faith, Sirro encouraged cooperation from all religions and congregations, throughout the western world.

Next to Sirro was a young stranger of fourteen who sought no cooperation, and gave none in return. Under a dusty hood, the stranger's wavy, dishwater blonde hair was parted in the middle. His ruggedly handsome face displayed a keen, fearless determination, intimidating onlookers in subtle ways. Like whispers voicing of a terrible doom, the stranger's ghostlike movements were as silent as a grave. His presence caused the hair on Garry's neck to stand on end, as the guide's mountain superstition took hold.

Lazing on the riverbank, Copenhaver and Schlender drank whiskey and insulted their guides. Shimura, Sirro, and the stranger approached this small, motley crew. "You were hired to take men into Sykes," Shimura told the smugglers, "not to lie here like flatulent swine in the sun."

Copenhaver stormed at Shimura with his man-killin' stick. "Who gave you the call to order me about?" he growled. "Them damn, ungrateful guides got us lost in this windblown pisshole."

"We ain't lost!" cried Garry. "It's just that . . . I was never here, before!"

Davy turned to Garry, nervously. Garry's claim was a lie, and both boys knew it. They prayed that the smugglers didn't.

"You see that big, wet thing snaking from an even bigger wet thing to the west?" asked Shimura. "It's a river. Follow that, and it'll take you straight into Sykes."

"You must think we're stupid!" yelled Schlender, placing one hand on a sword hanging from his leather belt.

"That's right," responded Shimura, undaunted. "I *do* think you're stupid."

"I don't take to no sons of whores talkin' to me like that," said Copenhaver, shaking his man-killin' stick at Shimura. "I ain't never taken it from no one, and I ain't takin' it from you!"

Shimura laughed in Copenhaver's face.

That did it. Copenhaver didn't care if Shimura was a Branellian naval officer, and much larger. He aimed to teach the gook a lesson he'd never forget.

Without fear of reprisal, Copenhaver swung the man-killin' stick at Shimura's face.

Blocking Copenhaver's attack with his left hand, Shimura sent his right fist into the smuggler's nose. Slamming into the rocky soil, Copenhaver lay there, motionless.

Schlender unsheathed his sword, and moved against Shimura.

A split second later, he had a sword pointed at his gullet.

It was not Shimura that threatened Schlender, but the young stranger at his side. His eyes glued to the stranger, Schlender carefully dropped his own weapon.

"I have orders too," the stranger said, carrying no malice in his voice. "They say you are to leave us alone. Counter me again, and I'll slit your throat."

The guides smiled, yet refrained from laughing.

Cautiously, Schlender knelt to Copenhaver. "Copper?" he asked, as his partner failed to regain consciousness. "Talk to me, Copper . . . Copper? *Copper!*"

Shimura snickered.

"Yellow bastard!" screamed Schlender. "You killed 'em!"

"I didn't kill the slob," answered Shimura. "I only wanted to."

Slapping Copenhaver's hairy cheek, Schlender gradually revived his groggy cohort. Struggling to sit up, Copenhaver shook his aching head as he remained on the cool, damp ground. Seeing double, the smuggler wondered how he got there, in the first place.

"Spare me some of your clothes," the stranger said to Garry and Davy. "And no squawks from either of you."

Garry was nearly a foot taller than the stranger, and unsuitable to provide his own clothing. Instead, he found a smaller version of the attire in Marc's backpack.

The stranger blushed as he examined the fluffy, long-sleeved dress shirt and flashy kilt that Garry handed him.

"My, won't you look simply divine?" kidded Shimura. "You'll be the envy in the King's royal bedroom."

"They're perfect, for what I've got to do," the stranger said, reluctantly. "May I pay you for these? There's no way I can return them."

"Go on, take them," offered Garry, nervously. "Right, Marc?"

"Right," agreed Marc, fearfully.

Tucking the clothes under one arm, the stranger departed with Shimura.

Sirro motioned for Garry to follow him, with Shimura and the stranger.

Once they were out of the two smugglers' sight, Sirro turned to Garry. "Some can afford to throw caution to the wind," he said in a calm, velvety voice. "I cannot. If this mission gets bloody, we must depend on each other to get through it alive." Pointing at the stranger, he added, "I'll escort him into Sykes tonight, and will return before your raid into the city tomorrow. I'll do what I can to assure your survival, and I ask the same from you."

"What're you gonna do with him?" asked Garry, staring at the stranger.

"No questions!" snapped Shimura. "The less you know, the better. Do exactly what Sirro tells you, and you and those other boys might just make it. Embrians don't like Branellians in their country. They'll be onto your checkered skirts before you even know it."

Garry was afraid. His presence in Embrey only added fuel to the fires of war. He realized that his chances of getting through this were slim.

"Do exactly what I say," urged Sirro, clutching Garry's hand, "and we'll live."

As Shimura and the stranger focused their attention upon the blustery Agron Ocean, a breeze parched their weathered faces. Seeking answers for their reasons for being in Embrey, Garry listened in on their conversation.

"You're not letting those pigs on the Browning, when this is over?" the stranger asked.

"Hell, no," replied Shimura. "I don't want them near my ship. Sirro and I are in contact with a high-ranking Embrian Councillor. He'll arrange for their capture and execution. Those goons will hide out on the beach, thinking I'll be here to pick them up. In truth, they await the hangman's noose."

Garry's hands and legs shivered in the wind. Fear swept over him, as he wished he would have stayed in Warren Dale, living in a stone and mud hut.

Shimura noted Garry's apprehension. "Not you. I'm talking about the rogues you came here with. The Embrians have wanted them for a long time. I give the Embrians what they want, while that Embrian Councillor compensates me with a well-deserved . . . *retirement.* Well, why not? He can afford it. Made his riches in publishing, or so I heard."

"Congratulations," the stranger said.

"Just the same, you keep your mouth shut," Shimura warned Garry. "Or I will see you hang. It don't matter to me if you are Branellian. I was a guard for a powerful warlord in Kokashima, before joining the Branellian Navy. I'll soon be a lazy, fat Embrian, getting drunk and watching the sunset in my old age."

"Just do as I say," Sirro advised Garry.

Keeping an eye on Shimura and the stranger, Garry mouthed *okay.*

"What you give the Embrians is far greater than what I can ever promise them," Shimura said to the stranger, warmly. "It's a long shot, my friend, yet all Branell rests its hope on this long shot."

"I'm not expected to live," the stranger said, flatly.

"Yes, but I'm fond of you," said Shimura, alarmed by the stranger's fatalistic attitude. "If you accomplish this mission, then get out with your hide and your head, I trust you'll see fit to visit an old, retired sea-dog."

"I've had a knife to my throat for so long, I'm unaware of no other existence," the stranger said. "Captain Maliek instructed us to love Embrey, more than our own lives. 'To die for the Motherland is to gain immortality!'" The stranger laughed. "I wonder what Maliek thinks of me now, since I've surrendered my allegiance to his Embrian Motherland, to fight and possibly die for Branell."

"I know Maliek too, remember?" said Shimura. "He sold himself to other nations than Embrey. Kokashima, Agron, Corapal . . . *Branell.*"

The stranger smiled. "I'm so honored that you'll see fit to invite me into your home, Captain Shimura."

"And I'm honored to call you a brother-in-arms." Shimura placed a meaty palm on the stranger's shoulder. "For what it's worth, I wish you the best of luck, Tim."

18

That same dewy morning found Bradley raking leaves near Lord Kelly's Administrative Building. This chore took his mind away from mounting concerns.

Bradley once enjoyed visiting with Brother Antoine. However, Antoine's cold treatment of Kenichi, along with his new uniform and curriculum, gave him a sleepless night. It didn't help when Fritz turned his own hearing into a circus.

The familiar, comforting chimes of Lord Kelly's bells announced the time of eight. Leaning on a rake, Bradley drank refreshing, cold water from a canteen. Why worry? This was, after all, the advent of a new day.

"Sven wants to see you," someone said, from behind.

Bradley turned to see Fritz, whose swagger was more pronounced than usual. The sleeves of his tunic were ripped free at the shoulders, baring his sinewy arms. Fritz had also split his tunic open at the chest. Short, black hair dotted his muscular frame.

Bradley wiped his sweaty brow. "What did you say?"

"Sven wants to see you," repeated Fritz, displaying his modified tunic. "Whadda ya think?"

"Why did you do that?" asked Bradley, in shock. "Someone else could have worn that uniform."

"Not with my stink still in it," laughed Fritz. "Well, I'm s'posed to see Karl and Pancake Head, here real soon."

"Who's 'Pancake Head'?"

"Y' know, yer buddy from Lord Billy's," answered Fritz. "The guy with the pancake on his head."

Bradley liked Fritz's nickname for Antoine, but didn't say so.

Excited that his life at Lord Kelly's was drawing to a close, Fritz also revealed hints of regret and sadness.

"Are you going to be okay?" asked Bradley.

"I'm a'ways okay." said Fritz. His eyes watering, he offered Bradley a handshake.

Strangely, Bradley felt kind of sorry for Fritz. Reluctantly, he shook the ruffian's hand. "Take care," he said, equally bearing sorrow and grudges.

Bradley watched as Fritz disappeared around one corner of the Administrative Building. He never thought to see the troublemaker again. Life was like that at Lord Kelly's. Brothers come and go. Some remained in Sykes, while others merely faded away.

Bradley leaned the rake against a tree, then went inside to see Sven. Entering the hallway, he heard shouting from the Head Leader's office. It was Giorgio and Karl going rounds, as the commotion disturbed everyone in the aging structure. Bradley pitied Kenichi, who had a 'front row seat' to the conflict.

Bradley spotted Sven behind his desk, reading a verse or two while indulging in a bottle of Lord Kelly's wine. "You asked to see me," he said, standing at the doorway.

"Come in," slurred Sven. His eyes were bloodshot, and clothes ragged and filthy. "Have a chair, Brad. I've got an errand for you."

Bradley sat at a bench, then motioned toward Karl's office.

"Pathetic," commented Sven. "That's been raging, since Giorgio got back this morning."

"Where was he?"

"Councillor Theo's. Giorgio's mad because he wasn't at Fritz's hearing. Karl's mad, just because he's Karl. Both see the writing on the wall, but have to get their licks in before Giorgio packs his bags."

Bradley's heart sank. "Where's Giorgio going?"

Sven snickered. "He's got an internship with the Embrian Council. Giorgio's lucky. Fritz thinks he's outa here. What he doesn't know is that Antoine's taking him to Lord William's."

"What for?"

"To kick his ass into submission!" giggled Sven. "Poor Fritzy don't know what's coming to him . . . Neither do I."

Bradley sought illumination.

"I'm not around for much longer, either," confessed Sven, saliva caking his beard. "Karl's had his fill of me, too."

"Sven!" cried Bradley. "Please don't go!"

"I ain't got no choice, Brad. Demon rum's what beat me. It used to be a good friend. Now it's a grumpy, nagging old hen!"

"Oh, Sven," whined Bradley. Who'd be left at the school, once the dust settled? Maybe Kenichi was right. Lord Kelly's was a sinking ship! "Now what am I supposed to do?"

"Stay true to the faith," said Sven. "Stay true to yourself. Weather the storm, Brad."

"What's going to happen to you, Sven?"

"I've got a sharecropper uncle in the north. Maybe I'll work for him until I get it figured out . . . *if* I get it figured out."

Overwhelmed with grief and sadness, Bradley rested his head on Sven's desk.

"Don't act that way," urged Sven. "That's life. It usually works out in the end."

"What difference does it make?"

Sven smiled. "Even the bad days pass. Soon, you'll be a Leader here. I'll just know you'll be the best we've ever had!"

Bradley wiped away a tear. "I'll never forget you."

"We'll live in our hearts, and our thoughts." Sven reached into his desk for a bundle of coins. "I've got much to do today, and I need to pay an overdue bill."

"What for?"

"*Shh!*" whispered Sven, handing Bradley the money. "It's a secret. I'm in enough trouble, as it is."

"Where do I take this?"

"A small market, about a mile away toward Port Sinclair on Cameron Street. A little place called *Erickson's Imports*. I've got a balance which has to be settled. Pay the bill, then go. There's somebody at Erickson's who'll promise you Heaven, but . . . Just pay the damned bill, then go!"

"I'm not sure if Karl will let me go. But if I can find another Leader to . . ."

"I'll take you to Erickson's," said Giorgio, stepping into Sven's office. His squabble with Karl had just ended. "Officially, I'm still on duty until tomorrow noon. That should be worth something."

"Is it okay if I go with Giorgio?" asked Bradley.

"You're in good hands with Giorgio, even if Karl doesn't think so," said Sven.

"Thanks, Giorgio."

Giorgio patted Bradley's shoulder. "It's my pleasure."

"Remember what I told you about Erickson's, Brad," warned Sven. "And I'll see you when you get back."

Exiting Lord Kelly's main gate, Bradley and Giorgio strolled through the hectic venue of Cameron Street. The poisonous atmosphere in the Administrative Building was exhausting. For the time being, it was enough just to get a breath of fresh air.

"I'm sorry you're going," moped Bradley, looking up at Giorgio.

"It would've been great, the two of us as Leaders," said Giorgio.

"Yeah."

"It's not happening, though. Karl thinks he'll live forever! Doesn't he realize that his old ideas have failed? I wanted to move Lord Kelly's to a more socially conscious agenda. I want to help everyone, not just Brotherhood members."

"Is that why you're friends with Councillor Theo?"

"Of course!" shouted Giorgio. "At least Theo has goals. Things were different when Karl was our age. Back then we weren't ruled over by a pervert! And what if things get worse, instead of better? Karl's just going to stand back and watch everything fall apart!"

"He cares about Lord Kelly's, too," argued Bradley.

"Sure, as long as he's in charge. We would've been a great team, Brad. I just know it! A blind man can see that you really love the school."

"Well, so do you, Giorgio."

Painfully, Giorgio resigned himself to his fate. "Guess I'll just have to do my 'loving' somewhere else."

Giorgio and Bradley squeezed their way through a busy lane until they reached a modest, brick, two-story establishment called Erickson's Imports. As they entered the dimly lit room, the sickening sweet smell of incense hit their noses. Shelves were filled with an assortment of liquors. Sawdust covered the floor, to catch the grease drippings of a freshly slaughtered beef.

The boys were the youngest patrons in Erickson's. The clientele was a rough looking bunch, with unshaven faces and decaying teeth. Bradley, in particular, felt out of place. He heard everyone laughing at him, asking why an innocent entered the business.

Or was he so innocent?

Bradley soon understood why Sven suggested to pay the bill, then go. Erickson's Imports was not for God-fearing youth! With that in mind, why did Sven trade there? Apparently, he had an affliction for booze. What other failings did he possess?

"What c'n I do for ya?" asked a grizzled old man, standing behind a counter.

Bradley dropped the coins on the counter. "This is from Sven," he whispered, conscious of muffled laughter directed at him.

"Whatcha say?" the old man asked.

"Sven asked me to pay this," said Bradley. "You know . . . Leader Sven, from Lord Kelly's Academy . . ."

The old man was amused, and offended. "He sent *you?*"

"Religious types," said a fat, husky woman, slicing bloody strips from the beef. "Getting a boy to do their dirty work."

With a strained smile, Bradley silently agreed with the woman. Sven should've completed this transaction, himself! Shame brought a man like Sven into Erickson's. And shame was the reason why Bradley had to make this final payment. Bradley was both angry, and sympathetic, with Sven. Like everyone else, Sven had weaknesses. Bradley still cared for him. This was, indeed, a lesson in life.

As the old man scribbled out a receipt, Giorgio was diverted by Erickson's products. Like a kid in a candy store, he sampled the company's beverages, while engaging in smutty conversation with the other customers. Bradley was dismayed. Sure, Giorgio was now free to do what he pleased. He took advantage of his liberties, by turning his back on God.

"What's that?" asked Giorgio, drawn to a thin, tattooed man inhaling smoke from what appeared as dried leaves, rolled in a thin paper cylinder.

"Somethin' we just got in," the old man answered. "Tobacco."

"Tobacco?" inquired Giorgio, curiously. "Where'd you get it?"

"The west," the tattooed man said, evasively.

"Agron?" guessed Giorgio.

"Hell, no," another customer laughed. "The west! A lovely little paradise known as Izwe Enquaba . . ."

"Izwe what?" Giorgio snickered. "Say again . . .Izwe *what?*"

"Shut your stinking mouth!" the tattooed man hollered. "He don't need to know where I'm from!"

"You shut up, Paransky!" the customer growled, sipping illegal Branellian whiskey. "This is my country, y' damned Agronian freebooter! And if ya don't like it, then get the hell out! You and that Mucker guy, upstairs!"

Giorgio ignored the fiery dispute. "Can I try it?"

"You want one?" asked Paransky. "Good. Twenty Embrian shillings."

Giorgio eagerly reached into his pocket for the money. *A guy only lives once!*

Handing Giorgio a cigarette, Paransky said, "Hold it tight between your lips. When I give it a light, suck it in!"

As Giorgio placed the item in his mouth, Paransky ignited it with the burning end of his own cigarette. "Now! Suck it in, *hard!*"

Taking a drag, Giorgio was overwhelmed with smoke entering his lungs. Coughing and gagging, tears drained from his eyes as he nearly dropped the tobacco. Ashes from the cigarette drifted onto the floor. For the exception of Bradley, everyone laughed.

"Takes a little getting used to," chuckled Paransky. "Not so hard next time, sport."

On his second go-round, Giorgio allowed the smoke to swirl around his teeth and tongue. The taste was equally pleasing and bitter.

"Like it?" the old man asked.

"Like it? I love it!" cheered Giorgio, taking another drag. "Care to try this, Brad?"

Bradley wanted no part of the tobacco, and wondered if he still had a place in his heart for Giorgio. As the old man gave him the receipt, he hoped never to pass through those doors again, when . . . from behind, he heard a soft, feminine voice say, "I need help moving that table."

Turning, Bradley saw a blonde-haired young lady, standing at a doorway leading to a backroom. The girl was around Bradley's height but older, around eighteen or nineteen. She was dressed in a black, silky robe. As the garment dragged across the floor, Bradley caught a glimpse of the girl's thighs. A number of men snickered. Even Giorgio was humored by the girl's presence.

"Move that table yourself!" the fat woman ordered. "That's what you're paid for!"

Bradley assumed the girl was hired to perform Erickson's more tedious, physical labor. The girl was undoubtedly overworked and underpaid! She was also the most beautiful person Bradley had ever laid eyes on.

Instinctively, Bradley had an urge to assist her. "How big is that table?" he asked, invoking nervous laughter from Giorgio.

"Will you help me?" the girl asked, a smile highlighting her face.

Bradley sought Giorgio's permission. "Sure, Brad," said Giorgio, chugging a shot of brandy. "I'll wait for you."

"I'll help you move that table," offered Bradley, pocketing the receipt.

As he followed the girl into the backroom, Bradley noticed the customers' expressions. Certain patrons viewed him with wonderment, while others grinned maliciously. Cutting steaks from the beef, the fat woman sneered at the girl. As a moral obligation, Bradley only wished to lend a hand.

The young lady led Bradley into a storeroom. Cool, damp autumn air dominated the musty quarters. The storeroom was cluttered with boxes, barrels, and pouches of the smoking weed hanging from rafters. The sole light came from a small window, blotched by soot, dust, and cobwebs. In one corner sat a narrow feather bed.

Bradley's eyes focused on a large cottonwood table, crowding the storeroom's center. Switching his attention to the girl, he held off temptations of staring at her. Bradley could not ignore, nor deny, her magnetic beauty. Her blonde hair and fair skin were enticing!

The girl pushed open a heavy, thick door, leading to an alley. "Is that where you want the table?" asked Bradley, pleasantly.

"You don't mind?" the girl asked.

"No, not at all!" said Bradley, lifting the table's front end to study its weight. It'd be a job, all right. Such obligations were expected of a good Samaritan.

The girl ran her hand along Bradley's waist and torso. "I've never seen clothes like that, before."

"You haven't?" asked Bradley, aroused by the girl's touch. "I'm a Brother at Lord Kelly's Academy. This . . . this is my school uniform."

"You're very cute in it," the girl giggled.

Blushing, Bradley hoisted the table, then began lugging it outside. The girl was of little help, and permitted the furniture's legs to skid across the stone floor. As Bradley hauled the table outside, his fingers scraped the edge of the doorway. *"Ouch!"* he cried, dropping his end.

"I'm sorry!" the girl apologized. "Are you all right?"

Bradley examined his sore knuckles. "I'm fine," he sighed. "Just lemme get a better grip on this."

As Bradley negotiated the table outside, the girl exerted no real effort. He was better off doing the job by himself! In truth, Giorgio should have also lent a hand. Even though it took no time to place the table against a brick wall, Bradley was winded.

"You look so tired!" the girl said.

"I'm all right," gasped Bradley, reentering the storeroom.

"Please sit down." The girl motioned to the bed. "Thank you so much! I don't know what I would've done, without you!"

Bradley relaxed on the feather bed. "No problem," he said. Breathing heavily, he removed the skullcap to wipe his sweaty forehead. "Have you worked here long?"

"Since I was thirteen. By the way, I'm Leni."

"I'm Bradley," he said, shaking Leni's hand.

"Can I get you a drink?" asked Leni.

"No, wait!" exclaimed Bradley. "I rarely drink wine or distilled . . ."

"I just made a pitcher of lemonade. Want a glass?"

"Sure, I guess," accepted Bradley, wondering if he hadn't already taken advantage of Leni's generosity.

Bradley smiled, as Leni ran to the storefront. As one friend went out, a new friend stepped in. *Goodbye Giorgio, hello Leni.* All of Bradley's chums were guys. With Leni, perhaps he'd be free to confide issues that he wouldn't dare speak to a buddy. Bradley gathered that most of Leni's associates were cutthroats and criminals. He hoped to introduce her to a whole new world, filled with goodwill and decency.

However, Bradley wanted something more from Leni. Thoughts, which were deemed as forbidden, corrupted his heart and soul. No, he reminded himself, this is wrong! Leni was an acquaintance, nothing more! And anyway, Bradley had pending duties at the school. There were still plenty of leaves to rake!

No matter. Bradley wanted Leni next to him. He craved her body while hoping, maybe, she felt the same for him.

Leni returned to the backroom with a pitcher and two glasses. "I hope you like this," she said, filling Bradley's glass.

Consciously, Bradley looked away from Leni as he sipped the lemonade. "Thanks."

Leni placed the pitcher on a night table and sat beside Bradley. Without invitation, she casually rubbed her hand across his bare knee. "Is it good?" she asked, taking a drink.

"G-good," stuttered Bradley, aware that Leni softly caressed his leg.

"You're a brother at . . . where again?"

"Lord . . . Lord Kelly's," answered Bradley, nervously teetering back and forth on the bed.

"How many brothers do you have?"

"About a hundred-and-sixty."

Leni giggled. "Wow, your mother must be really old! And busy!"

"No, no, I meant . . . my *spiritual* Brothers!" stammered Bradley, his heart racing. Was this a sign of stress, fatigue, or panic? The last time Bradley experienced such emotions, he obsessed over an oil painting of a nude woman at a Sykes art gallery. As a laugh slipped past his lips, he thought the lemonade was drugged, or tainted. But no, it was his hunger to envoke this reaction, as he ran his fingers through Leni's long, blonde hair.

Leni petted Bradley's thigh. "Tell me about Lord Kelly's," she requested, in a melodic voice.

As Bradley chattered away, his speech grew slurred and nonsensical. Who cares about the stupid leaves at Lord Kelly's, or even the school, itself? As Bradley gulped down a second glass of lemonade, he willfully neglected his responsibilities. The only thing he cared about now was Leni.

As Bradley told his life story, Leni snuggled against him. Sneaking one hand beneath the tunic, she sent her fingers into his undergarment. Peeking at her breast, Bradley realized Leni wore nothing under the robe. He dropped his glass, which shattered onto the stone floor. He couldn't have cared less. Neither did Leni. Without hesitation, Bradley planted his lips to Leni's.

Untying Bradley's undergarment, Leni welcomed herself inside. Bradley tore away the undergarment, and thoughtlessly discarded it to the floor. Eagerly, he lifted the tunic to his waist, and exposed himself to Leni. Unstrapping the robe, Leni provided Bradley a full glimpse of her body.

Leni reached down to pleasure Bradley. Bradley released a low moan, then dug his fingers into the mattress, as one leg involuntarily jolted forward. Closing his eyes, he allowed Leni to perform her magic. His left arm flailed wildly, as if to have a life of its own.

Heart, body, and soul centered between Bradley's legs, as Leni continued her skillful act. Passionately, Bradley kissed Leni's face and lips. His fingers delicately massaged, and occasionally entered her vagina. Bradley was at Leni's mercy. He belonged to the girl, her loyal servant and slave.

This went well beyond desire. In truth, it was quite celestial. It felt so vital, so wonderful, and so meaningful! Nothing outside of the backroom mattered. So what if the backdoor was left open, allowing a voyeur to see everything? This moment was the total of human endeavor, the reasons for the sun and the moon and the stars.

It wouldn't have been so enjoyable, had God not wished it so!

Once again, Bradley released a deep, guttural moan, as this plea drifted into the storefront and humored Erickson's customers. Leni fondled Bradley's scrotum, then gave it a firm, tight squeeze. Bradley gasped. But no, Leni wasn't finished. Lowering her head, she greeted Bradley's manhood into her warm, wet mouth.

Lacking forethought, Bradley lifted the pitcher of lemonade above his head, then doused himself with it. The drink splashed into his hair and face, streamed through his tunic sleeves, and drenched Leni. With a loud, gleeful shriek, Bradley threw the empty pitcher across the room, where it impacted a wall. Glass shattered everywhere, but failed to distract the teenagers' adult play.

Expressions resembling agony, but indeed ecstasy, painted the emotions. The action built to unspoken levels, engulfing Bradley's entire being. As the pressure multiplied, Bradley curled his toes in.

Go on, go on, go on . . .

I love you, my Leni, I love you . . .

Be mine forever . . .

With clenched fists and gritting teeth, Bradley prepared for the eruption. Here it comes, here it comes, here it comes! Attempting to voice his appreciation and gratitude, a screeching howl spilled from the throat. No escaping it, now!

Oh no, oh no, oh no . . .

Oh, yeah!

The explosion heightened the greatest journey of Bradley's young life. Surrendering, he went the distance, and was left exhausted and exhilarated.

Wearing a lopsided grin, he panted, "How did I do?"

Leni kissed Bradley, leaving traces of semen on his cheek. "You were the perfect gentleman."

Bradley wrapped his arms around Leni. He dreamed of making love to her, from now till the end of time. The couple had shared a special moment of intimacy, never to be coveted by anyone.

"Brad!" shouted Giorgio, from behind an unlocked door. "Bradley, what's going on?"

Laughing as she pulled away, Leni pointed to the door, which led to the alleyway. "You've had your fun . . . now *go!*"

Bradley frowned. He was equally hurt and confused, as Leni's behavior quickly turned cold. This was replaced by sudden panic, as the door to the storefront slowly crept open. Bradley lowered his tunic then darted through the back door. Gripped by fear, he cleared two city blocks on Cameron Street, before coming to a halt.

Catching his breath, Bradley's thoughts were trapped between what had just taken place, and what might happen next. Gradually returning to his senses, he evaluated how this event could affect him. Though it was good *(damned good!)* what price was he to pay for his lack of judgment?

What have I done?

This question repeated in Bradley's mind, until it nearly drove him mad. He didn't intend for Leni to give him oral sex, despite the fact that he savored every moment of it. He was unable to avoid the impending guilt and remorse, tearing at his everlasting spirit. How could I be so stupid?

Bradley's tunic was covered with lemonade, as his groin and upper thighs revealed clues of immoral activity. He struggled to get his head together. First things first! Bradley had to get home, wash the evidence away in a hot bath, then replace his soiled uniform.

Was it possible to wash away sin? Or was he condemned to eternal damnation?

Bradley swore never to be influenced by flesh. Alone, at night, he fought against the solitary joys of masturbation. That day, he destroyed a solemn oath. He could argue that Leni was entirely to blame. In his heart, he still thirsted for her.

All men carry secrets with them. Bradley hoped to conceal this one from everybody! It didn't matter. God had just witnessed a moral catastrophe. There was no way to dispute or deny it. "Forgive me, Father!" Bradley wept, staring up at the skies above. "Please forgive me!"

"What are you running away from?" asked Giorgio. He jogged toward the frightened sixteen-year-old, the smell of tobacco and brandy on his breath.

Desperately, Bradley searched for an answer. Even a dumb response was better than none at all! "I . . . uh . . . have to go rake the leaves . . ."

"You forgot this," said Giorgio, dangling the undergarment in Bradley's face.

Bradley's eyes widened. "What . . . what did you see?"

"Everything, Bradley old boy!" laughed Giorgio. "There's a peephole in the wall at Erickson's Imports. Man, you were really going at it!"

"We didn't go all the way!"

Giorgio shook Bradley like a rag doll. Instead of playing the role of the kindhearted, understanding sibling, he was a crazed, fanatical inquisitor. "Maybe you didn't go all the way," he said. "But you went too far!"

Bradley attempted to break away. "No Giorgio, please! Don't say anything! *Please!"*

Giorgio roared in laughter. Bradley wasn't the only guy from Lord Kelly's to receive Leni's 'gift.' Sven had, and so did Fritz! Rumor had it that even Geoffrey spent a few minutes with her, in hopes that he had no real taste in men. Half of the boys on the dorm's third floor fooled with Leni, at one point or another. It was enlightening to learn that Bradley, too, had fallen under her spell. Little Bradley! Darling little Bradley, the Leaders' favorite son, and heir apparent to Karl's throne! Well, not now! Not anymore!

Overruling Bradley's cries for salvation and redemption, it was Giorgio's privilege in announcing this shocking news to the student body and staff of Lord Kelly's Academy . . .

19

"The hell you say!" shouted Fritz, sitting on a bench in Karl's office. "Y'ain't haulin' me to Lord Billy's!"

"We've already made the arrangements," said Karl. "There's nothing you can do about it."

Minutes before, Fritz went into the Administrative Building, certain he'd soon receive his discharge papers, from Lord Kelly's. Pancake Head was there too, decked out in his shiny new school uniform. Contrary to his nature, Fritz was courteous and kind. Bowing to Karl, he often addressed the Head Leader as 'sir.' He never expected to be placed under Antoine's authority.

"I told you yesterday I ain't putting up with all yer goddamn rules!" cursed Fritz. "Do us all a big favor, and lemme go!"

"The Embrian government doesn't think you're old enough, and surely not mature enough, to make your own decisions," explained Karl. "Since we're unable to control you here, maybe they'll straighten you out at Lord William's."

"Oh, we'll straighten him out, all right," said Antoine. Standing at a window, he tossed a bundle of clothes in Fritz's lap. "Put these on, then we'll go."

"Wanna know what you can do with 'em?" growled Fritz.

Antoine answered Fritz's defiance with a swift blow to the chin.

After getting slammed to the floor, Fritz saw lightning bolts and stars. For a beanpole, Pancake Head sure packed a mean wallop!

"Don't do that!" shouted Karl, leaping from his chair.

"Why not?" asked Antoine. "He asked for it."

Slowly, painfully, Fritz got to his feet. His eyes warned of an attack against Antoine. In response, Antoine presented a knife from his tunic. Fritz smiled, and spit a wad of bloody saliva to the floor. "Feel better, now?" he asked, sarcastically.

"Put those clothes on!" snapped Antoine, impatiently.

Returning to the bench, Fritz unraveled the bundle of clothes to see the insignia of the rattlesnake and the sword. "I don't like snakes," he mumbled in a lame stab at humor, even as panic swept over him. "I'm sorry, Karl! Can't I just stay here, please?"

Antoine frowned. "I told you to . . ."

"Now wait," interrupted Karl. "It's not my desire to send you away, Fritz. But you deliberately violate our rules, and goad the younger boys to follow your poor example."

Fritz shrugged. "I try."

"Maybe, just maybe, I'll give you one last chance," sighed Karl. "In return, give me your word that you'll do as you're told."

Fritz wiped his bloody mouth. "Why are you so worked up about me? I take care of myself!"

"You do?" argued Karl. "What if I tell Brother Antoine about our first meeting?"

Fritz stopped dead in his tracks, unable to make a wise comeback.

Karl leaned against his desk. "About eight years ago, while performing missionary work in the south, I rode into one of the country's more impoverished villages. It was in the middle of winter, with more than a foot of snow on the ground." Karl took a deep breath. It was nearly impossible to get this story out.

"When a small boy, wearing nothing but his sister's dress and no shoes to speak of, begged me to check on his father."

Antoine smiled.

"I followed the boy into a tiny stone hut." Karl paused. "When a foul stench almost knocked me over."

"What did you find?" asked Antoine, in anticipation.

"The boy's father was already dead. By then, rats had already gnawed away at the corpse . . ."

"Shut yer filthy mouth!" cried Fritz, teary-eyed. "Ain'tcha said enough?"

"No, I want to hear more!" said Antoine, still brandishing the knife. "So you wear your sis' dress, eh Fritzy? I had no idea!"

"Quiet, Antoine!" ordered Karl. "To make a long story short, there were a half-dozen of those kids, all starved and frozen. I asked to save all six, but the church hierarchy allowed me to adopt only one." Karl pointed at Fritz. "With that in mind, you'd think he'd show me a little kindness and respect."

"You treated me like dirt, ever since!" sobbed Fritz.

"I gave you a home!" said Karl, emotionally. "I gave you love, discipline . . ."

"Why didn't you take the others, instead?"

"I took you." Karl crossed his arms. "Now, are you really capable of fending for yourself?"

"He might be," said Antoine, smugly, "if this school was any good."

Karl glared at Antoine. "What did you say?"

"I was at the hearing, yesterday," reminded Antoine. "You let Fritz walk all over you."

Karl wagged a finger at Antoine. "Do you think my job is easy?"

"Honestly, I can't see that you're doing your job, at all."

"You have no idea how difficult it is to monitor a hundred-and-sixty boys!"

Antoine laughed. "And you do?"

"Don't come into my school and . . ." Karl was at a loss of words. "Just who do you think you are? Don't you dare come into my school with that attitude!"

"That's it, Karl!" laughed Fritz. "Kick his ass!"

"Maybe you've been in charge here for too long," taunted Antoine. "Youth must be led by youth. It's time for you to step aside, Karl."

"And make room for you?" questioned Karl. "You think it's easy being a Leader? You'll get an education yet, mister!"

"Please Giorgio, *don't!*" a high-pitched voice screamed, from outside. "I'll do anything, I swear! Just don't tell Karl . . ."

"You'll get what's coming to you!" yelled Giorgio, shoving Bradley into the office.

Tears spilled from Bradley's eyes, like rain. Although it was a real battle forcing Bradley to face the music, Giorgio looked forward to giving Karl this sour tune.

Already at wit's end with Antoine, Karl was mortified when Giorgio arrived with Bradley. "What's the meaning of this?" he demanded.

"Are you going to tell him?" asked Giorgio, clutching Bradley's arm. "Or will I?"

Bradley whimpered, when his eyes met Karl's.

"Talk to me," pleaded Karl, nervously. "What happened?"

As Bradley tried to explain, words failed him. "I'm so *sorry!*" was the best he could possibly say. Throwing his arms around Karl, he begged for understanding, compassion, and forgiveness.

"What's going on?" inquired Kenichi, standing at the doorway.

"None of your business!" snapped Karl. "Get back to work, Kenichi!"

Kenichi's complexion reddened. "This is my business."

"Who invited the Oriental mongrel?" insulted Antoine.

"Quiet!" Karl stared at Giorgio. "Very well, big shot. What's this all about?"

Giorgio searched for the right words. "I escorted Bradley to Erickson's Imports, when . . ."

"Erickson's Imports?" Karl gasped. "What were you doing, there?"

"Take one goddamn guess," snickered Fritz.

Giorgio grinned, sheepishly. "Paying a bill . . . for Leader Sven . . ."

"Sven?" Karl turned to Kenichi. "Get Sven in here."

Kenichi refused Karl's orders.

"Kenichi!" shrieked Karl. "Get Sven in here, immediately!"

Reluctantly, Kenichi went to retrieve Sven.

"Oh, this'll be good," commented Fritz.

"Go on," Karl said to Giorgio, impatiently.

Giorgio cleared his throat. "We went to Erickson's to pay a bill for Sven, when . . . this girl asked Bradley to help her move a table in the backroom . . ."

"Leni!" blurted Fritz, equally surprised and tickled. He slapped Bradley's back, and giggled. "Good boy! Someone finally made a man outa ya!"

"Shut up, Fritz!" cried Bradley.

"Just who is Leni?" asked Karl. "Well? Speak up!"

Giorgio blushed. "She's a worker."

"Yeah," agreed Fritz. "You can say that, again."

"What do you mean?" asked Antoine.

Giorgio sighed. "Let's just say that Brad and Leni weren't in there, just a move a table."

"It's not as bad as the liquor you drank!" screeched Bradley, in a lame defense. "Or . . . or that evil, smelly stuff you were inhaling!"

"Oh?" Giorgio shot back. "How does that compare to what you let Leni suck on, a few minutes ago?"

Karl shoved Bradley away. He couldn't accept or believe what he just heard. Bradley had always been an outstanding, decent lad. Now this! Slumping against the desk, Karl grew faint. "Did she? . . . were they? . . ."

"I went in there, and caught Bradley running through a backdoor." Giorgio tossed Bradley's undergarment onto the desk. "I found this lying on the floor."

"Is that yours?" Karl asked Bradley, staring at the undergarment as if it derived from Hell.

Giorgio confirmed Karl's fears by lifting Bradley's tunic.

Concealing his embarrassment beneath the tunic, Bradley sought forgiveness from both Karl and the Lord. "I didn't know what I was doing!" he bawled.

"Bet ol' Leni gave you a pretty good lesson," said Fritz.

Bradley shivered. Despite this one error, he still believed in the spiritual values he learned at Lord Kelly's. He'd do anything never to violate a one of them, again! Did he deserve a second chance? And how would everyone at the school view him, now?

Karl ripped Bradley's necklace loose, then threw it to the floor. The item was a gift, not only speaking of love for Lord Kelly's, but also of mutual respect between teacher and pupil. That day, it signified nothing but broken hearts, faded memories, and betrayal.

To the onlookers' shock and horror, Karl backhanded Bradley in the mouth. As Bradley crashed to the tile floor, Karl turned away from the others, to hide the tears dripping from his own eyes.

Bradley rolled himself into a ball and wept. He didn't care that, in his present position on the floor, he exposed his bare bottom. Did it really matter at that point?

"The weak must be chiseled away," said Antoine, in contempt. "A young Embrian must be as swift as a greyhound, and as tough as leather!"

"You know what you and your buddy Gornick can do with that line of bullshit?" suggested Giorgio, realizing now that Bradley forged a tragic sight. Instead of a potential rival, Giorgio saw only a friend who required his unconditional love and support. It was wrong, indeed *vile,* to squeal on Bradley. Giorgio admired Bradley, but was also envious of him. He played a part in Bradley's fall from grace, and therefore shared in this moral crisis.

"He who owns the youth, owns the future!" added Antoine, with glowing fervor. "With you at Lord Kelly's, and me at Lord William's, just think what we'll accomplish for a new Embrey, Giorgio!"

Giorgio shook his head. "You can go back to Lord William's, or straight to hell, Antoine."

Antoine's jaw dropped. *"What?"*

"When you take Fritz, take this one as well!" Karl told Antoine, pointing at Bradley. "I never want to see him, again!"

Kenichi returned to the office with Sven, who carried a full bottle of the school's wine in one hand, and a second bottle he just emptied in the other. Terrified to see Bradley on the floor, Kenichi pushed Giorgio aside and knelt beside him. "Brad!" he called, anxiously. *Brad!"*

"Get to work, Kenichi!" barked Karl. "I'm in charge, here!"

Kenichi lifted Bradley in his arms, and looked straight into Karl's eyes. "You're in charge here, all right," he said, angrily. "Come on, Brad. We're going."

"I'm no good," sobbed Bradley, burying his face against Kenichi's chest. "I'm no good!"

"It's all right, I promise," whispered Kenichi, carrying Bradley to the door. "Don't let anyone call you a failure. I don't care what you did, buddy. You're the best."

"And just where do you think you're going?" questioned Karl.

"I'm leaving," said Kenichi, "and Bradley's coming with me."

"Can I go, too?" asked Fritz.

Karl blocked Kenichi's path. "You're not going anywhere!"

"What's up?" burped Sven, having trouble staying on his feet.

"Did you send Bradley to Erickson's Imports?" asked Karl, in an accusatory manner.

"Well yeah, but I don't . . ." Sven sat a bottle on a desk. "What happened?"

"It's not what you did," said Fritz, fearful of the tense situation but unwilling to admit it. "It's *who* he met at Erickson's."

"Leni?" asked Sven, amused at the anger drawn against him. "Aw, well. Bradley coulda done a lot worse'n that. I oughta know. . ."

Karl hit the roof. He had spent more than fifty years at Lord Kelly's Academy, where his time and labor were willfully given to the Almighty. He believed the institution was under siege, from within its own ranks and through outside interference. He refused to tolerate it, especially from someone like Sven.

Without warning, Karl smashed the unopened bottle over Sven's head. Wine and shattered glass flew everywhere. This event took place so quickly that it was initially viewed with mirth. Fritz released a mischievous cackle, until he noticed blood trickling from Sven's forehead and nose.

"Oh, god," breathed Giorgio, sickened by the grisly display.

Sven stood motionless. Attempting to make a feeble jab at humor, he instead collapsed to the floor in an unnatural, contorted shape. Lying there, he looked up at Bradley with two cold, lifeless eyes. Bradley leaped from Kenichi's arms, and shrieked.

For several seconds, Kenichi and Karl glared at each other. Neither said a word. Kenichi was caught between notifying the authorities of Sven's death, or rushing away with Bradley.

Infuriated with the self-righteous look on Kenichi's face, Karl grabbed onto his ponytail. "Let go!" screamed Kenichi, squeezing Karl's nose the same way he detained Andre, days before.

"Unhand me!" demanded Karl. Dropping the jagged remains of the wine bottle, he wrapped his legs around Kenichi's shins.

As onlookers stood idly by, no one stepped forward to break the two up. Rather, they awaited the outcome, which forever haunted them to their dying day.

One leg tangled around his opponent's, Kenichi tried to shove Karl into the desk. Instead, Karl fell backward, his hand still clutching Kenichi's hair. As the combatants toppled over, Karl's head slammed into the desk with an explosive *thud!*

Resembling a chicken with its head cut off, Karl convulsed in a wild, spastic fit. Releasing Karl, Kenichi allowed him to drop onto the floor.

Silence. Kenichi first looked at Karl, then at Giorgio.

"You killed Karl," whispered Giorgio, in disbelief. "Kenichi, you *killed* Karl."

Kenichi grabbed Bradley by the arm, then fled from the office. Karl let out a final breath, as Giorgio, Fritz, and Antoine exchanged nervous glances.

Once the reality of this had finally set in, Antoine was determined to apprehend Bradley and Kenichi. "Help get them back!" he ordered Fritz.

Confusion ruled over Fritz. His attention was placed on Karl's lifeless body, sprawled on the floor next to Sven.

"Fritz!" screamed Antoine, slapping the bully's face.

Despair was replaced by sudden, red-hot anger. Fritz swung the empty wine bottle at Antoine. As the bottle brushed harmlessly across his beret, Antoine stepped backward, failing to comprehend the meaning of Fritz's assault.

Believing the bottle had shattered against Antoine's head, Fritz plunged it into his belly. Unsheathing the knife, Antoine slashed Fritz's left thigh.

Fritz cursed as he reached for the raw, bloody wound. Once more, he swung the bottle at Antoine.

Ducking, Antoine jabbed the knife at Fritz's chest, but missed. Furiously, Fritz slapped Antoine's cheek with the blood-smeared palm of one hand. "Think yer real smart!" he roared. "Don'tcha, Pancake Head?"

Off-balance, Antoine thrust the knife at Fritz, yet failed to make contact.

Even if he disliked Fritz, Giorgio despised Antoine that much more. Throwing his arm around Antoine's throat, he strangled the zealous Gornick supporter. Gasping for air, Antoine released the knife.

Fritz removed the beret, and whacked the bottle against Antoine's head.

The bottle refused to break. Antoine's skull did not. Antoine's face twisting to a bizarre, near-comical mask, before he fell across Sven's torso.

Fritz's tough-guy persona altered to that of a frightened child's. "Let's get outa here!" he whined, his voice raspy and jittery.

Giorgio knew that he and Fritz had to make a run for it. His breathing swift and shallow, panic gripped him like a vice. For a brief, fleeting moment, he thought of taking this matter to Royce. At the same time, he could not involve an innocent man into this mess. The lazy, neglectful city constable would likely jail Royce, simply for being there.

Giorgio saw only one venue, which he prayed was open to him. Would Theo grant him a safe haven? Assuming Theo did help, then what? Giorgio dreaded the possibilities of being arrested, then facing a harsh interrogation. Though he took no part in Sven and Karl's death, he assisted in sending Antoine to the pearly gates. Like it or not, Giorgio feared he'd have to leave the country. But where to? Kusch? Agron?

Branell?

One idea, which never left Giorgio's mind since he first pondered it, meant accompanying Major Kohl on a planned mission to Insula Infernus . . .

20

As Bradley and Kenichi ran from the Administrative Building, they encountered a world unaffected by the incident in Karl's office. Most students carried on, as if their lives were unchanged.

Bradley was more of a hindrance than anything. Kenichi had to practically drag him to the gate. Before leaving the campus grounds, Bradley fell to the turf. There, he wept like an infant.

Kenichi was afraid of everyone and everything around him. In the shadow of his hatred for Karl, was he entirely at fault for what happened? He couldn't flee from images of Karl falling into the desk, or the overpowering sensations of guilt sweeping over his entire body.

I killed Karl! I didn't mean to . . .

. . . but I did!

Karl killed Sven! Would it have been better, to let him kill Bradley or me? Karl hated toward me! But was it worth killing? . . .

Killing . . .

Accidentally killing him?

Karl's dead, because of me!

Because of me!

Paranoia was only one of the dangers facing Kenichi. For Bradley's sake, he kept it together. The two boys required a decent shelter for the night. There was a constant need for food. Finally, the nights grew steadily colder. Kenichi wanted to shed his tunic for a wool shirt and some long breeches. The school uniform, a source of humility and embarrassment, now linked him to a crime.

Lifting Bradley in his arms, Kenichi dashed past the gates to enter the crowded, hectic streets of Sykes. Tiredly, he slipped into a darkened alley separating two buildings, and stopped at the corner of a brick tavern. In the distance, he heard the rowdy, boisterous camaraderie from the tavern walls.

No one was in sight, as Bradley and Kenichi sat near a scattered pile of decaying fish. "Brad," whispered Kenichi, catching his breath. "I can't tell you how truly sorry I am . . ."

"It's my fault!" whined Bradley. "If I didn't go into that room with . . . Kenichi, do you hate me?"

"Hell, no! If I hated you, would we be together? I'd be half way to Kusch by now!"

"But I did wrong, by . . ." Bradley tried, yet failed to explain himself. "I thought the spirit was stronger with me, Kenichi. I promised God and Karl that I'd never do anything like . . ."

"God will forgive you," sighed Kenichi. "Karl never would."

"But he wouldn't have killed Sven, if . . ."

"If Karl really loved you, he wouldn't have treated you that way!" argued Kenichi.

Bradley rested his head on Kenichi's shoulder. He had to accept the fact that Karl and Sven were dead. How could that be? The two men were alive and well in Bradley's heart and mind, an irreplaceable part of life. Despite Karl's uncompromising attitudes, it was impossible to loath the man. And, regardless of Sven's mistakes, Bradley admired his kindhearted nature.

Numbness, denial, anger, sadness, and fear fought for possession of Bradley. This was no dream or fantasy found in a dusty old library book, or drama staged at the Falcon Theatre. It was a harsh, inescapable reality! Though he didn't yet know how to take it, Bradley knew that Karl and Sven were dead. He watched them die!

Whenever he needed answers, Bradley usually went to Giorgio or Sven for solutions. If they couldn't help, the next in line were Karl or Royce. If nothing more, there was always God to fall back on. Where was God now, to counsel and comfort him?

Bradley allowed the pain and sorrow to drain out, in a flow of tears.

With the exception of his mother or Leader Lionel, Kenichi usually distanced himself from others. Even if it cost him his freedom or life, he was determined to look out for Bradley. Kenichi couldn't have cared less about what happened between Bradley and someone named Leni. Bradley wasn't necessarily weak, only human. "Was she good?" asked Kenichi, with a strained smile.

Bradley wiped his eyes. *"What?"*

"Leni?" Kenichi asked, mischievously. "Was she good?"

Bradley grinned, with a fiery blush.

Kenichi snickered. "She *was,* wasn't she?"

"Sort of," admitted Bradley, recalling the moment he wandered into the backroom of Erickson's Imports with Leni. Would he take it all back? Yes, and no! He tried never to cave into such desires, and lost.

Oh hell, yeah, Leni was good! Bradley wanted to lay her down on a bed and thrust himself into her, over and over and over, for all eternity! At the same time, he held himself accountable for the bloodshed in Karl's office. Perhaps it was Heavenly retribution for his lack of moral courage and conviction.

Perhaps Bradley was destined to burn in Hell for it.

Bradley felt betrayed by those he cared about. Karl lobbied for him to become a Leader. Giorgio claimed to uphold him. Antoine was once a loyal, trusted friend. Maybe all three had revealed their true colors.

Then again, so did Bradley . . .

After getting to their feet, Bradley and Kenichi darted through the narrow alleyway, until they found a decaying, heavy wooden door, leading to the lower level of an abandoned building. Working their way through thick dust and spider webs, they spotted a corner with a small window. For Kenichi, this was the hideaway he so desperately needed. For Bradley, it was a dank, disgusting mess. "I'm not staying here," he complained.

"Why not?" asked Kenichi. "I've been in worse."

"But I won't!"

"That's because you've never been homeless!" shouted Kenichi, knowing that Bradley had to get tough, or die. "That is, until now."

Bradley's feelings were hurt, from Kenichi's scolding.

"We've got no choice but to stay here," said Kenichi. "We're on our own. It's only for tonight. We'll start out, first thing tomorrow morning."

"Where are we going?" asked Bradley, hopelessly.

"The hell out of here! As soon as we reach the country, we'll find work on a farm . . . I guess. Around here, our stupid uniforms give us away."

Bradley resented Kenichi's attitudes about the school tunic. Stupid or not, he'd keep his.

Hunting through the basement, the boys found piles of loose straw, buried under a few wool blankets and quilts. Not far from this makeshift bed were stacks of empty liquor bottles. Kenichi saw this as a fortunate discovery. However, it made Bradley yearn for his warm, clean dorm room. "Why would someone fix a bed in here?" asked Bradley, in disdain.

"The same reason you went into that backroom with Leni," joked Kenichi.

"What do we eat?" asked Bradley. He was angered at Kenichi's remark, but didn't say so.

Kenichi dug into his tunic pocket. "I've got thirty shillings."

"Twenty-six," said Bradley, holding his meager savings in the palm of one hand.

The boys rganized the straw and blankets, then shaped it into a modest bed. Kenichi was aware of their grim situation. Winter was coming! Was it smart in expecting Bradley to carry his weight? There were no feather beds, unwavering generosity, or hot meals on the road. Although he hated falling back on it, Kenichi saw theft as a solution. It was dog-eat-dog, from here on out.

"Keep making this bed, and tidy up," said Kenichi. "I'll get something to eat."

"Can't I go with you?" whined Bradley, afraid to be alone in that dark, desolate basement.

"I won't be gone for long, I promise."

"We'll be okay . . . won't we?"

Kenichi clutched Bradley's hand. "There's nothing we can't do, if we stick together."

Bradley gulped. He trusted Kenichi, but was worried. The city constable was probably investigating the Administrative Building. Kenichi wasn't popular at the school. What if Giorgio, Fritz, or Antoine pinned the blame squarely on him?

"Be careful," said Bradley, giving Kenichi a hug.

With a reassuring smile, Kenichi left the basement.

To keep busy, Bradley spread the quilt and blankets upon the loose straw. It was deplorable! That morning, Bradley woke up in the comfortable, predictable surroundings of Lord Kelly's. That night, he'd slumber in a cold, miserable basement, struggling to keep his spirits up.

What reasons did Bradley have in shaping that bed? Karl and Sven were dead! Who could sleep, after that? Even with their frailties and weaknesses, the two Leaders filled a necessary void for Bradley. On his own, he was scared.

Bradley rolled himself in a fetal position, covered his face in the palms of both hands, and cried for more than an hour.

Entering a bustling avenue leading downtown, Kenichi tried to disappear amongst the crowd. He kept a watchful eye for the law, suspecting those who so much as gave him a passing glance. If only he'd get rid of that stupid uniform!

"Kenichi!" someone called, in the noise and chaos of the busy street. "Kenichi!"

Kenichi froze. Looking in all directions, he saw a couple of familiar schoolmates waving at him.

Trevor and Derek snaked their way to Kenichi, who needed no extra mouths to feed. It did no good eluding the youngsters. With his ponytail and clothing, he stuck out like a sore thumb.

"Kenichi!" greeted Trevor. "We looked everywhere for . . ."

"I'm running errands for Leader Royce," fibbed Kenichi. "What . . . what are you guys doing here? You know you're not supposed to leave campus, without permission."

"Haven't you heard?" asked Trevor.

"Heard what?" asked Kenichi, too jumpy for his own good.

"Karl and Sven got killed!" announced Trevor.

Kenichi feigned shock and surprise. *"Killed?"*

"Someone murdered them," said Trevor, sadly. "Them, and Brother Antoine."

Kenichi's mouth dropped open. *"Antoine?* You sure? Antoine?"

"Someone mashed his brains in," said Derek.

"No they didn't!" argued Trevor. "They just broke his head real bad."

"Well," mulled Derek, absently. "Looked like his brains was mashed in, to me."

Trevor rolled his eyes back. "Moron."

With a deep breath, Kenichi sat at a bench in front of a butcher shop. Derek plopped down next to him and said, "The constable's looking for you."

"Me?" gasped Kenichi. "What does he want with me?"

"He thinks you know who done it," said Trevor, kneeling upon the sidewalk.

"How could I know?" questioned Kenichi, betraying himself with a jittery voice. "I've been running errands for Leader Sebastian!"

"Sebastian?" asked Trevor, rubbing an annoying sunburn on his thigh. "I thought you said Royce."

That cinched it. Kenichi started for the basement.

"Where are you going?" asked Derek.

"Nowhere," answered Kenichi, vaguely.

"Can we go with you?" begged Trevor. "We got nowhere else to go!"

"They closed the school," said Derek, "and made us leave without our stuff. Now what're we s'posed to do?"

Kenichi knew he couldn't properly care for Trevor, Derek, *and* Bradley. Under the circumstances, his conscience refused to turn them away. "Do you guys have any money?" he asked.

"I got my yo-yo," said Derek, retrieving the toy from his pocket.

"That's not quite what I had in mind," said Kenichi. "Well, I guess you'd better come with me . . . I guess."

"Where to?" asked Trevor.

"To a nice . . . spacious room for the night," said Kenichi. "We've got a good friend there, waiting for us!"

21

"I can't believe it!" cried Giorgio, pacing back and forth in Councillor Theo's study. "Everything was fine, and then Karl broke that bottle over Sven's head!"

Generally, life was calm and tranquil at Theo's country home. Not now. Minutes before, Theo received an unexpected visit from Giorgio and Fritz. Accustomed to Giorgio's rants about Lord Kelly's, he wasn't prepared to hear about the deaths of two Leaders, along with a student from Lord William's.

Theo liked taking long walks in the warm afternoon sun, to clear his head and ease his spirit. That day, he stayed in the enclosed section of his home. Based on Admiral Kraig's directives, dozens of soldiers were deployed to "protect" Theo and Kohl. For the sake of privacy, all doors and windows were kept shut.

As Giorgio relayed this disturbing episode, listeners said nothing. Theo urged Giorgio to sit still. Meanwhile, Yuri obediently filled everyone's glasses with Campens Rose'.

While Giorgio knew everyone in the room, Fritz was a total stranger. He made a comical sight in his tunic, with both sleeves missing and the chest ripped open. After Yuri and Linus treated and bandaged his wounded leg, Fritz sat in one corner of the study. Requesting more hooch, he tried to ignore Theo's weird little stepson. The Kuschan's mere presence gave him the creeps. What was that brat's name, again?

Yerree? Yoo-Ree?

Urine?

Fritz sought oblivion by chugging the rose' like there was no tomorrow. He wanted to be freed from Lord Kelly's jurisdiction. He finally got his wish. Now what?

Unable to ease his fraying nerves, Giorgio nursed his drink. "Everything was fine," he whimpered, "until Karl broke that bottle over Sven's head . . ."

"Sit down, Giorgio," ordered Theo, keeping his own emotions in check. "Have another drink, then we'll come up with a plan of action. Yuri, more Campens Rose'!"

Giorgio only wanted a sip, while Fritz demanded a full glass.

Once again, Giorgio paced back and forth like a trapped animal. "Everything was fine," he repeated, "when . . ."

"The hell!" slurred Fritz, not caring whether his language offended anyone. "Nothin' was fine back there, goddamn it! First, Pancake Head got ol' Karl all riled up, and then you went an' shoved Bradley into the room, which got Karl even more riled . . ."

"Excuse me," interrupted Theo. "Just who exactly is 'Pancake Head'?"

"Brother Antoine," sniffled Giorgio, "from Lord William's Academy."

Kohl and Vix turned to each other. *Pancake Head?*

"He's a Gornick supporter," said Giorgio, "or was, until Fritz and I . . ." Waving his arms in the air, he accidentally splashed Theo and Yuri with Campens Rose'. "Fritzy and I aren't killers! I mean, Antoine had that knife . . . But I didn't mean for him to die!"

"Better him than me," said Fritz, hiding his own remorse under a cloud of intoxication.

"Neither of you will return to Sykes," said Theo. "As a matter of fact, I'd better arrange for you to leave Embrey, right away."

The study grew quiet, as Giorgio and Fritz exchanged glances. Like it or not, the two were fugitives. Where could they go? The Branellian Empire was out of the question! Agron, with its notoriously renegade and rebellious nature, already had its share of expatriates from the mainland. That backward nation remained neutral on most issues outside of its shores. Although Theo had positive ties with Kusch, neither Giorgio nor Fritz understood the language.

Because Embrey was a large nation, it was possible for the two teens to change their names and reside in other provinces. While that idea appealed to Fritz, Giorgio hoped to make a name for himself in society and politics.

"Major Kohl, do you need more men for your voyage to Infernus?" asked Giorgio.

"Here we go again," sighed Theo.

"I can use all the good men I can get," answered Kohl, excitedly. "Are you man enough to join me on this quest?"

"Not likely!" exploded Vix. "If he ain't man enough to face the consequences of his actions, then by god . . ."

"What was I supposed to do?" asked Giorgio, defensively. "Wait around to get arrested?"

Vix left the chair and approached Giorgio with his fists clenched. Theo stepped between them. "None of that!" he shouted.

The two antagonists glared at each other. Neither budged, nor backed down.

"Theo's right," said Kohl, wearing a smile that agitated Vix. "Go outside, Sergeant, and cool off."

In Vix's mind, leaving the room signified a retreat. He wanted to kick Giorgio's butt for sassing a grownup. Too angry to voice his contempt, he deliberately overturned his chair. Storming outside, he slammed the door behind him.

There was little regard between Theo and Vix. Lately, they agreed more now, than ever before. For an expedition to bear fruit, Major Kohl required brave, experienced, competent men.

With a deep breath, Theo asked, "I ask you to stay here with me, Giorgio. You too, Yuri. Neither of you have any business going to Infernus."

"But you just said that I'll have to leave the country!" argued Giorgio. "I'm an adult, Councillor Theo. If I must leave Embrey, isn't it my decision where I go?"

Knowing nothing about Infernus, or Kohl's projected mission there, Fritz threw his hat into the ring. "I ain't got nothin' better to do. Whatever you got goin', Major, I'm goin' too!"

Kohl roared in laughter. He had Giorgio's leadership, Fritz's brawn, and Yuri's prowess with weaponry. Not perfect, maybe, but a promising start!

"Are you boys aware of the dangers on Infernus?" asked Theo.

"What about the dangers here, in Embrey?" asked Giorgio.

"I know several good lawyers in Sykes," said Theo. "I'm sure you'll be acquitted for what . . ."

Giorgio shook his head. "No, sir. I don't want you jeopardizing yourself, or your career, on account of Fritzy or me."

"Major Kohl!" cried Theo. "I offered to pay for a second voyage to Infernus. I will not be responsible for the loss of innocent blood!"

This statement brought objections from Giorgio, Fritz, and Yuri, who hated being referred to as 'innocent blood.' Kohl enjoyed watching the trio debate Theo, each fighting to get their feelings out. Though it sounded like gibberish, he admired the spunk and drive motivating these young men to greatness.

"Giorgio," said Theo, organizing his chaotic thoughts. "You abhor violence, you said so yourself. Didn't you just get done saying that you're not a killer? Don't forget that your parents died in the Border War."

"How can I forget that, Councillor Theo?" replied Giorgio. "Yes, I hate violence, just like I hate what . . ." His throat tightened. "I just don't want to be thought of as a coward. Maybe by the time we return from Infernus, our crimes will be forgiven."

"It's not cowardice I'm talking about!" shouted Theo. "You didn't like watching your Leaders die this afternoon. As far as that young man from Lord William's, well . . . Under the circumstances, I'm not sure whether to fault you or not. After all, he did injure Fritz."

"Damn right!" agreed Fritz.

"I ask you to reconsider going to Infernus with Major Kohl," said Theo. "You're liable to see more death on that campaign than you can ever imagine. What will you say, when you watch men fall by the dozens?"

Giorgio didn't answer.

"You tell them, Major Kohl," said Theo. "How many casualties did you suffer on that last trip? I beg you, don't take these boys with you!"

"You left home at age fourteen to make your fortune on merchant ships," reminded Kohl. "Cut these fellows some slack. Let them grow up, like the rest of us."

"If this expedition is worth funding, isn't it as important to provide men?" asked Yuri. "You always said that we should help others, in their time of need. Major Kohl needs my help."

Enthusiastically, Giorgio, Fritz, and Kohl affirmed Yuri's sentiments.

Theo's face sagged. "Is it justified for you to come to a friend's aide, even if it runs contrary to my better judgment, as well as breaking my heart?"

"I'm not doing this to break your heart," said Yuri. "I want to be the man you expect me to be, the sort of man you are, Father! Not only for us, but for the nation of Embrey! I can take care of myself, as well as anyone!"

"I know you can, son," admitted Theo, painfully, "It's just that . . ."

"And I'm an adult, too!" claimed Yuri. "I'm fifteen!"

"Bullshit!" commented Fritz, as if it was a sneeze.

"If you truly expect great things from me," added Yuri, "then let me do them!"

"You will, Yuri, in good time," said Theo. "And not in the battlefield, but in the Embrian Council."

"Everything you have is going to me, right?" asked Yuri. "Not only your property, but your title and all the privileges with it?"

"Of course, son," said Theo. "You already know that."

"Then let me earn them," said Yuri. "Why simply give them to me?"

Justified, for the good of all . . .

Theo rushed from the study. "Linus, ready my wagon!" he called to his manservant.

As Theo departed, Kohl stayed behind to discuss the mission with his recruits. It tickled him to see such bright-eyed youngsters, eager to prove themselves. "There's a treasure hidden on Infernus," he fibbed. "And I've been assigned to bring it here, to Embrey."

This caught Fritz's attention. Giorgio was also intrigued. With the closing of Lord Kelly's Academy, why not go somewhere promising adventure, new experiences, fame and, most of all, a second chance?

"I won't say it's not dangerous," warned Theo, though his tone was inviting. "I must raise an expeditionary force to locate the treasure, while collecting rare species from the island."

"I'm ecstatic!" said Giorgio. "But why not take trained soldiers with us, too?"

Kohl was stumped. He thought to have locked three brave, scrapping young warriors, and didn't want them slipping away from him. "This mission is of the utmost secrecy," he boasted. "Even my brother, Admiral Kraig, isn't aware of it."

The more Kohl described this venture, the more Giorgio and Fritz wanted in on it. "Who else you got on this crazy boat ride?" asked Fritz, nearly falling from his cot.

"Can you get me more men?" asked Kohl, thrilled with prospects of a larger army.

Giorgio thought about his many schoolmates, all lacking shelter, blowing like leaves in the wind throughout Sykes. He felt responsible for his younger charges. Some of the guys weren't "men" at all, and unsuitable for Kohl. On the other hand, there were certain guys Giorgio would lay down his life for, or depend on in a crisis.

Shame gnawed at Giorgio, as he fretted over Bradley. He had no right harming a friend that way! So why did I do it? Why did I drag Bradley into Karl's office?

'Cause I was jealous of him, that's why!

It made Giorgio look superior to deliver news of Bradley's disgrace to Karl. At what cost? Karl went nuts and killed Sven! Then Kenichi killed Karl!

And then . . .

A severe, sharp pain hit Giorgio's gut. Don't think about it! Just don't think about it!

If at all possible, Giorgio had to make an amends to Bradley. How? God only knew where Bradley was, at that hour! Sykes was a huge city. Looking for the one kid was like searching for a needle in a very large haystack. Giorgio knew of Bradley's friendship with Kenichi and, with luck, the two were together. Giorgio had no malice toward Kenichi, and saw a need for him in Kohl's army.

Giorgio also wanted Bradley in on the mission. First he had to find him, along with a good number of other students. "I'll get you some men," he said. "It means having to go into Sykes to get them."

Kohl slapped his leg, and laughed. "I'm sure you will find me some very fine men, Giorgio! I'll pay you ten shillings a piece for each one!"

Encouraged by this challenge, Fritz swallowed the rest of his drink. Releasing a loud burp, he staggered to the door. "What're we waitin' for?" he asked, bumping his knee into the table, and nearly spilling the expensive Campens Rose'.

"I'll go, too!" volunteered Yuri.

Kohl patted Yuri's back. "That's the spirit!"

Giorgio never really liked Fritz. That didn't matter. Kohl was happy with Fritz. Therefore, the miscreant was also enrolled in the expedition.

Giorgio was also uncertain of Yuri's participation. Still, he needed all the help he could get! "Do you have anything to sober Fritz?" he asked.

"I'll get a canteen of coffee!" suggested Yuri, running to the kitchen.

Coffee! Giorgio drank a cup of it the last time he dined with Theo, and stayed awake most of the night!

As Kohl and Yuri collected provisions, Giorgio eased Fritz outside. Stepping into the warm autumn sunlight, they saw Vix leaning against a fencepost, whittling a slab of firewood. No words were exchanged. Yet, Vix's scowl warned of potential fireworks.

"Urine comin'?" asked Fritz.

"Who?" asked Giorgio.

"Y' know . . . The politician's creepy little brat!"

Giorgio frowned. "I'm afraid so."

"Aw, hell," griped Fritz. "We'll have to carry 'em around on our backs!"

Yuri left the house with an emergency kit, which included dried fruits and meats, along with first aid supplies. What puzzled Fritz and Giorgio were the bows and arrows he had with him. "What's he think we're gonna run into?" asked Fritz. "Branellians, or bears?"

Vix watched the trio march through the muddy path leading to Sykes, and didn't like what he saw. Dropping the slab of wood to the ground, he brushed loose shavings from his clothes, and went to confront Major Kohl.

Vix entered the study to find Kohl sprawled on a cot, sipping on a pint of rose'. The major seemed quite pleased with himself.

"Just whadda ya think your doing?" demanded Vix.

"I sent Giorgio to amass an army," said Kohl, put off with Vix's harsh tone.

"Giorgio? What kinda men you think he'll get? A kiddies' brigade?"

"It's an army, isn't it?" Refusing to look up to an inferior, Kohl got to his feet. "Who else can we get, on such short notice?"

"If you want me to stick my neck out, get some men with experience, and a backbone," argued Vix. "As it now stands, Major Kohl, I ain't going to Infernus with you."

Kohl's mouth gaped open. "Why, of course you are, Sergeant Vix."

"No sir. Heading back to that hell hole's bad enough. Taking a buncha kids is just plain stupid."

"How dare you turn your back on me?" Kohl clutched Vix's arm. "You have to come with me. It's the only way!"

Vix sighed. "Sir, if Theo's willing to give them boys safe passage to another country, maybe we oughta leave, too."

"For God's sake, Sergeant Vix! Not only are you deserting me, but Embrey as well!"

"I ain't no deserter," growled Vix.

"Fine, then go! That is, if you can still live with yourself. Frankly, I don't want the air around me spoiled by a lazy, malingering, sniveling coward!"

Neither man caved in, nor made concessions. Finally, Kohl broke the stalemate by slapping Vix's face.

That did it. Before Kohl negotiated a second attack, Vix slugged him in the nose.

As Kohl flew into the table, he sent the bottle of Campens Rose' crashing to the floor. Blood filled his nose and mouth.

"Head back to the island, if you want to!" yelled Vix. "Or to Hell, for all I care!

You'll get there before I will!"

With that, Vix stormed from the study. After slamming the door, he drifted from Councillor Theo's home and Major Kohl's life.

"Vix!" screamed Kohl, desperately. "Vix, I'm ordering you back here! *Vix!*"

An auburn-haired, peach-fuzzed corporal burst into the study, and was alarmed to spot Kohl on the floor. "Major!" he cried, taking Kohl's hand. "Are you all right?"

"What's your name?" asked Kohl, in humiliation.

"Corporal Rupert, sir!"

"It's *Sergeant* Rupert now! Help me to my feet, soldier!"

Anxiously, Kohl limped outside. His leg hadn't yet healed from his encounter with the unknown assailant who killed Salazar's men. So what? He just had to catch up with Vix. But all he saw was the dust stirred by the sergeant's horse.

"Vix!" Kohl called out, equally frustrated and forgiving. "Get back here! I . . . we have to talk!"

"Should we apprehend Sergeant Vix?" asked Rupert.

"No," answered Kohl, figuring that Vix would return, in time. Vix was too reliable to simply ride away, without explanation or apology.

Rupert retrieved a handkerchief from his pocket, and gave it to Kohl. Urgently, Kohl wiped blood from his nose and mouth. "How old are you, son?" he asked.

"Nineteen," answered Rupert. "How old are you?"

Kohl didn't say. Instead, he patiently awaited Vix. Once the sergeant had a change of heart and returned, everything would be the same as before.

After waiting a minute, there was still no sign of Vix. A cruel, overbearing sensation crept into Kohl's stomach. How can I possibly undertake the mission, now?

"Major Kohl?" asked Rupert. "Anything I can do for you? Sir?"

Wild-eyed, Kohl screamed, "Sergeant Vix! Damn you, get back here! *Vix!*"

Since his late-night meeting with Yuri, Strunk obsessed over rendering payback on the nasty little Kuschan and his fat, politician daddy.

Nobody ever whipped Strunk in a fair fight. Nobody! Prior to that evening, Strunk had never once tasted the bitter fruits of defeat. When it came to a stand-up, toe-to-toe brawl, Strunk came out as the winner. With his small, barrel-shaped frame, opponents learned it never paid to tangle with him. Strunk loved seeing an enemy's reaction as they were struck by his sharpened steel. He never tired of blood from a gashing wound, whether it was from the belly, the lungs . . .

. . . or a cut off head.

As Strunk sat on a stump in front of his shed, feeding them mangy chickens, melancholy tormented him. His glory days were at an end, and lost in fading memories.

Goddamn Theo's bloated hide . . .

Goddamn Theo, for taking away the best job a man could ever ask for . . .

Goddamn Theo, for that queer-eyed Kuschan he brung around here . . .

Waking on that chilly morning, after his late-night meeting with Yuri, Strunk suffered from a terrible headache. The misery was compounded with heartache and despair, brought on by his first whipping in life . . .

. . . against a sneaking, limp-wristed, Kuschan fairy!

Endlessly, Strunk fantasized about destroying Yuri and that disgusting, bloated, fat politician father!

As Strunk tossed seed to them mangy chickens, his anger was more than he could fathom. On that sunny afternoon, he thought of nothing but using his considerable talents on the fat politician, and his cowardly, limp-wristed Kuschan. Why not wipe out their whole goddamn household staff? After decorating his cramped, cold shed with their rotting heads, he'd then sell himself to those willing to pay for his grisly skills.

What good was thinking about it? Thinking ain't no good! Strunk still had to work a crappy job, live in that cold shed . . .

Which, added to the memory of the night when a cowardly, limp-wristed, queer-eyed Kuschan got the best of him!

Strunk endured the ill-effects of an unceasing headache and heartache, after Yuri sent both feet into his grimacing face. What few teeth he had hurt like a dirty son of a bitch! His neck bones was never quite the same, neither! Thoughts, which Strunk regarded as unthinkable, stated that Yuri done permanent damage with the cowardly, chickenhearted, blind-sided blow! He figured himself goddamn lucky that the Kuschan queer never tried nothing unnatural, or finish him off in the front of his shed.

Goddamn Kuschan prob'ly thought about it . . .

Yuri spared Strunk's life. Regrettably, Strunk was left with the knowledge that someone bested him in a fight. Especially a goddamn fairy who laid him out at the door of the shed.

Strunk made promises that Yuri's win would be short-lived. He failed to stop thinking about sending a blade between Yuri's ribs, watch blood spurt outa the innards, chop the goddamn Kuschan's head off . . .

. . . and keep it as a fuckin' trophy.

What good was thinking? Thinking was a curse, a disease, a poison! The worst affliction of all! Thinking don't get nothin' done! Thinking only got Strunk that much more madder! And Strunk was tired of thinking about it, over and over and over!

One of them days *(if one of them days ever come!)* Strunk'd pay Yuri back permanent, and give the fat politician a horrid memory he'd never shake!

Memories to torment the fat man, clear to the grave . . .

Theo traveled by wagon with his manservant Linus and a half-dozen guards to see Strunk. Stepping from the wagon, Theo cautiously approached the executioner. No Yuri. Just as well. Strunk might get a lucky shot against the fat man, maybe even the Kuschan in a stand-up brawl. Then he'd have to tangle with them guards. Strunk'd make one last stand before dying at his goddamn shed. Be one helluva fight, one that ever'body in Embrey knowed about!

This wasn't the day for Strunk to lash out against the fat man. It didn't prevent him from getting in a few licks with a saucy tongue. "I hear tell that Gornick's lookin' to legalize beheadin's," greeted Strunk, with a smirk. "Whadda ya gotta say about that?"

Theo pasted on a strained smile. "I've got a job for you."

"Yer wantin' me to clear out them lodge pole in that back forty," groaned Strunk.

"No." Theo ran one finger across his neck. "You'll make good on it, just the same."

"Think so? Why don'tcha get that ghoulish houseboy of yers to do it?"

Theo frowned. "You know I don't like it when you refer to Yuri that way."

Strunk thought about commenting on cowardly, sneaking Kuschans doing bodily harm on lowly-paid workers. Judging by Theo's facial expressions, Strunk guessed the fat man was unaware of Yuri's assault on him. Not one to openly boo-hoo on such infractions, he buttoned his lips. "What?" laughed Strunk. "The little cutthroat? He did a helluva job on Salazar's men. Makes ya right proud, don't it? Wonder what Gornick'll do with you and yer ankle-biter, after he dispenses with that pervert king?"

Theo turned away. "I should've known better than to take this up with you."

"Now wait just a minute!" Strunk grabbed Theo's arm. "What is it you wanna see me about?"

Theo pulled away from Strunk's filthy paw.

"Aw, c'mon," snickered Strunk, offering Theo a bottle of ale. "Take a snort, let's talk."

Theo refused Strunk's hospitality. "Do you know of Major Kohl's plans of returning to Infernus? I've tried talking him into hiring men on this mission, but he won't. Now he wants to hire boys . . . including my son."

"Yuri?" asked Strunk, disparagingly.

"Yes, Yuri!"

"Aw, I reckon the Kuschan'll take care of himself. Might do me a bit o' good to see him in a real fight, instead of all that cattin' around in the dark."

Theo glared at Strunk. "What do you mean?"

"Nothin'." Strunk swigged the ale. "Just makin' a bit o' conversation."

Theo's assignment required those of low moral character. Praying to never resent this deal, he said, "I'll pay you a year's salary if you get Major Kohl and his team to Infernus, and safely back home. Including Yuri."

Giggling, Strunk accidentally spit ale on Theo's robe. Would the guarantee stick, if an arrow, sword, or pink monkey got the best of a cowardly, sneaking little Kuschan?

Sick and tired of crappy wages, Strunk sought to challenge himself, once more, on the battlefield. Sure, he was interested *(goddamn interested!)* in the job, with the understanding that Kohl and his team got safely home.

Save one cowardly, limp-wristed Kuschan.

And the loss of that one Kuschan would torment the fat politician for the rest of his greedy, gluttonous life!

In the heat of combat, what prevented Yuri from dying in a real man's brawl, toe-to-toe against a worthy foe? Strunk would do the boy a favor by battling him upfront, instead of that cowardly sneaking around or shooting arrows from behind rocks, trees, or bushes. After Yuri had the honor of dying like a real man, Strunk would do him the honor of givin' 'em four feet of lovely, worm-infested dirt *(based on head size!)* at a prize location on Insula Infernus!

Strunk danced a jig, to Theo's annoyance. "Helluva bargain there, Councillor! I'm lookin' to take you up on it. How'm I s'posed to manage it all on my lonesome?"

The contract required not only Strunk, but others of that same, loathsome ire. "Very well," said Theo, grudgingly. "I'll allow you a few sailors of your choosing, to coordinate the mission."

Spitting in his right hand, Strunk gave Theo a firm, steady handshake. "Got yerself a deal!"

"But remember this, Strunk," added Theo, sternly. "The lives of those boys, including my son, lie squarely on your shoulders. Don't you forget that."

Strunk laughed. He wasn't forgetting his obligations to Theo, anymore than he could easily forget about a cowardly, queer-eyed Kuschan sneaking up on him in the dark. Nor would he forget to pay Yuri back, for sneaking up against lowly-paid workers. "Hell no, sir," said Strunk, happily. "I ain't forgettin'!"

22

Once Vix got to the Ministry of War, he was promptly reassigned to a "pup."

Vix had never met Captain Willowby, but knew that the young officer came from an illustrious military family. Vix had the distinction of serving with Willowby's father, grandfather, and various cousins and uncles. As a whole, they were courageous warriors who never shirked their duties to Embrey.

Vix approached this new appointment, still suffering from thoughts of abandonment and disloyalty to Kohl. He had been the major's right-hand man since their days at the Wilderness, and wondered if it was best to bury the hatchet. Was that even possible? Kohl was a damned fool, for his plans of going to Infernus with a bunch of schoolboys!

As the sun neared the western horizon, streaks of light beamed through darkened clouds in hues of fiery reds, yellows, and oranges. Traveling to Fort Cooley, a minor outpost at the city's edge, Vix considered on resigning from the Army, and settle down at the homestead where he spent his childhood.

On the banks of the Ember River, Fort Cooley had been a vital installation, when Sykes was under siege from brigands and rival armies. It was now a recruit and training center. Consisting of a few scattered log cabins over a meager four acres, Cooley was staffed by a couple of officers and a hundred troops. Entering the fort, Vix figured he'd serve as a sword master.

Leaving his horse at a livery stable, Vix was dismayed to find the area populated by motiveless, undisciplined brats. These 'soldiers, all under the age of eighteen, loitered aimlessly throughout the facility, lacking order and purpose. Vix saw no pride in the recruits' faces, actions, or wrinkled, soiled uniforms. The grounds were littered with trash and horse dung.

Searching for the commanding officer, Vix met two snot nosed lads of fourteen, leaning at the entrance of a barracks. Neither saluted Vix, and failed to acknowledge his presence. It mattered little to Vix whether they were seasoned veterans, or raw recruits. These two hooligans needed their butts kicked! Barely containing his anger, Vix asked for the CO.

"Huh?" the boy to the right grunted. "What about him?"

Vix grabbed the boy's throat and shoved him into the door. "You're choking me!" the boy gagged.

"I ain't choking you," snarled Vix. "If that was the case, you couldn't talk!"

The other boy thought of challenging Vix to fisticuffs. Instead, he stood by to watch Vix rip his best friend a new one. Gritting his teeth, Vix asked to see the fort's head honcho.

The boy with Vix's hand around his gullet, pointed to a small structure to the left. As Vix released him, the insolent teen crumbled to the ground.

Vix stormed into the headquarters, determined to set things right at Fort Cooley. Entering through a narrow doorway, he peeked into an office to find a third kid working behind a large desk. One wall featured a portrait of Count Fossbinder, a noted war hero and one of Willowby's esteemed ancestors. Decked out in his finest dress uniform, his graying whiskers curried and combed, Fossbinder was the model of what each and every Embrian soldier hoped to be. A small fire in a corner wood stove held off an early evening chill.

The boy at the desk was a slightly plump fellow, with sandy hair, a chubby face, round eyes, and buckteeth. Vix thought he looked like a chipmunk. Knocking at the door, he asked for Captain Willowby.

The boy stepped around the desk and, wearing a goofy smile, offered Vix his hand. "I'm Captain Willowby," he said, with a slight lisp. "The commander of Fort Cooley."

"You're Captain Willowby?"

"Yes," the boy said, taking note of Vix's field-worn uniform. "I'm Captain Willowby. And you are? . . ."

"Sergeant Vix." Grudgingly, he saluted Willowby.

"It's a pleasure to meet you, Sergeant Vix," said Willowby, returning to his chair. "Won't you please sit down?"

Vix declined Willowby's hospitality. "How old are you, Captain Willowby?" he asked, pointedly.

"I just turned sixteen."

Vix refused to abide this upstart, or his neglect of Fort Cooley. The Embrian military was fraught with this level of incompetence. It was typical to place someone in charge, based only on their names and political connections.

Most of Willowby's forbears had tremendous courage, valor, and fortitude. Vix was proud to have fought alongside them. In time, Willowby might be of that same caliber. Not yet. Not today.

Initially, Vix planned on bypassing Willowby's authority, to bring about a semblance of order. His greatest obstacle sat before him, in the form of a baby-faced charlatan.

Vix stared at Willowby. "Permission to speak candidly, sir."

Getting to his feet, Willowby did not appear as a daunting or imposing figure. In a high-pitched, quivering voice, he said, "Permission granted."

"Sir, when'd you assume command here?" asked Vix.

"Pardon?"

"How long have you commanded Fort Cooley?"

"Two weeks," answered Willowby, quietly. "Why do you ask?"

"I was a soldier, long before you was even born."

"Your point?"

Vix almost asked what gave Willowby the right to be an officer. That sort of talk usually ruffled feathers. If Willowby was a mere glimmer of his lineage's eyes, he'd hear Vix out. "I fought with your pa at the Wilderness, your grandpa at Mount Patten, and your Uncle Alistair more times than I can count."

"I'm so honored that you knew them, Sergeant Vix," said Willowby, with a blank expression.

The dumb look on Willowby's face made Vix want to cuff his ears. "Would you be 'so honored' if they saw the mess you made here?"

"Explain yourself!" the captain whined, sheepishly. "This is hardly my fault!"

"Hell, this joint's so deep in horseshit a man can't go nowhere without tramping in it!" hollered Vix. "Your men got no respect for me, the Army, their uniforms, or themselves! Not one damn bit! They don't even respect you, if they even knew you was here. They oughta be whipping this place into shape, and you oughta be out there, telling 'em how it's done! Now sir, I got a lotta respect for your kin. An awful lotta respect. And I'd like to give it to you. I will, soon as you take control of this fort, instead of sitting on yer ass in here."

Willowby pounded his fist onto the table. "You can't speak to me that way!"

"I just did."

"And what do I get from you, in exchange?" asked Willowby, sounding more like an adolescent than an Army officer.

"The men don't look like soldiers, and they don't act like it. That's 'cause they ain't soldiers! We'll remedy that problem right now, or at four in the morning. It's your call." Vix stood at attention and saluted.

Willowby asked for a capable, qualified sergeant and, like it or not, that's what he got. He knew that Vix was the right man for the job, the man he so prayed for. "You may stand at ease, Sergeant Vix," he said.

"Thank you, sir."

"General Chang sent me here a short while ago and, believe me, it's no picnic," sighed Willowby, apologetically. "Some of the men are conscripts from work farms, orphanages, or jails. They know nothing of what is expected of the Embrian infantry. To be honest, they scare me." Willowby shrugged. "Enough of that. I've hidden out here for days. I'm not a brave person, Sergeant Vix. Several of the men assigned to this base wouldn't blink an eye to run a knife in me."

Vix shook his head, in astonishment. "You ain't no officer, if you fear your own men."

"I deserve that comment, in no uncertain terms." Willowby frowned. "As it now stands . . . Well, you see, I have no NCOs at all, not until now. I wished to acquaint myself with my shortcomings, as time goes by. But I need your help, and I'll grant you free reign as you please."

"I ain't gonna take your place at this fort, and I don't want to," said Vix. "I'm just a sergeant, but by god you're the commander! You don't need an old warhorse like me. What you need are a couple o' balls hanging between them skinny legs."

Willowby behaved like a cornered rat. "Are you saying that you won't help me, Sergeant Vix? All I need is a little more time, and . . . and . . . Please, Sergeant! I beg of you!"

"A'right then, boy," said Vix, regarding Willowby for what he was, a frightened kid. "But you ain't gonna hide in here no more!"

"I never intended it to turn out this way!" cried Willowby. "I've not even completed my training! At the Embrian Military Academy, they told us that certain facts must prevail in the Army. Men are properly trained. There's a defined chain of command. All soldiers know their duty. The only thing I know is that we're bound for the front in one month, regardless of our combat readiness."

Vix felt that his placement at Fort Cooley was more of a curse, than a godsend. Heading to Infernus with a bunch of schoolboys, or heading to the eastern front with lazy ones, was about the same.

"What did you do before you joined the Army, Captain Willowby?" asked Vix.

"Me? I . . . uh . . . attended Lord Conway's Academy. It's a parochial school, not far from here in . . ."

"I know where it is. Passed it a few times headin' to the War Ministry." Vix glared at Willowby. "Here's how I see it, Captain. You got two options. You can either give up your commission, and finish up your schooling at Lord Conway's. Or you can take command of Fort Cooley. What's it gonna be?"

Willowby hesitated. "Well, I . . . I want to stay here, at Fort Cooley."

"Goddamn it, you wasted two weeks hidin' behind that desk a'ready!" shouted Vix. "It ain't my place to tell you what to do, but your gonna have to prove yourself. Better get at it, right here and now!"

"How?" gulped Willowby.

Vix smiled. "That's up to you, sir. When we hit the border and meet up with a horde o' savage Branellians with checkered kilts and screeching bagpipes, the men ain't gonna look to me for answers, but to you."

Despite his reservations of what Vix told him, Willowby needed him on his side. "I wondered if you'd have dinner with me, tonight?" he asked, in a plea to win Vix's favor. "I'd love to hear about your wartime exploits . . . and that of my family's, too!"

Vix laughed. Willowby's father also spoke in an uppity, *snoot-i-fied* manner. Like father, like son. Occasionally, Willowby even resembled his daddy. Based upon his loyalty to the descendants of Count Fossbinder, Vix aimed to do his utmost in getting Willowby and the recruits of Fort Cooley in proper fighting form.

"Yes, sir!" Vix said, graciously. "I'm hungrier'n a bear, and I'd like to get off my feet to tell you a good lie or two!"

23

"Don't worry," Geoffrey said to his four friends on a quiet Sykes street corner. "I'll get us a place to stay."

It was an empty promise. Geoffrey had no idea where he and his chums were going to spend the night. No longer in charge of the dormitory basement at Lord Kelly's, he assumed a leadership role over those few chums who followed him from Lord Kelly's. This small group consisted of twelve-year-old twins Sergio and Giuseppe, Sister Judith's assistant Eduardo, and Geoffrey's companion, Randy.

Hours before, the Sykes constable announced the murders of two Leaders and a student from Lord William's, then closed the school until further notice. This sudden calamity forced the entire student body into homelessness. While Geoff, Eduardo, and Randy were notified of the deaths, they didn't share this information with the twins. Oblivious to the reasons why they were sent packing, Sergio and Giuseppe wandered the city alone, until Geoffrey decided to look after them.

Geoffrey also had to look out for himself. Accustomed to the role of a facilitator, despite crippling self-doubts and anxiety, he lacked the security and assurances his former post had afforded him. Many schoolmates knew of his relationship with Randy, a source of unceasing fear and bad jokes. Geoffrey spent long days and nights in torture, while gradually accepting his love for another boy. He prayed never having to face damnation for it. As much as he enjoyed the facade of authority that his job provided him, Geoffrey required Randy's affections that much more.

Even with his demeanor and posturing, Geoffrey lacked essential survival skills. Randy and Eduardo did their part to help him. Nightfall was upon them, and the cold breeze was piercing. The need for a hot meal and warm beds weighed heavily on Geoffrey's mind.

Geoffrey turned to one of the twins. "I'll see to it that we get something good to eat, Sergio."

"I'm Giuseppe," the confused child said, pointing to his brother. "That's Sergio over there."

Geoffrey was infuriated with himself. Identical in their height, blue eyes, and pug noses, the twins differed in their hair styles and personalities. Outgoing and often audacious, Sergio had short locks, shaped as a bowl. Reserved and naive, Giuseppe had long, wavy hair hanging to his shoulders. Geoffrey prided himself in knowing most of the guys living in the basement. Mistaking Giuseppe with Sergio only augmented his insecurities.

"Why were we told to leave the school?" asked Sergio, shivering. "I'm freezing!"

Geoffrey couldn't lower himself to tell a lie, and his silence rattled the youngsters. He hoped that Eduardo or Randy had an answer.

"Didn't you hear, Sergio?" asked Eduardo, smiling. "We graduated!"

"Graduated?" asked Sergio. "Me and Giuseppe never graduated!"

Upholding the fabrication, Eduardo asked, "Weren't you at the ceremony?"

"Hell, no!" yelled Sergio. "Nobody told us about no damn ceremony!"

While Eduardo gave the twins a cock-and-bull story, Geoffrey stepped away with Randy. "What am I going to do?" he whispered.

"What are you going to do?" asked Randy. "What are *we* going to do?"

Geoffrey shrugged. "I . . . I just don't know . . ."

"Did they even say who murdered Sven and Karl?"

Geoffrey shook his head. As the wind grew stronger, so did his fears. "I don't know what we're supposed to do, Randy."

"Maybe we'll get jobs and earn our keep," suggested Randy. Running his fingers through Geoffrey's thick, coal-black hair, he held off temptations of kissing him on the lips. "If anyone will help us, Geoff, it's you."

"I can't help anyone."

"You helped me! Where would I be, without you? Before I got to Lord Kelly's, I was nothing more than one of Ogden's playthings. I didn't know what love was, until I met you."

"What . . . what if we go to Joel's shop?" pondered Geoffrey.

Randy swallowed, nervously. "You already know what your brother thinks of me."

"But will he feel the same about Eduardo, or the twins? Sure, he's got no use for either of us. I swear he won't turn them away!"

"I dunno," mumbled Randy, doubtfully.

"We're staying at my brother Joel's," said Geoffrey. "His shoe shop's not far from here. I'm . . . if anyone will give us lodgings, I'm sure he will."

"You see!" laughed Eduardo. "We just graduated from Lord Kelly's, and now we're shoemakers for Geoffrey's big brother!"

Giuseppe gave Eduardo a look of horror. "But I don't wanna make shoes! I'm just a little kid!"

"Yeah," agreed Sergio. "I a'ready thought you was a shoemaker, Ed, after last night's clam chowder."

Eduardo twisted Sergio's ears until the boy cried, *"Uncle!"*

Geoffrey led everyone to his brother's shop, several blocks away. Not far for the older boys, it seemed like a tremendous journey for the twins, who complained of empty stomachs, sore feet, and the windy weather. The lads soon reached a two-story, brick and mortar building, featuring the name *JOEL'S* painted in bold calligraphy.

As Geoffrey went to the door, an older man stepped outside. This was the proprietor, who resembled his younger sibling for the exception of bushy black sideburns covering his cheeks. Surprised to see Geoffrey and his four schoolmates, Joel's dour expression was none too inviting. "Geoff," he said, neither hostile nor hospitable.

"How are you, Joel?" asked Geoffrey. "How's business?"

"Not bad," answered Joel, in a voice that unnerved Randy. During their last meeting, the cobbler gave no prior warning before splitting Randy's upper lip. "You're still with *him*," said Joel, pointedly. "Does Leader Karl know you ruffle the sheets with 'Loverboy,' there?"

Geoffrey's throat tightened. "Leader Karl's dead."

Joel was bowled over with this news. *"Dead?* What's going on?"

"They closed the school," said Geoffrey, evasively.

"What happened, Geoff?" insisted Joel.

"He . . . Karl was murdered," answered Geoffrey, sadly. "Karl, Sven, and a kid from Lord William's."

Joel grew pale.

"The constable closed the school," said Geoffrey. "We need a place to stay for the night . . . that is, until we get on our feet."

Joel stared at Randy, menacingly.

"Listen, Joel," begged Geoffrey. "We need a place to stay. We've got nowhere else to go!"

"Geoffrey," said Joel, forcefully. "The proudest day of my life was when I adopted you, after Mom and Dad died. The saddest day of my life was when you brought him here." Joel pointed at Randy.

"But he's my best friend!" claimed Geoffrey.

"That's not all he is to you!" shouted Joel. "When I enrolled you into Lord Kelly's, I hoped they'd get your head straight. Looks like I was wrong."

"What's with Geoff and his brother?" Giuseppe asked Eduardo. "Why can't we go in? I'm cold!"

"I know you hate Randy and me," whimpered Geoffrey. "But my friends need a place to stay, and something to eat. The twins are hungry!"

"I don't hate you!" argued Joel. "I never hated you! You're my brother, Geoff. This shop was going to be partly yours, after you finished your schooling."

Geoffrey shed tears over broken ambitions, dreams, goals, and promises. As a small boy, he imagined himself with a good vocation, responsibility over his many employees, and pride in a job well done. What else was he to do on that late afternoon, but rely on Joel? He made these concessions, not only for himself, but for Eduardo, the twins . . . and Randy. It was a mistake asking Joel for anything. The five students were leaving, with no hope, no prospects, and no certain future!

All on account of loving another boy . . .

Joel sobbed, in betrayal. "You're my brother, Geoff. Do you think I want to turn you away?"

"Who says you've got to?" asked Geoffrey. "Turn me away if you must, but what about my friends?"

"I'd let you stay, but not them." Joel voiced the toughest words he ever shared with kin. "I don't know them, but I know you. I don't ever want to know that one," he directed at Randy. "It's best for you to get shy of him. Maybe God can forgive you, in time. As long as you live like that, you're not welcome under my roof."

Geoffrey almost fell to his knees. Yes, he was Joel's younger brother, and always would be! Joel may have loved Geoffrey, but refused to tolerate that which he regarded as an abomination. "Why can't you get your head straight?" he asked, harshly. "It'd break Mom heart if she found out about you and him! And I can't believe that you held as important a job as dorm assistant, and get away with that! We were raised to be God-fearing, and Lord Kelly's is a God-fearing school! You get yourself a job as dorm assistant, then get away with that!"

Geoffrey wept, as he knelt before Joel. "How can you do this to me?"

Joel might have held influence over Geoffrey. Not Randy, who refused to watch Joel abusing one so dear to him. He loathed ideas of homelessness. His only consolation was to share this miserable strait with three buddies, and a life partner.

Randy approached the door, to fetch a wounded spirit.

"Get out!" barked Joel, blocking his path. "You're not welcome here!"

Randy cautiously backed away.

Joel lifted Geoffrey up by the collar. "Look at me when I talk to you, and think about what I got to say," he said. "The folks didn't raise us up as sissies!"

Geoffrey shook like a leaf.

"And they didn't raise us up to be the thing that you become!" added Joel. "I do want to let you into my home, believe me. That's what Mom and Dad asked of me. You'll always be my brother, and nothing can ever change that. The shop's partly yours, but not until you get your head straight, and surely not for *him!*"

"But I love Geoffrey!" screamed Randy. "I love him more than you ever will!"

"You call *that* love?" snapped Joel.

Eduardo was torn between taking the twins from Joel's shop, or refereeing a fight. He imagined himself as a fly on the wall, and resented every minute of it. Perhaps it was best that Sergio and Giuseppe not be subjected to this. Reluctantly, Eduardo stayed close, just in case Joel made mincemeat of Geoff and Randy.

Joel fetched some coins from his pocket, and slapped them into Geoffrey's hand. "You won't get far with this pittance, but it's a start if you spend it wisely. I don't want to turn you away, and you got no idea how sorry I am for Sven and Karl." Joel embraced Geoffrey, as a tear seeped from his eye. "You're my brother, Geoff, but you can't stay here unless you get your head straight."

With that, Joel turned around, entered the shop, and closed the door behind him.

This was among the most humiliating experiences of Geoffrey's life. It wasn't just the language spewing from Joel's mouth. Eduardo, the twins, and Randy saw everything! Eduardo was a trusted and understanding confidante, while the twins generally respected his stewardship of the dormitory basement.

Randy threw his arm around Geoffrey. "We don't need his help. Let's just go."

Geoffrey's emotions proved too great of a burden. Upholding his obligations and responsibilities to his buddies, he blew it. He wouldn't have blamed the others, had they left him as an empty shell on the street.

Geoffrey dropped to the cobblestone walkway, and sobbed.

Randy sat next to his lover. *"Geoff,"* he spoke, in an equally assuring and scolding manner.

"Does this mean we don't get to make shoes?" asked Sergio, sarcastically.

"It means we're in a world of hurt," whispered Eduardo. "It also means the shoemaker's a jerk!"

"I'm hungry," whined Giuseppe, the breeze stinging his skinny thighs. "Can't we go somewhere to eat?"

Digging in his tunic pocket, Eduardo had enough change to buy the twins each a pastry or an apple. With that scant amount, he'd go without supper. He had no idea how much money Joel gave Geoffrey, but knew it wouldn't sustain everyone.

Eduardo wasn't afraid to work. Sister Judith blessed him with confidence and experience in Lord Kelly's busy kitchen. Eventually, he'd have to earn the bread, and not just bake it.

"Sergio and Giuseppe's starving," said Eduardo, knowing that Geoffrey and Randy wished to be alone.

Walking away with Eduardo and Sergio, Giuseppe turned to see Randy plant his lips to Geoffrey's. In confusion, he asked Eduardo about it.

"They're . . . close, Giuseppe," explained Eduardo, guardedly. "Aren't you close to Sergio?"

"Not that close!" gasped Giuseppe.

"They're queer, Giuseppe," snickered Sergio.

"Queer?" asked Giuseppe.

"Don't say 'queer,'" mumbled Eduardo. "Geoff and Randy like each other. They like each other, a lot."

"Yeah," remarked Sergio. "Geoff likes playing with Randy's pee-pee."

"Why?" asked Giuseppe.

"Because they're queer," repeated Sergio, mischievously.

"You got any clue how many times I caught you playing with your pee-pee, Sergio?" kidded Eduardo. "Does that make you queer, too?"

"Look!" said Giuseppe, excitedly. "It's Giorgio and Fritz!"

Eduardo was relieved to spot two familiar figures on the street, and eagerly escorted the twins toward them. Giorgio and Fritz were joined by a short, blonde kid, carrying a bow and some arrows.

Waving his arms in the air, Eduardo called, "Over here! Hey, over *here!"*

24

"Have a nice evening," said Pastor Dimitri, as members of his congregation left the church after a night's study session.

Standing at the front stoop, with a cool breeze in his face, Dimitri watched the Kuschan immigrants walk away in the moonlight. Like their pastor, these folks departed their native soil for a new life in an unknown land. While they all missed their old country, few planned to return, and were content to remain in Embrey.

Dimitri's eyes drifted from the starry skies above, to the lights of the nearby metropolis, when he saw eight young men coming toward him in the darkness. He easily recognized the individual taking the lead. "Yuri!" greeted Dimitri. "What on Earth are you doing here?"

"My friends need a meal, and a room for the night," said Yuri.

"Your friends?" questioned Dimitri.

Stepping forward, Giorgio introduced himself as a Leader-Trainee. "Or I was," he said, evasively. "Now, the school is . . . *finished.*"

Dimitri eagerly allowed the visitors into his humble church, and home. His wife would be another story. Yana was leery of those belonging to opposing faiths. However, Dimitri's conscience wouldn't permit him to neglect cold, hungry boys. His faith in the Kuen motivated him to grant them food and shelter.

Dimitri opened his doors to the outsiders. His one reluctance came from the ruddy-faced kid in the tattered clothing, who smelled of liquor. As the students entered the church, Dimitri asked them to sit at the pews and await supper.

Even with a need for warmth and sustenance, a few of the boys felt threatened by this Kuschan house of worship. Karl and Sebastian regularly voiced their contempt of that "heathen religion." This animosity carried itself mainly with the twins, who were told that Kuschans committed atrocities on children. Their appetite was greater than fears of dying over a fiery pit. Sergio relaxed in a rear pews, while staring at the candle lanterns lining the church walls.

Everyone's attention was drawn to the painting of a nude male, the Kued, impaled on a winged demon's sword. As Giorgio studied the artwork with wonderment and awe, his schoolmates viewed it with humor, horror, or grotesque pornography. "What the hell's that crap?" cursed Fritz, loudly.

"Keep it down, Fritz," warned Giorgio. "We're their guests."

"I don't give a damn if Ol' Scratch lives here!" snapped Fritz. "Who'd paint that sick, hairy-assed shit o' some naked kid getting gutted by a green guy?"

"*Shh!* We're here on their charity."

Fritz sat down, with a demeaning smile.

"Make yourselves at home," said Dimitri, heading to the living quarters he shared with Yana and their three children. "I'll have my wife fix supper."

"Dimitri," said Giorgio, as he and Geoffrey approached their host. "May we have a word with you?"

"Yes?" asked Dimitri.

"Lord Kelly's closed this afternoon," whispered Giorgio, nervously.

"Closed?" asked Dimitri. "What for?"

"Two of our Leaders were killed," said Geoffrey, "along with a student from Lord William's."

Dimitri was alarmed. "Who'd do such a thing?"

Giorgio's suspicious behavior was concerning.

"Well?" insisted Dimitri, staring at Giorgio. "Do you want to tell me what's going on?"

"It was awful!" cried Giorgio. "I mean . . . I . . . I dunno what happened! I went into Karl's office when I saw . . . It was just awful!"

"Karl?" asked Dimitri. "Is he dead?"

Giorgio nodded. "Yes, and Leader Sven."

Dimitri wanted to give Giorgio the benefit of the doubt. Yet, the expression on Giorgio's face made him shutter. Giorgio probably knew more than he willingly admitted. "Have Yuri come to my office," requested Dimitri. "I need his help in the kitchen."

Geoffrey shook Dimitri's hand. "Thank you, sir! You have no idea how much this means to us!"

"That's all right," said Dimitri. "Once you're fed, we'll scrounge together enough bedding for everyone. You'll make due on the floor. Very well?"

"Yes, sir," agreed Geoffrey, running to fetch Yuri.

Giorgio sensed Dimitri's mistrust. *What's wrong with me?* Giorgio asked himself. *What's wrong with me?*

Giorgio put himself in charge of finding recruits for Major Kohl. It was more than just ten shillings a man motivating him. Here was an opportunity to help out some of his friends, while serving Embrey. Giorgio wished to rectify his many mistakes, while upholding righteous values and ideals. He hoped to eventually reside in Embrey, working with men like Theo to reshape it into a nation where citizens were free to make their own decisions, rather than to be mere subjects to the crown. He'd work as an aide and, in time, become a legislator for the new nation. By assisting Kohl to retrieve a treasure hidden on Infernus, he'd finally be able to hold his head up, once more.

Giorgio also wished to reconcile with a dear friend, if at all possible. He thought he knew better than to indict someone on issues of morality, especially Bradley! He also felt that his judgment prevented him from taking part in acts of violence, even with an antagonist like Antoine. He was caught between hiding his face in shame, or pursuing a long, narrow path to redemption.

What was Bradley's sin, compared to mine? Giorgio was no virgin, while Fritz proudly boasted of his sexual conquests! And what about Geoff and Randy? Aware of their love for each other, Giorgio tried keeping their relationship a secret. He only saw two chums who required his support and devotion.

So, where was Bradley? Heaven help me, if I never see him, again!

Heaven help me, if I never make an amends to him!

Yuri explained the Kued painting to Eduardo and Randy, when Geoffrey informed him of Dimitri's needs in the living quarters. Promising to resume this conversation later, Yuri went to see Dimitri.

Geoffrey inhaled, deeply. He swore an oath to the Brotherhood of Faith, and to God, in caring for his peers. Now was the time to fulfill that pledge.

"Are you feeling all right?" Eduardo asked Geoffrey.

"Never felt better!" answered Geoffrey, feigning self-confidence. "Anything I can do for you?"

"Are we really wanted here?" asked Randy, recalling his earlier conflict with

Joel. "I hope we don't wear out our welcome."

"If anyone rocks the boat, it'll be Fritz," said Geoffrey. "Keep your noses clean, and we'll be okay."

Nodding in agreement, Eduardo and Randy chatted quietly between themselves.

Geoffrey tried to relax. Outcast from kin, he had to face the possibilities that his life choices meant forever being misunderstood and hated. Why couldn't Joel accept Geoffrey for what he was, while accepting Randy as a member of the family?

All for the love of another boy . . .

All for the sake of love . . .

Giorgio checked on his younger schoolmates. As Sergio assimilated himself to this environment, Giuseppe fought to stay awake. Sitting down between the twins in the back pews, Giorgio patted Sergio's knee. "Hanging in there, kiddo?" he asked, warmly.

"This place gives me the creeps," admitted Giuseppe.

"Why?" asked Giorgio. "We're perfectly safe here. What are you afraid of?"

"Do Kuschans eat children?" asked Giuseppe.

Giorgio laughed. "Who told you that? Karl, or Sebastian?"

"Both, Leader Giorgio." Giuseppe smiled. "You are a Leader now, aren'tcha?"

Giorgio was flattered, and floored, by the rank Giuseppe afforded him. "I sure hope so. I'll do my best, I promise!"

"Then why wasn't me and Sergio invited to the graduation?" asked Giuseppe, tiredly.

Graduation, Giuseppe?" asked Giorgio.

"Eduardo said that we graduated today," said Giuseppe.

"Yeah," added Sergio, "to become shoemakers for Geoff's lousy brother."

"Oh, really?" asked Giorgio. "Well, I've got a better idea. Let's go search for a treasure on Insula Infernus."

"Infernus?" questioned Sergio, in disbelief.

"What kinda treasure?" asked Giuseppe, barely keeping his eyes open.

"I don't know," sighed Giorgio. "We'll know when we find it. Who wants to stay here and make shoes for Joel? Come with me to Infernus! How about it, guys?"

"Why?" asked Giuseppe.

"Because it won't be any fun without you." His eyes welling in tears, Giorgio kissed Giuseppe's forehead. "I love you and Sergio very much. You do know that, don't you?"

Giuseppe curled himself in a ball, and propped his head against Giorgio's shoulder. "I love you, too," he said, then dozed off.

Entering Dimitri's cramped, messy study, Yuri found the pastor sitting behind a handcrafted, oak desk. For a moment, he thought he'd done wrong, by leading the Brotherhood members to a Kuschan church.

Dimitri reached across the desk to confiscate Yuri's bow and arrows. "I'll take these. You don't need them in my home."

Yuri obeyed Dimitri.

"I wouldn't mind so much," explained Dimitri, placing the weaponry in a closet. "Yana will have my hair, if she sees them. Then she'll have yours."

Yuri smiled at his own expense.

"Sit down, Yuri," requested Dimitri. "How's Theo?"

"Good," answered Yuri. "He worries about me. Father worries about everything."

"I'd worry too, if you were my son." Dimitri leaned forward. "We've been friends for a long time, and are honest with each other. I expect your honesty, tonight. What do you know about the murders at Lord Kelly's Academy?"

Dimitri was an advisor and a confidante, someone Yuri freely shared secrets with. Yuri was expected to be forthright with him. It troubled him to know that, poker-faced, he'd lie to the pastor. "I only know what Giorgio told me," said Yuri, seemingly oblivious.

"Can you rely on Giorgio?" asked Dimitri, doubtfully.

"His parents died in the Border War. He hates violence. Father wants him on the Embrian Council. Giorgio's not Kuschan, but if anyone enters Paradise, it's him."

"What about that big, stupid looking kid who trashed his uniform?"

"Fritz talks tough," said Yuri. "He's just a loud, obnoxious drunk."

"He won't be a loud, obnoxious drunk here. I've got two sons, and I don't want them near a bad influence." Dimitri snickered. "I'm glad you're making friends your own age. It's not healthy for you to be around old fuddy-duds like your father and me. You'll only get stodgy and dull."

"I have another friend, an Army officer named Salazar." Obviously, Yuri failed to mention that he killed three of Salazar's men.

"I knew Salazar's papa," informed Dimitri. "Yana and I worked at Romero's for a few months to raise the money to build this church. A very decent, moral man, but a little uppity. If Salazar's a shadow of his dad, he'll do Embrey well."

"My friends and I will only be here for the night," said Yuri, "then go to Father's in the morning."

"You're in charge of those boys." Dimitri smiled, cleverly. "If they get out of line, I'll give you those weapons back. Right now, I've got another problem on my hands. She'll tell me about it, when I go to the kitchen."

Mustering his courage, Dimitri left to go deal with the boss.

Yuri returned to the fellowship hall, to find Dimitri's kids acquaint themselves with their Embrian counterparts. Alexei was a tall, slender lad of twelve who inherited Dimitri's sinewy physique and Yana's blonde locks. As he crouched on the floor with Eduardo, Geoffrey, and Randy, eleven-year-old Grigori sat in the pews with Giorgio and Sergio, setting up a chess board. While Alexei's features were a bit rough around the edges, Grigori had a smooth, unblemished quality to his appearance.

Sasha, the pastor's daughter, was thirteen. She wore a long, black dress, had a round, cherub face, and usually kept her hair in a bun. Sitting next to Giorgio, she willfully rested Giuseppe's head in her lap. Sleeping peacefully, Giuseppe was unaware that Sasha caressed his brown, curly hair, while admiring his thin, masculine frame.

Fritz sat in a far corner of the room, with his arms crossed. Bored silly, he wanted something to drink and someone to screw. He was uncomfortable in this "heathen joint," especially with the likes of that weird *Urine* brat, and those of that same strange, foreign breed.

For the exception of Fritz, no one paid attention to the ethnic, political, or religious differences separating them. They were youngsters at play, quietly enjoying their camaraderie and company.

This scene wasn't all peaceful, however. From behind the apartment door, Yuri heard Dimitri arguing with his wife Yana, their language alternating from Embrian to Kuschan, then back again.

Yuri sighed. Dimitri had to be a man of undying virtue, faith, and understanding, to cope with that . . .

25

Bradley regarded Trevor and Derek as nuisances, until they found their way to that dark, dank basement with Kenichi. Left alone for what seemed like an eternity, he had made a lackluster bed from filthy blankets, quilts, and straw. He later found a few wax candles, and a rusty candle holder.

Hopelessness nearly got the best of Bradley. He wondered if Kenichi had abandoned him, or was arrested. He now had to depend on himself. He considered on either going back to Lord Kelly's, or seeking help from the authorities.

What if there's no one out there I can count on?

Bradley slapped away a bug crawling up his left shin, and screamed.

That did it! Bradley refused to spend another minute in that horrible basement! He refused to sleep on that degrading straw bed, or pretend that nothing bad ever happened. Out of fear and frustration, he released a second, hair-raising shriek. He never felt so dirty, down-and-out, or desperate in his entire life. He was trapped in a nightmare reality, from which there was no escape.

Karl and Sven are dead! What's the point to keep on living?

On the verge of spilling more tears, Bradley was relieved when Kenichi returned with Trevor and Derek. Lifting himself from the floor, he happily welcomed the two youngsters into that grimy shelter. Each boy then worked to make the place seem a bit more livable. After lighting a candle, they ate a modest supper of venison, which Kenichi bought from a butcher shop.

To keep everyone's spirits up, Kenichi chatted about everything but the day's events. It was better to discuss a future, even a fanciful one, than to face a harsh truth. "I'm signing onto the biggest ship I can find, then sail the open seas!" said Kenichi, enthusiastically.

"Me, too!" cheered Trevor. "I'm gonna take a trip around the world!"

"That's impossible, dummy!" argued Derek. "Nobody can sail around the world. You'd fall off!"

"Uh-uh!" stated Trevor. "The world's round, moron!"

"No it ain't, retard!" shouted Derek. "It's flat!"

"Leader Sven says it's round!"

"Said," reminded Derek, sadly. "Leader Sven's dead. Remember, dummy?"

The quartet silently evaluated Sven's demise. Despite his shortcomings, Sven cherished his students. Even though Kenichi never really got to know the man, he still comprehended the others' loss.

"What're we gonna do now, Kenichi?" asked Trevor. "Where are we gonna go?"

"You let me worry about that," answered Kenichi, hastily moving onto another topic. "Then I'm going to search for buried treasure!"

"What if you get caught by pirates?" asked Derek.

Kenichi laughed. "Then I'll whip out my sword, and cut them in half!"

"I'd like to catch a whole buncha pirates!" said Trevor, swinging an imaginary sword in the air.

"From whose pirate ship?" asked Bradley. "Fritz's?"

"Fritz has to first build a ship," said Kenichi. "He's too dumb and lazy for that."

"I'm scared of the ocean," admitted Derek, quietly. "What if we run into sea serpents?"

"Don'tcha mean whales?" snickered Trevor.

"Uh-uh!" argued Derek. "I heard of lots of people getting ate by sea serpents!"

As the candle slowly faded away, Trevor and Derek grew tired. It had been a long day, and the four boys needed rest. Kenichi and Bradley traded nervous glances, knowing they'd face a sleepless night. Preparing a spot for Trevor and Derek at the end of the bed, the older lads gave them each a blanket. This left Kenichi and Bradley with a couple of torn, wool quilts.

Wrapping himself in a dusty shroud, Kenichi leaned against the mortar wall and closed his eyes. The light from a nearby street lamp shined through the sooty window, as a draft swept through the basement. Kenichi heard rodents scurrying around the room, as he brushed away a spider. Disturbing images repeated, over and over, in his head.

Forget about it! You can't change a thing, so just forget about it!

Think only of the good things . . .

What good things?

My goals and ambitions . . . my friendship with Bradley . . . By   this   time tomorrow, we'll be far, far away from here!

Unless the constable catches me, first . . .

Tears began to stream down Kenichi's cheeks. The night was so long.

So long, lonely, unforgiving, and cold . . .

I didn't mean to kill Karl! Nothing stopped him from killing Sven! I had to do something, before he turned on Bradley and me!

Like it or not, Kenichi was responsible for Trevor, Derek, *and* Bradley. What were they to do, for the mess they were in?

And just how did he get there, in the first place?

Yes, the night was so long, lonely, unforgiving, and cold. Kenichi wondered if he'd ever see the sunrise again. Darkness closed in, until it practically smothered him. There was no end to it! Why don't the morning come, and relieve me of this torture?

Of those terrible thoughts I can never run from?

Life was never easy. Kenichi spent fourteen years in a brothel. That ended with his mother's death, an attempted rape, and murder.

Murder! I murdered that sailor, just like I murdered Karl!

I murdered Karl!

Accidentally murdered . . .

Killed . . .

Accidentally killed . . .

Kenichi lived on the streets and roadways, under bridges, in empty warehouses, factories, and barns. The basement he shared with his three roommates was luxuriant, compared to some of those pits! Kenichi survived by begging, stealing, and selling himself to rich, widow women.

Life changed for the better, when Lionel adopted Kenichi. The kindly Leader taught Kenichi how to read and write, while granting him inspiration and hope.

Life changed for the worse, when Lionel died on Mount Patten, and Kenichi was sent to Lord Kelly's.

Kenichi wept for the woman who bore him, and died while performing the world's oldest profession. He wept for a beloved father figure, who gave him an appreciation for languages and the wonders of nature, while reminding him that all things are possible if only he put his mind to it. Kenichi's heart now broke for a dear pal, the closest thing to a sibling. Bradley was one of the few honorable people Kenichi ever knew.

Weeping on behalf of himself, Kenichi never asked to be brought into this world. Thanks to Lionel, he once believed that his life carried truth and meaning. Where was truth and meaning of sleeping in a basement, with three naive children?

And then, to make matters worse, Kenichi was being hunted by a corrupt Embrian lawman!

Kenichi wanted to be on his own. How could he possible succeed, with Trevor and Derek tagging along? They were better off without him! Kenichi figured it was best to place them in another school, which meant the risk of blowing his cover.

Because Kenichi was a wanted man, who said that Bradley was safe with him? Perhaps Brad was also better off to enroll into a new school *(but not Lord William's!)* and eventually obtain his Leadership.

Assuming General Gornick gained power over Embrey, he'd turn the kingdom's youth into mindless, savage zombies, dressed in black uniforms featuring the sword and snake, their souls filled with bigotry. Bradley wouldn't prosper under such conditions. Like Kenichi, he too had to flee to the countryside. Away from such strife, Bradley and Kenichi were free to marry lovely brides, raise beautiful children, and be unaffected by outside troubles and interference.

Kenichi had to be free! The only way to arrange that meant giving his account to the constable, then walk away clean and clear. What if the constable don't believe me? Surely, they'll have to believe Bradley! What if he can't handle their manipulation, and interrogation?

Who says I'm strong enough to handle their interrogation?

A whimper, slipping from Bradley's lips, snapped Kenichi out of his self-imposed hell. Running his fingers along Bradley's legs and torsos, Kenichi learned that he was without a blanket, and froze in the cold, autumn air. "Brad!" he said, urgently. "Where's your covers?"

"I gave them to Trevor and Derry," said Bradley, his teeth chattering.

Resting Bradley's head against his chest, Kenichi shared a blanket with him. "What's your problem, bud?" he scolded, rubbing his hands against Bradley's shivering body to warm him. "Trying to kill yourself?"

"No!" said Bradley. "I just thought . . ."

"I know, I know. You're concerned with Trevor and Derry. Well, I'm concerned for you."

"Why?"

"Why? Because you're my best friend, that's why!"

Bradley smiled. "Sure wish I was there when you clobbered Andre and Bentley."

"I got a great roommate out of the deal," laughed Kenichi. "The best roomy a guy could ever ask for!"

"Really?"

"What do you think? We're going to Mount Patten next summer, aren't we? I hope you come with me! Want to race me to the top?"

"Why not?" agreed Bradley. "Anything's better than putting up with Trevor and Derry lagging behind, griping about their tired, aching legs . . ."

"Brad . . ." whispered Kenichi. "I don't think we should take them with us. They have to stay with those who'll take better care of them."

"But we just can't leave them with someone like Antoine!"

Kenichi took a deep breath. "Antoine's dead."

"Dead?" gasped Bradley.

First Sven, then Karl . . .

And then Antoine!

Antoine's dead?

Bradley's thoughts ranging between denial and disbelief. "What happened?"

"I don't know. Trevor and Derek told me." Kenichi sighed. "Not only that, but the constable's looking for me."

"What for?"

"Because of Sven and Karl. I'd better go talk to the constable, and . . ."

"Kenichi," warned Bradley. "The constable's an idiot! What if he locks you up?"

"Why don'tcha all shut up?" someone muttered, in the dark. It was Derek. "I'm tryna sleep."

Bradley nearly jumped from his own skin. "Derek?" he said, worrying about how much of this conversation the youngster heard. "Derry?"

Snoring . . .

It was pointless to discuss such matters, under clouds of fatigue and stress. "Sleep any?" Bradley asked Kenichi.

"What do you think?"

"Me, neither."

Locking his arms around Bradley's slight frame, Kenichi closed his eyes. "Good night, Brad," he yawned, as sounds from a nearby saloon faded to a dull roar. Seconds later, a couple of drunkards passed by the basement door, singing bawdy songs and laughing.

"Good night," whispered Bradley, using Kenichi's shoulder as a pillow.

Resting against the unyielding, stone wall, Kenichi fought to shut off an exhausted, overworked mind. He had lost two very special people in his life. He refused to part with a third.

There were so many things Kenichi had to tend to, that following morning. He had to find a suitable school for Trevor and Derek, then contact the constable. By day's end, Kenichi and Bradley were to be on the open road, seeking a path to their own lives and future.

What if everything falls apart? What if I don't make the right decisions?

What if the constable jails me, without rights or privileges of a hearing? What will the younger boys do, then? Is Bradley strong enough to care for them, as well as himself? Am I even strong enough to care for them? What if we freeze, or starve to death, because I failed to do my best?

What if I'm no longer able to properly care for myself?

26

"My saying this is of little help," Sirro of Vladistan told the young stranger next to him. "But I wish you luck."

The stranger, who entered Embrey with Sirro and Captain Shimura early that morning, said nothing. He stared at the bright moon above, wondering if he'd live to see another day. In the cool night air, he found himself outside of King Ogden's royal palace, on the verge of changing history forever, or becoming a pathetic footnote in Embrian propaganda by dying for Branell.

In embarrassment and humility, the stranger also focused upon the fancy dress shirt and kilt he had on. This was the first time he wore such clothing, since growing up under the shadow of Mount Patten. Home to a fair number of Branellian refugees and expatriates, their food, customs, and attire influenced that region of Embrey. The stranger learned to imitate the Branellians' accents, slang, and mannerisms.

On occasion, the stranger figured he was, at heart, a Branellian spirit trapped inside an Embrian body.

While working for Captain Maliek, the stranger was placed under the temporary command of an ambitious Embrian colonel. Their mission was to conduct a murder raid within Branell. This covert operation served only the colonel's social and political agenda. It also secured the colonel's reputation, promoted him to the rank of general, and a vital position in Ogden's inner circle.

That colonel's name was Gornick.

In western Branell, a physician named Tenant made strides in curing an illness which ravaged its victims' skin. Moved to an isolated, remote colony, those suffering from the illness dealt with ignorance, superstition, and scorn. Tenant's critics never viewed his efforts as acts of mercy. Rather, they were in league with the Devil.

Acting upon these fears, and with the full support of King Ogden, Gornick was to terminate Tenant, wipe the disease's carriers from the face of the Earth, then sanitize the colony in a baptism of fire.

The stranger was to murder Tenant in the name of God, humanity, and Embrian purity. Upon meeting Tenant, and obtaining an appreciation of his work, the stranger soon had other ideas. Saving Tenant's life, then helping him move the colony to an area safe from Gornick's reach, the stranger surrendered his allegiance to Embrey.

It also brought him to the Embrian capital of Sykes on a chilly, windy autumn night, to set things right for both Embrey and Branell.

The stranger swallowed his pride, and convinced himself that the fluffy shirt and plaid kilt were necessary to access Ogden's attention and favor.

"Are you well?" asked Sirro, his voice lacking concern.

Yes, the stranger mouthed, his face creased with worry. It wasn't a question of carrying out his grisly deed, but whether he'd die in the process.

Death would come as no surprise. The stranger regularly taunted it, first for Captain Maliek, then for the Branellian Empire. Assuming he met his demise that evening, the stranger preferred doing so with bravery, than do go out like a whiny, whimpering coward.

Who cared if the stranger served Branell with distinction, but no recognition?

He was told never to boast, brag, or lament his work. He was not to speak of it, period! Even if his accomplishments had saved thousands of lives, he accepted no credit for it. He rejected such credit, whenever it was granted him.

Of all the jobs the stranger did in his fourteen years, tonight's was the most vital, the most elusive, and the most dangerous.

So there he was, standing outside of the royal palace, examining his target who blissfully got drunk on a third story balcony, above. In the nude, King Ogden looked down upon his subjects as if he was God Almighty, perched upon a Heavenly throne.

As the stranger struggled not to reveal emotions, Sirro was afraid for him. On the long journey from Kentworth to the Embrian coast, he exchanged few words with the stranger. Both shared desires for peace.

Sirro also believed that the stranger silently craved the warmth and security of companionship.

Sirro drank from a bottle of wine which derived from the vineyards of an Embrian parochial school. Had his contacts in the United Westerland Brethren known that he savored beverages from the hated Brotherhood of Faith, he'd be excommunicated, perhaps marked for death.

The price to pay for an open mind!

Why drink to oblivion? The strange had a role to play, as did Sirro of Vladistan.

Corking the bottle of Lord Kelly Academy's finest brew, Sirro whispered, "I'll be leaving, shortly."

The stranger merely nodded.

Sirro breathed out a sigh. "When I'm able, if I'm able, I'll deliver King Josiah's correspondence to Councillor Theo."

The stranger smiled as he contemplated Theo's adoption of a former student of Captain Maliek.

Yuri, of St. Alexandrov . . .

Of all the boys to win love and support from a man of Theo's stature, why Yuri?

The stranger never forgot the day when Yuri got expelled by Maliek. Very few students liked Yuri, and even fewer admitted it! Refusing to play ornery tricks on Yuri, the stranger never went out of his way to befriend him. He made little effort to befriend anyone under Maliek. In his line of work, friendship was hazardous!

Who could forget that afternoon when Yuri finally took enough abuse, and lashed out against Marietto? It was the stranger who rushed into the barracks to drag Yuri from Marietto. Jesse claimed that he detained Yuri. *Yeah, right!* Jesse did nothing but stand to one side, screaming of the "dastardly homo slaying my best *friend!*"

And then what? Yuri and Jesse were now in the tall cotton. One had an enviable post under Admiral Kraig, while the other was to inherit Theo's land, power, and title. And here I am, freezing in the cool Embrian breeze, on the verge of making history, or becoming a pathetic footnote in Embrian propaganda!

Slightly intoxicated, Sirro mumbled, "Like I said, this is of little help to you, but . . ."

The stranger embraced Sirro. "Just in case . . . just in case I never see you, again," he said, with a smile.

Sirro bowed. "If we are to enter the gates from which there is no return, let us do so together!"

The stranger laughed.

"Farewell, Timothy, my brave young friend!" cheered Sirro. Like Shimura, he too had grown fond of the stranger. "Goodbye, and good luck!"

King Ogden of Embrey relaxed on his bedroom balcony, overlooking Sykes. He sipped a glass of champagne, and awaited his next nocturnal companion.

The cold, harsh wind nearly curbed Ogden's ritual of loitering on the balcony, naked. Advisers and family members viewed this behavior with disdain and contempt. Ogden paid them no mind. Who were they to order him around? He was the King! What was so wrong about letting the evening air bless and caress his nude shell? Regrettably, the breeze motivated Ogden to throw a quilt over himself, as he rested on an an easy chair, admiring the full moon in the eastern sky.

Upon the death of his father, Ogden ascended to the throne at the age of eighteen. He was unprepared for this sudden rise to power, as friends and allies questioned his ability to rule. Would Ogden find a suitable queen and raise children, to maintain the royal bloodline? It was debatable. Even in his early teens, Ogden invited boys to his place of slumber.

His father, King Marco, was renowned for a violent, intolerant nature. He planned to kill Ogden, while choosing his second son, Rudolph, to succeed him. A mother's intervention prevented Marco from carrying out this sanction, as Prince Rudolph was groomed for the reigns of authority.

Upon Marco's death, Ogden was hastily pushed to the top. Days later, Rudolph died in a "polo accident."

Oddly, no one explained the gaping wound in Prince Rudy's throat.

That was five years ago. At twenty-three, Ogden was unmarried, yet still cherished young, masculine figures. Marriage never ended his mind. There was, however, an illegitimate son, born from Ogden's practice of lifting a maid's skirt to have his way with her. This was not a lustful act, but punishment exacted upon the maid's mere existence. Ogden's brutality was legendary. His various lovers, male and female, were often carried away with dislocated joints and broken bones.

Standing barely five-feet in height, Ogden was a scrawny, awkward fellow who sported a lame excuse at growing a beard. Where Marco was a huge, burly man with a voracious appetite, Ogden ate very little, yet squandered the nation's wealth. He took kudos for good news, ignored negative dispatches, and permitted his military and roads to decline. The Border War was a minor headache. It was too far away to personally affect Ogden. However, the skirmish did prove useful in disposing of peasants and hobos.

Political enemies called for Ogden's resignation. Their numbers were legion! What right did anyone have in asking Ogden to step down? He was the King! God Himself decreed that Ogden was to rule over Embrey. And only God determined when it was time for others to assume power!

Chief among the rivals was that self-righteous fatso, Councillor Theo. Ogden despised Theo with every ounce of his fiber. Thousands of Embrian subjects wanted Theo to sit upon the throne. Like a fanatical, arm-waving evangelist, Theo exalted hot air on the virtues of a representative government. From Ogden's standpoint, such disloyalty called for the spilling of blood!

With General Gornick's assistance, Theo would soon be no more. Rubbing a finger across his thin mustache, Ogden wondered what it would be like to have Theo brought to him, trussed like a pig. He entertained thoughts of injecting his manhood into Theo, then garotte him from behind. A displeasing whim, to be sure, but one to serve Theo right. Afterward, the Embrian Council would be dismantled, and Theo's publishing house destroyed.

Marco respected Theo, but he didn't like him. Despite their differences, the two men forged an alliance which worked to Embrey's advantage. This arrangement may have prospered in the past, but Ogden had no use for it. His place for Theo was on public display, the legislator's entrails hanging like a grotesque sideshow attraction.

"My liege," a well-dressed manservant addressed. "You have a visitor."

"Yes, Kane," said Ogden, expecting a delicious, preteen boy. Instead, a muscle-bound, well-decorated Army officer entered the balcony.

"General Gornick's here to see you," announced Kane, leaving the officer to speak with Ogden in private.

Wrapping the quilt around himself, Ogden reluctantly welcomed Gornick to his favorite spot. "Sit, General. Will you have a glass of champagne with me?"

"Just one," answered Gornick, sickened by the pipsqueak he bowed down to. Because this false admiration furthered his own agenda, he willfully played the game. Ogden and Gornick shared certain goals for Embrey's future. Once these measures were secured, Gornick aimed to dispose of Ogden.

Sitting in an uncomfortable chair, Gornick poured a glass of the rat piss Ogden drank. He rarely consumed alcohol, and treated public intoxication as a social plague. Gornick watched Ogden babble on, as it to drive someone away from forced boredom. For Gornick, evil was all-too-real, located in idle hands and hearts. What passed as an imperial presence was a spoiled brat, whose mother ruined by leniency, as well as the childish teachings of Leader Karl. Karl meant well, but was no expert on human nature. Too often, he rattled on about the mythology of dignity.

Dignity. What bullshit! Dignity was only to be spoken of, but never practiced. Dignity was a lie which Gornick hated, intensely! Promise men a harsh life, and demand more than they can possibly deliver. Reward them with praise and positions of honor. Hand power to those who have obtained "truth," but never trust them. "Truth" states that man is nothing but a bug, to be trampled upon if he fails to pledge his life to the flag and kingdom of Embrey.

Ogden lubricated himself to the point where any qualms he had about defiling boys had diminished. Like most in the inner circle, Gornick loathed Ogden's sexual misconduct, but remained silent. He simply wanted to be the one to send the pervert to the infernal regions.

Somehow, Gornick earned Ogden's respect and reliance. No one ever got that close to King Marco, not even the Queen Mother. Gornick could have easily butchered the disgusting little son of a bitch, then walk away without suspicion.

Later . . .

Tonight, let's be nice . . .

"I bring ill-news," said Gornick, hoping this information gave him permission to strike against the populace.

"Oh?" inquired Ogden.

"Your spiritual advisor was murdered this afternoon."

"*Leader Karl?*"

"Yes, sir."

"By whom?"

"Unknown. But my men will bring the culprits to justice."

"Any clues?"

"A few." Gornick cleared his throat. "My liege, you must step up your security."

"Leader Karl . . . the poor, poor man . . ." whispered Ogden, mourning this sudden loss. No matter what others thought, he listened to Karl's suggestions on living a wholesome life. Patiently, Karl allowed Ogden to speak candidly about his infractions against the Heavenly Father. Karl faithfully counseled Ogden, recited a prayer or two, then sought God's forgiveness of the monarch.

Ogden never obeyed Karl's rulings. Instead, he supported Lord Kelly's Academy with his own coffers, as restitution for Karl's service to the crown.

Gornick frowned. "Sir?"

"Yes, General Gornick?" asked Ogden, slipping out of a trance.

"Your security?"

"What have I to fear?"

"Didn't I just tell you that Leader Karl was murdered?"

"*Karl . . .* What a kind, understanding man! Who'd murder him?"

Gornick ignored Ogden's foolish rambling. "You have a good many things to fear. What about that morbid little Kuschan Theo keeps as a bodyguard?"

"*Yuri . . .*" mused Ogden, thinking that the Kuschan was extraordinarily cute. Creepy, but cute! If Theo had any sense, he'd penetrate Yuri to the point of tainting him. Just my luck Theo nabbed him, first!

Theo had been quite a ladies' man in his youth, and held no interest in Yuri other than as a watchdog, and heir to a substantial fortune. Well, if Theo doesn't want Yuri, why can't I have him? What I'd do for just one night of Yuri's affections!

"That Kuschan's a crafty little bastard," warned Gornick. "Crazy, too. I can't trust his boss, as far as I can throw him."

"Neither do I," agreed Ogden.

"Sir, I urge you to post my men here. I also advise you to crack down on the commoners, until we apprehend those who murdered Karl."

"Have you consulted with Chang and Kraig?"

Gornick planned to arrange for his colleagues early retirements, or untimely deaths on the battlefield. Unfortunately, both men had loyal troops. Removing those old warhorses would only create a bloody conflict within the ranks. If Gornick persuaded them to join his side, he'd restore stability to Embrey.

Chang and Kraig had reservations about the Border War. Were their hesitations brought on by caution, or cowardice? At any rate, the two senior officers loved Embrey, and Gornick couldn't afford to ruffle their feathers.

King Marco was a hard man, but he had good ideas. Under his domain, the military was strong, and prided itself. The commoners knew their place. Theo published only those volumes that didn't threaten national security. Marco upheld honor and order, not chaos and rebellion!

With a pansy on the throne, the military fell into disarray. Crime grew rampant in the larger cities. Entire neighborhoods were overrun by vice. Youth no longer upheld authority. Theo rallied scores of followers to his cause. The subversive bastard!

"General Chang and Admiral Kraig see it my way," lied Gornick. "Sir, I must insist on posting my finest men here, right away!"

"First thing in the morning," yawned Ogden.

"But, sir . . ."

"That is all, General Gornick," interrupted Ogden, impatiently awaiting his special guest. "Did you enjoy your drink?"

"Yes, Your Majesty." Gornick placed his glass on the table, and got up. "I wish you'd reconsider. Please allow me to . . ."

"That will be *all*. Good night, General Gornick."

"Good night, King Ogden." Grudgingly, Gornick stepped from the balcony to the bedroom, then went into a dimly-lit hallway.

Sure enough, a youngster was at the bedroom door, undoubtedly ignorant of Ogden's intentions for him. Gornick glared at the slight figure in the fancy shirt and kilt. A Branellian? He's sharing his bed with a Branellian? Probably another stinking refugee! Embrey's got no room for anyone of that foul nationality! They oughta be killed, every last one of them!

Gornick shook his head and walked away.

"My liege," announced Kane. "You have a visitor."

Alas! Throwing his quilt to the balcony floor, Ogden displayed his nude body to the city before going inside. There, he spied upon a blonde-haired boy of thirteen or fourteen, dressed in a long-sleeved dress shirt and kilt. The boy stood beside a bed, wide enough to accommodate a large-scale orgy. Ogden stopped dead in his tracks, and licked his lips. "Are you Branellian?" he asked, in anticipation.

"Y-y-yes, sir!" the boy stuttered, shuffling his feet like a timid virgin.

"Hmm . . . a Branellian?" Ogden jumped onto the bed, rolled to one side, and smiled. He never slept with a Branellian, and the boy looked quite delicious! "Please sit down, love," invited Ogden. "Here, on the bed. What's your name?"

"Tim . . . Timmy!" the boy sighed, doing what he was told. Looking away, he feigned a sheepish insecurity to arouse Ogden.

Ogden rubbed the boy's bare thigh. "And what may I do for you, Timmy?"

"I want . . . I want . . . I want to stay in Embrey! They said you'd help me!"

"Oh, I'll be more than happy to help you." Ogden hated needless chatter. Talk was cheap, and he wished to make memories for a lifetime! "Lift up your kilt, darling," he commanded, eagerly. "Now! Show me what you've got!"

Timmy got to his feet and screamed, "I know what you are! You're a sissy man!"

Ogden nearly allowed rage to defeat him. Forcing a grin, he slowly extinguished his anger. "Surely, you know what lies ahead of you. It's the price you must pay for my generosity."

"I . . . I understand, kind sir." Hesitantly, Timmy gave Ogden a quick peek under the kilt. "But why must I do this?"

Ogden lunged at Timmy, determined to peel the kilt away and throw him onto the bed. As Timmy eluded him, Ogden only snatched a few strands of the boy's blonde hair. Deprived of a royal privilege, he shouted, "Get back here! Comply, or my guards will kill you!"

Timmy stood less than ten feet away, his back to the wall. He began to speak.

"Quiet!" snapped Ogden, caressing his own genitals. "Take your clothes off, and come to me."

Timmy produced a knife from under his shirt, then approached Ogden. "I'm one of Captain Maliek's former students," he said, menacingly. "Not your cheap little strumpet . . ."

Collecting his horse from the castle's livery stable, Gornick started toward the drawbridge with a dozen armed men. Seconds later, a muffled, high-pitched scream caught his attention. Alarmed, Gornick dismounted from his horse, rushed to the nearest entrance, and ran inside. His men weren't far behind.

Gornick dashed into Ogden's quarters, and found the monarch lying on the floor, next to the bed. Ogden stared at a chandelier above, a knife lodged deep within his chest. Blood covered his face, where it gushed from the nose and mouth. Kane's attempts to save Ogden had failed. The King had fallen into a sleep, from which there was no awakening.

Gornick had long believed that assassination was the only way to dispose of King Ogden. He regretted that Ogden was slain prior to his convenience, and that it wasn't his blade driven into the bastard's hide. It infuriated him to know that Ogden was killed by a stinking Branellian.

A lousy, stinking Branellian . . .

Gornick sneered. Was this merely an isolated incident, or the advent of a much greater attack? Where there's smoke, there's also fire. The presence of one Branellian indicated there were more, about to invade Sykes.

The Branellians are invading Sykes!

Gornick was more determined than ever to strike out against the populace, escalate the Border War *(since he now had a valid reason to do so)* and assume control of the government. While unprepared to take such bold actions, Gornick realized he had to make his move. Ogden's assassination justified his brutal tactics.

"General Gornick," Kane spoke tearfully, holding a purple, bloodied armband in one hand. "This was on my liege's body."

"Give me that!" shouted Gornick, ripping the armband from Kane. With a quick glance, he read two words embroidered on the armband, and was puzzled by their meaning.

For Embrey.

27

"If ya don't like shoveling horseshit," Sergeant Vix screamed at his recruits, in the early hours of the morning, "then why'd ya let it get so deep?"

Vix got the recruits of Fort Cooley out of bed at four a. m. After a quick breakfast of eggs and bacon, he ordered them to clean the grounds. Fetching every pitchfork, rake, shovel, pick, and wheelbarrow on the post, he began turning these boys into men. Vix wanted Fort Cooley transformed to a place of distinction and honor, while shaping soft, lazy children into lean, tough Embrian soldiers.

The recruits worked with excessive complaints. Prior to Vix's arrival, the fort grew lax. No more. Even Willowby, exerted himself. For those lacking tools, bare hands were essential. Once the grounds were in tip-top shape, Vix planned to render repairs on the buildings. Most had leaky roofs, broken windows, loose door hinges, and rough, splintery floors.

By six o'clock, the sun was up. Already, the young army complained of calloused hands, aching joints, and sweat pouring into their eyes. Vix gave them no sympathy. Determined to teach these malcontents what swords were for, he watched the runts turn Fort Cooley into a viable military base. It prided himself knowing his efforts had a positive effect.

Willowby leaned against a rake, and sighed. With the breeze sweeping through his sandy hair, he already earned a good workout. He received an officer's commission for his sixteenth birthday. He never dreamed that Army life involved tough manual labor. His rank gave him an ability to shirk such responsibilities, and go back to bed. However, Vix stood over everyone like a hawk, jumping on those showing little drive or spunk. That included Willowby, who was motivated by Vix's words of "upholding the family honor." That phrase cut to the bone. It angered, upset, troubled, and finally reminded Willowby that he alone was accountable to his soldiers. If nothing more, he hoped to prove that he met his kin's patriotic traditions.

Why was it so difficult?

"Don't let 'em see you lean on that rake, sir," warned Vix.

Tiredly, Willowby scooped loose hay and manure into an orderly pile.

Vix rested his hand on Willowby's shoulder. "You're doing good, sir. Real good."

Willowby frowned. "My father was killed at Buford's Pass, against the Branellians."

"I was there."

"I never heard, Sergeant Vix . . . how did he die?"

"Like an Embrian soldier," said Vix. "Some officers do all the telling from the rear, then stand back and watch their men catch hell. Not your pa. If he got orders to go into a fight, he'd be right there at the front, sword in hand."

"You told me to uphold my family's honor!" cried Willowby. "How can I do that, if I'm not as good as my father?"

"Just keep doing what you're doing now, sir."

A scrawny, thirteen-year-old boy left his post at the fort's lookout. "Hey, Willowby!" he called. "There's an . . ."

"Address him as 'Captain Willowby,' or 'sir'!" roared Vix.

The kid stepped away, nervously.

"What is it, Private Calvin?" asked Willowby, politely.

Calvin swallowed. "Sir, me and Billy Joe . . . *Corporal* Billy Joe, I mean . . . We seen a buncha men heading this way, from the riverbank."

Willowby looked to Vix for guidance and support.

"How many?" asked Vix.

Calvin shrugged.

"Damn it!" cursed Vix. "How many?"

"I . . . I dunno." Calvin's lips quivered. "Around twenty or so . . . I think."

"What's so extraordinary about these men?" questioned Willowby. "Maybe they're just out fishing."

"Sir," reported Calvin, anxiously. "They got weapons."

Willowby gasped. *"Weapons?"*

"Yes, sir," answered Calvin, "and some of them are wearing kilts!"

"Mister Copenhaver," Garry whispered to the smuggler, as the small band of Branellians entered the outskirts of Sykes. "See them buildings over there?"

"What about 'em?" growled Copenhaver, annoyed at his chickenhearted guide.

"That's Fort Cooley," informed Garry. "It's an Embrian Army base."

Copenhaver laughed. "That? Ain't nothin' there but pups, just off their mamas' tits."

"I know," said Garry, "but . . ."

"It's a recruit depot, goddamn it!" Copenhaver shook the man-killin' stick at Garry. "You think they'll send them shirt-tailed boys against us? Them sons of whores ain't no kinda army. One look at us, they'll run on home cryin' 'Momma'!"

Garry turned to Sirro. The night before, the Vladistani diplomat went into Sykes with the young stranger. Garry knew nothing of Sirro's character, but felt safe with him. Along with his fellow guides, Garry hoped to break away from Copenhaver and Schlender, to win his freedom.

The tiny village of Warren Dale was no paradise. It amounted to little more than dirt and stone huts, nestled against a steep hillside in a narrow mountain pass. Residents froze in the winter, and fried in the summer. It was muddy in the spring, and bone dry in the fall. Its rocky soil was unsuitable for most crops. On occasion, Garry still yearned for his life in that secluded canyon. Despite the hazards he faced while hauling cargo over steep mountain ranges and across swift-moving streams, he never walked straight into a battle, especially with the likes of Copenhaver!

At dawn that morning, Copenhaver and Schlender divided their team into two. They were assigned to create disturbances throughout Sykes, while robbing it blind during the ensuing confusion and chaos. It wasn't yet time for Garry to flee from the smugglers. As Marc and Harold stayed with Copenhaver, Ivor and Davy left with Schlender.

Garry feared losing track of Davy. Growing up together in Warren Dale, the two boys were like brothers. Sensing Garry's apprehension, Sirro patted his shoulders. This did nothing to ease Garry's cautious nature.

"I want to go home!" a whiny voice cried from the rear. It was Harold, who never stopped moping since leaving Warren Dale.

Copenhaver approached Harold, slapping his hand with the man-killin' stick.

"Told ya what I was gonna do, if ya didn't shut that up."

Marc was unsympathetic to Harold. It was Garry and Davy's idea to take the crybaby with them. Harold's endless bawling put everyone at risk. Let the sniveling little wimp stay in Branell, picking rocks while eating crawdads and taters!

"What's wrong?" Garry asked Harold.

"I want to go *home!*" screeched Harold, slugging Garry's unprotected gut.

"Gonna shut that up?" questioned Copenhaver. "Or am I gonna shut you up, permanent?"

"That's enough, Harold," spoke Sirro, in a caring but stern voice. "You're too old to act that way."

"But I want to go *home!*" sniffled Harold, snot dripping from his nose.

"You're here!" shouted Sirro. "So take it like a man!"

Harold glared at Garry in betrayal.

Nearly a hundred yards from Fort Cooley, the Branellians arrived at a small cottage, sitting alone on a cobblestone street. Smoke bellowing from the chimney, along with candlelight shining through a window, told Copenhaver this dwelling brought easy pickings. "Bjorn, Wilde," he said to a couple of lowlife associates. "This here's as good a place, as any."

Excitedly, Bjorn and Wilde stepped toward the cottage. Bjorn was a tall, skinny man with a bald scalp, crooked jaw, and Van Dyke beard. Short and fat, Wilde's entire body was matted with thick, black coats of greasy hair.

"What do you think you're doing?" questioned Sirro, blocking a picket gate into the cottage's yard.

"We ain't getting paid for this invasion," explained Copenhaver. "Something wrong with us paying ourselves?"

Wilde brushed past Sirro, on his way to the cottage. "Outa my way, y' brown-hided bugger," he grunted.

Sirro objected to the smugglers' criminal actions, but felt helpless.

Unsheathing their swords, Bjorn and Wilde kicked open the cottage door, then invited themselves inside.

Garry was unnerved by sights and sounds of the candle being extinguished, chairs overturned, and terrified screams of the residents struggling not to be dragged outside. Sirro's thoughts resembled Garry's, while Marc remained silent. Harold crouched onto the street, buried his face in both hands, and wept. A dozen Branellian Army regulars, assigned to Copenhaver, were baffled. Were they to help the ruffians in this raid, or passively ignore it?

Seconds later, Bjorn and Wilde carried two towheaded youngsters from the cottage; a girl in her late-teens and a boy of twelve. Both were still in their nightgowns. Where the girl fought back against Bjorn, the boy in Wilde's arms shrieked.

Garry's heart sank. He had watched similar crimes play out before. He wasn't so much a witness to these horrors, as an unwitting partner. Garry turned his head away, in revulsion.

"Get her legs!" shouted Bjorn, as the girl kicked and slapped at him.

Latching onto Bjorn's beard, the girl pulled out a few locks of hair. About to release his trophy, Bjorn again hollered, "Get her legs!"

Copenhaver entered through the gate, shaking his man-killin' stick at Bjorn. "Sons of whores! If I knowed you was gonna have this much trouble . . ."

Bjorn's eyes widened. "Well, I . . ."

As Copenhaver reached for the girl's flailing legs, she sent both feet into his head.

Copenhaver staggered backward, and nearly toppled to the ground. A few of the soldiers, along with Marc, found humor in this incident. Only Garry and Sirro were alarmed. Fearing that Copenhaver would use the man-killin' stick on the girl, Sirro dared to intervene on her behalf.

Garry had known Copenhaver his entire life, and was deathly afraid of him. Thoughts of watching the girl get her head crushed in sent chills down his spine.

Clutching her fingers into Bjorn's ears, the girl head-butted him, then broke free.

Bjorn spit out a wad of bloody saliva, as Copenhaver shouted, "Catch her! Someone catch her, goddamn it!"

The girl screamed as she sprinted toward Fort Cooley.

Seconds later, the gates of Fort Cooley swung open, and out charged more than a hundred recruits, and one veteran sergeant.

The smugglers were horrified as soldiers from a measly recruit depot charged at them with rakes, hoes, pitchforks, axes, and shovels.

Marc and Harold were hired to haul goods in and out of Embrey, not to die from garden tools. They made a beeline to the Ember River, as Wilde dropped the boy. Following Marc and Harold's example, the Branellian infantry hightailed it from the cottage, their flashy kilts fluttering in the early-morning breeze. Meanwhile, Garry and Sirro disappeared through a deserted side street.

While the Branellians made good their escape, the boy joined his older sister with the Embrian recruits. Racing into Vix and Willowby's arms, they embraced their saviors as scores of recruits followed the enemy. "Look at those kilted fools go!" cheered Willowby.

"Yeah, but you better get our boys back," warned Vix. "We scared that rabble off, a'right. Who knows what's hidin' in the brush?"

With his arms around the girl, Willowby asked, "They *were* Branellians, weren't they, Sergeant Vix?"

"Don't know what else they coulda been. No other race of people dresses that dumb."

As her brother's sobs cut through the stillness of the dewy morning air, the girl said, "We were having breakfast, when they bust into the house and dragged us outside."

"The sex trades," said Vix. "Rampant all over Branell. Rampant all over everywhere. Lucky we got here when we did."

Willowby's elation of scaring those few combatants away surrendered to doubt and uncertainty. Looking at Vix, he asked, "So . . . just how many more Branellians do you think there are?"

28

Kenichi opened his weary eyes and yawned, as sunlight sneaked through the basement's smudged window. Morning was a blessed sight.

Kenichi pushed the quilt away, stretched his stiff, aching legs, and woke Trevor. "How'd you sleep?" he asked.

"Horrible!" griped Trevor. "I had mice crawling all over me!"

"Me, too," said Kenichi. "I can't imagine how bad we must smell."

In the faded light, Trevor looked around the basement. Like the others, he took little notice of the low, rumbling sounds from outside. Sliding free from his blankets, he uncovered Derek, lying next to him. Buried under the blankets, Derek was hesitant in leaving the sack. "It takes a whole army to wake Derry," explained Trevor.

"Let's go," said Kenichi, giving Bradley a gentle nudge.

"What time is it?" asked Bradley, brushing dust and dirt away as he got up.

"Time to go," said Kenichi, slapping Derek's arm. "Come on, Derry. Let's go."

"No!" argued Derek, muffled under the blankets. "I wanna sleep!"

Kenichi winked at Bradley and Trevor. "Fine. You'll miss all that good food I ordered at the restaurant. Eggs, bacon, apple cider."

"Yeah!" fibbed Trevor. "Ice cream and cookies for dessert!"

This rousted Derek from bed. "Where?" he asked, eagerly.

"I lied," said Kenichi, handing Derek a slice of venison.

"This is jerky, you jerks!" whined Derek, examining the venison with disdain. "Why's it so cold in here?"

"We forgot to pay the coal bill," joked Trevor.

As Trevor and Derek went outside, the older boys stayed inside. "Do we really got to leave them at another school?" asked Bradley, sadly.

"They'll only slow us down," insisted Kenichi. "I can understand why you'll miss them. Me, too. But its for the best."

Thoughts of saying goodbye to his younger roommates tore Bradley apart. Life goes on, as it usually does. Too bad.

"Kenichi," said Bradley, nervously. "I don't want you to get arrested."

"I guess," sighed Kenichi. "The same for you."

"Please don't go to the constable. I think we'd better just get out of town, before they find out . . ."

The two teens were jolted by a woman's loud, shrill scream, from beyond the basement's door. "What was that?" asked Bradley, his heart skipping a beat.

Kenichi reacted with a snicker, as Trevor and Derek sprinted back inside. Both were as white as sheets. "We ain't going out there!" cried Trevor, shaking like a leaf.

Initially, Kenichi thought the youngsters were pulling a prank. Leaving the basement, he glanced through the cluttered alleyway, toward a nearby avenue. He stood there motionless, frozen in his tracks.

"Kenichi?" whispered Bradley, joining Kenichi at the door.

There, he spied upon an event, best described as a bloodbath . . .

An early riser, Pastor Dimitri sat in his cramped little office, working on a few scrolls as his wife and three children prepared for studies. Along with many other

Kuschans living in Embrey, Yana educated the kids at home. That was fine with Dimitri, who'd finish his chores without the boss' constant nagging.

Dimitri had mixed feelings about the students from Lord Kelly's. Oh, the twins were generally well-behaved. While Giuseppe slept much of the time, Sergio played quietly with Sasha, Alexei, and Grigori. Dimitri liked Eduardo, who was handy in the kitchen. Without asking to do so, Eduardo set up the table, cleaned up after supper, and washed dishes.

Dimitri had little opinion, good or bad, about Geoffrey and Randy. He suspected they were "different." Neither caused trouble, were polite, and obeyed house rules.

Dimitri disliked Fritz, who never went out of his way to befriend the pastor or his family, complained about the food, and remained standoffish.

Dimitri's greatest concern was Giorgio. Sure, Giorgio took charge of the younger boys, and was cordial. Still, Dimitri couldn't shake concerns that Giorgio was somehow involved with the murders at Lord Kelly's. This wasn't something Dimitri knew, but rather what he *felt*.

Members of the Brotherhood of Faith weren't usually fond of the Kuschan religion. While the Embrian students never raised any awkward, divisive issues, Dimitri and Yana were on eggshells throughout the night.

Dimitri stretched his stiff, aching back. Writing under the light of a single candle, his eyes grew tired. After tossing another slab of wood in the fireplace, he smiled at the assuring sounds of pops and crackles, stemming from the controlled inferno.

Dimitri dedicated his life to the native faith, which had existed longer than the Kuschan nation itself. Within the past decade or so, his religion had given way to science and self-centered desires. Since King Leonid assumed power over Kusch, the country became more secular and "progressive." Kusch forged ahead in technological and artistic advances, at the expense of spiritual values which placed others above self. Younger Kuschans disavowed or ignored the ideals and beliefs of their ancestors. Concepts as the Kuen, the Kued, and Soraq were treated as superstition. No higher intelligence created the Universe, it inception simply *happened* by random chance. Instead of placing wisdom and hope within a celestial being, Kuschans now emphasized their own personal needs, dreams, and wishes.

Under this social and political climate, Dimitri relocated to Embrey, where his fellow Kuschans held onto the old ways. There were always lingering questions as to whether Embrey greeted these new citizens, or merely tolerated them. Cooperation between churches was not among Embrey's virtues. The Brotherhood of Faith hated the United Westerland Brethren, the Brethren hated everyone, and Kuschans were often caught in the middle.

"I need my weapons back!" cried Yuri, sprinting into the office.

"Good morning," chuckled Dimitri, humored by Yuri's urgency. "Where's the fire?"

Yuri pointed to a window, above Dimitri's desk.

Dimitri casually left his cozy chair. To his shock and horror, entire blocks of Sykes were in flames. Recognized structures and landmarks, within the cities infrastructure, were engulfed as fire shot hundreds of feet in the air. Black clouds of smoke loomed over Sykes, and often blocked the sun.

Dimitri opened the window, unwilling to believe his own eyes.

Even from a distance of more than a mile, Dimitri had a clear view of the destruction and panic streaming from the nearby metropolis. He shook his head, in utter disbelief and denial. He wondered if this catastrophe was the result of a terrible accident, or man-made as Yuri suspected.

The answer came from a large group of men and women heading toward the Kuschan church, shouting angry slogans as they carried fiery torches in their hands . . .

As Sykes erupted in mass hysteria and violence, Bradley and Kenichi caught a small glimpse of the insanity, from the basement door. The morning sky was clouded with thick, dark smoke. As black-clad soldiers marched through a nearby street, each slammed their sword pommels onto their shields. The loud, booming racket of a rhythmic *thud! thud! thud!* echoed through the dusty corridors. Alternately, these soldiers used their weapons for their true purpose, that of spilling blood. Innocent men, women, and children were cut down. From the rooftops, archers sent a rain of arrows into the frightened masses, below.

During this frenzy, hundreds of civilians rushed through the crowded, claustrophobic lanes. Those who fell were trampled to death. A few brave souls fought the marauding soldiers, by throwing stones and Molotov cocktails at them. Most were annihilated in the grisly onslaught. This civil unrest included acts of assault, rape, and looting. The dead and dying scattered the streets, storefronts, and sidewalks.

A kilted cavalryman rode his horse through the alley. Bradley and Kenichi ducked back into the basement. Angry citizens were in pursuit of the cavalryman, armed with scythes, axes, and bare fists. All shouted threats and obscenities at him.

As the men cornered him at a dead end, the cavalryman thrashed at them with his saber. Within seconds, both horse and rider were forced upon the ground. The cavalryman pleaded for his life as he was slowly beaten to death. Meanwhile, scores of civilians battled over the horse's flesh. The alley was avoided by all but a few people who stood idly by, viewing the carnage.

Trevor hid in a back corner of the basement, with tears streaming down his cheeks. Derek huddled next to him, shivering. Bradley paced back and forth, searching for answers that did not come. All three boys were grilled in beliefs that the end of the world was near. They felt that time was now upon them. None were prepared to leave their rat-infested shelter.

Kenichi preferred to take his own chances by escaping, despite doubts as to his own survival. Initially, he thought only of himself. Yet, his conscience refused to permit leaving the others behind. "Let's go!" he shouted.

"No!" cried Bradley.

Kenichi shoved Bradley against a brick wall. "Trevor and Derry need us, and I'm not about to leave here without you!"

Bradley embraced Kenichi, afraid to meet the end alone.

Desperation motivated Kenichi to throw himself and Bradley into harm's way. He began by pushing Bradley outside. Bradley hit, knee-first, into the narrow, stone path of the alley. Looking everywhere, he saw nothing but doom and destruction.

"Get going, Brad!" ordered Kenichi. *"Move!"*

Ignoring a bruised hand and scraped knee, Bradley sprinted around one corner, into an enclosed stoop. Kenichi wasn't far behind, dragging Trevor and Derek with him.

Bradley glared at Kenichi, as the four boys hid at the entrance of a hotel. Love and respect were the only things keeping him from slugging his new roommate. Fire and smoke surrounded the four boys. With the smell of death and decay in the air, Bradley wondered if the Almighty had already condemned him to Hell. "You idiot!" he screamed at Kenichi. "You really think we're better off out *here?*"

"We are, if we keep moving!" shouted Kenichi, seeking any means of reaching the outskirts of town . . .

. . . *if* they reached the outskirts of town!

Bradley held onto Trevor and Derek. Any illusions he had of dying courageously had evaded him.

Kenichi spotted the mutilated bodies of two men, who had fought to the death. One was dressed in a blue, double-breasted tunic and kilt. On the other soldier's uniform, Kenichi noted the image of a rattlesnake, coiled around a sword.

Gornick . . .

Sweaty palms, a racing heart, and hyperventilating betrayed Bradley. Blinding dust and smoke, the sounds of galloping horses, shrills screams, and breaking glass were enough to motivate any nonbeliever into begging for salvation. Not ten yards away, two armed men dragged a woman under a darkened stairway.

Trevor turned the door handle, leading into the hotel. "It's locked!" he screamed. "Kenichi, it's locked!"

Kenichi fetched an eroded brick from a dead man's hand. "Cover your eyes!" he ordered, shattering the door's window. He carefully reaching through the jagged glass, and grasped onto the interior handle . . .

When the door flew open, and out came a frightened old lady. "Get out!" she ordered, whacking a broom across Kenichi's head. "Get out!"

As the four teens backed away, Bradley cried for the old woman to allow them inside. The old woman said nothing. Instead, she jabbed Derek's belly with the blunt end of the broom handle. Derek doubled over, and collapsed to the cobblestone lane. "Get *out!*" the old woman repeated, coming a fraction of an inch from nailing Trevor with the broom.

Kenichi lifted Derek into his arms, and ran from the hotel. Bradley and Trevor hastily took the rear.

The four boys dashed through a maze of winding alleys and streets, until exhaustion forced them to crawl into another hiding place, long enough to catch their breaths and forge on.

At a heavily-traveled thoroughfare, the boys witnessed the fiery destruction of a bordello. Before them, The Rooster's Beak was burning to the ground. Flames shot straight into the hazy, black sky. The extreme heat from the bordello was unbearable. Prostitutes lay dead around the structure. Some were decapitated. Scores of Gornick supporters waved banners, celebrating the bordello's razing. The smell of smoldering flesh choked onlookers.

A few blocks away, a number of armed men under General Gornick rounded up more than a dozen women and children, who were then ordered to strip naked. Those refusing the command were murdered on the spot. Detainees slow in removing their clothes were cursed, kicked, and spit upon.

Then, one-by-one, they were flogged with leather whips.

This proved too much for Trevor and Derek, who took off like spooked rabbits. Bradley threw his arms around Trevor, and tackled him.

Bradley held Trevor to the ground. Both wept. Derek was another story. He wished only to flee from the ensuing brutality, by zipping into a narrow pathway. Kenichi chased Derek through a canyon of cobblestone, dust, smoke, and brick, until he lost track of him. "Derry!" he shouted, at his own peril. *"Derry!"*

"Hey there, boy!" a familiar voice called, in the distance. "Don't go kicking at me!"

Andre . . .

The strong aroma of fresh meat and liquid smoke caught Kenichi's attention. Cautiously, he peeked into the open door of a butcher shop. Dried beef and a slaughtered hog dangled from the rafters. Andre's darkened silhouette struggled to gain control of Derek. The smaller boy kicked at Andre's bare shins and knees. "Hold it there, boy!" shouted Andre. "Hold it!"

"Lemme go!" screamed Derek, biting Andre's hand.

As Andre released Derek, teeth marks creased his fingers.

Squeezing through the door, Derek tripped over Kenichi's feet and somersaulted outside. Kenichi locked his arms around Derek's waist and carried him into the butcher shop. "Lemme go!" screamed Derek, thrashing at Kenichi.

Kenichi pushed Derek against a wall, and shook him. "Stop it, Derry! Just stop it!"

Slowly coming to his senses, Derek gave Kenichi a cheesy grin. *"Okay . . ."*

"Why don'tcha take your little bitch somewhere else to screw, 'Itchy'?" taunted Andre, angrily.

Kenichi grabbed onto Andre's hair and lifted him off the ground.

"Hey!" screamed Andre, slapping blindly at Kenichi.

Kenichi slammed Andre against a butcher's table. "One more remark like that and I'll make you wish you'd never been born, 'Just Plain White'!" he threatened.

"What are your plans then, boy?" sighed Andre, thinking twice before flying into Kenichi.

"Getting the hell out of town," growled Kenichi. "Just what do you think, boy?"

Have you seen my brother Bentley?" asked Andre, with a sigh. *"Kenichi?"*

"What makes you think I've seen your stupid brother?" asked Kenichi. "Speaking of which, is he still a moron, or just plain stupid?"

"Bentley ran off," said Andre, emotionally. "I can't find him anywhere! For all I know, he's probably dead! Happy now, 'Itchy'?"

"Don't worry," said Derek, nervously. "We'll find him . . . won't we, Kenichi?"

Kenichi shrugged.

"After the school closed down, we slept in the boneyard," said Andre. "When I got up this morning, Bentley was gone. I looked everywhere for him, until this crap started!"

"I haven't seen Bentley since lunch yesterday," said Derek.

"It was my job to look out for Bentley," whined Andre. "I promised Dad I'd take care of him."

"Sorry," said Kenichi. "But we have to get back to Brad and Trevor."

"Who?" asked Andre.

"Bradley and Trevor," said Kenichi. "Look, maybe your brother was picked up by the law."

"I'm staying right here," said Andre, defiantly. "We go traipsing around, they'll kill us out there!"

"Or kill us in here," argued Kenichi. "But if you want to stay, fine by me. It's your funeral, and I couldn't care less, 'Just Plain White.'"

Andre retrieved a meat cleaver from the table.

"Don't even think about it," warned Kenichi.

"It ain't for you, 'Itchy,'" laughed Andre. "It's for some Branellian or Gornick boy who gets in our way."

"Give it to me," ordered Kenichi, sternly.

"It's mine," said Andre. "I'm fixing to stay alive."

"So am I!" yelled Kenichi. "Just make sure you don't hurt yourself or somebody else with it, or I'll make sure it'll accidentally on purpose get shoved up your ass."

Moments later, the trio found Bradley and Trevor kneeling behind an abandoned produce stand, reciting a prayer. Spoiled fruits, vegetables, and loose change scattered the ground. Bradley caressed Trevor's hair, as both stopped weeping. Derek embraced Bradley and Trevor, then joined them in a Heavenly plea. Andre considered on taking part in this vigil. Vanity disallowed it.

"After the cathouse . . . I mean The Rooster's Beak burned down, those kooks left," said Bradley, gaining inner strength from Trevor and Derek's presence.

Trevor looked to Kenichi for support and answers. "What are we going to do?" he asked.

It was a tough question, and Kenichi had no solution.

"Why ask *him?*" whispered Andre, with resentment. "He don't know."

"And *you* do?" snapped Kenichi. "One more remark like that, and you'll be wearing that meat cleaver."

Taking note of Bradley's missing undergarment, Andre joked, "What happened to your underpants, boy? Nasty yourself, or what?"

"Getting a cheap thrill by looking up my tunic, *boy?*" asked Bradley, crossing his legs in embarrassment.

Derek giggled. "Yeah, bitch!"

Andre's face reddened in a blush.

Kenichi collected the coins lying within the produce stand, then asked his schoolmates to follow him. Bradley, Trevor, and Derek willfully took his advice. Staying close to the ground, the four boys kept their eyes peeled for any and all dangers, as they hurried toward a residential area of town.

Andre debated the wisdom of tagging along. What other choices did he have? With no alternatives on hand, Andre hesitantly followed everyone from the produce stand and, with his fingers crossed, to safety.

29

Yuri fetched his weapons from the closet in Dimitri's office, then dashed out of the Kuschan house of worship. Outside, he was mortified, and strangely *mesmerized,* by the sight of flames looming over Sykes. His thoughts soon returned to Theo. I shouldn't have left Father! I should've stayed home to protect him!

More pressing to Yuri, and everyone else, was the angry mob coming their way. Yana led the students from Lord Kelly's, along with her own children, to a secluded shelter in the nearby woods.

Yuri considered on challenging the mob who threatened the church. At best, he'd only nail a few of the antagonists, before they stopped him. Yuri was torn. He didn't want to die, but could not allow the mob to harm everyone.

Justified, for the good of all? . . .

"Yuri!" shouted Dimitri, tugging at the young assassin's robe. "Forget it! It's only a church!"

"But it's your home!" argued Yuri.

A mob, consisting of more than two dozen men and a few supporters and onlookers, charged into the church.

Yuri obeyed Dimitri's orders to flee, while granting the enemy this one victory. More than anything, he wanted to lash out at the mob. He didn't care if his intentions served the Kued, the Kuen, Soraq, or humanity in general. He didn't debate on how it was to affect his conscience, later on. Assuming he did confront the mob, he'd justify it as payback for the hatred inflicted upon Dimitri and his family.

Rage finally motivated Yuri to take action. At a distance of around fifty yards from the church, he positioned himself behind a decaying log. Lying on his stomach, he had a good view of the lunatics, now surrounding the church. Grinning mischievously, he took aim at a fat oaf who barged to the church's main doors, with a torch. Holding his breath, he prepared to unleash an arrow at the oaf's backside.

"Yuri!" scolded Dimitri. "Don't do it!"

"Why not?" questioned Yuri, in the Kuschan tongue to reflect pride in his nationality.

"Stay here then, if you want to!" snapped Dimitri. "But you're not endangering my family, or your Embrian friends!"

Yuri grudgingly followed Dimitri's orders.

A quarter of a mile through a twisting, overgrown trail, Yuri and Dimitri reached a dugout, carved into a hillside behind morning glory vines and thick brush. The shelter was supplied with burlap sacks of beans, grain, and parched corn. It was furnished with a table, two chairs, a wood stove, and feather mattresses.

Yana, her three kids, and the Embrians were already there. Their emotions ranged from anger, to confusion, to sadness, to fear. As Giorgio and Geoffrey assigned themselves to calm the younger children, Eduardo, Randy, and Alexei kept brave faces, despite adversity. Grigori, Sasha, and Giuseppe sat together on a mattress. As Yana fixed a humble meal, Fritz and Sergio sat at the table, sharing a bottle of Campens Rose'.

Years before, Dimitri built the church with his own two hands, and the assistance of dedicated volunteers. Whether his enemies liked it or not, he was determined to stay in Embrey, and construct a another house of worship.

"When're we gonna go kick ass?" slurred Fritz, not wanting this infraction to go unpunished. "We ain't gonna just sit back and let 'em do us this way, are we?"

Ripping the bottle from Fritz's hand, Dimitri took a drink. "Next time you share," he said, wiping his mouth after handing the bottle to Yuri.

"There's too many of them," added Yuri, bitterly. He still wanted to exact vengeance on the mob, and dismissed Fritz's words as empty and cheap. He sipped from the Campens Rose' which had been lifted from Theo's study, then threw it at Giorgio.

"Why are they doing this?" whined Geoffrey. "Why do they want to hurt you?"

"Why not?" sighed Dimitri. "They don't know us, they don't understand us, they don't like us."

"Then let's go kick their asses," said Fritz.

"I told you, there's too many of them," said Yuri, his anger flaring at both Fritz and the mob.

"Maybe for you, *Urine,*" insulted Fritz. "But not for me."

"That's great, Fritzy," said Giorgio, handing the bottle to Eduardo. "Go ahead and kick their asses. Sell tickets, while you're at it. Just don't do us the favor by leading them here."

"You Embrians are lucky!" said Yana, laying out plates of parched corn. "You can leave here, anytime you want. Those fools will kill us, only because we're Kuschans."

Giorgio turned to his schoolmates. Dimitri had to protect his family. That didn't include anyone from Lord Kelly's.

"Embrians are our brothers, too," said Dimitri, sitting with his son Grigori, daughter Sasha, and Giuseppe on the mattress. "We're all equal in the eyes of God, and to the Kuen."

"Those are Gornick men out there," said Yuri, helping himself to a handful of Giorgio's corn. Slowly, he accepted Dimitri's decision to retreat. "No one's safe from them."

"We don't want to be any trouble, ma'am," said Eduardo, giving Yana the bottle of Campens Rose'. "That meal we had last night was delicious."

"Why, thank you Eduardo," said Yana, taking a drink. "I'm just not used to be driven from my house by crazy people, Embrians or not."

"How long must we stay here, Mother?" cried Grigori. "When do we go home?"

"Not too soon," answered Yana. "Not soon enough for my liking."

"When do we go home, to St. Alexandrov?" asked Alexei, rebelliously.

"'St. Alexandrov?'" questioned Dimitri. "Son, we're not going to St. Alexandrov."

"Why not?" asked Alexei. A toddler when he left Kusch, Alexei had vague memories of his birthplace. "No one wants us here, Father!"

"I'm not turning tail to run!" yelled Dimitri. "This emergency can't last forever. We came here for the long haul. We're Embrians now, Alexei. If you don't believe me, just ask your mother."

"Dimitri!" shouted Yana.

"Well, from one damn Embrian to another," said Fritz. "I say let's go stomp mudholes in . . ."

"And I say for you to shut up!" barked Dimitri. "You think I like what's going on outside? You think I like being forced from a place I built with my own sweat and sacrifice? No matter how much work I put in it, I'd rather see it burn than have my children get harmed! The church is wood and mortar, we're flesh and blood. I value life above any man-made object. That goes for your schoolmates, too!"

"Go ahead and stir that hornets' nest up, Fritz," said Yuri. "We'll bury what's left of you . . . *maybe*."

Fritz pouted, refusing to acknowledge Yuri or Dimitri's words.

"That's all right," said Geoffrey, handing the bottle to Fritz. "Sit this one out, like the rest of us."

Fritz realized that the bottle was now empty. He dropped it to the floor and scowled.

"How long are we staying here?" asked Sasha, her arm around Giuseppe.

"I don't know, sweetheart," said Dimitri. "Until spring, if that's what it takes."

"There's plenty of room at Father's," said Yuri. "I know he won't mind . . ."

"Councillor Theo's already got enough to worry about," said Dimitri.

"You can't stay here until spring!" argued Giorgio.

"We spent our first Embrian winter in this dugout," said Yana. "Our children were all tiny, then. No one said it was fun."

"We'll kill a buck or two," said Dimitri. "Alexei's old enough to hunt wild game. We'll make due by our own hard work, and from the blessings of the Kuen."

Alexei, Sasha, and Grigori looked at each other, in dread.

"Dimitri!" balked Yana. "We can't stay here straight to the new year."

"What choices do we have, dear?" asked Dimitri, knowing that Yana would badger him to death.

"Father will house you," said Yuri, speaking in Kuschan. "We have a secret compound, in our woods behind the house."

"You've already got a heavy load, with your Embrian friends," answered Dimitri, also in Kuschan. "And Theo's got too much on his plate, as it is."

"But Father!" cried Sasha and Grigori, in unison.

"Stupid assed Kuschan gibberish," whispered Fritz.

"I'm head of this house!" hollered Dimitri, in perfect Embrian. "It won't be easy, but whoever said life is easy? Our move from St. Alexandrov wasn't easy, either. We'll make it, if we cinch our belts and get tough about it. As Kuschans, we'll stick it out in our adopted country, if it's the will of the Kuen. And we Kuschans must stick together."

Giuseppe hopped to his feet and pointed to a small window on the shelter's door. "Look!"

Dimitri and Giorgio both peeked through the window, to see thick, black smoke rising above the trees. The enemy had won, after all. Dimitri's hopes, dreams, and ambitions went into the church, which would soon be rendered to ash. The pastor grieved, despite his rhetoric about staying the course and starting over. For everyone's sake, he never showed it.

Alexei put his arm around Dimitri's shoulder. *"Father,"* he whispered, feigning strength and courage.

"Yana, boys, Sasha," Dimitri said to his family. "Gather around. You too, Yuri."

Obediently, the Kuschans formed a circle within the dugout. Clasping hands while lowering their heads, they spoke a prayer in their native language. Four of the Embrians, Giorgio, Geoffrey, Randy, and Giuseppe, welcomed themselves into the circle.

Remaining at the table, Fritz and Sergio viewed this as idiotic superstition to a heathen god. "I dunno about you, Serge," mumbled Fritz. "But I ain't bowing down to no bare ass kid with a sword stuck in 'em, or ugly green bastard with wings!"

That afternoon, Yuri and Dimitri examined the charred remains of the church, from behind thick brush and trees. Most of the vandals were gone. A few stragglers remained behind, laughing heartily at their actions against the Kuschans.

The church was history. Little was salvageable, other than a few items. Every piece of furniture and clothing was destroyed. A small section of the pews could be preserved, assuming it was placed in the dry, cleaned, and then repainted. Part of the east wall still stood, though it was smoldering. The smoky air and dank odor were atrocious.

Dimitri had difficulty accepting any of this. What was there to do, now? Were there reasons for even trying? Maybe Alexei was right. Maybe it was best in returning to St. Alexandrov. On the other hand, was it all right to passively allow this crime to go unpunished? For a brief moment, Dimitri nearly gave Yuri permission to kill the stragglers.

Dimitri collapsed to his knees. What a waste! Mouthing a prayer, he contemplated his duties to the congregation, to his kin, and finally to the Kuen. What was the greatest sin, staying in Sykes, or moving on? Did self-respect allow Dimitri to leave his fellow believers in Embrey? The mob wanted blood. What if a number of Kuschans had already fallen victim to their intolerance?

What if Dimitri was all alone, in a hostile nation?

Yuri knelt beside Dimitri. "Please don't spend the long winter here. Come with us, to Father's."

"How can I do that?" questioned Dimitri.

Yuri fought back tears. "I'm worried about you and the kids. Yana, too."

"Listen to me, Yuri," sighed Dimitri. "Just listen. Years ago, a group of Kuschans immigrated to Embrey, with goals of settling down while staying true to their faith. We built a church, then. We'll build another one, now."

"Nothing stopped them from destroying this one! What's to keep them from finishing the job, by killing you and your family?"

"If any of our countrymen wish to stay in Embrey, then I must stay, too."

"Why ask your wife and kids to stay in that dugout, while you rebuild something which will likely get burned down, anyway?"

"You're right, Yuri," said Dimitri. "By staying, I put my family's life at stake. If I go, I break my pledge to the Kuen. Our earthly bodies die only once. It's inevitable. By upholding the faith, we live forever in Paradise. What kind of a man am I, for running every time life gets rough? How can I serve mankind, the Kued, or the Kuen, if I cannot handle adversity? The Kued dies in his sacrifice to mankind. I'd better do the same, if that's what's asked of me. Admit it, Yuri, you feel the exact same way."

"But, Dimitri! I won't leave you! Come with me, please! My own family threw me out, because I'm . . ." Yuri choked up. "You're family to me, the same as with Theo! Please don't stay here, Dimitri! Come with me!"

There were no guarantees of anyone reaching Councillor Theo's compound, alive. Dimitri didn't know if the civil unrest was targeted at a specific ethnic or religious group. Everyone was "fair game," including Brotherhood members. Thoughts of residing in that dugout were miserable, even if well-stocked with plenty of bedding. Yana and the kids were wise in their hesitations to winter there. At the same time, Dimitri hated to burden Theo.

And what if Theo was already dead?

Dimitri was ashamed to rely on Yuri. The boy could easily defend himself. Was he able to protect everyone else? Well, there was nothing left at the church, but warm memories and deep resentment. "All right, Yuri," agreed Dimitri. "I will . . . I *will* go to your father's."

Giorgio sat on the dugout floor, enjoying a humble meal of parched corn and beans. His nerves gradually subsided, after his sudden departure from the church. To stay calm, he made sure that his fellow students had enough to eat.

Yana wanted her kids to think of themselves as Embrians, though they rarely socialized outside of their "comfort zone." Even if she personally disliked the Brotherhood of Faith, it didn't diminish her attitudes about the majority of boys in present company. Her maternal spirit didn't begrudge Eduardo, who was helpful, or Sergio and Giuseppe, who befriended her own children. Apparently, Sasha was under the spell of puppy love, when it came to Giuseppe. She seemed perfectly happy and content, with her arm around him.

"How was the food, Giuseppe?" asked Giorgio, smiling as Sasha cuddled next to the youngster.

With a mouthful of food, Giuseppe voiced his approval with a nod.

After finishing his meal, Geoffrey requested Giorgio to step outside with him. "What is it, Geoff?" asked Giorgio, leaving the dugout.

"Are you sure there's room for us at Councillor Theo's?" asked Geoffrey. "Are you sure he's even around? For all we know, he's been taken prisoner, or . . . *something.*"

"He's at this hidden compound," said Giorgio, inadvertently revealing doubt. "Or so, that's what Yuri thinks. Did you see Brad anywhere, before we met with you yesterday?"

Geoffrey shook his head, 'no.'

"I've been worried about him, since . . ." Giorgio paused. "Sure wish I knew his whereabouts, right now!"

"By the way, thanks for getting me that dorm assistant's job," said Geoffrey, secretly.

"I didn't give it to you, Geoff. You earned it. Royce did more to set that up, than me. I'm glad you got my old job in the basement. Too bad you couldn't keep it, though. Frankly, you look real snazzy in that green tunic!"

"And I'm sorry Karl opposed you as a Leader." Geoffrey hesitated. "I also want to thank you for keeping Randy and me a secret."

"Royce already knew. So did Sven."

"They *did?*"

"Royce respected you for being a good student, and a good guy," explained Giorgio. "He knew that you and Randy had nowhere else to go. Sven was usually too drunk to care. Let's pray that Royce gets together with his fiance, and they're both all right."

"Amen to that," sighed Geoffrey.

"Collect your things," ordered Dimitri, wandering to the dugout with Yuri. "We're going to Councillor Theo's."

"Anything's better than that." Giorgio pointed at the dugout.

Dimitri frowned at Giorgio, but held his tongue.

"Are you sure your father's at his compound, Yuri?" asked Giorgio.

"Father had it built, in case of moments like this," said Yuri.

"Well, this might not be wise on my part," mumbled Giorgio, sick with fear, "but I'm going into Sykes."

"What on Earth for?" asked Dimitri.

"To find a close friend of mine, named Bradley," informed Giorgio.

"There were more than a hundred-and-sixty kids in that school," said Dimitri. "Forgive me for asking, but what's so special about this Bradley kid? What makes you think you'll even find him?"

For a second or two, Giorgio nearly confessed his role of the murders in Karl's office. "It's not just for Bradley. I was recently appointed as a Leader. I've got to help as many students as I can. Please try to understand, I've just got to find Brad."

"You mean *we've* got to find Brad," insisted Geoffrey.

"I'll go," volunteered Yuri.

"You don't even know what those boys look like, Yuri!" argued Dimitri.

While Dimitri appreciated Giorgio and Geoffrey's convictions, Sykes was no place for any God-fearing youth, at that particular time. Neither had any business searching for their buddies, in the middle of a battlefield. "No, Yuri," said Dimitri. "We're going to Theo's, together. Wait for the military to secure the area. I don't know about the rest of you, but I'm paying my way at Theo's. There's no reason to keep food and supplies in the dugout. We'll need help taking it with us."

"We both believe in God, in our own image of Him," said Giorgio. "God tells me to seek out my Brothers, trapped in the city."

"Stay with the Brothers you've got here," said Yuri. "Stay with your wife and kids, Dimitri. I'll find more of their friends."

"Each of us had loved ones in Sykes," spoke Dimitri. "Sadly, a few are already dead. That's the harsh, painful truth. Why gamble your life, any further?"

"Your schoolmates are all dressed in those same skirts and funny little hats, right?" Yuri asked Giorgio, failing to heed Dimitri's warning.

"Yeah, that's right," answered Giorgio, humored by Yuri's description of the school uniform. "That same color and insignia on the chest and buckle."

"Yuri, there's a very good chance we'll never see you again, except in Paradise!" shouted Dimitri, emotionally.

"Or in Heaven," added Geoffrey.

"I'm doing this for the good of all," said Yuri. "Isn't that what the Kuen expects of us?"

Dimitri resigned himself to Yuri's choice. "You're part of the family now," he said, with a grin. "Remember that."

"Thank you, Dimitri," said Yuri. "Giorgio, what does Bradley look like?"

Giorgio gave a brief description of both Bradley and Kenichi, along with Lord Kelly's vicinity. Silently, he questioned whether Yuri was able to fight his way out of anything, especially a nightmare scenario like Sykes. Ashamed of not accompanying Yuri into the city, Giorgio said, "I'm being selfish by asking you to go look for my pals."

"If they're out there, I'll find them," said Yuri, with certainty. "I'll bet you ten shillings on it. Is that a deal, Giorgio?"

"What does he mean?" asked Geoffrey, curiously. "'Ten shillings'?"

Giorgio was unwilling to disclose his arrangement with Major Kohl. "Just a dumb . . . in-joke, between Yuri and me."

"Don't do anything you'll be sorry for," Dimitri told Yuri. "If you have to, make sure it's for the right reasons."

Yuri was touched by Dimitri's concern for him.

"Look, Yuri, you've been to this secret compound," sighed Giorgio. "We haven't. How do we find it?"

"It's in our backwoods, three miles west of the house," explained Yuri. "A wagon road next to the barn will take you to it. It's overgrown with brush and weeds, but follow the wheel ruts. You'll find what's left of an earlier settlement, a few old buildings and an outhouse. Stay on that road, and you'll be fine."

30

After helping chase a few Branellians away, Sergeant Vix regained a sense of calm and tranquility at Fort Cooley.

As Captain Willowby penned a report of that morning's incident, Vix returned the recruits to cleaning the grounds. The youngsters who were nearly kidnapped by Copenhaver and his crew had breakfast in the commissary, then gave their accounts to Willowby. A sentry, Corporal Bergman, delivered Willowby's dispatch and the siblings to General Chang in the War Ministry.

Alone in his office, Willowby couldn't prevent his hands from shaking. His breathing grew increasingly shallow, as panic swept over his entire body.

Branellians . . . What are Branellians doing here?

The war's in the eastern provinces, not here on our western shores!

Were those Branellians part of a small raiding party, or a fraction of a much greater force?

What if Embrey's on the verge of collapse?

It did nothing to ease Willowby, once he learned that sections of the city were under siege, as civilians left the area in droves.

Willowby tried to behave in a commanding fashion. Still, it was impossible to project confidence in the face of potential doom. What were his responsibilities to Fort Cooley, now? What about responsibilities to himself? Did his ancestors' esteemed histories mean a thing in a crumbling society? Assuming Willowby was captured, the Branellians would likely make an example of him, due to his family's reputation.

Willowby went outside, to gain assurances from Vix. In the warm autumn sun, the veteran sergeant showed no fear. The recruits were sure scared! Whether it did any good or not, Willowby wished to be at Vix's side. "Captain Willowby," addressed Vix, undeterred.

Willowby chose his words, carefully. "Sergeant Vix . . . shouldn't we . . . do something?"

"Like what, sir?"

"I don't know." Willowby shrugged. "Go see what's happening . . . or, you know . . . evacuate the fort?"

Vix glared at Willowby. "What the hell for?"

Willowby nearly fainted. "What? . . . What if the Branellians surround us? You know, like what happened at that old Brotherhood mission in southern Embrey?"

"You're talking about a volunteer army of two-hundred men, fighting five-thousand Branellians."

"Yeah, but . . . they died!" cried Willowby. "All of them! What if we're surrounded, like they were?"

"Shut that up!" yelled Vix. "Wanna lose your soldiers' respect?"

"Sorry," moped Willowby, his emotions at odds with themselves. "I want to see what's going on in town, and fight the enemy there, wherever they are! We can't just wait around here!"

"You think the boys are up to it?"

Willowby smiled, nervously. "They were, this morning."

"We got lucky this morning. There wasn't that many Branellians. What if we meet a trained army of superior numbers? First sign of trouble, most of our boys'll run, and get themselves and everyone else killed in the bargain. Boys got no place in that sorta slaughter."

"But we're trapped here! I think we'd better leave the fort and do something, not just stand behind these walls, waiting to die!"

"You wanna do something, act like you know what the hell you're doing!" commented Vix. "Give the recruits someone to look up to."

"I thought that was your job, Sergeant Vix," mumbled Willowby.

"If you wanna be an officer, then act like one! Either that, or I'll take command. You like that?"

Willowby addressed a freckle-faced, fifteen-year-old recruit, stationed at the eastern ramparts. "Corporal Billy Joe," he said. "What do you see, from there?"

"The sky, Cap'n Willowby!" answered Billy Joe. "Nothin' but blue sky!"

"What?" questioned Vix.

"N-nothin'!" stuttered Billy Joe. "Nothin' this way, Cap'n Willowby! Nothin', Sergeant Vix!"

"Thank you, Corporal," said Willowby, unsure whether to be relieved or frightened by this news. He had ordered Corporal Bergman out, more than an hour ago, with no return. A lack of answers was scary. Not knowing what took place away from Fort Cooley was so aggravating! Willowby imagined himself alone, isolated, and abandoned. Assuming his tiny post was attacked from all sides, who'd come to his rescue? Would anyone know, or care, of Fort Cooley's last stand?

"Cap'n Willowby, sir!" cried Billy Joe.

"Yes, yes!" responded Willowby. "Report!"

Riders from the northeast!"

"Well?" asked Willowby, impatiently. "Who are they?"

"Looks like a . . ."

Silence . . .

"Who?" screamed Willowby. "Who? *Who?*"

"Sir . . ." warned Vix.

"Cap'n Willowby!" shouted Billy Joe. "Corporal Bergman's back . . . with Colonel Owensby and some other fellas."

Willowby groaned. He disliked Colonel Owensby, intensely. Vix's opinion of Owensby was even worse.

Riding behind Owensby, an aide and a few guards, sixteen-year-old Corporal Bergman appeared exhausted and browbeat. His sensitive, deep-set eyes were teary and reddened from Owensby's constant berating. Owensby had graduated with Major Kohl at the Embrian Military Academy, and was reputed to win promotion through cronyism and backstabbing. He also wore the hated rattlesnake and sword, revealing an allegiance to General Gornick.

Vix and Willowby stood at attention and saluted, as two small boys collected the newcomers' horses. "Colonel Owensby," greeted Willowby, wearing a strained smile.

"Captain Willowby," spoke Owensby, harshly. "Why are you still here, when the whole country's crawling with Branellians, as thick as fleas?"

Willowby looked to Vix for support. "Sir, my duty is to Fort Cooley."

"Your duty is to Embrey, not to sissies hiding behind these flimsy, matchstick walls." Owensby examined the fort with disdain. "Today may just be your lucky day, Captain Willowby. Today you'll become famous, like your father and grandfather before you."

"Yes, sir?" asked Willowby, curiously.

Owensby offered his dark, tricorn hat to an aide, as downtrodden as Corporal Bergman. "I won't stand here in the wind. Your office, Captain Willowby?"

Vix and Willowby directed Owensby to the office.

"Who asked the sergeant to this meeting?" griped Owensby, his complaint aimed at Vix.

"Words intended for me are to be shared with Sergeant Vix, sir," explained Willowby.

Owensby regarded an enlisted man's presence as an infraction of his own code of conduct. Even if he had the right to dispute Willowby's ruling, the colonel reluctantly agreed to it. "Very well," he huffed, scooting his fat gut through the door. "As you were."

Once everyone entered the office, Willowby offered Owensby a chair and a glass of brandy. Out of courtesy, Owensby accepted Willowby's generosity. Sitting behind the desk, Willowby requested the purpose of Owensby's visit.

Owensby leaned across the desk. "The Branellians had the audacity to launch a strike against us, from the sea."

Willowby turned to Vix, who stood to one side of the room. "They *were* Branellians this morning," he said, quietly.

Vix nodded.

"Rather than stage an inland invasion, the rotters hit us where it counts." Owensby grinned. "Fortunately, we were ready for them, and are now in control. We're certain the Branellians' rendezvous point is the mouth of the Ember River. Ships from their navy, led by that slant-eyed mongrel Shimura, are to retrieve those ranks who've survived our military's warm hospitality."

"Thank you," said Willowby. "What does that mean to Fort Cooley?"

"We'll surprise the kilted ghouls, before they have a chance to leave our fair Embrey," said Owensby. "We need men stationed at the mouth of the Ember River. *Your* men, Captain Willowby."

Vix cleared his throat. "With all due respect to Captain Willowby, our soldiers ain't up to it."

Owensby raised one eyebrow. "It's not a request, Sergeant Vix. It's an order. You of all people should understand the necessity of killing Branellians, before they get away."

"Colonel Owensby," said Willowby, diplomatically. "I support Sergeant Vix's assessment of the men. This is a recruit depot. We lack the skills and training for that operation."

"Not only that," added Vix, "but we're under General Chang, not General Gornick as you are, Colonel Owensby."

"What difference does that make?" argued Owensby. "Embrey's in a state of martial law, and we require every man on the field." Owensby laughed. "I suppose Major Kohl's childishness and incompetence has rubbed off on you. Eh, Sergeant Vix? Or are you man enough to handle the truth?"

Vix nearly hit the roof. He wanted to leave the room, but felt a need to remain with Willowby.

"Excuse me, Colonel Owensby," said Willowby. "What makes you so sure the Branellians are to meet at the mouth of the Ember River?"

"We captured a few of the gluttonous swine," said Owensby, proudly. "They get very loose-lipped when the heat's on, these Branellians. Not a lick of couth, courage, or sand to their character. We obtained a good deal of information from that sniveling horde."

"And then what?" asked Willowby.

"And then what?" laughed Owensby. "We stretched their necks from only the finest Embrian ropes, that's what!"

"Sir," said Willowby. "I must agree with Sergeant Vix. "We're not the right squad . . ."

"No other squad is available," interrupted Owensby. "Are you to carry out my orders, or must I relieve you of your command, then direct your men to this destination?"

"These are boys, not men," stated Vix, tiredly. "Boys got no place ..."

"Cowards, you are!" screamed Owensby, leaping to his feet. "Nothing but old women and cowards at Fort Cooley! Captain Willowby, I gave you the opportunity to prove that you are indeed of an esteemed military family. So what do I find when I get here? A lily-livered cur, and lazy, good for nothing sergeant!"

"I protest your language against Sergeant Vix and me!" shouted Willowby.

Owensby snickered. "You may protest it. Still, you deserve every word of it. Are you the descendant of that man in the portrait, Embrey's legendary Count Fossbinder? I doubt it! I'm of the mind that you're not of his noble stock, but the result of your mother's infidelity with a black-skinned peasant boy, in the backroom of a cheap, riverside brothel."

Willowby was devastated. He forgot his role as an officer, and evolved into the frightened, overburdened child he truly was. He rested his head onto the desk, and released a whimper.

"Sergeant Vix!" shrieked Owensby. "I order you to take command of this post, and ready your soldiers for a march to the mouth of the . . ."

"No, sir!" yelled Vix. "Captain Willowby won't lead our troops to that destination and by god neither will I. And by god neither will you!"

"Call in the guards!" Owensby shouted at his aide. "Are you refusing my orders, Sergeant Vix? If so, then I'll place you and that sorry excuse at the desk under arrest. Once this is over, I'll see you hanged from the same ropes I used on those Branellians!"

Anger nearly got the best of Vix. Whoever thought that Willowby had the experience or maturity to run an Army base needed to be hurt. Willowby's crippling fear, along with his melancholy from Owensby's caustic tongue, told Vix that the captain had to know what it meant to be a man, before taking on such responsibilities.

"Colonel Owensby," said Vix, with a deep breath. "Our boys ain't properly armed. Hell, they wouldn't know what to do with a sword, if they had one."

"What about that ruckus, this morning?" asked Owensby. "I heard all about it from your Corporal Bergman."

"We shooed them Branellians off with picks, shovels, and rakes. Rocks too, when the boys found them."

"If you succeeded in shooing Branellians off this morning, then perhaps we'll talk them into surrendering, tonight. Will you come with me on your own accord, Sergeant Vix? Or must I drag you into battle, on chains?"

Vix's dedication to Embrey, Captain Willowby, and Fort Cooley made that decision for him. He felt no obligation, whatsoever, to Colonel Owensby, and didn't pretend to. "I don't wanna take the boys into no mess," he answered. "I don't want it on my conscience. I don't like your mission, and I sure as hell don't like you. But I'll go."

Owensby couldn't care less if Vix liked him, or not. He required the sergeant's cooperation, not his love or admiration.

Owensby retrieved his hat from the aide, and placed it on his head. "Be ready in fifteen minutes. The sooner we reach our destination, the sooner we'll intercept the enemy." Owensby turned to Willowby, who was still stinging from the insult. "What about it, Captain? I give you one final chance to redeem yourself, in my eyes and in the hearts of the Embrian race. Will you come with me, or must I kick you like a lazy porch dog?"

"He's coming," answered Vix, before Willowby responded. "The troops of Fort Cooley need him, and he won't let 'em down."

"We'll just see about that." Owensby stepped from the office. "Be ready in fifteen minutes!"

Once Owensby left, Willowby looked up at Vix, sadly. He disgraced himself in the company of a superior officer! Why did Vix defend him, now? Why did Vix continually grant him his unfailing support?

Vix lifted Willowby up from his chair. "Don't ever lemme see you crawl around like a worm, again!" he growled.

It mattered little how badly Owensby may have upset Willowby. Vix's words hurt that much more.

"I can't stand Owensby, not one damn bit," said Vix. "If anyone gets killed, I hope it's him. If we're lucky, them Branellians'll give up. If we're damn lucky, Kraig or Chang's men have already got 'em."

"I . . . I shouldn't be a part of this," stuttered Willowby.

"I know that. Me, neither! Looks like we're in it, though. No one's putting me in chains! Only reason we're going is that I don't wanna give that bastard the satisfaction."

"Yes, Sergeant Vix," mumbled Willowby.

Vix popped his heels together and stood, ramrod straight. With a salute, he asked, "Your orders, Captain Willowby?"

31

An hour after meeting Andre at the butcher shop, Kenichi led Bradley, Trevor, and Derek to a quiet neighborhood, seemingly unaffected by the mayhem of the inner city. Even then, they couldn't afford to relax. Each boy carried on as if danger lurked within every building, around street corners, and at open windows.

Near the outskirts of town, the five students were greeted by a hundred Embrian Rangers, under General Chang. Dressed in faded tan shirts and hoods, the Rangers were armed to the teeth with sabers, knives, bows, and arrows.

A young lieutenant approached the boys. "Hello," he spoke out. "I see you're from a school, but which one?"

"Lord Kelly's Academy," answered Kenichi, pleased to see the Rangers.

The lieutenant sighed. "Good. A few minutes ago, we met a few school kids who weren't so nice, not at all. Those hooligans pulled knives on us! You believe that?"

"We need some food, and a place to rest," said Bradley.

"Yeah," added Andre, "and some underpants for Brad."

"Stay on Riley Street," said the lieutenant. "Admiral Kraig and General Chang have set up their new headquarters, about a mile from here."

"New headquarters?" asked Kenichi.

"Gornick overran the Ministry of War," the lieutenant informed. "He went ballistic when he found out there were Branellians roaming the streets."

"Branellians?" gulped Bradley.

"Yes," the lieutenant said. "I think most of them were captured, killed, or skedaddled. They weren't as bad as Gornick's lame-brained men. Not only is he fighting the Branellians, but our own citizens! You believe that?"

Kenichi rolled his eyes back. If Gornick had secured the War Ministry, what other chambers of government were under his thumb?

"They'll give you lodgings at the new headquarters, at least for the night," the lieutenant said. "I'm not sure if you can stay there, long-term."

"Thanks," said Kenichi. "We'll be okay on our own."

"Just watch your backs," the lieutenant advised.

"Won't you take us there?" begged Trevor. "Please?"

"Yeah," shuttered Derek. "We might get lost!"

The lieutenant laughed. "Stay on Riley Street, and you won't get lost. Be careful, just the same."

"You see my little brother at your headquarters?" asked Andre. "His name's Bentley."

"There's a few school kids around there," the lieutenant said. "I didn't catch their names. The place is filling up with refugees."

Andre feared the worst, and nearly gave up on Bentley.

"How long do you think this will go on?" asked Bradley.

"It can't end soon enough, for us," the lieutenant said. "Get out of Sykes, boys! This town is Hell on Earth."

While Bradley didn't like everything about Sykes it was, after all, his home.

"We won't be back," said Kenichi. "At least I won't be. Thanks, lieutenant."

"Good luck," the lieutenant bid, as the Rangers marched away.

With greater optimism, the five students headed toward the War Ministry's current headquarters. Trevor and Derek imagined a hot feast, steaming hot baths, and soft, warm beds there. In particular, Kenichi felt confident and assured . . . until he spotted the church steeple of Lord William's Academy.

Derek skipped through Lord William's main gate. "Derry!" yelled Kenichi, afraid of the reception the youngster might receive.

"It's all right, Kenichi!" laughed Trevor. "We got friends here!"

Kenichi looked at Bradley. Trevor and Derek were unaware of the drastic changes taking place at Lord William's.

Lord William's campus was empty, as Derek entered the facility. Seconds later, he encountered four young men, leaving a cafeteria. Like Antoine, all wore black berets, heavy boots, and tunics featuring the rattlesnake and sword.

"You got no idea how happy we are to see you!" cheered Derek.

Three of the four students from Lord William's brandished knives, similar to the one Antoine had. Derek stopped. There were always rivalries between their two schools, but nothing like this!

Bradley recognized three of the four students. Terry and Quinn were among them. Samuel was seventeen, had thick, dark eyelashes, and was built like an ox. Both Samuel and Terry held daggers. Quinn was the only one without a weapon.

"What do you think you're doing here?" asked Samuel, in a deep, baritone voice.

Though he disliked Samuel and Terry, Bradley hoped Quinn's presence eased tensions. It didn't help when Andre showed up with the meat cleaver. "Hey, guys," said Bradley, softly.

"I asked you a question," demanded Samuel. "Just what are you doing here?"

"Leave them alone," said Quinn, ashamed of his schoolmates. "They didn't come here for a fight."

"Quinn's right," said Bradley. "We're not looking for any trouble."

"You're from Lord Kelly's," said Terry.

"So?" asked Kenichi.

"You killed two of your Leaders, and Antoine," accused Samuel. "One of you did! I think it was the gook!"

Bradley looked at Kenichi, wondering what Samuel knew. Kenichi said nothing, despite his objections to Samuel's racial slur.

"We ain't got nothing to do with that, boy," argued Andre, waving the meat cleaver at Samuel.

While this alarmed Quinn, Samuel and Terry didn't know whether to be intimidated, or humored, by the meat cleaver. Neither feared Andre, and regarded him merely as a joke.

"They just need somewhere to rest," suggested Quinn, anxiously.

"And I say they killed their own Leaders!" cackled a measly little weasel, standing between Samuel and Terry. This mouthy troublemaker, who was even shorter than Derek, had beady eyes and a long nose.

The weasel stepped toward Trevor. As Trevor cowered behind Bradley, the weasel laughed hysterically.

Defiantly, Andre positioned himself between Bradley and the weasel.

"Put the meat cleaver down, Andre!" ordered Kenichi.

"No, sir," refused Andre, facing the weasel. "They ain't telling me what to do."

"Don't be a retard!" warned Derek.

"Yeah, Andre," the weasel snickered. "Don't be a retard."

"Screw this," said Kenichi, shaking his head in frustration. "C'mon, guys. We're outa here."

"Keep out of this, 'Itchy,'" said Andre, gritting his teeth at the weasel.

The weasel jabbed his dagger at Andre, hoping to frighten him. Andre shoved his hand into the dagger to block the weasel's attack, and received a severe gash across the palm.

Andre backed away, blood dripping from the wound. It was bad enough, getting bitten by Derek earlier. Now this! Staring at the wound, Andre nearly passed out. The pain was excruciating.

"Ooh!" gagged Derek, his eyes glued to the wound. *"Gross!"*

"Happy now?" asked Kenichi, sarcastically.

The accident shocked everyone, including the weasel, who placed the dagger in a sheath hanging from his belt. "Say, um? . . . What's your name, again?" he asked, apologetically. *"Andre?* I . . . uh. . . look Andre, I'm really sorry about that . . ."

Andre's anger was greater than his common sense. With a manic yell, he struck the weasel's neck with the meat cleaver. Blood spurted onto Andre's face, legs, and tunic, like a geyser. Bradley, Trevor, and Derek screamed, as Quinn turned away.

With the cleaver still embedded in his neck, the weasel dropped to the ground, convulsing like a farm animal at butchering time. Twitching wildly, he kicked his undergarment out from under his tunic, as urine sprayed onto his feet and legs.

Kenichi removed the cleaver from the weasel's neck. Covering the gaping wound with his skullcap, he tried to halt the bleeding. It was no use. Blood splashed onto Kenichi's cap, tunic, and hands.

Seconds later, the weasel released a final breath.

"Son of a bitch," whispered Samuel, in disbelief.

Silence wedged the two camps, as no one made a move. Kenichi slowly got to his feet.

To even the score, Terry and Samuel circled Andre.

"I didn't mean it!" cried Andre, backing away. "If that boy hadn't cut me like that!"

Andre turned to his schoolmates for help. Bradley and Kenichi thought of intervening, yet neither stepped forward in Andre's defense. As Terry hesitated to make a fight of it, Samuel was determined to square things up for the weasel.

Andre was blinded by the pain in his injured hand. He wondered if he deserved to die, as payment for killing the weasel. He feared the Hereafter . . . or the lack of it. "Brad . . . *Kenichi* . . ." he whined. "Someone help me . . ."

As Samuel lunged at Andre with a dagger, Quinn halted his advance by leaping in the way.

A split second later, Samuel drove his dagger into Quinn's chest.

Staggering like a drunk, Quinn tried to speak. Instead, blood gurgled from his mouth, as crimson bubbles emerged from the chest wound. Quinn collapsed to the grass, his breathing labored and erratic. "Quinn!" screamed Bradley, kneeling to the wounded boy.

Oddly amused, Samuel refused to take responsibility for Quinn. Rather, he chose to pin everything on his counterparts from Lord Kelly's.

Kenichi wanted to run, but his legs failed him. He knelt down to check on

Quinn. Trevor and Derek stood by, petrified. Weeping, Bradley ran his fingers through Quinn's fiery, red hair.

Terry dropped his dagger, sickened by what happened to Quinn and the weasel. "Why did Quinn do *that?*" he gasped.

"What difference does it make?" yelled Kenichi. "It's over!"

"Not with me it's not," said Samuel, locking Derek in his sinewy arms. Shoving his dagger against Derek's throat, he glared at the others. "Say your prayers, you scrawny little turd!"

Derek kicked and bit at Samuel, to no avail. Struggling to break free, he cried to somebody, *anybody,* to save him. "Kenichi!" he screeched, his tiny voice echoing throughout the schoolyard.

"Let 'em go, boy!" ordered Andre, favoring his bleeding hand.

"Hold still, Derry!" urged Kenichi. "Let him go, and we'll get Quinn to a doctor!"

"We're not doing any good," Terry spoke to Samuel, his voice cracking. "Let's just help Quinn, all right?"

"An eye for an eye!" roared Samuel, ready to thrust his dagger into Derek.

Derek traded glances with Trevor, and let out a wicked, high-pitched scream.

From out of nowhere, an arrow pierced Samuel's back.

Samuel dropped Derek, as he squalled like an injured cat. Meanwhile, Terry retreated into the cafeteria. Derek dashed into Trevor's open arms.

Samuel took a clumsy step toward the cafeteria, when a second arrow impaled his throat. His knees buckling, Samuel fell and lay motionless at the cafeteria door.

As Kenichi held Derek down upon the ground, Bradley and Trevor threw themselves across Quinn. Too worked up about the weasel, along with his injured hand, Andre stayed on his feet.

"Make it stop!" cried Derek, slapping at Kenichi, Panic-stricken, he wished to run, as fast as he could, away from Lord William's Academy. "Somebody make it *stop!*"

"Stay put, Derry!" ordered Kenichi, looking all around.

"Are you from Lord Kelly's?" a distant voice inquired, in a thick Kuschan accent.

"No one move," whispered Kenichi.

"But what if he shoots us?" whined Trevor.

"Are you from Lord Kelly's?" the voice repeated. "I was sent to find you!"

"Don't shoot!" shouted Kenichi. "We're from Lord Kelly's!"

"Kenichi," warned Bradley.

A small-framed young man with blonde hair jumped from a stone wall next to the school's gate. Wearing a long, burgundy robe, the young man carried a long bow, some arrows, and a pouch around his neck. Initially, the five students didn't know if this individual was male or female.

Kenichi slowly returned to his feet, and cautiously dusted himself off. "We're from Lord Kelly's," he said, hoping not to provoke the newcomer.

"Giorgio sent me out to find some more of his friends," the Kuschan said.

"Giorgio?" questioned Kenichi, with mistrust.

"I'm Yuri, son and loyal servant to Councillor Theo. Giorgio's a frequent guest at our home."

"Theo's son?" asked Kenichi, in disbelief. Yuri's appearance and weaponry forged an unlikely combination. Kenichi's first impression stated that Yuri was incapable of killing. Yet, Samuel was taken out with two, well-placed arrows. "Councillor Theo's *son?*"

Yuri glanced at Samuel. He didn't intend to end the brute's life, but saw no alternative in saving Derek. Considering the dagger Samuel clutched in his cold, dead hands, along with the insignia of the rattlesnake and sword, Yuri wanted to believe that maybe, just maybe, his actions were justified.

"And who are you?" asked Yuri, shaking Kenichi's hand.

"Kenichi . . ." he answered, wiping sweat from his forehead. "Nothing, to nobody."

"Is there one here named Bradley?" asked Yuri.

Kenichi pointed at Bradley, still kneeling beside Quinn. Wondering what Yuri wanted from him, Bradley swallowed nervously but said nothing.

Andre showed Yuri his bloody hand. Motioning toward the weasel, he lowered his head in shame.

"Oh, so *that's* why you struck him with that cleaver?" asked Yuri.

Crouching next to the weasel's body, Yuri began to nurse Andre's hand. Obediently, Andre allowed Yuri to clean the wound, then bandage it. Andre's one complaint came when Yuri dabbed smelly, burning alcohol on the gash.

"Do you use your right hand or your left?" asked Yuri, to ease Andre's frayed nerves.

Andre shrugged, in confusion.

"For solitary pleasures," explained Yuri.

Andre blushed.

"I want to make sure these bandages don't spoil it for you," said Yuri. "Right hand, or left?"

Self-consciously, Andre mouthed *right.*

"Quinn," sobbed Bradley. "Oh, Quinn."

Drowning in his own blood, Quinn was unable to speak.

Yuri ripped open Quinn's tunic. Firmly, he pressed both hands against the chest. "Hold his feet off the ground," he told Kenichi. "I can't save his life, but this may give him a few more minutes."

Andre's idea of playing the tough guy brought on much of this tragedy. Attempting to make explanations or apologies, the words never came. Stepping away from everyone, Andre leaned against the cafeteria wall and cried.

"Pray with me, Quinn," requested Bradley. "Will you please pray with me?"

Quinn coughed out an inaudible answer, and nodded.

Trevor and Derek joined Bradley in his solemn plea to the Almighty.

"Oh, Heavenly Father," whispered Bradley, failing to muster the courage for this spiritual obligation. All he saw, through his vision, blurred by tears, was Quinn.

Am I worthy of God's Kingdom, and His love? Are any of us deserving of eternal life, with our Lord and Savior? Does Heaven even exist? Bradley saw no evidence of it in Sykes, or in the hearts of most men.

"Amen," whispered Quinn, knowing Bradley was unable to finish. "God bless you, Brother Bradley . . ."

"God bless you, Brother Quinn," said Bradley, watching another friend drift into eternal sleep. Clutching Quinn's hand, he made a silent, vain request to spare the dying teen.

As Quinn ran his hand across Bradley's cheeks, he left faint smudges of blood. Leaning forward, Bradley kissed Quinn's forehead. His eyes fluttering, as consciousness gradually slipped away, Quinn took in one last breath.

Unable to accept what he had just witnessed, Trevor buried his face against Kenichi's shoulder and wept.

Seconds later, Brother Quinn was dead.

32

"I didn't join the Army for this," voiced Patrick, overwhelmed by the gruesome scene around him.

In the past, Lieutenant Commander Salazar looked forward to his first taste of combat. Not now. Instead of basking in honor and glory, he dealt with insurmountable sadness, despair, and anger. He once argued that General Gornick would restore pride, order, and sanity to the Embrian people. He didn't think that Gornick, or his loyal supporters, were capable of committing atrocities.

The city was a nightmare! It wasn't enough to see how the urban landscape was changed, forever. Salazar coped with the lingering smell of smoke, death, and decay. Admiral Kraig was right! Gornick was a butcher and a madman!

Patrick handed Salazar a canteen of water. "I mean it, sir. I didn't join the Army for this."

"We're in the Navy," reminded Salazar. "Remember, Pat?"

Currently, Sykes was divided by two warring factions. The south was under Gornick's rule, while the monarch's troops retained the northern sections of town. Small numbers of Branellians hid in the back streets and allies. Most had assimilated themselves into the population. They weren't nearly as much of a threat as Gornick's overzealous troops, bent on wresting control of a crippled nation.

Understanding that Embrey had its tail kicked weighed heavily upon Salazar. There wasn't a thing he could do about it! Embrey, as the man once knew it, no longer existed. Fears of civil war were meaningless. That day, it became an unspeakable reality.

Salazar was assigned to consolidate royalist forces, then proceed with subsequent mop-up operations. With his aide Patrick and bodyguard Jesse, Salazar and his regiment organized scattered units to clear out pockets of resistance. For the most part, these men were busy collecting the dead, for cremation or burial.

Corpses scattered the avenues, boulevards, and alleys, as feral dogs fought over the remains. The deceased were laid out in extended rows, awaiting their resting place, not far from where they fell. In more extreme cases, bodies were placed onto large fires, for immediate disposal. There wasn't time for memorial services, or to identify the victims. Those under Salazar's command, many hardened by battle, found it difficult to handle their frail emotions. Even the toughest of warriors shed tears.

Not far from the smoldering ashes of a small home, leveled by fire, a small family was massacred. A woman, in her early-thirties, was raped prior to having her throat cut. Her nude body lay next to a preteen girl, who received the exact same treatment.

A boy, who was little more than ten years of age, was handcuffed to a fence post. After his pants were pulled down, the boy's genitals were cut off, and taken as a trophy. Dried blood caked the boy's shirt, hips, and thighs, as his frightened eyes remained wide open. It was as if the boy called for vengeance, even in death.

Salazar sent Jesse to apprehend those guilty of this crime. Yet, he expected no justice to be served. The evildoers were probably bragging about it, over pints of ale. "Cut that boy down," Salazar told a corporal. No longer could he stomach the horrific sight. "Bury him with the others, as soon as you can!"

"Whoever is at fault for this, we'll stop them, sir!" said Patrick, barely containing his rage. "I swear, we'll stop them!"

"Who, Pat? Branellians, or Gornick?" groaned Salazar, slapping Patrick's back. The aide was a decent man, who rated higher than to be subjected to this disgusting detail.

It will take an eternity for these wounds to heal, Salazar thought as he splashed cold water in his face. As a child, he studied history courses on how metropolitan areas were decimated during times of war and strife. Those texts were read in the comfort and safety of classrooms and libraries, detached from the grim facts. What occurred in Sykes that day was a daily routine on the Embrian-Branellian border, hundreds of miles to the east. The war suddenly hit painfully close to home. Pray our children and grandchildren never suffer this same fate!

"Here comes Jesse," announced Patrick.

Salazar returned the canteen to Patrick as he awaited Jesse, riding on a white stallion. As usual, Jesse was decked out in a Cavalier hat, sky-blue cape and tunic, tights, and riding boots. Above his head was a violet parasol, fluttering in the afternoon breeze.

With Jesse were three men. One voluntarily surrendered, pulled along on a rope tied to the saddle. The other two men were face down over a burro, shot full of arrows.

Though Salazar had not warmed to Jesse, he acknowledged that that bodyguard was good for something. "Who are they?" he demanded, unwilling to grant Jesse a pleasant greeting.

"Those who did this," answered Jesse, pointing at the murdered family.

"What makes you so sure?" questioned Salazar.

Jesse turned to the boy, as he retrieved a small pouch from his saddle bag. "This item's previous owner."

"'Previous owner'?" asked Patrick, peeking into the small pouch. What he saw made him gag. "Good Lord! Have a look for yourself, Commander Salazar!"

"Take it to the . . . previous owner," ordered Salazar, shaking his head.

Patrick urgently took the pouch to a soldier, who dug the boy's grave under a cherry tree.

Salazar stared at Jesse's prisoners. "What about them?"

"Those on the burro wanted to fight," reported Jesse, dismounting. Tugging on the rope, he dragged his one living hostage to Salazar. "After making expedient work of his partners, I changed this cad's mind."

A member of the United Westerland Brethren, Jesse's captive was only a teen, himself. As with his cohorts, he wore a pointed hat and a long, black robe. Brown clumps of hair dotted his lips, cheeks, and chin.

"I should finish you off, right where you stand," threatened Salazar. "How old are you?"

"Huh?" the prisoner asked, in fear and confusion.

"How old are you?" repeated Salazar, impatiently.

"Seven . . . seventeen!"

"And those on the burro?"

"Seventeen," the prisoner answered. "I think . . . I think they were seventeen, too!"

"Did you murder these innocent people?" asked Salazar, suspiciously.

When the prisoner failed to answer in a timely manner, Salazar backhanded him. Jesse giggled. "Tell me!" shouted Salazar. "Did you murder these innocent people?"

"It's not my fault!" the prisoner cried. "It's not my fault God made me this way!"

"God?" gasped Salazar. "You sick son of a bitch, God had nothing to do with this!"

"God told me to eliminate the nonbelievers!" the prisoner explained. "They belonged to the Brotherhood of Faith, and supported Theo. I'm only following His commandments!"

Salazar squinted. "And just who is your god?"

The prisoner dug through a pocket for a medallion, with the rattlesnake coiled around a sword. Salazar and Patrick were speechless. Only Jesse seemed unaffected by this development. "God is everywhere, and in everything," he said, sarcastically.

"It's not my fault!" the prisoner argued. "God told me to eliminate the nonbelievers!"

Salazar ripped his sword from its scabbard. "Did he also tell you to keep that little boy's privates as a souvenir?"

"No, sir!" Patrick reached for the handle of Salazar's sword, and prevented him from taking matters into his own hands.

"You're absolutely correct, Patrick," breathed Salazar, looking the prisoner in the eye. "I'd just as soon kill you, myself. However, my orders state that you must be tried in a court of law."

With that, Salazar drove his fist into the prisoner's gut.

As air rushed from his mouth, the prisoner doubled over. "Does your high and mighty rules forbid me to do that, Patrick?" growled Salazar.

"Forbid what?" laughed Jesse. "I didn't see a blessed thing. What about you, Pat?"

Patrick couldn't entirely fault Salazar for that one violation. At any rate, Salazar's actions weren't worthy of comment. Who'd the admiralty believe?

"I'll enjoy watching you hang," Salazar told the prisoner. "Where will your god be, then? Swinging next to you, with a rope around his neck! *Jesse!*"

"Sir?" asked Jesse.

"Take this animal to Admiral Kraig and General Chang. Patrick, fill out a charge slip, so the brass knows what this is about."

"What about them?" asked Jesse, pointing to the men on the burro.

"Leave them here, so the dogs and worms can fight over them. At least they won't testify on their own behalf."

Jesse unhitched the dead men from the burro, and let them drop into the dusty street.

It had been a long day, never to be forgotten or forgiven. All Salazar wanted to do was relax, open a bottle of Romero's finest Scotch, and get drunk.

Embrey is dead . . . My beloved Embrey is dead!

"I'll be at headquarters by sundown," informed Salazar. "Get that bastard out of my sight, Jess, before I earn a court-martial offense, and upset Patrick's sensitive idealism. One more thing, Jess. Don't let him get away. You may follow that order any way you want, but I don't care to report on it . . ."

33

"Where is General Gornick?" the interrogator demanded, dunking the prisoner's head into a whiskey barrel filled with water. Seconds later, the prisoner was yanked up by his hair, for a quick breath. *"Where* is General Gornick?"

"I don't know!" the prisoner screamed, sucking in needed oxygen.

"Then where is God?" the interrogator asked, again lowering the prisoner's head into the barrel.

Once the Ministry of War fell under Gornick's command, Embrian loyalists fortified themselves in a makeshift tent community, at an empty field outside of town.

The location was a hotbed of activity. Officers and staff mapped out strategies of ousting Gornick from the War Ministry, while also ridding themselves of the Branellian invaders. Soldiers and civilians constructed four high walls of mortar, stone, and log poles. The fortress engulfed an area of nearly ten square acres. While it gave combatants a minor level of protection, the fortress was also regarded as a deathtrap.

Jesse arrived at this post, with his one prisoner. Within minutes, the prisoner was stripped naked and chained to a fifty-gallon barrel of water, used to extract information. The interrogator was a giant of a man with long brown hair, and a gray mustache. Smiling, he beat the prisoner with a leather strap. The prisoner's spine, legs, and backside were marked with red, bloody stripes, as his nude body burned in the hot sun.

Lazing in the shade of the parasol, Jesse drank brandy and treated the interrogation as a joyous spectacle.

Gaining admission by two guards, Salazar and his men entered the fortress. As their horses were taken to a hastily-crafted livery stable, he wandered to a set of long tables outside a large canvas tent, where the general staff were.

Patrick was drawn to the interrogation. He was torn by what he saw at this 'fact finding' mission. Horrified by the prisoner's criminal activities, he couldn't approve of this form of punishment. Carefully, he approached Jesse and the interrogator.

"You don't know where General Gornick is?" the interrogator questioned, harshly. "How can you not know?"

"I don't know!" the prisoner gagged, water dripping from his face and hair. "I told you, I don't *know!"*

"Keep telling me you don't know until you miraculously find out!" the interrogator shouted, again dunking the prisoner. "I'll bet you do know where I can find General God or Lord Gornick? Where is He?"

"God knows all and sees all," said Jesse, swigging the brandy. "The Father, the Son, and the Holy Gornick."

"What's going on?" asked Patrick, disapprovingly.

"Just enjoying the show." Jesse handed Patrick the bottle. "Pull up a chair, and take a snort."

"If I'm not mistaken, didn't the Embrian Council ban this barbaric practice?" asked Patrick.

"Barbaric?" argued Jesse, as the interrogator laughed. "You saw what this nutjob did today. You call what we're doing 'barbaric'?"

"Then what you're doing is illegal," said Patrick, nearly losing his cool. "Councillor Theo has ruled that flogging is . . ."

"Councillor Theo can kiss my fat ass," the interrogator cut in. "Too bad he ain't here."

"Yes," said Patrick, anxiously. "But his son is."

As Yuri entered the fortress with five students from Lord Kelly's Academy, the interrogator shot a nervous glance at Patrick. Jesse hopped to his feet, sporting a grin.

"Help me unshackle him!" the interrogator ordered Patrick.

Fetching a set of keys from the ground, Patrick unlocked the chains bonding the prisoner. The prisoner collapsed, in extreme pain and exhaustion.

Yuri went the interrogation site. Things grew tense. Jesse and Yuri stared at each other, in a mute challenge to end their differences, once and for all. "Yuri," addressed Jesse, breaking the silence.

"Jesse," replied Yuri.

"Are you . . . *friends?*" asked Patrick, quietly.

"We go way back," answered Jesse, refusing to turn his back on Yuri. Somehow, he maintained a calm facade. "Moving up in the world, Yuri? An Embrian Councillor's son? Not bad. Not bad at all."

Yuri ran his fingers along Jesse's cape and tunic. "Who's your tailor?" he asked, feigning interest.

"A eunuch from Corapal. To my grave misfortune, he died of a nasty snake bite, a few weeks ago."

Yuri snickered.

"You have nice taste in clothes, too," said Jesse, admiring Yuri's robe. "If you don't mind my saying."

"Father makes sure I'm well-groomed." Yuri looked at the prisoner. "What is this?"

Jesse chuckled. "Oh, just a little harmless fun. Surely you'd approve, if you knew what the fiend did to deserve this."

"Father will be most disturbed by this torture," responded Yuri, pointedly.

"Let's make it our little secret, Yuri," proposed Jesse. "You know, between friends. I doubt if this wretched fool would have survived the jaunt here, had he been under your loving care."

Yuri found it difficult to conceal his hatred of Jesse.

"My, but who are the skirted lads with you?" asked Jesse, referring to the students from Lord Kelly's. "Choirboys?"

"Friends of mine."

"*Amazing!* You have friends, now! My, what a lovely surprise!"

"Yes," answered Yuri, getting hot under the collar. "Much nicer than the ones we knew at Maliek's school."

"*Hmm . . .*" mulled Jesse. "I rather enjoyed our old chums there, most especially Marietto."

"Marietto was your friend, not mine," said Yuri, awkwardly. "I never liked him."

Jesse grinned. "I gathered that, after what you did to him."

Yuri frowned.

"Pray tell, how did that chap get so bloody?" asked Jesse, pointing at Andre.

"Surely, you'd approve," mocked Yuri, "if you knew what his opponent did to deserve it."

"Commander Salazar needs me," said Patrick, hastily leaving the interrogation site.

"You know, Yuri, I've got my orders to hunt you down." Jesse smirked. "Somehow, you always eluded me! I believe the idea was to make you *disappear*. Regrettably, your adoption by Councillor Theo makes that a tad inconvenient, perhaps even impossible."

"For you," said Yuri, no jest in his voice. "What makes you think I committed the crimes of which I'm charged?"

"Don't insult my intelligence."

"What intelligence, Jesse?"

"Well, just think, Yuri. Who else is twisted enough to carve poor Macready into itsy-bitsy pieces?"

"It wasn't me!" stated Yuri. "For all we knew, it was Tim or Conrad who murdered . . ."

"Surely, you're far brighter than that," taunted Jesse. "Timmy wouldn't, and Conrad couldn't."

Yuri sighed. "I'm telling you, why would I kill Macready?"

"Oh, it matters precious little, now. Your status in Embrian society forbids me to take action against you . . . for the time being."

Yuri gritted his teeth. "For the time being."

"Well, congratulations are in order, for Theo's adoption of you." A twinkle sparkled in Jesse's eye. "What are you offering Theo, in exchange? The same favors you gave that lovely pageboy in Kentworth, before separating him from his beating heart?"

"That's a lie!" screamed Yuri. "Why do people keep saying that about me?"

"Calm yourself, Yuri dearest. Rumors, that's all. Just nasty little rumors. I shouldn't worry myself over it. At least, *I* shouldn't."

This conversation had gotten too scary, even for the interrogator, who also departed. The prisoner also wished to go, but suffered from the interrogator's uncompromising discipline.

"Captain Maliek taught us many things," said Yuri. "Too bad he didn't teach you to shut your mouth, or how to swim!"

"Unkind!" laughed Jesse, unwilling to admit that Yuri's remark was painful. "Is that any way to speak to an old friend?"

"We were never friends!" said Yuri, and walked away.

"Ta-ta," whispered Jesse, effeminately. "Later."

"You'd better hope not," said Yuri, unable to hide his anger and frustration.

From a distance, Bradley witnessed Yuri's exchange with that weird kid in the fancy clothes. He wondered what had gotten Yuri so riled up. At Lord William's, Yuri killed Samuel. Yet, a trading of barbs moved him to tears. "You all right?" asked Bradley.

"It's nothing," moped Yuri. *"Nothing!"*

Bradley frowned, but kept still.

"Sit down," Yuri told the students. "Please, sit! I'll see to it that we get something to eat, while I arrange an escort to Father's."

"If it's all the same to you, Brad and I can look out for ourselves," said Kenichi.

"No, no," insisted Yuri. "Your friends await you, at my father's."

Kenichi squinted. "Just who are you talking about?"

"Giorgio," answered Yuri. "Eduardo, Geoff, Randy, the dumb-looking one in the torn clothing."

As Yuri went to chat with members of the general staff, Kenichi said to Bradley, "As soon as we get to his father's, let's get out of there."

"What about Trevor and Derek?" asked Bradley.

"They'll be in good hands with Theo, and we're better off on our own."

Bradley sneered. It was wrong to leave his spiritual family, in a time of crisis.

"Trevor," Kenichi told the younger boy. "I don't want you or Derry leaving. Stay together."

"Don't worry," assured Trevor. "We're not going anywhere!"

Andre sat on the ground, at one corner of the fortress. He knew that Bradley and Kenichi blamed him for the conflict at Lord William's. In grief and sadness, he isolated himself from everyone.

Needing to chat in private, Bradley and Kenichi rested at a secluded patch of receding grass. "You're not having second thoughts about coming with me?" asked Kenichi. "Are you?"

"No," answered Bradley, uneasily. "But what about Trev and Derry?"

"What about them? I told you, they're better off without us, and we're better off without them. We'll be on the road soon. Best of all, we'll be far away from here! I'm still going to Mount Patten next spring, and I want you with me!"

As Derek fell right to sleep, Trevor stared up at the deep, blue sky. Recurring images continued to haunt him.

Bradley had developed a much greater appreciation of his chums, and wasn't ready to let go. He was as dependent upon Trevor and Derek, as they were upon him. Under the circumstances, Bradley should've granted words of support and kindness to Trevor, who found it impossible to sleep. By helping Trevor, Bradley also helped himself. As much as he loved and respected him, Bradley thought that Kenichi was acting selfishly, for abandoning Trevor and Derek.

On the other hand, Bradley pinned Quinn's death squarely on Andre. To bad it wasn't Andre smothering to death on his own blood!

No, don't say that! Andre just screwed up! He didn't mean to screw up!

Just like I screwed up, by going into that backroom with Leni!

Maybe I should have died, instead of Quinn!

No one's worthy of God's love and forgiveness! Everyone *and* everything's screwed up, in this ugly world!

Bradley felt sorry for those who lost their lives. Karl, Sven, Antoine . . . he even felt badly for Samuel and the weasel! Most of all, he was sorry for Quinn! Why did Quinn have to die? Why him? Why not me?

His insides twisted around like a pretzel, Bradley didn't want to face what he regarded as horrifying truth. Karl, Sven, and Quinn were dead! There was no denying it! Entire neighborhoods were destroyed, with shattered buildings and shattered lives, of human depravity and human despair!

Kenichi wanted to leave Sykes, and his younger roommates, as if nothing ever happened. Naturally, Bradley had to keep going, like the survivor he was destined to be. But how?

Bradley had no idea where most of his schoolmates were. In all likelihood, a few had perished in the slaughter. But not Trevor and Derek. The two boys were alive. *Alive!* And, because they were alive, Bradley and Kenichi had to take care of them!

"You can still serve God, if you want to," said Kenichi "I think you should, Brad! If there really is a god, He's lucky to have you on His side!"

Bradley had to start over. Lord Kelly's would not reopen for a long time, if ever. Bradley didn't want Kenichi calling all the shots. He had a say in his own destiny! No matter the path Bradley and Kenichi took in the coming days, weeks, and months, Trevor and Derek were tagging along.

Bradley patted Kenichi's knee. "I'll go anywhere with you, I promise," he said, hesitantly. "But are you willing to go anywhere with *me?*"

"Good afternoon," greeted Yuri, to members of the Embrian general staff.

Admiral Kraig, General Chang, and other top dogs in the brass glared at Yuri. Their opinions of him ranged from disdain, to distrust, to outright contempt.

"Yuri!" cheered Salazar, leaving his chair at the table to give the boy a warm handshake. "How are you, my young friend?"

"Very well," said Yuri, smiling. "Congratulations on your promotion, *Lieutenant Commander* Salazar."

"Thank you."

The majority of officers at the table were astounded with Salazar's ignorance and naivete. Salazar had no idea who he was dealing with! Patrick already held negative feelings about Yuri and Jesse, and thought it best to walk away.

"Does everyone here know Yuri?" Salazar asked his superiors.

"We know him," said Chang, flatly.

"State your business, Yuri," demanded Kraig.

"I'm with those students from Lord Kelly's Academy," said Yuri. "We need a meal, and an escort to Father's."

"Oh, I'm sure we can arrange that," answered Salazar, cordially.

"We can give you some bread, a little venison," said Chang, hesitantly. Supplies were low, and were to be rationed for an indefinite period.

"We appreciate anything you can give us," said Yuri, put off by Chang and Kraig's tone.

Admiral Kraig got to his feet. "As to the escort to Councillor Theo's, I'm not so sure . . ."

"I'll take them," offered Salazar. He did this, not for Theo's sake, but for his own. He had endured unimaginable humiliation, from the death of Reginald and the two guards. He needed the opportunity to demonstrate his leadership skills, while reminding Theo and Kohl that he was still around. This, for his pleasure, and their discomfort.

"Are you sure, Commander Salazar?" warned Kraig. "It might be dangerous."

"If we depart under the cover of darkness, we'll make it," assured Salazar.

"Oh, we'll make it, all right," said Jesse, welcoming himself to the table. "You're in very good hands, Commander, with me and my old pal, Yuri."

Jesse's intrusion aggravated Yuri. It was just like that jackass, to butt into everyone's affairs. Jesse was just begging for a fight!

In due time, Jesse, in due time . . .

Then we'll see who's laughing!

"Thanks for your help," snickered Kraig, amused by Yuri and Salazar's sour reaction to Jesse.

"All in the line of duty, Admiral Kraig," said Jesse, grinning.

Yuri frowned at Jesse, but said nothing.

"I'd like a word with you, Yuri," said Kraig, sternly. "If you don't mind."

As an Councillor's son, Yuri didn't merit unwarranted disrespect from anyone! Reluctantly, he left the table with Kraig.

Salazar wanted to remedy Jesse's rude behavior. Before he got a chance to reprimand the insolent teen, Jesse wagged a finger at him. *"Ah, ah, ah!"* scolded Jesse, like a mother correcting her small child. "You of all people should know better than be fooled by Yuri's effete nature and loving mannerisms."

"What's that supposed to mean?" questioned Salazar, angrily.

"Watch your back around the darling little Kuschan," advised Jesse. "Trust me, just watch your back."

Insulted by Jesse's demeaning attitude, Salazar retreated to his tent, where a bottle of liquid encouragement awaited him.

It wasn't Romero's, but who cared? It'd do . . .

"You've got a lot of gall coming here," Kraig told Yuri, as the two stopped beside a horse stall.

"I was told to take those students to Father's," said Yuri, defensively.

"Why? I should think that would be the last place to take anyone, especially now."

"I have my orders!" shouted Yuri. "Why must I explain myself to you, Admiral Kraig? My father outranks you, and your colleagues at that table!"

"In a state of war and martial law, the military outranks everyone," said Kraig. "Don't forget that. What makes you think your father's even home? For all we know, either Gornick or the Branellians have apprehended him."

Yuri had already pondered that very question. He was still willing to risk a long trip in the dark. "He's probably at his secret compound, in our backwoods."

"I've been there," said Kraig, tempering his heavy-handedness. "Your father and I rarely agree on anything, but he is an Embrian Councillor. As such, I'll see to it that his wishes are carried out."

"Thank you, Admiral Kraig."

"But, as for you, Yuri. It's not safe for you to be here, especially since you are Theo's adopted son."

"I didn't kill Macready, if that's what you're thinking," said Yuri.

"You've been accused of it."

"Why would I kill Macready? Father tried negotiating a peace deal with the Branellians, long before he adopted me. He sponsored Macready's trip into Kentworth, the same as you did!"

"Then who did assassinate Macready?" asked Kraig. "I know it wasn't Jesse."

"Jesse," commented Yuri. "What a boastful, arrogant clown! Why couldn't you find someone better than Jesse to protect Salazar?"

"Why should that matter to you?"

"I like Lieutenant Commander Salazar."

"Is that why you killed three of his men?" asked Kraig, pointedly. "But you were only following orders. Right, Yuri? Well, General Chang and I ordered Salazar to collect my brother, Major Kohl. Theo's orders and your actions violated my directives!"

"You've done your share of killing too, Admiral Kraig," reasoned Yuri.

"Yes," agreed Kraig, "but you're regarded as a loose dagger. Some day it'll catch up with you."

"Tell me, Admiral Kraig," said Yuri, tiredly. "Have you given Jesse that same speech, or is it meant for only me? Let me guess . . . Jesse works for you now, doesn't he? You approve of that particular loose dagger, but not me."

"I'm doing Councillor Theo and those schoolboys a favor," said Kraig. "That doesn't include you. I can detain you for as long as I want. You got any more smart remarks, or should I make Jesse's day by placing you in irons?"

Yuri said nothing.

"Very well, then," said Kraig. "I'll allow Salazar to escort you and those boys to your father's. I'll assign a company of men, as convoy."

"Thank you," said Yuri, bowing graciously.

"Be ready at two in the morning," said Kraig. "And Yuri . . . your father may be an Embrian Councillor, but you're nothing to me. Once you leave this fortress, I never want to see you again. Is that understood?"

"Yes, Admiral Kraig," agreed Yuri, knowing he'd never win the naval officer's respect or approval. Well, so be it! "Understood . . ."

Circling the area around Councilor Theo's home, Giorgio and Dimitri were unnerved, not by what they saw, but what they couldn't see.

Nothing. Not a sign of life or movement anywhere on the property. Usually, workers were busy in the fields and orchards. Admiral Kraig had recently placed infantrymen on the facility, to "protect" Major Kohl and Theo.

That afternoon, not a soul was there.

Giorgio expected to see the yard littered with bodies of the household staff, soldiers who died fighting Branellians or Gornick loyalists, shattered windows, doors smashed in, and Theo or Kohl hanging from the flagpole. The home remained intact. Overhead, an Embrian flag fluttered proudly in the wind.

All was quiet. *Too* quiet. The only sounds came from chirping birds, a calm breeze, and a donkey braying in the distance. As Giorgio and Dimitri debated on searching the house, their family and friends awaited at the graves of Salazar's former aide, and the two guards.

Dimitri sighed. "Well, there's nothing more to do here than to follow Yuri's orders, and go to that compound where, presumably, Councillor Theo is."

"We hope," mumbled Giorgio. "If that compound's really there."

"It better be!" exclaimed Dimitri. "I didn't drag my family out here for the fun of it!"

Giorgio glanced through a narrow, overgrown lane. "What if Yuri directed us to a dead end? No shelter, or anything? What if Yuri lied to us?"

"Why would he lie? Yuri's dedication to Councillor Theo is . . ."

"It's just that . . ." Giorgio shrugged. "I don't know. I'm not sure if I can trust Yuri."

"Why not? He trusts you!"

"But he gives me the creeps!" admitted Giorgio.

"I've known Yuri since he was a small boy in St. Alexandrov, long before he had to fend for himself, and long before that Maliek character . . ." Dimitri stopped. It was best never to mention Yuri's life as an assassin. "I'm aware that Yuri's different."

"Very!"

"But make no mistake about it," added Dimitri. "I love Yuri like a brother. I'd trust him before I'd trust most anyone." Dimitri glared at Giorgio. "if there's someone here I don't trust, it's you!"

Giorgio's heart skipped a beat.

"I don't think you've been entirely honest with me," continued Dimitri, sternly. "Something tells me you know more about those murders at Lord Kelly's than you're willing to say. You, and that drunken lout in the tattered school uniform."

Giorgio shook his head, as his throat tightening. He wanted to confide with Dimitri, yet considered speaking half-truths, or half-lies. "I went in Karl's office," he said. "What I found there, I . . . I just had to keep it from Geoffrey and the younger boys!"

"What about Fritz?" asked Dimitri. "What's he know?"

"I . . . I don't know."

Dimitri's head and heart were conflicted. It wasn't in his nature to pounce upon a suspected wrongdoer. Still, once they reached Theo's compound, he planned to keep watch over Giorgio and Fritz. Truth had a way of unearthing itself, in time. "If you'd like to talk, feel free to do so," offered Dimitri. "As for Yuri, I'd stake my life on him. Not just my life, but that of my wife and kids."

Nodding, Giorgio mouthed *okay.*

As Dimitri went to the others, Giorgio caught sight of someone opening a rear window of Theo's home, then crawl inside.

Fritz . . .

*S*neaking through a narrow hallway of Theo's house, Fritz thought of himself as an adventurer, in search of booty. Similar to his quest in Sven's quarters, this journey had its share of dangers.

The fat politician probably hightailed it, once he learned that Branellians and guys with snakes on their shirts aimed to knock him off. Why did he leave without first collecting personal items and treasures, left there for the taking by those lucky enough to find the joint, unattended?

Such as Fritzy?

Fritz had an opportunity to liberate all sorts of goodies from the premises. Too bad. In his modified school uniform, he couldn't take anything of real value. There were a few paintings which could be sold on the black market. Fritz wasn't interested in that. Instead, he looked for items to share with his buddies, even that heathen preacher and his nagging wife. He'd be doing Theo a huge favor, by taking a few bottles of liquid refreshment to its rightful owner.

He sought to salvage any and all of the Campens Rose', which was left behind.

So, just where did Theo keep the good stuff?

Fritz slipped into Theo's room where a modest bed sat in one corner. He figured the fat politician would've owned a lavish bed, featuring gold-plated posts and costly blankets. There was only a single straw mattress, a wool quilt, and a stained, cottonwood frame. The walls were adorned with bookcases, filled with volumes of world literature, antique weaponry, and cast iron statuettes.

But no booze . . .

Theo's room was fancy, when compared with Urine's. All Fritz found in the little freak's bedroom was a teensy bed, a Kuschan flag with its single blue star against a white backdrop, and a painting of the fat politician and queer stepson. Like Giorgio, Fritz was afraid of the weirdo! Just being in Urine's room made him shutter!

Get a move on it, Fritzy! No time to lose!

Fritz figured he had a social and moral duty to preserve any of the Campens Rose' left on the property. Not to mention that he was dying for a drink!

Was that a door that just opened, and then closed?

And what about those footsteps, coming his way?

Fritz didn't know whether to laugh, scream, run, or crap himself. Who else was traipsing around the house? Fritz smiled at his own expense. He'd either get several years in the pokey or a trip to the gallows, for breaking into a VIP's house! He didn't conceal nor deny fear, as chills ran down his spine.

Screw the hooch . . .

I'm outa here!

As Fritz sprinted from Urine's room, his path was blocked by someone wearing a long, brown robe, along with a sour expression.

Giorgio!

Giorgio wanted to beat Fritz's butt, for infractions real, imaginary, or merely guessed at. In response, Fritz acted like a kid with his hand in the cookie jar. As he shuffled his sinewy legs, both eyes revealed criminal intent.

"Just what do you think you're doing?" demanded Giorgio.

"Me?" asked Fritz, innocently. "What about you?"

"I always knew you were a thief, but I thought you'd never stoop so low as to steal from an Embrian Councillor!"

"It wasn't stealing!" argued Fritz. "And besides, what difference does it make? What makes a guy like Theo any better'n you or me? He's just a fella, as far as I can tell . . ."

"But he's my friend!"

"So whatcha gonna do about it?" cackled Fritz. "Drag my sorry ass to Karl, like what you did to Brad yesterday? Betcha feel real good about yerself. Don'tcha, *Leader* Giorgio?"

"Dimitri's onto us!" whispered Giorgio.

"Huh?"

"Dimitri's onto us!" repeated Giorgio. "He knows we had something to do with . . . With what happened to Sven, Karl, and Antoine . . ."

"The hell I did!"

"The hell you didn't! What about that bottle you whacked over Antoine's head?"

Fritz pointed at the scar on his thigh. "What was I s'posed to do, let 'em cut my balls off?"

Giorgio sighed. "So, what do you think you're doing, sneaking around in here?"

"I gotta use the crapper."

"The crapper? Fritz, can't you see that small building, not thirty yards from here?"

"This is only my second time at this joint. How am I s'posed to know? . . ."

"All right, just forget it!" screamed Giorgio, impatiently. "Let's go, before we get caught . . ."

"Too late!" a low, booming voice shouted, from one end of the hallway. "You're done caught!"

Fritz and Giorgio turned to see a tall, heavyset soldier, clad in a black uniform featuring the rattlesnake and sword.

With a nervous chuckle, Fritz ran to the open window, from where he first entered the house . . .

. . . only to spot a second Gornick man, blocking his path.

The first soldier grinned, as he waved a saber at both teens. "Too late, boys," he laughed. "You're done caught . . ."

Giorgio and Fritz were dragged from the house by two brawny soldiers, then ordered to stand at the gate. They were joined by their fellow students, along with Pastor Dimitri and his family. All had been apprehended by a number of infantrymen, under General Gornick's command.

The students and Kuschan immigrants watched as the soldiers stormed through the house, taking everything of value while disregarding the rest. A few men conducted themselves in an orderly manner. Others carelessly smashed windows and furniture. As antiques and jewelry sat in one corner of the yard, "unworthy" items were thrown in a pile, then torched. That included tables, chairs, cots, and hundreds of books. The Embrian flag was cut loose from its pole, and replaced by a banner displaying the rattlesnake and sword.

A couple of soldiers celebrated their crimes, while trading a bottle of Campens Rose'. Occasionally, they made racial slurs at the Kuschans, who had no choice but to suffer this indignity. As Dimitri faced this adversity in a stoic fashion, Yana and the children were visibly upset. To appease his father and the Kuen, Alexei dared to look his persecutors in the eyes.

Giorgio feigned a calm demeanor, despite his dry mouth, sweaty palms, and racing heart. Sergio and Giuseppe were confused by the soldiers' actions, as Eduardo stood at their sides, whispering words of comfort and encouragement. Geoffrey clutched Randy's hand, as he fought an urge to weep. Meanwhile, Fritz spouted idle threats under his breath. He didn't care about the literature, furnishings, or that ugly painting of Urine and his fat step-daddy which was tossed into the flames.

He was pissed off at the grunts who selfishly hoarded all that fine booze!

An older man stepped toward the detainees. With piercing eyes, a hooked nose, and a dress military uniform, he quietly evaluated his captives. His cocky, arrogant demeanor infuriated or frightened the prisoners.

As Fritz held off desires to spit in the man's face, Giorgio attempted to meet this situation with a stiff upper lip. Thoughts of seeing his friends executed nearly make him break down.

Giorgio was scared. *Damned scared!* It was bad enough to die. He preferred doing so alone, if it spared the others. Or so he told himself. If given the chance, would Giorgio sacrifice himself for his schoolmates? Surely, he'd take a blade for the twins, Eduardo, possibly even Geoffrey and Randy.

But Fritz?

Giorgio wished to speak on everyone's behalf. With his luck, it'd come out a whines and pleas. He was afraid of appearing as a crybaby or a fraud. Turning to Giuseppe and Sasha, he offered nothing more than a shrug.

The man introduced himself as Major Conroy. "And if I didn't mind the waste of a good rope," he added, assuredly, "I'd hang the filthy Kuschans."

"For your information, I speak Embrian!" shouted Dimitri. "As for hanging the 'filthy Kuschans,' you'd better start with me!"

"Dimitri!" cried Yana, as Sasha and Grigori cuddled to their parents.

Conroy stared at Dimitri, in grudging respect disguised as contempt. "Spoken like a pure Embrian, which you are not," he commented. "You're a Kuschan holy man, scaring your meager congregation with fables of winged men and nude boys impaled upon swords."

Fritz smirked.

"Me and Giuseppe ain't no Kuschans!" yelled Sergio. "We're Embrians, working as shoemakers for Geoffrey's stupid brother!"

"You show the fine courage and savvy of an Embrian," stated Conroy, motioning at Eduardo. "However, I suspect that your friend is the bastard child of a loin-clothed, Actonian savage and fair-skinned whore, best suited to serve pastries and tea for wealthy landlords. Just like the niggers my family own."

Eduardo wiped away the tear, sneaking from one eye.

"And a blind man can see that *you'll* never be of pure Embrian stock," said

Conroy, taking notice of Geoffrey's hand, clutched tightly around Randy's. "Your perversions are not the will of God, but a weakness deriving from your own godless souls!"

Geoffrey released Randy' hand and stepped away. It was no use. His nervous eyes had already revealed his tender feelings for Randy.

"You and your associate belong in the King's royal bedroom, not within the hallowed walls of Lord Kelly's Academy!" laughed Conroy

"I had to spend two years with Ogden!" informed Randy, painfully. "No one said I liked it!"

"Well now, at least you fess up to it." Mockingly, Conroy rubbed his palm across Randy's face, as his fingers caressed the boy's hair. "General Gornick has stated that we don't have that phenomenon in Embrey, which can only mean one thing. You're Branellian spies, trading in your kilts for . . ."

"Leave them alone!" screamed Giorgio, expecting a harsh reprimand for daring to speak up. "I . . . *I* was the one who brought these people here!"

"Why?" questioned Conroy. "This home belongs to a degenerate criminal, posing as an Embrian Councillor."

"Councillor Theo's a very honorable man!" argued Giorgio. "Better than the racist pig you bow down to!"

"An honorable man?" debated Conroy. "Better than the racist pig I bow down to? And to think I took you for an educated man! Very well, then. Allow me to educate you on the innocent lives taken by that honorable man, with the help of his treacherous, Kuschan bodyguard."

"I don't know what you're talking about!" claimed Giorgio, his voice high-pitched and raspy.

"Really?" snickered Conroy. "You don't know that your very honorable man and his horrid stepson are responsible for the deaths of three Embrian soldiers, buried at the very spot we picked up the Kuschan dogs and your Embrian cohorts?"

"Liar!" snapped Giorgio. "Councillor Theo loves this country too much to commit . . ."

"You suggest that Councillor Theo loves his country, and I don't?" questioned Conroy. "You don't know the man as well as you think. Let me clue you in on something, smart guy. Presently, Embrey's in a state of martial law, as we eliminate those advocating lawlessness. It's about time we restored Embrey to its former glory."

"You're talking revolution," said Dimitri, "with Gornick in charge."

"Why not?" asked Conroy. "General Gornick is an uncompromising man, and will rule Embrey in an uncompromising manner. Despite your foolish notions of equality and justice, a revolution is not a literary event or a social dinner, and can never be carried out with eloquence or courtesy. A revolution is an act of violence."

"Does that give you a right to come here and take whatever you want?" asked Giorgio.

"To the victor go the spoils." Conroy smiled. "You're obviously educated enough to understand my reasons for this looting. What brought you here?"

Giorgio didn't answer.

"Come on, tell me," insisted Conroy. "Why are you here? Is it to kiss the honorable man's fat ass, or to steal from him? What did you expect to find in his home? Antiques, or a bit of priceless jewelry, stashed here and there?"

"Campens Rose'!" said Fritz. "Woulda had me some too, but yer men are too greedy to share!"

"Well, now!" laughed Conroy, slapping Fritz's shoulder. "Perhaps you're the closest thing we have to a pure Embrian, in the whole rotten lot. A powerful physique, the ruggedly handsome face."

Fritz grinned.

"Yet, what does the ruined school uniform say of your true character?" questioned Conroy.

"A damn sight more than the ugly-ass snake on yers!" growled Fritz, his drunkenness getting the better of him.

Conroy frowned. "From what I see, you lack pride in your nation, as much as you lack faith in your spirituality."

"And what's your idea of a pure Embrian?" asked Giorgio, as fear slowly took charge. "You?"

"Sergeant Munro," Conroy said to an enlisted man. "Bring that boy to me. This high-minded moralist wants to know what a pure Embrian looks like."

After saluting Conroy, a pug-nosed sergeant went into the house, then returned with a male child of twelve. The boy was dressed in a black beret, and a long-sleeved tunic draped above two bare, knobby knees. As expected, the tunic featured the insignia of the sword and rattlesnake. The "pure Embrian" grinned as he noticed a few buddies among the detainees.

Violating Conroy's orders to stay put, Giuseppe broke rank and embraced the pure Embrian. *"Bentley!"* he cheered, happily. "I thought you was a goner!"

Bentley hugged Giuseppe, in response.

"Pure Embrian, my ass!" cursed Sergio. "Bentley's whacko, and his brother Andre's worse! My dumb brother's dumb for liking them!"

"Him?" Fritz sneered at Bentley. "What makes you think he's such hot shit?"

Conroy took Bentley under his arm. "Note the blue eyes, the blonde hair, and the fair complexion," he explained. "Even if God failed to bless him with the sharpest of minds or the quickest of wits . . ."

"You can say that again," whispered Eduardo.

" . . . In appearance, this boy is precisely what we desire in the Embrian race," said Conroy, as Bentley's eyes drooped and his jaw fell slack. "He is a prime example of what we seek in future generations. Your imperfections in heart, mind, and body only upholds my defense of him."

"How'd you like my imperfect Embrian foot up yer fat Embrian ass?" threatened Fritz.

"Maybe you'd like to try it," responded Conroy, belting Fritz across the face.

In retaliation, Fritz sent a clenched fist into Conroy's chin.

Practically everyone in sight responded with gasps and moans, as Conroy soon found himself on the ground.

As a trio of soldiers surrounded Fritz, Conroy struggled to get back on his feet. Comprehending the severity of his actions, Fritz's thoughts shifted from surprise, to mute horror, to awkward, shrill laughter.

Giorgio witnessed this occurrence with fear, mixed with envy and amazement. He wondered if he had it in him to save Fritz's life. Even if he disliked Fritz, he contemplated on accepting punishment for the bully's aggression against Conroy . . . if only he possessed the courage and convictions to do so.

"Hang that dirty bastard!" demanded Conroy, as Bentley helped him to his wobbly feet.

"If you're so high on the idea of hanging someone, why not me?" argued Dimitri.

"Dimitri, *no!*" screamed Yana, as Sasha and Grigori openly wept.

"What do you expect from me, Yana?" asked Dimitri, with growing anger and resentment. "For that matter, what does the Kuen expect from me? This morning, our home and church was burned to the ground. Must I forgo my dignity, as well?"

"What about our children?" cried Yana.

If Dimitri was willing to make the final sacrifice on Fritz's behalf, what concessions would Giorgio now have to consider? Assuming the Kuen called for Dimitri's death, did God ask the same of Giorgio?

His hands shaking uncontrollably, Giorgio knew what he had to do. What assurances were there that Conroy stopped with only Dimitri or Giorgio? What if he proceeded to kill Yana, Geoffrey, Randy, Eduardo, the twins, or even the pure Embrian himself, Brother Bentley? "Me," whispered Giorgio. Stepping forward, he was unable to look Conroy in the eye.

"Out of my way," ordered Conroy. Pushing Giorgio aside, he staggered to a spindly apple tree.

Two guards locked Fritz's arms behind his back, then led him to Major Conroy. A third positioned himself as a barrier against the students and Kuschans. Meanwhile, Bentley remained oblivious to it all. Tugging at Giuseppe's sleeve, he asked, "What're they gonna do to Fritzy?"

Normally, Fritz wouldn't have had it in him to challenge someone like Major Conroy. His thirst and intoxication from Campens Rose' had gotten him into trouble, before. Savoring the effects from indulging in expensive, bootleg elixir, Fritz quickly sobered up as he pondered the wisdom of striking Conroy.

As a soldier shaped a rope into a noose, others grabbed Fritz's flailing legs. Fritz struggled to break free. Obscenities spewed from his mouth.

"You're not so ruggedly handsome, now," giggled Sergeant Munro. "Are ya, tough guy?"

"I'm sorry!" apologized Fritz, in mounting terror. "You don't gotta hang me, I didn't mean it! Goddamn it, I'm sorry! I'm *sorry!*"

What is death? That question repeated in Fritz's head, as the rope was tossed over a limb. Frantically, Fritz weaved and bobbed his head to avoid the noose. He wondered what he'd know *(if anything!)* or where he'd go *(if anywhere!)* once the end came. Was there pain, a conscience sense in closure of one life, with the emergence of another? Or was it unknown, and unexplainable? Evaluating his life's choices, Fritz didn't especially care where his spirit was likely to go, if it even existed beyond death.

Not one to accept the existence of Heaven, Fritz suddenly believed in the possibilities of Hell. "Help me!" he screeched, his bad-boy image eroding to that of a panic-ridden, cowardly wretch. As the rope tightened around his gullet, he uttered frightened, nonsensical pleas to a celestial being he previously rejected. Was it too late to win God's approval?

And what was worse, spending an eternity in a fiery pit?

Or nothing?

Nothing . . . nothing . . .
NOTHING!

As Fritz let out a loud, ear-shattering shriek, the soldiers laughed as schoolmates witnessed his impending doom. His eyes darting in every direction, Fritz caught blurred images of the sky, the apple tree, the dome-shaped house, Giorgio and Eduardo and Dimitri and the silly, little pure Embrian. As the words "Son of a bitch!" shot from his mouth, frightened onlookers expected those to be his final words.

"Halt!" someone called, from the nearby forest. "*Halt!* Stay right where you are!"

Two dozen Embrian Rangers left the darkened woods from the west, and marched onto the homestead. They were led by a heavyset officer with a thick, brown beard, shaggy hair hanging over the ears, and three stars at each shoulder. The officer carried himself with poise and confidence, as he approached Major Conroy.

As Giorgio grinned in recognition of the officer, Dimitri recited a silent prayer.

Conroy wandered over to the officer and introduced himself.

"I'm General Gronky," the officer said.

"*Gronky?*" Conroy scratched his head. "Why, I've never heard of a General Gronky."

"I've never heard of you, either," answered Gronky.

"General Gronky, we caught two of these rotters breaking into Councillor Theo's home," explained Conroy.

"And that gives you the right to hang them from Councillor Theo's tree?" questioned Gronky. "Or steal from Councillor Theo? Or burn Councillor Theo's furnishings and books?"

"Sir, by the time General Gornick takes full command of the armed forces and government, Theo won't amount to a thing," said Conroy.

"Does that mean we no longer conduct ourselves like Embrians?" asked Gronky.

"I . . . I don't understand, General Gronky," mumbled Conroy.

"Is this vandalism the work of Embrians, or crimes committed by enemies of the Embrian state?" asked Gronky. "No decent Embrian stoops so low, as to hang Embrian children."

"Children?" Conroy pointed at Fritz. "Him?"

"Yeah!" whined Fritz. "I'm an Embrian children!"

"Major Conroy," said Gronky. "I need men to build a foot bridge across a river. I'll take these boys off your hands. Those Kuschans, too. They're as reliable of slave labor as I've ever known."

Conroy smiled. "If it's men you want, my men and I will be glad to throw in."

"No," said Gronky, flatly.

"But why? . . . why not, sir?" stuttered Conroy. "I'm sure my men will . . ."

"No," repeated Gronky. "I need weak minds and stout hearts. Your men possess certain necessary qualifications, but their fingers are too sticky for my trust."

"Very well," sighed Conroy. "You may have the prisoners. But if it's bridge builders you want, one of my lieutenants is a trained engineer."

"That will be all, Major Conroy," said Gronky.

Removing a knife from his belt, Gronky cut the rope loose from the tree. "I give you the opportunity to live, and prove your worth to a new order in Embrey," he told Fritz. "Will you give me a good day's work, and learn a useful trade? Or do I satisfy Major Conroy, by letting him watch you die like a petty thief?"

"I'll kiss yer ass from here to the Branellian Empire, if it means I don't get hung!" said Fritz, tossing the rope to his feet.

"A simple 'yes' or 'no' will suffice," said Gronky.

"I promise to do my best for you!" promised Giorgio.

"My family and I haven't an idle bone in our bodies," said Dimitri. "If it's a bridge you want built, we Kuschans . . ." He turned to Yana. "We *Embrians* will see it through."

"I've never doubted the integrity of Kuschans, or Embrians," said Gronky.

"Sir," said Conroy, hoping to gain Gronky's good graces. "If there's anything I can do?"

"What makes you think I want anything from you?" asked Gronky. "From what I've seen, those aren't soldiers you command, but thugs. I'd appreciate it if your men left this house alone. I personally lay claim to it, upon General Gornick's victory."

Conroy frowned. "Yes, sir."

"So do me a favor," demanded Gronky, "and get your thugs out of *my* house."

Conroy walked away in disapproval and disappointment.

"What about him?" Giorgio asked Gronky, pointing at Bentley.

"What about him?" questioned Gronky. "Looks mighty pea-witted to me."

"He is. But I want him in Major Kohl's army."

"Yeah," said Fritz. "Don'tcha know he's a pure Embrian? If you don't believe me, just ask him."

"As you wish," said Gronky, calling Giorgio and Dimitri to one side. "Where's my son?"

"He volunteered to find more of my schoolmates," informed Giorgio. "In Sykes.

"Sykes?" whispered Gronky, in horror.

"We tried talking him out of it, but you know Yuri," said Dimitri. "If he's not trying to please you or me, he'll lend a hand to his new friends, from Lord Kelly's."

Gronky scratched at the irritating beard. "I'll have Linus prepare a meal for everyone. I'll let the students sleep in the bunkhouse, at my compound. I hope that meets with your approval, Giorgio."

"It does," said Giorgio, putting an arm around Gronky's broad shoulders. "Thank you for coming to our rescue, *Councillor Theo*."

35

The recruits of Fort Cooley, led by Colonel Owensby, marched toward the mouth of the Ember River to catch "chicken-thieving Branellians" on the run. Owensby rode at the head of the pack, next to Captain Willowby and Sergeant Vix. Meanwhile, the recruits tagged along on foot, carrying an arsenal of garden tools.

Vix said little on this trip, as Owensby's lips never stopped flapping. Endlessly, the colonel boasted of his countless adventures, during his three decades in the Embrian Army.

Arriving at their destination, the recruits set up camp while keeping their eyes peeled for Branellians, coming by land or by sea. Discipline was a challenge, as the boys initially treated this excursion as a day at the beach. As a result, Vix and Willowby ordered them to do calisthenics. Even if the recruits complained, it kept Owensby off their backs.

As everyone prepped for dinner at four in the afternoon, the sky threatened rain. Vix tossed a dry log into the fire, next to the tent he shared with Willowby, and began cooking chow. He ignored Owensby's hot air and hooey, while placing sliced onions into a fry pan with venison and eggs. It was easier to fix the loudmouth's meal, while calming the Captain Willowby. As Owensby sipped from a pint of bourbon, Willowby sat quietly by the flames.

Owensby chided Vix and Willowby for their hesitation to take part in this mission against the "beady-eyed Branellians." He then shared a story of his heroism in the Wilderness, twenty years before. He claimed that, as a first lieutenant under then Colonel Chang, his platoon held off an attack at a frozen wasteland known as Sisko Canyon.

"I remember seeing Chang at Sisko Canyon," said Vix, staring into Owensby's nervous, flinching eyes. "Just like I remember Willowby's Uncle Alistair, *and* Major Kohl. But from my recollection, you wasn't at Sisko Canyon."

"I was too!" claimed Owensby. "Don't you dare contest my war record!"

"What war record?" asked Vix. "Them nights you got your ass thumped by Marines and sailors in cheap, waterfront whorehouses?"

"Sergeant Vix!" protested Owensby. "You haven't the right to dispute my account of Sisko Canyon!"

"How can I dispute it, if you wasn't there?" snickered Vix. "So you was under Chang's command? Me, too. What part of the canyon was you stationed?"

"At the base of Smelcer's Butte," blurted Owensby. "Where that creek drained into the river."

"I'll be damned. Never knew you was a prisoner of war. Branellians held that point the whole time. We never got nowhere near Smelcer's Butte."

"Damn you, Vix! I was too at Smelcer's Butte! What qualifies you to say I wasn't?"

"The river was covered with ice. I don't know how you coulda got that far."

"I . . . my men sneaked across it on foot, in the middle of the night," stuttered Owensby.

"Yeah, Chang did make a mistake by sending men across the river. Them poor boys stuck out like sore thumbs in the moonlight, and was sitting ducks for Branellian archers. None of them got back alive. They just laid out there on that ice 'til spring, when the river thawed out and swept 'em off."

Willowby laughed at the embarrassed expression on Owensby's face.

Put off by Vix's sharp memory, and lacking ammunition of his own, Owensby asked, "What did *you* do at Sisko Canyon?"

Vix rolled his sleeve up to reveal the wicked scar, still visible after twenty years. "I was with Kohl in one of them caves on the west bank, when a Branellian gave me this." He ran his finger along the length of the scar. "Damn near lost my arm and my life, on account of it."

Willowby whistled in amazement.

"Kohl," mumbled Owensby disparagingly, his jealousy revealing itself in his burning eyes and quivering lips. "What a joke."

"I wouldn't be here, if it wasn't for Major Kohl," argued Vix. "He saw more men fight and die defending Embrey, than you'll ever know."

"Oh, I doubt that very much," said Owensby, in a snotty tone.

"To hear you tell it, you took on entire Branellian regiments all by yourself," growled Vix. "Forget them who got killed, just so you can tell lies. It'd be one thing if you was at Sisko Canyon, but you wasn't. Had you been there, you wouldn't be so eager to talk about it."

"Why not?" asked Willowby, curiously.

"Wouldn't want to." Vix flipped over slices of bacon, sizzling in the pan. "Colonel Owensby, your damn lies are a slap in the face to those of us who was there. Go ahead and call Major Kohl a joke if you want to. I know his service to Embrey, so shut up about it."

"Take that back, or I'll have you up on charges!" hollered Owensby.

"Have me up on charges! General Chang knows what kinda man you are, and so do I. He also knows what kinda man Gornick is, and that's the worst kind!"

Vix had bested Owensby in front of Willowby. Even then, Owensby's rank gave him an advantage over an enlisted man, which he now utilized. Grinning maliciously, he said, "Despite your loud, blustery talk, you're a coward, Sergeant Vix. An insubordinate coward, at that."

"And you're a lying sack of shit," answered Vix. "You know it, I know it, Captain Willowby knows it, and so does ever'one else around here."

With a deep breath, Willowby imagined that Owensby's penalty against Vix would be stiff, and unyielding.

"That's all right," snickered Owensby, salving a bruised ego. "I may be a liar, but you're still an insubordinate coward. You and your pimple-faced captain. You proved it this morning. And I know exactly what to do with insubordinate cowards." Owensby pointed to a nearby hillside, overlooking the river, with a lone tree and a huge boulder on the horizon. "I'm placing you and *Corporal* Willowby on guard duty, upon that ridge there. What do you have to say for yourself now, *Private* Vix?"

36

The afternoon was drizzly, as tired men rested a few miles from their rendezvous point at the mouth of the Ember River.

News quickly spread along the coastline that King Ogden was murdered by a lone assassin. Although the Branellians' invasion had furthered the Embrians' hatred and fear, it also divided them. Not only did General Gornick wage war against the Branellians, he also fought his own citizens, which he planned to control through terror.

Scores of Branellians fled to the Agron Ocean, where Captain Shimura was expected to take them home. Instead of coming together as an organized unit, splinter groups scattered the region. Some perished in the fighting, while others were captured, interrogated, and executed. A few disappeared in the vast Embrian countryside, or began their long trek eastward.

Abandoned by the soldiers assigned to accompany him into Sykes, Copenhaver realized his part in the invasion had fallen apart. Hoping to steal goods and human cargo for buyers in Corapal and Branell, the smuggler had an empty sack. The last thing he expected was to be attacked by an army of boys with picks, hoes, rakes, and shovels. Copenhaver and his two partners, Bjorn and Wilde, were left with their own youthful guides. He wondered if Schlender, who led a separate party into Sykes, had fared better.

In five short years, Copenhaver and Schlender were among the most wealthy and accursed figures in the continent's underworld. Initially working for others, they now called the shots. People answered to them. Those challenging their power and dominance were either paid off, or eliminated. The two criminals owned several mayors and magistrates in Branell, and made life quite comfortable for corrupt leaders in Embrey, Campens, Kusch, and Corapal. With the snap of a finger, Copenhaver and Schlender got things done through their subordinates' sweat, toil, and effort.

Copenhaver now found himself near the windblown Embrian coast. More than anything, he needed a way back to Branell. Was it best to rely on a gook naval officer? Copenhaver didn't become an influential voice in the black market, simply to die in a goddamned war! Could he survive the long journey home, while burdened with idiot guides following him around like lost, sad-eyed puppy dogs?

At a bare hillside overlooking the ocean, Copenhaver decided to lessen his load by removing those he viewed as liabilities. He had to free himself from the brain-dead guides, along with two lazy, good-for-nothing bums named Bjorn and Wilde.

In the hazy fog and drizzle, Copenhaver approached Garry with his trusty man-killin' stick.

Garry knew what Copenhaver had in mind. Copenhaver was a ruthless bastard, all right. But was he really *that* mean?

Bjorn and Wilde leaned against a decaying fence post. Drinking whiskey, they were content to watch Copenhaver murder Garry in cold blood. Neither had a clue they were also on the hit-list. Even then, Garry shot a glance at the two lowlifes, pleading for their intervention. What good was that? Bjorn and Wilde smiled in anticipation of Copenhaver's grisly deed with the man-killin' stick.

Garry thought about running away. Who could he possibly depend upon, in a foreign land? If Copenhaver didn't nail him with that big club, what prevented Embrian sharpshooters from nailing the hapless guide?

Copenhaver began to swing the stick at Garry when, unexpectedly, his intended target was sent to the ground by a surprise tackle from the rear.

Since leaving Warren Dale, twelve-year-old Harold never once laughed, joked, made plans for the future, or passively accepted his ill-luck. The crybaby whined and complained throughout the entire trip, while constantly yearning for his harsh existence in the Branellian highlands.

Harold blindsided Garry with a clenched fist to the ear. Garry landed in the deep, damp grass, where he was practically buried in thick, gray and green foliage.

Before Garry even knew what hit him, Harold straddled him across the waist. Crazed from unceasing fear and panic, Harold pounded on Garry with erratic, clumsy shots to the head and torso.

Garry thought that Harold was no match for him. The little sissy hit like a girl. Regrettably, that same little sissy had Garry down on the ground, smashing his face. Garry lay there in a helpless daze. Looking up at a dark, overcast sky, he heard the smugglers giggling at him. Awkwardly, he retaliated against Harold with a few lucky shots to the chest or chin. For the most part, Harold had the upper hand over him.

As Garry attempted to shield himself from Harold, consciousness gradually faded away. He refused to hold it back. His life was little more than a nightmare, anyway. Never once did he paddle his own canoe, or have a say in his own decisions or future. He was conceived only to satisfy another person's needs and desires. He didn't ask for this existence in the cruel, violent world of the trades. He'd now pay the ultimate price, for trying to escape his pathetic fate.

A lousy end, to a lousy life.

Seconds before the lights went out, Sirro dragged Harold away from Garry.

Lying flat on the dewy ground, Garry was rattled. Every inch of his body hurt like sin. Inhaling quick breaths of moistened air, he rolled himself into a ball and wept.

Harold screamed like a spoiled brat, and slapped at Sirro.

Tired and fed up from a lack of food and sleep, Sirro shoved the terrified child against a tree.

Copenhaver stood to one side. He didn't want Sirro knowing his intentions to finish off the "dead weight." Anyway, Schlender had finally arrived with a couple of guides and a squad of Branellian infantrymen.

As the smugglers quietly chatted between themselves, Davy cradled Garry in his arms. "What happened?" he asked, caressing Garry's swollen face.

"Harold went nuts, and . . . and Mister Copenhaver tried killing me with his man-killin' stick!" sobbed Garry.

"What?" asked Davy, in disbelief.

"It's your fault, you bastard!" screamed Harold. "Why did you make me come here with you?"

"Pipe down, Harold!" shouted Ivor.

"You guys wanna stay in Embrey, not me!" bawled Harold.

Marc then planted a fist into Harold's stomach.

Doubling over, Harold dropped to the ground, as air rushed out of his mouth. "Shut the hell up, or I'll hit you harder next time!" threatened Marc, pulling

Harold's hair. "One more word, you won't have to wait around until Copenhaver whomps on you, 'cause I'll do it myself!"

Harold sat on the ground and whimpered.

Sirro crouched next to Garry and Davy. "I must deliver an important message to Councillor Theo," he whispered.

"He'll kill us if you go!" informed Garry.

"Who?" asked Sirro.

"Mister Copenhaver came at me with that man-killin' stick of his!" said Garry, wiping his bloody nose.

Sirro and Captain Shimura were to hand the smugglers over to the Embrian authorities, in exchange for political asylum. Sirro hoped that Garry and his young friends also benefitted in this arrangement. He possessed a secret letter for Councillor Theo from Branell's King Josiah, calling for peace between the two rival nations. He wanted to take the guides with him to Theo's compound, rather than leave them at the smugglers' mercy. In their kilts, who among the five boys passed as anything other than Branellians? "I can't risk taking you with me," informed Sirro.

"Why not just Garry?" suggested Davy. "That'll work out, won't it?"

"Can you handle those goons by yourself?" questioned Sirro. "Don't forget, you're still on foreign territory!"

"You gotta meet up with that Theo guy, right?" said Davy. "Take Garry with you, and put in a good word for us. Do you think Theo will hear us out?"

"He's been very good to me," acknowledged Sirro. "Garry, can you walk?"

Garry nodded, as Sirro and Davy lifted him to his feet. Teetering like a drunk, he nearly vomited. He remained dizzy and disoriented from the thrashing he took from Harold.

"How will you explain our disappearance?" Sirro asked Davy.

"Play dumb," answered Davy, brushing loose grass and dirt off of Garry's clothing. "I'm good at that."

Garry saw no humor in Davy's remark. The two boys were inseparable. It was troubling to know that, once more, they had to part. "Be careful, Dave," said Garry, thinking he'd never see his best friend, ever again.

"That goes double for you," said Davy. "Chin up, Garry! Take care of yourself, and bring us good news!"

Garry followed Sirro to Theo's compound, hidden deep within an evergreen forest. He had no idea where he was going, and felt out of place, and definitely out of step, in unfamiliar country.

Fear nearly drove Garry away, as desperation pushed him forward. He hoped he wasn't a burden on Sirro, as they ran toward this secret hideaway.

In a fiery glimmer of sunlight through darkened clouds, Sirro sprinted through the thickest, deepest brush Garry ever saw. Where Sirro was confident and sure-footed, Garry often tripped over low-lying limbs and vines. His clothes got caught in branches, which scratched his bare legs. An "expert guide" at the age of fourteen, Garry was a babe in these particular woods.

Garry released a tired sigh.

"Do you want to stop?" asked Sirro.

Garry was exhausted. Still, there was no time to lose. Peace was at stake! To play even a minor role in history wasn't so much exciting, as it was humbling! Still, there were probabilities of Theo refusing Garry any aide or sympathy. Why should an Embrian Councillor bother himself with a few dumb kids in kilts? They were only Branellians, so why bother?

Garry tried to keep his spirits up, by convincing himself that he was on the track to liberty and freedom.

Garry and Sirro spotted an outhouse overlooking several cottages, two bunkhouses, and a barn. A welcome sight for Sirro, the compound nearly motivated Garry to turn tail. Even fear prevented the boy from expressing fear.

Who knew that a man of Theo's importance and stature housed himself in such meager surroundings? Garry expected Theo to own a majestic castle. Instead, the compound resembled a sharecropper's home, not a sanctuary for one of great influence. The houses were unpainted, and the yard unkempt. Chickens helped themselves to measly strands of weeds and grass, as horses ran freely in an open field.

Garry felt so strange, so awkward, so *foreign*. He noted the looks of those who wandered around, outside. Was this a sign of curiosity, bewilderment, or danger? Many were Embrian soldiers, who were experienced in fighting those of Garry's nationality. If Sirro was scared, he never showed it. Already, Garry was thinking around corners.

An Embrian Marine, dressed in a red tunic and white pith helmet, his face covered with sideburns, stopped Garry and Sirro. What business would a Branellian and Vladistani have in a restricted area? The Marine hated Branellians and the United Westerland Brethren. More than anything, he despised men in kilts! The Marine considered on shooting first and asking questions later. After all, the two outsiders were likely worth more dead, than alive!

"Where do you think you're going?" the Marine asked.

"To see Councillor Theo," said Sirro, in urgency and annoyance.

"Why?" the Marine asked. "What do you got for Councillor Theo that's so important? A dart, a sharp, pointy thing, or an explosive device?"

"I won't stand out here haggling with you!" shouted Sirro. "I must see Councillor Theo, immediately!"

The Marine pointed his sword at Sirro's nose. "And I'm ordering you to surrender, *immediately*. Otherwise, I'll have a mess to clean up after I spill your blood, then eat the Branellian's heart for supper."

"Sirro!" someone called, from one of the cottages. "So, help me, I'm happy to see you!"

Garry and Sirro turned to see Pastor Dimitri, coming to greet them.

The Marine had a particular spite for practitioners of weird religions. Embrey was no place for those of alien descent, especially during a war. And most especially for boys in kilts! "They ain't going anywhere," the Marine said, "without Councillor Theo's consent and permission."

"I'll vouch for their character," said Dimitri.

"That's not good enough!" The Marine shook his head. "How can I vouch for their character? They ain't even got the proper authorization!"

This unfriendly behavior cinched it for Garry. One way or the other, he'd make his way back home to Warren Dale! There, he'd resign himself to living in thatch huts, eating crawdads and taters, and escorting smugglers and bootleggers into neighboring countries. Anything was better than dealing with ornery Embrian Marines!

A former Branellian officer, barely sworn into the Embrian Navy, left the exact cottage Dimitri came from. Garry recognized him as Captain Shimura who, at seven feet in height, towered over everyone around him.

The Marine's judgment warned him never to trust Shimura. He was intimidated by the Kokashima-turned-Branellian-turned-Embrian immigrant. Badly outnumbered by alien races, the Marine swore to live or die by protecting the three legislators currently residing at the compound. Furthermore, he refused to salute Shimura. In his mind, the Oriental was still a Branellian, and undeserving of respect.

"What's the problem?" Shimura asked the Marine.

"These cretins say they're here to see Councillor Theo," the Marine answered.

"Address me as 'captain' or 'sir' when you speak to me," insisted Shimura. "What cretins are you talking about?"

The Marine was tempted to give Shimura a degrading, racial insult. Councillor Theo was wrong in trusting someone like that! The Marine gritted his teeth. "Sir, these cretins . . ."

"That Vladistani's no cretin!" laughed Shimura, slugging Sirro's shoulder.

Garry was deathly afraid of Shimura. Though he didn't yet know Dimitri, the boy somehow felt secure with him.

Shimura motioned at Garry. "How did you get him away from those scallywags?"

"It wasn't hard," explained Sirro. "They were too busy drinking and bragging about themselves to pay attention to us. I'm here to deliver that message to Councillor Theo. Garry wants the same thing we do. A better life."

Shimura practically drilled holes through Garry, with his two piercing eyes.

"I didn't wanna be in the trades!" cried Garry. "My mom and sister made me!"

"Don't worry, I'm just glad to see a former countryman," said Shimura, calmly. "What about those other boys? Are they safe?"

"They won't be, if Copenhaver has his way," said Sirro. "He tried killing Garry with that big stick, a few moments ago. He'll murder the others, so he and those scoundrels can get away."

"Is that how you got those bruises on your face?" asked Shimura. "By walking into that man-killin' stick?"

"No," mumbled Garry, in embarrassment. "By walking into Harold's fist, three or four times."

"Well, I'm not sure if you're any good or not," Shimura told Garry. "You're no good on an empty stomach."

"What am I supposed to do?" asked the Marine, frustrated by the preferential treatment Shimura gave Sirro and Garry.

"I don't care what you do," said Shimura. "Just act like you know what you're doing."

The Marine resented taking orders from a man who turned his back on Kokashima royalty, years before. Now, Shimura had turned his back on Branell. Who was to say that he wouldn't eventually betray Embrey? The Marine prayed he never regretted giving Garry and Sirro access to the compound. Admiral Kraig might hang him, simply to make an example out of someone.

As Garry entered the small cottage, he didn't know what to expect from it. By Embrian standards, it was a modest home, furnished sparingly, and lacking in frills. A small candle lantern hanging from the wall illuminated the room, as wood crackled and popped in a fireplace.

In Garry's opinion, the humble cottage was splendid! This was the first time he'd been under a roof, since leaving Warren Dale. The house was lavish, when compared to the sheds, shacks, and barns he called home. If this was the way most Embrians lived *(and it was quite marvelous!)* then Garry was eager to stay

. . .

Assuming he was allowed to.

Shame swept over Garry. He should've stayed behind with Davy, or taken his friends with him! Except Harold. The smugglers could keep him!

"It's good to see you, Sirro," someone spoke, from the end of the hallway.

Garry caught his first glimpse of Councillor Theo. A heavyset man who matched his own height, Theo was dressed in a long, burgundy robe. Even with little sleep, Theo was an impressive figure to those of Garry's social standing.

Sirro shook Theo's hand. "Today, we'll finally make needed changes, to benefit both Embrey and the Branellian Empire."

"Do you have the letter from King Josiah?" asked Theo.

Sirro reached into a pocket for the scroll. Quietly, Theo read through the document. After a minute or two, he looked at Garry. He wanted to trust the boy. His suspicions said otherwise. He knew better than to take kindly toward strangers, even one as seemingly docile as Garry. Having met some of the kids trained by Captain Maliek, there were others he was unfamiliar with. Most of those assassins were two-faced, crafty, and had the ability to enter the tightest security, undetected. They came in many shapes, sizes, costumes, and nationalities.

"This is Garry," introduced Sirro, "from the Northern Branellian Mountains."

"How well do you know my son, Yuri?" Theo asked Garry, cautiously. "What about Jesse . . . Tomas . . . Conrad?"

Garry shrugged.

"Garry's harmless," assured Sirro. "He never met Maliek."

In a stern tone, Theo asked Garry to voice his reasons to be in Embrey. Without saying so, he was already won over by the kid's soft, sensitive eyes and shy, awkward nature.

"I worked the trades, and I don't wanna go back," said Garry. "Don't I get to stay in Embrey? *Please?*"

"The 'trades'?" asked Theo.

"The black market," explained Sirro. "This kid and four others were hired to traffic nefarious characters in and out of Embrey, from Branell."

"My mom and sister made me," said Garry. "But I didn't want to, and I don't wanna go back!"

"He came with our old friends, Copenhaver and Schlender," said Shimura, with a sly grin.

"Copenhaver and Schlender?" Theo gasped. "Where are they, now?"

"We was supposed to meet him at the mouth of the Ember River!" Garry pointed at Shimura.

Shimura laughed. "Won't they be in for a big surprise, when they find out I'm not there? That's as far as they go, before they get a rope around their necks."

"Not my friends!" exclaimed Garry.

"No, not your friends," said Theo. "We'll make sure nothing happens to them."

"Garry's sincere in his wishes for Embrian citizenship," said Sirro. "Those scoundrels treated him badly."

"I'll do what I can to grant you political asylum," said Theo, exhausted by the day's event. He had just peeled off the wig and fake beard used to deceive Major Conroy, and enjoyed a short break when Sirro and Garry arrived. "While I visit with Sirro and Captain Shimura, please make yourself at home," he told Garry. "I'll have Linus cook you a meal, fit for a king."

Garry sat down at an oak dining table and chair. He never once saw such nice furniture, and didn't want to dirty them.
He worried that he had already imposed upon Theo's generosity.

Dimitri sat down next to Garry. "It's all right," he said, politely. "I'm sure you'd like a good meal, and a bath. Are you new to Embrey?"

"I been around here lots of times, but never to stay."

"I moved here from Kusch, years ago. It was tough, at first. It's never easy to leave your own people." Dimitri sighed. "I just hope that my family and I don't have to leave. My wife . . . the *boss,* nags me about one thing or another. My church was burned down this morning, and my children endangered. Right now the kids talk about returning to St. Alexandrov. Grigori, my youngest, doesn't even remember the city. He was a baby when we came here. But when I can, I'm going to rebuild my church, better than before."

"What made your house burn down?" asked Garry.

"Intolerance and stupidity," remarked Dimitri. "Don't worry, you'll see that too, if you haven't already. With faith in the Kuen, and my family's support and love, I'll stick it out. It's not easy living in Embrey. But if I can do it, so can you, Garry."

"What made you come here?"

"I was obligated."

"By who? The boss?"

Dimitri laughed. "No, not really. There are a fair number of Kuschans living in Sykes, not just my family and me. The king of Kusch doesn't approve of our faith, so for me to serve the Kuen I moved here." Dimitri gently rubbed Garry's calloused hand. "You say your mother and sister forced you into smuggling. What were they doing, while you hauled freight over the mountains?"

"Getting rich."

Dimitri smiled. "I'll put in a good word for you."

Even with the promise of freedom, Garry was afraid of the changes it brought. What was expected from him, in return? Aside from the village of Warren Dale, the trades were the only life he knew.

Theo's manservant Linus entered the room with a meal. The smell of chicken soup, strips of bacon, and goat's milk were overwhelming. The only food Garry had on the trail was salty venison, and whatever he stole. He thought the feast was for Dimitri, until Linus gave it to him. *"Me?"* he inquired.

"Will this do?" asked Linus, handing Garry a set of wooden utensils. "Or may I bring something else?"

"Are you sure?" asked Garry.

"Councillor Theo's orders," explained Linus, warmly. "No reason for a new Embrian citizen to go hungry."

Accustomed to eating with his fingers, Garry fumbled with the knife, fork, and spoon. He didn't know how hungry he truly was, until he swallowed that first mouthful. After sipping the goat's milk, he needed sleep.

Garry ate quickly, as Dimitri and Linus watched. After finishing, Garry thanked Linus, and complimented him for his culinary expertise. Retrieving the empty dish, Linus offered seconds. Clearly, Garry hadn't eat that well, in ages!

Linus and Dimitri surmised that Garry hungered for another valuable commodity . . .

That of *love*.

Once Linus refilled his dish and cup, Garry apologized for the inconvenience of feeding him. Consuming the soup and bacon, he couldn't take his mind away from Davy. Was it right to sit by a warm fireplace, letting an old man wait on him, as his best friend shivered in the cold wind, on an empty stomach? Garry sneaked a cinnamon roll in his leather sporran, to share with his best friend later on.

"Still hungry?" asked Dimitri.

Garry shook his head, 'no.'

"You're nervous about something," noted Dimitri. "What's on your mind?"

Garry frowned.

"Talk to me, Garry," begged Dimitri. "What's wrong?"

"What do I gotta do, if I get to stay in Embrey? Where are me and my friends gonna live?"

"I don't think the authorities will cast you out on your own, though I'm sure you'd do just fine. You'll probably go to a parochial school."

"What's that?"

"A school owned and operated by a church," said Dimitri. "What congregation do you belong to? The Brotherhood of Faith?"

"Never went to church."

"Do you believe in God?"

"If there is one, he's really mean," said Garry.

Dimitri controlled his flaring anger. "Why is God mean?"

"He just sits around on his throne all day, watching us hurt each other! Why don't he make us stop it, if he's that powerful and mighty?"

"Well, Garry, maybe it's up to us to stop it," said Dimitri.

"But what can I do?"

"Assume that Councillor Theo lets you stay in Embrey. What will you do, to keep other children from working for men
like Copenhaver and Schlender?"

"I can't do nothing! How can I stop it?"

"We must depend upon ourselves, and not God, to solve our problems," said Dimitri. "It wasn't God that brought you here, was it?"

"No," said Garry. "It was Sirro."

Dimitri laughed. "My god, the Kuen, will grant me the strength to build my house of worship. I don't expect Him to buy the boards, the hammers, or the nails. I know He won't lend a hand in erecting the new structure."

From behind an office door, Theo, Sirro, and Shimura engaged in a fiery yelling contest, each struggling to shout down the other.

Where this racket frightened Garry, Dimitri snickered. "Politicians. They'll agree to disagree for a while. If we're lucky, they'll agree to agree, then maybe we're better off. Mainly it's posturing and chatter. If you wish to accomplish something, do it yourself. Don't just talk about it. And don't expect government to be of much help, subsidy, or support."

"Father," someone spoke, entering the cottage. It was Dimitri's daughter Sasha, with twin brothers Sergio and Giuseppe.

"Yes?" asked Dimitri.

"We can't find our chess set, anywhere," said Sasha, feeling awkward and shy around Garry.

"It was lost in the fire," said Dimitri. "I'll see if Omar or Fumiko have one. Sit down, and acquaint yourself with Garry."

As Dimitri left, Sasha, Sergio, and Giuseppe hesitantly approached Garry. Their thoughts ranged from curiosity to contempt. As Sergio checked out his clothes with disdain, Garry held the exact same regard of the twins' school uniforms.

"Are you a Branellian?" asked Sasha.

Garry didn't answer.

"Do you damn Branellians eat babies?" asked Sergio, angrily.

"No!" yelled Garry, defensively. "Do you damn Embrians hump sheep?"

While Sergio and Garry sneered at each other, Sasha defused the situation by asking, "Do Branellians play chess?"

Garry wrinkled his nose. *"Chest?* What's chest?"

"'Chest'!" giggled Sergio. "Told you he was a dumb Branellian!"

"Leave him alone, Sergio!" scolded Giuseppe. "He can't help being a dumb Branellian! They're all dumb!"

Garry hopped to his feet, torn between fighting the twins or leaving the cottage. Both ideas endangered his citizenship status. In the end, he'd only get into trouble. If he went outside, the ornery Marine would beat him up. If he took a swing at Sergio or Giuseppe, he'd risk alienating Sirro and Dimitri.

Standing up, Garry towered over the twins and Sasha. His complexion reddened, from anger. Severe fatigue, mixed with anxiety, nearly sent him over the edge. Resolving problems through fisticuffs was common in the trades, and in Warren Dale. Garry hated fighting. Chances were, Theo didn't tolerate brawls in his house.

Affectionately, Sasha threw her arms around Garry's wiry torso. Her body was warm and comforting. Garry blushed, unaccustomed to being touched by a member of the opposite sex. This, to the twins' amusement.

"I hoped you kids were getting friendly," said Dimitri, returning to the cottage. He wasn't sure about letting Sasha embrace Garry. "I'm afraid you already *have*."

Setting up a chessboard and pieces at the table, the twins and Sasha taught Garry the fundamentals of the game. This wasn't without a bit of gentle ribbing and a few crass remarks. Initially, Garry was confused by the separate players and their roles. This confusion led to frustration, then despair as the twins, then Sasha made mincemeat of him. Dimitri coached Garry by giving him pointers. As Sergio took pleasure in belittling him, Sasha and Giuseppe eventually gave their former enemy needed approval and compassion. Garry was insecure, harmless, and occasionally whiny. No one felt threatened by the 'dumb, baby-eating Branellian.' As Giuseppe took Garry's side against his twin brother, Sergio continued making waves concerning the boy's kilt.

Theo, Sirro, and Shimura left the office, their differences expressed through strained smiles. "Having fun?" asked Theo, his voice hoarse and raspy.

The twins and Sasha nodded. Garry merely shrugged.

"I'll write a letter, recommending you and your friends for political asylum in our fair nation," Theo told Garry.

"What's 'political asylum'?" asked Garry.

"It means you don't have to live in Warren Dale, anymore," said Shimura. "The same goes for Copenhaver and Schlender, but under different circumstances. Where they're going, you don't want to follow."

"Where's that?" inquired Garry.

"A tall tree with a couple of short ropes," answered Shimura. "Their necks will snap, they'll do a funny little dance in the air, then fill their pants."

"And their troubles are all over," added Sirro. "In this world, at least."

Garry shuttered. "What about me and my friends?"

"You let me worry about that," said Theo. "As an Embrian civilian, you're expected to find a sponsor, then perform a duty, either for the military and civil service."

"Mister Theo . . . *Councillor* Theo, I mean . . ." Garry frowned. "What's a sponsor?"

"Someone to cover your expenses," explained Theo. "We want to make sure your transition to Embrian citizenship is a smooth one. It's been my privilege to meet thousands of men and women from around the globe, who left their homelands to make their fortunes here."

"He's making speeches again," Sirro whispered to Dimitri.

"Look around this room, Garry," said Theo. "Sirro's from Vladistan, Captain Shimura's from the faraway land of Kokashima, and Pastor Dimitri and his daughter Sasha are from Kusch."

"What about me and Sergio?" asked Giuseppe, feeling left out.

"Today, it's my pleasure to greet a fine young man from the Branellian Empire," said Theo. "Tell me, Garry, what made you decide in emigrating to Embrey?"

"Nothing made me decide," said Garry. "Davy and me came up with the idea, all by ourselves. Now that I'm here, I ain't going back. I'm tired of sleeping in barns, getting bit by bugs and fleas, and shoveling other peoples' horses' shit."

Dimitri and Sasha were shocked by Garry's language, while Sergio and Shimura roared in laughter.

"Well, that's as good a reason to leave Branell, as any," agreed Theo.

"I hauled freight and people all over them mountains, since I was a little kid," said Garry. "My mom and sister made me."

"Excuse me," interrupted Theo. "Did you say you hauled *people?*"

"Flesh peddlers," said Sirro. "Copenhaver and Schlender made their fortunes, not only by trafficking illegal goods, but from kidnapping women and children for prostitution."

Theo glared at Garry. "You were involved with that?"

"I didn't want to!" exclaimed Garry. "Can't I stay in Embrey, please? I'll do everything you want from me!"

"I'm sorry," apologized Theo. "I don't mean to imply that you're responsible for what the smugglers did. Under the circumstances, you're the perfect candidate for Embrian citizenship."

"I must report to the Browning," said Shimura. "My cabin boy, Gruffydd, is boiling a chicken for the captain's table. Will you have dinner with me tonight, Sirro?"

Sirro graciously accepted.

"What about me?" asked Garry, afraid to stay in the compound, without Sirro there to protect him.

"I don't think you should leave, Garry," advised Theo.

"I don't think I should stay, neither!" argued Garry.

"You'll be all right," said Dimitri. "I'm sure Sergio and Giuseppe's pals from Lord Kelly's would like to make your acquaintance."

"Just don't tell Fritzy you're a dumb Branellian," kidded Sergio.

"What about my friends?" cried Garry. "They're still with them smugglers!"

"I'm glad you're so concerned about them," said Theo. "We hope to rescue your friends, while apprehending Copenhaver and Schlender. For right now, I can't spare any soldiers without compromising my own security."

"I shouldn't have left them, Sirro!" cried Garry. "I oughta go get them, myself!"

"I'll go with you, Garry," offered Giuseppe.

"You try that, you'll both end up dead, or worse," said Shimura. "What makes that pig Copenhaver think he'll get to Branell, if he offs his guides? He can't even locate a commode in broad daylight."

"He'd slit his own mother's throat, if it meant saving himself," stated Sirro. "He's murdered better men than us, just for sport. He'll murder Garry for slipping away with me."

"Apprehending the smugglers is a job for the military," said Theo. "There are squads of Embrian Marines and Naval Infantry, spread along the coastline. It's their duty to stop those criminals, not ours."

"What if my friends are dead?" moped Garry.

"Casualties of war," said Shimura. "You knew the risks, Garry, or you should have."

Garry almost wept.

"Once I get aboard, I'll search the mouth of the Ember River," proposed Shimura. "The best thing for you is to look out for yourself." Shimura looked deep into Garry's eyes. "Congratulations, we're now citizens of Embrey. I just replaced my Branellian colors with Embrian ones, and I need a midshipman. I'd be proud to have you serve with me. If that's what you want, you'll know better than to raise your voice to Councillor Theo, or to me. I've given my allegiance to him, and I ask that you give your loyalty to me, a newly-commissioned Embrian naval officer."

"Don't worry," assured Sirro. "If anyone can find Davy and the others, it's Shimura."

"I'm got an important meeting in the morning, and cannot be disturbed," Theo told the children. "Go outside with Sasha and the twins, Garry. Once again, I welcome you to Embrey. I just know you'll love it here!"

"You're a survivor, and I know you'll make good in your new home," added Dimitri, leading Garry outdoors.

Garry hoped that everything would be all right. Maybe, just maybe, his concerns added up to nothing. However, images of seeing his friends with their heads bashed in, as the smugglers got away, were too horrible to bear. Not only would Garry blame Copenhaver and Schlender for it, he'd blame himself!

As the sun sank below the horizon, Sasha and the twins joined Grigori and Alexei in playing fetch with Yuri's terrier, Boris. Absently, Garry stood to one side, watching. While the Kuschans shouted commands to Boris in their native language, Sergio made fun of their "tongue-tied gibberish."

As Dimitri had said earlier, it was up to Garry, and not God, to solve his problems. Someone had to free his buddies from those two cutthroats . . .

. . . and that someone was Garry!

As the twins tossed a tennis ball back and forth, Sergio overthrew and sent it above Giuseppe's head. After hitting the ground, the ball rolled away and disappeared behind a cottage. "I'll go get it," said Giuseppe.

"No, I will!" volunteered Garry, running after the ball. Seconds passed, as he failed to return with the tennis ball.

"Dumb Branellian!" cursed Sergio. "I told you he was dumb, Giuseppe!"

Wandering past the cottage, Giuseppe found the ball lying in a mud puddle. Looking around, he searched for the gangly kid in the turtleneck sweater and flashy kilt. "Garry!" he shouted, his tiny voice cracking in the afternoon dim and quiet. *"Garry!"*

But Garry was nowhere to be found . . .

38

"Need a drink, *Corporal* Willowby?" Vix asked his *(former)* captain. Posted on a hillside overlooking the Ember River, the two soldiers guarded their men, camped down below.

"No thank you, *Private* Vix," answered Willowby, unhappy because he and his *(former)* sergeant had kept watch, since the late afternoon. It was almost sundown, now!

Vix and Willowby were given only a canteen of water and a few pieces of jerky, sneaked to them by Corporals Bergman and Billy Joe. A full moon, beaming across the ocean, was occasionally blocked out by thick clouds and fog. Damp, miserable, and freezing, Vix stayed warm by pacing back and forth, while sharing his wartime exploits with Willowby.

Willowby huddled behind a huge boulder, under a wool blanket provided by Bergman. Shivering, he took his mind away from the blustery conditions by listening to Vix's account of Army life. The cold air seemingly clung to him. There was no getting away from it!

Willowby was awestruck by Vix's stories. Some were heroic, several bawdy, others comical and a few tragic. He was like a student, taking lessons from a respected teacher. Vix's tales were hallowed treasures! Willowby also spoke of his own family's experiences, in uniform. While these accounts were shared with pride, they detailed others' lives. It troubled Willowby knowing that his service had meted very little. What did he do, to match up with Vix? Where Vix was a giant among men, Willowby viewed himself as a measly little insect, unworthy of praise. He had no wounds to show. What valor or courage did he possess? Sure, the recruits of Fort Cooley had scared off a few Branellians that morning. So what? No blood was shed. No one gave the ultimate sacrifice, for king or for country.

"How she hangin' there, Sarge?" a voice asked in the twilight, as Bergman and Billy Joe strolled from camp.

"*What?*" growled Vix.

Bergman and Billy Joe stood at attention, their arms filled with blankets and finger foods. "Holding up, Sergeant Vix?" asked Bergman. "You, Captain Willowby?"

"As well as can be expected," answered Willowby, accepting the provisions. "Thank you."

"They ain't just from us, Cap'n," said Billy Joe, struggling to maintain a straight face. Vix made him so nervous, it was almost funny. "The boys're all with you, sir. Ever'one pitched in to get you them things."

"Give everyone my gratitude," said Willowby, his teeth chattering.

"Thank you, sir," said Bergman.

"How's it going at the riverbank?" asked Willowby.

"Very well, Captain Willowby," said Bergman. "It's just that. . . we're worried about you, and Sergeant Vix, too! Are you holding up, well?"

"Corporal Bergman, I stood watch in colder weather'n this," said Vix. "I stood watch, long before you or Billy Joe was even born! Rather be in a cathouse right now, a glass of beer in one hand and a cheap floozy in the other!"

A laugh slipped from Billy Joe's mouth.

"Be a lot better, soon as we get home," said Vix. "Ain't no sense in us standing out here like a couple of damned fools."

"Believe me when I say that my heart, and my devotion, belong to the men of Fort Cooley," said Willowby, visibly moved by the recruits' generosity.

Vix cleared his throat, in disapproval of Willowby's sentimentality.

"Thank you, sir," said Bergman, his voice cracking.

"So, where's King Owensby?" asked Vix.

"In bed," said Bergman. "I wish he'd take a hike, Captain Willowby! Why did he order us to come to such a place? There's nothing here but wind and fog!"

"Yeah," added Billy Joe, "and a big buncha water, out west."

"One more thing, Sergeant Vix," said Bergman, hesitantly. "When you first showed up at Fort Cooley, some of us didn't like you very well."

"Yeah," said Billy Joe, "and some of us didn't like you, at all."

"You might be a hard ass, sir," said Bergman. "You're still better than that fool colonel we're dealing with, now!"

"I'm buying the drinks, soon as we get back," offered Vix. "You fellas better just settle on sassafras tea. You're still too young for the good stuff!"

Bergman and Billy Joe smiled in anticipation.

"Is that all?" asked Willowby, wishing his two corporals stayed to keep him company.

"No, sir," said Bergman. "Anything more we can do for you?"

"Get some rest," ordered Willowby. "I'll see you in the morning."

As Bergman and Billy Joe returned to camp, Vix and Willowby sat against the boulder and wrapped themselves in wool blankets. "You didn't have to tell the boys that," mumbled Vix, slicing off pieces of venison.

"What?"

"That crap about your heart and devotion belonging to 'em."

"Why not? I only thought . . ."

"Their respect's worth a damn sight more than that."

"Sorry," sighed Willowby. "What else am I supposed to say?"

"Got any dirty jokes?" said Vix, turning to the east. A line of fiery red, beneath a foggy haze, stated that buildings still burned in the heart of Sykes. Vix didn't care if the damage was caused by Gornick, Branellians, or a cow kicking over a lantern. He wanted the culprits' heads in a sack, and wondered why Owensby led the recruits away from Fort Cooley.

Well, his recruits weren't real soldiers. They weren't men, at all! The boys needed far more discipline and training, before they were remotely prepared for battle!

"What happened at Sisko Canyon?" asked Willowby.

"Ain't you a'ready heard enough about that?" asked Vix. "Some of your kin was up there."

"Yeah, but they never talk about it."

Vix groaned.

"So, you're not talking, either," mumbled Willowby.

"Ain't got nothing to talk about."

"Please? What was it like?"

"Pretty horrible," said Vix. "It's always horrible in the Wilderness. Guess that's why it's a wilderness. A man's gotta have more sense than to fight over a place like that. I fought in some god-awful country, but Sisko Canyon's the worst.

Snows all year 'round up there."

Willowby begged to hear more.

"If that fatgut Owensby really was up there, he wouldn't wanna talk about it, neither," said Vix, more guarded than usual. "There's a lotta men on both sides still up there, frozen where they croaked. Some just gave up and died. I knew a few fellas who killed themselves, just so they wouldn't have to face it no more."

"Weren't they given proper burials?"

"Yeah, in the snow and ice! That is, until spring, when they bloated up and stunk."

"Bloated?"

"Bloated up so big they popped right outa their shirts," said Vix.

Willowby felt sick.

"I don't even know why we was up there," groaned Vix. "Ain't a damn thing up there to fight over. Half the time we wasn't fighting, just freezing."

"Who won?"

No one. Ever'one just packed up and left." Vix smiled, weakly. "Sure hope you don't end up in a mess like that."

"Sergeant Vix?" asked Willowby. "Am I a good officer?"

"Aw, your workin' on it."

"But am I now?"

"You think I went into the Army, knowin' everything? It's like any job. Takes time to get good at it."

Willowby sighed. "Maybe I shouldn't have joined the Army. Maybe I should've followed in the footsteps of Mom's family."

Vix frowned.

"They're gravediggers," explained Willowby, "and own the more highbrow cemeteries in western Embrey. I'll bet I won't have a hard time breaking into that profession."

"You're in the Army now, so forget about it."

"What if the gravediggers need me more than the Army?"

"I dug plenty of graves in the Army, more'n I care to talk about." Vix put his arm around Willowby's shoulder. "I a'ready know how good you ain't with a shovel. You're better off in uniform."

"Yeah, but they get really busy in cemeteries, whenever there's a plague or . . . a war."

Vix nudged Willowby as he pointed to a trio of riders, heading into camp from the riverbank. Dressed in brown khaki shirts, wide-brimmed felt hats, and tight breeches tucked into their boots, the newcomers were led by an aging Army officer, mounted on a spotted horse.

"Uncle Alistair!" cheered Willowby, waving at the riders.

Vix and Willowby sprinted into camp. Once they reached Alistair with two guards, both saluted.

"I thought you was retired," said Vix, grinning.

"I thought I was, too," said Alistair, dismounting. Nearly sixty, he had graying sideburns and a thick mustache. His face and forehead were creased and leathery. "Old soldiers never die," he added. "They just smell like it. Nor are they allowed to die, without the proper paperwork and consent forms."

Vix had heard that same joke countless times in the past. Taking note of the two stars on Alistair's shoulders, he asked, "Who'd ya bribe into promote you to general?"

"Chang," said Alistair, in frustration. "It's only temporary, until they get this straightened out, or someone kills me first. No need to worry about that, Sergeant Vix. Men like us are too ugly and stupid to die. Where's Major Kohl?"

"Ain't working for him, no more," said Vix, with regret and sadness.

"Who, then?" asked Alistair.

Vix put his hand on Willowby's shoulder. "This runt, here."

After the death of Willowby's father, Alistair became something of a father-figure to the young officer. "What do you think you're doing, son?" he asked, removing Willowby's hat to ruffle his hair.

"I'm the commanding officer of Fort Cooley," said Willowby, hoping to meet Alistair's approval.

"That figures." Alistair rolled his eyes back. "If you're the CO of Cooley, why are you lollygagging with an old baboon like Vix?"

Willowby found it hard to explain.

Owensby stepped out of his tent in a fancy, silk robe, carrying an expensive bottle of booze in one hand. On his robe was a crest, in the form of a shield decorated with lions, unicorns, and castles. "What are you doing down here?" Owensby barked at Vix and Willowby. "Get back on that hillside, or I'll have you up on . . ."

"They're with me," interrupted Alistair, crossing his arms. "And I haven't got the time nor inclination for your stink-water attitude."

Owensby frowned. *"General* Alistair? *You're* a general?"

"General Chang's orders," said Alistair.

"But . . ." Owensby scratched his head. "I thought you just retired, with the rank of lieutenant colonel."

"That's none of your business," said Alistair. "General Chang has ordered that I take eighty of these recruits off your hands."

"Not on my authority, you won't," stammered Owensby. "I brought these men out here to make sure those gutless Branellians don't leave our shores, alive."

Alistair retrieved documentation from his pocket, and handed it to Owensby. "Let someone else deal with the Branellians," he said, tiredly.

"I was informed by a group of Branellian prisoners that we're at the rendezvous point for those curs to join up with that gook sailor, Shimura," argued Owensby.

"Shimura won't be here," said Alistair, vaguely.

"How do you know that?" asked Owensby. "What makes you so sure?"

"He won't be here," repeated Alistair, failing to disclose Shimura's defection from Branell. "General Chang ordered me to order you to cut eighty of these men loose. Get to it."

Owensby sneered as he skimmed through the dispatch. Wanting to rip the letter to shreds, he thought better of it. "These men are needed here! Are there not enough men in Sykes to satisfy Chang's demands?"

Alistair sighed. "General Chang feels, as I do, that it's too risky to post unsupervised recruits in harm's way."

"Unsupervised?' disputed Owensby. "They're under *my* supervision!"

"Those were Chang's exact worries," said Alistair, as Vix and Willowby stifled laughs. "However, he is willing to leave twenty of them here tonight, to satisfy your unharnessed ego. At first light tomorrow, you are to place them under General Chang's command, for his satisfaction. Will you cut eighty of these recruits loose for my satisfaction, or must I apply my boot up your ass to motivate you?"

"They're Corporal Willowby's, not mine!" snapped Owensby, retreating to his tent. "Let him take care of it!"

Willowby grinned. "Thank you, Uncle Alistair . . . General Alistair!"

"I'm still your uncle, whether you like it or not." Alistair patted Willowby's back. "You should be in school, son. What convinced your mother to let you play soldier boy, especially at a time like this?"

"I'm sixteen!" argued Willowby.

"That's right," said Alistair, stone-faced. "How stupid of me. You're sixteen! You know everything!"

Willowby frowned.

"You should be in school," repeated Alistair. "After that, university."

"My duty is to my men," explained Willowby, nervously.

"My duty is to place eighty of your men under General Chang's jurisdiction," said Alistair. "If I had my choice, I'd relieve you and Owensby of them all. Cut eighty of your men out for me. I'm not asking again. Get to it, son."

Though Willowby never said so, it was a tremendous weight lifted from his shoulders to comply with Alistair. He preferred releasing all of the recruits to his uncle, away from a pompous windbag like Owensby.

"Sir," said Vix. "I request to stay with them twenty you're keeping here."

Alistair gave Vix a lopsided grin. "Can you handle Owensby?"

"I handled him earlier," said Vix. "That's what got me and Captain Willowby stuck up on that hill. Owensby don't like the way I handled him."

"How's that?" asked Alistair, curiously.

"I reminded him that he wasn't at Sisko Canyon."

"Request granted, Sergeant Vix!" laughed Alistair. "I feel safer leaving some of these boys in your care. The odds of them surviving have just doubled."

"I also request that Captain Willowby go with you," added Vix.

"Request denied!" shouted Willowby.

"Request granted, son," stated Alistair. "I was about to make that very suggestion. No matter how much I respect General Chang, my orders for your return home come from a higher authority than his."

"Who?" asked Willowby, angrily.

"Your mother," said Alistair. "If I go against Chang, I risk disciplinary action and a court martial. That's nothing compared to my sister-in-law Audrey's wrath. I've got orders from Chang and your mother. I intend to carry them out, and so will you."

Willowby's lips quivered. "But what about those twenty men we leave here?"

"You were ordered to cut eighty of your men out," scolded Alistair. "Get to it."

"Them eighty men headin' out with Alistair need you, Captain Willowby," said Vix. "Them twenty staying here are in good hands, with me."

Family history and tradition told Willowby to remain at the mouth of the Ember River. His gut, along with an intense disliking of Colonel Owensby, urged him to accompany Alistair and eighty recruits into Sykes.

Willowby looked at his men. A few of the boys stood around campfires talking, while others played an improvisational game of rugby on the beach. So what if they wore Army uniforms? Willowby knew in his heart they weren't full-fledged soldiers, but youngsters.

He also faced a major dilemma. Which recruits were going home, and which stayed with Vix and Owensby? Willowby understood that he, alone, had that decision to make.

With his back to the setting sun, Willowby saluted Alistair, then went about his business.

"I can't imagine a better sergeant for my nephew than you, Vix," said Alistair.

"Thank you, sir," answered Vix.

It's my opinion that Willowby has to serve a former CO, his mother. General Chang agrees with me. Like you, I never got married, or raised kids. It hasn't stopped me from thinking of Willowby as my own son. He's a fine boy, but I think he still needs his mom. And she needs him."

In the short time he got to know him, Vix not only liked Willowby, but grew to love him. If Willowby required a tough parental figure, why not a rough and rugged career grunt named Vix?

Alistair took a deep breath. "If my sister-in-law wants him back under his wing, I won't argue with her about it. Let her take care of him, Sergeant Vix, for just a little while longer . . ."

39

"If I catch up with that black-hided booger or lily-livered Garry," an angry voice said, in the fog and darkness, "I'm gonna kill 'em, Davy. Then I'm gonna kill you."

"No, Mister Copenhaver!" another voice cried out. "Honest, sir, I dunno where they went! One minute I was talking to Sirro and Garry, the next they was gone!"

"Lyin' son of a whore!" the first man cursed. "You know where they run off to, don'tcha? Yer fixin' to run off too, soon as yer able."

Vix wasn't asleep on guard duty. Rather, his mind had drifted away from his lonely post, overlooking the mouth of the Ember River. With the cold wind sweeping over him, he sat under a wool blanket. His back propped against the boulder, he struggled to stay warm, and awaited sunrise.

Alone in the dark, Vix couldn't avoid thinking of his estrangement from Major Kohl, or wonder if he'd ever whip his recruits into top shape. It was a cinch they'd never amount to a thing, assuming they answered to Owensby's hair-brained schemes, or get dragged into lousy mop-up operations for Chang and Alistair. Vix just knew he could mold the boys into excellent soldiers! The Army was his home, and by-god he'd make it theirs, too! Those unwilling or unable to cut it would be discharged, but only after Vix was convinced they'd never make it. The old sergeant needed this experience, as much as the recruits needed him. More than anything, he had to reaffirm his place in the armed services of Embrey.

Even then, Vix wondered if he still had a place in the Army. He spent twenty years with Major Kohl, and was determined to grant that exact same dedication to Captain Willowby. Regrettably, Alistair thought that Willowby had to go home to Mommy and, in time, a lousy job burying people. Vix hoped to shape Willowby into a formidable Embrian warrior, in the tradition of the boy's father, grandfather, Uncle Alistair . . .

. . . and Count Fossbinder!

Panic nearly seized Vix, as he snapped out of his trance by the sounds of voices, coming toward him in the dark. Peeking over the wool blanket, he spied upon a group of men. Some were dressed in the uniforms of Branellian Army regulars. Vix began to speak, but thought better of it. He saw the Branellians, all right. Were they able to see him?

To Vix's horror, the Branellians entered camp, where Colonel Owensby and twenty recruits were asleep in their tents.

Owensby slowly, *painfully* sat up, after lying on a cot which was too small for his large frame. Suffering from a severe backache, he caught a slight chill from the damp night air, beating against the canvas walls of his tent. He missed the huge feather bed, on the second floor of his Sykes mansion.

He also obsessed over the lowly Branellians, slithering around his fair nation.

Owensby rubbed his weary eyes and yawned. The only light came from a small lantern beside the cot, along with the blurred moonlight through the thin canvas. Glancing at a gold pocket watch, Owensby learned it was a few minutes past midnight. There was no sign of the mangy Branellians. Even then, Owensby was certain they'd show up at the mouth of the Ember River, unless they were already apprehended.

Were those few recruits under his command sufficient to force the enemy's surrender? Hell, no! Alistair left Owensby with his ass hanging out! In the likelihood of a disaster, Owensby intended to prefer charges against Alistair, then watch the old bastard swing for his negligence. Might as well string up Vix and Willowby too, just for the hell of it!

That'd teach 'em! That'd teach 'em all!

With any luck, General Gornick had already executed most of the dirt-eating Branellians, while displaying their rotting corpses hanging from the trees! If so, Owensby was sorry for not being there to see it!

Owensby fetched the bottle of bourbon stashed under the cot, and took a sip. He'd show that disorganized rabble from Fort Cooley what Embrian soldiers were supposed to be, by ordering them to do calisthenics in the tidewater! Private Vix was right. Those recruits weren't men! They didn't look like men, and sure didn't act it! They were the most undisciplined, shameless gutter trash to wear Army uniforms!

Men, real men, were in the sack long before sunset, then up and at 'em before sunrise. That mess from Fort Cooley handled this mission like it was a camping trip! This was a military campaign, not fun and games!

Taking a second drink, Owensby dropped the bottle when he heard shrill screaming, from outside. He left his cot, buck-naked, and reached for his breeches when a big, bearded man with a club barged into the tent.

Owensby froze, as he failed to comprehend the meaning of this intrusion. He began issuing a protest against the brute. Instinctively, he reached for his saber, leaning against the cot.

Seconds later, his brains were splattered onto the tent walls . . .

Vix did not see what happened at the campsite, but he heard it.

From a distance of more than two-hundred yards away, Vix listened as his boys were being slaughtered. Most were killed in their beds, or died trying to escape. They met their deaths from sharpened steel, arrows, or a man-killin' stick. With the brisk wind and tide washing against the shoreline, Vix heard his charges cry out in the night, as their assailants roared victoriously. Those recruits pleading to surrender were executed.

Within a few short minutes, the Branellians had secured the campsite, as the corpses of twenty recruits littered the area.

This wasn't the first time Vix had "witnessed" such an event. What made this so damning was knowing that these lads were so childlike, full of energy, enthusiasm, and life.

Well, what difference did it make, now? Twenty of his recruits were dead. There wasn't a damned thing he could do to change it.

Vix shivered from the cold air and bloodshed. Anger, sadness, and despair set in. Vix assured Willowby these twenty recruits were safe with him. Now, he had just failed his commanding officer, his responsibilities as a sergeant, the Embrian Army . . .

. . . and finally himself.

Corporal Bergman fell next to Billy Joe on the damp, sandy ground. Slowly dying from the gashing wound in his left shoulder, he heard the revelry and laughter stemming from the Branellians who overran their hapless victims.

Bergman knew he was a goner. Weakened by the cold weather and loss of blood, he had to get in one last lick against the enemy. Nudging Billy Joe, he whispered for his fellow corporal to assist in this grisly deed. Too late. Billy Joe was already dead, with a Branellian dirk in his heart.

Bergman held back a whimper, aware of his impending doom. Quietly, he clutched onto an arrow and a sword, lying beside him in the sand. Growing increasingly lightheaded, he mustered the will to strike against the Branellians. Looking around, he spotted the four smugglers celebrating their win, by sharing a bottle of Agronian whiskey.

The Branellian guides stood to one side, sickened by the massacre of the Embrians. They took no part in this debauchery, and prayed they'd never be indicted for it. Davy, in particular, loathed the extremes of depravity the Branellian infantry used in securing the campsite. Was it necessary to kill everyone? Surely the Embrian recruits, all around the guides' same ages, would've given up.

Davy turned to Marc and Ivor . . .

. . . as Corporal Bergman got up and ran an arrow deep into his shin, just inches below the knee.

Davy released a crazed, high-pitched shriek. Desperately, he tried but failed to remove the arrow. Backing away, he stumbled to the ground and cried for help.

Staggering around on two wobbly feet, Bergman drove his sword into Wilde's hairy gut. With a howl to drown out Davy's hair-raising screams, Wilde staggered sideways and tripped over a tent peg.

All eyes now centered on Bergman, as he downed another opponent. The vengeful corporal paid no mind to the Branellian soldiers charging at him . . .

. .. until a dagger was thrust into his chest.

Gasping for air, Bergman gutted the combatant who knifed him. In agony he pushed on, the dagger still dangling between his ribs.

Bjorn was oddly amused as he watched Wilde die, a few scant feet away. It was far too absurd and dreamlike to accept Wilde's sudden downfall. As everyone watched in disbelief, only Copenhaver took evasive action against Bergman.

Bjorn's mirth ended when, in a last ditch effort to even the score, Bergman swung the sword into his throat. Bjorn's blood splashed onlookers like a geyser. Moments later, Copenhaver collapsed Bergman's ribcage with the man-killin' stick.

Bergman wore a look of bewilderment, as air rushed from his gaping mouth. He made a feeble stab at Schlender, before dropping his sword to the ground.

His final thoughts were of the big oaf, slamming a heavy club into his face.

Vix expressed no open feelings of sorrow. There was time for that later on, in quiet contemplation and a pint or two of ale. The only thing to do now was to report this disaster to superiors, then await further orders.

Boys got no place in war! That rule especially applied to the twenty fallen recruits from Fort Cooley, who lived only in myth, legend, and lies told by loudmouths and braggarts who weren't there when they died.

Two Branellian grunts announced their arrival on the hillside with two bloodcurdling yells, as they ran toward Vix. Vix pushed the blanket away and drew his own sword.

One Branellian was more determined to fight, than the other. The second preferred not to shed more blood. He missed long days working the wheat fields of central Branell, balmy nights at a local alehouse, and nights in a warm bed.

Vix answered the first Branellian's aggression by decapitating him. The Branellian's body staged a macabre dance in the moonlight and fog, as he swung his arms and legs like a headless marionette. Vix bared his teeth and waved the crimson sword at the second Branellian.

That did it. The second Branellian carelessly threw his weapon to the grass, turned tail, and sprinted to his brothers-in-arms.

Vix ran more than a quarter of a mile from the river, across muddy springs, and through waist-deep grass. A full moon above was his only guide, through unfamiliar territory. Out of breath, Vix was tortured by thoughts that he left the recruits' bodies behind, on the beach.

Vix crouched beside a roaring creek. All around him, he heard men speaking in the cold, dark night. He saw a number of silhouetted figures against the blackened sky. He concealed himself behind thick brush and remained still, until the Branellians passed him by, or gave up the chase.

Vix held his breath as he watched the Branellians search everywhere for him, the lazy mountain dialect rolling off their tongues like rancid butter. He debated on knocking off a few of the Branellians, as payback.

Just how would he explain this tragedy to the brass? And why, just why, did he alone survive?

Once he was able to do so, Vix began his long, arduous journey to Sykes. Stumbling through a narrow, stony canyon, he suffered from a palpitating heart, as his breathing grew erratic and shallow. During his two decades in the Army, he watched thousands of men die. What made this event any different?

Vix put considerable distance between himself and the scene of a moral catastrophe. He was equally blessed and cursed to live another day. For whatever reason, his respect and passion for the military meant damned little to him, now.

"Shut the hell up!" Copenhaver hollered at Davy, who sat on the ground with an arrow lodged in his shin. "The whole country's swarmin' with Embrians! You wanna rot in their goddamn dungeons?"

Davy struggled to silence his own cries. It was impossible. Whenever he moved, the arrowhead struck a raw nerve, not far from the bone. Resting on a blanket furnished by the Branellian infantry, he could not ignore the blood seeping onto his leg, sock, and kilt. The campsite was cluttered with the dead. There was no time for burials, as Branellian soldiers carried the corpses to the Ember River, where they drifted into the sea.

Davy's sole comfort came from his buddies. As Ivor secured a tourniquet around his leg, Marc gave him water from a canteen. Davy shivered, even as he was covered in a heavy blanket. With the shin swelling, the pain got increasingly worse. He soon grew feverish and delirious. While Harold carried on about his family in Warren Dale, Davy occasionally forgot where he was. A ceaseless, throbbing sensation stemming from the injury was the only thing preventing him from going off his head. "Where's Garry?" he asked. *"Where's* Garry?"

"Go to sleep," urged Marc, rubbing a damp cloth across Davy's forehead.

Attempting to relax, Davy concentrated on more uplifting, positive thoughts.

He returned to a more carefree, blissful time with his best friend, Garry. When they were not involved with the trades, the two boys spent long summer days in the hills above town, skinny dipping in crystal-clear streams, hunting crawdads, watching the sunset, and imagining life away from the dreary sameness of their remote community. Neither boy harbored any specific dreams for the future. All they truly understood was the harsh existence around them. Both boys were ignorant when it came to reading, writing, or arithmetic.

Such goals were elusive. What reasons were there to seek a better life, now? Perhaps it was divine intervention for them to fail. It was foolish to break free from their roles in God's plan. The guides were all going to die, just to spend eternity in purgatory or hellfire.

Once more, Davy asked for Garry, fully aware that his dearest friend wasn't there. It was his heart, and not his head, to make this vain request. Soothingly, Marc again asked Davy to rest. In time, the injured boy would ease into a deep sleep, never to awaken.

Copenhaver and Schlender fought two separate foes. One was the Embrian military, while the other was fear. Neither planned to die like Bjorn and Wilde. Apparently, Shimura was a no-show. The smugglers had to seek another route to Branell, thousands of miles to the east.

"You mean that lame-brained teamster rolled his wagon on top of Wiley?" whimpered Davy, delirium gradually overtaking him. Tears covered both cheeks like rainwater on a stormy day. "Oh God, no! You mean we gotta haul all that stuff over them mountains, by ourselves?"

"*Shh*, Dave," whispered Marc, to calm the dying teen. "It's just a bad dream. Get some sleep . . . Please Dave, just get a little . . ."

"Wiley's got one eye popped out of its socket, where the wagon split open his skull!" shrieked Davy. "What're we s'posed to do for him, now? How's he gonna live out the night, suffering like that? Just what are we s'posed to do for him, Garry?"

"Why don't we kill that miserable bastard, and be done with it?" screamed Schlender. "Look at 'em, Copper. He's as good as dead, a'ready! I can't stand watching 'em bleed like a stuck hog! I say let's kill 'em, and be done with it!"

Schlender was right. Why carry a decrepit boy through the rugged Embrian countryside, just to let the gangrene slowly end him? Them guides wasn't worth the trouble, anyway! Best to do 'em all in! Let the Branellian Army go one way, and the smugglers go the other.

Every man for himself!

Copenhaver decided to carry on with his earlier plans of mashing the guides' heads in. How to go about it? Them boys wouldn't passively take a head-crushin', no matter how scared or stupid they was. Killin' Davy was a cinch. Harold was also an easy mark. Neither had the will or ability to fight back. Why, that crybaby Harold practically begged to die!

What if Marc and Ivor made a fight of it? Copenhaver was damned talented with the man-killin' stick, and had the victims to prove it. Even if them pups tried to go rounds with him, he knew exactly how to make quick, easy work of them.

The deaths of his partners in crime rarely bothered Schlender. He made an exception with Bjorn and Wilde. Copenhaver couldn't have cared less. It was their own fault getting chopped by a sawed-off Embrian corporal.

An aging Branellian colonel, who had escorted Schlender into Sykes the day before, chose to lead his army from the beach. The infantry had its fill of this mission, and were even more frustrated with the smugglers. The colonel and his men weren't eager for another battle against the Embrians. Like the smugglers, the colonel also awaited Shimura, and had to find another way home. He dreaded thoughts of trekking over the mountains. Winter was fast approaching, and he held scant hope of surviving.

Out of civility, the colonel shook hands with the smugglers. "We're moving out," he said, with a tired, deep breath.

"Then move out, ya sorry son of a whore," growled Copenhaver, waving his man-killin' stick at the colonel.

Without another word, the colonel did an about-face and returned to his men.

"Whadda ya say, Copper?" asked Schlender, anxiously.

"Hell do ya think?" answered Copenhaver, impatiently. "Hijack a goddamn boat. We got a mess o' garbage that needs throwed out, first."

"What?"

Copenhaver pointed at the guides.

Eagerly, Schlender unsheathed his sword to assist in this gory task.

Sensing what the smugglers had in mind, Marc and Ivor stood their ground.

"Think that's gonna stop me?" asked Copenhaver. "That Embrian corporal thought he had the bull by the horns, when he killed Bjorn and Wilde. What he didn't know is that I had 'em by the balls. Got his head mashed in, didn't he? Well, now I'm gonna mash yer's."

Ivor shook his head, in defiance. "No . . . no you won't."

"You're a'ready pissin' yer kilts, ain'tcha?" laughed Schlender. "Y' got a yellow streak runnin' down yer backs, and yer legs!"

Marc forced a weak smile. "What if we just leave with the soldiers?"

"They'll be dead before they even get outa the province!" argued Copenhaver. "How far you think yer gonna get with them kilts on? If the Embrians get a hold o' you, were gonna wish I did ya in. When they're done carvin' red stripes up and down yer spines, they'll getcha down on the ground an' butt fuck ya! Then when they're done with that kinda fun, they'll nail y'all to posts and watch ya die, slowly!"

Harold released a mournful whine.

"Someone please pull this arrow out of my leg!" screamed Davy.

"You want that thing outa yer leg?" asked Schlender. Maliciously, he wiggled the arrow lodged in Davy's shin. Blood and puss shot from the wound.

Davy screamed as loud as he could.

In response, Ivor slugged Schlender in the mouth.

Staggering backwards, Schlender stumbled over Wilde's body, crawling with hundreds of bugs who enjoyed the massive feast.

Marc and Ivor fetched large stones to defend themselves. They knew better than to expect any help from Harold. The younger boy sat down, crossed his legs, and resigned himself to his fate. "I want to go home!" he wailed, expecting death to liberate him from a cold, dank prison. "I want to go *home!*"

In the howling wind, birds called overhead. Even with the unceasing tide, one could hear a pin drop.

"Gimme half a chance," threatened Schlender, wiping his bloody lip as he got to his feet, "I'm killin' all you flea-bitten, egg-sucking sons of bitches!"

"Aw hell, don't get yer dander up," said Copenhaver, smiling at Marc and Ivor. "If we don't finish the job, the Embrians'll be more'n happy to. What's the rush? Them boys gotta sleep, sometime . . ."

40

Derek had no trouble sleeping on the bare ground, despite the terrible events from that long, eventful day. Unlike his schoolmates, he wasn't haunted by thoughts, dreams, or images of death and destruction.

The boy rested well until he heard Kenichi say, "C'mon, Derry, we have to go . . ."

"No-o-o!" yawned Derek, wrapping himself in the blanket he shared with Trevor.

"Derek!" shouted Kenichi, tiredly. "If you don't get out of bed, we won't give you any fried chicken or mashed potatoes."

Derek sat up to see Kenichi's darkened silhouette above him. Cool air rushed across his face and hair. The world around him was colored in hues of transparent blue. Torches lit the War Ministry's interior. Scores of men constructed the structure's walls, even in the middle of the night. "Where?" asked Derek, anticipating a hardy meal.

"You tell me," said Kenichi, lifting Derek from the bedding, into the chilly night air.

"I wanna sleep!" whined Derek. "It's cold out here!"

Yuri offered Derek a long, lightweight jacket, which draped below the knees. "Put this on," he said.

All around, Derek saw only shapes of people darting back and forth, within the military post. Soldiers prepared for a possible assault, either from Branellians or Gornick supporters. Derek hastily slipped on the jacket, which covered the arms, torso, and most of his skinny legs. "You said there was fried chicken and mashed potatoes!" he griped.

"Shut up, moron!" ordered Trevor. Like Kenichi, Bradley, and Andre, he also wore a similar jacket provided by the War Ministry.

"You shut up, retard!" snapped Derek. "What time is it, anyways?"

"Time to leave," answered Kenichi, vaguely. "We have to go to Councillor Theo's compound . . . wherever that may be."

Derek was afraid.

"Don't worry, Derek," said Bradley, inadvertently revealing his own apprehension.

"Can't we just go back home?" asked Derek, missing his old dorm room at Lord Kelly's.

"Go right on ahead, boy," suggested Andre, invoking nervous laughter from Trevor. "If we're lucky, the school's been burned down."

"Quiet!" whispered Kenichi.

"You quiet, Itchy," groaned Andre.

"I'm hungry," complained Derek, shivering. "Can't we eat?"

Kenichi reached into his tunic pocket for a small piece of jerky.

"I hate you guys," responded Derek, in disdain.

"What else is new?" asked Kenichi.

The scene was nerve-racking and confusing, as Derek saw only shapes of his friends' faces. Aside from torches illuminating the fortress, the only light came from the full moon, above.

A mustachioed naval officer and young man with red hair approached the five students. "I'm Lieutenant Commander Salazar," the officer said. "This is my aide, Patrick."

"Glad to meet you," said Patrick, warmly.

"Same here," greeted Bradley, watching Jesse perform fencing practice in a showy manner, by torchlight.

"I'm your escort to Councillor Theo's," informed Salazar. "His son Yuri will lead us to this destination."

"Oh, yippee," said Andre, favoring his injured hand which agonized him in the cool air.

"I'll dress that again, when we get to Father's," Yuri told Andre.

Andre cursed under his breath, preferring to have the wound checked right away. The injury kept him awake all evening. To keep his spirits up, he asked Yuri, "Right hand or left?"

"What?" questioned Yuri.

"You know," said Andre, simulating masturbation. "'For solitary pleasures'? Right hand or left?"

Yuri refused to answer.

"Stay close to Brad and me," Kenichi said to the younger boys, as the wind pierced his face, hands, and shins. What price he'd gladly pay for warm shoes and long breeches! "Mount Patten?" he said, slapping Bradley on the back.

"Mount Patten," answered Bradley, his teeth chattering.

"I'm scared!" cried Derek, loudly.

"We'll be all right," spoke Kenichi. His tone said otherwise.

"But . . . what if we run into something?" questioned Derek.

"What're we gonna run into?" asked Andre. "A tree?"

"He believes in monsters!" laughed Trevor.

"No, I don't!" argued Derek. "Moron!"

"You're the moron, retard!" shouted Trevor.

"Are you morons and retards ready to go?" asked Jesse, rubbing his hand across Bradley's skullcap in a demeaning manner. "Nice hat, choirboy! You buy it in a flea market?"

Bradley frowned. His opinion of Jesse mirrored Yuri's.

"There are no monsters," said Kenichi. "If there were, you think I'd be going?"

"Maybe," admitted Derek, realizing he was acting childishly. Still, he couldn't deny the dread of what awaited everyone, beyond the fortress gates.

"Hold on," warned Yuri, a mile from Theo's compound, which was tucked away behind evergreen and cottonwood trees in the Embrian foothills.

The small band, consisting of five students from Lord Kelly's and three dozens soldiers, spent nearly four hours marching through rural flat lands, bare fields, and fruit orchards. The only sounds came from hooting owls and howling coyotes. Conversation amounted to whispers and muted laughter. Andre and Derek griped about their injured hand or tired, cold legs. For the younger boys, this was a long, mysterious journey.

Beams of light streaked across a partly cloudy sky, as the sun gradually peeked over the horizon.

"What is it, Yuri?" asked Salazar.

"I'd like to have a look around," said Yuri. "May one of your men come with me, Commander Salazar?"

"Jesse?" suggested Salazar.

"No, not him!" argued Yuri.

"All right . . . what about you, Pat?" asked Salazar.

Patrick didn't have to voice his reluctance. His frightened eyes said it all.

"Kenichi?" asked Yuri, hopefully.

Salazar was offended with Yuri's desire in using a schoolboy, rather than a trained soldier. "I'm sure one of my men will . . ."

"Kenichi?" interrupted Yuri. "Will you come with me?"

Kenichi had mixed feelings about Yuri. The Kuschan had an ability to fend for himself, a trait which Kenichi admired. In this case, this often meant ending the life of another human being. However, if Yuri's request brought everyone closer to safety, then Kenichi was obligated to help. He only hoped Salazar's small contingency was enough to deter any opposition.

Kenichi dropped his jacket to the ground, as the early morning breeze chilled him.

"Kenichi," begged Bradley. *"Don't . . ."*

"Nothing to worry about," said Kenichi, with uncertainty. "I wouldn't be doing this, if I thought something bad might happen."

"Don't worry, I'll take very good care of him," said Yuri, sarcastically.

"Look," Kenichi whispered to Bradley. "It anything does happen, run for the trees and stay there until sunrise."

As Kenichi followed Yuri in the ominous twilight, Bradley motioned for his friends to kneel onto the stony path. Trevor and Derek obeyed him. Meanwhile, a number of soldiers leaned against their sword sheaths, or sat down for a short break.

From out of nowhere, a long, thin object struck one of the soldiers. With a mournful cry, the soldier collapsed.

"What was that?" questioned Salazar.

"Vanzetti's been shot!" someone yelled.

"Check on his condition!" ordered Salazar, in alarm.

"He . . . he's dead, sir!"

"Bradley," whimpered Derek. "I'm scared!"

A split second later, a second warrior was shot.

"We're gonna die!" someone screamed, as soldiers sprinted in all directions.

"Repel attack!" shouted Salazar.

Bradley panicked. He was forced to look out for his buddies, and resented Kenichi for leaving with Yuri. "Hurry!" he called, leading Trevor, Derek, and Andre god-knew-where into the forest.

Seconds later, Jesse tackled Bradley at the edge of a thicket. "Lay flat!" he said. "And hush your skirted girls down!"

Salazar watched helplessly as a third man, then a fourth, died before his own eyes. "What are we going to do?" asked Patrick.

"Keep it down!" shouted Jesse, hidden in the cottonwoods. "Remove the targets, and make the enemy comes to us!"

"What?" asked Salazar, failing to understand Jesse's directives.

"Just do it, Commander Salazar," said Jesse, angrily, "or die with the others!"

It didn't take long for Kenichi and Yuri to realize that Salazar was under attack. Crawling on their stomachs, the two peeked over a log, at the nearby skirmish. Black images, sprawled with in a clearing, were dead and wounded soldiers.

"How can they shoot in the dark?" asked Kenichi, turning away from the carnage.

"Those silver buttons on the uniforms give our men away," said Yuri. "It's up to us, Kenichi. We have to put a stop to this!"

Kenichi followed Yuri toward a clicking sound, where a skilled archer sent a rain of arrows into the clearing. Kenichi grew faint. This wasn't a silly game of 'hide and seek,' but rather a desperate fight for survival.

Yards away, Bradley, Trevor, Derek and Andre knelt in the brush, near a dried creek bed. Bright moonlight gleamed upon large, pale stones. Tears streamed down the younger boys' cheeks, and neither kept still. Bradley also wept. Derek covered his head, and closed both eyes.

"Itchy sure knew what he was doing when he up and run off like that!" commented Andre.

"Shut up!" said Jesse, in the misty darkness.

"Get over here, Jess!" ordered Salazar. "Where the hell are you? Answer me!"

"You're asking for it, aren't you?" laughed Jesse, at his own peril. "Didn't I already tell you to shut your mouth, Lieutenant Commander Salazar, *sir?*"

Circling the clearing, Kenichi and Yuri sneaked through the trees, until they spotted the location of the clicking sounds. Moonlight revealed an outhouse, where a camouflaged archer was. The smell of dried excrement lingered in the brisk, autumn air. Kenichi and Yuri flanked the murderous figure, who fired arrows at will against Salazar's men. Adrenaline sprinted through Kenichi's veins like greased lightning.

Yuri removed a knife from under his robe, and crept upon the sniper. Kenichi held his breath. As Yuri approached the archer, Kenichi silently egged him on, knowing the results were unspeakable and bloody.

Closer, closer . . .

Closer . . .

Closer . . .

Yuri locked onto the sniper's chin, and turned his head to one side. Kenichi closed his eyes, sickened by that which hadn't yet occurred. Yuri shoved the knife from behind the sniper's ear, as blood spewed upon the outhouse wall and trees. Once Yuri released the sniper, he struggled to make sense of what he'd just done, and what he had yet to do.

Justified, for the good of all? . . .

Kenichi got to his feet when, in the corner of one eye, he detected movement. A second assailant, brandishing a stiletto in one hand, leaped toward him.

As Kenichi backed away, the assailant's weapon got caught into his tunic. Breaking free, Kenichi sent his fist into the opponent's face, as the stiletto fell to the ground. Kenichi fell backward, catching his feet into thick brush. Within seconds, the assailant was on top of him, forcing the stiletto toward the jugular vein.

The assailant wasn't an especially large person, but had tremendous strength in the arms and legs. Kenichi saw only the form of the assailant's face, along with the comical pageboy haircut. Blood dripped from the assailant's nose, where Kenichi hit him.

Wrapping his legs around the assailant's waist, Kenichi attempted to get the upper hand. No good. The assailant was less than an inch away from slitting his throat. Kenichi shouted in fear and defiance. Briefly, he thought about his friendship to Bradley, their plans of relocating to the country, and climbing Mount Patten in the spring. It was not to be. For all Kenichi knew, Bradley was already dead.

Kenichi screamed, once the stiletto pressed against his neck . . .

As Yuri drove his own blade between the assailant's ribs. Releasing the stiletto, the assailant's body went limp.

"Are you all right?" asked Yuri, lifting the assailant off of Kenichi.

Kenichi groaned as he slowly got up. Brushing grass, dirt, and twigs from his clothing, he limped away with a bruised shin, and scratches on both legs. Leaning against the outhouse, he let out a deep breath and gradually regained control of his shaky nerves. He rested his hand on Yuri's shoulder. "I am, now . . ."

"Look out!" Yuri called out, and swiftly ducked.

As Kenichi lowered his head, a whisk of air brushed past his face.

A large, heavy object slammed into the outhouse wall with a loud, echoing *thud!* Splinters flew from the aging structure. Crawling away on all fours, Kenichi saw the broad head of a splitting mall, lodged into the wall.

"Conrad!" shouted Yuri. *"No!"*

Kenichi turned to see a darkened figure, working to free the mall from the outhouse.

"Drop it, Conrad!" ordered Yuri. "Do it, now!"

"Yuri?" the fellow spoke, unhanding the mall. He smiled in recognition. "Is that you? . . . Hey, long time no see, buddy!"

Yuri laughed as he took his friend Conrad's hand. Tears of joy seeped from his eyes.

Just then, an arrow pierced Conrad's back, and exited from the chest. Conrad vomited blood as he staggered away and fell, the splitting mall still embedded into the wall.

Firing many questions at his rattled mind, Kenichi lacked answers for the inquisitive brain. Who were the three killers, awaiting Salazar? Were they hired to perform this crime, or acting as free agents?

And who sent that final arrow into Conrad?

"Conrad!" cried Yuri, kneeling to his dying comrade.

Kenichi's throat tightened, once he realized that all three assassins were in their teens. Stepping away, he sat next to a stump and sobbed.

"I didn't know it was you," whispered Conrad, blood trickling from the corners of his mouth.

Yuri softly ran his fingers through Conrad's dishwater blonde hair, cut in a shape of a bowl. Educated in the art and craft of killing, Yuri was never to endear himself to his classmates. He was an outsider, unpopular with most everybody.

Yuri and Conrad became sparring partners, while enrolled in fencing courses. Their competitive spirit eventually grew into support, mutual respect, and cooperation.

Yuri knew that a few former colleagues were under Gornick's command. He never imagined Conrad being swayed by the renegade general's fanatical spell. Yuri was caught between ending Conrad's life or, in futility, trying to save it.

"Yuri," breathed Conrad. "Helen and I killed Macready."

"You?" questioned Yuri, in shock and as a fierce accusation.

"I heard you got fingered for it," explained Conrad, his eyes clouding. "I can't help you now, but I never wanted you to . . ."

"Dead men tell no lies," interrupted Jesse, stepping from the shadows with a bow and a quill of arrows. As usual, he sported a smug, self-assured grin. His cruel, thoughtless statement prevented Conrad from saying more, as the assassin died in Yuri's arms.

Yuri cradled his friend's body. "Did you hear what he said, Jesse? It was Conrad and Helen who murdered Macready!"

"So?" asked Jesse. "They can't say diddly-squat, now. Let them tell it to the Devil."

"Please, Jesse! Make a report to Admiral Kraig!"

"Maybe I will, and maybe I won't," snickered Jesse.

Yuri glanced at the other two killers, who also served with him in the past. The first, who masterfully targeted Salazar's men, was Clive, the oldest student in Maliek's school. The second was the sole female member of the training. A short, stocky girl, Helen beat every boy in arm wrestling. It was Helen who nearly killed Kenichi with the stiletto.

"I never liked that dyke bitch, anyway," said Jesse, standing above Helen's corpse.

"Jesse," said Yuri. "You know the truth about Macready."

"I never liked you either, Yuri," said Jesse. "You wretched little fairy."

"I'm not a fairy!"

"Then do something about it," taunted Jesse. "Go ahead, if you feel that bad. Come on! Let me get you out of my misery, so you can join your friend Conrad in the Promised Land. Or do you Kuschans call it Paradise? Think of it as retribution, for what you did to *my* friend Marietto."

Yuri wanted to go a few rounds with Jesse, when someone barked, "What do you think you're doing?" It was Salazar, angrily approaching the outhouse. "Six of my men are dead, and here you are . . ."

As Yuri wiped his teary eyes, Jesse said, "It's okay, sir. We took care of it. You won't lose any more men."

Salazar stared at the three assassins. "Who were they?"

"Those who planned this massacre," smirked Jesse.

"God Almighty!" yelled Salazar, discovering that his opponents were kids, hired by Gornick to wipe out his small contingency. "What's the matter with you damned people, Jess? Do you enjoy killing? Do you think it's fun?"

"It's my job," explained Jesse, flatly. "That's it, sir. Nothing more."

Salazar released a sigh. "I don't know how you boys are about manual labor, but we've got graves to dig. Sorry, Yuri. That goes for you, too."

"I understand, Commander Salazar," said Kenichi, biting his bottom lip.

"What shall we do with these fiends, and the ones who almost stopped you, sir?" asked Jesse.

"There were more?" asked Salazar. "Where?"

"Behind that berm, where you were hidden. They were Agronians, dressed in loin clothes and painted as leopards. Don't concern yourself with them. They're as dead as my grandmother's first pet cat."

Salazar grew faint. "Why did they fire on us?"

"They were probably after Councillor Theo, which is splendid news," said Jesse. "That means he's still alive. Those Agronians are showy, but prone to stupidity. They're known to kill an entire village, just to get at one man. There's nothing you could have done any differently. Write this down as experience and move on, Commander Salazar."

"Very well, then," Salazar told Jesse. "While I 'move on,' I want you to drag these three into that privy, then set fire to it. They deserve no better than that."

"*Moi?*" gasped Jesse.

"Yes you, Jesse! And be fast about it!" With both fists clenched, Salazar returned to the clearing.

"You heard Commander Salazar!" snapped Jesse. "Get to work, you foul Kuschan dog! That goes for you too, lovely Oriental schoolmarm!"

"You get to work!" Kenichi shouted back. "I've got better things to do, than take your guff."

Jesse giggled. "Oh? One of those sweet, innocent kiddies in the brown dress? Who died and made you God?" Jesse squinted both eyes as he strutted toward Kenichi. "Hey baby, me real horny! Me real *horny.* You want *fucky?* You want *sucky?* Me love you, long time!"

Kenichi gave Jesse a menacing glare.

Mischief pushed Jesse to make another joke. Instead, he grudgingly followed Salazar's orders.

Yuri attempted to walk away, when Kenichi cautiously approached him. "Don't follow me!" bawled Yuri. "Please go away, Kenichi. I'm just . . . counting my arrows."

"Thanks for helping me," whispered Kenichi. "I thought she was going to kill me."

Yuri faced Kenichi, conscious of his teary eyes. *Justified, for the good of all?*

"Who is he?" asked Kenichi, pointing at Jesse.

"A bastard!" responded Yuri. "What do you think?"

"*Ah, ah, ah!*" Jesse wagged a finger at Yuri. "It takes one to know one, Yuri dearest. Is that any way to speak of a friend?"

"We were never friends, Jesse!" screamed Yuri. "And why did you have to kill Conrad?"

"Why did Conrad turn against us?" retorted Jesse. "Admiral Kraig assigned me to watch Commander Salazar's back. I'm only doing my job, so sue me."

It devastated Yuri knowing that his one buddy at Maliek's school was gone. What propelled Conrad to take Gornick's side, or to kill Macready? Was it love, money, idealism, or merely a "good idea" at the time?

Yuri wished he had been a typical boy, living a typical life, and passing the time of day in a typical fashion. "Why did we ever get mixed up with a man like Captain Maliek?" Yuri asked Jesse. "Why?"

Jesse grinned. "I'm not complaining."

"But I'm sick of this!"

"Now, now," said Jesse. "The sight of blood never bothered you, not in the least! Admit it. You enjoy killing, don't you? Maybe more than me."

"Kenichi?" asked Yuri. "Have *you* ever had to kill anyone?"

Kenichi thought about the sailor who tried to rape him, after slaying his mother. That was hard enough to deal with! And what about that incident, less than two days ago, when he killed . . .

. . . *accidentally* killed Karl?

There was nothing Kenichi could do to change what happened in the bordello, or at Lord Kelly's. He only hoped that neither event had any ill-effects on his friendship with Bradley.

Bradley!

Kenichi sprinted into the clearing, to encounter a scene mired in tragedy. By now, daylight had overtaken the long, cold, merciless night. Shrubs, grass, and soil were dampened by clammy films of dew, as the blurry shadows of trees lined the forest floor.

Searching for the jacket he left with Bradley moments before, Kenichi learned it was used to blanket a wounded soldier. Ignoring Salazar's orders, he focused on locating his best friend. "Brad!" he called, his throat sore and dry. *"Bradley!"*

No answer, as fear seized Kenichi. Images of his roommates lying dead were unimaginable. Surrounded by a tiny military force, Kenichi felt alone and isolated.

A solitary figure, dressed in a brown tunic and skullcap, wandered through the trees. One hand was shrouded in yellowed bandages. Although he disliked Andre, Kenichi found comfort and safety in familiarity. "Hey boy," addressed Andre, scowling.

"Andre?" asked Kenichi, hesitantly. "Where . . . where's Brad?"

"Yonder."

"Is he? . . . Are they? . . ."

"They're okay. No thanks to you, Itchy."

Kenichi ran through the dark, murky forest, until he arrived at a dried creek bed. He spotted his three roommates, huddled together behind a decaying log. "Bradley!" shouted Kenichi, his voice echoing in the stillness of the early morning.

"What's going on?" asked Trevor, wiping his runny nose.

"Come on out," said Kenichi, evasively. "We . . . took care of it . . . I mean . . . Commander Salazar and his men. They took care of it."

Trevor and Derek cautiously left the creek bed and went to the clearing.

Kenichi was exhausted. It had been a long night, concluded by a brutal, hellish dawn. Was there time, and opportunity, for anyone to rest or collect their chaotic thoughts?

Kenichi was only one of nearly a billion souls, stranded on an often vicious, mean-spirited world. There had to be a refuge from all this madness! Kenichi yearned for the day when he'd reside in an unspoiled land, where a handshake was as good as gold, and a man's word his code of honor.

In the distance, Jesse ignited the outhouse to cremate the bodies of his treacherous comrades and two Agronian mercenaries, who died serving General Gornick.

Bradley stepped toward Kenichi, then stopped. As the two boys looked at each other, neither made a sound. Then, as if to speak telepathically, Bradley reached out to hug Kenichi. In a friend's arms, he had assurances that all was well. At the same time, Kenichi held onto the sibling he so begged for.

In the harsh, bone-chilling breeze on that hazy autumn day, Bradley and Kenichi kept warm in their loving embrace.

"Lieutenant Salazar?" a young enlisted man said, entering the clearing with a half-dozen soldiers.

"That's Lieutenant *Commander* Salazar," the officer corrected. He had just placed another body into a humble, shallow grave, with Patrick's help.

"I'm sorry," the enlisted man stuttered. "I . . . I was sent to find ..."

"Who are you?" demanded Salazar. "Give me your name, soldier."

The man wore a strained smile. "Sergeant Rupert."

"*Sergeant* Rupert? Your insignia's that of a corporal."

Rupert swallowed, nervously. "Major Kohl promoted me two days ago."

"Major Kohl?" Salazar shook his head, in disgust. "Very well, *Sergeant* Rupert. What do you want?"

"Councillor Theo wanted me to check on the fire." Rupert glanced at the outhouse's smoldering remains. Five charred bodies highlighted the gruesome scene. Jesse stood by the ruins, preventing them from burning out of control.

"I was escorting Councillor Theo's son and five boys from Lord Kelly's Academy, when we ran into . . . this," explained Salazar, sadly.

"We've been expecting Yuri's arrival," said Rupert, pleasantly.

Yuri took notice of the conversation between Salazar and Rupert. "How is Father?" he asked.

"He's fine," informed Rupert. "The Embrian Council, what's left of it, is holding an emergency session in the executive room of the compound."

"Thank you, Sergeant Rupert," said Salazar. As an officer and a gentleman, he behaved as such. "My men need a moment of silence, before pushing on."

As Rupert left, Salazar and Patrick shared a canteen. After planting six more men in the earth, Salazar was beat. "I don't know how to tell you this, Pat," he confided, splashing cold water in his face. "I just don't think I'm the right man for the job."

"Don't say that," argued Patrick. "I know your worth, sir, even if you don't."

"But you saw what happened this morning! What good am I, always getting caught with my pants down?"

"Captain?" asked Andre, approaching Salazar.

"What did you call my superior officer?" asked Patrick, defensively.

Andre shrugged. "Well hell, boy, I didn't mean nothing by that . . ."

"I'm a lieutenant commander," explained Salazar. "Can't you tell by my uniform?"

Andre laughed. "I ain't never been in the Army!"

"*Navy,*" spoke Salazar, impatiently. "We're in the . . . Oh, forget it! What do you want, Andy?"

"*Andre,*" the boy said. "That weird kid by the fire says he wants to talk to you."

Salazar snickered. "Well Pat, shall we meander yonder to converse with the 'weird kid'?"

"If you say so," said Patrick.

Salazar strolled to the outhouse's ruins with Patrick. "Are you the weird kid who desires in chatting with *moi?*" he asked, mockingly.

"Commander Salazar, this fire's almost out," said Jesse, annoyed with his superior officer. "How long must I detail it?"

"Go ahead and extinguish it," answered Salazar. "Then I'd like a word with you."

"How shall I go about extinguishing it?"

"Oh hell, I don't care. Piss on it, if you have to."

Minutes later, Salazar and Patrick sat in the shade of an evergreen tree, quietly welcoming the sunrise. As birds chattered away in the warming air, the two men caught sight of a doe and her spotted fawn, peeking at them from a distance of less than twenty-five yards away.

"I've always enjoyed the dawn," commented Salazar, tiredly.

"Yes, sir," agreed Patrick. "Me, too."

"Pat, when the war ends, if the war ends, are you willing to come to work with me at Romero's?"

"You're not leaving the Army, are you?"

"The Navy, remember?"

Patrick frowned. "Sir, the country needs us!"

"I don't know, Pat. When old Kraig hears about this, my name won't amount to a thing in the War Ministry."

"Don't talk like that. You're a good man, sir. Where can I hope to find as worthy an officer, as you?"

Before Salazar answered, he was interrupted by Jesse. "Your humble servant," addressed Jesse, bowing with a silly grin.

Salazar got to his feet. "Jess, I can't trust Theo as far as I can throw him," he whispered. "As soon as we get to that compound, keep an eye open for . . ."

"It's not Councillor Theo you need to worry about," said Jesse. "Sir."

"Oh, really?" asked Salazar, infuriated. "Then just who do I 'need to worry about'?"

Jesse smirked. "The Kuschan daisy you've taken such a liking to."

"Patrick," spoke Salazar, sternly. "I will speak to my bodyguard. *Alone.*"

Patrick left, relieved not to hang around for the upcoming fireworks display.

"Take that goddamn hat off," Salazar ordered Jesse, containing his fiery temper.

Jesse did as he was told.

"I want to know something, and I expect an honest answer," insisted Salazar. "Why do you hate Yuri so much?"

"He's much too sensitive," explained Jesse. "It's in my nature to exploit weaknesses I find in an opponent."

Opponent? Yuri? Hell, he can't even hurt a fly!"

"Maybe not a fly, but most certainly you. Sir."

Salazar resented Jesse for rarely coming to the point. "You know what I think?" he said. "Your hatred of Yuri is based on his nationality, along with his . . . *peculiarities.* If I didn't know better, I'd swear you're jealous of Yuri. Are you two stinging from a childish lovers' quarrel? Feeling a tad jealous, are we Jess? Did Yuri *dearest* find himself a new beau?"

"My heart is reserved only for the ladies," stated Jesse, concealing his growing anger. *"Sir!"*

"Then what is it, ladies' man? Give it to me straight, and not in your coy mannerisms or riddles."

"Commander Salazar," said Jesse, somberly. "Yuri is colder than you can possibly imagine, even with his petite appearance and behavior. There are few in this world that I'm truly afraid of, and Yuri's one of them."

"I don't believe it! Do you really think I'm that stupid?"

"I didn't mean to imply . . ."

"When Reggie and my favorite horse were murdered, not far from this very spot, neither Theo nor Kohl gave me the time of day! So, who do you think went out of his way to help me? *Yuri!*"

Jesse laughed.

"Jesse," scolded Salazar, fed up with the bodyguard's attitude. "I see myself as a fair judge of character, and trust me when I say the 'Kuschan daisy' is all right. I don't care about your petty slanders or prejudices, and neither will you while you're under my command. Is that understood?"

Jesse sighed. "I've known Yuri much longer than you, and believe me . . ."

"Is that *understood?*" repeated Salazar.

"Have it your own way," said Jesse, in a demeaning manner. "But allow me to give you some advice, Commander Salazar. You only think you know Yuri. You don't know enough to be scared."

41

"Good morning, everyone," greeted Theo, at the opening of an emergency meeting. This crucial event, undignified by its surroundings, was held in a small shack, hidden away in the backwoods of Theo's secret compound. The meeting room, which had no windows, resembled a shoddy storage building.

While some believed that the compound was the last refuge of a scoundrel, for Theo it meant the difference between life and death. It also meant the life and death of Embrey. There were cartloads of vital documents, under guard in a storeroom, to be destroyed if the compound fell under enemy hands. Assuming General Gornick found these papers, heads would surely roll.

Theo was met by two of his fellow legislators. An older woman, Fumiko was a former princess from the eastern nation of Kokashima. Even with her slight frame, Fumiko still carried a loud, influential voice in national affairs. Omar, a dark-skinned, handsome man was, at twenty-nine, the Council's youngest member. He started out as Theo's intern. Through exposure to the legislative process and his own ambitions, he was chosen as one of five councillors.

Theo awaited two other Council members, Elias and Wilhelm. No one had saw hide nor hair of either man, since the fighting started. Both were missing and presumed dead.

Theo also felt Yuri's absence. The boy left with Giorgio and Fritz to find more men for Major Kohl's mission to Infernus. Theo imagined the worst. Based on dispatches delivered by sentries and a minor spy network, Sykes remained a kill-zone. No telling how many people were dead. It terrified Theo to think that Yuri was among the deceased. His anxieties multiplied when he saved a few schoolboys, along with Pastor Dimitri and his family, from Major Conroy. Breaking away on his own, Yuri hadn't been seen, since.

Finally, Theo worried about Garry, who disappeared minutes after he went outside with Sasha and the twins. Theo wrote a letter on Garry's behalf, to be endorsed by the Council. He knew that Garry sweated over his fellow guides. The region was no place for a shy, awkward kid in a kilt.

However, Theo managed to stay calm. Even with the extreme body count, the upheaval was a blessing of sorts. With the cards strewn across the table, they could be stacked to a more favorable position. Timing was everything.

Theo smiled as he faced those gathered in the meeting room. Omar and Fumiko, his manservant Linus, Pastor Dimitri, and a couple of pageboys sat in on the conversation. This structure included a fireplace, candles lining the walls, and a round table.

Theo stood to speak. Normally, his oratory was jovial and high-spirited. As a marked man, his authority granted him no room for uncertainty or weak nerves. "My dear friends," he spoke, "Embrey's destiny lies in our hands. With the displaced Ministry of War, we must fully support our armed forces, to battle those advocating tyranny. Once victory is achieved, we will again boast of our proud nation. On some brighter day, may we salve our wounds, then reconstruct Embrey to become a mightier nation than she's ever known."

Omar got to his feet, hoping his voice didn't crack or reveal overwhelming fright. "Councillor Theo, there are rumors that our sovereign is dead, and the government is deteriorating. Based on what we now know, can we restore the monarchy?"

"My dear Omar," said Theo. "Does the monarchy truly serve the people? Should we even bother to restore it?"

Omar shrugged. "I don't understand. What are you proposing?"

"Does Embrey require a king to squander its wealth, or lead the nation into self-centered whims and debauchery?" questioned Theo. "We have a chance today for bold action. You know of my plans in forming a representative government. It's up to us in deciding if we're ready for such a plan. I believe in a government which grants its citizens greater privileges, and the rights of self-determination." Theo turned to Dimitri. "Along with religious freedoms for all Embrians, nationals and immigrants."

Dimitri nodded, in affirmation.

"Councillor Theo," said Fumiko, standing to have her say. "Embrey is a vast nation. How do you expect your reforms to work in the outlying region, where our security is at its weakest?"

"Good point," said Theo. "Due to the King's failings, those are dangerous, lawless provinces. However, a solution is easy. The outlying areas hold provincial capitals. Their lords are nothing more than tax collectors, who depend on us to administer the laws. They'll be replaced by men which the landowners have chosen to govern. Through the advice and consent of these new governors, may we do what's right for the separate regions." Theo snickered. "Especially if the province is delegated by one of greater wisdom and knowledge . . . such as a woman."

"What if a particular region or province is sympathetic to General Gornick, and not us?" pondered Omar.

"Another good point," said Theo. "I'd hate to see Embrey divided into warring factions and confederations, working to gain dominance over the other. I tell you, Omar, it is not a problem. The landowners have the most to lose. Our rewards to them are surely more generous than what they can hope to achieve from Gornick."

"Your proposal also depends upon mutual respect and trust between neighboring countries," said Dimitri. "If your borders aren't secure, neither are your ally's. Only from fair trade and cooperation with foreign partners, will your ideas succeed."

Theo laughed. "Why else did I ask you to sit in on this meeting? Embrey has warm ties with our southern neighbor, and will uphold this bond. We cannot persevere without Kusch's blessing and support."

"Naturally," agreed Dimitri.

Everyone's attention was diverted, when the door popped open and in ran Yuri. Happily, the boy leaped into Theo's arms.

Although the display of tender emotions humiliated him, Theo was moved to tears from Yuri's homecoming. "I've missed you so much, my son!" he cheered.

"I've missed you too, Father," said Yuri, with his arms around Theo's shoulders.

Omar, Fumiko, and Dimitri had friends and family who were unaccounted for. They did not begrudge Theo for the return of his stepson. Yuri's homecoming gave them encouragement and hope, in a potentially hopeless scenario.

42

"Bradley!" shouted Giorgio, leaving a bunkhouse at Theo's compound. *"Brad!"*

Commander Salazar and his group reached their destination, as Yuri ran into one of the buildings to see Theo. Everyone else was standoffish. No one imagined that a man of Theo's stature would house himself in such humble structures. Salazar, in particular, looked down his nose at the compound.

Bradley and Kenichi glanced at each other. Why did Yuri lead them here?

Yuri's black terrier, Boris, snarled at the newcomers. As Trevor attempted to pet him, the dog refused his kindness.

"You have no idea how happy I am to see you!" shouted Giorgio, approaching his five schoolmates.

Trevor and Derek threw themselves into Giorgio, and nearly tackled him. The trio laughed, in celebration of their reunion.

"Hey, boy?" asked Andre. "You seen Bentley around, anywhere?"

"Sure, Andre." Giorgio pointed at the bunkhouse. "In there."

"I'm hungry!" whined Derek.

"Help yourself to lunch in the bunkhouse!" invited Giorgio. "We've got fried chicken, mashed potatoes, gravy . . ."

"Uh-uh!" Derek shook his head, in disbelief. "I ain't falling for *that* lie, again!"

Bradley backed away from Giorgio. He leaned against a tamarack, and struggled not to cry.

Bradley was not strong enough to face Giorgio. Kenichi had no trouble confronting him. "Trevor, Derry," he said, sternly. "Go inside."

"Okay," said Trevor, taking Derek into the bunkhouse. The two youngsters didn't know why Kenichi was so hostile with Giorgio, and didn't wait to find out.

Kenichi stepped toward Giorgio, who contemplated on runing away. Pride motivated the Leader-Trainee to stand his ground. Even then, it was impossible to look Kenichi square in the eye.

Kenichi grabbed onto Giorgio's robe. "Why did you tell Yuri to bring us here?"

"I . . . I've been worried about you!" stuttered Giorgio.

"Were you all that worried when you got Brad in trouble with Karl?"

"Wait . . . *Kenichi* . . ."

"Six of Commander Salazar's men are dead, and I almost got my throat cut this morning!" screamed Kenichi. "Do you have any idea just how dangerous it was coming here? Guess that shows you how worried you are!"

"How . . . how was I supposed to know? . . ."

Kenichi backhanded Giorgio's face. It wasn't an especially heavy blow, but still injured Giorgio in its intent.

"Stop it!" ordered Patrick, throwing himself between Kenichi and Giorgio. "Listen, isn't it in your best interests just to talk this over?"

"No!" snapped Kenichi.

"Kenichi, wait," begged Giorgio. "Please, just wait!"

"What did you and Fritz do to Antoine?" asked Kenichi, as an accusation.

"Who?" asked Giorgio, his eyes betraying him.

"Which one of you killed Antoine?" questioned Kenichi.

Giorgio's face altered to an ashen gray.

"What are you talking about?" asked Patrick, wondering if he should take this matter to Theo or Salazar.

A loud, shrill scream from the bunkhouse agitated an already tense situation. Bentley fled from the bunkhouse, still wearing his uniform with the sword and snake. Andre was in hot pursuit. "I don't give a damn if you are a 'pure Embrian', boy!" hollered Andre, chasing Bentley into the forest. "I'll kick your ass 'til your nose bleeds!"

Patrick followed the two brothers, leaving Giorgio at Kenichi's mercy.

"Well?" demanded Kenichi. "What happened after Brad and I left Karl's office? Which one of you killed Antoine?"

Giorgio gulped. "Who . . . What makes you think he's dead?"

"The constable thinks I did it!"

"Antoine stabbed Fritz, and I . . . we had to do something!" claimed Giorgio.

"Why didn't you tell the constable it was in self-defense?"

Giorgio was fed up with this interrogation. "You think you're so special, *Brother* Kenichi? Why didn't you stay, after you murdered Karl?"

Kenichi was speechless. Karl's death was an accident . . . wasn't it? Maybe so was Antoine's. Kenichi had no way of knowing. Even then, he didn't want to let Giorgio off the hook. "What was the big idea, blabbing to Karl about Brad and that girl?" he asked. "Don't tell me you've never been with a woman!"

"I have," admitted Giorgio, who took great pride in being a trusted confidante to the boys. In his heart, he had blown it. Giorgio loved Bradley more than anything, and prayed they were still close. "Can we talk, Brad?" he begged. "Please? There's something I have to tell you!"

"Now what are you trying to do?" questioned Kenichi. "Humiliate him in front of everyone else."

"How can you say that, Kenichi?" asked Giorgio. "You don't know how much Brad means to me! We've been friends for over five years!"

Kenichi smiled, maliciously. "With friends like you, who needs enemies?"

Kenichi's words were offensive. Maybe, just *maybe,* Giorgio deserved them. He was never really *there* for the students, once he became a Leader-Trainee. He spent too much time at Theo's, griping about Karl's tenure at Lord Kelly's. In Giorgio's absence, Kenichi took his place as a role model and big brother for some of the guys.

Finally, Karl's glowing praise for Bradley and ceaseless criticisms of Giorgio pitted them against each other.

Giorgio's eyes met Bradley's. Had Bradley not admired and respected Giorgio, the incident in Karl's office would've meant little. Bradley expected more from Giorgio, who should have been the last person to bring injury upon him. In doing so, Giorgio brought injury upon their friendship. Bradley wanted to forgive Giorgio, while also forgiving himself.

In a world gone straight to hell, there were no constants to rely on. Bradley hated thoughts of resenting Giorgio. Such feelings weighed heavily upon the heart, body, and soul. It evolved into a prison where Bradley was judge, jury, and executioner. Never could he escape the one who pressed him into bondage.

Never could he escape the one holding the key, which set him free.

Giorgio buried his face in the palms of both hands, and cried. It was a deplorable sight. Bradley recalled lying on the floor of Karl's office, pleading for everyone's   forgiveness. That day, Giorgio required the exact same considerations.

The jail sentence was over, as Bradley embraced Giorgio. The two boys needed each other, to forget the past and become whole, once more.

Kenichi saw nothing good in Bradley's reconciliation with Giorgio. How stupid could Brad be, to align himself with a wolf in sheep's clothing? Sure, Kenichi appreciated Bradley for his kindness and good will to most everybody. Those very traits were also his undoing.

Perhaps it was jealousy or envy, but Kenichi loathed seeing Bradley with Giorgio. A sense of one-upmanship gave him superiority over the Leader-Trainee. Indeed, it was pleasing to hate Giorgio's guts!

Trevor and Derek entered the bunkhouse, where a gust of warm air greeted them. Not only did they find several of their friends there, but a tasty meal which Eduardo prepared on a wood cook stove, in one corner of the room. The aspiring chef had fried chicken, potatoes, and gravy awaiting them. The arousing smell of poultry sizzling on the griddle was comforting to Derek. Where most of the boys were now dressed in thin shirts, vests, and wool breeches, Eduardo remained in his school uniform, to work at the hot fire.

The bunkhouse was constructed of logs, with a straw roof. Twenty bunks lined the interior. Lanterns dangled from the rafters, above. Wood smoke blackened the walls, furnishings, and windows.

Geoffrey hopped from a top bunk. "Make yourselves at home," he said, relieved to see Trevor and Derek.

Derek made a beeline to the chow. He fetched a steel dish and wooden fork, stacked with pieces of silverware on a nearby table. Eagerly, he stabbed his fork into a juicy chicken breast, still sizzling in the pan.

"That's not done, yet," said Eduardo.

Derek didn't care. He sat on a bunk between Sergio and Giuseppe, and gorged himself on the meal as everyone laughed at his lack of manners.

"Well, Trev?" asked Randy. "Coming in?"

Trevor wore a lopsided grin, as his knees buckled. Taking a small step inside, he collapsed at the bunkhouse door, in exhaustion. Carefully, Eduardo and Randy placed him on a top bunk, above Sergio's bed.

"Is he dead?" asked Giuseppe.

"How would you feel, if you had nothing to eat but jerky for two days?" asked Kenichi, entering the bunkhouse.

"What took you so long?" asked Eduardo, handing Kenichi a dish.

Kenichi refused to speak of the events from the past two days. After filling his plate, he returned outside. He relished food over conversation.

"Too good to eat with the white folks," commented Sergio, slightly intoxicated.

Derek looked forward to a second helping of lunch, along with several hours of sleep, until . . .

"Grub tastes a lot better with this," someone spoke, offering him a tin chalice with cold, bubbly liquor.

Derek looked up to see Fritz, with a bottle of Campens Rose'. The bully was still clad in his ruined tunic, which exposed his sinewy frame. "What's this?" asked Derek, curiously.

"Treats," snickered Fritz.

Derek hesitated to take a drink.

"If he don't want some, I want s'more!" demanded Sergio.

"I can't approve of you letting them drink that," said Geoffrey. "You're not being a positive role model, by providing children with alcohol . . ."

"Aw, just shut the hell up, Geoff!" screamed Fritz. "What kinda role models are you and Randy?"

Geoffrey said nothing, in his own defense.

Fritz laughed. "Why don't you and yer friend go outside and prance neckid around the trees, birds, and flowers, or whatever you homos do in the deep, dark woods?"

Geoffrey shot a nervous glance at Randy. For the exception of Trevor's snoring, the room grew deathly quiet. Geoffrey and Randy thought it best to leave.

"Get back here!" ordered Eduardo. "He doesn't have the right to boss you around!"

"See you later, Eduardo," said Randy, leaving the room with Geoffrey.

"If you was any kinda man, Ed, you wouldn't be doin' woman work!" remarked Fritz.

"And if you were any kind of man, you wouldn't have screamed like a little girl when they tried to hang you yesterday!" shouted Eduardo, slamming the bunkhouse door behind him to join Geoff and Randy.

"Where's the treats?" asked Derek, scooping more potatoes and gravy into his dish.

"You'll get some, as long as ya keep yer mouth shut," promised Fritz, slowly recovering from Eduardo's remark. "Bottoms up, Derry! Put a little hair on yer chest!"

Derek examined the chalice as he sat down. Cautiously, he took a sip.

"Goddamn, that ain't no way to drink it!" roared Fritz. Swigging the bottle, he let booze drip from the corners of his mouth. "Like that!"

Derek bravely downed the Campens Rose'. The liquid fire burned clear to the stomach, and hit the boy like a stampede. Derek swayed back and forth, almost dropping the chalice. His eyes watered as he bumped against the twins. Was this really a treat, or just another one of Fritz's ornery tricks?

As Derek emptied the chalice, everyone cheered as Sergio patted his slight shoulders.

"Well?" asked Fritz. "Whatcha think?"

"That's horrible!" gagged Derek, handing the chalice to Fritz. "Hurry it up, Fritzy! I want s'more!"

Bradley and Giorgio strolled along the foothills surrounding Theo's compound, as they celebrated a renewal of their friendship. Saying little, they admired the beauty of the Embrian countryside, in autumn. Plant life, which had been full and lush just weeks before, now resembled the dark, gray colors of the soil from which it grew. Already, trees had shed their leaves, or altered them to an array of bright red, yellow, and orange. A slight breeze was relaxing.

"I'm sorry, Brad," whispered Giorgio, breaking the silence.

"Me, too," replied Bradley.

On a bald hillside, the two boys had a vivid look of Sykes, in the distance. A haze of smoke lingered over the crippled city. The community once burst with energy. Now it was in shambles. Noted landscapes, such as the Falcon Theatre, were no more. On the Ember River, large sections of the waterfront smoldered, as ports were destroyed. The bells of Lord Kelly's, which were heard from miles around, had not chimed for more than two days.

"Will you come on an adventure with me?" begged Giorgio.

"Where?" asked Bradley. "Mount Patten?"

"Mount Patten?" laughed Giorgio. "No, Insula Infernus!"

"What?"

"I'm serious! We've been hired to find a treasure on Infernus, with an Army officer named Major Kohl. There's nothing left for us, here. But if we retrieve this fortune, it may help finance our country's rebirth."

Bradley knew little about Infernus, but heard a great deal of its legend and unsavory reputation. Based upon his earlier discussion with Leader Royce, King Auric IV and a small number of followers traveled to that faraway land, never to return. Royce suggested that Auric's descendants were still there, thriving in this new world. Rumor also claimed that traders sold the island's various goods, through the black market. Bradley doubted these accounts. In his mind, Auric and his men died of starvation, despair, or far worse.

Bradley knew of Giorgio's opposition to the Border War, which was among his countless disagreements with Karl. If Infernus was as scary as people thought, what propelled Giorgio to go there?

"What happened to Antoine?" demanded Bradley.

Giorgio hesitated. He owed Bradley the truth, at least his version of it. "Antoine was your friend," he sighed. "Mine too, until he drew a dagger on Fritz and me. In time, he would've drawn a sword on you and Kenichi."

It upset Bradley to see Antoine brainwashed by Gornick. Similar to Karl, Antoine was open in his hatred of Kenichi.

"My parents are dead," said Giorgio, misty-eyed. "I have no idea where my brothers and sisters are. I . . . I had no right getting you into trouble, Brad. I wanted to get back at Karl, but hurt you instead. For that, I'm truly sorry."

"I'm sorry, too," said Bradley. "I want to believe that everything will work out in the end, but I can't!"

"We're both in hot water, unless we sway public favor on our sides."

"What if we can't?"

"You still want to be a Leader, Brad?" asked Giorgio.

"I don't think I'm qualified. Not anymore."

"Why not?"

Bradley shrugged. "Well . . . you know . . ."

"You're not the first guy from Lord Kelly's to be with Leni," said Giorgio. "She was my Thursday night ritual. Believe me, I went a lot further with her, than you did."

Bradley glared at Giorgio.

"I know, I know, I'm a hypocrite!" Giorgio's throat tightened. "Not only do I owe you an apology, but God as well."

"Me, too." Bradley was unable to look beyond this one error. Would he regret it to his grave?

"I have something to give you." Giorgio reached into his pocket, cupped a round, metallic object, and placed it in Bradley's hands. It was the necklace featuring Lord Kelly's insignia, a gift from Karl to Bradley. The last time Bradley saw it, Karl had ripped it from his neck, and threw it on the floor.

"I know how much this means to you," explained Giorgio. "I prayed of returning it to its rightful owner. In my worst dreams, I thought you were dead!"

Bradley's lips quivered. "I can't keep it!"

"Why not, Brad? It's yours!"

"It was a present from Karl. It broke his heart when he found out . . ."

"Well, now it's a present from me." A tear streamed from Giorgio's eye. "Your sins are nothing, compared to Karl's. He was never your friend! He cast you off for a mistake which he undoubtedly made, himself! Karl saw his grace and redemption through you, not from his own accomplishments. You've never broken my heart, and I do hope we do become Leaders, some day."

"How?" pondered Bradley. "The school's closed!"

"Maybe we'll reopen it, once we return from Infernus. We'll have earned our Leadership, by then. Didn't King Auric try to colonize Infernus?"

"That was four-hundred years ago!"

"But if there are Embrians living there, don't we have an obligation to deliver the word of God?" asked Giorgio. "For all we know, Auric may have left the treasure there. In that case, it's got historical, as well as monetary value. Just think! We'll redeem ourselves to God, if we share our beliefs to those cut off from civilization! Faith and prayer will get us through anything. Will you pray with me?"

Bradley frowned. "After what I've seen lately, I'm not sure if I have faith in anything."

"Don't say that, Brad. If we lose faith, we lose everything! Sometimes faith is all we've got!"

"But where is God, when we need Him? What if He was never there, to begin with?"

"We need God now, more than ever," said Giorgio. "Please, Brad. Will you pray with me? There's nothing I want more from you, than that."

Whether his faith was tested or not, Bradley agreed that prayer was necessary in the act of forgiveness. As he rested his hand in Giorgio's, the two knelt to the ground. Lowering their heads, the two boys recited in unison, "Oh, most righteous on high . . ."

Kenichi sat on a chopping block at the bunkhouse door, enjoying his first decent meal in days.

Kenichi appreciated the warm food and tranquility at the compound. Even then, he still hoped to leave soon. Bradley gave his word to tag along, a promise Kenichi began doubting. Bradley was chummy with his other schoolmates, long before Kenichi's arrival. Kenichi had no claims to Bradley, or anyone else from Lord Kelly's. No matter. Bradley was a real pal, when Kenichi thought he'd never have another.

Friendship was disposable, and Kenichi could find new buddies. He even thought about returning to Lord Charles, to see if the old gang was there. How? Kenichi had little money, no food, and only his school uniform to wear. He didn't like the idea of going on a road trip, dressed in a measly school tunic, without the luxuries and assurances of companionship. With a nation at war, Kenichi put himself in harm's way, by venturing out alone. On the other hand, he had depended upon himself, before meeting Leader Lionel.

In the past, he didn't have to worry about Branellians, or kooks with swords and snakes on their clothes . . .

Was it selfish for Kenichi in asking Bradley to accompany him? It wasn't just that he cared about Bradley. He *wanted* to care about him! Bradley needed a keeper, and Kenichi hated to see him swayed to Giorgio's side. It was wrong for Bradley to leave with that self-righteous jerk! The numbskull believed what everyone had told him, be it Giorgio, Fritz, Karl, Sven . . .

Or *Kenichi.*

As Kenichi finished lunch, a few hens scratched for something to eat. Three youngsters, the children of a Kuschan pastor, played fetch with Boris. That was, until the dog took an interest in the chicken bone on Kenichi's dish. Boris sniffed at Kenichi's leg, and snarled. "Here," said Kenichi, giving Boris the prize as he smiled at the Kuschans. "Go away, mutt. They like you more than I do."

After cleaning the dish, Kenichi thought about starting his long, lonely trek before sundown. Was he allowed to do a bit of work at the compound, in exchange for some provisions and clean clothes? After his brief stay at Lord Kelly's, Kenichi grew fond of a few schoolmates, and hated to bid them adieu. It was a scary, uncertain jaunt without a buddy at his side.

With his heart breaking, Kenichi wondered if he was better off without Bradley . . .

. . . and if Bradley was better off, without him.

Kenichi broke free from self-pity when he saw Yuri coming his way. "Kenichi!" greeted Yuri, happily. "Where's Bradley?"

"He left with Giorgio," said Kenichi, unable to conceal his animosity and jealousy.

"Father wants to meet you," said Yuri.

"Who?"

"Come with me!" urged Yuri, patting Kenichi's shoulder.

Kenichi had recently spent a night in a filthy basement. That morning, he was nearly killed by a trio of assassins. He'd now acquaint himself to one of the most powerful men in Embrey!

Kenichi placed his dish on the chopping block, then followed Yuri. Entering the meeting room, he met Theo, Omar, Fumiko, and Pastor Dimitri. Social, political, and religious status usually meant nothing to him. The bordello, where he and his mother worked, served several mayors, magistrates, and spiritual leaders. However, once he laid eyes upon the three Embrian Councillors and a Kuschan holy man, Kenichi was in awe.

Already, Kenichi was impressed by Theo. The legislator was just a man, but an important one! Kenichi suddenly grew conscious of his every word, move, and gesture. Out of formality and politeness, he bowed.

"We never garner that level of respect from those emptying the pots in the parliament building," laughed Theo. "Good morning, young man. I'm Theo, Yuri's father."

"I'm Kenichi, no one's father . . . I hope."

"Please sit down." Theo pulled up a chair for Kenichi, as he introduced everyone at the table.

Aware of his skinny, bare legs, Kenichi discreetly kept them together.

Theo sat between Kenichi and Yuri. "I've heard many good things about you," he said.

"From who?" asked Kenichi, awkwardly.

"Oh, first from Giorgio, then from Yuri."

Kenichi rolled his eyes back. He doubted if Giorgio had anything nice to say about him, now.

"Where are you from?" asked Fumiko, drawn to Kenichi's heritage.

"Marks," answered Kenichi, jittery.

"Is that where your parents are from?" asked Fumiko, her eyes glued to the thin figure in the immodest brown tunic.

"No, Ma'am," said Kenichi, covering his thighs under both arms. "My mom was from Kokashima. I never knew my father."

"Relax," said Fumiko, casually rubbing Kenichi's knee. "My youngest son Hiroyuki attends Lord Werner's Academy in Griffith, and their uniforms are similar to yours. I assume he's still there. I've yet to hear from him."

Kenichi sighed. "It's just that . . . I don't like this tunic."

"Oh?" questioned Fumiko. "I think boys are quite handsome in that style of clothing."

"That makes one of us," commented Kenichi.

"Hiroyuki looks very dashing in his uniform," said Fumiko. "What do you think, Councillor Omar?"

"I wore those same kinds of clothes when I was a boy," said Omar. "Commander Salazar is a friend of mine, and we went to Lord Conway's, together. He'll agree with me. Those tunics are uncomfortable, especially in the wintertime."

"Well, I don't like Commander Salazar, and his opinion doesn't count," said Fumiko. "I immigrated from Kokashima, when Hiroyuki was still a baby."

"Fumiko's the daughter of Ko, a former warlord," informed Omar.

"Oh, that was years ago," dismissed Fumiko, as if her royal background amounted to nothing. Sipping a cup of tea, she added, "I don't care to go there. The country's new regime will pay handsomely for my head. So Kenichi, what does your mother do?"

Theo had heard what Kenichi's mother did for a living, and hastily changed the subject. "I'm sorry!" he said, giving Kenichi a cup and small pitcher. "Do you want some coffee?"

"Coffee?" asked Kenichi.

"Try some!" encouraged Yuri. "You'll love it!"

Once Theo filled his cup with hot java, Kenichi took a drink. The fluid swirled around in his mouth, went down his throat, and gave him a quick jolt. The coffee was preferable to Lord Kelly's wine, which often brought on drowsiness and stupidity. Kenichi felt more alert and alive.

"Yuri and I are from St. Alexandrov," said Dimitri. "Have you ever been to Kusch?"

Kenichi shook his head, 'no.' "I'd love to visit it! I hope to travel, some day."

"I understand you can read and write," said Theo.

"Yes, sir," said Kenichi, taking another drink. "Leader Lionel taught me at Lord Charles'."

"You're fortunate," said Theo. "Most Embrians don't know their letters or numbers. After spending my early years as a merchant marine, I brought the first printing press into Sykes. You've probably read some of the volumes I've published."

"You were a merchant marine?" asked Kenichi, in fascination.

"When I was your age."

"Where did you go?"

"Everywhere," laughed Theo. "Well, everywhere the charts revealed."

"I'd like to serve on a merchant vessel," said Kenichi, excitedly.

"I'd still be hauling freight around the world if I was half my age, and thirty pounds lighter," said Theo. "More coffee?"

"Yes, sir."

"I wonder if I may have a few words alone, with Kenichi?" asked Theo, to the others in the room.

"It's a beautiful fall day," noted Omar. "Will you join me for a walk, Councillor Fumiko?"

"If you'll excuse me," added Dimitri, leaving the meeting room. "My wife, the *boss,* has lunch ready in my cottage."

"We'll talk, later," said Fumiko, resting Kenichi's hand in hers. "It's very nice to meet you, Kenichi."

"You, too," said Kenichi, smiling. "I look forward to seeing you, again."

"That's delightful," agreed Fumiko, as she followed Omar outside.

"Goodbye, Father," said Yuri, kissing Theo's cheek.

"Later, Yuri," said Theo, warmly. "It's nice having you home, son."

Yuri's eyes were teary as he left Kenichi with Theo.

"So, what do you want to be, when you get older?" asked Theo, refilling Kenichi's cup.

"Alone," answered Kenichi. "I want to be alone."

"I appreciate that," chuckled Theo. "My current situation doesn't allow that privilege. I hate to break this to you, but you won't be alone on a ship. It's pretty cramped aboard merchant vessels."

"What I really want is to travel with my friend Bradley," explained Kenichi. "Next spring, we're climbing to the summit of Mount Patten . . . At least, I am."

"You've been to Mount Patten?"

"Yes, sir. Four or five times."

"Amazing! I envy you! What do you have planned, after that? You don't look like a soldier, farmer, or clergyman."

"I'd like to share my knowledge and education."

"To the children of the upper crust. Those opportunities aren't open to serfs. I dream of giving all Embrians a good education. It won't happen in my lifetime, I'm sorry to say." Theo paused. "What do you think of Yuri?"

Silence. Honesty and dishonesty were equally perilous. "Your son saved my life, sir," whispered Kenichi. "He saved everyone, including Commander Salazar and his men."

"I was notified of that," sighed Theo. "As you can guess, Yuri's a trained assassin, along with the well-dressed boy working for Salazar. That was the only opportunity afforded them, unfortunately. Initially, I hired Yuri as a bodyguard. I never married, and had no heir to my property and fortune. I now regard Yuri as my son."

Kenichi smiled, weakly.

"I wished Yuri had the chance to a normal childhood, what's left of it." Theo beat his fist to the table. "It's a disgusting practice, teaching boys to kill. I'm just as guilty as using Yuri's skills as others intended, for their own greedy motives."

Considering the grisly events near the compound, Kenichi was lucky that Yuri and Jesse were there. With that in mind, he was indebted to Yuri. What was expected, in return?

"Yuri doesn't have many friends his own age, for the exception of Dimitri's children," said Theo. "They're ignorant of his profession. I prefer to keep it that way."

Such was life for those like Yuri and Jesse. Trust led to an early death, and Kenichi was afraid of befriending Yuri. He was afraid of him, altogether! He also felt sorry for Yuri. Both Kenichi and Yuri knew what it meant to be outsiders, in a misunderstanding society and culture.

"I hope to give Yuri every advantage in life," said Theo, in desperation and determination. "Everything I own will be his, and I must shape him into a man of title and property. I admire you, Kenichi, for lifting yourself up from humble beginnings."

"The same can be said of most everyone from Lord Kelly's," replied Kenichi. "I'm not the only one there who's had it tough."

Theo smiled. "Eduardo sure knows his way around a kitchen. I plan to hire him, full time. My manservant Linus is getting up in age. Are you willing to stay with us . . . that is, until the nation gets back on its feet? I need someone of your education and character, and I'll pay you a good wage."

Kenichi was flattered by the tempting proposition. While not as *liberating* as pursuing his dreams on the road, he looked for anything which opened doors for him. Were there any strings attached? "Is it all right for Brad to stay, too?" asked Kenichi. "He doesn't stand a chance on his own."

"I don't see why not," said Theo. "That may work out even better. You see, I want Yuri to hang up his weapons. I believe he wants that, too. I think your presence, and Bradley's too, will have a positive effect on him."

Theo failed to point out that his idea might also prevent Yuri and the other boys from accompanying Major Kohl to Insula Infernus. He still saw necessity in the mission. However, the civil unrest in Embrey changed everything. Every worthwhile soldier or mercenary had likely taken one side or another in this fight, and were unavailable for Kohl.

Theo's mind was jumbled. He didn't know which path to take. Who had been spared the sight of bloodshed and murder? Was it best to get those lads out of the country, on an extended sea voyage, with a seasoned crew?

Theo knew the skipper of an Agronian schooner, the *Tyree James*. He believed that Captain O'Toole was a capable man, who supplied him with goods such as Campens Rose'. A few of O'Toole's men had already been to Infernus. The first mate Fernandez was involved with a disastrous attempt at colonizing the strange, faraway land. Perhaps Major Kohl and the boys would be safe on the Tyree James, although Theo hated placing them with Agronian rabble!

Kenichi was uncertain about accepting Theo's offer. It wasn't a question of Theo's heartfelt love for Yuri. While Kenichi owed Yuri a great deal, he saw nothing in the Kuschan's future but a tragic end. He also wondered if Yuri was unpredictable, and insane.

"How dare you draw a sword on me!" shouted Commander Salazar, from outside. "I'll have you in chains by nightfall, Kohl!"

Theo and Kenichi ran outside.

Near the meeting room, Major Kohl aimed his sword at Salazar. The young naval officer wasn't afraid of Kohl, but rather outraged. To most observers, this clash's outcome was apparent. Even with a weapon in his hand, Kohl was terrified of Salazar.

What scared onlookers was the possibility of an escalating conflict. Not only did Salazar's men back him, but Kohl had his supporters on hand. Jesse and Yuri stared at each other, as if they'd soon grapple. Nearly everyone currently residing at the compound played witness to this incident.

"How dare you challenge my rank?" Salazar questioned Kohl.

"You haven't earned that esteemed commission!" argued Kohl. "What idiot promoted you to lieutenant commander?"

"Your brother!" informed Salazar. "And if Admiral Kraig had any sense, he'd arrest you for impersonating an officer!"

"Stop this, or I'll have you both decommissioned!" spoke Theo.

"You have no right to break me!" screamed Salazar, still in the belief that Theo and Kohl were responsible for the deaths of Reginald, two guards, and a horse. Once more, his temper had gotten the best of him, and it wasn't worth trading barbs with someone of Kohl's lowly caliber. It humiliated Salazar to lose his temper. On a recurring basis, he reminded himself that he was, after all, an Embrian military officer. "My apologies," he said, swallowing his pride. "I'm expected at the War Ministry, and must take my leave of you, Councillor Theo."

"*Aw,*" said Jesse, with a snotty grin. "Just as I was getting so comfy."

Cautiously, Kohl placed his sword in its sheath.

Theo disliked Salazar, yet saw the necessity in treating him fairly. "I haven't compensated you for bringing my son home," he said, choosing his words judiciously.

"Just doing my job," mumbled Salazar, his tone hollow and insincere.

"It's commendable that you're mindful of your duty, *Lieutenant* Salazar," smirked Kohl. "Once I get back, you won't be fit to lick my dirty shoe."

"Major Kohl!" scolded Theo. The aging officer nearly spilled the beans about his covert mission to Infernus.

Get back from where?" demanded Salazar. "Get back from *where?*"

Kohl gulped. "I . . . I'm not at the liberty to say."

"You're up to something, aren't you?" laughed Salazar. "Aren't you?"

Kohl shook his head, in denial.

"Oh, yes you are," accused Salazar. "And when I find out, I'll see you hang."

Kenichi wanted no part of this squabble. More than anything, he had to break free from the expectations of others.

"Let's go, Pat," ordered Salazar. "I've had my fill of their Embrian hospitality."

"Commander Salazar," said Kenichi, stepping forward to shake the officer's hand. "I wish you well, sir. Thank you for your sacrifices to my friends and me."

Salazar nodded, flattered by Kenichi's gratitude.

"Please be careful, Commander Salazar," said Theo, in a conciliatory manner.

"You'll see to that, won't you?" answered Salazar, sarcastically. "Collect the men, Pat. We're leaving immediately!"

"Yes, sir," said Patrick, bowing to his host. "Good day, Councillor Theo."

"What did Major Kohl say to get Commander Salazar so riled up?" Kenichi asked Theo.

"Who knows?" answered Theo, secretly. "They're like banty roosters, striving to be the coop's top cock."

Kenichi frowned. *Okay, so don't tell me!*

"Make yourself at home, Kenichi," said Theo. "Feel free to explore the grounds, at your luxury. I'll give you time to mull things over. I do hope you consider staying on. You'll be a real asset."

"Thanks for the coffee," said Kenichi, once more dreaming of the snow-covered peak of Mount Patten, shining in the bright, afternoon sun. *I have to be free!*

"Major Kohl!" snapped Theo, angrily. "Step into my office!"

Kohl went into Theo's cottage, like a whipped puppy dog.

"Commander Salazar," addressed Theo, diplomatically. "There's something I'd like to tell you."

"There's something I'd like to tell you, too," responded Salazar, "but it may be construed as treasonous."

"Hold on, I must speak to you!"

"Funny, I sure don't have to speak to you . . ."

"Stop that, *Ensign* Salazar!" barked Theo. "That's an order!"

Salazar did as he was told.

"Much of the upheaval was the work of a significant raiding party from Branell," informed Theo.

Salazar laughed. "Councillor Theo, my men and I were all over Sykes, yesterday. Let me tell you, Gornick and his fanatics were responsible for most of the casualties." Ashamed, Salazar knew that he, too, had previously been a loyal Gornick 'fanatic.' "If you don't mind, I have to be at the Ministry of War by nightfall."

"I'm not finished!" exploded Theo, fed up with Salazar's cold shoulder.

"Yes?"

"Since you already know the price of failure, I give you my word of honor to General Chang, Admiral Kraig, and to you. More importantly, I give my word of honor to our beloved Embrey."

"Very well," said Salazar, hesitantly. "You have my attention."

"According to my . . . sources, a number of Branellian ships had recently departed from our shores, but left some of their men behind. Stragglers are situated at the mouth of the Ember River. I suspect they're looking to steal a small craft, to make good an escape. You'll be granted your due, if you succeed in capturing them. I claim no knowledge of this dispatch." Theo smiled. "The glory will be yours, Commander Salazar, and yours alone."

"I'll check it out," responded Salazar, fearing he was being drawn into a trap. "It'll please you to know that we may not get home with our lives, based on my luck."

"I bear you no ill-feelings," said Theo. "I know you don't like me. However, my son speaks quite highly of you. I ask that we put aside our differences, and work together to preserve our nation. Will you agree to that?"

With a nod, Salazar walked away.

Theo watched this small contingency march away from the compound. He prayed that Salazar followed his directions, but had his doubts.

Theo entered his cottage where Major Kohl awaited him, and angrily slammed the door.

44

After circling the compound, Kenichi cracked open the bunkhouse door to catch a few schoolmates singing bawdy, barroom songs. In the center of this revelry was Fritz and Derek, sitting on an upper bunk, sharing a bottle of Campens Rose'. Rocking back and forth, the duo roared out the ballad's filthier lyrics. Both were drunk. The smartest kid in the room was Trevor, who managed to sleep through it all.

Kenichi wondered if it was time to go wherever fate, opportunity, and the winding road took him. He had made it on his own before, and would so again. However, after what Leader Lionel taught him at Lord Charles', did he have what it took to steal, reside in abandoned buildings, sell himself for another person's pleasure, or eat decaying food?

Face it . . .Kenichi was obligated to Bradley, Trevor, and Derek.

Kicking at a white hen, Kenichi cursed himself. Why didn't I keep to myself at Lord Kelly's? It was a mistake to make friends! It was a mistake to love Bradley like a brother!

Face it . . . I'm stuck with that dumb kid, and he's stuck with me.

Kenichi hiked across a bald ridge when he met up with Bradley and Giorgio. As he had feared, the two were on speaking terms. Bradley, that numbskull! How long will it take before Giorgio screws him over again? And where does Bradley stand, when it comes to the future?

Is Mount Patten still in the works?

Giorgio and Kenichi traded caustic glances. Both teens were worried about Bradley. Would they use him as a pawn, to get their own way? Kenichi wasn't interested in being cordial with Giorgio, yet upheld warm ties with Bradley.

Likewise, Giorgio had difficulty maintaining eye-contact with Kenichi. It was nearly impossible for him to get these words out. "You were right about confronting me . . ." His throat tightening, Giorgio finished by mouthing, "Sorry."

For Bradley's sake, Kenichi shook Giorgio's hand. With that, Giorgio disappeared to lick his wounds, consider the error of his ways, or fantasize about beating Kenichi's butt.

"Are you hungry?" asked Kenichi.

"I could eat a bear!" sighed Bradley.

"There's chicken and potatoes in the bunkhouse, unless Fritz let it burn on the stove."

"Fritz?"

"Yeah," said Kenichi. "Good ol' Fritzy. Seems we'll never get shy of him, will we?"

"Kenichi?" asked Bradley, nervously. "We still going?. . . You know, to Mount Patten?"

Kenichi's heart sank. Did this conversation lead to saying 'goodbye'? "You're coming with me, aren't you?"

Bradley fidgeted. "Well, yeah . . ."

"'Well, yeah' what? What's going on?"

Bradley's silence was unnerving.

"Look," sighed Kenichi. "Theo offered me a job, but I'm not sure whether to take it. If it's all the same to you, I'm moving on, and I want you with me. I may be gone by tonight, or tomorrow morning at the latest."

"No!" cried Bradley. "Me and Giorgio thought you'd go to Infernus with us."

"What?"

"I know this sounds crazy," explained Bradley. "But Giorgio says there's a treasure somewhere on Insula Infernus, and we need your help finding it."

"That's the dumbest thing I ever heard, Brad!" argued Kenichi. "There's no treasure on Infernus, and even if there was, who says we're the ones to fetch it?"

"All I know is what Giorgio told me!"

"And if Giorgio said the sky was falling, you'd believe that, too?"

"Don't talk to me like I'm stupid!" shouted Bradley. "You're the one saying he wants to see the world. Great, then let's go see the world!"

Yes, Kenichi was curious about Insula Infernus, a place of myth, legend, and tall-tales. He preferred traveling there with experienced, toughened sailors, not guys like Fritz, Andre, and Giorgio!

"I have to do this," defended Bradley.

"What for?" questioned Kenichi. "Giorgio?"

"No, for God!"

"What's God have to do with it?" Kenichi snickered. "That Leni thing? Learn from your mistakes."

"I knew you'd never understand."

"Look, I can see why you want to stay with your buddies, especially if they go on that stupid trip."

"That's exactly why I have to go!"

In desperation, Kenichi sought to change Bradley's mind about Infernus. "I was wrong about Trevor and Derry," he said. "Maybe we are the ones to take care of them, instead of leaving them at another lousy school. They're better off with us, instead of hopping a ship with guys like Fritzy, or . . ."

"Whatcha doin', fellars?" slurred Derek, staggering outside from the bunkhouse. "Where ya been? Lookin' all over for ya!"

The last time Bradley saw Derek drunk was on a Sunday evening, when the gangly youngster indulged in too much wine. That night, Derek was just slightly tipsy. Now he was totally sloshed!

Derek leaned against the bunkhouse door, barely staying on his feet. "C'mon in, boys!" he laughed, slugging Bradley's shoulder. "More where 'at come from!"

It didn't take a genius to figure out who gave Derek the liquor. Bradley was afraid of Fritz, but he also despised him. He stormed into the bunkhouse, in time to catch Fritz handing Sergio the bottle of Campens Rose'.

Despite his tumultuous history with Bradley, Fritz was happy to see the little do-gooder. "Hey!" he cheered. "Never congratulated you on Leni . . ."

Bradley sent a clenched fist into Fritz's face.

Fritz bounced into an upper bunk, where Trevor was asleep. Trevor woke up, as the bunk teetered.

Painfully, Fritz examined his throbbing nose, as blood dripped from both nostrils. He hoped to let bygones be bygones, and welcome Bradley into the bunkhouse. Not now! Fritz couldn't excuse a bloody nose, or what he regarded as a needless act of aggression. In retaliation, he shot a right undercut at Bradley. It was a slow, clumsy move, which Bradley easily diverted.

Derek wasn't so lucky, as he meandered into the bunkhouse. As Fritz missed Bradley, he inadvertently nailed the drunken boy square into the forehead.

Derek flew across the bunkhouse, just barely missing the stove. "I only wanted 'nother drink!" he screamed.

Fritz lifted Bradley above his head. Fighting back, Bradley nearly slid out of his tunic, and revealed his bare backside to everyone in the room.

"Put him down!" ordered Kenichi, sprinting into the bunkhouse with Yuri.

Once Fritz did as he was told, Bradley fled to Yuri and Kenichi.

"That's right," growled Fritz, blood trickling into his mouth. "Hide behind the half-breed's skirt, why don'tcha?"

"What's going on?" demanded Kenichi.

Fritz pointed at Bradley. "That chickenshit hit me!"

"Is that any excuse to clobber Derry?" questioned Trevor, leaving his bunk to check on his best friend. Along with the twins, he carried Derek to a lower bunk.

Fritz glared at Yuri. "Hell do you think yer starin' at, Urine?" he demanded.

Yuri lifted one eye, puzzled by Fritz's odd nickname for him.

"Well, if ya got nothin' to say," grunted Fritz, "then get the hell out. And watch out for them neckid boys and green guys with wings!"

"Major Kohl wants to meet with us tonight, at seven o'clock," announced Yuri, wondering if he should 'correct' Fritz. Why bother? Fritz was nothing more than hot air, and posed no real threat.

As Yuri left the bunkhouse, the only sounds came from Derek's sobs.

Overwhelmed with guilt, Fritz downed the last of the Campens Rose', then threw the bottle to the floor. "Outa my way," he said, brushing past Bradley and Kenichi to the door.

"How's Derry?" asked Bradley, anxiously.

"Nothing a good night's sleep, an ice pack, and tonic water won't cure," said Trevor, smiling at Derek. "How's it going, buddy?"

His eyes bulging, Derek vomited on Trevor, Sergio, and himself.

"Screw this!" cursed Sergio, backing away. "You sober 'em up, Trev. I'm outa here!"

Bradley pinned much of the blame for Derek's mishap on himself. He regretted slugging Fritz, and wanted to resolve problems in a more passive, godly fashion.

"It's okay, Brad," said Kenichi. "I'm proud of you for standing up to him."

Bradley lowered his head. How well did he sit with the Lord, now?

"I'm glad to see Fritz get his comeuppance," said Kenichi, leading Bradley outside. "But how do you feel about getting stuck on a ship with him for several days?"

Seconds passed, as Kenichi allowed this question to soak in. "Sure you really want to make that trip to Infernus?"

45

As he raced to the location where he left his friends with the smugglers, it was apparent that Garry, an experienced guide, was lost.

Garry attempted to retrace the steps he took with Sirro the day before, and got turned around. He was surrounded by rolling hills layered in deep grass, and faded, blue skies with hazy clouds above. He searched for any recognizable man-made or geographical site. All he heard was the tide from the nearby ocean, as the harsh breeze parched his face, hands, and legs. Breathing heavily, he thought he'd go mad with fear.

Calm down!

Calm down, and figure out . . .

Where am I?

Garry sneaked away from Councillor Theo's compound, and spent a long, lonely, sleepless night in a dry irrigation ditch. He was hungry, thirsty, slightly feverish, and exhausted. Despair had gotten the best of him. What good was it to wander aimlessly through the bland, gray countryside and thick grass, higher than his waistline? The only certainty was that a frightened, confused kid was lost in western Embrey. Assuming he stumbled upon a farmhouse, its inhabitants would probably attack him, simply because he was a Branellian.

A dumb, dirty, stupid Branellian . . .

The Branellians and Embrians shared a common language and a past, when they were part of a much larger empire. The two nations fought over mostly worthless terrain, usually steep granite mountains and arid steppe country. Thousands died over mere inches of land.

There were men who sought reconciliation and peace, such as Theo. Too often, they were ignored.

Garry hadn't laid eyes upon another human being, since leaving the compound. More than anything, he craved the sound of another person's voice.

From a distance of more than a hundred yards, Garry caught sight of an image he was doomed to remember, for the rest of his life. Hanging from a sturdy branch of an apple tree, like overripe fruit in the sun, were three men.

They were wearing kilts.

Two of the men were already dead. Their heads draped over their shoulders in an unusual, contorted manner. The third barely clung to life, as he thrashed his feet out while gasping for air. The man's clothes fluttered in the wind, as both hands were tied behind his back.

For a brief moment, the man gazed at Garry. Struggling to speak, his words came out as *"Urghh!"*

Garry stared at this horrific spectacle. He was torn between coming to the man's rescue, or running away. The wretched soul was as good as dead, anyway. For several seconds, Garry looked at the three men. He had no idea who had executed them, and wondered if the culprits were still around.

Shrieking, Garry ran blindly through the stark Embrian hills, leaving his countryman to die.

Fear was in charge, as Garry knew that he'd soon join the three Branellians in the gallows. He became even more disoriented and lost, as he staggered through the grass. Wild-eyed, with his heart beating rapidly, he felt that death was inevitable, a faceless reality never to escape.

Garry tripped over his own clumsy feet, and slammed to the ground. Trapped in an unknown, bleak landscape, he yearned for his home in Warren Dale. His friends' welfare meant nothing to him now, as he sought only to save himself. Under the shade of a passing cloud, he lay on his stomach and wept.

"Hold it!" someone called, from behind.

Garry turned to see a big, burly man, dressed in an Embrian Army uniform. The man kept one hand upon a sword, hanging from his belt.

Garry leaped to his feet. He pulled out a knife from its sheath, next to the sporran. "Go away!" he ordered. "Go away, or I'll . . . I'll kill you!"

"With *that?*" the man asked, more annoyed than intimidated. "You're a Branellian, and a damn young one at that. The Branellian Army must be pretty hard up to enlist the likes of you."

"What . . . what makes you think I'm a Branellian?" stuttered Garry, backing away.

"That dress you got on. Only Branellians're dumb enough to wear that sorta getup."

"I'm a guide!"

The man snickered. "You are, huh? Then guide your ass on home. You don't know where the hell you are, do ya?"

"I'm from Embrey, and I . . . I live at the base of Mount Patten!"

"A'right, so where's Mount Patten?"

Guessing the wind's direction, Garry said, "That way!"

"I never knew Mount Patten was in Kusch," the man laughed. "And I never knew of any Kuschans who wore kilts, neither. You don't look like no Kuschan to me, and you damn sure don't sound like one."

Garry was stumped.

"Don't that beat all," the man said. "A Branellian guide, and he don't know his way home."

"Go away!" cried Garry, like a cornered animal.

"Gimme that knife before you hurt yourself!" the man ordered. "I ain't never killed no runts, except them who tried killin' me . . . or them I took into a war zone. I seen too many boys die a'ready, and I ain't gonna hurt ya, so gimme that knife."

Garry shook his head.

"Hell're you doin', way over here?" the man asked. "Fightin's clear over at the border. Or was, 'til yesterday."

Garry wanted to trust the man. Self-preservation warned against it. "My mom and sister made me come here."

"Why didn't you tell 'em to go to hell?"

"I worked the trades since I was little, and don't wanna go back. Mister Theo . . . *Councillor* Theo, I mean . . . he said me and my friends can stay here, in Embrey. I went out looking for them."

"Councillor Theo? The hell!"

"Go ask him!"

"Gimme that knife, and we'll both go."

"N-no!"

"Hell're you doing in the trades?" the man asked. "Boys got no place doing that kinda work. If you're an Embrian, why're you so scared of me?"

"You'll hang me!" whined Garry. "Like what you did to them other Branellians!"

"'Them other Branellians'?"

Garry gasped.

"I had nothing to do with that!" the man claimed. "So you're a Branellian. I can tell, by that skirt you got on."

"It's my *kilt!* And I like wearing kilts!"

"What the hell for?"

"What for? *Because!*"

The man gritted his teeth. "I ain't standing around here all day, haggling with you. Had one helluva day, a'ready. Gimme that knife, and I'll give you a drink from my canteen. You look awful tired and thirsty to me."

"I gotta go find my friends! Don't come after me, or I'll . . ."

Without finishing his sentence, Garry turned tail and ran in the opposite direction. It was futile. In no time, the man tackled him to the ground. Garry kicked and clawed at the man, as if his life depended on it.

As the man latched onto Garry's kilt, he slapped the knife from the boy's hand. The knife landed feet away, in thick grass and brush. Terrified, Garry managed to wiggle out of his kilt. Nude from the waist down, he retrieved the knife. Meanwhile, the man stood just feet away, pointing a sword at him.

Garry held the knife in a defensive position, unaware that his genitals revealed themselves from a thin clump of pubic hair.

The man laughed, as he held Garry's kilt as ransom.

"By god, you ain't going nowhere like that!" the man shouted. "Gimme that knife, I'll letcha have the skirt back, *and* a drink from my canteen!"

As Garry waved the knife in one hand, he concealed his groin under the other. "Go away!" he shrieked, his complexion a fiery red.

"How far you think you're gonna get, runnin' around like that? Get your ass sunburned, then froze off by morning. That is, if you don't get caught, or croak first." The man frowned. "No knife, no skirt!"

Garry debated on whether or not to surrender. What difference did it make? The man was right, so what other choice did Garry have, now? He was a prisoner of war, doomed to be executed like the three Branellians hanging from that tree. In defeat, Garry dropped the knife to his feet. The man fetched the knife, then offered Garry the kilt.

Garry fell to his bare bottom and sobbed. "My mom and sister *made* me go into the trades!"

"Stop that damn cry babying!" the man scolded, sitting next to Garry. "Put your skirt on, I'm tired of seein' you all bare-assed like that. Then I'll give you a drink."

With both hands shaking, Garry slipped the kilt on. His words spilled out in nonsensical whimpers and gibberish, as he took a drink. "I gotta get my friends to Mister Theo . . ."

The man took pity upon the lanky runt in the wool sweater and plaid kilt. Wiping away tears from Garry's face with a calloused hand, he asked, "When'd you go see Theo? This morning?"

"Yes . . . yes . . . *yesterday!*" stuttered Garry.

"You ain't no Maliek boy?"

"I ain't no Maliek boy! I ain't never heard of no Maliek! My mom and sister made me . . ."

"Yeah, I know," the man yawned. "Made you go into the trades. Who are ya, boy, and where'd you come from?"

"Garry," he said, wiping his runny nose. "Garry . . . from Warren Dale."

"Hell, your way outa your own territory! Well, we gotta find a way to get you home . . ."

"I don't wanna go back! Mister Theo said me and my friends can stay in Embrey. Please don't make me go back to my mom and sister!"

"That ain't up to me," the man said. "I can't speak for Theo, and Chang and Kraig might see it different. I'll see what I can do for you, soon as we get to the War Ministry."

Garry nodded.

"I'm a sergeant in the Embrian Army," the man said. He reached into his pocket, and handed Garry a thin slice of venison. "The name's Vix."

46

"So how'd a runt like you get mixed up with that mess o' thieves?" asked Vix, sitting under a lone pine tree as he shared his canteen with Garry. "Boys got no place in the flesh trades."

"You don't gotta worry about me!" cried Garry. "I didn't ask to be in this war, and I don't wanna go back to Branell, neither."

"That's good," said Vix, in a threatening tone. He took a liking to Garry, but still wanted to instill respect and fear in him. "I'd just as soon cut you from nuts to nose, then bury you with them Branellians we unhitched from that tree."

"No . . . no sir! I wanna stay with you!"

"Whatcha gonna do about that silly getup you got on? Won't make a convincing Embrian with them clothes on. I don't know why you people think you gotta dress up like women."

"But I like kilts!"

"Why hell, you ain't even got no under britches on!"

Garry crossed his legs, and blushed. "I didn't ask to be here, any more than you did."

"Any more than I did?" snapped Vix. "This is my country, by god! I was born and raised, not a mile from this here spot!"

Garry bugged his eyes out, thinking that Vix was going to murder him.

Vix slapped Garry's knee. "Well, if some Embrian squad shows up, keep your mouth shut and go along with what I say, or I'll beat you to a frazzle."

For twenty long years, Vix served with Major Kohl. This, to his detriment and folly. He wondered where his career would have gotten him, had he been under a more capable man.

On the other hand, Vix wished he hadn't turned his back on one who'd been like a father to him! Why did he choose to make such a terrible decision? 'Cause Kohl got some hair-brained idea of heading back to Infernus, that's why! Worst of all, he hired some dumb schoolboys to find a treasure which didn't even exist!

That's why he rode away from Major Kohl . . .

. . . and why he had yet to forgive himself for it.

Vix was torn. He'd never abide Kohl's plans of collecting specimens from the island, or using kids to assist him. Was it smarts, or disloyalty, preventing him from making peace with an old comrade? The aching in Vix's heart was more than he could stand!

Vix and Garry saw Lieutenant Commander Salazar marching toward them, accompanied by a large number of soldiers.

"Better get up," advised Vix, standing. "That son of a bitch thinks he's God. If you don't believe me, just ask him."

Garry stood at attention.

"Fancy meeting you here," said Salazar, none-too-thrilled with seeing Vix in the flat lands. "I thought you'd be out saving Kohl from winged men and pink monkeys."

"Major Kohl ain't my superior officer, no more," said Vix, staring at Salazar's uniform. What's *he* doing, dressed like a naval officer? Who pulled the strings for that sweet deal?

"Then who is?" inquired Salazar.

"Captain Willowby, from Fort Cooley."

"Address me as 'sir'!" insisted Salazar. "Where may I find Captain Willowby?"

"Probably in Sykes, with his Uncle Alistair," said Vix. "Twenty of his men got killed by Branellians, last night."

Patrick turned as white as a sheet.

"Say again?" requested Salazar.

Vix gritted his teeth. "Twenty of his men got killed by Branellians last night."

"Branellians?" asked Salazar.

"Yes, sir," said Vix. "Colonel Owensby sent us out here yesterday, thinking we'd meet up with some Branellians at the mouth of the Ember River. Alistair showed up last night, needing men for mop-up duty, and left a few boys for Owensby and me."

"And where may I find Colonel Owensby?" asked Salazar.

"Reckon he's dead, too," answered Vix. "Him, and everyone else Alistair left out there . . . except me."

"And you alone survived?" asked Salazar, disgustedly.

Vix resented Salazar's tone. "Well, there was too many of them to fight single-handed. But if I can get me a few good men, I'll pay 'em back for what they done."

"What were the Branellians doing here?" asked Patrick, anxiously.

"Sightseeing," said Jesse, sipping from a canteen filled with Campens Rose' that he 'borrowed' from Theo. "I trust they'll go away with fond memories of our beloved Embrey."

"Jesse!" scolded Salazar. "I'll ask the questions! So, what were the Branellians doing here, Sergeant Vix?"

"Killing twenty of mine and Captain Willowby's men," answered Vix. "Whadda ya think?"

"What about the boy with you, Sergeant?" asked Salazar, motioning at Garry.

"One of ours, sir," fibbed Vix. "He got away, too."

"Why is he dressed like a Branellian peasant?" asked Salazar, suspiciously.

"You're right, sir," said Vix. "He is dressed like a Branellian runt. When the Branellians was killing our men, he up and crapped himself, *bad.*"

"Yes, sir!" agreed Garry. "I . . . I did crap myself . . . bad!"

"He's the other sole survivor, besides me," said Vix. "He took them clothes off a dead Branellian."

"Hah!" laughed Salazar. "Who are you, boy? And why are you in Embrey?"

"I . . . I'm Private Garry, from Mount Patten! These are the only clothes I can afford!"

"That's enough," breathed Salazar, tiredly. "Where are the Branellians now, Sergeant Vix?"

"They was camped out at the mouth of the river," said Vix. "Think they might still be there."

There was little reason to dispute Vix. While most everyone questioned his reasons for serving under Major Kohl for two decades, the sergeant's courage, integrity, and battlefield exploits were unmatched.

However, when it came to the boy in the kilt . . .

Salazar had to take charge. He was, after all, an Embrian military officer. He assumed his soldiers were up to it. Could the same be said about him?

"I've got need for you and your sword, Sergeant Vix," declared Salazar, taking an authoritative stance. "That goes for you too, *Private* Garry."

"We going after them Branellians?" asked Vix, eagerly.

"We are now, and you're a part of it," ordered Salazar. "Understood?"

Vix had scant regard for Salazar. Yet, he had unfinished business with the Branellians. "Me and my sword are ready!"

"Thank you," acknowledged Salazar.

"Sir, I know this country," added Vix. "I was born yonder, and hunted quail in this here field."

Salazar grinned. "Then you're just the man I want!"

"We're going to capture the Branellians?" asked Patrick, anxiously.

"We can't just let them get away," spoke Salazar, sharing Patrick's animosity.

"Oh, goody!" cheered Jesse. "This will be fun!"

"Go with Sergeant Vix," Salazar told his men. "I've got a word with *Private* Garry."

"Sir, this runt deserves a commendation," said Vix. "He showed great courage in last night's fight."

"Even if he did crap himself, bad?" questioned Salazar. "Very well, I'll take it under advisement. Carry on, Sergeant Vix."

As Vix led the soldiers toward the river, Salazar, Patrick, and Jesse stayed behind with Garry.

As Garry attempted to speak on his own defense, words failed him.

"I expect honest answers from you, and I expect them now," demanded Salazar. "Who are you, and what are you doing in Embrey?"

"Please, sir!" begged Garry. "Don't hurt me!"

"We're not going to hurt you, but I can't guarantee your safety, unless you cooperate. You are a Branellian, aren't you?"

Garry swallowed. *This is it. This is the end.*

"What's the meaning of this invasion?" questioned Salazar.

"I had nothing to do with it, Commodore!" screamed Garry.

Jesse giggled, while Salazar merely blushed.

"My officer is a lieutenant commander, not a commodore," explained Patrick, sympathetically.

"All I know is that he's in the Army," said Garry

"Navy," snickered Salazar. "Let it go this time, Pat."

"He's pathetic, Commander Salazar!" laughed Jesse. "Vix is right, he did crap himself, *bad*. I smelled him clear from Commandant Theo's house!"

"I got nothing to do with the invasion!" cried Garry. "I was forced into it, same as my friends."

"Let me guess . . . you went along for the ride," said Jesse, tugging at Garry's kilt. "My, but what lovely fabric! Pray tell, who is your tailor . . . *hmm?*"

Garry dropped to his knees. "I gave my knife to Sergeant Vix! I worked the trades, when they threw the lot of us together for this raid. I don't wanna go back to Branell! I wanna stay in Embrey, me and my friends both! I need political asylum, whatever that is."

"Calm down," urged Patrick. "You help us, and you'll gain your amnesty."

"I'll tell you what I told Vix!" said Garry. "I don't like fighting Embrians, or anything else. I was only supporting my mom and sister, by working . . ."

"Who threw you together for this raid?" interrupted Salazar, kneeling beside Garry. "Who brought you here?"

Hoping this confession didn't bring harm upon himself or his comrades,

Garry said, "Mister Copenhaver and Mister Schlender."

"Copenhaver and Schlender?" asked Jesse, excitedly. "*The* Copenhaver and Schlender?"

"I guess." Garry shrugged. "I didn't know there were others with them same names."

"Who exactly are Copenhaver and Schlender?" asked Salazar, noting Jesse's elation.

"Only the two most ruthless cutthroats on the entire continent!" explained Jesse, happily. "They traipse back and forth into Embrey, not only searching for bootleg delights, but to peddle flesh. Our naval intelligence forces have pursued that scurvy for years. Why, just the other day, Admiral Kraig jumped me for not apprehending them! Even the Kuschans and Agronians want a piece of those meany-heads. The Kuschans for violating their borders, the Agronians because they hate the competition."

Salazar took a deep breath. Theo had told the truth about the Branellians, after all. Salazar had to prevent the two smugglers from leaving Embrey. Fear seized him. Duty forced him to get tough about it.

"Sir, I trust this boy," said Patrick. "We're not going to hand him over to the interrogator, are we? He'll be tortured."

"He won't be tortured, if I have a say in it." Salazar lifted Garry to his feet. "But we're obligated in capturing Copenhaver and Schlender. I just hope they're still at the Ember River, and don't put up too much of a fight."

"Sir, if we do take those rogues, believe you me, it'll be a feather in our caps!" said Jesse, frothing at the mouth. "Oh, happy day! Won't Admiral Kraig be so proud of me! I'm finally going to nab Copenhaver and Schlender!"

"*We're* going to nab Copenhaver and Schlender, and not just for Admiral Kraig's pleasure," stated Salazar. "Tell us what you know, Garry, and I'll do everything I can to make sure you'll win your amnesty."

"Yes, and whatever else you need," added Patrick, with Garry's best interests at heart. "Stay close to me, and you're in good hands..."

Two miles away, and a half-an-hour later, Salazar, Vix, Jesse, Garry and Patrick peeked over the large boulder overlooking the mouth of the Ember River. A cool, damp breeze chilled them, as darkened storm clouds blew in from the Agron Ocean.

A few of the bodies belonging to Willowby's recruits still canvassed the area. More than a hundred yards from the Embrians were a half-dozen Branellians, consisting of two desperate men and four kilted boys.

As Salazar squinted at the Branellians through a spyglass, Garry wondered if his cooperation with the Embrians endangered himself and his young countrymen.

The two smugglers victimized their guides by kicking, demeaning, or dragging them around by the ears. A big, bearded man threatened the youngsters with a heavy club. One of the guides was sprawled on a blanket, an arrow in his shin. Neither man made an effort to help him. If the boys complained of their treatment, the smugglers responded with pranks and insults.

"Can we expect a contest if we try to apprehend them?" asked Salazar.

"The grownups will," answered Garry. "They'd rather die than go into the hoosegow. My friends will give up, like I did."

Salazar wanted to trust Garry. Past experiences urged him to use discretion. "There's little work for us here," he whispered. "However, let's proceed with caution."

"Oh, Sergeant Vix and I can easily manage this," snickered Jesse, in anticipation.

"Why not?" agreed Vix, who surmised that Jesse was a former disciple of Captain Maliek's. Eventually, he'd corner the punk about it. For the moment, there were bigger fish to fry.

"Now, wait just a moment!" advised Salazar, as Vix and Jesse readied their swords. "Don't go rushing down there!"

"Yeah!" agreed Garry, frightened by the sight of sharpened steel gleaming in the faded sunlight. "Some of them are my friends!"

"Copenhaver and Schlender aren't," laughed Jesse.

Salazar glared at Jesse. "Now, wait just a minute . . ."

Jesse waved his sword, released a high-pitched yell and ran toward the Branellians. Vix was not far behind. Encouraged by their lead, most of Salazar's men joined in the fight.

If you can't beat 'em, join 'em! "Let's go!" shouted Salazar, following Vix and Jesse.

Marc and Ivor scattered, while Harold and Davy threw their arms up in surrender. Schlender reached for his sword, still in its sheath.

Before Schlender's weapon even cleared leather, Vix slashed into the smuggler's belly. Blood gushed from Schlender's mouth, as his intestines dropped to the ground.

Although it failed to bring back the dead, Vix stared at Schlender with an odd sense of justice, satisfaction, and glee. The humane thing meant finishing the smuggler off. Instead, Vix enjoyed watching the scraggly bastard die, slowly.

Harold and Davy shrieked. Neither had ever watched someone crawl around, dragging his innards behind him. Schlender opened his mouth, to beg for help which did not come. As Schlender exhaled a mournful groan, his eyes glazed over.

Copenhaver ran for his man-killin' stick, awaiting him beside a backpack. Too late. "Looking for this, old boy?" asked Jesse, happily waving the club in Copenhaver's face.

"Son of a whore!" cursed Copenhaver, realizing that Jesse had gotten the better of him. Thinking the fop would now use the man-killin' stick on him, he backed away.

"Nice," complimented Jesse, examining the man-killin' stick with awe and admiration. "Very *nice*. Mind if I keep it as a souvenir?"

"The rest of you give up!" ordered Salazar, entering the campsite. It was a pointless command, since there was little spunk or argument in Harold and Davy.

Garry threw both arms around Davy.

"Garry," whispered Davy, weakened by the loss of blood which caked his leg, sock, and the blanket. His teeth chattered from fever. Tenderly, he rubbed his hand against Garry's face.

"Giving you a problem?" Jesse asked Davy, in a self-assured manner.

Davy nodded, painfully.

Clutching the arrow protruding from Davy's leg, Jesse gave it a quick pull. Davy screamed, as the crimson arrowhead exited from the wound.

Jesse hastily ripped Davy's sock apart, then secured a tourniquet around the injured leg, below the knee. "You won't be attending tonight's masquerade ball, I'm sorry to say," he kidded. "But you'll live."

"Patrick," ordered Salazar. "You and Sergeant Vix collect those two kilts that ran off."

Copenhaver glared at Garry, determined to get even with the cowardly traitor. When he thought no one was looking, he attempted to retrieve the man-killin' stick, lying next to Jesse and Davy on the ground.

Salazar pointed his sword at Copenhaver. "Sit down," he spoke, forcefully. "And keep those greasy paws to yourself."

"A'right, so y' got us," growled Copenhaver, doing what he was told. "Now, whadda ya gonna do?"

"Nothing, as long as you cooperate," answered Salazar.

"Spare us," cried Davy, allowing Jesse to doctor his leg.

"Granted," assured Salazar. "Treat them with decency and honor, men."

"What about me?" asked Copenhaver.

"According to my bodyguard, you've got an impressive price tag on your head," stated Salazar. "You'd be wise to keep your mouth shut, and maybe you'll get a fair trial."

"Fair trial?" argued Copenhaver, defiantly. "The hell you say. I know how you Embrians are with prisoners. Yer gonna beat us!"

Harold whimpered.

"Put a lid on it, flesh peddler," warned Salazar.

"Yeah, Harold, there'll be scars on yer skinny little ass, 'fore nightfall," laughed Copenhaver. "Embrians are born killers, a'right. I seed it with my own eyes."

Patrick returned with Vix and the two delinquent Branellians, catching the tail-end of Copenhaver's spiel. It was true that Embrians had a reputation for abusing and torturing detainees. Because of that, Patrick planned to speak on the Branellian guides' behalf.

"My officer told you to clam up," Jesse said to Copenhaver.

"What for?" snickered Copenhaver, getting to his feet. "I'll talk all I want, don't make no difference to me now. Yeah boys, first they'll beat you down like dogs. An' when they're done havin' that kinda fun, they'll ram their peckers into ya, all the while laughin' at yer hollerin' and screamin'!"

"Sit down and shut up!" yelled Salazar. "Or I will compel you to do so."

"Compel me then, goddamn it!" taunted Copenhaver, spitting in Salazar's face. "Whatcha gotta say about that, y' damn yellow-bellied spick?"

Salazar intended to handle his prisoners with the highest regard and dignity, including Copenhaver. He was frustrated by his poor showing in uniform, and angered by the earlier dispute with Kohl. Copenhaver had just crossed the line, and Salazar refused to let it go unpunished.

With a shout of contempt, Salazar took out his sword and cut Copenhaver's arm off at the elbow.

Copenhaver screamed, as blood showered mortified onlookers. He attempted to flee an inescapable fate, by sprinting away. Collapsing a few yards from the riverbank, he joined Schlender in the Hereafter.

"I couldn't have said it better, myself!" giggled Jesse, slapping his leg.

"Tie the rest of those Branellians together!" hollered Salazar, furiously. "And let's get on the road!"

"Please, sir!" whined Garry. "You said you'd help me if I brought you to Mister Copenhaver and Schlender!"

"Surely not Garry!" added Patrick, disturbed by Salazar's violent reaction to Copenhaver. "Sir, you gave him your word!"

Salazar took a deep breath. "Fine, then *don't* tie them up," he said, wearily. "Just make sure they can't get away. Happy now, Pat?"

"Yes, sir," said Patrick, believing he'd never look at Salazar in quite the same way, again.

"You asked me about amnesty, and your amnesty has been granted," spoke Salazar. "Make good on it, *Private* Garry."

"Thank you!" cheered Garry, taking Salazar's hand.

"No need to thank me," groaned Salazar, wondering how to explain himself in a report to Admiral Kraig.

"What about Davy?" asked Garry.

"He poses no threat of evasion," said Salazar. "How soon can he be moved, Jess?"

"Better that we get him to a military hospital," said Jesse, wrapping a bandage around Davy's shin. "If he stays here, gangrene will set in."

Salazar nodded. "We'll have to carry him."

Vix lifted Davy in his arms. "No sweat, sir. He's as light as a feather."

Garry was moved by Vix's kindhearted gesture.

"You've earned a promotion in my book, Sergeant Vix," complimented Salazar.

"What about the others?" asked Patrick. "Are they to be tortured, once we get to the War Ministry? They're just boys, Commander Salazar."

"I can see that!" snapped Salazar. "I've got eyes, don't I? What about those Embrian boys who were killed last night? Have you got anything to say about that?"

Patrick was offended by Salazar's fiery outburst.

"How they're treated when he get to Sykes, that's up to them," said Salazar, diplomatically. "I'll do what I can, but first we must *get* to Sykes."

"Yes, sir." Patrick saluted Salazar, then walked away with Garry.

As everyone prepared to leave, Salazar summoned Jesse. "I've got a crucial task for you," he whispered, secretly.

Jesse presented himself to Salazar, conscious of his boozy demeanor. "Yes, sir?"

"Are you trained in the fine art of . . . spying?" asked Salazar. "Those criminals are up to something."

"Criminals? What criminals?"

"Theo and Kohl," explained Salazar. "Just who do you think I was talking about?"

"Copenhaver and Schlender," said Jesse, with an impish grin.

"Theo and Kohl," repeated Salazar. "I don't know what they've got brewing, but I'd like to find out."

Jesse was on the verge of laughing. "Yes, sir."

"Are you going to do what I ask of you?" asked Salazar, impatiently. "Or must I kick your ass, first?" It was an empty threat. In a knockdown, drag-out brawl, Jesse would have likely trounced Salazar. Provided he wore an officer's uniform, Salazar demanded obedience and respect from those under him. That rule applied even to killers.

Jesse removed his hat, and stood at attention.

"Kohl made an asinine remark about when he got back, I wouldn't be fit to lick his dirty show," relayed Salazar, still stinging from the insult.

"That's right, sir," said Jesse. "I was there when he said it."

"Yes, but get back from *where?*"

"I pondered the same thing. I too am curious."

"Thank you. Theo's also in on it. I can tell by the way he was acting, after that fool shot his mouth off. I need answers, Jess. Are you qualified to get them for me?"

Jesse smiled. "I'm ready, willing, and able to carry out your wishes."

"I figured as much. I'd appreciate it very much, if you do carry out my wishes."

"Sir, what about Copenhaver and Schlender?"

"What about them?" asked Salazar. "They're dead."

"Yes, but I need help in delivering them to Admiral Kraig. What should I do? Remove their heads for the War Ministry's satisfaction?"

"Jesse, you deranged little bastard!" exclaimed Salazar, in horror.

"You don't understand!" laughed Jesse.

"I understand enough to understand that what you're suggesting is a court martial offense! Do you want me to face a war crimes tribunal, just so you can have trophy mounts on your wall?"

"Admiral Kraig harangued me over those two fiends for the longest time, sir. Will he believe that we actually nabbed them, without physical proof?"

"Does it matter that much to you?" questioned Salazar. "What other body parts do you want, to appease your bloodthirsty ego?"

"Don't you see, Commander Salazar? We're heroes! If you knew the full extent of these cads' activities, you'd think so too."

"If that's what it takes to be a hero, then I don't want it." Salazar stretched his aching back. "Very well. If Admiral Kraig wants their filthy carcasses, I'll offer them a prize."

"Thank you, sir," said Jesse, proudly. "Believe me, their deaths are a huge weight off my shoulders."

"Not to mention a feather in your cap," groaned Salazar. "What about the dim-witted Branellian boy who brought us here? Does he get any recognition for the smugglers' capture, or are you too selfish to share in this glory?"

Jesse frowned. "Whatever you say, Commander Salazar."

"You'll be too busy spying on Theo and Kohl to pack two maggoty heads around. I'll have the men construct a couple of stretchers to transport those stiffs." Salazar wagged a finger at Jesse. "If it pleases you that much, I'll tell Kraig you killed them both. As for me, I refuse to take the credit."

47

Yuri sat on a grassy hillside above the compound, as the sun sank in the west. He rested his head in the palms of his hands, lost in his own thoughts.

The compound was usually abandoned and quiet. That evening, it resembled a school grounds or city park, not a covert government installation. There were almost as many kids there now, as adults. Theo's home was often a place for boring, intellectual discussion or political dissent. That evening, it was populated with the carefree, childhood games of youth. Along with Dimitri's three kids, the students from Lord Kelly's enjoyed the tranquil, rural setting by tossing balls, exploring the surrounding countryside, playing fetch with Boris, or daydreaming. Leery of strangers, the terrier soon warmed to Trevor and the twins, who teased him with rambunctious pranks and laughter.

Assuming Major Kohl's plans came to fruition, the students were to create a small expeditionary force to the faraway island of Infernus. Did they know what was expected of them? Were they smart enough, disciplined enough, and brave enough to fulfill their obligations? Some of the boys were perhaps too naive or innocent for the rigorous, hard work of military life and combat.

Renown for its unpredictable, dangerous reputation, Infernus promised adventure. It also threatened thrill seekers with sudden, horrible death.

Kohl required an army, and that's what he got. For what was an army, asked Captain Maliek, than the initiation of shaping boys into men? Evaluating the students, Yuri saw them as distinct individuals, with separate hopes, dreams, and ambitions. Together, they forged a unit based on love, affection, and camaraderie. Most of them got along well, and were cooperative. The greatest problem was Fritz, and the bickering siblings, Andre and Bentley. However, Andre's concerns for Bentley demonstrated that he'd willingly give up his own life, if it meant saving his kid brother.

Under Maliek, Yuri was grilled on the necessities of a strong force, united in their desires to fight and possibly die for Embrey. Most of the captain's followers were zealous in their dedication to the nation. The team was glued by common initiatives.

Regrettably, certain members of the team, Jesse and Marietto in particular, upheld a common initiative of bringing insult upon injury to Yuri.

Even with attempts to fit in, Yuri was an oddball, an object of ridicule. He was too weird, too foreign, too short, too sensitive, and too "different." Jesse rallied the others to turn Yuri's participation into a nightmare. Among those refusing to take part in Jesse's shenanigans were Conrad, Yuri's one true friend, companion, and confidante.

And now Conrad was dead.

Yuri grieved the loss. It was impossible to accept the painful truth of Conrad's demise. Yuri tried to make sense of it, come to terms with it, then find his own separate peace. Throughout the day, he wished to discuss the matter with Theo or Dimitri. Theo was busy mapping out plans for Embrey's future, while Dimitri tended to his family *(mainly the boss!)*. Therefore, Yuri looked to himself for answers. He only found more pressing questions.

What swayed Conrad to General Gornick's side? And why did he target those with Commander Salazar, including five students from Lord Kelly's?

And why did Jesse kill Conrad, when he had just surrendered to Yuri?

Conrad's passing left Yuri asking if he had any friends his own age. He hoped the Lord Kelly's guys accepted him on their team.

Or would they also find him too weird, too foreign, too short, too sensitive, and too "different"?

From experiences and perceptions, Yuri felt he was safe with most of the students. He felt assured with Kenichi, who was self-sufficient, and had a good head on his shoulders. Yuri had developed a healthy rapport with Andre, by nursing the injured hand. Due to his associations with Theo, Giorgio was already an ally.

Because of his loudmouth and overbearing characteristics, Fritz had the potential of endangering the mission. Brawn, not brains, was Fritz's asset. In a wicked, no-holds battle against a worthy foe, such attributes might come in handy.

Despite Fritz's off-colored comments, no one made waves against Geoffrey and Randy. Geoffrey held a leadership role at Lord Kelly's, while Randy was forced into being a "plaything" for King Ogden. Few among the students minded that the two were "different."

Would they give Yuri that same consideration and respect?

Like all adolescents, the boys remained within their own groups or cliques. Trevor and Derek were usually together, while the twins were seemingly inseparable. Eduardo adjusted himself to most everyone, while Fritz had a strange, magnetic effect on the younger boys, to the chagrin of the older ones. Like Giorgio, Geoffrey wished to facilitate and accommodate the team.

Kenichi was a bit standoffish and aloof, and something of an outsider, except when it came to Bradley. For whatever reason, Kenichi endeared himself to the one kid who fretted over each and every one of his schoolmates . . .

. . . except Fritz.

Yuri was drawn to Bradley, who wore his school uniform like a badge of honor. He was attracted to Bradley's warm smile, blonde hair, and slight frame. Unwilling to openly admit it, Yuri wanted to run his fingers through Bradley's hair, while smothering him with loving kisses. He fantasized about long nights in Bradley's arms, sharing a bed as they shared their lives, locked together as one spirit.

Were Yuri's desires for Bradley appropriate for a future Embrian Councillor? Bradley would never, could never, succumb to such urges. Bradley wasn't "different."

Yuri felt alienated and alone. He had needs for emotional and physical love, and the comforts of a life-partner to cherish for the remainders of his days. Yuri envied Geoffrey and Randy, who managed to find one another, satisfy their companion's hunger, and fill once hollow, empty voids.

There had to be someone out there for Yuri. Or was he even too weird, too foreign, too short, too sensitive, and too "different" for that?

Lost within his own thoughts, Yuri failed to notice Eduardo strolling up the hill toward him. "Yuri?" asked Eduardo, mindful of the Kuschan's solitude.

Yuri broke free of his trance. "Y-yes?" he stuttered.

"Linus and I made dinner for everybody." Eduardo motioned at the bunkhouse. "Your father wants you to join us."

"Why?" asked Yuri, surprised by the invitation.

Eduardo smiled. "Why not? It's rabbit and chicken. A few men pitched in with the fish they caught this afternoon. We're supposed to meet with Major Kohl, after dinner."

Slowly, Yuri got to his feet. "Eduardo?" he asked, wondering if the cook ever felt out of place, based on his spiritual background and ethnicity.

"Yeah?"

Yuri quietly followed Eduardo to the bunkhouse. He was starving, not only for food and drinks, but for acceptance and tolerance. "Thank you, Eduardo," he said, anxiously.

"You okay?" asked Eduardo, perplexed by Yuri's behavior. "You seem worried about something."

"It's nothing." Yuri patted Eduardo's shoulder. "Thank you . . . all right? Thank you."

Eduardo smiled. "What for?"

"Never mind," said Yuri, as he breathed in refreshing, cool autumn air. "Just thanks . . ."

48

The students from Lord Kelly's crammed into the meeting room, for their engagement with Major Kohl. The table and chairs were pushed to one corner, accommodating a larger number of participants. The room was lit with wax candles at each wall of the tight, claustrophobic space.

The boys either stood, or sat on the floor, as they awaited Kohl. Yuri quietly observed his shipmates. Recruited to help coordinate the mission, Sergeant Rupert acquainted himself to the team. He remained friendly and cordial, despite his new status as a non-commissioned officer. As Derek recovered from a hangover, Fritz prevented one by drinking more liquor, provided by the fat politician. On occasion, he glared at Bradley and Kenichi, who stood together. As Fritz mouthed idle threats, they were countered by Kenichi's smartass grin.

At the hour of seven in the evening, Kohl entered the building. A few boys had first taken notice of him, from his confrontation with Commander Salazar. Keeping his spine ramrod straight, Kohl stood at attention, as if to be inspected by the heavens above. Overall, the boys were awed by this daunting figure, with his graying brow and salt-and-pepper goatee.

Kohl gave everyone a fatherly smile. He didn't appear as a harsh, strict disciplinarian. Rather, he was pleased by the enthusiasm afforded the mission. His warm expressions gave everyone needed assurances and confidence.

"Well, I'm delighted to see you all here," stated Kohl. "I've only got one question which must be answered, not to my satisfaction, but within your own hearts and minds." Kohl cleared his throat, then spoke in a loud, baritone voice. "Are you man enough to undertake a mission of destiny? A mission of such importance as to make the ongoing war pale by comparison? Who will say aye? Are you man enough to go to Infernus with me?"

There was a pause. Certain boys laughed or made disparaging remarks to the pals. Others internalized the inquiry by questioning their own courage and abilities.

"Prior to this meeting," continued Kohl, "I overheard some of you commenting on how dangerous this journey will be. Yes, men, the expedition will be very dangerous! Need I remind you that we live in dangerous times? Embrey, our beloved Embrey is in the grips of a madman. You know of whom I speak. He is a man who'll stop at nothing to gain the absolute power of a dictator. He seeks no justice, but rather to inflict his will upon all Embrians. He'll sway our nation from prosperity and wisdom, then turn it into a concentration camp!"

Bradley rested his hand on Kenichi's shoulder, recalling the incident at Lord William's. The minds of those kids were poisoned by intolerance and hatred. How many more youngsters were brainwashed by Gornick?

"Boy!" shouted Kohl, motioning to Bentley, who still wore the uniform furnished by Major Conroy. "You, boy! Come to me."

Bentley turned to his brother Andre, then squeezed his way through the crowd to Major Kohl.

"I see you wear the snake and sword," said Kohl, in disapproval.

Bentley looked to his schoolmates for guidance and support. "I dunno," he mumbled.

"How dare you wear that heinous symbol on your uniform?" growled Kohl.

"Our nation's at war, and here you wear . . ."

"Pardon me, Major Kohl," said Geoffrey, joining Bentley at the front of the room. "He didn't mean to wear it, sir . . . He was forced into it."

The others supported Geoffrey's claim.

"Is that true?" Kohl's features changed from hostility, to that of regret and sadness. He ran his weathered fingers through his goatee. "I see . . . you wear that gaudy insignia, involuntarily?"

"I guess," whispered Bentley, nervously shuffling his feet.

Kohl stared at everyone. "Are you content to see your friend wear that vulgar uniform? Will *you* wear such clothing? How can you possibly call yourselves upstanding Embrians, if you're ordered to carry that disgusting emblem with you?"

"You can't," agreed Geoffrey.

"Damn right you can't!" shouted Kohl.

"Major Conroy said I was a pure Embrian," said Bentley.

"And *that* makes you a pure Embrian?" questioned Kohl. "I think not. Know now that we'll all be forced to wear that vulgar emblem, if Gornick has his way. If we don't, then we will die! Look within your own hearts, and not to fanatics, to see if you are indeed a pure Embrian. Let this divisive symbol be stamped out today, stamped out tomorrow, and stamped out forever! Let it be so removed from our memories, from now to the end of time!"

This was met with approval and applause.

"Make no mistake about it," said Kohl, gravely. "This only proves that our country needs you. If we fail in our obligations, we fail not only ourselves, but our families, our friends, our neighbors, and Embrey itself. If we're unable to secure the treasure, hidden within Infernus' interior, the more enlightened forces of reason will go lacking. All will be lost."

The boys' moods had changed. Instead of voicing callow jabs and insults, the began to understand the gravity of their situation. Were they up to the formidable task? Were they indeed 'man enough' for Kohl's lofty expectations?

"I dread to imagine what will happen, if Embrey falls into the hands of a madman," said Kohl, pretending to wipe away a tear from one eye. "No one will be safe! Not only won't we adequately protect ourselves, those closest to us will be at the mercy of those wishing to do them harm. Do we embrace such a future, from failure to act? Do we embrace a future where our mothers, our sisters, our sweethearts are violated by brutes? Do we live in a society where our fathers, our brothers, and our friends are butchered, their severed heads displayed on blood-soaked pikes?"

Kohl's rhetoric disturbed a few lads, many who had already witnessed varying atrocities. What was at stake, if they chose not to accompany Major Kohl on this perilous assignment? How bad would things truly get?

"Sorry, men," apologized Kohl. "I meant to frighten you, but now I see my own folly. How can any of you refuse to embark on an adventure, where the hazards are far less than those we leave behind? You each come to me from places of service, and I know why you were brought here. It was through divine intervention, and the promise from God of our righteous cause. I am a soldier, and my duty is to a nation I have defended, time and again. Looking at my military career, I realize I have accomplished nothing. Yet, a power from on high bade me for the chosen to come forward. And here you are, the righteous saviors of our fair Embrey! How can we fail? In your eyes, failure is an impossibility! It's been my privilege to lead men into combat. I say now that I've never been blessed with such as you, until this very day!"

Kohl wandered into the crowd. "I made this inquiry, at the beginning of our meeting. Are you man enough to follow me to Infernus? Of course you are! No doubt about it . . . you were not summoned by me, but selected by the very hand of God!"

That statement invoked hearty cheers from most everyone. Bradley now believed this quest had the potential to bring him closer to the Almighty. Moved to tears of happiness, Giorgio embraced Sergeant Rupert, in a spirit of unity and companionship.

It was a lie to stay that Kohl's speech wasn't stimulating. In Kenichi's mind, how much of it was motivation, and how much of it was *manipulation?*

"You'll soon all be heroes to the Embrian people," said Kohl. "I ask you to embark on a journey for which you'll always be remembered for. From now one, you bow down to no one. No, others will bow down to you! May your story reign eternally in the annals of Embrian lore? Proudly, you'll share your experiences with your children, and later on with their children. They, too, will boast of your adventures! These tales will be known to everyone, within our great nation. Schoolboys will read of your selfless devotion to the homeland! Centuries from now, your exploits will be the stuff of myth and legend! No one can take that away from you . . . my boys, my heroes, my chosen men!"

This brought further applause. The boys' jovial outbursts were contagious, as they spread throughout the room. Who among them wished to stay behind, when offered with promises of immortality?

"You come to me from varying backgrounds and lifestyles," said Kohl. "That makes no difference to me. There's little reason in thinking yourself as isolated or inferior, tonight. Each and every one of you is very special to me! Your might is my shield, and mine yours! You are my rock, my anvil, my sword! We are equal in death, and in the heart of God. Who cares if you're tall or short, or of another race or religion?" Kohl faced Yuri. "Does it matter if you come from another country, or Hell itself? Trust me, you'll distinguish yourself in this quest! If we believe in ourselves, and trust in God or the Kuen, may be accomplish anything!" Slapping Bentley on the back, Kohl added, "And that, my boy, makes you a pure Embrian!"

Kenichi was troubled by the speech and its thunderous reception. Even Bradley was caught up in the fervor, as a sense of euphoria painted his smiling face.

Kohl had somehow managed to win the boys' support, as he held them in the palms of his hands. Regardless of doubt and animosity, he had secured an army. Now, he had to maintain their respect and loyalty in the coming days and weeks. Briefly, his mind returned to a distant past, to a time and place which forever defined him.

Kohl Kuen . . .

Anumun . . .

Anumun . . .

Oh, if only Sergeant Vix stood with me, now!

"I will be so honored to fight alongside you," said Kohl, holding a clenched fist in the air. "Will you so honor me? You refer to each other as 'Brother.' Please, allow me to be your Brother." Raising both arms like an evangelist minister,

Kohl's voice echoed throughout the room. "Allow me to be your Brother, in this noblest of endeavors! Those who value justice, you are my Brother! Those already in the service of Embrey, you are my Brother!" Kohl pointed at Kenichi. "You, most honored son of the Orient, you are my Brother! Those holding faith in the Lord, you are my Brother! To those wishing to live your lives as you choose, you are my Brother! You of minor size or stature . . . you – you – you are my Brother!"

Everyone cheered. Even Kenichi, who was mentioned in this spiel, now felt honored by Kohl's explosive rhetoric.

"We make this effort, this commitment, this sacrifice to our fellow Embrians!" shouted Kohl. "We must vow never to lie under the oppressive rule of tyranny! While in battle, we fight with a sword in one hand, and the love of God in the other! For truly He loves you. Better to die in glorious battle, than to live as slaves in bondage! Are you man enough to join me?"

Those in the room were under Kohl's spell. Who dared to refuse him, now? Yet, questions still lingered in the minds of a few. Were they involved in the mission because they had faith in Major Kohl, or because they feared their friends' rejection and reprisal? Did they sign on for their own sake, or to appease the kid next to them? Who'd return, safely home? And who'd perish in that mysterious land, hundreds of miles away?

Kenichi was afraid, not only for himself, but for his roommates as well. Did they know what they were getting themselves into? Considering their reactions to the bloodshed on the streets of Sykes, and then at Lord William's, what were they to expect once they saw a friend die?

Kenichi was obligated to stay with his roommates. There was no denying it! Even then, he knew that some of his friends were going to die.

"God bless our homeland!" declared Kohl, his arms waving high in the air. God bless Embrey! God bless you, one and all!"

"Y' got any good women and hooch on that island?" asked Fritz.

Kohl smiled at Fritz. "They are the most beautiful and ripest berries ever to be picked!"

The students' mirth and merriment were short-lived, when someone from behind hollered, "A'right, y' sorry, tit-suckin' sons o' bitches! Listen here!"

Everyone saw a short, bald, stocky man with an untrimmed beard storm into the room. His squinting eyes, sinewy arms, and toothless grin (*or was it a grimace?*) intimidated the lads. This newcomer stared at the team, as if it was his personal plaything to be mistreated at will. As he focused on Yuri, the two exchanged caustic glances.

This was Strunk, the former state executioner. And he was scary. His mere presence gave most everyone reasons to shutter. "Major Kohl's in charge of this rat-killin', but yer ass belongs to me!" he yelled. "When I tell ya t' jump, ya better jump good! Are you bastards man enough to do what I say, or do I have to kick yer asses 'til yer nose bleeds?"

The sounds of a barking terrier were drowned out by the team's groans of grumbles. That is, until the dog's warning evolved into a shrill, ghastly whelp. The piercing, high-pitched shriek cut into the minds and souls of those unlucky enough to hear it. The terrier released a final shriek, then was forever silenced.

"What was that?" asked Trevor, with a nervous laugh.

"Boris?" whispered Yuri. Frantically, he sprinted outside into the brisk, windy darkness. Bradley and Kenichi followed him.

A soldier, posted to guard the facility, lay unconscious a few feet away from the door. Yards away, the three boys found Boris' bloody remains. The dog's fir and guts splattered the grounds. Bradley turned away, sick to his stomach.

Yuri knelt to caress his dog. His feelings ranged from sadness, to fury, to outright contempt. A gift from Councillor Omar, the terrier was among Yuri's prized possessions. The boy often took Boris for long walks in the fields behind Theo's home.

Yuri covered his eyes, unable to conceal his fragile, raw emotions. Burying his face into Kenichi's chest, he sobbed. "He killed him! He killed *Boris!*"

"It's all right," said Kenichi, with his arms around Yuri. "It's all right, I promise."

"But he killed my dog!" cried Yuri. He did not resemble one capable of sending two arrows into Samuel at Lord William's, or stopping two of the three assassins, that morning. Rather, he was a soft, sensitive child, mourning the loss of a cherished companion.

"I don't understand," sighed Bradley. "Who'd do such a thing?"

Yuri screamed, "Jesse!"

49

Commander Salazar returned to the Ministry of War in the late afternoon. The Branellian guides were loose-lipped about their roles in the invasion. Salazar made sure they were treated well. Davy was to stay in a hospital, until his leg healed. Copenhaver and Schlender's bodies were identified, then placed in unmarked, shallow graves near the Ministry's gates.

Placing ink to paper, Salazar worked on his report to Admiral Kraig. He was tempted by sleep, which refused to come. Images of the family's massacre the day before, the loss of six men that morning, and the smugglers' capture were far too sobering.

Salazar was not permitted to go home, a massive, three-story mansion he shared with his aging mother, brother Enrique, and a number of servants. The residence sat on the other side of town. Salazar was afraid the estate had been destroyed, or occupied by Gornick supporters. He was concerned for his mom and brother, as certain neighborhoods were still under siege. Unless authorized by General Chang or Admiral Kraig, leaving the fortress was restricted.

The War Ministry filled with refugees, seeking shelter from the civil unrest. Hunched over a desk in his tent, Salazar ignored the constant drone of citizens' boisterous conversation. Food consisted mainly of meat, delivered by soldiers, farmers, or hunters. Liquor, rations, and medicine were limited, tempers grew short, and communications from the outside were nil. Around the clock, sentries and guards kept watch for a potential attack.

Salazar undressed, then slipped into a leisurely robe. There was little reason for formality. After lubricating himself in low-grade bourbon (and not *Romero's*) he waited at the entrance of Kraig's tent, with a written statement.

"Come in, Salazar," said Kraig, opening the flap of his tent which doubled as his home and office. Filled with a cot, provisions, a lantern, and weaponry, the tent was in disarray. Due to a hectic schedule, Kraig had no time to make it more livable. "Sit down, anywhere. On the ground, if you want."

"Thank you, sir," replied Salazar. "I prefer to stand."

"You look like hell, Commander Salazar. Sit down before you fall down. That's an order."

"Yes, sir." Salazar smiled, at his own expense. Dropping to the turf at the end of Kraig's bed, he crossed his tired legs.

"Congratulations on your victory," said Kraig, handing Salazar a shot of brandy. "It may have been only a minor skirmish, but you bagged two valuable birds for me, today. A win, just the same."

"Jesse did it," explained Salazar. His one comfort was seeing an open bottle of Romero's finest brandy on Kraig's desk. "Actually, Sergeant Vix and that Branellian kid did more to apprehend Copenhaver and Schlender, than me. I just happened to be there."

Kraig chuckled. "I appreciate your modesty, but those miscreants had been thorns in my side, for quite a while. Together, they ran one of the largest smuggling and prostitution rings on the continent."

"Yes," yawned Salazar. "Jesse told me all about it. He's pretty proud of himself."

"The high-ranking officers get the glory, while the grunts do the work. Show yourself a little kindness. You've made the country a much safer place."

"It will be, when and if we stop General Gornick." Salazar frowned. "You were right, Admiral Kraig. Gornick is a butcher and a madman. You were right, and I was wrong. I'm very sorry about that, sir."

"You did well this afternoon," said Kraig. "Savor the moment while it lasts. A few days from now, it'll be forgotten and you'll go back to being just another Navy man." Kraig cleared his throat. "I heard you ran into some trouble, this morning."

"Who . . . who told you that?"

"Patrick. Oh, don't be angry with him. I chatted with Pat, earlier. I'm sure there's mention of it, in your report."

Salazar's face sagged. "I have sir, in explicit detail. I'm not down on Patrick. How can I be? He's too good a man to be under my shoddy command."

"Why are you so hard on yourself?"

"I'm a damned fool, sir! I walked straight into an ambush!"

"I shouldn't have let you go," said Kraig. "It was a mistake for anyone to leave at that time of night, especially with children in tow. You did your best. Don't forget you apprehended a couple of important crime lords, and that alone is worth a great deal. Not to mention, those Branellian guides are talking, plenty."

"Six of my men are dead!"

"You didn't kill them."

"No, sir. It was . . . three of Maliek's former students."

"Some of those rogues have assimilated themselves into Embrian society, by handling security for dignitaries," said Kraig. "Or, in Jesse's case, they work for me."

"That's another thing, Admiral Kraig. I wanted to talk to you . . . about Jesse."

"What about him?"

Salazar didn't know how to respond. He'd been through this with Kraig before, and got absolutely nowhere.

"Jesse's your bodyguard, not your friend," reminded Kraig. "I suggest you keep it that way."

"He's an insubordinate ass! Sure, I concede he's good at his job, too good! I simply can't stand him, sir! I hate his mannerisms, his cocky attitude, that goddamned hat!"

Kraig snickered. "You dislike Jesse, but you rave over Yuri. Why is that, Commander Salazar?"

"What's there not to like about Yuri. I admit he's a bit . . . *strange,* but very gentle."

"There are many things you don't know about Yuri."

"I know what he is, Admiral Kraig," defended Salazar. "Jesse and I had that same discussion this morning and, frankly, I don't care if Yuri has a hard-on for guys. That's his story, not mine. I won't harass him over it."

"You voice your disdain for Jesse. Common sense reasons that you must dislike Yuri, that much more."

"Why?"

"As you already know, Jesse was one of Maliek's pupils." Kraig paused. "So was Yuri."

Salazar shook his head, in disbelief.

"This will be hard for you to swallow," said Kraig, in a matter-of-fact voice, "but Yuri's one of the most bloodthirsty persons I've ever met."

"You lie!" snapped Salazar, forgetting that he blew up at a superior officer. "Jesse said the same thing, and I don't believe him, either!"

"Calm yourself, Salazar, or I'll have you in chains!"

"I . . . I'm sorry, sir."

Kraig took a deep breath. "Please accept what I have to say. Around the same period that Jesse was . . . *educated,* so was Yuri. While Jesse excelled with Maliek, Yuri was undisciplined, prone to melancholy, and rarely got along with anyone."

"He's just a boy, Admiral!"

"You're right. Yuri is just a boy. I won't dispute that. On one level, Yuri is a sweet, sensitive child who loves Councillor Theo. It didn't take long before everyone, including Maliek, was afraid of him. He got expelled for almost killing a classmate over a prank. We also have reason to think that Yuri was involved in the assassination of a Campensian diplomat named Macready."

"Why did they teach boys to kill?" questioned Salazar, having grown fond of that odd, beautiful waif living under Theo's roof. "What did Embrey achieve by it?"

"Don't bother yourself with that. I'm telling you as it is. Take it as a bitter pill. Or must I call the guards in, to help you swallow it?"

"No, sir," mumbled Salazar, in humility.

"Very well, then. Where is Jesse?"

"I sent him to spy on Major Kohl and Councillor Theo."

"What the hell for?"

"I believe that Theo, and your brother, are up to something," whispered Salazar. "I got into a war of words with Kohl, earlier. He said something that . . . well, it sticks in my craw."

"Go on," requested Kohl, his smile infuriating Salazar.

Salazar gambled on the potential of wiping egg off his face. "Your brother told me that . . . well, when he got back, I wouldn't be fit to lick his dirty shoe."

"Get back? Get back from where, Salazar?"

"When I confronted him about it, he wouldn't answer. The look on Theo's face tells me that something's brewing between them both."

"Are you sure?" asked Kraig. "Perhaps Kohl is just posturing. He's notorious for blowing his mouth off at the worst times."

"Let's just say it's a hunch, sir. Please, Admiral Kraig, something just tells me . . ."

"Thank you," interrupted Kraig. "It may be worth looking into."

"I sent Jesse to see if he could find any pertinent information on the matter. I . . . I hope that was appropriate. I think Theo bought me off, by informing me of the smugglers' whereabouts. Theo's not treasonous, just conniving."

"How did he know where Copenhaver and Schlender were?" asked Kraig, curiously.

"I didn't ask, and Theo didn't tell. I thought he was full of it, until I met up with Sergeant Vix and that Branellian kid."

"It might not mean anything, but you never know. When Jesse shows up, I'd like to see the two of you, right away."

"Yes, sir!" Salazar got to his feet, saluted Kraig, and began to leave.

"Have you been dismissed?" asked Kraig.

"No . . . no, sir!" Salazar stood at attention.

"I debated on telling you this, but I think you ought to know." Kraig stepped from behind his desk, to pat Salazar's shoulder. "I'm sure your life in the Embrian military hasn't always been very rewarding."

Salazar groaned. So far, military life was terrible!

"I trust you'll take this as a grown man," said Kraig, diplomatically. "Hear me out, Salazar, not with passion, but as an Embrian naval officer. If you plan to stay in uniform, you must learn to control your emotions."

Salazar wrinkled his brow. "Yes, sir?"

"Those in power are gamesters, as much as anything else. They think they're right all the time. We're simply caught in the middle. Our power is limited, our actions and reactions scripted by others. Our time isn't wasted, however. We can make a crucial difference, if we await the right moment to be decisive, then act upon our own good intent. I know this game all too well, and won't take part in its pettiness. And neither will you, Commander Salazar. Understood?"

"Yes, sir . . . Understood."

"It's our belief that Yuri killed Reginald and your two guards at Theo's."

Salazar's eyes widened.

"What did I just get done telling you?" asked Kraig.

"Yuri may have killed those three men!" shouted Salazar. "But it was Theo who gave him the orders to!"

"*Salazar . . .*"

"Give me the word, Admiral Kraig, and I'll arrest Major Kohl and Councillor Theo for murder!"

"One more request like that, and I'll arrest you!" warned Kraig.

"But they were my men!" cried Salazar. "How can I stand back and? . . ."

"I can't add up the number of men who died following my orders! Some of them didn't die in the hands of our enemies, either! Trust me, you'll watch more of your men die, in due time. It's a reality of our profession."

"But, sir . . ."

"That'll be all," yawned Kraig. "It's late, and I'm very tired. Good night, Commander Salazar."

"But . . ." Salazar swallowed. "What about Reggie and those guards? Not to mention, my horse?"

"Casualties," answered Kraig, flatly. "*Good night,* Commander Salazar . . ."

Salazar went outside. He was exhausted, all right, yet sleep eluded him. The march to Theo's, his fight with Kohl, and finding the two smugglers would keep him awake. Then, to hear that Yuri was a killer, linked to the deaths of three men and, perhaps, even a vital diplomat . . .

Finally, there was the chaos in Sykes. Salazar was outraged as he examined darkened silhouettes of familiar landmarks in the moonlight, rendered to debris and rubble. The smell of decaying bodies turned his stomach. Among the more important cities on the globe, Sykes grew desolate and dead. Would it ever be rebuilt? Could it ever be rebuilt? It'd be years, if ever, before the metropolis was a thriving mecca of trade and commerce.

Salazar had his first win that day. It was a lopsided victory, involving a few boys and two lowlife scoundrels. It didn't prove a thing! Several men under Salazar's command were dead, because he failed to keep an eye open for miscreants, lurking within the darkest shadows, or masquerading as friends. Why was I so stupid, to trust Yuri? Why am I so blasted stupid? Do I even belong in the service? Do I possess the temperament, maturity, or cold-blooded willingness to send men to their deaths? Am I willing to die, in order to preserve the nation? How can I resign my post, when Embrey needs me the most?

My family's got a business and small fortune, unless it too is lost or plundered. What if I use my talents and abilities to help the country, in more peaceful ways? I'm making no progress as a naval officer! All I'm doing is getting people killed!

"Sir!" a guard spoke, in the night.

Salazar assumed the facade of authority and leadership. The guard was old enough to be Salazar's father. He was ready, willing and able to meet his doom by an officer's decree.

Salazar wished to tear down the limits of rank and stature, and enjoy a warm conversation with the guard. Wisdom, insight, and truth were often beheld by elders. "At ease," ordered Salazar, upholding protocol. "Where are you from, soldier?"

"Sykes," the guard answered. "I've lived here, my whole life."

Salazar and the guard both regarded the city as home. Each watched the community torn apart by cruel human intervention. Both had loved ones, unaccounted for. Salazar wanted to relieve the guard, and allow him to check on kin. Regrettably, duty locked Salazar and the guard behind the confines of the fortress walls.

"I've been gone all day," said Salazar. "Any sign of mischief?"

"All quiet today, sir," the guard answered. "Just a little trouble. Nothing like yesterday."

"Wonderful." Salazar nearly smiled, but thought better of it. "Well, you're doing a splendid job, soldier."

"Thank you, Commander. The same goes for you."

Salazar almost buckled under the strain of his play acting. "Carry on," he said, then slowly walked away.

Salazar wandered toward his own quarters. The aging guard treated him with the highest kindness and courtesy. Too bad. Salazar thought of himself as a fraud or a phony, unworthy of his rank or the guard's respect and esteem.

50

"How's the chow?" asked Vix, sitting on the floor of his tent at the Ministry of War. Drinking a bottle of raspberry wine he watched, by faded candlelight, as Garry had supper.

"Great!" said Garry, with his mouth full. "Can't eat another bite."

Vix frowned. "Well hell, you only had three plates!"

Garry responded with a sheepish grin, as Vix handed him the bottle.

"What is it?" asked Garry.

"Wine!" growled Vix. "Whadda ya think, a goddamn snake?"

Garry sipped the wine, then handed it to Vix.

"How do you aim on getting home?" asked Vix.

"I want to stay here," said Garry.

"But you're the enemy! You, and them other runts!"

"We didn't mean to be the enemy, Sergeant Vix!"

"That ain't my doin's," yawned Vix. "Well, reckon it'll be safe to share my tent with the likes of you. Think I better sleep with one eye opened, though. You try anything, I'll cut your head off and sell it to a friend of mine in a carnival."

"You ain't got nothing to worry about! I ain't gonna try nothing! This is the best I ever had!"

Vix laughed. "If this is the best you ever had, then you ain't had it worth a spit."

Garry frowned. "I ain't, Sergeant Vix."

"Anyway, we still gotta find a way to get you home."

"But I wanna stay in Embrey," said Garry, his soft, sad eyes melting Vix's heart. "With you."

"*What?*"

"I wanna stay with you."

"What the hell for?"

"You're my friend!" said Garry. "No grownups were ever as nice to me as you, except Sirro, Mister Dimitri, and Mister Theo's cook. Can't I stay in Embrey, please?"

"But you're the enemy! What about your ma and sister?"

"I didn't ask to be in the trades. I was made to work in the trades. Theo said he'd give me asylum, or something like that. Do you really want me to go back?"

"Well, don'tcha wanna go back?" asked Vix.

"My ma and sister can get by without me. I didn't ask to be in the trades. All I got out of it was a buggy pile of hay to sleep on in the loft, and moldy bread to eat. Do you really want me to go back?"

"Hell, no," groaned Vix. "But what am I supposed to do with a runt, and an enemy runt, at that?"

Garry smiled. "I'll cook and clean for you."

"What if I get my head cut off, and have it sold to a friend of yours in a carnival?" snickered Vix.

Garry didn't appreciate Vix's humor.

"I can't go looking out for no kid," argued Vix. "I don't know why you wanna stay here, since we're your enemy."

Garry hoped to establish a positive relationship with Vix, and feared he wasn't welcome in the tent.

"Well, if you're gonna stay here, we oughta figure out what to do with ya," said Vix. "The War Ministry can't have no idle mouths to feed. You'll get put to work digging a latrine."

"I'll do what you ask of me!" cried Garry.

"No, you'll do what Kraig or Chang ask of you." Vix corked the wine bottle. "I'm asking you to blow out that candle, shut your mouth, and get to sleep."

Garry extinguished the candle, crawled into the blanket Patrick gave him, and closed his eyes. "Sergeant Vix?" he asked, rolling on his side.

"Yeah?"

"What's a latrine?"

"It's a fancy way of saying shithouse," explained Vix. "Now, get to sleep."

Vix sighed as he rested his head on the backpack which doubled as a pillow. That Branellian runt was a mess of trouble! Vix was in no position to keep a foreigner under his wing. Without a commanding officer, he would likely be reassigned at any time, perhaps even to the border. It was a cinch that Garry wouldn't fight his own people. It didn't matter, anyway. The Army was no place for Garry! In no time, he'd get himself and someone else killed!

Maybe even Vix . . .

Still, Vix realized that his life had grown empty and meaningless, since his departure from Major Kohl. Despite his better judgment, he wanted to reconcile with the old officer. He'd never stoop so low as to lead a stupid kiddy brigade to certain death. It was bad enough playing witness to it, the night before.

To Vix's concern, Garry's presence began filling a void left by the slaughter of twenty recruits, along with his estrangement to Major Kohl.

Vix waited until Garry dozed off, then quietly left the tent for a walk through the War Ministry. Outside, he found the installation crowded with soldiers and civilians alike, seeking refuge from the chaos of a shattered city. The Ministry had to house and feed all these people. Eventually, they'd be forced to turn them away. Vix wondered how long it'd take before the tense situation boiled over.

"Sergeant Vix?" a familiar voice called, from the shadows.

Vix spotted a young man, standing next to a horse stall. The boy was dressed in a uniform belonging to Lord Conway's Academy, a long-sleeved, bright gold tunic, tight leather boots, and skullcap. The tunic featured an image of a white dove in flight, across the chest.

At first, all Vix saw saw in the torchlight was a scrawny kid with skinny, bare legs and knobby knees. He soon learned that it was his commanding officer. Vix laughed as he wrapped one arm around the kid's torso. "Captain Willowby!"

"No, it's just Willowby," the boy said, his tone carrying a mixture of regret and relief.

"What'cha doing in that getup, sir?" asked Vix. "You look like some kinda no-nothing, shirt-tailed schoolboy."

"Well, because . . . because that's all I am, now," answered Willowby, his knees nearly buckling. "Uncle Alistair met with General Chang, and they . . . decommissioned me."

Vix sneered.

"I'm not Captain Willowby, anymore," the boy sighed. "Just Willowby. Plain old Brother Willowby."

"What the hell?"

"It's for the best, I suppose," said Willowby, frightened by Vix's sudden anger. "I just don't think I'll ever become an officer, like others in the family. You were more in charge of Fort Cooley, than I ever was."

Vix glared at Willowby. "You ain't qualified to run no fortress, not yet. Not yet with the mess going on right now. But don't go thinking that just because you got your feathers ruffled, you ain't good enough to be an officer. Give me half a chance, I'll get you and the other boys squared away . . ."

"They're dead, aren't they?" interrupted Willowby. "The men we left with you and Owensby. They're dead, aren't they?"

"There wasn't a damn thing I could do to stop it," said Vix, thinking he too should have died alongside those twenty young recruits, *and* that damned Owensby. "I said I'd look out for 'em, all right. But there wasn't a thing I could to do . . ."

"Bergman and Billy Joe, too?"

Vix nodded, yes.

Willowby leaned his head against a post and released a high-pitched sob. He concealed his eyes under one hand, not knowing whether to hold back the tears or allow them to spill, freely. "What happened?" he asked.

"Them Branellians Owensby waited on finally showed up."

Willowby wiped the tears from his face, tucked on his school uniform, and feigned courage. It was unmanly to cry! "I should have stayed behind too, Sergeant Vix."

"You're damn lucky you didn't. I'm sorry it was them to catch hell, sir."

Well, what difference did it make? It was wrong to place Willowby in command, or allow a stupid son of a bitch like Owensby to position inexperienced soldiers in harm's way. It was typical for the brass to give someone like Willowby the responsibility of overseeing an Army base, simply because of his background and ancestry. What else was new?

Willowby wanted to believe that Bergman and Billy Joe died standing up, bravely facing the enemy. He had known the two boys since the first grade, and found it difficult to accept that both were gone. He sought illumination to the events leading to this disaster on the beach, for the sake of closure. Perhaps it was best not knowing how they fell.

Willowby embraced Vix, like a son requiring love and affection from a caring father. He grieved over the casualties, most of which were his closest friends.

There were no words of comfort to ease the pain. Under the circumstances, Vix wanted to get drunk, and drown his own sorrows in a bottle of the foulest rotgut he could find. For the moment, it was enough to stand beside Willowby, in his time of need.

"Willowby!" someone shouted, in the darkness. *"Willowby!* Mom wants you!"

Vix and Willowby were joined by a lad of ten or eleven, who wore a similar school uniform as the former captain. Once he made eye-contact with Vix, the lad stopped dead in his tracks.

Once again, Willowby wiped away the tears which streamed down his face. He didn't want the younger boy to see him like that. Once he regained his composure, Willowby led the boy over. "Zach," he said, softly. "This is the guy I told you about, my top sergeant, Vix. Vix, this is my brother Zachary."

Vix held out his meaty paw, as Zachary timidly shook hands. "Glad to meet you," the sergeant spoke, with a grin.

Zachary smiled, but said nothing.

"I have to go," said Willowby, with resentment. "Mom wants me. I'm so glad I found you, Sergeant Vix. When I heard what happened last night at the mouth of the Ember River, I was afraid that you were also . . . you *know* . . ." Willowby was unable to say more.

"I'd hate to think you was all tore up over Colonel Owensby," responded Vix, sarcastically.

"Take care of yourself, Sergeant Vix," mumbled Willowby. "I hope we'll meet again, in better days."

Vix smiled. "I'd like that, Captain Willowby."

"No, no. Not Captain Willowby. Just Brother Willowby. Plain old Brother Willowby."

"Whatcha gonna do now, after your done with school? Think you'll try the Army again, or go to work in a boneyard, with your ma's kin?"

"I don't know," said Willowby. "But if I do return to the military, I hope it's with a man like you. A sergeant of your qualifications, your experience, and your courage. I can't think of a better man to serve with, than you."

As Willowby started to walk away, his brother Zachary in tow, Vix called him back. "Yes, Sergeant Vix?" he asked.

"If I ain't dead or retired in a year or two, gimme the word, and I'll be there." Vix stood at attention, to give his former CO a fond salute. "Your orders, Captain Willowby?"

Returning the salute, Willowby smiled and said, "As you were, Sergeant Vix!"

51

Early that next morning, Yuri's dog Boris was buried upon a hillside above the compound. Officiated by Pastor Dimitri, this "memorial" was attended by Yuri, Theo, Fumiko, Omar, the pastor's three children, Bradley and Kenichi.

Kenichi felt he still owed Yuri a huge favor, so he helped "pray" Boris into Canine Heaven. Later on, he aimed to talk Bradley, Trevor, and Derek into leaving the compound with him, to seek their fortunes elsewhere.

Meanwhile, the others prepared for their voyage to Insula Infernus.

Dimitri read a verse from *The Song of Carlos,* speaking of the beauty, magnificence, and splendor found in nature. Yuri openly wept, as he stared at the burial mound. Theo did his best to console his stepson.

Yuri was convinced that Jesse knocked the guard out, then killed Boris. Jesse never held back in harming Yuri in the past! What stopped him from adding insult to injury, now?

As Dimitri closed with a final prayer, the service ended. This small congregation then returned to the compound, where a breakfast of eggs and sausage was served. "Stay strong," Dimitri urged Yuri, then followed everyone from the tiny grave site.

This left Yuri and Theo to contemplate the loss of their dog. The two sat on a thin patch of dried grass, then stared out across the valley. Dark clouds blocked the sun, as a cool breeze swept over the hillside.

Finally, Theo broke the silence. "I'd like you to reconsider on going to Infernus."

"But why?" asked Yuri, dealing with severe heartbreak.

"They don't need you," said Theo. "When it comes to discipline or security, I'm sure Major Kohl or Strunk can . . ."

"But I want to go! Major Kohl needs me!"

"You don't understand, Yuri. I'm asking you to stay here, with me."

"What for?" asked Yuri. "Don't you think the soldiers Kraig posted here can adequately protect you?"

"It's not that," sighed Theo. "I need you, not only as a bodyguard, but for companionship."

"That's what Omar's for," laughed Yuri. "To catch the bigger fish, or beat you at cards. If you get tired of losing to him, what about Dimitri?"

"Omar and Dimitri are my friends. Yuri, you're my son."

"I love you too, Father," said Yuri, predicting Theo's next words. "But Major Kohl needs me, especially after Sergeant Vix left."

"I need you more than Major Kohl! I'm an old man . . ."

"You're not that old!" snickered Yuri. "You're the same age as Major Kohl!"

Theo rubbed Yuri's cheek. "I never dreamed we'd be so close."

"I'm all right, Father. I know you're worried about me. I'll be fine."

"You'll be all right, without me. Will I be all right, without you?"

"You're the bravest, most generous man I've ever known," said Yuri. "I can never repay your kindness to me."

"Then repay me by staying!" begged Theo. "Please understand. In my old age . . ."

"In your old age . . ." mocked Yuri.

"Please Yuri, hear me out! In my old age, I can't imagine parting with you, not even for a minute. Those days you were away, finding new recruits for Kohl, I constantly fretted over you. Thoughts that you'd been captured or killed nearly put *me* in the ground. I'm worried sick about you, now!"

"You don't have to worry about me."

"But you'll worry about me. Won't you, son?"

"That's different!"

"How's it different?"

"As soon as I get home, I promise never to leave here, ever again," said Yuri. "You always lectured me on giving to those in need. I must help Major Kohl."

"You've already helped Kohl, by finding those recruits. The best way to help me is by staying."

"Dimitri and you want me to have friends my own age," said Yuri. "What about Brad, Kenichi, or Giorgio? I want to be with them when they land on Infernus. They need me, too! For the longest time, you were the only one who cared for me!"

"That's not true! There are lots of people who care . . ."

"When I was at the War Ministry, I found out how much those officers hate us! They said the worst things about you!"

"My policies aren't very popular with the Ministry of War." Theo ran his fingers through Yuri's hair. "Many officers dislike me, intensely. But I love Embrey, and its potential, more than their opinions of me. And as much as I love Embrey, I love you that much more."

"They say our relationship is . . . unnatural."

"Politics," said Theo, containing his anger. "It's difficult being in a position of authority and power. If your opponents can't beat you one way, they'll defeat you in another."

"It's not fair! Everyone hates us!"

"Yuri . . ."

"Just like when I was at Captain Maliek's school," cried Yuri. "No one liked me, except this one kid. Conrad was my only friend, there. And now he's dead."

Yuri tried to befriend fellow students at Clive, Tim, Tomas, Marietto . . . and *Jesse*. It got him nowhere. In the end, he always lost. In his profession friendship netted little, other than the means of securing a target. Sure, he got "chummy" with a pageboy in Kentworth, though it wasn't as Jesse and Strunk described it. Not entirely. Yes, the pageboy encouraged an "unnatural relationship" with Yuri. And yes, after giving in to the pageboy's wishes, Yuri murdered him in an extremely gruesome manner. This was not achieved for hate's sake. It furthered Theo's goal of terminating a Branellian legislator who got rich from the Border War. The pageboy was simply an obstacle, and undeserving in his fate.

"People say I'm weird," said Yuri. "And everyone knows that I'm . . ."

"Do you know what I think?" interrupted Theo. "You're special, Yuri. You're unique."

"I'm different, Father. Is that it?"

"'Special,' 'different,' 'unique'! Words, just words! So you're different? You're my son and heir, that's what makes you different. Those who hate me hate you, too! Why should I care? It's the hardship I face, for my stewardship of Embrey." Theo smiled. "You do get along with Kenichi. Right, son?"

"He's really smart! That's another reason I want to go on the trip. It's not only for the treasure, or for Major Kohl. If I'm going to be friends with Kenichi and the others, then I have to go. I can't stay behind."

"I love you more than all the treasures in the world," said Theo.

"If you really love me, then let me go with Major Kohl. If you want me to be the man that you and Dimitri expect of me, I have to earn the respect of the Embrian people. Maybe my going to Infernus will be justified, for the good of all."

"It will be dangerous."

"I know, but . . ."

"Some of those boys will be killed!" shouted Theo. "That is, if they even make it to Infernus! I was a merchant marine, Yuri. If the ocean doesn't get you, then pirates and enemy vessels will. I've lost many friends out there. It's no place for childhood whims."

"Then maybe I can keep someone from getting killed."

Yuri was almost a grown man, a fact which agonized Theo. The legislator had no way of holding Yuri back, any more than his own parents stopped him from leaving home at age fourteen. If Theo did indeed love Yuri, he owed him an opportunity of proving himself, beyond working as a hired sword.

"I'll make sure you have plenty of coffee," said Theo, removing a ring from one finger. "Please put this on, Yuri."

"Why are you giving it to me?"

"It will guarantee your safe passage, to Agron. It's an violation to assault any member of an Embrian Councillor's family, in international waters. Once you display this ring, it's a declaration of war for those bringing harm upon you."

"Thank you," said Yuri. "I'll wear it with dignity and honor."

"This property is mine," added Theo. "Someday, it will be yours. Everything I owe I bequeath to you, including my title and the privileges which comes with it." Theo kissed Yuri's forehead. "Bring this ring, and yourself, back home to me."

"I will," said Yuri. "Don't worry, Father. I'll be home soon, I promise!"

"Go on," said Kohl, smiling. "Take them."

Giorgio stared at the coins spread across Theo's dining room table. "What are these for?" he asked.

Kohl rubbed his fingers across a fifty-shilling gold piece. "The reward for securing an army," he said. "Go on, take them. You've earned it."

Giorgio silently counted out the money. "One-hundred-and-thirty shillings?" he whispered, in disbelief. "That much, sir?"

"Thirteen, fine scrapping young soldiers, at ten shillings a piece," explained Kohl. "I counted you in, too. Is that what we agreed on?"

Giorgio shook his head. "I can't accept this, Major Kohl."

"Why not? You've earned it!"

"You don't have to pay me, Major Kohl," said Giorgio, nervously. "I didn't go out and find those guys, for money."

Kohl slid the coins across the table. "Nonsense! You promised me an army, and that's what you brought me. Is this not enough?"

"No sir, it's plenty! It's just that . . ."

"Reap the rewards of your efforts," urged Kohl.

"That's right," agreed Sergeant Rupert, joining Kohl and Giorgio at the table with a cup of hot coffee. "From what I heard, you risked life and limb to . . ."

"I didn't do it alone." Giorgio's throat tightened. "Yuri went with me . . ."

"So did that big oaf in the torn school uniform," said Kohl. "I made a deal with you, not Fritz or Yuri."

Giorgio sighed. "Yuri did more to get everyone here, than me."

"Don't tell me you did nothing to bring the boys together," commented Kohl. "I know better than that."

"I was there, Major Kohl," said Giorgio. "That's all I can say."

Kohl and Rupert quietly awaited Giorgio's explanation.

"Yuri found us a place to stay, the night before last," said Giorgio. "That next day, after that mob burned down Dimitri's church, he went out alone to find more of my friends."

"*Hmm . . .*" Kohl squinted. "Well, anyway . . . You delivered eight, brave young men to me, including yourself. Good work! Pat yourself on the back."

"And I wouldn't have gotten some of those guys, without Pastor Dimitri," added Giorgio.

"Your contributions amounted to more than just being there," said Kohl. "You did more than just stand around with your hands in your pockets, when you spotted those five boys in town."

"I should give Geoffrey credit for that," said Giorgio. "He took Sergio and Giuseppe under his wing. Randy and Eduardo helped out too, I guess. It was only by the grace of God that Yuri and I found them, when we did. We were blessed when Yuri took us to that Kuschan church!"

"Are you man enough to give yourself any credit for bringing those young men here, to me?" asked Kohl, with increasing anger. "What about that stupid-looking kid, wearing the heinous Gornick Youth uniform?"

"Bentley," laughed Giorgio. "We wouldn't have gotten him, either, had it not been for Major Conroy."

"Conroy?" snapped Kohl. "What's he got to do with it?"

"I don't know how Conroy found Bentley, before raiding Theo's home." Giorgio smiled. "For what it's worth, I'm glad he had Bentley with him."

"Well, you spared that youngster from a life of worshipping a madman," said Kohl. "Good for you, Giorgio!"

"Show yourself a little kindness," said Rupert, "and take the money."

"Honestly!" cried Giorgio. "I don't want it! No offense, sir, but . . . Why . . . why don't you just give it to Yuri, instead?"

"Yuri don't need it!" shouted Kohl. "As Theo's son and heir, he has more money than you and I can ever dream of!"

"Yeah, well . . . Maybe he earned it," mumbled Giorgio. "I didn't."

Kohl frowned. "Tell me, Giorgio. Just how did you finagle your way into the Leadership at Lord Kelly's, with so little confidence in yourself?"

Giorgio bit his lip. Kohl was quite fond of him, and the money only supported that. Whether Giorgio was indeed a Leader, or held any real authority over his Brothers, did his selfish actions and behavior garner their respect?

"The boys look up to you, Giorgio," said Rupert. "Believe me. I talked to most of them, and that's what they said."

"Kenichi and Fritz don't," sighed Giorgio. "Look, Major Kohl. I appreciate what you're doing, but you don't have to pay me. I had nothing to do with finding the five guys that Yuri and Commander Salazar brought here, yesterday."

"It'll be a cold day in Hell before I give Salazar anything more than a swift kick to the ass!" roared Kohl, impatiently. "I've got no more time for your nonsense, Giorgio! We've got to get ready for our long sea voyage, to Infernus. Take the money. You're under my command now, and that's an order. Enjoy the fruits of your labors."

Reluctantly, Giorgio pocketed the shillings. "Yes, sir."

"Sergeant Rupert?" requested Kohl. "Bring me those clothes from my quarters."

Rupert went into Kohl's bedroom, and returned with bundles of clothing in his arms.

Kohl smiled. "Your school tunics look very grand on the men, but are inadequate for life on a seagoing vessel. Give these sailing clothes to those who don't have any, so they'll be dressed more suitably for our adventure. I know you're man enough to do that."

"I can tell already that we'll be lifelong friends!" said Rupert, excitedly. "I can't wait to board the Tyree James. Can you?"

Giorgio saluted Kohl and Rupert, placed the clothes under one arm, and left Theo's cottage.

Giorgio stepped outside, to a warm day. The shillings were burdens he could not ignore, nor deny. Although the money motivated him to search for his schoolmates, he was simply happy to be reunited with some of them. Regaining Bradley's good graces was a tremendous weight off his shoulders. Giorgio vowed never to hurt the kid, ever again! Having Bradley along on the voyage was better than all the treasures on Infernus!

So, what about those coins jingling in Giorgio's pocket? He had already determined that they weren't rightly his. What was he to do with that amount of money, in the company of Agronian sailors? Naturally, he wanted to be rewarded for shaping an army on Kohl's behalf. What if he gave his buddies equal shares of it? What good was that? Fritz was liable to swipe the younger boys' portions! What if Giorgio just gave it to Dimitri, to cover certain expenses for a new church? Dimitri was too proud and stubborn to accept it.

However, it was impossible for Giorgio to keep the money. The Brothers from Lord Kelly's Academy were worth far more than ten shillings a piece!

Giorgio held the money in one palm, thinking of the good things he'd do with it. Yuri and Fritz were well-aware of this financial arrangement with Kohl. What if Giorgio shared it with them, at the risk of alienating those who truly cared for him, be it Geoffrey, Bentley, Eduardo, the twins . . .

. . . or Bradley?

Lacking an easy solution, Giorgio yelled out a string of curse words.

Seconds later, he dropped the one-hundred-and-thirty shillings into a round, stone-lined well.

Seconds later, he cursed himself for doing such a stupid thing.

Giorgio was torn, as he listened to the echo of coins clanging against the bricks, before splashing into the water below. He was angry and relieved, liberated and imprisoned, happy and sad. *A hundred-and-thirty shillings! And look what I just did with it!*

Staring into the darkened abyss of the well, Giorgio debated if he did the right thing by throwing that much loot into the drink. It was too late to retrieve it. Assuming the well was drained, some lucky person would find the money, and wonder how it got there while celebrating their good fortune. As he glanced at his own reflection in the well, was Giorgio supposed to feel better, or worse, by making that sort of sacrifice?

What the hell good was money, on Insula Infernus?

"Brad?" asked Kenichi, swallowing his last bite of breakfast. "Do you really want to go on that voyage?"

"Yeah, Kenichi," answered Bradley, decisively. "I really want to go."

The two boys sat outside of the bunkhouse, enjoying a lovely fall day. Kenichi wanted no part of the trip to that mysterious land, far to the west. As for Theo's job offer, he began having second thoughts about that, too. "What about spending long days on a ship with Andre and Fritz?" he pondered, aloud.

Bradley frowned.

"The more I think about it, the more that trip scares me." Kenichi slapped Bradley's knee. "Let's sit this one out, okay?"

"But I gave my word to Giorgio!" yelled Bradley. He hated conflict, but saw no way to avoid it.

"Will you still give your word to Giorgio, if he asked you to jump off a cliff?" questioned Kenichi. "I don't think I'm man enough to follow Major Kohl into Heaven, Hell, or Infernus."

"What am I supposed to do?" asked Bradley. "Stand back and let others serve our country? Don't you want to be a hero, Kenichi?"

Moments later, Giorgio arrived with the bundles of clothes under one arm. "Hey, guys," he greeted, feeling uneasy around Kenichi. "Major Kohl asked me to give you these." Grinning, he added, "The major wants you dressed in something more suitable for our journey."

Bradley and Kenichi unraveled the clothes to find lightweight, long-sleeved shirts, silk underwear, and long, wool breeches. "Where can we go to take a bath?" asked Kenichi.

"There's a creek over there," said Giorgio, pointing. "It's probably too cold to bathe in though, I'll bet."

Smiling eagerly, Kenichi and Bradley sprinted toward this secluded water hole.

"Like I said," mumbled Giorgio, "the creek's too cold. If you don't mind, we've got warm tubs in the bunkhouse . . ."

Bradley and Kenichi disappeared into the woods, new clothes in hand. Giorgio pouted. It made him jealous to see them together. So what? He still had to furnish Trevor, Derek, Andre, and Bentley with their sailing clothes.

Less than a hundred yards from the bunkhouse, Bradley and Kenichi found a swift-moving creek, lined on both sides with oak and cottonwood trees. "Hope you don't mind seeing me naked," said Bradley, resting his sandals and skullcap on a boulder. Taking a deep breath, he shed his tunic, then cautiously stepped across small, tiny stones to examine the creek's temperature. The autumn breeze against his nude body was refreshing.

"If you don't mind, I don't mind," said Kenichi, quickly removing his soiled uniform. Carelessly he threw his tunic and skullcap into the stream, and watched them float away.

"Why'd you do that, for?" asked Bradley, placing one toe into the crystal-clear stream.

"You got no idea how glad I am to get rid of those!" laughed Kenichi.

Bradley watched at Kenichi dropped his loincloth to the rocks. Normally, it didn't bother him to see his friends in their birthday suits. One particular characteristic of Kenichi's anatomy made him blush. Kenichi was hung like a horse!

"How's the water?" asked Kenichi.

"Freezing!" said Bradley, slowly inching into the creek.

Kenichi let out a cheer as he leaped into the current with a thunderous *splash!* "Jump in, Brad!" he laughed, shivering in the waist-deep water. "It's great!"

Bradley entered the creek to his knees. His teeth chattered, as goosebumps pocked his pale skin.

Adapting himself to the creek, Kenichi scrubbed his chest, underarms, and groin. Water dripped from his hair like rain.

Bradley threw himself into the current. Crouching on his backside, he relished the fresh, chilly water flowing over his scrawny shell.

Bradley treated this relaxing experience as a personal baptism. He suddenly felt like a new man, while struggling to free himself from a troubling past. He'd never live to escape from his mistake with Leni, as memories of the bloodshed at Lord William's continued to haunt him. If nothing more, this bath took the edge off. As Bradley lay in the stream, the only sounds came from the wind, streams of water beating against the rocks, and chirping birds.

Bradley closed his eyes and concentrated on a wall of solid, fiery reds, oranges, and pinks, as sunlight hit his face. During this brief period of tranquility, he reevaluated his faith in God. Was this a whole new deity, or simply another version of the same Heavenly Creator?

Oh, Father . . .

Grant me courage to undertake the journey before me. Give me this one opportunity to follow Your commandments and Your will, in the service of all mankind. Give us fair weather during our long journey. Guide us in seeking the treasure, to restore civility and freedom to the people of Embrey.

Oh, Father!

Stand beside me! We cannot hope to succeed on our own! Lead us through this perilous voyage, and assure our survival, so all who accept this challenge may return safely home. With Your love and guidance, let us obey that which pleases you . . .

Amen . . .

"How is it, Brad?" asked Kenichi.

"Terrific!" answered Bradley. "You, Kenichi?"

"Great!" laughed Kenichi, dunking himself.

Bradley opened his eyes to a cloudless, turquoise sky above, while he basked in the pleasures of solitude. More than anything, he was glad to share this time with a friend. In the warm autumn air, he wasn't ready to draw a close to this calm, pleasant swim.

At the same time, Bradley was trapped between Giorgio's hopes of redemption on Infernus, and Kenichi's plans of reinventing himself in the Embrian countryside. More pressing, he wondered if his involvement in Kohl's endeavor would make any real difference, in the long run.

What if our mission ends in disaster?

"The constable's coming!" someone cried from the bank.

Trevor and Derek sprinted to the creek, still in their school uniforms.

"What did you say, Trev?" asked Kenichi.

"The constable's here!" said Trevor, winded. "He's looking for anyone who knows what happened to Karl, Sven, and Antoine."

"We don't know anything!" screamed Bradley, glancing at Kenichi.

"All the constable said is that he was mostly looking for you, Kenichi," said Derek.

Kenichi raced to his new clothes, as Derek's mouth gaped open. "Holy crap!" the youngster gasped, staring at Kenichi's naked body. "That thing ever get in your way?"

"Shut up, moron!" yelled Trevor, slugging Derek's arm.

"You're the moron, retard!" responded Derek, favoring his sore arm.

Trevor rolled his eyes back. "Kenichi can't help it if it's that long! Quit being so inconsiderate, Derry!"

Without waiting to dry off, Bradley and Kenichi put their new clothes on.

"Whatcha doing?" asked Trevor, in confusion.

Bradley looked at his younger roommates. There was no reason to jeopardize them. Bradley gave Trevor a hug, then kissed the boy's cheek. "Take care, Trevor," he said, his voice cracking. As he threw his arms around Derek, tears seeped from both eyes.

"Don't go!" begged Trevor, as Derek sobbed.

Bradley saw a need to grant words of comfort to the boys. There was no time for it. Bradley fetched his skullcap and tunic from the rocks.

"Leave them!" ordered Kenichi. "The same for that damned necklace!"

"But why?" questioned Bradley.

"They link us to a scene of a crime!" stated Kenichi, impatiently. "Toss them, and let's go!"

Bradley tucked his skullcap and tunic into his new shirt. With his heart sinking, he followed Kenichi. Without so much as a 'goodbye,' the two boys disappeared behind a thick growth of trees, toward the advent of another life.

"I know nothing about the killings at Lord Kelly's Academy," Theo told the mounted constable. Along with Kohl and Yuri, he disputed the lawman's investigation on his property. "How do we even know these boys were in Karl's office, that afternoon? There are children here from Lord Kelly's, all right. But no one fitting that description."

The constable was a man in his mid-forties, with a black eye patch, thick sideburns, a dark hood and a double-breasted, blue jacket. He was accompanied by five armed deputies.

"I've been directed to apprehend those charged with the deaths of two Leaders from Lord Kelly's, and a student from Lord William's," the constable said. "We were notified that Lord Kelly's secretary is here. He's our prime suspect. Now, if you don't mind, Councillor Theo, I'd like to take a look around."

"I do mind!" shouted Theo. "I'm an Embrian Councillor, not a pimp or petty thief! On whose authority do you make this search? You have no right here, without a written warrant!"

Smiling, the constable reached into his jacket for an official document. "With Councillors Omar and Fumiko, you are to relocate to the Ministry of War. General Chang and Admiral Kraig's orders. If you are not there by noon tomorrow, I will take you by force."

"Give me that!" demanded Theo, ripping the document from the constable's hand. It was a decree for the three legislators to move to the present site of the Ministry of War, on the outskirts of Sykes. Below were the signatures of Kraig and Chang.

"This compound is not a government post, and is considered unsafe," the constable said. "If you wish to serve the sovereign nation of Embrey, then you must . . ."

"I already know my duties to Embrey!" yelled Theo. Not only was he outraged at the constable, but the brass' command to leave the compound. But Embrey was in a state of martial law, and Theo had no choice but to obey the decree's order.

The constable stepped off his horse. "My men and I will look around for the suspect."

"I tell you, he's not here!" argued Theo.

The constable laughed. "Then you won't mind if we have that look around, will you?"

"You've got more urgent business than to violate the sanctity of my home," said Theo, impatiently. "Sir, your time is wasted here. What about Sykes' security? What about the fate of King Ogden?"

"King Ogden's been assassinated," the constable announced.

Theo was shocked, despite the fact that he disliked Ogden, both as a ruler and as a man. Regaining his composure, he asked, "And what are you doing about that? You can't tell me that Ogden's killer is on these premises!"

"That particular investigation is under the War Ministry's jurisdiction." The constable knelt to Theo, as did the other peace officers. "For all we know, you may now be Embrey's king," he said. "Even with my support of General Gornick, I mean no disrespect to you, Councillor Theo. I've been given my orders, nothing more. Now sir, may we have that look around?"

"Yes," agreed Theo, grudgingly. "You may have that look around. Upon your return to Sykes, give General Chang and Admiral Kraig my compliments. Inform them that I will arrive at the Ministry of War, this evening."

"It's my honor to be in your service," the constable said, standing. "Is there anything I may do for you?"

"No," answered Theo, storming away with Yuri and Kohl. "Make your damned search, then go!"

Theo entered the meeting room, and slammed the door behind him. "If I am indeed Embrey's new king, as that clown says, why must I take orders from Kraig or Chang?"

"They have no call treating you that way," said Kohl, in a posturing manner.

Theo sighed. "I must arrange for a trip to the Ministry of War. You'd better leave for Infernus, as soon as possible." Theo put his hand on Yuri's shoulder. "Do you understand, son? We go our separate ways, this very afternoon."

Yuri was anxious to begin his journey. He was also saddened. "I understand," he said, keeping his emotions in check.

"I'll get our supplies together," said Kohl, shaking Theo's hand. "My old friend, I cannot thank you enough for your support and subsidy of this valiant quest! I promise never to let you down."

"I've got the greatest confidence in you," said Theo, silencing any doubts he had about Kohl. It was too late to fret over that, now. Theo chose to sponsor a second expedition to Infernus, and placed his hopes and faith in this venture. "You've never once disappointed me, Major Kohl."

Kohl smiled as he left the room.

"Where's Giorgio and Fritz?" asked Theo, nervously.

"I hid them in the outhouse," answered Yuri. "That two-holer, upon the hill."

"Pray the constable doesn't look there. What about Brad and Kenichi?"

"They went to take a bath in our creek. I sent Trevor and Derek to warn them."

Theo maintained the facade of authority. "Go help Major Kohl, son. Get the twins and Eduardo to assist you. Above all, stay calm. I don't want to give the constable any suspicions."

"Can they arrest someone, simply on a hunch or a whim?"

"You know those municipal stooges," said Theo. "They'll apprehend Kenichi, because they can. That racist scoundrel from Sykes thinks he's better than everyone else. No one dares obstruct his screwy concepts of fairness and justice. Whether Brad or Kenichi had anything to do with the murders, I don't hold them personally responsible, under the circumstances." Theo forced a smile. "You see, Yuri, I like those boys, too."

"Stinks in here," whispered Fritz, as he hid in an outhouse upon a hillside above the compound. The stall smelled atrocious in the warm sunlight. His only view outside was through a tiny crack in the wall. Worst of all, he needed a stiff drink! "How long we gotta stay in here?"

"I don't know," said Giorgio, in the stall next to Fritz's. Occasionally, he peeked through a crescent moon, carved in the door. Assuming he was caught, Giorgio feared he wouldn't stand up under the constable's heavy interrogation. His hopes of traveling to Infernus were fleeting.

White knuckles and shallow breathing revealed Giorgio's growing panic. He considered on telling lies to satisfy the constable, and needed a suitable fall guy. Who? Not Bradley! What about Fritzy, who was custom-made for the rap? No one liked him, anyway. Who'd come to that cretin's defense, especially after his break-in at Councillor Theo's house?

Then again, it was Kenichi who slammed Karl into that desk . . .

Giorgio lowered his head, in shame. Not only was he jealous of Bradley, but Kenichi as well! Indicting Kenichi for the trouble in Karl's office might get Giorgio off the hook. In return, it meant losing Bradley's love and respect!

One thing was certain; it was impossible to stay in the outhouse for much longer. The smothering heat was unbearable!

Giorgio's nerves nearly failed him, as two lawmen stepped toward the commode. Crouching behind the door, he held his breath and prayed. Better just to give in, fess up to my guilt, and take it like a man!

I'll take Fritzy down with me!

"Goddamn joint smells," mumbled Fritz. "I'm getting outa here ..."

"No!" warned Giorgio.

"Why not?"

"Someone's coming!"

"What?"

"Someone's coming!" repeated Giorgio.

"Aw, shit," said Fritz. "I gotta piss . . ."

Inadvertently, Giorgio laughed. The outhouse is the first place they'll search! What now? Drop my drawers and claim ignorance?

Me? I'm taking a dump, what's it look like?

Then I'll really get caught with my pants down!

"We got 'em!" someone called, from the opposite side of the outhouse.

"Say again?" one of the deputies asked.

"Well, I'm not sure," another said. "But we got the gook!"

Giorgio sighed. It was better for Kenichi to take the heat, than him!

However, it wasn't Kenichi who cried out, "But we're innocent!" It was Bradley.

"If you're innocent, then why were you running?" the constable asked, as he and a deputy dragged Bradley and Kenichi to their fellow peace officers. The two boys' hands were tight behind their backs.

"Who'd they get?" asked Fritz.

"Brad and Kenichi," answered Giorgio, thinking strongly about taking Bradley's place. Was it worth endangering himself, to save a friend?

"We're not getting much out of these hooligans," the constable laughed. "As soon as the interrogator applies leather to their backs, they'll say plenty!"

"But we didn't do it!" whimpered Bradley.

"Do what?" the constable asked, forcefully. "Tell me, boy. Do you know why you're under arrest? I know you're involved with a crime, by the way you up and ran when we saw us. What's this 'it' you didn't do?"

Bradley shrugged.

"Brad didn't do anything!" said Kenichi, defiantly. "He wouldn't hurt a fly!"

"And you would?" the constable asked. "Let me guess. You didn't do 'it' either."

"We're Councillor Theo's guests," said Kenichi. "We were given permission to pick wild strawberries in the woods."

"Oh, so that's why you tried to run away?" the constable laughed. "Wild strawberries are in high demand this time of year. Too greedy to share with us! Where are the buckets, to carry these wild strawberries to Councillor Theo?"

Kenichi frowned at his lousy alibi.

"Tell it to the interrogator, when he rips those clothes off to decorate your shoulder blades," the constable said.

Kenichi looked at Bradley. Guilt and innocence meant nothing. It was over for them.

Once the law officers took their prisoners away, Giorgio carefully slipped out of the stall.

"Are they gone?" asked Fritz.

Giorgio nodded 'yes,' as sucking in a deep breath. He had to do something, *anything,* to get Bradley and Kenichi out of this mess!

Brushing himself off, Giorgio heard the sounds of Fritz urinating, from behind the outhouse door. "Fritz," he said, his hands shaking from weak nerves. "We've got to help Brad and Kenichi."

"What's this 'we' crap?" questioned Fritz. "Why should I go outa my way to save Kenny Slant-Eyes, and the little do-gooder?"

Giorgio hit the roof. Yeah, it was easy to let Bradley and Kenichi take the blame for everything. It was convenient for Giorgio to walk away, allowing others to carry the weight for his own failings and shortcomings. But was it right? Fear prevented Giorgio from sacrificing himself, for Bradley's sake. Fear also motivated him to come forward, on Bradley's behalf.

More than anything, Giorgio wanted to get back at Fritz, for the recklessness and stupidity that troublemaker inflicted upon everybody.

Once Fritz left the stall, Giorgio planted a clenched fist into his chin.

Fritz flew into the outhouse door. "That's for breaking into Theo's home!" explained Giorgio, angrily.

Fritz began to speak out, when Giorgio slugged his unprotected gut. "And that's for getting Sergio and Derry drunk, yesterday!" snapped Giorgio.

Fritz staggered backward, this time landing upon the stall.

Giorgio's face was a fiery red, as he stepped forward to grant Fritz another dose of the bad medicine. "And this is for what you did to Antoine!" he growled, wishing to pound Fritz's face into ground beef.

Blinded by his own rage and hostility, Giorgio failed to see Fritz cock both feet back . . .

. . . until they were unleashed upon his head.

Giorgio impacted the grassy hillside with a bone-crunching *thud!* His nose and mouth filled with blood. A surge of pain sprinted throughout his entire body, from the massive jolt of Fritz's blow. His thoughts alternated between Brad and Kenichi's dilemma, to a sense of irony found only in self-deprecating humor. Giorgio forced a strained smile, as he attempted to crawl away from Fritz.

Fritz bolted from the outhouse, and lifted Giorgio up by the hair.

Frantically, Giorgio waved his arms for Fritz to cease fire, while spitting out bloody saliva. "Why do you always have to be a jerk, Fritz'?" cried Giorgio. "Why don't you try to help somebody, once in your life?"

Fritz laughed. It was empowering to watch that pompous big shot crap his pants. "Why don't *I* try t' help somebody, y' chickenshit bastard?" asked Fritz, victoriously. "Why don't *you?*"

"You have no right to take those boys, without my consent!" Theo shouted at the constable and his five deputies.

The past few days had been stressful for Theo. He was an important figure in Embrian politics, and carried the weight of the world upon his shoulders. He often found himself in situations greater than his own personal strengths and abilities.

While household staff and soldiers collected items for their relocation to the War Ministry, Major Kohl got ready for his journey to Infernus.

At that given moment, Theo had to rescue Bradley and Kenichi. According to Embrian law, detainees were to be legally arraigned for their alleged crimes. Such procedures were rarely administered. In all likelihood, the two boys would be coerced into making false confessions, discarded into filthy jail cells, and forgotten. Like many elements of a corrupt judicial system, it was a negligent practice which Theo worked to remedy. Reforms were slowly enacted, but more had to be done.

Theo was determined to hold Bradley and Kenichi in his custody, rather than subject them to the constable's cruel handling. Rules were to be obeyed, even in martial law.

"What makes you so sure these boys are the murderers?" questioned Theo. "What gives you the authority to barge in here and and grab anyone who vaguely resembles the suspects' descriptions?"

"I'm following my orders," said the constable. He pointed at Bradley and Kenichi, who sat on the ground. "I was told that one of the killers was a gook. The blonde had a Lord Kelly's uniform under his shirt, and a pretty little necklace linking him to the crime."

Kenichi remained quiet, as Bradley openly wept. A number of schoolmates stood idly by. Derek threw himself upon a bunkhouse cot and cried, while Trevor clung onto Eduardo. Their sobs cut deeply within the hearts of most everyone at the compound. Even a few of the deputies debated the validity of this arrest, yet refused to voice their concerns. Eduardo held his arms around Trevor, searching for words of solace and comfort which eluded him.

"That's right, you're only following orders," said Theo, sarcastically. "Do your orders order you to imprison those I know to be innocent? I'm sure General Kraig and Admiral Kraig didn't specifically implicate these two lads. Or do your orders come directly from General Gornick?"

"I'm a very busy man," the constable said. Mounting his horse, he tugged at the rope cinched to his prisoners. "I haven't got all day."

"But we didn't do anything!" bawled Bradley, getting to his feet. In a last ditch effort to save Kenichi and himself, he gave Theo a silent plea to intervene. His wet, dewy eyes said what words could not.

Kenichi had spilled Karl's blood. Now he'd pay for it. He wept as he took Bradley's hand in his. He shed tears for a dear friend who was totally blameless. Unable to speak, he mouthed *sorry*.

The constable saluted Theo and grinned. "Good day, Councillor!"

"Wait!" interrupted Theo. "You're so high on the idea of taking orders. Well, I'm ordering you to place them in my custody!"

"*Your* custody?" the constable argued. "How can you watch over these hoodlums, when you're expected at the War Ministry? You've got your duty to

Embrey, and I've got mine. My duty says that I'm doing right by arresting this gook, and that other one. Out of the way, sir, before I have the mind to arrest you!"

"What do you think you're doing with my son?" someone hollered, from a nearby cottage.

It was Fumiko, who marched toward the constable and Theo. Wagging a finger at the lawmen, she demanded, "Just what do you think you're doing with my darling Hiroyuki?"

"Mother!" exclaimed Kenichi, figuring it best to play along with Fumiko. "I thought never to see you!"

"Did you have a pleasant trip from Griffith?" asked Fumiko, kissing Kenichi's lips.

"Yes, Mother," said Kenichi. "That is, until we got stopped by a highwayman at the Kingston River."

"What purpose do you have with my son?" Fumiko asked the constable. "What has he done to you?"

The constable swallowed. "He's *your* son?"

"What's he look like to you, a prophylactic?" asked Fumiko. "Is this your idea of a joke? Untie him immediately, before I report you to a superior!"

"But I've got my orders!" the constable whined.

"Mother?" asked Kenichi. "Do you remember my best friend, Jarvey?"

Bradley despised the ridiculous, phony name Kenichi just gave him, but had no way to counter it.

Jarvey? Jarvey?

JARVEY?

"Why, of course I do," said Fumiko. She kissed Bradley, and left traces of lipstick on his cheek. "My goodness, Jarvey, you've lost weight since your last visit! What do they feed you?"

"Gruel," answered Bradley. "On holidays we get lard and a dry, moldy biscuit."

"That's *your* son?" the constable repeated, his complexion growing pale.

"Is that lawman an imbecile?" asked Fumiko.

"He must be," said Theo. "The penalty for the wrongful incarceration of an Embrian Councillor's family member is death."

"Then I'll see him hang!" screeched Fumiko. "Get down off your horse, mister! I don't fancy looking up to the likes of you! Get down, so I can have a word with you!"

"I didn't know he was your son, ma'am," the constable apologized, slowly dismounting.

Fumiko slapped the constable's face.

For a moment or two, the constable was intimidated by Fumiko's audacity and strength. While the deputies said nothing, one fought back the urge to laugh.

"Cut my son and Jarvey loose, or I'll throw a rope around your neck, then find a stout tree limb!" demanded Fumiko.

"Travers!" the constable called to a deputy. "Give me your dagger . . . *Now!*"

A deputy leaped from his horse and gave his weapon to the constable. "Why didn't you tell me he was Councillor Fumiko's son?" the constable asked, releasing Bradley and Kenichi.

"You didn't ask," snickered Theo.

Once the boys' hands were freed, they both hugged and kissed Fumiko.

As this drama played out, onlookers kept their fingers crossed. They displayed their approval, quietly. A celebration was to come, later on.

"You look starved!" said Fumiko, leading Bradley and Kenichi to her cottage. "Let me make you each a raspberry jam sandwich."

Once the trio reached Fumiko's quarters, Bradley glared at Kenichi. *"Jarvey?"* he asked, angrily.

"I . . . I honestly didn't know he was Councillor Fumiko's son," the constable stuttered.

"Let this be a lesson to you," scolded Theo. "Now, ride on."

"I meant no offense," the constable said. "If there's anything I can do, please give me the word."

"As a matter of fact, there *is* one thing I want from you," requested Theo. "This very day, if you please."

"Sir?" asked the constable, eager to make an amends.

Theo grabbed onto the constable's shirt. "Your resignation!"

Giorgio and Fritz ran to the compound yard, as Bradley and Kenichi went into a cottage with Fumiko. As the constable rode away with the deputies, lacking the prisoners they so desired, the expressions on everyone's faces told Giorgio that all was well. As Theo sighed in relief, Kohl ordered his men to prepare for their mission.

Giorgio was pleased, very pleased, to learn that Bradley wasn't on his way to a dungeon. Regrettably, he couldn't flee from emotions of disappointment and frustration. *He* wanted to be the one to save Bradley and Kenichi, and regarded himself as a failure for not being there when the detainees needed him the most.

Well, what difference did it make? Bradley and Kenichi were safe! And where was I most of this time? Hiding in a shithouse, or getting the shit beat out of me by Fritz!

Geoffrey was alarmed by the sight of the severe swelling and bruises on Giorgio's face. Fritz grinned as he shot a glance at Giorgio, concealing a secret not to be shared by anyone. "What's going on?" asked Geoffrey. "Where were you guys?"

"Don't ask," whispered Giorgio, walking away.

"We had a pissing contest," chuckled Fritz, evasively, "and he won."

As Fritz went to fetch supplies, Geoffrey scratched his head in confusion.

Bradley and Kenichi dined on a snack of raspberry jam sandwiches and apple cider in Fumiko's guest cottage, and relaxed after their run-in with the constable.

Most witnesses saw humor in Fumiko's antics. It was also dangerous. Thankfully, the constable never caught on. The two boys hoped Fumiko never got any negative backlash for helping them. With luck, she'd soon be reunited with her actual son, Hiroyuki.

Kenichi spent the last few days trying to make sense of Karl's death. He also understood that he had to get far away. But where? Assuming the constable discovered that Kenichi wasn't Hiroyuki, and Bradley wasn't Jarvey, it spelled trouble for Fumiko!

"Are you feeling well?" Fumiko asked Kenichi. "You don't seem to be enjoying the sandwiches and cider."

"I can't thank you enough for saving Bradley and me," said Kenichi.

"We'd be goners," added Bradley, "if you didn't say that Kenichi was your son."

"I have three sons and a daughter," laughed Fumiko. "My youngest, Hiroyuki, is a student at Lord Werner's. You remind me a great deal of him, Kenichi. I'd never stand by and let that incompetent fool take you to jail."

"What if he learns the truth?" asked Kenichi.

"The constable?" questioned Fumiko. "That bum? Half of the prisoners in Sykes have no business being locked up. He arrests anyone he thinks is a likely suspect."

"Why don't they just fire him?" asked Bradley.

"He's General Erik's brother-in-law," said Fumiko. "Or was. I heard that General Erik's head was forcefully removed from his body, two days ago. The fool deserved it. Erik was a staunch supporter of General Gornick. When the dust settles, if the dust settles, the constable won't be anything, anymore. I might recommend him for a job scooping horse poo from the streets, though."

Kenichi wanted to confess his role in Leader Karl's death. Was it wise to trust Fumiko? No matter what, Kenichi had to liberate himself from guilt! With his self-appointed responsibilities to his roommates, he feared buckling under the strain. Like it or not, his only choice meant boarding that Agronian schooner, then sailing to Infernus. Neither Brad, Trevor, or Derek would fare well, if they had Giorgio or Fritz taking care of them!

Kenichi's fate was set. Like an actor on a stage, he lacked the freedom of breaking away from the confines of a script. He'd now secure his dreams of life on the sea. He hoped it wasn't a one-way trip.

"The sandwiches and cider are terrific," said Kenichi. "When Brad and I return, maybe things will be different. Maybe things will be better."

"You mean you're coming with us?" asked Bradley, in anticipation.

Kenichi nodded. "Yeah, Brad . . . I'm coming."

"You had me scared!" sighed Bradley. "I don't know what I'd do, without you!"

"May we call on you, at a later date?" Kenichi asked Fumiko, politely.

"I'd be offended if you didn't!" said Fumiko. "I pray, keep yourselves safe."

"Don't worry," said Kenichi. "As long as Brad and I are together, no harm will come to us."

"Oh, I'm sure you'll be fine," said Fumiko, giving Kenichi a kiss. "You boys should stay together. It looks to me like you really need each other."

54

Commander Salazar was summoned to Admiral Kraig's tent, that morning. Jesse had arrived at the War Ministry earlier in the day, then requested a bottle and a bed before meeting with Kraig. Salazar was anxious to find out what Kohl and Theo were scheming. He wasn't eager to be in the same tent with Kraig and Jesse. He felt badly outnumbered with those two!

Salazar removed a spot of lint from his uniform, took a deep breath, then entered Kraig's quarters. Jesse was already there, sitting on a bench with a glass of brandy. He was dressed in his sky-blue cape, tunic, and tights, along with the Cavalier hat which infuriated Salazar. In Jesse's lap was Copenhaver's man-killin' stick, a thrilling addition to his spoils of war.

"Admiral Kraig," addressed Salazar, standing at attention.

"Commander Salazar," greeted Kraig. "Have a seat."

Salazar cleared his throat. "If you don't mind, sir, I'd rather stand . . ."

"Sit down!" barked Kraig. "Have a glass of brandy. It was confiscated from Copenhaver and Schlender's things."

"Not to mention, it's Romero's," said Jesse. "Not as good as Galbraith's, mind you, but a worthy substitute just the same."

Salazar sat next to Jesse, and fixed himself a drink.

"Let's have it, Jess," said Kraig, sitting at his desk. "What do you know?"

Jesse giggled like a mischievous child. "Councillor Theo is paying for your brother, the redoubtable Major Kohl, to partake in a second mission to Insula Infernus."

Kraig jumped to his feet. "What the hell's he thinking? Why would he pull a stunt like that?"

"That's not all, sir," added Jesse, coyly. "Major Kohl hired those darling little lambs from Lord Kelly's Academy to assist him in this endeavor. He also invited Councillor Theo's nasty little Kuschan along, for the ride."

"Admiral Kraig!" shouted Salazar. "We can't permit Major Kohl from leaving the country! I demand to be given a reactionary force to Theo's compound, immediately! With your authorization, I'll place those criminals in chains!"

Kraig chewed on his mustache, and said nothing. For once, Salazar was right. Kohl was an idiot for taking kids on such a perilous journey. He was known for his childish attitudes concerning honor and glory. He really took the cake, now!

Kraig contemplated on his brother's military record. Kohl was a decade older. In his youth, Kraig idolized Kohl as a wise, noble individual. The tables had turned. Who was behaving as a responsible, level-headed sibling, now? Even then, Kraig wanted to uphold Kohl, whose career was uninspiring and, more often than not, indefensible.

Major Kohl faced court martial charges, an ugly blotch on his service to Embrey. Taking a second trip to Infernus was an act of desperation, the means of proving his case and restoring his name. While Kraig couldn't condone Kohl's intentions, he refused to further condemn the man. General Chang was liable to agree with Kraig, while Gornick had no say in the matter. Kohl was to be handed a meaningless job, retire with the rank of lieutenant colonel, and spend the rest of his life telling lies by a fireplace.

Salazar paced the floor, while Jesse fidgeted with the man-killin' stick. "Well, sir?" asked Salazar, impatiently. "What are we going to do about this?"

"What I do is my business, Commander Salazar," responded Kraig. "What you're going to do is sit down and shut up."

"But, sir . . ."

"Sit down and shut up!"

Salazar did as he was told, wearing his whipped puppy dog look.

"Yes, something has to be done," sighed Kraig. "Councillors Theo, Omar, and Fumiko have been ordered, by my decree, to locate themselves into the War Ministry, no later than noon tomorrow. Theo won't like it, but I don't care. It'll be necessary to grant assurances of their safe arrival, to this post. That's your bit, Commander Salazar."

"Yes, sir," said Salazar, still upset with Kraig's earlier outburst.

"We must also assure that Major Kohl is unable to go through with this mission to Insula Infernus," said Kraig. "Jesse, do you know anything about their departure time?"

"No," answered Jesse, "but I'm sure it's later today. Theo chartered an Agronian schooner, the Tyree James."

"Then we've got no time to lose," said Kraig, decisively. "Commander Salazar, you're to accompany the Embrian Council into Sykes. With good fortune, Major Kohl may still be at the compound. He will accompany you here, along with his young charges. You may use any means at your disposal to guarantee their safety and security."

"Yes, sir!" Excitedly, Salazar turned to leave the tent.

"Have you been excused?" questioned Kraig, sternly.

"No, sir!" corrected Salazar. *Damn it, I did it again!*

"Major Kohl will be under your command, and your jurisdiction," explained Kraig. "He'll pull rank on you, but tell him to go to hell. Remember always that discretion is the better part of valor. The last time I checked, I still have a brother named Kohl. Don't forget that, Salazar. If I hear about you abusing the man, you're in a midshipman's berth. Understood?"

"Yes, sir." Salazar swallowed. "Understood."

"Good luck." Kraig shook Salazar's hand. "Let's have dinner, sometime. I'm buying."

"I . . . I look forward to it," stuttered Salazar. "Thank you, Admiral Kraig."

Once Salazar left the tent, Jesse sought Kraig's favor. "What else do you have for me?" asked Kraig.

Jesse eased himself on the bench. "Well, sir . . ."

"Stand at attention when you speak to me!" ordered Kraig. "And take off that hat! Your head isn't cold."

Jesse did as he was told.

"Go on," said Kraig.

"The Kuschan daisy isn't responsible for Macready's untimely demise," informed Jesse.

"So, who is?"

"A couple of old friends, named Conrad and Helen."

"And where are they?"

"The Great Beyond," snickered Jesse. "Yuri and I saw to that."

"Very well. It clears that up."

"Admiral Kraig?" asked Jesse. "How well do you sleep, knowing Yuri's not far away? Frankly, I find myself slumbering with one eye open."

"I already know Yuri's a scary sort," agreed Kraig. "What of it?"

"What if Major Kohl's already left on that jolly boat ride to the scary place?"

"He won't get far."

Jesse smiled. "As I've stated earlier, our darling little Kuschan's been invited on Major Kohl's grand adventure. I'm not allowed to do much, while Yuri dearest's in the country. I can't do much outside of Embrey, either. But, when did I ever fret over the legalities of my actions?"

Kraig glared at Jesse. "Get to the point."

"Supposing . . . just supposing, tragedy befell Yuri on his way to Infernus?"

"Yuri is Councillor Theo's son!"

Jesse laughed. "Yes. But as I've said before, how well do you sleep nights? If Yuri had his way, we'd both we six feet under. Is that not true?"

"Carry on, Jess."

"Yuri's not guilty of killing Macready, but *still!* The Fairy Queen has done in a number of undeserving souls, based on Daddy's desires. Not to mention what he did to my friend, Marietto. Why, if Theo told him to do so, what's to say that Yuri wouldn't run a knife through you?"

"What you're suggesting is a violation of international treaty."

"Boo-hoo."

"Drop that saucy line, goddamn it!" hollered Kraig. "You and I both know it's an act, and a damned annoying one at that. If I didn't know any better, I'd take you for a bigger fairy queen that Yuri."

"Sir," said Jesse, straight-faced. "Yuri poses a threat. I've known him for years and, believe me, he's not right in the head."

"I know that."

"Yuri is Councillor Theo's son, providing him immunity from all misdeeds, foreign and domestic. However, is Embrey better or worse with someone of his caliber, traipsing around as free as you please?"

"The same can be said of all you Maliek boys."

"Touche." Jesse paused. "Sir, I am an Embrian, and loyal to the monarchy."

"Boo-hoo. And what if our new monarch is King Theo and Prince Yuri, the Fairy Queen? So Yuri poses a threat? What do you want me to do about it?"

"For the exception of Councillor Theo, who do you think will miss Yuri, should his heart suddenly stop beating?"

"What do you propose to do?"

"Arrange an accident. *Sir.*"

"You'd like that, wouldn't you?" said Kraig, sardonically. "I don't like Theo or Yuri. But my job doesn't give me the right to remove those I don't approve of."

"But you have removed certain barriers from your path. Right, Admiral Kraig? If memory serves me, Johanek also enjoyed certain immunities, bought and paid for from the Branellian Empire and Corapal."

"If, somehow, Major Kohl does leave Embrey with those boys, he won't get far," whispered Kraig. "Mark my words! And, if you are involved in the process of halting Kohl's advances, I can't personally stop you from arranging an accident. As for your request, I can't say yea or nay to it. If it comes back on you, I don't want it coming back on me. I have no knowledge or approval of your plans against Yuri."

"Yes, sir," said Jesse, barely containing his frustration. "Admiral Kraig is free and clear of any mishap, resulting in the death of Yuri, Kuschan son of Councillor Theo."

"However," concluded Kraig. "If you can arrange an accident, then by all means arrange it. Like you, I too have had trouble sleeping."

55

Garry woke around eight in the morning. He learned that Sergeant Vix had left the War Ministry, without telling him. Garry stepped out of Vix's tent to an area filled with refugees and warriors. Despite the massive scores of people around him, he felt isolated and alone.

Most everyone lined up for a breakfast of bacon and eggs. Garry refused to wait his turn. In his turtleneck sweater and kilt, he was viewed with curiosity and disdain. Garry was an outsider, a foreigner, the *enemy*. As he sat in the entrance of Vix's quarters, his mind drifted from boredom, to alienation, to fear. By noon, he was starving.

"Hungry?" asked Patrick, kneeling beside Garry.

"Sorta," answered Garry. "I don't think it's okay for me to go eat."

"Why not?"

"'Cause I'm a Branellian."

Patrick smiled. "Well, as soon as we get the papers signed by General Chang and Admiral Kraig, you'll be an Embrian."

"I won't look like one."

"If we get you out of those clothes, who'll know the difference?"

"But I like kilts!"

"Don't you wear breeches?"

"Nope." Garry shook his head. "Never have. Just kilts."

Patrick ran his fingers along the fabric of Garry's kilt. "I'm not sure I'd like wearing these. Anyway, if I say it's all right for you to have lunch, then it is."

"Where's Sergeant Vix?" asked Garry.

"He left on patrol. He'll be back shortly."

"What about my friends?"

"They were put to work sitting up tents and digging latrines."

"Not Davy!" cried Garry.

"No, not him. He's still in the infirmary." Patrick slapped Garry's back. "Don't worry. Our surgeon's a top man, and Davy's receiving the finest care."

"Can't I go see him?"

"Not yet," answered Patrick. "He needs rest. I'll make sure you get the chance to visit him, sometime today. But, for right now, you better get in the chow line. It's all right, Garry, if I say it is."

"What's going to happen to me, Pat?" asked Garry. "Colonel Salazar told me I'd get to stay here, after him and Vix killed Mister Copenhaver and Schlender."

"That's *Commander* Salazar," laughed Patrick. "Just think of yourself as an honored guest of the Embrian nation. You'll receive political amnesty for helping capture the two smugglers. I tip my hat for what you've been through, Garry. Don't worry. As soon as I return, my first order of business is to see that you obtain full citizenship."

"Where are you going?"

"I have to leave with Commander Salazar, to escort three Embrian Councillors here."

"Can't I come?" whined Garry.

"It's a long way, and you'll get tired and hungry."

"No I won't! If I can haul stuff up and down the Branellian Mountains, then who says I can't? . . ."

"Right now, you need a meal," insisted Patrick.

"Pat? Why ain't I out helping my friends dig latrines?"

"Sergeant Vix specifically asked for you not to do menial labor." Patrick smiled, warmly. "He won't say so, but I think old Vix is quite fond of you."

"Pat? . . . What's a latrine? Sergeant Vix said it's a fancy way of saying 'shithouse.'"

"Well . . ." snickered Patrick. "That's pretty much of the size of it. Anyhow, I have to go with Commander Salazar, and you've got to go eat."

"So my friends are out digging shit holes?"

"I guess so," said Patrick, walking Garry to the chow line, where a few refugees gave off bad vibes.

Noting the onlookers' animosity, Garry tried to retreat into Vix's tent.

"Don't worry," said Patrick, silencing his own concerns. "You'll be fine until I return. Make yourself at home. Who knows? You might even make friends. Enjoy yourself, and I'll see you soon."

Garry stood in the chow line, knowing he wasn't wanted there. He wished to hide out in the safe confines of the tent. A number of refugees voiced their malice toward the "primitive," by whispering behind his back. Awkwardly, Garry kept to himself.

A trio of boys, each younger and shorter than Garry, approached him. They weren't part of a welcoming committee. Garry tried to ignore the boys, while hoping they'd simply go away.

"Who invited you?" a fat, pug-nosed kid asked.

"Look at us when we talk to you!" a lazy-eyed, dishwater blonde kid asked, as he poked one finger into Garry's chest.

"Them dumb Branellians can't hear a word you say," a freckle-faced twerp said. "Real stupid, too."

"Yeah," the pug-nose said. "They smell like pigs, and breed like hares."

"I'm not a Branellian!" screamed Garry, knowing it was a mistake to get in the chow line.

"Then why you got that dress on?" questioned lazy-eyes, as onlookers laughed. "You a boy or a girl, Branellian?"

"He ain't got nothing on under this!" pug-nosed giggled, peeking under Garry's kilt.

"Get outa our country, Branellian!" someone shouted.

"To hell with that!" another cried. "Let's just kill the bastard!"

It made no difference what Garry said, in his own defense. He'd take a beating. The tent was only twenty yards away. It might as well have been twenty miles. Even if Garry did reach this sanctuary, what prevented this angry group from violating his privacy? They'd probably just rip the tent to shreds, then assault Garry for the fun of it. Garry wasn't risking his life over dried meat, a cold potato, or a tin of goats milk. Without Vix or Patrick there, his presence within the Ministry of War invoked hostility. Garry had no choice now but to leave the chow line, the fortress, and Embrey altogether! He didn't care where he went, as long as it was away from those awful words and ugly faces.

What about Captain Salazar or Mister Theo's promises of letting him stay? And what about his friends, out digging shit holes? That was fine for a crybaby like Harold! What about Marc, or Ivor, or Davy?

With a sigh, Garry faced the harsh reality that he was stuck in the War Ministry, dealing with those who wanted him dead.

As Garry started for the tent, he was shoved to the ground. In no time, he had a boot heel to his chest. The next thing he knew, seemingly everyone around punched and kicked at him.

These wrongdoers had absolutely no thought or regard for Garry's emotional, spiritual, or physical well-being. Obscenities spewed out of their mouths like venom. Garry tried, in vain, to deflect the attacks with his hands and bare legs. Laughingly, the three boys grabbed onto Garry's kilt, to strip it away from him.

Garry released a shriek, both in defiance and as a cry for help. He drove his fist into pug-nose's face, and drew blood. Pug-nose ran away, protesting the injury given to him by the filthy, Branellian sow.

Garry's face, limbs, and torso were on fire, where the Embrians lashed out against him. Growing faint, he sent both feet into lazy-eyes crotch, when . . .

"Get off o' him!" someone ordered, grabbing the freckle-faced twerp and throwing him like a rag doll. It was Sergeant Vix.

As the freckle-faced twerp hit the ground, he ran screaming for his momma.

"What's wrong with you damned people?" hollered Vix, dragging Garry away from the mob.

Admiral Kraig sat hunched over his desk, when he was distracted by the explosive racket outside. Tensions were running high in the War Ministry, from a lack of food and shelter. While most refugees conducted themselves with patience and restraint, others did nothing but complain. Kraig feared the potential of a riot. Apparently, tempers had finally reached a breaking point.

Kraig dashed from his quarters, and caught sight of a half-dozen refugees pulverizing Garry. This, as Vix fought them back. There were plenty of guards on hand. Regrettably, most witnessed this disturbance with leg-slapping mirth. Only when Kraig left the tent, did they take action.

"Move it!" shouted Kraig, pushing civilians and soldiers out of the way. "Move it!"

As a few Embrians backed away from Garry, several were ruthless in their handling of him. This, even with Vix and Kraig around. As five guards threw themselves into this ruckus, did Ministry personnel finally gain the upper hand.

Vix cradled Garry in his arms, as an old lady pulled the boy's long, unruly hair. Vix's fiery temper refused to abide such shenanigans. He placed his full weight into a right undercut to the crazed woman's head, where she collapsed to the ground.

Garry covered his face under both hands and wept, as Vix rushed him to the tent.

"What's the meaning of this?" demanded Kraig, approaching the chow line. "Speak up! Who's responsible for this disruption?"

"He's a Branellian!" a teenage student spoke, dressed in the black beret and tunic of Lord William's Academy. "We're here to teach him a lesson!"

"Branellian or not, he's just a kid, and afforded the same rights as the rest of you," said Kraig.

"To hell with Branellians!" another crowed, shaking his fist as cheers rang out. "To hell with all Branellians!"

"Kill 'em all!" the student declared.

Kraig frowned. "There are days when I'm ashamed to be an Embrian."

"Better to be an Embrian, than a dirt-dwelling Branellian!" someone yelled.

"That Branellian's here on my authority!" stated Kraig, pointing to the Ministry gates. "Those of you who fancy yourselves too good to eat with him, aren't fit to be in my company. If you don't like it, then go!"

"You can't turn us away!" the old lady screamed, getting back on her feet. A black eye and wobbly knees failed to deter her. "You can't take the side of a damned illegal alien over someone born and raised in this country!"

A large number of refugees cheered in support of the old woman.

"Can't I?" snickered Kraig, surprised by the old woman's stubbornness and spunk. "Maybe General Chang's got something to say about that. We're in charge here, and I say who stays and who goes. And the Branellian stays!"

"And maybe General Gornick has got something to say about that!" the student argued, displaying a tattoo of the snake and sword on his forearm.

The mob grew deathly quiet.

"You support my former colleague?" questioned Kraig, in disgust.

"And proud of it!" the student responded. "Whadda you gotta say about that?"

The old lady fetched a whiskey bottle sitting near a cauldron of boiling potatoes, and smashed it over the student's head. The student fell, as the mob then turned their aggressions upon him. In no time, the guards were forced to support the loudmouthed student.

As Kraig returned to his tent, he called a young corporal into his tent.

"Yes, sir?" the corporal asked, standing at attention.

"See to it that the Branellian kid gets a meal," said Kraig. "Make sure he's served double-rations."

"Yes, sir."

"I also want the surgeon to examine the Branellian," added Kraig. "Once his stomach's full, and his injuries treated, I'd like a word with him and Sergeant Vix."

"Quit all that crying!" yelled Vix, resting Garry on a quilt in his tent. "Act like a man, and quit that damn crying!"

Garry couldn't help it. His tears weren't just brought on by pain, but the cruelty inflicted upon him. It came out as sobs, whines, and gibberish.

"Y' act like they damn neared killed you out there!" growled Vix. Even then, he wanted to murder those who attacked Garry. "Lie down," he urged, softly. "You ain't dead, yet."

"Thank you," whispered Garry. His legs and torso were black and blue, and his left cheek was swollen.

"What'd you do to provoke 'em?" asked Vix.

"I didn't do nothing but get in the chow line, like what Mister Pat told me!"

Common sense and experience told Vix to keep his distance from Garry. It never paid to let others get too close, or grow dependent upon him. Vix had already made that mistake with Kohl and Willowby! However, this incident at the chow line motivated him to protect and nourish Garry. "Lie down," said Vix. "I won't let 'em getcha. You hungry? Want something to eat?"

"I ain't ate since last night," said Garry, struggling to sit up.

"I can't see why they done you like that. They're tough when there's a buncha them, and only one of you. Bet they ain't got the guts to face you, like men."

"I don't like fighting."

"I don't care if you like it or not. A man's gotta fight! You better learn how to stand up for yourself."

A portly man with a silver mustache and piercing eyes entered the tent, carrying a tray of food and a medical pouch. "Can I come in?"

"That for Garry?" asked Vix, examining the grub and supplies.

"That's right." The old man sat next to Garry. "I'm a military surgeon, assigned to the War Ministry."

"I seen you around," said Vix, suspiciously.

"After I perform the examination, I'll let him eat." The surgeon sat the tray on the ground. "Right now, I need the boy to . . ."

Look sawbones, forget about cutting on 'em," warned Vix. "I know what you butchers do . . ."

"Admiral Kraig's directives," the surgeon insisted. "You don't want gangrene to set in, do you?"

"If it's gangrene, I'll kill 'em myself," argued Vix. "Be a lot quicker and humane than you."

"Don't fret over me!" screamed Garry. "I'll be good, as soon as I eat!"

The surgeon fetched a heavy saw from the pouch.

"You gonna use that on me?" questioned Garry, his sad, sensitive eyes glued to the grisly tool.

"I doubt it," the surgeon mumbled. "It wouldn't be right. I had to take off more than a dozen arms with it, day before yesterday. It hasn't been cleaned yet, and it's duller than a hoe."

"Vix!" screamed Garry. "Don't let him cut on me!"

"If you care for this boy as much as I think you do," the surgeon said, "you'll let me perform this examination. I need you to stay and help me. Can you do that, Sergeant?"

Vix agreed.

The surgeon smiled at Garry. "The first thing I'll need is for you to strip, son."

Garry refused.

"See here," the surgeon spoke, pointedly. "I've seen plenty of folks in the raw, men and women. Some of them homelier than you. Nothing to get worked up over. I won't laugh if you got a tiny pecker."

Garry looked to Vix for support.

"Better do as he says, or he'll take them clothes off, himself," said Vix. "If he gets too friendly, I'll stomp 'em."

"Start from the bottom up," the surgeon told. "First the socks and brogans, then the skirt, then the blouse."

Slowly, painfully, Garry kicked off the shoes, as the surgeon removed both socks. With a blush, he hesitantly peeled out of the kilt. He sat on the quilt, holding his breath, wearing nothing but his sweater and a fiery complexion.

"I've worked in your neck of the woods a time or two," the surgeon said, to calm Garry's nerves. "What part of the Branellian Empire are you from?"

"Warren Dale," whispered Garry.

"Say again, son?"

"War . . . *Warren Dale . . .*"

"Mountain folk," the surgeon mumbled. "No shame, as I see it. I've known huskier men with shorter jocks than you. Except an infantryman in the Battle of

Mount Patten, who got his lopped off with an ax."

Garry rolled his eyes back, doubting the surgeon's qualifications.

"Did they do any damage down here?" the surgeon asked, running his hands along Garry's feet.

"No."

"I've got to work on your legs, though." The surgeon dabbed Garry's left knee with a thin cloth, soaked in grain alcohol.

"That burns!" cried Garry, in agony.

"Hold this bandage to his knee," the surgeon told Vix. "It'll hurt, before it heals. You'll thank me for this, later."

Garry was far from voicing his gratitude.

"Now the right knee," the surgeon said, doctoring the sore joint.

"Hey!" griped Garry.

"Don't feel like it's broken," the surgeon mumbled, rubbing his hands against Garry's thighs. Tossing the saw to one side, he added, "Won't need this, after all."

Despite his throbbing joints and the foul smell of alcohol, Garry sighed in relief.

"I'm worried about that face," the surgeon whispered. "Looks like they had a grand old time beating on your nose and chin. Open up, let's see your teeth."

Garry followed the surgeon's orders, craving sympathy and support from Vix.

"Wonderful!" the surgeon said, contorting Garry's face and mouth in every imaginable shape. "Not a spot of yellow or decay on them! It's that clean, pristine water in the upper elevations! Embrians have got the worse teeth! I've pried more choppers from the dirtiest mouths! But there's nothing wrong with yours!"

Garry tried to speak, but instead uttered nonsense.

"I'd like to get that puffiness down," the surgeon said. "I say, though! You've got the most beautiful teeth I've ever laid eyes upon!"

"How's Davy?" asked Garry, uncomfortably.

The surgeon stared at Garry. "Who?"

"Another Branellian runt," explained Vix. "Shorter, with blonde hair, wearing the same kinda dumb clothes as this one. Took an arrow in the leg."

The surgeon's eyes revealed concern.

"He's my best friend, and I want to see him," said Garry. "Is he okay?"

"Only time will tell," the surgeon answered, evasively. "The best thing for him is bed rest."

"That's what Patrick said!" cried Garry.

"You let me worry about the patients," the surgeon spoke. "You worry about yourself. Very well, then. Let's get that blouse off, shall we?"

Garry wondered if his nude body was under scrutiny. As he attempted to remove the sweater, he gave out a bloodcurdling howl.

"What's wrong?" asked Vix, lifting the sweater to reveal a severe bruise, under the right arm. "Doc?"

The surgeon cautiously pressed his fingers against the bruise. "I feel no broken ribs," he noted. "If your lungs are punctured, I hope you say your prayers at night, because there's nothing I can do for you."

"Am I going to die?" whined Garry.

"Sooner or later."

"Huh?"

"None of us are getting out of this one, alive," the surgeon snickered. "I'm sorry to say it, but you'll live a long, healthy life."

Garry figured the surgeon gave all his patients this much trouble. Or was it reserved mostly for Branellians?

"I'd like for you to breath deeply, then exhale," the surgeon requested. "Tell me if you experience any sharp pain."

"A little," answered Garry. "Am I okay?"

"You're okay by me," the surgeon kidded, dabbing a moist cloth against the bruise under Garry's arm.

"Ouch!" screeched Garry, glaring at the surgeon.

"Like I said, you'll thank me later," the surgeon repeated. "Hold that to the bruise, Sergeant Vix. I'll check his chest, back, and belly." With that, the surgeon poked and prodded Garry's tummy. "Tell me if this hurts . . ."

"Yeah!" snapped Garry.

"Where?"

"Everywhere!"

"Sorry," the surgeon apologized, reaching behind Garry's shoulder blades. "Oh, heavens . . . I don't like this . . ."

"What?" asked Vix, anxiously.

"Lay down on that quilt," the surgeon ordered Garry, "and turn over on your left side."

"No!" argued Garry.

"Look, we're almost done," the surgeon spoke, diplomatically. "I just need to check your spine, and that's it. When that's done, you may put on your skirt on, and eat."

Garry refused.

"Do what he says," said Vix, "then he'll leave you alone."

Garry whimpered as he rolled to his side.

The surgeon raised the sweater above the shoulder blades, and gazed upon a hideous sight. "Mother of mercy!" he gasped.

"Goddamn!" cursed Vix, gritting his teeth in rage.

Zigzagging across Garry's backbone, like a grotesque tic-tac-toe board, were a countless number of scars.

56

"Hell're ya waitin' for?" cackled Strunk. "Get this cathouse on the road!"

The pace at Theo's compound was usually laid back and calm. That afternoon, everyone hurried to put their needed supplies into wagons. While the majority of those at the compound were leaving for the Ministry of War, a few began their long journey to a strange land, far to the west.

Within an hour, the compound would be empty, desolate, and lifeless.

Theo sat in his meeting room, claiming to be writing a letter for Admiral Kraig and General Chang's eyes only. In truth, he sought a moment of solitude to consider his life's choices, before saying goodbye to a beloved stepson. In these most crucial of times, Theo concentrated on one he regarded as his own flesh and blood.

Throughout his years as a merchant marine, in publishing, and finally in the Embrian Council, Theo never married. Oh, there were women, lots of women, along with plenty of wine and song. Love and commitment never played a role in his busy schedule. Never were there biological children, to carry his genes or legacy.

And no one to keep an old man company, in the autumn of his life . . .

The autumn of his life . . .

When Theo first met Yuri, the boy was cold, ragged, and scared. After being expelled from Captain Maliek's school, Yuri participated in a rescue mission to save the institute's founder. Few knew of his involvement in his covert action.

When Theo took Yuri in, it was originally for personal security. Occasionally, he engaged in casual small talk with the youngster. Yuri was open to Theo's ambitious dreams for Embrey, learned how to read, then became an advocate for the legislator. While he furthered Theo's goals through intimidation and violence, the legislator had loftier goals for Yuri. In time, Theo gave Yuri affection, companionship, and love.

Theo dabbled with the ladies, many ladies. These conquests amounted to little more than good times. Theo had no partner in his old age, and no one to comfort him in his old age.

And no children.

Yuri gave Theo hope that his words and deeds carried through to a new generation. Theo prayed that his influences and philosophies remained immortal, timeless.

Eventually, he hoped that Yuri made a name for himself, as an emissary of peace. Great men are often forged from personal histories of strife and instability.

Theo had known Yuri for just a short period of time. He couldn't imagine life without the boy at his side. In a few minutes, Theo was to leave for his new headquarters at the Ministry of War, while Yuri left for destinations unknown.

Theo struggled to be confident, courageous, and strong. In truth, he was mired in doubt, uncertainty, and despair. Considering the shakiness of the Embrian nation, there were no guarantees that his own future was bright. General Gornick was still out there, along with scores of Branellian soldiers. The next few days, weeks, and hours were dire. What assurances were there that Theo would even see Yuri, again? This question tore at Theo's heart, mind, and soul.

Theo caught a glimpse of Kenichi sprinting past the open door, and felt envious. Like Yuri, Kenichi came from humble roots. He did something Theo only fantasized of, by climbing to the top of Mount Patten. Theo had traveled the world, and witnessed events most men were oblivious of. He never once reached Embrey's highest geographical point!

Theo was also jealous of the one element Kenichi still possessed, which he no longer enjoyed the taste of:

Youth.

How totally unfulfilled and lonely Theo felt, in the autumn of his life. How empty and meaningless it now seemed. Was it too late to call off Major Kohl's mission to Infernus, move everyone to the Ministry of War, then shape a new Embrey?

"I'm going, Father," someone said, from the doorway.

Theo glanced up from the table to see Yuri. "I . . . I trust you'll have a safe journey," he stuttered. "Take care of the crew, son. They need you."

Yuri didn't say so, but his heart was breaking. He was far more concerned for Theo, than for himself. As much as he wished to travel to Infernus, did it bring about an emotional betrayal against Theo? "Major Kohl needs me," said Yuri, "and I must be with my new friends. For the good of them all."

Theo got to his feet. "They're in good hands with you," he said, his voice cracking.

"Will you be all right, without me?" asked Yuri. "I mean . . . are are threats out there, Father. I hope I'm not being too selfish, by . . ."

"You're a grown man, Yuri," said Theo, in resignation. "I can't expect to keep you here, forever."

"But I promise never to leave you, upon my return! You said this land is partly mine! I've got to look after what's rightfully ours!"

"Before I joined the merchant marines, my mother told me that if you love something, let it go. If it comes back, it's yours. If it doesn't, it never was."

"But I will be back, Father! I promise!"

"When I left home at fourteen, I never saw my parents for five years. There was always more freight to haul, more places to go, more adventures to boast about. I don't think I've been to my birthplace a half-dozen times, since then. My parents are dead, now. I've got no idea where some of my siblings are, if they're even still alive."

Yuri bit his bottom lip. "This morning, you were afraid to let me go. Now, you're eager to get rid of me!"

"I'm not eager to get rid of you, son!" said Theo. "I'd trade every year on those ships, my first printing press, even my stewardship of Embrey if it meant keeping you here. I love you more than anything! I thought I was being selfish for not wanting you on that voyage!"

Yuri threw his arms around Theo.

Theo caressed Yuri's face. "Of course I'll miss you. If I were half my age, and at least thirty pounds lighter, I'd go, too!"

"Why don't you?" asked Yuri, hopefully.

"My responsibility is to Embrey. And your responsibility, for the time being, is to board the Tyree James with the other . . . men."

"Eduardo told me that you're hiring him as our new cook, when we get home."

"You know me, Yuri," laughed Theo. "I want only the best."

"You mean *we* want only the best." Yuri smiled. "What about the other guys?"

"Well, if I can, I'll place them all on my payroll. I still want Giorgio as my intern, Kenichi as an educator for less fortunate Embrians, and maybe hire everyone else as groundskeepers. We'll just have to see."

"Then we have to clean out those woods behind the house!" said Yuri, excitedly. "That's where I'll build my cabin. We'll build one for Kenichi, one for Brad, and another for Giorgio."

"I'm tuckered out, already!" laughed Theo. "I haven't even rebuilt Embrey, and now you're talking about placing new houses on the property!" Theo frowned. Realizations of letting go were daunting. He didn't want Yuri to leave, and still considered putting a halt to the mission. However, if Theo had to go out into the world to make his fortune, then Yuri had to follow his own path. Even if Yuri eventually resided on the land, Theo owed him a chance of proving himself.

Youth is fleeting.

"Get the lead outa yer ass!" Strunk hollered, at an unknown *(and undeserving!)* recipient, from outside. "Dead people fuck faster'n you haul shit, goddamn it!"

"Keep an eye on Strunk, son," warned Theo. "Don't you dare turn your back on him."

Yuri never told Theo of his late-night meeting with Strunk, just days before, and aimed to keep it a secret. "He can behead condemned men, Father, but I'm not afraid of him. Not anymore."

"Strunk's a very dangerous man!"

"Don't worry, I'll take care of myself." Yuri squeezed Theo's hand. "I only hope you'll be all right."

"I'm fine," sighed Theo. *Get this over with!* "They're ready for you, Yuri, and I've got to collect a few more things, for my move into Sykes."

Yuri found it increasingly harder to speak. The time had arrived for him to join his new friends, and make good on this undertaking for Major Kohl.

Without facing Theo, Yuri reached out, as if to give the man a handshake. He didn't want his father to see the tears. Too late. Even Theo's vision had blurred, as he looked at Yuri. There was no opportunity for a long, drawn out farewell, to break bread at the dinner table, or create warm memories by a campfire or fishing hole.

Theo kissed Yuri's teary cheek. "We'll have a provisional government in place, when you return. Then we'll clean out that back forty, so you'll have a home of your own."

"I know, Father," whispered Yuri. "I'll make you proud of me!"

Theo nearly voiced regrets that Yuri was unlikely to bear any biological children. The teen's preference for his own gender made it unlikely, for the rearing of offspring. Whether Yuri was "different" or not, his impending absence remained an open wound.

"I'm already proud of you, Yuri," said Theo, walking his son to the door. "Good luck, my boy. Bring yourself, and some exciting stories of adventure, home to me!"

As Yuri stepped into the bright afternoon sun, he suddenly grew weak. As his companions hopped aboard a wagon taking them to a dock, he was indecisive, having to choose between staying with Theo, or joining those on their way to

Infernus.

"Yuri!" a voice called, in a thick Kuschan accent. It was Dimitri.

As Yuri faced his countryman and mentor, he never attempted to conceal the tears.

"Yuri?" asked Dimitri. "Homesick, already?"

"Dimitri," whined Yuri. "Am I doing right by going away?"

"I don't know. Are you?" asked Dimitri. "Only one person can answer that. What do you want, Yuri?"

"I promised Major Kohl I'd go to Infernus with him, but Father . . . Will you take care of him, while I'm gone?"

Dimitri snickered. "I think it'll be Theo taking care of everyone in Embrey. You've got it easy. All you've got to do is look out for those guys on that wagon. You've also got to look out for yourself. I won't pretend that I'm not concerned, but, well . . .somehow, I just know you'll be fine."

"What about you and your family?" asked Yuri, wondering if anyone on the mainland needed him, now.

"For the time being, we're stuck in the War Ministry, and they're stuck with us," sighed Dimitri. "Soon, we'll lick our wounds, figure out what we've got to do, then build a second church."

"You've got your hands full," said Yuri, harboring fears of abandoning Dimitri.

"You'll be home before we even start construction," said Dimitri. "If you want to help, I can use you. Alexei and Grigori will get an education in hammers, saws, and nails."

"I'm not much for manual labor," admitted Yuri, recalling his failure to assist Commander Salazar on the burial of three Embrian soldiers. "But I'll do what I can . . ."

The two Kuschans embraced, as Yuri sobbed.

"B'fore you queer-eyed Kuschans get all kissy-assed," growled Strunk, getting in the wagon, "we got pink monkeys and winged men to kill!"

"I'd better let you go," said Dimitri, softly. "I've got to run, too. Your friends need you, more than a couple of fuddy-duds like your father and me. They'll need your abilities, your . . . *survival* skills. Make sure that, whatever you do, it's for the best, and justified for the good of all."

Yuri smiled. "We never did have dinner together, did we? Except for the night I brought my friends over."

Dimitri sucked in a deep breath. "Stay out of harm's way, and I'll see you in a few months."

"We'll always be friends," said Yuri, mustering up every ounce of courage to fulfill the job at hand.

"I wouldn't have it any other way," said Dimitri, on the verge of choking up.

Yuri jumped in the wagon, and crowded himself between Bradley and Kenichi. Giving Dimitri a wave, he called out, "Remember what you always told me. We Kuschans must stick together!"

A few miles northwest of Sykes, Lieutenant Commander Salazar and two dozen men met of contingency of soldiers and household staff, from Councillor Theo's compound. Linus drove one of the wagons, heading toward the Ministry of War. Joining him were Omar, Fumiko, Dimitri, his wife Yana, and their three children.

Surrounding the wagon were several guards, ready to give their lives for the two Embrian Councillors.

As he blocked the afternoon sun from his eyes, Salazar saw nothing of Major Kohl, Yuri, Theo, or the youngsters from Lord Kelly's Academy.

"Do you think they've already left for Infernus?" asked Patrick.

"Probably," mumbled Salazar, in disappointment. "I'll bet Theo went with them."

"Why would he?" questioned Patrick.

"To avoid the consequences," stated Salazar. "The consequences of murdering three of my men, of letting Kohl blow his big mouth yesterday, or allowing those schoolboys to go with the moron."

Salazar turned to Jesse, who usually responded to bad news with annoying, childish remarks. Having 'personal business' with Yuri, Jesse was also let down. The Kuschan Fairy Queen was still out there, *somewhere*. Jesse didn't care if his nemesis was in Embrey, or whether his self-appointed plans of terminating him were a violation of international law. Dead was dead, and Jesse wanted Yuri stuffed in a body bag. One of them had to permanently go bye-bye. It was simply a question of who got in the first lick.

Jesse shuttered, as he imagined Yuri hiding behind a rock, tree, or thick brush, waiting to strike.

Salazar chuckled, pleased to see Jesse so down in the dumps. "Cheer up, Jess! An empty sack, for the both of us! What did you expect?"

"It's not over, Commander Salazar, *sir,*" vowed Jesse. "It's not over, until I say it's over."

"Oh, you never know," mulled Salazar. "I'll wager that Kraig let Kohl leave the country."

"What makes you say that?" asked Patrick.

"Kohl can't even wipe his own ass, without someone's blessings or financial subsidy," said Salazar. "It's not just Kraig or Theo's hand in that one. It's also the *dahling* Kuschan choirboy. Right, Jess?"

Jesse managed a weak smile.

Salazar released a tired sigh. "Theo even bankrolls somebody to hold onto Kohl's shlong, when he has to take a piss."

This invoked laughter from everyone, including Patrick.

"Well, slap on your brown-nose paint," whispered Salazar, "and act nicely to Omar and Fumiko."

Salazar and his men stepped toward the wagon.

On behalf of those with him, Omar got out of the wagon to greet Salazar. "It's a pleasure to see you, Commander," he said, politely.

Salazar had no qualms about Omar. He hoped the Junior Councillor soon bypassed Theo in rank and importance. Salazar and Omar were former schoolmates, and represented a new generation of Embrian leaders. "The pleasure is mine," addressed Salazar. "Where may I find Councillor Theo?"

"For reasons of security, Theo took another route into Sykes," answered Omar, uneasily.

"Another route?" questioned Patrick. "I thought this was the only route."

Omar's nervous eyes betrayed him.

Patrick was right. There were no other roads from the compound into Sykes.

Omar's explanation was a lie! Theo was too much of a coward to answer for his many crimes! Rather than owning up to them, he was in hiding, or fled to Kusch with Yuri! Salazar wanted to think the two were on their way to Infernus. *Hah!* May they meet their deaths, at the hands of winged men and pink monkeys! Similar to a rogue scoundrel named King Auric IV, perhaps Theo was to spend his final days on that wicked island.

But what about those students from Lord Kelly's? Did Salazar wish for them to die?

"Admiral Kraig requested that I escort you to the Ministry of War," informed Salazar. "I trust that's to your satisfaction."

"Thank you," said Omar. "We appreciate that."

"Meals, beds, and tents will be set up for everyone," added Patrick.

"It won't be quite like home," chuckled Salazar, "but at least you're safe."

"Splendid," said Omar, graciously.

"I was to lead Major Kohl and those schoolboys into Sykes, as well," said Salazar, choosing his words carefully. "Are they with Councillor Theo?"

"To be honest with you, I cannot say," mumbled Omar, suspecting that Salazar already knew the truth.

Salazar did not blame Omar for concealing Kohl's whereabouts. Theo likely put Omar up to it. Salazar was slowly growing accustomed to such dishonesty. Both Omar and Salazar found themselves in loathsome professions, and still had much to learn.

"We'll see them at the Ministry of War," responded Salazar. "Is there anything more I can do, Councillor Omar?"

"No, thank you, Commander Salazar," answered Omar. "We value your service and commitment to Embrey."

"Very well." Salazar shot a quick glance at an aging figure, standing next to the wagon. There was something vaguely familiar with this old man with the long, hooded robe, walking stick, and thick, gray beard. "Pardon me, Councillor Omar," mumbled Salazar. "Who is that elderly gentleman, standing near Pastor Dimitri and Councillor Fumiko?"

"Councillor Theo's head gardener," answered Omar, warmly.

"Hmm . . ." Salazar squinted. "Why is he walking, and not in the wagon?"

"He likes to walk, that's all," replied Omar. "We asked him to join us, but he won't."

"Huh," pondered Salazar, wandering away with Patrick.

"We're traveling with Commander Salazar," said Omar, returning to the wagon.

"Of all the officers Admiral Kraig could have sent us, why must we settle for him?" complained Fumiko.

"Salazar's not a bad sort," said Omar, sitting between Grigori and Sasha. "We went to Lord Conway's together. Even as a boy, he was always heavy-handed and serious. An excellent rugby player, though. Very intense on the playing field."

"Did he have a mustache then?" asked Sasha, smiling admirably at Salazar.

"No, except one out of milk," chuckled Omar.

"If you ask me, he's in dire need of a personality, *and* a sense of humor," said Fumiko.

The aging gardener grinned.

"How are you?" Dimitri asked the gardener. "I hope this severe heat isn't getting to you."

"I'm fine," the gardener said, scratching his chin and lips. "I'll sure be glad when I take this beard off."

Out of courtesy, Omar handed the gardener a canteen filled with water.

"Much obliged, Councillor Omar," the gardener said.

Omar laughed. "You're very welcome, Councillor Theo."

57

Bradley was no expert on ships. Never once had he been on the ocean, in any seagoing craft. However, his first glimpse of the Tyree James gave him equal thoughts of anticipation and apprehension.

As Kohl and his party reached the abandoned dock, the Tyree James' crew was ready for the upcoming voyage. Secrecy was a priority, as Kohl's disappearance was sure to raise suspicions. Kohl was due at the Ministry of War with Theo by noon that next day.

As the wagon came to a halt, everyone began hauling their provisions onto the schooner. Once Kohl paid him a small token, the wagon's driver left for Sykes.

Bradley turned to Kenichi. "Mount Patten," he said, as a cool breeze swept through his hair.

"Mount Patten," answered Kenichi, also evaluating the ship's seaworthiness. He guessed the Tyree James' length at thirty yards, its width a third of that. Two masts, boasting four sails of varying sizes, pointed skyward. The hull was of sturdy pine, cottonwood, and oak. The schooner usually held a crew of six men, including the captain, first mate, and cabin boy. Their numbers had doubled, due to this mission.

Those assigned to the Tyree James were a rough-looking bunch, most with tattoos and untrimmed facial hair. Those catching Bradley's attention were the three standing at the quarterdeck. O'Toole, the skipper, barked orders in a dialect which lazily rolled off his tongue. His white shirt and wool breeches, tucked inside cleat boots, were soaked in sweat. O'Toole's tanned, weathered face was covered with thick, gray whiskers.

Fernandez was the first officer. He had a dark complexion, coal-black hair, and a receding goatee. Years before, he took part in an ill-fated attempt to colonize Infernus. The creases in his forehead spoke of his concerns over this endeavor.

Willie, the cabin boy, was a lad of thirteen. He wore a thin, loose-fitting shirt, cutoff pants which bared his wiry legs, and no shoes. He had long, red hair and a freckled face. Occasionally, he handed O'Toole a bottle of something which likely induced intoxication. The language spewing from Willie's mouth was enough to make even Fritz blush.

Bradley wondered what was on his schoolmates' minds. Were they motivated by adventure, service to their country, or (in Fritz's case) greed? Most already dreaded the schooner's dismal eating and sleeping quarters, as accommodations were badly cramped. For the next few weeks, the Tyree James was home.

Yuri said nothing, as he retrieved his weapons. His eyes were still red and dampened from his farewell to Theo and Dimitri.

Trevor released a nervous chuckle, while Derek glared at the vast, expansive ocean in front of him.

"Ready?" asked Giorgio, eagerly. Despite the lumps on his face from his dispute with Fritz, he conducted himself in an encouraging manner.

Derek backed away, and bumped into Geoffrey.

"What's wrong?" asked Geoffrey, curiously.

As Derek stuttered, Trevor, Andre, Bentley, and Sergio giggled.

"*Shh!*" scolded Giorgio, kneeling to the frightened boy. "What is it, Derry?"

"He thinks we're going to sail off the world!" laughed Trevor, slugging Derek's shoulder.

Derek shook like a leaf, as he latched onto Giorgio's sleeve.

"We're not going to sail off the world!" assured Giorgio, battling his own mirth.

"Boy!" snapped Kohl, glaring at Derek. "Do you see your comrades shying away from this? Aren't you man enough to follow them to Hell and back? You dishonor them, as you dishonor me, with your petty fears!"

"Aw, just leave the little bastard here!" growled Strunk. "As for the rest o' you, them wantin' in on this rat-killin' had best grab their shit, an' haul ass!"

Everyone stopped to evaluate Strunk's order. Eduardo took Derek's hand and walked him to the ship, granting words of understanding and support.

Bradley exhaled. *This is it. Time to prove ourselves to God and country* . . .

. . . Or die trying.

"Mount Patten," Bradley repeated, resting a burlap sack of dried beans on his shoulder.

As he stepped toward the schooner, Bradley recalled those events leading to his enrollment in Major Kohl's mission. Turning toward land, he wondered if his involvement would make any difference. *What could he do, to change what had already taken place? This was no carefree school outing. What if it ends in disaster? What if we don't find the treasure?*

What if we all die in the strange, faraway land, simply to be forgotten?

Days before, Bradley woke in his soft, warm bed at Lord Kelly's Academy. That was the last time he knew what it meant to live a normal life. That afternoon at the dock, he redefined the word "normal," and questioned if his life was to ever be *normal* again.

Normally, Antoine didn't dress in a shiny black uniform, featuring a disgusting image of a rattlesnake and sword, or spout angry, bigoted slogans.

But he did.

Normally, Sven never purchased goods from a back-alley company called Erickson's Imports.

But he was.

Normally, Bradley never succumbed to temptations of the flesh, in the form of a beautiful, blonde girl.

He did, and would do so again if given the opportunity.

And then what? Karl and Sven were dead! So was Antoine, Samuel, the weasel, and Quinn. Entire neighborhoods of Sykes were decimated, as warring factions clashed in the streets, leaving thousands dead, injured, or homeless.

And what about the massacre near Theo's compound, the grisly demise of Yuri's dog, or Brad and Kenichi's arrest? Bradley wanted to think of it as merely a bad dream, and easily discarded.

He feared never to comprehend the meaning of "normal."

What point was there in denying the truth? Karl and Sven were dead! So was Antoine, Samuel, the weasel . . . and poor Quinn. Never again would Bradley skinny-dip in the Ember River, attend stage productions at the Falcon Theatre, or hear the predictable, hourly chimes of the bells of Lord Kelly's.

Bradley was trapped in a reality, not of his own making. He was ill-prepared to stand up and take it like a man. His eyes glued to the Tyree James, as he was overwhelmed with a sense of impending doom. His world had gone totally insane, leaving him a sad, confused soul, lost in a torrent of change. Life was no longer calm, predictable, or "normal."

Bradley glanced at his buddies, as his illusion of reality was torn to pieces. With the world slipping out from under him, he was sent whirling, downward, in a free-fall. His breathing grew erratic and shallow, while his heart beat wildly out of control.

He was on his way to Infernus, perhaps never to return.

Bradley dropped the sack of beans onto the dock. Clumsily, he knelt to retrieve it. A fog of doubt and uncertainty flooded his consciousness. Frozen in place, Bradley's hand lacked the ability to touch, feel, or grasp. He suffered from an odd, disembodied *something,* which was not his. All around him, shadows drove out the sun, replacing that which made sense with that lacking sanity or reason.

Panic-stricken, Bradley swayed from side-to-side. He stared at the beach, the ship, the ocean, his friends' faces, and the sky. His throat tightening, and the air cut off, Bradley thought he was going mad, choking, dying.

"Brad?" asked Kenichi, placing a sack of potatoes to the decaying planks, below.

Bradley glared at Kenichi, seeing nothing more than horror.

"Brad, you all right?" asked Giorgio.

Bradley was afraid of death. Worse yet, he was afraid to die alone, in the company of those dearest to him. His body was totally engulfed in an unseen, unknown fear. Thinking the end was near, Bradley embraced Kenichi, with tears welling in his eyes. *"Kenichi!"* he wailed, his voice high-pitched and jittery.

"What's with him?" asked Giuseppe, wrinkling his nose.

Giorgio put his hand on Bradley's shoulder. In the past, Bradley always went to him for guidance, help, and answers, and not to a newcomer like Kenichi. Giorgio begged for redemption and forgiveness, not only from Bradley or the Almighty, but from himself. More than wealth or fame, he craved self-respect and honor, threatened by a spiteful envy of a brother in faith and love. Conflicting with anger and pride, Giorgio knew he had to put aside his differences with Kenichi, for everyone's sake.

"Quinn . . ." wept Bradley, refusing to let go of Kenichi. "Oh, Quinn . . ."

Kenichi threw his arms around Bradley. Under the circumstances, Bradley needed a good cry. Who was Kenichi or anyone else to judge him unfairly, or belittle displayed weakness? Bradley's life was shattered, the same as when Kenichi lost his mother and Leader Lionel. Bradley took the weight of the world upon his shoulders, and had to let it all out.

"I'm sorry, Brad!" cried Giorgio, nearly buckling under the strain. "I'm so sorry! Even if you forgive me, how can I ever forgive myself?"

"What the hell's your malfunction, soldier?" shouted Kohl. He shoved Giorgio out of the way, then took Bradley to the side. "Answer me when I talk to you!" he ordered, spitting hot breath in Bradley's face.

Onlookers idly stood by, watching Bradley get berated by Kohl.

"You gave me your word that you were man enough for this valiant quest!" screamed Kohl. He pointed a finger at Derek, who stood aboard the schooner. "Now to learn that you and that little worm aren't men at all, but pathetic, thumb-sucking babes, still thirsting for your momma's tit!"

"Leave them alone!" yelled Kenichi. "They're men enough, damn it, so just leave them alone!"

Kohl was startled by Kenichi's outburst. Knowing what happened once he slapped Sergeant Vix, he thought twice about tangling with Kenichi. Cautiously, he backed away. With his own doubts and anxieties, buried just slightly below the surface, his face evolved into an idiot's mask.

Kohl Kued . . .

Kohl Kued . . .

Anumun . . .

"I'm sorry, Major Kohl," apologized Kenichi. "It's just that . . . well . . . they're drunk, sir! They had a few too many, before we left Councillor Theo's!"

Kohl's mouth gaped open. *"Drunk?"*

"Please, sir, they've had a pretty hard time of it," explained Kenichi. "Brad and Derry lifted a bottle from Theo's cupboard, after our run-in with the constable . . ."

"It's my fault," interrupted Fritz, to everyone's amazement and surprise. "I wasn't happy with that pissy little canteen of Campens Rose' the fat politician . . . I mean what Theo gave me, so I lifted s'more for the trip . . ."

Schoolmates wondered what motivated Fritz to make a false confession, which potentially threatened his participation in the mission. What punishment would Kohl now give him, let alone Bradley or Kenichi? The silence was unbearable.

Kohl had the wind knocked out of his sails. For a moment, he strongly considered canning every soldier in the whole rotten lot. But how could he? Like it or not, he had the army he so desperately called for. He needed the boys, as much as they needed him.

Kohl stuck his nose up, let out a caustic *"H'm!"* then stormed onto the Tyree James.

Fritz released a self-satisfactory laugh. This once, just this once, he had the upper hand over Giorgio, Bradley, *and* Kenichi. Jabbing Giorgio's chest with his knuckles, he whispered, "Y' owe me, *Leader* Dumbshit!"

With that, Fritz stepped aboard the deck of the Tyree James, then quickly disappeared through an open door to the lower quarters.

Bradley slowly gained control of his frayed emotions. Crippling fear was replaced by humility, inadequacy, and worthlessness. What good was he, now that his buddies had seen him fall apart? Bradley first proved what a failure he truly was, in the backroom of Erickson's Imports. That afternoon, he demonstrated what a disappointment he had evolved into. What were the guys to think of him, in the heat of battle?

"See you on the ship, Giorgio," insisted Kenichi.

Insulted by Kenichi's suggestion to get lost, Giorgio stammered, "But I . . ."

"See you on the ship, *Giorgio,"* repeated Kenichi, not as a request but as a demand.

Giorgio slumped. When would Kenichi finally let him off the hook? Wasn't it enough to drop that money Kohl gave him into the well, or take a beating from Fritz? Weren't kind words and gestures worthy of gratitude or consideration? Eventually, Giorgio aimed to follow them up with good deeds, self-sacrifice, and honor!

What if Kenichi begrudged Giorgio throughout the entire voyage? What could Giorgio do, to earn Kenichi's approval and favor? Was Kenichi bent on undermining Giorgio's obligations as a facilitator, "big brother," and role model? What if it really was too late for Giorgio to fully mend fences with Bradley and Kenichi? What if he was already viewed as "damaged goods," in the minds of his schoolmates?

Giorgio gave Bradley's hand a gentle squeeze, as he mumbled, *"Sorry."* This, without looking Kenichi in the eye.

"Me, too," whispered Bradley.

Giorgio lifted a box of dried fruit from the dock, and slowly boarded the schooner.

Bradley was perplexed by Kenichi's cold treatment of Giorgio.

"You didn't just get yourself into this mess, you know," said Kenichi, angrily. "You got me into it, as well."

"But I thought you wanted to be a sailor!" whined Bradley.

During his brief stay at Lord Kelly's, Kenichi waited impatiently to turn eighteen, then rid himself of the school and its stupid uniform. He'd then sign onto the first ship, leaving Embrey. Well, he got what he wanted, along with Bradley's companionship in the bargain. What right did he have to complain, now?

"You probably think you need me," sighed Kenichi. "Why, I'll never know."

"Don't say that," said Bradley. "Where would Trevor, Derry, or I be without you? Not only did you save us, but Andre, too."

"I guess," sighed Kenichi. "Look, Brad . . . as much as you need me, I need you that much more."

Bradley sought illumination.

Kenichi had difficulty getting his words out. "It wasn't my idea getting sent to Lord Kelly's, anymore than when my mom or Lionel . . . I thought I'd hate every minute of it at Lord Kelly's! But you were always there for me, and that made all the difference in the world . . ." Kenichi fought back temptations to get all mushy, sappy, and sentimental.

Eduardo stepped off of the schooner, and approached Bradley and Kenichi. "Major Kohl told me to tell you to get a move on it, or be left behind," he snickered. "'Left behind with all the other cowards and shirkers! Tell them to get on board, or forever be denied their glory!'"

"Thanks," said Kenichi.

Strunk cackled, as he passed Bradley and Kenichi on the dock. "You ain't drunk," he said, with a scary, toothless grin. "You lost yer goddamn marbles, you an' that goddamn, crazy-ass major! Well, boys, you'll be spinnin' on a winged man's spit, soon enough! That's what you get for joinin' a real man's fight! Go lookin' for Hell, you'll find it!"

As storm clouds loomed overhead, Bradley and Kenichi understood what was expected of them. Now was the time to carry it out.

"If you want to be a Leader, then act like one!" said Kenichi, forcefully. "Are you man enough to follow me to Hell and back, soldier?"

Bradley sucked in a deep breath, clenched his fists, and got his head together. He was scared. *Damned scared!* He was also ashamed of the poor example he gave everyone, and was determined to salvage himself in the coming days and weeks. He had to search within himself, for the wisdom and courage to handle his chores on the Tyree James. On occasion, he had to look to his shipmates, for their unyielding support and guidance. If necessary, he had to become that Leader he so wanted to me.

More than anything, the boys had to take care of each other, united in their quest to retrieve a sought-after treasure and return, safely home, to Embrey.

Bradley threw the sack of beans over his shoulder, and smiled.

"Mount Patten?" asked Kenichi, excitedly.

"Mount Patten," responded Bradley, as he boarded the Tyree James. Whispering to himself, he added, "*Insula Infernus . . .*"

58

"I'm aware of your intentions to obtain Embrian citizenship," Kraig said to Garry, in his cluttered tent at the Ministry of War. "From what Sergeant Vix and the doc told me, you're a strong candidate to remain in our country."

"I don't care what I gotta do," said Garry, unsure of the proper manner to address Kraig. Standing in front of the admiral's desk, he turned to Vix for support. "I don't wanna go back to the trades."

"According to your own report," said Kraig, examining an official document on his desk, "Councillor Theo said he'd write a letter on your behalf. You didn't stay at the compound long enough to receive it. Surely you've got to have more sense than to leave a safe refuge, during a battle."

"I had to go find my friends!" explained Garry, defensively. "I thought them smugglers was gonna kill them!"

"Good thing Sergeant Vix found you, and not some trigger-happy private!" scolded Kraig. "Still, you were influential in apprehending Copenhaver and Schlender, so I'll take that into account."

"I didn't apprehend Mister Copenhaver and Schlender," said Garry. "Sergeant Vix and Corporal Salazar killed them."

"That's *Commander* Salazar!" laughed Kraig. "You were there when the Embrian Navy, and . . ." Kraig smiled at Vix, sitting next to the surgeon in the tent. "*Army* got them."

"In other words, you're a national hero," the surgeon spoke.

"A national hero or not," said Kraig, "granting this boy citizenship status isn't as easy as all that."

"Garry was a guide, nothing more," the surgeon stated. "He wanted no part of the Branellians' invasion. Based on a physical examination of him, he'll benefit greatly from residing in our fair nation."

"Looks to me like someone come awful close to doin' 'em in with a leather strap," added Vix.

"Not only must we consider what is in Garry's best interests, but also the best interests of Embrey," argued Kraig.

"I'd say that lots of people took part in scarring this child, and that it went on for years," the surgeon said. Leaving his chair, he lifted Garry's sweater to give Kraig an inspection at the teen's back.

Garry groaned, in objection of this humiliating exhibition.

"I don't care to look," said Kraig. "I'll take your word for it. From the bandages on him, I can tell that Garry was abused. He requires our protection and care, not only from the Branellian Empire, but also from disgruntled Embrians."

"Garry poses no security risks," the surgeon agreed. "He only wants to be happy. Based on his part in locating Copenhaver and Schlender, we owe him that."

Kraig smiled. "Thank you, doc, you're excused. Sergeant Vix, you and Garry will stay. I've got more questions for you."

Vix nodded.

"I do want to grant you permanent status in Embrey," Kraig told Garry. "However, you must clarify your exact contributions to the Branellian invasion."

"It wasn't my idea!" cried Garry, intimidated by Kraig.

"I'm sure of that!" laughed Kraig. "The conflict between our two countries started long before you were even born. Long before I *was* even born!"

"Admiral Kraig," interrupted Vix. "You ain't gonna get much outa him."

Kraig saw validity in Vix's words. However, several hoops still had to be jumped through. \

Skimming the scroll before him, Kraig said, "I take no pleasure from asking these questions, but relax. It won't take long."

Garry fidgeted.

Kraig cleared his throat. "You worked the black market."

"I never worked no black market!" shouted Garry. "I never sold no kinda black people!"

"That's not what I meant," said Kraig. "You shipped illegal cargo from Branell, into Embrey. It's appalling! Why did your family force you into it? Just how did you fall in with that company?"

"My mom and sister made me," answered Garry. "I thought everybody did that sorta work."

"Not hardly." Kraig hesitated. "This will be difficult, and I don't want to upset you. I do expect you to be honest with me. Who did that job on your back, son?"

Garry refused to answer.

"Admiral Kraig!" shouted Vix. "Ain't it bad enough that he was whipped, bad? Reckon we're doin' him a big favor, by gettin' 'em outa . . ."

"It's not important," said Kraig, embarrassed by the list of questions in the inquiry. "Tell me, Garry. What types of goods did you bring into our country?"

"Mainly hooch from Corapal and Campens," said Garry. "We picked up lots of things, to take back into Kentworth and Hamblin."

"No weaponry? Small arms, bows, arrows, swords?"

"No."

"What did you move from Embrey, into Branell?"

"Stuff that we swiped from rich folks. You know, stuff like jewelry."

"Have you ever murdered an Embrian?" questioned Kraig, sternly.

Garry shook his head. "I never killed nobody!"

"Not even in self-defense?"

"What makes you think he's capable of murder?" snapped Vix.

"I'm asking the questions!" Kraig shouted back. "Garry, did you kidnap Embrian women and children?"

Garry swallowed. *"Maybe . . ."*

"Well?" asked Kraig, impatiently. "Did you, or didn't you?"

"What would he want with our women and children?" argued Vix. "That was them smugglers' doin's, not his."

"You can't possibly be that naive, Sergeant," said Kraig. "They sold women and children into prostitution."

"I never," said Garry, sadly. "But them smugglers did, all the time."

Kraig looked straight into Garry's eyes. "Were you or your friends exploited by prostitution?"

Garry sobbed.

Vix leaped to his feet. "Does he gotta answer *that?*" the sergeant asked, angrily.

"I believe he already did," answered Kraig, apologetically. "You must understand, I don't think these questions are of any use. Their sole purpose is to let some damned public official justify his own existence. I only want to know the details of the Branellians' attack, who masterminded it, and to learn the identity of King Ogden's assassin."

"A'right," said Vix, returning to his chair. "Then ask it."

"So Garry," continued Kraig. "How were you involved in this attack on Embrey?"

"We was working the trades," explained Garry, "when they snatched the whole lot of us up, and made us . . ."

"Slow down, son," urged Kraig. "Who snatched you up?"

"Them smugglers, Mister Copenhaver and Schlender. They was the meanest men I ever knew."

"No point looking for them, after me and Salazar settled their hash," noted Vix.

"I know that, Sergeant Vix," said Kraig. "Our nation's intelligence forces have pursued them for years. You and Salazar did the right thing by 'settling their hash.' What I don't understand is why the Branellian government recruited men like that."

"Captain Shimura told this scary kid he made a deal with an Embrian Councillor so you guys could hang them," said Garry. "That's all I know."

This news grabbed Kraig and Vix's attention.

Leaning back in his chair, Kraig smiled. "And what did Captain Shimura want, in exchange for all that?" he asked, in anticipation.

Garry shrugged. "Something about him giving you guys Mister Copenhaver and Schlender, and this Councillor guy giving him a retirement."

"Theo!" shouted Vix. "The two-faced, sorry son of a bitch!"

Kraig shook his head. "I'm sure Councillor Fumiko's also got something to do with it," he theorized.

"What makes you say that?" asked Vix.

"Shimura was a bodyguard for the royal court in Kokashima," said Kraig. "He's known Fumiko for years. When Fumiko migrated to Embrey, with Theo's assistance, Shimura joined the Branellian Navy. He wanted to align himself with us but my predecessor, Admiral Marsden, turned him down."

"Mister Copenhaver said the only way to end the Border War is by scaring the hell outa Embrians," said Garry.

"Well, the invasion most certainly did that." Kraig rubbed his mustache. "Please, Garry, tell us more about this scary kid you saw with Shimura."

Garry scratched his leg, afraid of hurting his chances of staying in Embrey. "All I know is that he wanted me to give him some clothes for a job he had to do."

"Clothes?" asked Kraig.

"Like . . . like what I got on," stuttered Garry.

"A kilt," whispered Kraig. "Ogden's servant told me the assassin wore a kilt."

"It wasn't me!" screamed Garry. "I only gave him some of Marc's clothes!"

Kraig wagged a pen at Garry. "I want the truth from you, and I want it now. Are you sure you're not more involved with the invasion, than you claim?"

"I swear!" cried Garry. "I never saw that scary kid or Shimura, until then. I don't know 'em, and I don't wanna know 'em! Please don't make me go back to the trades!"

"You're not going back into the trades, that's for sure," said Kraig. "You'll stay in Embrey, either as a freeman or as a prisoner of war."

"I hope I didn't do nothing wrong by giving that scary kid Marc's clothes," whined Garry.

"No," answered Kraig. "Embrey was ruled by an evil man. Since you were considerate enough to give this *scary kid* one of your friend's kilts, you probably did us a bigger favor than you know."

"Well?" asked Vix. "What more do you want from Garry? Don't you think his help gettin' them two smugglers is worth some kinda amnesty?"

Kraig knew of Shimura's hopes of defecting from Branell, into Embrey. Clearly, certain members of the Embrian Council were also privy to this. Both Garry and Shimura had won their rights to Embrian citizenship. However, they were to perform a service to the nation.

"A few more questions, Garry," said Kraig, leaning against his desk. "Were Copenhaver and Schlender the ones who tortured you?"

"No!" bawled Garry, hoping Kraig would finally let up on this inquiry. "It was my mom!"

"Your mom?" asked Kraig, in revulsion. "Well, son, I can assure you that your mom will never harm you, ever again. There's no need to go on. Congratulations, Garry, you're now an Embrian citizen, once I get General Chang in here so you may swear an oath of allegiance."

Vix proudly clasped Garry's hand, as the boy wiped his teary eyes and smiled.

"Don't get too excited," said Kraig. "We first have to figure out where to place you. You'll need a sponsor, then fulfill a term of civil or military service."

"I want to stay with Sergeant Vix," said Garry.

"That's right, sir," agreed Vix, wondering what he was getting himself into. For twenty long years, the Army was his home. Most of that time was spent with Major Kohl. Regarding his estrangement with the major, Vix felt lost and aimless. If taking Garry under his wing led to his retirement from the military, then so be it.

"That's very commendable of you," said Kraig. "And allow me to thank you personally for your hard work and dedication to my older brother."

"Yes, sir," said Vix, in humility.

"Yet, need I remind you of your duty to the Embrian Army?" asked Kraig. "You're a fine soldier, Sergeant Vix. How do you propose to care for Garry?"

"My folks owned a parcel, not too far from here," said Vix. "They're dead and gone, so I reckon it's mine, if the house ain't fell in. I never liked ideas of takin' up the plow. Looks like that's what I'm gonna do."

"You don't look to me like a farmer," noted Kraig.

"Farmer or not, I'm taking Garry with me. If Theo can adopt that crazy little Kuschan, figure I can adopt this Branellian runt."

"That's all well and good," said Kraig. "But I've got an important assignment, which General Chang and I discussed. We'd like to offer you a well-deserved promotion. First, I've got a series of questions for you, concerning Insula Infernus."

"It'll be a cold day in hell before I set foot there, again!" hollered Vix. "Right now, I gotta get me and Garry settled in, and find me a job 'til plantin' time."

"You may change your mind, after we chat a while," said Kraig. "You're not tired of the Army, are you? Is that why you're retiring?"

"I ain't gettin' no younger," chuckled Vix. "Where's it gotten me, all these years?"

"You've been passed over for promotion, far too often," said Kraig. "I'm sure your loyalty to Major Kohl is partly to blame."

"Major Kohl saved my life," sighed Vix. "I wouldn't be here, if it wasn't for him. If anybody's to blame for my rank, it's my bullheadedness."

"Perhaps I can remedy that, today," suggested Kraig. "With a stroke of my pen, I can solve your problems. What do you say about that, *Master Chief Vix?*"

59

Salazar delivered Councillors Omar and Fumiko to the Ministry of War, cut his men loose, and went into his tent. Similar to Kraig's present quarters, Salazar's home and office was cluttered, impersonal, and disorganized.

"Home" was a memory, no longer a noun. Salazar didn't even know if "home" existed anymore, and remained ignorant of his family's fate and whereabouts.

Salazar pulled off his sweaty boots, poured a glass of Romero's Bourbon, and fell onto the cot. Unable to sleep, he questioned his right to wear the uniform of an Embrian naval officer. He thought he understood his reasons for entering such a prestigious, if risky career field. His dreams of glory were a fabrication, and he alone was liable for pushing himself into it.

A child of wealth and privilege, Salazar spent his youth at Lord Conway's Academy, getting an education as well as the word of God. After graduation, his parents sent him abroad for "real world" experience. Salazar had an opportunity to visit places few Embrians heard about. He used his father's name, money, and influence to party, chase women, and prolong adolescence into his late-twenties.

Upon his return to Sykes, Salazar was to accept employment at Romero's, his family's distillery. By then his father was six feet under. Salazar had no desire in being his brother Enrique's number two man in the business. Rather, he sought a life in the military.

Salazar managed to pull the right strings, and was commissioned as a second lieutenant, without first possessing the proper aptitude and teachings for such responsibilities.

Salazar was exhausted, to the point of despondency. Warily, he sat up and rested his head in the palms of both hands. He had last seen his family, the morning Sykes evolved into a bloody nightmare. Were his mother and Enrique safe, or lying dead somewhere on the streets, as so many other unnamed statistics? Salazar wanted to get on a horse, ride across town, and check on his loved ones. Unfortunately, leaving the War Ministry was "restricted, until further notice.

"Commander Salazar?" asked Patrick, entering the tent.

"Come on in, Pat," yawned Salazar. "What is it?"

"Admiral Kraig wishes to see us."

"Now what?" asked Salazar, stretching his aching back.

"I'm not sure what it's all about, but Kraig asked to see us, right away."

"Well, whatever it is," responded Salazar, stepping outside with Patrick. "I'm sure we'll live to regret it . . ."

Kraig tapped his fingers upon the desk as he stared up at Senior Master Chief Vix. "You mean to tell me that Major Kohl's stories about the . . . purple simians and winged men are true?" he asked, in disbelief.

Vix crossed his arms as he stood before Kraig's desk. "Every word of it," he said, unflinchingly.

"You honestly expect me to buy that crap?" questioned Kraig.

"I don't give a damn if you buy it or not," responded Vix, refusing to budge from his account of Infernus. "I'm telling the truth, Admiral."

Garry sat in one corner of the tent, oblivious to what was being discussed.

"I don't know why Kohl and you had a falling out, but he sure thought the world of you," said Kraig. "I don't think it was just his negligence that got those men killed on the island. Either you're right, or covering up for his incompetency."

"Everything Major Kohl said at that hearing was true."

"Then why didn't you say so?"

"I did!" said Vix. "Me and them other survivors! You acted like we was all stupid!"

Kraig took a deep breath. Yes, Vix had testified to the existence of strange creatures on Infernus. No one on the tribunal, Chang, Kraig, or Gornick, accepted those tall-tales.

"Well, my young *Embrian* friend," said Kraig, turning to Garry. "What have you got to say about all that?"

"I dunno what you're even talking about," answered Garry. "I wasn't there."

"As an Embrian citizen, you are to perform a duty for the nation," snickered Kraig. "Chief Vix and you seem to get along. It'll do you good to stay together. Chief Vix's on his way to Infernus. He's got no choice in the matter. As to the question of your service, Garry, how do you feel about tagging along?"

"I'll tell you what he thinks!" yelled Vix. "He ain't going! If I had my druthers, I wouldn't be neither!"

"You are going!" snapped Kraig. "You've been to Infernus. You know the terrain. And, more important, you know Major Kohl, far better than I do. This arrangement wouldn't be necessary, had you reported Kohl and Theo's hair-brained scheme to us in the first place!"

Vix knew he should have informed the brass about Kohl's covert operation. Out of habit, he learned never to trust them.

"At least Garry spilled his guts of his role in the Branellian invasion," lectured Kraig. "He's a sight smarter than you or me, put together. Since you've taken such a fondness of him, which I admire, he'll learn a great deal from you."

"Only thing he'll learn from Infernus is how to have his guts spilled, then eaten," argued Vix. "It's suicide, if y'ask me! We was damn lucky to get outa there that last time! Damn it, I tried talking Kohl outa making another voyage over there!"

"It's too late for that," said Kraig. "For all we know, Kohl has already left. So, while you and I are chatting pleasantly, allow me to thank you for volunteering, Chief Vix. I'm so happy you agreed to the assignment of intercepting my brother. It's so much easier than having to draft someone."

"Wherever Master Sergeant Chief Vix's going," said Garry, "I'm going, too!"

"Splendid!" laughed Kraig. "This is better than I imagined! You've already got the makings of a fine Embrian citizen. Guts, spirit . . ."

"I'm a dead man, a'ready," said Vix. "I don't see why Garry's gotta throw in, just because I got to. All yer gonna get outa that runt is to have his guts and spirit torn to shreds by them damn winged men!"

Garry responded with a giggle.

"What's this nonsense about a treasure Major Kohl's retrieving from Infernus?" asked Kraig.

"There ain't no treasure," said Vix.

"That's what I thought," said Kraig. "If any of those schoolboys die on that expedition, I'm holding you personally responsible. Once more, you'll answer for your silence."

"Major Kohl aims to collect evidence for the military tribunal!" roared Vix, fed-up with Kraig's self-righteous tone. "It was the only way to prove his case in court!"

"Well, then, I hope he does manage to collect proof of those creatures," sighed Kraig. "I take no pleasure in punishing my brother, any more than I already have."

"Thank you, sir."

"But it won't make any difference," said Kraig. "You must stop Major Kohl, before he reaches Infernus."

"So, who you got to run this show?" asked Vix.

Kraig smiled. "He'll be along, any minute."

Seconds later, Salazar entered Kraig's tent, with Patrick and Jesse. With them was a barrel-chested Marine in his mid-forties, wearing a red tunic and white pith helmet. The Marine never exceeded the rank of first lieutenant, despite his advancing age. He smelled like vodka, while his uniform was soiled and wrinkled. He released a loud belch as he sat next to Garry.

Salazar saluted Kraig, and stood at attention. "Reporting to duty, sir!"

"At ease, men," ordered Kraig. "How was your march to Theo's compound?"

"Not good," answered Salazar. "I found Omar and Fumiko, a Kuschan pastor and his family, and the guards you posted there. But no Theo. I'm afraid that Major Kohl's gone, too. I'm guessing he took those students from Lord Kelly's with him."

"That's why I asked to see you, Commander Salazar," said Kohl.

"Sir?" asked Salazar.

In the likelihood of Major Kohl's departure from Embrian soil," said Kraig, "I'm securing a frigate to pursue them. You six men will board it, at first light tomorrow morning."

"Us?" gasped Salazar. For the exception of Vix and Jesse *(and, by God's graces, the drunken Marine!)* no one was remotely qualified for the job. A novice naval officer, timid Branellian guide, and pacifist aide would likely cause more harm than good. Salazar noted Vix's anger, Patrick's animosity, and Jesse's smartass grin. Garry had no ideas what lay before him, and the Marine probably didn't care. Thoughts of sailing hundreds of miles with this crew frightened Salazar. What he expected to find at the end of this trip was even more scary. That evening in Kraig's tent, he suddenly believed in purple apes and men with wings!

"Us?" repeated Salazar. "Sir, the six of us?"

"I've reassigned Vix as a master chief in the Navy," said Kraig. "He is to answer to you, Commander Salazar, and you alone."

"What if I'm dead?" questioned Salazar. "Who will he answer to, then?"

"It's my opinion that Chief Vix's knowledge of the territory is the difference between life and death," said Kraig.

"I ain't got much faith in your opinion of me," commented Vix, gravely.

"I stand by that opinion," asserted Kraig. "Garry has asked for, and will receive citizenship status, as a naval recruit. Patrick, you and Jesse are to serve Lieutenant Commander Salazar to the best of your abilities. Understood?"

"Understood, sir!" said Patrick, as Jesse laughed.

"Understood, Jess?" asked Kraig, sternly.

"Yes, sir!" said Jesse. "Understood!"

"You are to intercept Major Kohl, before he gets to Insula Infernus," explained Kraig. "If you fail to secure that goal, I've assigned twenty Marines to assist in apprehending Major Kohl and his army. These Marines are expert bowmen, and handle the ax with deadly precision." Kraig grinned at the Marine. "Lieutenant Thomson?"

The Marine stood and greeted Salazar with a lackluster salute. "It's an honor to meet you, sir."

"The honor is mine," answered Salazar, his voice lacking conviction.

"My men will do their utmost for you!" promised Thomson, cheerfully.

"I'm sure they will," said Kraig. "Now, fall in line."

"Sir!" responded Thomson.

"As for your mission," said Kraig. "It is my plan, gentleman, that no one from your team or Major Kohl's team will be harmed in any way. Is that clear?"

"Do I have permission to hang the silly son of a bitch from the yard arm?" asked Salazar, soon regretting his choice of words. "I . . . I'm sorry, sir!" he stammered, as Jesse giggled like a disobedient child. "Like you said, you have a brother named Kohl."

"That's right, *Commander* Salazar," growled Kraig. "I do have a brother who answers to the name of 'Kohl.' My rule applies tonight, as it did this morning. Don't forget that. Kohl may be a silly son of a bitch, all right, but what does that make me?"

"I'll do my very best, sir," assured Salazar. "You've got my word on that."

"When you get back, let's have dinner together." Kraig slapped Salazar's back. "I'm buying!"

"Looking forward to it," said Salazar, fearing this assignment was a prerequisite to a horrible death or, like Kohl, a court martial.

"Patrick, give your finest effort to Commander Salazar," said Kraig. "He couldn't have found a better right-hand man, than you."

"Thank you, sir," said Patrick, his thoughts resembling Salazar's.

"Jess," said Kraig, in a secretive tone. "As for the request you made of me today, it's your call. I urge you to use discretion."

Jesse said nothing. The twinkle in his eyes spoke volumes.

"Chief Vix," said Kraig. "This mission's success lies squarely on your capable shoulders."

Vix was quiet. He hoped to make a man of Garry. With luck, he'd have a chance to mold the shy Branellian into a confident, self-sufficient person. But not on Infernus! The only positive element was the potential of reuniting with Major Kohl.

"Garry, our country is better with you, than without you," said Kraig. "You're an Embrian, now. I expect you to conduct yourself as such. Do everything Commander Salazar and Chief Vix ask of you. Take pride in the service of your country."

"Okay," answered Garry, shrugging his shoulders.

"If I'm not mistaken, we fought together at Agron Bay," Kraig said to Thomson.

"And on the shores of Kusch, against the very man we sail with tomorrow," added Thomson.

"It's good to know he's finally on our side!" laughed Kraig.

"He'll soon learn the superiority of the Embrian fighting man!" boasted Thomson.

"I expect nothing less than your finest efforts," Kraig told everyone. "I must point out that none of you are real sailors. You're Naval Infantry. Leave the seagoing to the professionals, and their experienced captain."

"Excuse me, sir?" asked Salazar. "On whose ship do we sail?"

"A seasoned officer named Captain Shimura," answered Kraig. "That's all I can tell you."

"Him?" protested Vix. *"Shimura?* The hell?"

"Captain Shimura?" inquired Salazar. "I've never met him."

"Lieutenant Thomson and I share personal knowledge of Captain Shimura," said Kraig, withholding certain information. He first encountered Shimura in combat on the open seas, and had the scars to prove it. Kraig respected this former adversary. Like Garry, if Shimura was to become an Embrian citizen, he had to earn it! "You've got nothing to fear from Captain Shimura," said Kraig. "He's a good man."

"Thank you, Admiral Kraig," replied Salazar. "Anything more?"

"Nothing, really." Kraig stepped from behind his desk. "Other than to wish you luck. Keep yourselves safe, and I'll see you when you get back. That's all."

Everyone saluted Kraig, then left the tent.

"Sergeant Vix," Salazar spoke, as everyone went outside to a cool, autumn breeze. "Forgive me . . . *Chief* Vix."

"Yeah," said Vix, flatly.

"We got off on the wrong foot," said Salazar. "Whatever problems we may have had in the past, I'd like to bury the hatchet and work together. Is that tangible with you?"

Vix grudgingly saluted Salazar.

Noting the tension, Salazar smiled. "Thank you," he accepted, approaching the drunken Marine. "Lieutenant Thomson, I'd like you at my tent, at six tomorrow morning."

"That I will do," said Thomson.

Salazar debated Thomson's qualifications. Still, he wished to forge a strong working relationship with the man. "I look forward to serving with you, Lieutenant Thomson. Is there anything you ask of me?"

"A tall ship," answered Thomson, his breath foul enough to choke a horse, "and a first-rate officer at the helm."

"We're in good hands with you, Lieutenant Thomson," said Salazar. "I'll see you in the morning."

Thomson gave Salazar a final salute, then staggered away.

Salazar started to his quarters with Patrick.

With an annoying grin, Jesse began to follow the two men, until Vix called him back. "Yes?" asked Jesse.

"You're a Maliek boy," accused Vix. "Ain'tcha?"

"Well now, for the time being it appears that I'm a *Salazar boy*, and so are you," retorted Jesse. "What of it?"

"I got no say whether you're on this mission or not," said Vix. "But you keep your distance from me. And while you're at it, keep your distance from Garry."

Jesse upheld his cocky attitude, despite feeling intimidated by Vix. "And how do I keep my distance on a Branellian . . . beg pardon, *Embrian* frigate, Chief?”

"I don't care! I don't like you, and I don't like your kind.”

Vix's words cut to the bone. Jesse respected Vix, and hoped it was mutual. Oh, well. Jesse and his 'kind' rarely won approval, affection, and good graces. “So, why we're sailing merrily along on the frigate, what if I don't keep my distance from you, or the darling kilt?” he challenged.

“Then you won't be on the frigate,” warned Vix. “You'll be swimming back. If you know what's good for you, keep away from us!”

Jesse removed the Cavalier hat, and bowed. “You really love the kilted laddy,” he said, mockingly. “Don't you, Chief Vix?”

Vix didn't answer.

“You're a decent man, Chief Vix,” said Jesse, walking away. “And I'm sure the kilt's in excellent hands. Just make sure you don't love him to *death.*”

“What did he mean by that, Vix?” asked Garry.

“Never mind,” answered Vix, coldly. “Tonight, you can call me 'Vix' if ya want. By the time you crawl outa the sack, long before sunrise tomorrow, it better be 'Chief Vix' or 'Master Chief,' You'll do what I tell ya, and how I tell ya to do it.”

“Why?” asked Garry, in confusion. “What did I do wrong?”

“Nothing,” answered Vix. “But you wanted to be an Embrian. Now earn it, recruit. You're in the Navy, now . . .”

60

As Jesse entered his own tent, the smile which so defined him was gone. Undressing, he carefully laid the clothing onto a table, to avoid creasing and wrinkles. As the clothes came off, so did the facade.

Jesse sat on a narrow cot, his spirit as naked as his body. Thoughts of spending several days on a frigate, without poontang or a fancy drinking parlor, were unbearable.

Thoughts of spending several days on a frigate, surrounded by miles and miles of water, were worse.

Captain Maliek preached the need to control fear. Jesse failed to keep it together, when confronting the one thing which scared him the most. Alone in the dark, he lacked a target for his crude wit and humor, and was vulnerable. The tools he utilized to bury his phobia were his fancy clothes, a caustic personality, and liquor. One sustained the other.

Jesse wondered how much alcohol a Branellian frigate kept aboard. If their navy was as ill-equipped as the Embrians, then he was in real trouble. The Embrians were known for treating their sailors poorly by supplying cheap, rotgut whiskey, unworthy of his tastes. This meant that Jesse had to supplement himself! Was he able to sneak it on the Browning, without getting caught?

What if his booze was stolen by thieving, conniving, lowly Branellian sailors?

How far away was Infernus? How long did it take to get there? Dealing with a crew of stinking Branellians, while surrounded by the vast Agron Ocean, chilled Jesse's blood. Was there a way to get out from under his service to Salazar, and go back to being Kraig's blade-for-hire? Jesse had a long line of miscreants to remove for the Embrian government's convenience . . .

Howe Fat, Volonte' . . .

General Gornick . . .

Jesse was terrified. His hands shook while filling a chalice with Romero's second-rate whiskey. Why did he have to accompany Salazar to a land of horrors? The only thing he'd get out of the deal was to rid himself of a menace. With that in mind, what gave Jesse the greatest animosity? Spending long, countless days and nights on the water, or facing the adopted son of Councillor Theo . . .

Yuri of St. Alexandrov?

Jesse wanted Yuri dead! He was petrified of the creepy little Kuschan! He learned to be, the day Yuri nearly beat Marietto to death, with nothing but an unspeakable rage and two bare fists. It would've been more humane, had Marietto been killed outright. Instead, Yuri practically destroyed Jesse's best friend, now locked away in a filthy asylum.

Marietto spent most days screaming to the top of his lungs, or rattling the bars imprisoning him. Jesse once paid Marietto a visit, hoping to free him from the madness which devoured him. What he found in the loony bin forever tormented him. Furnished with a pot, Marietto still pissed and pooped himself, then wallowed in his own feces. Had Jesse been stronger, he would have gotten Marietto out of his misery.

Jesse was now left with unresolved grief.

Jesse was responsible for the majority of pranks, ranged against Yuri at the school. Marietto was merely a follower, who picked on Yuri because Jesse did.

Yuri never deserved the ill-treatment Jesse meted him. He was an easy mark, so who'd blame him for killing Jesse?

For that reason, Jesse had to kill Yuri.

Jesse poured another drink to sooth the nerves, as a draft crept into the tent. Straight-shooting the liquor, he slipped on a silk nightshirt. In the unforgiving darkness of the tent, Jesse looked within himself for the will to survive the journey to Infernus, on a frigate with a crew of stinking, thieving, conniving Branellians, surrounded by the vast Agron Ocean.

Chances were, the Browning had to stop at Agron, for trade and barter. Was there a chance of Jesse wetting his noodle in that vulgar, renegade nation? He'd only been to Agron once. From recollection, their women were butt-ugly and hairy!

Could he get a piece of tail in the War Ministry?

It was cruel for Admiral Kraig to send Jesse on a suicide mission, without getting drunk, or enjoying a little nooky. Jesse had to do something, *anything,* to extinguish the fire burning within his loins.

Without a female on hand, he chose to salve himself *manually.*

Jesse pulled up his nightshirt. Nursing a drink in his left hand, he fondled his bare crotch with the other. Caressing himself delicately, he failed to get aroused.

I'll die on that god-awful frigate, or go off my head from a fear of water!

What was there to do on the Browning, to ease the spirit or forgo the deep, dark ocean surrounding him? Was he able to feign the foppish persona? Could he stay drunk throughout the entire trip?

Was he even permitted to drink on the Browning?

Jesse had a reputation to uphold. He'd been grilled by Captain Maliek to always stay calm! What good was he to Salazar or anyone else, if he evolved into a wimpy, whiny coward? Why suffer defeat from a childish phobia? Why can't I just ignore it, get tough, and laugh?

I know! I'll divert my attention, by making light of Sergeant Vix's pet Branellian . . .

Escusez-moi!

Chief Vix's pet Branellian, a lanky, calloused, silly-looking scrub in a plaid kilt! Can I perform such merriment, on a ship crowded with that simpleton's own countrymen? Will Salazar, Patrick, or Vix tolerate my behavior toward that imbecile? Garry can't do anything to stop me, that's for sure! He's an even bigger pushover than Yuri! Jesse had nothing to worry about from Salazar or Patrick, other than their ranks. They were no match for him, in a fight.

Vix was another story . . . even if he was *old.*

Vix was more than twenty years Jesse's senior, with a number of dirty tricks acquired from his tenure in the Army. Where Jesse had education and skill, Vix had experience and brawn. One could not survive a long, harsh winter in the Wilderness without an unconquerable will to live. For that reason, Jesse was leery of Chief Vix!

After chugging his fourth shot of liquid courage, Jesse drank straight from the bottle. Not only did he have to silence his doubts and anxieties about the voyage, but temporarily quill his hunger for sex.

Feeling light and loose, Jesse toyed with the object dangling between his legs. He closed both eyes and licked his lips, while recalling a night in western Branell, when he and Tomas got their jollies with three *(three, mind you!)* high-priced strumpets, a piece! Jesse's sexual prowess most assuredly displayed itself that night! Minutes after spilling his seed, Jesse had mounted another woman. *Four times!* Four times did Jesse drill his hardened manhood into the females. As Tomas slumbered in the arms of two whores, Jesse went at it clear till morning!

Too bad he hadn't made it five, as the job called him away!

Too bad Tomas had no memories of this event.

Too bad that, according to Tomas, Jesse was still a virgin.

Jesse squeezed his majestic organ, ignoring obligations to a country he vowed to live or die for. Putting on his Cavalier hat, he embraced a pillow as if it were a hot-blooded lover. He passionately kissed the pillow, as five fingers massaged his pride and joy.

With a burning sensation in his stomach, and the taste of liquor in his mouth, Jesse exhausted himself in this act of self-pleasure. He worked it with the same ferocity and intensity, as if to savor the company of a call girl. On occasion, he sipped from the bottle.

Jesse's mind wandered from that fictional night in a Branellian brothel, to his trip to Infernus, to his plans of killing a Kuschan fairy. Not once did he permit a reprieve from this forced escapade. Who knew when, and if, he'd get another opportunity for solitary splendor?

Jesse clenched his teeth as he happily reached climax. Breathing heavily, he gulped down a swallow of whiskey and celebrated this delightful, masturbatory session. Alone in his tent, Jesse now felt he had the ability of taking on anyone or anything, from Commander Salazar, to Chief Vix, to pink apes and purple winged men, or a shipload of stinking, conniving Branellians! In his current state, he was prepared to challenge prancing Kuschan daisies, or a humiliating fear of water.

Providing that Jesse had his booze, his smartass wit, and his lovely Cavalier hat, there was nothing to stop him!

At sundown, Salazar and Patrick strolled through the Ministry of War. They were not pleased with their upcoming assignment. There was a mounting insecurity of not knowing what tomorrow might bring, or the number of tomorrows each man still had.

"Pat," said Salazar, outside of his quarters. "I have to go on this trip, but it doesn't mean you've got to."

"Sir?" questioned Patrick, as if Salazar had insulted him. "Admiral Kraig ordered me to . . ."

"If you'd like, I'll reassign you to another officer."

"But, Commander Salazar," moped Patrick. "I don't want to miss the party!"

"For all we know, it might be a one-way ticket. We might not return."

"I don't like it anymore than you do!" cried Patrick. "How can you ask me to sit this one out?"

Salazar had no answer.

"Sir," argued Patrick. "We're lucky to have Chief Vix with us. Even then, you'll need all the help you can get. Please don't ask me to turn my back on you!"

"Patrick . . ."

"How can you ask me to abandon you? I can't, sir. I won't!"

Salazar grinned. It was shortsighted for him to part with his finest man, even as the odds were ranged against them.

"You've already got your hands full," said Patrick. "And what about Garry?"

"What about him?"

"He can't read."

"Most Embrians can't read," reminded Salazar.

"Then I'll teach him, Commander. Anyway, Garry has to make a satisfactory adjustment into the Army."

"Navy," laughed Salazar. "The Navy, remember. Damned Naval Infantry."

"Please don't turn me away, sir!" begged Patrick. "I don't want to go to Infernus. I don't think any of us do. That's why you'll need me, more than ever!"

There was little point in changing Patrick's mind. At any rate, Salazar required the loyal aide's support and friendship. "I look forward to meeting Captain Shimura," he said, revealing animosity in his jittery voice. "Hopefully, we'll *both* make a good impression on him."

"I won't let you down," assured Patrick. "You can count on me!"

"I know," said Salazar, touched by Patrick's unfailing devotion. "I'm so honored to have you with me."

Patrick's eyes grew misty. "And I'm so honored to be at your side."

"Get some sleep," urged Salazar, "and I'll see you at first light."

As Salazar entered the tent, he wore that same phony grin used to appease Patrick. Placed in a leadership role, he had to infuse encouragement and confidence in the men. In truth, he was scared to death! Throwing himself upon the cot, he didn't know whether to laugh or cry.

Traveling by ship was nothing new to Salazar. He was accustomed to dining at the captain's table, but only as a passenger, and never in a position of authority.

Salazar chuckled, at his own expense. Kraig sure picked some winners to intercept those schoolboys and a half-witted major!

Mirth was soon replaced by apprehension. This was no time to show indecisiveness or weak nerves! Damn it, I made the choice of joining the service!

Salazar wondered what sort of man Captain Shimura was. Perhaps the Kokashima sailor was of a comical nature, prone to high spirits and whimsy. He was probably a strict taskmaster, tolerating no humor or frailty. Salazar assumed the worst. One thing was for certain. He couldn't come off as a fraud. At the same time, he questioned if he was on the verge of becoming the one thing he despised the most.

An officer of Major Kohl's foolish caliber.

61

Before sitting down to his first meal in the Ministry of War, Dimitri excused himself from the cramped tent he shared with his family, to go look for Alexei.

Dimitri searched everywhere for his oldest son, surrounded by scores of refugees crowding the military installation. There was no reason to call out the boy's name. The shout would be drowned out by the drone and conversation of those within the fortress.

Dimitri's emotions ranged from confusion, to worry, and finally to anger. Where could the twelve-year-old be, at that hour of the night?

Sick with frustration and fear, Dimitri prayed that Alexei had not left the fortress, or gotten into a fight with those who hated Kuschans. He heard what happened to Garry that afternoon, and dreaded ideas of his own flesh and blood getting tormented and beaten.

Dimitri found the boy standing at the fortress gates, separating him from the outside world. "Alexei!" he sighed. "Where in the world? . . ."

Alexei was a moody youngster, prone to wander alone in the fields and forest around the church, and be gone for hours at a time. His absence from supper wasn't much of a surprise for Dimitri. However, Dimitri hoped Alexei curbed such activities, for their duration at the War Ministry. It wasn't safe for anyone to get lost or astray, even behind four sturdy walls.

"It's suppertime," said Dimitri. "There's a plate of food waiting for you. You'd better come along, before it gets cold."

"I'm not hungry," said Alexei. Apparently he was afraid . . . but why?

"What's going on?" asked Dimitri, his tone both comforting and scolding.

"Father, how long must we stay here?"

"Not too long, I'm sure. When they say it's all right for us to do so, we'll pack up and go."

"Where?" questioned Alexei, in spite. "That ugly, muddy old dugout in our woods?"

Dimitri nearly came unglued. It was just like Alexei to challenge him! Dimitri knew he'd have trouble on his hands, once Alexei became a teenager.

Dimitri debated on consoling Alexei, or slapping the boy's face off. He kept his temper in check. "No," he said. "Councillor Theo has offered to let us stay with him, assuming the house hasn't been . . . When we can, we'll go to work building our new church, *and* our new house."

"I don't see why we have to stay in Embrey," whined Alexei. "Why can't we go home, to Kusch?"

Dimitri rolled his eyes back. "We already discussed this."

"So why don't we, Father?"

"Because Kusch isn't home, anymore."

"Neither is Embrey!" snapped Alexei, speaking Kuschan. He did this, not only to provoke Dimitri, but to see if the man answered in kind.

"We're Embrians, now," spoke Dimitri, in the language of his adopted country. "Not only because your mother says so, but because I say so, too."

"What if they kill us this time, then destroy *your* new church and house? I'll never forgive them for what they did to us, Father!"

Dimitri frowned. "I know it's hard . . ."

"I'm scared! You heard what they did to that Garry kid Sasha's got a crush on!"

Dimitri snickered. "I think your sister has a crush on every good-looking guy she meets. Garry, Giuseppe, Commander Salazar . . ."

"I hate Embrey!" shouted Alexei, loud enough for a passerby to hear him.

"Alexei . . ."

"And I hate those gates standing in my way! I wish I could just walk right out of here, and never look back."

"That makes one of us," said Dimitri. "Those gates are for our protection, son."

"What if they imprison us? Can't you see, Father? I'm scared! What if we get attacked, like what they did to Garry?"

"I understand, Alexei," said Dimitri. "I'm more afraid of what's beyond those gates, than what's in here. I don't believe that everyone's out to get us. I think the folks who lashed out at Garry thought he was the enemy. Give thanks that Kusch isn't at war with Embrey. It might not hurt if we try to make friends while we're here, and get some of these people on our side."

"No one's on our side, here," grumbled Alexei. "I still wish we'd go home, to Kusch."

"Well, if you're that determined to leave, I won't hold you back," said Dimitri. "I don't know how you'll make it all the way to St. Alexandrov, or what you'll do for money once you get down there. Your mother's liable to skin me for letting you go . . . not to mention, I can use your help on *our* new house and church. I was also looking forward to taking you hunting before winter. Too bad I'll have to take Grigori or Sasha with me, instead."

The wheels in Alexei's head began to spin.

"I'll sure miss you, Alexei," added Dimitri. "So will Grigori and Sasha. But I can't hold you back, if you're really that afraid to stay here."

"Are you trying to be funny?" asked Alexei, in contempt.

"I don't think it's funny to see you leave us. It wasn't funny saying goodbye to Yuri, or watching our church burn to the ground, or having that lunatic Army officer threaten us at Councillor Theo's." Dimitri patted Alexei's shoulder. "Listen to me. Kuschans of faith are to protect all mankind from evil, even at the cost of our own lives."

Alexei glared at Dimitri. "Do you really believe that?"

"If I didn't, then my life's work has been nothing more than a lie."

Alexei let out a deep sigh.

"I'll tell you what, Alexei," offered Dimitri. "If you won't have supper with your mother and me, why not with Grigori and Sasha? If you leave without so much as a 'goodbye' or a 'go to hell,' the boss won't let me hear the end of it." Dimitri smiled. "Will you please do what I ask? Or do you condemn me to Yana's constant nagging and complaining?"

After a moment or two, Alexei asked, "How old were you when you got your first buck, Father?"

"The same age as you," said Dimitri, recalling fond memories of his childhood in Kusch. "I'll never forget when your grandfather and I hiked up these foothills, just behind the house. It was freezing cold out there, but I didn't care. I was too excited to care! By noon it started getting balmy, and we hadn't seen much game." Dimitri laughed. "I took a couple of shots at this big buck, but missed by a mile. Your grandpa made so much fun of me!"

Alexei smiled.

Dimitri went on. "Heading home that night, we came across a herd of deer, grazing a few hundred yards from the house. Your grandpa gave me the first shot. Sneaking up on them, I was so nervous I almost peed my pants. I took aim behind an old red fir, with this crossbow your grandpa made me for my twelfth birthday, let go, and *whang!* Got one! As the others scattered, I ran up to slit his throat. My hands shook so badly I made a mess of it, but . . ." Dimitri looked into his son's eyes. "I don't know who was happier, your grandpa or me. I never slept a wink that night, I was so proud!"

"How big was the deer?"

Dimitri placed both hands above his head, and jutted his fingers out like they were antlers. "I nice four point," he said.

"Are you really taking me out hunting?" asked Alexei, in anticipation.

"What father doesn't want to spend precious time with his oldest boy?"

"But just me?" begged Alexei. "All right, Father? Grigori and Sasha can wait their turns!"

"There's no one I'd rather take hunting right now than you, Alexei."

Alexei rested his head against Dimitri's shoulder as they wandered toward the tent, where their family enjoyed supper. "Thank you," whispered Dimitri.

"Don't worry, Father, I'll do anything for you," promised Alexei. "I'd hate to see you get into trouble with the boss."

"That makes two of us," laughed Dimitri. "What changed your mind about walking back to Kusch?"

"It's too far away," said Alexei, fantasizing about his first day out in the woods, with Dimitri by his side. "Anyway, you're going to need my help, building *our* house and church. It's like what you keep telling me, Father."

"What's that, son?"

Alexei smiled. "We Kuschans must stick together . . ."

62

As Kraig read over stacks of tedious paperwork, he ate only a small portion of his dry cornbread and greasy bacon. He thought he'd never get caught up! He could have laid this chore on a clerk, but wanted to make sure it was done right. He disliked correcting other people's mistakes.

Soon after Salazar and his team left, Kraig was visited by an elderly, bearded man. "May I have a word with you, kind sir?" the old man asked.

"Please sit down, Councillor Theo," snickered Kraig, pointing at a chair. "Sorry I ran out of Campens Rose'. I think Salazar's damned bodyguard swiped it. A shot of whiskey?"

Theo removed the annoying fake beard, then sat across from Kraig's desk. "You have no idea how happy I am to be rid of that," he said. "And yes, I'll have a glass of your finest whiskey."

"I don't know if it's my finest," commented Kraig. "You don't mind Romero's?"

Theo nodded, in approval.

"As well, I don't know whether to salute you, Councillor, or condemn you," said Kraig, offering Theo a shot glass.

Theo's jaw dropped.

"Have they left yet?" asked Kraig.

"*Who?*"

"Have they left yet?" repeated Kohl, sternly. "My brother Kohl, your son Yuri, and all those schoolboys?"

"I don't know what you're talking about," stuttered Theo. It was no use. He had some explaining to do.

"There is no treasure on Infernus," informed Kraig. "Or so that's what Vix told me. Your subsidy of Major Kohl's folly is wasted."

Theo felt like a disobedient child, being sent to bed with no supper. He prided himself on making wise decisions, to benefit Embrey as well as himself. He'd been bamboozled by greed, and a lifelong friendship with Kohl. What price was he to pay for this blunder? "No treasure?" whispered Theo.

Kraig shook his head. "No treasure."

"Kohl told me there was a sizable treasure hidden there!" shouted Theo, to sway attention away from himself. "How was I to know? . . ."

"Oh, Councillor Theo, you've got to know Kohl better than that! His mishandling of the truth is the same with you, as it was with our parents! We'd get home late from fishing at a nearby river, and Kohl would say we got held up by bandits, or some other damned story. It never worked. We still got our asses beat, first for being late, then for lying!"

"How did you find out about that second voyage to Infernus?" asked Theo, his voice barely audible.

"Never mind. Why did you let those boneheaded boys go with Kohl?"

"One of those boneheaded boys is my son," said Theo, defensively. "I . . . I hired experienced sailors to oversee them. With any luck, they'll collect a few interesting plants and species, and do a bit of exploration in the name of Embrey."

"With any luck," interrupted Kraig, "no one will get hurt or killed. With any luck, the men I send to intercept Kohl will be successful. With any luck, we'll soon forget this and go about the business of forming a new government."

Theo deserved to get bawled out by Kraig. He also needed to cover his own butt. He already missed Yuri, and wondered if he'd ever see the boy again. "If I knew Kohl was lying, I would've never bankrolled that expedition!" he said, shamefully. "Who are you sending out to stop them?"

"Lieutenant Commander Salazar, and Kohl's top sergeant. I promoted Vix to the rank of Master Chief in the Navy."

"Vix is a good man. On whose ship do they sail?"

"A frigate of defecting Branellians, led by an old friend." Kraig grinned. "Which brings us to another subject. Which of you Embrian Councillors is making deals with Captain Shimura?"

"What makes you think I'm dealing with Shimura?"

"I ran into a new friend of mine, today. I assume he's also your friend. A tall, skinny kid with long, unruly hair, a dirty face, and a kilt." Kraig laughed. "You know who I'm talking about. You gave him and his cohorts Embrian citizenship, yesterday."

"Garry?" asked Theo.

"Uh-huh."

"For Heaven's sake, I'm worried about him! Is he all right?"

"A number of refugees took exception to his presence in this fortress. Otherwise, he's fine. I took the liberty of granting him political asylum and citizenship, with the condition that he serves in the Navy, under Commander Salazar and our old friend Shimura."

Theo said nothing.

"What I learned from Garry is that Shimura was hired to bring our old friends Copenhaver and Schlender to us," said Kraig. "In exchange, a particular Embrian Councillor was to compensate Shimura with a generous retirement."

Theo merely smiled.

"Was that your big idea, or Councillor Fumiko's?" asked Kraig.

"I'm afraid we're both involved." Theo cleared his throat. "So is Omar."

"Omar?"

"Omar went along to get along . . . with Fumiko and me."

"Who else is in on this scheme?" questioned Kraig. "Oh, and by the way, thank you for failing to notify us in the War Ministry. I can see why you left Gornick in the dark. Why not discuss this with General Chang and myself?"

Theo sipped his drink, without answering.

"Might as well tell me," insisted Kraig. "After all, I was only King Ogden's naval advisor. With Ogden out of the way, my job has been rendered null and void."

"You'll keep your job," assured Theo. "So will General Chang. The country needs men of your maturity and experience to protect our interests from all threats, foreign and domestic. As for Gornick, that's another story."

"Thank you, Councillor Theo."

"Through a Vladistani diplomat named Sirro, King Josiah of Branell and I were in communications to end the Border War, once and for all."

"Let me guess," said Kraig. "King Josiah wants peace, but had to get shy of a particular thorn named Ogden. A bit treasonous, isn't it? Going against the King?"

"You never liked the pervert, either," responded Theo, sick of Kraig's piety. "Face it, we're all better off without Ogden. The Ministry of War mourns his loss as much as the Embrian Council."

"Well, I can't say I've always agreed with the Council's rulings. It's not my place to dispute the legislative body of government, but simply to go along . . . to get along."

"Do you prefer your men protecting our shores and borders, or fighting and dying over a few pitiful yards in the eastern deserts?"

"Hmm . . ." mulled Kraig. "Garry also mentioned a 'scary kid' with Shimura, someone he gave a kilt to. Was that the same scary kid who turned Ogden into a pin cushion?"

"What do you think, Admiral Kraig?" asked Theo, exhausted with this interrogation. "That scary kid is a former student of Captain Maliek, who now freelances for King Josiah."

"Why hire an outsider?" asked Kraig, sarcastically. "Isn't Yuri fully qualified for that sort of thing? Surely, he could have accessed Ogden's favor, just as easily as anyone. Why, Ogden was quite candid in his feelings for your son."

Theo was offended. "I'd never put Yuri up to that butchery! I want to shape my son into a man of class, distinction, and honor."

"He still did a hatchet job on three of Salazar's men, who were simply following my orders. So, what did you promise Shimura, to convince him into switching sides?"

"He'll be well-cared for," said Theo, a hollow feeling in his stomach. "What are you offering him, to pursue Kohl?"

"I'll forget about the scar he gave me, fifteen years ago."

"Major Kohl set sail this afternoon on an Agronian schooner, the Tyree James," said Theo, to redeem himself. "The skipper's name is O'Toole."

"Thanks," said Kraig, who enjoyed watching Theo squirm. "That'll come in handy. Pour yourself another drink. It's not every day I sit down with the Interim Governor of Embrey."

Theo stared at Kraig. "Pardon me?"

"Chang and I discussed placing the nation under military rule." Kraig lifted his glass, in a toast. "We've got enough on our plates, as it is. You're far more qualified to run our country, than we are. We knew that would make your day."

Reluctantly, Theo drank his whiskey.

"We thought about handing you the throne," explained Kraig, "until we found out about Kohl's trip to Infernus."

"I prefer to stay in the Embrian Council," said Theo, in humility. "We've got our own candidate to wear the crown."

"I thought so. Who is he?"

"Hiroyuki."

"Hiroyuki? Fumiko's youngest son?" Kraig laughed. "Bet that makes her day!"

"She was ecstatic when Omar and I put it to her," said Theo. "Anyway, Hiroyuki will be predictable and easily controlled, unlike Gornick's little lapdog, Ogden."

Kraig sat both feet on his desk. "Once we put a chain on Gornick, I'll give him a menial job at some remote outpost in the east, where he can't cause any trouble. I'd like to hang the bastard, but that'd make a martyr of him."

"It's going to be a battle royal, muzzling his fanatical supporters."

"Hopefully, nothing comes of Kohl's expedition of Insula Infernus," yawned Kraig. "No worries, I'm sure Salazar will catch up with him. Get my brother back here, retire him as a gold-leaf colonel, then forget the whole thing. Right, *Governor* Theo?"

"That's right," agreed Theo, downing a full glass in one swallow. "Then we can turn our attention to more pressing concerns . . ."

A stagecoach, pulled by six powerful horses, was guarded by two dozen armed cavalrymen in dress uniforms. The cavalry formed a protective column around the coach. The coachman, a bull of a man with a full beard and a sinewy build, shouted at the team as they rushed through rural Embrey. Preparations were made at key locations to replace the convoy, which moved steadily at high speed, with fresh horses.

The coach's sole passenger was a former student of Lord Werner's Academy. Two nights before, he was whisked away from his dorm room. In a few short hours, he was to be given a rank he'd hold for life.

Still dressed in his school uniform, the boy had traveled for more than a day, nonstop except to eat and relieve himself. His sleeping accommodations were the exact vehicle he rode in. Leaning his head against the window to fixate on the bright moon, the boy contemplated his own future. Soon, he'd be crowned the King of Embrey.

He was only sixteen years old.

The boy looked out at acres of farmlands and orchards, as familiar sights and landmarks became hazy blurs. One moment he was in a safe, comfortable room, laughing and joking with his buddies. Then, without asking his opinion on the matter, he was thrown into the stagecoach, and notified of his new position.

That was night before last . . .

Why me?

Why did the Embrian Council, supported by two members of the War Ministry's Chiefs of Staff, grant me such power and privilege? Was their decision based upon political persuasion, "lucky sperm," or conceived from sheer desperation?

The boy was born of royal stock, in the Far Eastern empire of Kokashima. So be it. Wasn't the honor of wearing the crown usually bestowed upon the eldest child? The boy's older brothers were part of the diplomatic team in St. Alexandrov, while his sister was married to a prosperous merchant. Obviously, Councillor Fumiko's "baby boy" was the only possible candidate to serve as Embrey's King.

Who else was available? What about Theo's adopted son, Yuri? Not hardly!

Fumiko's youngest child was fond of Embrian history and political science. He excelled in drama and often placed first in speech tournaments. Despite his slight frame and alternating high-pitched-to-baritone voice *(puberty!)* he had a strong, commanding presence when addressing large crowds.

The strong, commanding presence was now a nervous wreck, bouncing around in a coach which made an emergency trip to Sykes. It took more than good acting and speech skills to excel in the nation's highest office.

Hiroyuki, King of Embrey, and Commander-In-Chief of his country's armed forces . . .

Hiroyuki was the youngest child of the Embrian Councillor Fumiko. His grandfather, the mighty warlord Ko, was ousted from the throne as the family was secretly transported west. This was achieved, with the help of Fumiko's personal bodyguard Shimura, and a merchant marine named Theo.

Hiroyuki stood only five-foot-one. He wore a white, plumed Tudor hat over short, black hair. Lord Werner's uniform was similar to those of other schools operated by the Brotherhood of Faith, a long-sleeved tunic hanging inches above the knees, with no tights or breeches to protect the legs. The light-colored garment featured a bronze star at the chest, a belt cinched tightly around the hip, and a flowing cape. Hiroyuki's Equestrian boots stretched over the calves. His youthful face, dainty hands, and hairless thighs were a smooth, olive tone.

Upon his arrival at Theo's compound, Hiroyuki was to speak to the Embrian Council, the Chiefs of Staff, local magistrates, and diplomatic corps from nearby sovereign allies. The speech was written and rewritten, as Hiroyuki sat alone in the coach. Less than an hour from his destination, he reached into his bag for his manuscript. Silently, he skimmed through the text, as his mounting anxiety and sweaty hands made the task nearly impossible.

Leaning out of the vehicle's window, the future King of Embrey called for the driver that he had to pee.

The convoy stopped at a dry creek, adjoining grassy fields filled with livestock. Without waiting for the coachman to open the door, Hiroyuki popped outside and dashed to the nearest tree. He was given no privacy as armed men watched his back. Hiroyuki knew that, from now on, he'd never go anywhere without an entourage imposing upon his every move.

What price he wouldn't pay to be an irresponsible, fun-loving teen in the secure confines of his dormitory at Lord Werner's Academy? Barely recalling the splendor and grandeur of the royal courts of Kokashima, he tried to bring back faded memories of those lost times.

Back on the road, Hiroyuki practiced the speech. What good was that? His nerves were shot! It wasn't the speech that frightened him. Hiroyuki had lectured to larger crowds than the one he faced that evening. The yellowed, sweaty scroll in his hand was of little use. The speech was already planted in his head. It's what it represented that scared him. The text was to carry weight, truth, and meaning, not only for those in attendance, but to each and every citizen of Embrey.

Trekking along a winding path in the hills overlooking Sykes, Hiroyuki spied upon various sections of the city. Certain neighborhoods and business districts were in shambles, while noted landmarks and buildings had been razed. Influential voices within the hierarchy questioned if Sykes would ever retain its importance as a vital international and commercial metropolis.

Shock, horror, and despair overwhelmed Hiroyuki. Familiar structures, etched into the mind like friends' faces, were severely damaged or destroyed. Days after the bloodbath, a haze of smoke, dust, and fog lingered over the shattered city. Hiroyuki's heart sank, as he reminded himself that he'd soon take responsibility for Syke's restoration.

Everything evolved into a strange, fuzzy, surreal dream . . .

But who was dreaming?

I can't be the King of Embrey! Why place me in charge of all this?

Hiroyuki always had butterflies in his stomach, prior to making public speeches. He felt it was necessary, and expected, to assure a strong performance. Hiroyuki knew almost everyone waiting at the compound, to see him. Most were like a cherished, extended family. Quite often, Theo played the role of the father figure, Admiral Kraig and General Chang were like his uncles, and Councillor Omar acted as a trustworthy cousin. Through channels, he learned that Theo's son was away on undisclosed business.

Although he loved Yuri, Hiroyuki kept his distance from him. Yuri once beat a hen to death by repeatedly slamming it into a decaying fence post, for no reason other than to vent his uncontrolled anger and rage.

Embrey required a monarch. Hiroyuki should've been flattered by this appointment. Surely, no one expected him to take on certain obligations, without the proper training and education. He'd be attended by the finest teachers, and have assistance in major decisions.

However, if things went awry, who'd take the blame for it? God forbid the potential for a coup. Then where would Hiroyuki go? Kusch? Campens?

Or, like King Auric IV, to the faraway island of Infernus?

Life, so predictable just days before, now grew daunting and heavy-laden. Two nights ago, Hiroyuki sat in his dorm room with three buddies, when everything was turned upside down by members of Embrian Secret Police, who barged in to take him away.

Hiroyuki entered the compound to encounter rows of familiar faces along with a few strangers, there to greet him. Tears fell from his eyes, as he saw Fumiko standing next to Theo. For a brief moment, he forgot his pending duties to the nation, and wished only to shower his mother with kisses.

As the coach came to a halt, Hiroyuki again refused to wait on his driver to open the door. Jumping from the vehicle, he embraced Fumiko, uncaring if his actions were dignified or childlike.

Fumiko planted her lips to Hiroyuki's cheek, and sobbed. Onlookers reacted with good-natured laughter and kindhearted applause.

Behold! Our new King of Embrey, standing a mere five-feet-one inches in height, his weight barely a hundred pounds, dressed as a schoolboy in his fancy hat and silly, shortened tunic.

Behold! King Hiroyuki I of Embrey!

After spending time with his adoring mother, Hiroyuki turned his attention to Theo. More often than not, Theo gave him a firm handshake and manly pat on the back. Not today. Hiroyuki threw his arms around Theo.

His heart aching from Yuri's absence, Theo held the same regard and affection for Hiroyuki, as he did his beloved stepson.

Hiroyuki ran the gauntlet of smiles and well-wishers, then was led to his mother's humble cottage. There, he was unceremoniously stripped from his school uniform, and bathed. Standing naked in a chilly, dark bedroom room, he allowed a tailor to take his measurements, then create suitable clothing for the night's festivities.

Hiroyuki said nothing, yet wondered if all great men were subjected to this level of humility and embarrassment.

An army of servants put the new clothes on Hiroyuki. The boy was no longer permitted to dress himself. Passively, he had his hair cut, curried, and shaped into a ponytail he absolutely despised.

Based on his own ideals, and with strict orders from Theo, Fumiko, and Omar, Hiroyuki wore a long, burgundy robe and skullcap, similar to those adorned by the Embrian Council. After years of the King dressing in flashy, gaudy attire, the Council agreed that the monarch must now be a representative of the people, accessible to their wishes, needs, and desires. That suited Hiroyuki. As he was given this position for life, he was just a man, and hoped to be remembered as a good one.

Hiroyuki left the cottage. Once more, he was greeted by scores of those wielding powerful offices throughout Embrey and abroad. Whether it was proper for one in high standing to do so, Hiroyuki smiled. Was this a sign of unbridled happiness, or humor directed at himself?

A podium and rows of chairs were set up in the area around Governor Theo's cottage. There were more security guards at this gala event, than dignitaries. Those issued to protect Hiroyuki revealed their approval through cheers, whistles, and uproarious applause.

Hiroyuki bowed politely, and thanked everyone in attendance. Nearing the podium, he realized that the speech was left in the stagecoach. It was best to wing the whole thing, and speak mainly from the heart.

Was he truly the King of Embrey, or merely a figurehead and patsy for covert minds and intentions? Hiroyuki had a loud, persuasive voice . . . didn't he? He planned to state his aspirations and goals for the future, then pray that advisers offered him guidance and support for such grand endeavors.

Waiting for the applause to die down, King Hiroyuki I of Embrey stood at the podium, stated his appreciation for those in attendance, then mapped out an agenda for the birth of a new nation, promising that his reign was to bring lasting peace and prosperity.

"Esteemed guests," opened Hiroyuki, "having assembled as a voice for the citizens and armed forces of Embrey, I welcome you.

"We live in a troubled time," he continued. "A time when our country's fate lies in our hands. You have entrusted me in guiding those hands to rebuild this great nation to what it should have always been, yet seldom was. No nation upholding the high and the mighty, as the expense of the poor, is worthy of endurance! With your blessings and hard work, we can boldly step beyond what has often been expected from government."

Meriting wisdom or not, Hiroyuki backed away from the podium, to venture into the crowd. "If I am to be King, by the will of those gathered here, so be it," he said, concentrating on certain members of the delegation as he spoke. "If I am to remain on the throne, I will not do so at the expense of our commoners and peasantry."

Hiroyuki paused for onlookers to digest this rhetoric. He noted tears on Fumiko's face, and expressions of impassioned fire in Theo's eyes.

"We have a long way to go, to reach a destination with an incomplete, sketchy, and unwritten map," said Hiroyuki. "Indeed, you must help finish that map! No one can truly rule without knowledge. And no one should follow without a well-designed map.

"I pledge to rule with my God-given abilities, and be the man you seek for this coveted post. I will not rule through favoritism, dishonest or unquestioning cronies, or with neglect. You must guide me but never, never intone a selfish pleasure at the fault of another. We must work together to shape well-hammered proposals to best serve Embrey, and never condone one person's greed . . . especially my own."

Hiroyuki stepped toward the three members of the Embrian Council, and asked them to stand alongside him. He then turned to face the crowd.

Placing his arms around Theo, Fumiko, and Omar, the King of Embrey smiled.

"Upon my formal coronation, the rigors of court must prevail!" shouted

Hiroyuki, his words echoing throughout the compound. "For now, let me approach you as the friends you are, and always will be! For this one fleeting moment, let us celebrate this peaceful transition, while we pray for a brighter day! God bless you!

"God bless you, one and all!"

THE END